DICK FRANCIS

DICK FRANCIS

WHIP HAND

TRIAL RUN

TWICE SHY

Bloomsbury Books
London

Contents

Whip Hand

Prologue

I dreamed I was riding in a race.

Nothing odd in that. I'd ridden in thousands.

There were fences to jump. There were horses, and jockeys in a rainbow of colours, and miles of green grass. There were massed banks of people, with pink oval faces, indistinguishable pink blobs from where I crouched in the stirrups, galloping past, straining with speed.

Their mouths were open, and although I could hear no sound I knew they were shouting.

Shouting my name, to make me win.

Winning was all. Winning was my function. What I was there for. What I wanted. What I was born for.

In the dream, I won the race. The shouting turned to cheering, and the cheering lifted me up on its wings, like a wave. But the winning was all; not the cheering.

I woke in the dark, as I often did, at four in the morning.

There was silence. No cheering. Just silence.

I could still feel the way I'd moved with the horse, the ripple of muscle through both of the striving bodies, uniting in one. I could still feel the irons round my feet, the calves of my legs gripping, the balance, the nearness to my head of the stretching brown neck, the mane blowing in my mouth, my hands on the reins.

There came, at that point, the second awakening. The real one. The moment in which I first moved, and opened my eyes, and remembered that I wouldn't ride any more races, ever. The wrench of loss came again as a fresh grief. The dream was a dream for whole men.

I dreamed it quite often.

Damned senseless thing to do.

Living, of course, was quite different. One discarded dreams, and got dressed, and made what one could of the day.

I

I took the battery out of my arm and fed it into the recharger, and only realized I'd done it when ten seconds later the fingers wouldn't work.

How odd, I thought. Recharging the battery, and the manoeuvre needed to accomplish it, had become such second nature that I had done them instinctively, without conscious decision, like brushing my teeth. And I realized for the first time that I had finally squared my subconscious, at least when I was awake, to the fact that what I now had as a left hand was a matter of metal and plastic, not muscle and bone and blood.

I pulled my tie off and flung it haphazardly on to my jacket, which lay over the leather arm of the sofa: stretched and sighed with the ease of homecoming: listened to the familiar silences of the flat; and as usual felt the welcoming peace unlock the gritty tensions of the outside world.

I suppose that that flat was more of a haven than a home. Comfortable certainly, but not slowly and lovingly put together. Furnished, rather, on one brisk unemotional afternoon in one store: 'I'll have that, that, that and that . . . and send them as soon as possible.' The collection had gelled, more or less, but I now owned nothing whose loss I would ache over; and if that was a defence mechanism, at least I knew it.

Contentedly padding around in shirt sleeves and socks, I switched on the warm pools of tablelights, encouraged the television with a practised slap, poured a soothing Scotch, and decided not to do yesterday's washing up. There was steak in the fridge and money in the bank, and who needed an aim in life anyway?

I tended nowadays to do most things one-handed, because it was quicker. My ingenious false hand, which worked via solenoids from electrical impulses in what was left of my forearm, would open and close in a fairly vice-like grip, but at its own pace. It did *look* like a real hand, though, to the extent that people sometimes didn't notice. There were shapes like fingernails, and ridges for tendons, and blue lines for veins. When I was alone I seemed to use it less and less, but it pleased me better to see it on than off.

I shaped up to that evening as to many another. On the sofa, feet up, knees bent, in contact with a chunky tumbler and happy to live vicariously via the small screen: and I was mildly irritated when halfway through a decent comedy the door bell rang.

With more reluctance than curiosity I stood up, parked the glass, fumbled through my jacket pockets for the spare battery I'd been carrying there, and snapped it into the socket in my arm. Then, buttoning the shirt cuff down over the plastic wrist, I went out into the small hall and took a look through the spyhole in the door.

There was no trouble on the mat, unless trouble had taken the shape of a middle-aged lady in a blue headscarf. I opened the door and said politely, 'Good evening, can I help you?'

'Sid,' she said. 'Can I come in?'

I looked at her, thinking that I didn't know her. But then a good many people whom I didn't know called me Sid, and I'd always taken it as a compliment.

Coarse dark curls showed under the headscarf, a pair of tinted glasses hid her eyes, and heavy crimson lipstick focussed attention on her mouth. There was embarrassment in her manner and she appeared to expect me to recognize her, but it was not until she looked nervously over her shoulder, and I saw her profile against the light, that I actually did.

Even then I said incredulously, tentatively, 'Rosemary?'

'Look,' she said, brushing past me as I opened the door more widely. 'I simply must talk to you.'

'Well . . . come in.'

While I closed the door behind us she stopped in front of the looking glass in the hall and started to untie the headscarf.

'My God, whatever do I look like?'

I saw that her fingers were shaking too much to undo the knot, and finally with a frustrated little moan she stretched over her head, grasped the points of the scarf, and forcefully pulled the whole thing forward. Off with the scarf came all the black curls, and out shook the more familiar chestnut mane of Rosemary Caspar, who had called me Sid for fifteen years.

'My God,' she said again, putting the tinted glasses away in her handbag and fetching out a tissue to wipe off the worst of the gleaming lipstick. 'I had to come. I had to come.'

I watched the tremors in her hands and listened to the jerkiness in her voice, and reflected that I'd seen a whole procession of people in this state since I'd drifted into the trade of sorting out trouble and disaster.

'Come on in and have a drink,' I said, knowing it was what she both needed and expected, and sighing internally over the ruins of my quiet evening. 'Whisky or gin?'

'Gin . . . tonic . . . anything.'

Still wearing the raincoat she followed me into the sitting room and sat abruptly on the sofa as if her knees had given way beneath her. I looked briefly at the vague eyes, switched off the laughter on the television and poured her a tranquillizing dose of mothers' ruin.

'Here,' I said, handing her the tumbler. 'So what's the problem?'

'Problem!' she was transitorily indignant. 'It's more than that.'

I picked up my own drink and carried it round to sit in an armchair opposite her.

'I saw you in the distance at the races today,' I said. 'Did the problem exist at that point?'

She took a large gulp from her glass. 'Yes, it damn well did. And why do you think I came creeping around at night searching for your damn flat in this ropey wig if I could have walked straight up to you at the races?'

'Well . . . why?'

'Because the last person I can be seen talking to on a racecourse or off it is Sid Halley.'

I had ridden a few times for her husband away back in the past. In the days when I was a jockey. When I was still light enough for Flat racing and hadn't taken to steeplechasing. In the days before success and glory and falls and smashed hands . . . and all that. To Sid Halley, ex-jockey, she could have talked publicly forever. To Sid Halley, recently changed into a sort of all-purpose investigator, she had come in darkness and fright.

Forty-fivish, I suppose, thinking about it for the first time, and realizing that although I had known her casually for years I had never before looked long enough or closely enough at her face to see it feature by feature. The general impression of thin elegance had always been strong. The drooping lines of eyebrow and eyelid, the small scar on the chin, the fine noticeable down on the sides of the jaw, these were new territory.

She raised her eyes suddenly and gave me the same sort of inspection, as if she'd never really seen me before: and I guessed that for her it was a much more radical reassessment. I was no longer the boy she'd once rather brusquely issued with riding instructions, but a man she had come to in trouble. I was accustomed, by now, to seeing this new view of me supplant older and easier relationships, and although I might often regret it, there seemed no way of going back.

'Everyone says . . .' she began doubtfully. 'I mean . . . over this past year, I keep hearing . . .' She cleared her throat. 'They say you're good . . . very good . . . at this sort of thing. But I don't know . . . now I'm here . . . it doesn't seem . . . I mean . . . you're a jockey.'

'Was,' I said succinctly.

She glanced vaguely at my left hand, but made no other comment. She knew all about that. As racing gossip goes, it was last year's news.

'Why don't you tell me what you want done?' I said. 'If I can't help, I'll say so.'

The idea that I couldn't help after all reawoke her alarm and set her shivering again inside the raincoat.

'There's no one else,' she said. 'I can't go to anyone else. I have to believe . . . I have to . . . that you can do . . . all they say.'

'I'm no superman,' I protested. 'I just snoop around a bit.'

'Well . . . Oh God . . .'

The glass rattled against her teeth as she emptied it to the dregs. 'I hope to God . . .'

'Take your coat off,' I said persuasively. 'Have another gin. Sit back on the sofa, and start at the beginning.'

As if dazed she stood up, undid the buttons, shed the coat, and sat down again.

'There isn't a beginning.'

She took the refilled glass and hugged it to her chest. The newly revealed clothes were a cream silk shirt under a rust-coloured cashmere-looking sweater, a heavy gold chain, and a well-cut black skirt: the everyday expression of no financial anxieties.

'George is at a dinner,' she said. 'We're staying here in London overnight . . . He thinks I've gone to a film.'

George, her husband, ranked in the top three of British racecourse trainers and probably in the top ten internationally. On racecourses from Hong Kong to Kentucky he was revered as one of the greats. At Newmarket, where he lived, he was king. If his horses won the Derby, the Arc de Triomphe, the Washington International, no one was surprised. Some of the cream of the world's bloodstock floated year by year to his stable, and even having a horse in his yard gave the owner a certain standing. George Caspar could afford to turn down any horse or any man. Rumour said he rarely turned down any woman: and if that was Rosemary's problem it was one I couldn't solve.

'He mustn't know,' she said nervously. 'You'll have to promise not to tell him I came here.'

'I'll promise provisionally,' I said.

'That's not enough.'

'It'll have to be.'

'You'll see,' she said. 'You'll see why . . .'

She took a drink. 'He may not like it, but he's worried to death.'

'Who . . . George?'

'Of course George. Who else? Don't be so damned stupid. For who else would I risk coming here on this damn charade?' The brittleness shrilled in her voice and seemed to surprise her. She visibly took some deep breaths, and started again. 'What did you think of Gleaner?'

'Er . . .' I said. 'Disappointing.'

'A damned disaster,' she said. 'You know it was.'

'One of those things,' I said.

'No, it was *not* one of those things. One of the best two-year-olds George ever had. Won three brilliant two-year-old races. Then all that winter, favourite for the Guineas and the Derby. Going to be the tops, everyone said. Going to be marvellous.'

'Yes,' I said. 'I remember.'

'And then what? Last spring he ran in the Guineas. Fizzled out. Total flop. And he never even got within sight of the Derby.'

'It happens,' I said.

She looked at me impatiently, compressing her lips. 'And Zingaloo?' she said. 'Was that, too, just one of those things? The two best colts in the country, both brilliant at two, both in our yard. And neither of them won a damn penny last year as three-year-olds. They just stood there in their boxes, looking well, eating their heads off, and totally damn bloody useless.'

'It was a puzzler,' I agreed, but without much conviction. Horses which didn't come up to expectations were as normal as rain on Sundays.

'And what about Bethesda, the year before?' She glared at me vehemently. 'Top two-year-old filly. Favourite for months for the One Thousand and the Oaks. Terrific. She went down to the start of the One Thousand looking a million dollars, and she finished tenth. *Tenth*, I ask you!'

'George must have had them all *checked*,' I said mildly.

'Of course he did. Damn vets crawling all round the place for weeks on end. Dope tests. Everything. All negative. Three brilliant horses all gone useless. And no damned explanation. Nothing!'

I sighed slightly. It sounded to me more like the story of most trainers' lives, not a matter for melodramatic visits in false wigs.

'And now,' she said, casually dropping the bomb, 'there is Tri-Nitro.'

I let out an involuntarily audible breath, halfway to a grunt. Tri-Nitro filled columns just then on every racing page, hailed as the best colt for a decade. His two-year-old career the previous autumn had eclipsed all competitors, and his supremacy in the approaching summer was mostly taken for granted. I had seen him win the Middle Park at Newmarket in September at a record-breaking pace, and had a vivid memory of the slashing stride that covered the turf at almost incredible speed.

'The Guineas is only a fortnight away,' Rosemary said. 'Two weeks today, in fact. Suppose something happens . . . suppose it's just as bad . . . what if he fails, like the others . . . ?'

She was trembling again, but when I opened my mouth to speak she rushed on at a higher pitch. 'Tonight was the only chance . . . the only night I could come here . . . and George would be livid. He says nothing can happen to the horse, no one can get at him, the security's too good. But he's scared, I know he is. Strung up. Screwed up tight. I suggested he called you in to guard the horse and he nearly went berserk. I don't know why. I've never seen him in such a fury.'

'Rosemary,' I began, shaking my head.

'Listen,' she interrupted. 'I want you to make sure nothing happens to Tri-Nitro before the Guineas. That's all.'

'All . . .'

'It's no good wishing afterwards . . . if somebody tries something . . . that I'd asked you. I couldn't stand that. So I had to come. I had to. So say you'll do it. Say how much you want, and I'll pay it.'

'It's not money,' I said. 'Look . . . there's no way I can guard Tri-Nitro without George knowing and approving. It's impossible.'

'You can do it. I'm sure you can. You've done things before that people said couldn't be done. I had to come. I can't face it . . . George can't face it . . . not three years in a row. Tri-Nitro has got to win. You've got to make sure nothing happens. You've got to.'

She was suddenly shaking worse than ever and looked well down the road to hysteria. More to calm her than from any thought of being able in fact to do what she wanted, I said 'Rosemary . . . all right. I'll try to do something.'

'He's got to win,' she said.

I said soothingly 'I don't see why he shouldn't.'

She picked up unerringly the undertone I hadn't known would creep into my voice: the scepticism, the easy complacent tendency to discount her urgency as the fantasies of an excitable woman. I heard the nuances myself, and saw them uncomfortably through her eyes.

'My God, I've wasted my time coming here, haven't I?' she said bitterly, standing up. 'You're like all bloody men. You've got menopause on the brain.'

'That's not true. And I said I'd try.'

'Yes.' The word was a sneer. She was stoking up her own anger, indulging an inner need to explode. She practically threw her empty glass at me instead of handing it. I missed catching it, and it fell against the side of the coffee table, and broke.

She looked down at the glittering pieces and stuffed the jagged rage half-way back into its box.

'Sorry,' she said shortly.

'It doesn't matter.'

'Put it down to strain.'

'Yes.'

'I'll have to go and see that film. George will ask . . .'

She slid into her raincoat and moved jerkily towards the door, her whole body still trembling with tension. 'I shouldn't have come here. But I thought . . .'

'Rosemary,' I said flatly. 'I've said I'll try, and I will.'

'Nobody knows what it's like.'

I followed her into the hall, feeling her jangling desperation almost as if it were making actual disturbances in the air. She picked the black wig off the small table there and put it back on her head, tucking her own brown hair underneath with fierce unfriendly jabs, hating herself, her disguise and me: hating the visit, the lies to George, the seedy furtiveness of her actions. She painted on a fresh layer of the dark lipstick with unnecessary force, as if assaulting herself; tied the knot on the scarf with a savage jerk, and fumbled in her handbag for the tinted glasses.

'I changed in the lavatories at the tube station,' she said. 'It's all revolting. But I'm not having anyone see me leaving here. There are things going on. I know there are. And George is scared . . .'

She stood by my front door, waiting for me to open it; a thin elegant woman looking determinedly ugly. It came to me that no woman did that to herself without a need that made esteem an irrelevance. I'd done nothing to relieve her distress, and it was no good realizing that it was because of knowing her too long in a different capacity. It was she who was subtly used to being in control, and I, from sixteen, who had respectfully followed her wishes. I thought that if tonight I had made her cry and given her warmth and contact and even a kiss, I could have done her more service; but the block was there, and couldn't be lightly dismantled.

'I shouldn't have come here,' she said. 'I see that now.'

'Do you want me . . . to take any action?'

A spasm twisted her face. 'Oh God . . . Yes I do. But I was stupid. Fooling myself. You're only a jockey . . . after all.'

I opened the door.

'I wish,' I said lightly, 'that I were.'

She looked at me unseeingly, her mind already on her return journey, on her film, on her report of it to George.

'I'm not crazy,' she said.

She turned abruptly and walked away without a backward glance. I watched her turn towards the stairs and go without hesitating out of sight. With a continuing feeling of having been inadequate I shut the door and went back into the sitting room; and it seemed that the very air there too was restless from her intensity.

I bent down and picked up the larger pieces of broken glass, but there were too many sharp little splinters for total laziness, so I fetched dustpan and brush from the kitchen.

Holding the dustpan could usefully be done left-handed. If I simply tried to bend backwards the real hand that wasn't there, the false fingers opened away from the thumb. If I sent the old message to bend my hand inwards, they closed. There was always about two seconds' delay between mental instruction and electrical reaction, and taking that interval into account had been the most difficult thing to learn.

The fingers could not of course feel when their grip was tight enough. The people who fitted the arm had told me that success was picking up eggs: and I'd broken a dozen or two in practising, at the beginning. Absentmindedness had since resulted in an exploding light bulb and crushed-flat cigarette packets and explained why I used the marvels of science less than I might.

I emptied the bits of glass into the dustbin and switched on the television again; but the comedy was over, and Rosemary came between me and a cops-and-robbers. With a sigh I switched off, and cooked my steak, and after I'd eaten it picked up the telephone to talk to Bobby Unwin, who worked for the *Daily Planet*.

'Information will cost you,' he said immediately, when he found who was on his line.

'Cost me what?'

'A spot of quid pro quo.'

'All right,' I said.

'What are you after, then?'

'Um,' I said. 'You wrote a long piece about George Caspar in your Saturday colour supplement a couple of months ago. Pages and pages of it.'

'That's right. Special feature. In-depth analysis of success. The *Planet's* doing a once-a-month series on high-flyers, tycoons, pop-stars, you name it. Putting them under the cliché microscope, and coming up with a big yawn yawn exposé of bugger all.'

15

'Are you horizontal?' I said.

There was a short silence followed by a stifled girlish giggle.

'You just take your intuitions to Siberia,' Bobby said. 'What made you think so?'

'Envy, I dare say.' But I'd really only been asking if he was alone, without making it sound important. 'Will you be at Kempton tomorrow?'

'I reckon.'

'Could you bring a copy of that magazine, and I'll buy you a bottle of your choice.'

'Oh boy, oh boy. You're on.'

His receiver went down without more ado, and I spent the rest of the evening reading the flat-racing form books of recent years, tracing the careers of Bethesda, Gleaner, Zingaloo and Tri-Nitro, and coming up with nothing at all.

2

I had fallen into a recent habit of lunching on Thursdays with my father-in-law. To be accurate, with my *ex*-father-in-law; Admiral (retired) Charles Roland, parent of my worst failure. To his daughter Jenny I had given whatever devotion I was capable of, and had withheld the only thing she eventually said she wanted, which was that I should stop riding in races. We had been married for five years; two in happiness, two in discord, and one in bitterness; and now only the itching half-mended wounds remained. Those, and the friendship of her father, which I had come by with difficulty and now prized as the only treasure saved from the wreck.

We met most weeks at noon in the upstairs bar of the Cavendish Hotel, where a pink gin for him and a whisky and water for me now stood on prim little mats beside a bowl of peanuts.

'Jenny will be at Aynsford this weekend,' he said.

Aynsford was his house in Oxfordshire. London on Thursdays was his business. He made the journey between the two in a Rolls.

'I'd be glad if you could come down,' he said.

I looked at the fine distinguished face and listened to the drawling non-committal voice. A man of subtlety and charm who could blast through you like a laser if he felt the need. A man whose integrity I would trust to the gates of hell, and whose mercy, not an inch.

I said carefully, without rancour, 'I am not coming to be sniped at.'

'She agreed that I should invite you.'

'I don't believe it.'

He looked with suspicious concentration at his glass. I knew from long experience that when he wanted me to do something he knew I wouldn't like, he didn't look at me. And there would be a pause, like this, while he found it in him to light the fuse. From the length of the pause, I drew no comfort of any sort. He said finally, 'I'm afraid she's in some sort of trouble.'

I stared at him, but he wouldn't raise his eyes.

'Charles,' I said despairingly, 'you *can't* . . . you can't ask me . . . You know how she speaks to me these days.'

'You give as good as you get, as I recall.'

'No one in their senses walks into a tiger's cage.'

He gave me a brief flashing upward glance, and there was a small twitch to his mouth. And perhaps it was not the best way of referring to a man's beautiful daughter.

'I have known you, Sid,' he said, 'to walk into tigers' cages more than once.'

'A tigress, then,' I amended, with a touch of humour.

He pounced on it. 'So you'll come?'

'No . . . Some things, honestly, are too much.'

He sighed and sat back in his chair, looking at me over the gin. I didn't care for the blank look in his eyes, because it meant he was still plotting.

'Dover sole?' he suggested smoothly. 'Shall I call the waiter? We might eat soon, don't you think?'

He ordered sole for both of us, and off the bone, out of habit. I could eat perfectly well in public now, but there had been a long and embarrassing period when my natural hand had been a wasted, useless deformity, which I'd self-consciously hidden in pockets. At about the time I finally got used to it, it had been smashed up again, and I'd lost it altogether. I guessed life was like that. You gained and you lost, and if you saved anything from the ruins, even if only a shred of self-respect, it was enough to take you through the next bit.

The waiter told us our table would be ready in ten minutes and went quietly away, hugging menus and order pad to his dinner jacket and grey silk tie. Charles glanced at his watch and then gazed expansively round the big, light, quiet room, where other couples, like us, sat in beige armchairs and sorted out the world.

'Are you going to Kempton this afternoon?' he said.

I nodded. 'The first race is at two-thirty.'

'Are you working on a job?' As an inquiry, it was a shade too bland.

'I'm not coming to Aynsford,' I said. 'Not while Jenny's there.'

After a pause, he said, 'I wish you would, Sid.'

17

I merely looked at him. His eyes were following the track of a bar waiter delivering drinks to distant customers: and he was taking a great deal too much time thinking out his next sentence.

He cleared his throat and addressed himself to nowhere in particular. 'Jenny has lent some money . . . and her name, I'm afraid . . . to a business enterprise which would appear to be fraudulent.'

'She's done *what*?' I said.

His gaze switched back to me with suspicious speed, but I interrupted him as he opened his mouth.

'No,' I said. 'If she's done that, it's well within your province to sort it out.'

'It's your name she's used, of course,' Charles said. 'Jennifer Halley.'

I could feel the trap closing round me. Charles studied my silent face and with a tiny sigh of relief let go of some distinct inner anxiety. He was a great deal too adept, I thought bitterly, at hooking me.

'She was attracted to a man,' he said dispassionately. 'I didn't especially like him, but then I didn't like you, either, to begin with . . . and I have found that error of judgement inhibiting, as a matter of fact, because I no longer always trust my first instincts.'

I ate a peanut. He had disliked me because I was a jockey, which he saw as no sort of husband for his well-bred daughter: and I had disliked him right back as an intellectual and social snob. It was odd to reflect that he was now probably the individual I valued most in the world.

He went on, 'This man persuaded her to go in for some sort of mail order business . . . all frightfully up-market and respectable, at least on the surface. A worthy way of raising money for charity . . . you know the sort of thing. Like Christmas cards, only in this case I think it was a sort of wax polish for antique furniture. One was invited to buy expensive wax, knowing that most of the profits would go to a good cause.'

He looked at me sombrely. I simply waited, without much hope.

'The orders rolled in,' he said. 'And the money with them, of course. Jenny and a girl friend were kept busy sending off the wax.'

'Which Jenny,' I guessed, 'had bought ready, in advance?'

Charles sighed. 'You don't need to be told, do you?'

'And Jenny paid for the postage and packing and advertisements and general literature?'

He nodded. 'She banked all the receipts into a specially opened account in the name of the charity. Those receipts have all been drawn out, the man has disappeared, and the charity, as such, has been found not to exist.'

I regarded him in dismay.

'And Jenny's position?' I said.

'Very bad, I'm afraid. There may be a prosecution. And her name is on everything, and the man's nowhere.'

My reaction was beyond blasphemy. Charles observed my blank silence and nodded slowly in sympathy.

'She has been exceedingly foolish,' he said.

'Couldn't you have stopped her? Warned her?'

He shook his head regretfully. 'I didn't know about it until she came to Aynsford yesterday in a panic. She has done it all from that flat she's taken in Oxford.'

We went in to lunch, and I couldn't remember, afterwards, the taste of the sole.

'The man's name is Nicholas Ashe,' Charles said, over the coffee. 'At least that's what he said.' He paused briefly. 'My solicitor chap thinks it would be a good idea if you could find him.'

I drove to Kempton with visual and muscular responses on auto-pilot and my thoughts uncomfortably on Jenny.

Divorce itself, it seemed, had changed nothing. The recent antiseptic drawing of the line, the impersonal court to which neither of us had gone (no children, no maintenance disputes, no flicker of reconciliation, petition granted, next case please) seemed to have punctuated our lives not with a full stop but with hardly a comma. The legal position had not proved a great liberating open door. The recovery from emotional cataclysm seemed a long slow process, and the certificate was barely an aspirin.

Where once we had clung together with delight and passion, we now, if we chanced to meet, ripped with claws. I had spent eight years in loving, losing and mourning Jenny, and although I could wish my feelings were dead, they weren't. The days of indifference still seemed a weary way off.

If I helped her in the mess she was in, she would give me a rotten time. If I didn't help her, I would give it to myself. *Why*, I thought violently, in impotent irritation, had the silly bitch been so *stupid*.

There was a fair attendance at Kempton for a weekday in April, though as often before I regretted that in Britain the nearer a racecourse was to London, the more vulnerable it became to stay-away crowds. City-dwellers might be addicted to gambling, but not to fresh air and horses. Birmingham and Manchester, in days gone by, had lost their racecourses to indifference, and Liverpool had survived only through the Grand National. Most times it took a course in the country to burst at the seams and run out of racecards; the thriving plants still growing from the oldest roots.

Outside the weighing room there was the same old bunch of familiar faces carrying on chats which had been basically unchanged for centuries. Who was going to ride what, and who was going to win, and there should be a change in the rules, and what so-and-so had said about his horse losing, and wasn't the general outlook grim, and did you know young fella-me-lad has left his wife? There were the scurrilous stories and the slight exaggerations and the downright lies. The same mingling of honour and corruption, of principle and expediency. People ready to bribe, people with the ready palm. Anguished little hopefuls and arrogant big guns. The failures making brave excuses, and the successful hiding the anxieties behind their eyes. All as it had been, and was, and would be, as long as racing lasted.

I had no real right any longer to wander in the space outside the weighing room, although no one ever turned me out. I belonged in the grey area of ex-jockeys: barred from the weighing room itself but tolerantly given the run of much else. The cosy inner sanctum had gone down the drain the day half a ton of horse landed feet first on my metacarpals. Since then I had come to be glad simply to be still part of the brotherhood, and the ache to be riding was just part of the general regret. Another ex-champion had told me it took him twenty years before he no longer yearned to be out there on the horses, and I'd said thanks very much.

George Caspar was there, talking to his jockey, with three runners scheduled that afternoon; and also Rosemary, who reacted with a violent jerk when she saw me at ten paces, and promptly turned her back. I could imagine the waves of alarm quivering through her, although that day she looked her usual well-groomed elegant self: mink coat for the chilly wind, glossy boots, velvet hat. If she feared I would talk about her visit, she was wrong.

There was a light grasp on my elbow and a pleasant voice saying 'A word in year ear, Sid.'

I was smiling before I turned to him, because Lord Friarly, earl, land-owner, and frightfully decent fellow, had been one of the people for whom I'd ridden a lot of races. He was of the old school of aristocrats; sixtyish, beautifully mannered, genuinely compassionate, slightly eccentric, and more intelligent than people expected. A slight stammer was nothing to do with speech impediment but all to do with not wanting to seem to throw his rank about in an egalitarian world.

Over the years I had stayed several times in his house in Shropshire, mostly on the way to northern race-meetings, and had travelled countless miles with him in a succession of elderly cars. The age of the cars was not an extension of the low profile, but rather a disinclination to waste money on inessentials. Essentials, in terms of the earl's income, were keeping up Friarly Hall and owning as many racehorses as possible.

'Great to see you, sir,' I said.

'I've told you to call me Philip.'

'Yes . . . sorry.'

'Look,' he said. 'I want you to do something for me. I hear you're damned good at looking into things. Doesn't surprise me, of course, I've always valued your opinion, you know that.'

'Of course I'll help if I can,' I said.

'I've an uncomfortable feeling that I'm being *used*,' he said. 'You know that I'm a sucker for seeing my horses run, the more the merrier, and all that. Well, during the past year I have agreed to be one of the registered owners in a syndicate . . . you know, sharing the costs with eight or ten other people, though the horses run in my name, and my colours.'

20

'Yeah,' I said nodding. 'I've noticed.'

'Well . . . I don't know all the other people, personally. The syndicates were formed by a chap who does just that – gets people together and sells them a horse. You know?'

I nodded. There had been cases of syndicate-formers buying horses for a smallish sum and selling them to the members of the syndicate for up to four times as much. A healthy little racket, so far legal.

'Those horses don't run true to form, Sid,' he said bluntly. 'I've a nasty feeling that somewhere in the syndicates we've got someone fixing the way the horses run. So will you find out for me? Nice and quietly?'

'I'll certainly try,' I said.

'Good,' he said, with satisfaction. 'Thought you would. So I brought the names for you, of the people in the syndicates.' He pulled a folded paper out of his inner pocket. 'There you are,' he said, opening and pointing. 'Four horses. The syndicates are all registered with the Jockey Club, everything above board, audited accounts, and so on. It all looks all right on paper, but, frankly, Sid, I'm not *happy*.'

'I'll look into it,' I promised, and he thanked me profusely, and also genuinely, and moved away, after a minute or two, to talk to Rosemary and George.

Further away, Bobby Unwin, notebook and pencil in evidence, was giving a middle-rank trainer a hard-looking time. His voice floated over, sharp with northern aggression and tinged with an inquisitorial tone caught from tele-interviewers. 'Can you say, then, that you are perfectly satisfied with the way your horses are running?' The trainer looked around for escape and shifted from foot to foot. It was amazing, I thought, that he put up with it, even though Bobby Unwin's printed barbs tended to be worse if he hadn't the personal pleasure of intimidating his victim face to face. He wrote well, was avidly read, and among most of the racing fraternity was heartily disliked. Between him and me there had been for many years a sort of sparring truce, which in practice had meant a diminution of words like 'blind' and 'creti-nous' to two per paragraph when he was describing any race I'd lost. Since I'd stopped riding I was no longer a target, and in consequence we had de-veloped a perverse satisfaction in talking to each other, like scratching a spot.

Seeing me out of the corner of his eye he presently released the miserable trainer and steered his beaky nose in my direction. Tall, forty, and forever making copy out of having been born in a back-to-back terrace in Bradford: a fighter, come up the hard way, and letting no one ever forget it. We ought to have had much in common, since I too was the product of a dingy back street, but temperament had nothing to do with environment. He tended to meet fate with fury and I with silence, which meant that he talked a lot and I listened.

'The colour mag's in my briefcase in the Press room,' he said. 'What do you want it for?'

'Just general interest.'

'Oh, come off it,' he said. 'What are you working on?'

'And would you,' I said, 'give me advance notice of your next scoop?'

'All right,' he said. 'Point taken. And I'll have a bottle of the best vintage bubbly in the members' bar. After the first race. OK?'

'And for smoked salmon sandwiches extra, would I acquire some background info that never saw the light of print?'

He grinned nastily and said he didn't see why not: and in due course, after the first race, he kept his bargain.

'You can afford it, Sid, lad,' he said, munching a pink-filled sandwich and laying a protective hand on the gold-foiled bottle standing beside us on the bar counter. 'So what do you want to know?'

'You went to Newmarket . . . to George Caspar's yard . . . to do this article?' I indicated the colour magazine, which lay, folded lengthwise, beside the bottle.

'Yeah. Sure.'

'So tell me what you didn't write.'

He stopped in mid-munch. 'In what area?'

'What do you privately think of George as a person?'

He spoke round bits of brown bread. 'I said most of it in that.' He looked at the magazine. 'He knows more about when a horse is ready to race and what race to run him in than any other trainer on the Turf. And he's got as much feeling for people as a block of stone. He knows the name and the breeding back to the flood of every one of the hundred and twenty plus horses in his yard, and he can recognize them walking away from him in a downpour, which is practically impossible, but as for the forty lads he's got there working for him, he calls them all Tommy, because he doesn't know tother from which.'

'Lads come and go,' I said neutrally,

'So do horses. It's in his mind. He doesn't give a bugger's damn for people.'

'Women?' I suggested.

'Uses them, poor sods. I bet when he's at it he's got his mind on his next day's runners.'

'And Rosemary . . . what does she think about things?'

I poured a refill into his glass and sipped my own. Bobby finished his sandwich with a gulp and licked the crumbs off his fingers.

'Rosemary? She's halfway off her rocker.'

'She looked all right yesterday at the races,' I said. 'And she's here today, as well.'

'Yeah, well, she can hold on to the grande dame act in public still, I grant you, but I was in and out of the house for three days, and I'm telling you, mate, the goings-on there had to be heard to be believed.'

'Such as?'

'Such as Rosemary screaming all over the place that they hadn't enough security and George telling her to belt up. Rosemary's got some screwy idea

22

that some of their horses have been got at in the past, and I daresay she's right at that, because you don't have a yard that size and that successful that hasn't had its share of villains trying to alter the odds. But anyway . . .' he drank deep and tipped the bottle generously to replenish his supplies,' . . . she seized me by the coat in their hall one day . . . and that hall's as big as a fair-sized barn . . . literally seized me by the coat and said what I should be writing was some stuff about Gleaner and Zingaloo being got at . . . you remember, those two spanking two-year-olds who never developed . . . . and George came out of his office and said she was neurotic and suffering from the change of life, and right then and there in front of me they had a proper slanging match.' He took a breath and a mouthful. 'Funny thing is, in a way I'd say they were fond of each other. As much as he could be fond of anybody.'

I ran my tongue round my teeth and looked only marginally interested, as if my mind was on something else. 'What did George say about her ideas on Gleaner and Zingaloo?' I said.

'He took it for granted I wouldn't take her seriously, but anyway, he said it was just that she had the heeby-jeebies that someone would nobble Tri-Nitro, and she was getting everything out of proportion. Her age, he said. Women always went very odd, he said, at that age. He said the security round Tri-Nitro was already double what he considered really necessary, because of her nagging, and when the new season began he'd have night patrols with dogs, and such like. Which is now, of course. He told me that Rosemary was quite wrong, anyway, about Gleaner and Zingaloo being got at, but that she'd got this obsession on the subject, and he was ready to humour her to some degree to stop her going completely bonkers. It seems that both of them . . . the horses, that is . . . proved to have a heart murmur, which of course accounted for their rotten performances as they matured and grew heavier. So that was that. No story.' He emptied his glass and re-filled it. 'Well, Sid, mate, what is it you *really* want to know about George Caspar?'

'Um,' I said. 'Do you think there's anything he is afraid of?'

'George,' he said disbelievingly. 'What sort of thing?'

'Anything.'

'When I was there, I'd say he was about as frightened as a ton of bricks.'

'He didn't seem worried?'

'Not a bit.'

'Or edgy?'

He shrugged. 'Only with his wife.'

'How long ago was it, that you went there?'

'Oh . . .' He considered, thinking. 'After Christmas. Yes . . . second week in January. We have to do those colour mags such a long time in advance.'

'You don't think, then,' I said slowly, sounding disappointed, 'that he'd be wanting any extra protection for Tri-Nitro?'

'Is that what you're after?' He gave the leering grin. 'No dice, then, Sid,

23

mate. Try someone smaller. George has got his whole ruddy yard sewn up tight. For a start, see, it's one of those old ones enclosed inside a high wall, like a fortress. Then there's ten-foot high double gates across the entrance, with spikes on top.'

I nodded. 'Yes . . . I've seen them.'

'Well, then.' He shrugged, as if that settled things.

There were closed-circuit televisions in all the bars at Kempton to keep serious drinkers abreast of the races going on outside, and on the nearest of these sets Bobby Unwin and I watched the second race. The horse which won by six lengths was the one trained by George Caspar, and while Bobby was thoughtfully eying the two inches of fizz still left in the bottle, George himself came into the bar. Behind him, in a camel-coloured overcoat, came a substantial man bearing all the stigmata of a satisfied winning owner. Cat-with-the-cream smile, big gestures, have this one on me.

'Finish the bottle, Bobby,' I said.

'Don't you want any?'

'It's yours.'

He made no objections. Poured, drank, and comfortably belched. 'Better go,' he said. 'Got to write up these effing colts in the third. Don't you go telling my editor I watched the second in the bar, I'd get the sack.' He didn't mean it. He saw many a race in the bar. 'See you, Sid. Thanks for the drink.'

He turned with a nod and made a sure passage to the door, showing not a sign of having dispatched seven eighths of a bottle of champagne within half an hour. Merely laying the foundation, no doubt. His capacity was phenomenal.

I tucked his magazine inside my jacket and made my own way slowly in his wake, thinking about what he'd said. Passing George Caspar I said, 'Well done,' in the customary politeness of such occasions, and he nodded briefly and said 'Sid,' and, transaction completed, I continued towards the door.

'Sid . . .' he called after me, his voice rising.

I turned. He beckoned. I went back.

'Want you to meet Trevor Deansgate,' he said.

I shook the hand offered: snow-white cuff, gold links, smooth pale skin, faintly moist; well-tended nails, onyx and gold signet ring on little finger.

'Your winner?' I said. 'Congratulations.'

'Do you know who I am?'

'Trevor Deansgate?'

'Apart from that.'

It was the first time I'd seen him at close quarters. There was often, in powerful men, a give-away droop of the eyelids which proclaimed an inner sense of superiority, and he had it. Also dark grey eyes, black controlled hair, and the tight mouth which goes with well-exercised decision-making muscles.

'Go on, Sid,' George said into my tiny hesitation. 'If you know, say. I told Trevor you knew everything.'

I glanced at him, but all that was to be read on his tough weathered countenance was a sort of teasing expectancy. For many people, I knew, my new profession was a kind of game. There seemed to be no harm, on this occasion, of jumping obligingly through his offered hoop.

'Bookmaker?' I said tentatively: and to Trevor Deansgate directly, added, 'Billy Bones?'

'There you are,' said George, pleased. 'I told you so.'

Trevor Deansgate took it philosophically. I didn't try for a further reaction, which might not have been so friendly. His name at birth was reputed to be Shummuck. Trevor Shummuck from Manchester, who'd been born in a slum with a razor mind and changed his name, accent and chosen company on the way up. As Bobby Unwin might have said, hadn't we all, and why not?

Trevor Deansgate's climb to the big league had been all but completed by buying out the old but ailing firm of 'Billy Bones', in itself a blanket pseudonym for some brothers called Rubenstein and their uncle Solly. In the past few years 'Billy Bones' had become big business. One could scarcely open a sports paper or go to the races without seeing the blinding fluorescent pink advertising, and slogans like 'Make no Bones about it, Billy's best' tended to assault one's peace on Sundays. If the business was as vigorous as its sales campaign, Trevor Deansgate was doing all right.

We civilly discussed his winner until it was time to adjourn outside to watch the colts.

'How's Tri-Nitro?' I said to George, as we moved towards the door.

'Great,' he said. 'In great heart.'

'No problems?'

'None at all.'

We parted outside, and I spent the rest of the afternoon in the usual desultory way, watching the races, talking to people, and thinking unimportant thoughts. I didn't see Rosemary again, and calculated she was avoiding me, and after the fifth race I decided to go.

A racecourse official at the exit gate stopped me with an air of relief, as if he'd been waiting for me for a shade too long.

'Note for you, Mr Halley.'

'Oh? Thanks.'

He gave me an unobtrusive brown envelope. I put it in my pocket and walked on, out to my car. Climbed in. Took out, opened, and read the letter.

Sid,
I've been busy all afternoon but I want to see you. Please can you meet me in the tea room? After the last?
Lucas Wainwright.

Cursing slightly, I walked back across the car park, through the gate, and along to the restaurant, where lunch had given place to sandwiches and cake. The last race being just finished, the tea customers were trickling in in small thirsty bunches, but there was no sign of Commander Lucas Wainwright, Director of Security to the Jockey Club.

I hung around, and he came in the end, hurrying, anxious, apologizing and harassed.

'Do you want some tea?' He was out of breath.

'Not much.'

'Never mind. Have some. We can sit here without being interrupted, and there are always too many people in the bar.' He led the way to a table and gestured to me to sit down.

'Look, Sid. How do you feel about doing a job for us?' No waster of time, Commander Wainwright.

'Does "us" mean the Security Service?'

'Yes.'

'Official?' I said, surprised. The Racecourse Security people knew in moderate detail what I'd recently been doing and had raised no objections, but I hadn't imagined they actually approved. In some respects, I'd been working in their territory, and stepping on their toes.

Lucas drummed his fingers on the tablecloth.

'Unofficial,' he said. 'My own private show.'

As Lucas Wainwright was himself the top brass of the Security Service, the investigative, policing arm of the Jockey Club, even unofficial requests from him could be considered to be respectably well-founded. Or at least, until proved otherwise.

'What sort of job?' I said.

The thought of what sort of job slowed him up for the first time. He hummed and hah'ed and drummed his fingers some more, but finally shaped up to what proved to be a brute of a problem.

'Look, Sid, this is in strictest confidence.'

'Yes.'

'I've no higher authority for approaching you like this.'

'Well,' I said. 'Never mind. Go on.'

'As I've no authority, I can't promise you any pay.'

I sighed.

'All I could offer is . . . well . . . help, if you should ever need it. And if it was within my power to give it, of course.'

'That could be worth more than pay,' I said.

He looked relieved. 'Good. Now . . . this is very awkward. Very delicate.' He still hesitated, but at last, with a sigh like a groan, he said, 'I'm asking you to make . . . er . . . discreet inquiries into the . . . er . . . background of one of our people.'

There was an instant's silence. Then I said, 'Do you mean one of *you*? One of the Security Service?'

'I'm afraid that's right.'

'Inquiries into exactly what?' I said.

He looked unhappy. 'Bribery. Backhanders. That sort of thing.'

'Um,' I said. 'Have I got this straight? You believe one of your chaps may be collecting pay-offs from villains, and you want me to find out?'

'That's it,' he said. 'Exactly.'

I thought it over. 'Why don't you do the investigating yourselves? Just detail another of your chaps.'

'Ah. Yes.' He cleared his throat. 'But there are difficulties. If I am wrong, I cannot afford to have it known that I was suspicious. It would cause a great, a very great deal of trouble. And if I am right, which I fear I am, we . . . that is, the Jockey Club . . . would want to be able to deal with things quietly. A public scandal involving the Security Service would be very damaging to racing.'

I though he was perhaps putting it a bit high, but he wasn't.

'The man in question,' he said miserably, 'is Eddy Keith.'

There was another countable silence. In the hierarchy of the Security Service then existing, there was Lucas Wainwright at the top, with two equal deputies one step down. Both of the deputies were retired senior-rank policemen. One of them was ex-Superintendent Eddison Keith.

I had a clear mental picture of him, as I had talked with him often. A big bluff breezy man with a heavy hand for clapping one on the shoulder. More than a trace of Suffolk accent in a naturally loud voice. A large flourishing straw-coloured moustache, fluffy light brown hair through which one could see the pink scalp shining, and fleshy-lidded eyes which seemed always to be twinkling with good humour, and often weren't.

I had glimpsed there occasionally a glint as cold and unmerciful as a crevasse. Very much a matter of sun on ice: pretty but full of traps. One for applying the handcuffs with a cheery smile; that was Eddy Keith.

But crooked . . . ? I would never have thought so.

'What are the indications?' I said at last.

Lucas Wainwright chewed his lower lip for a while and then said, 'Four of his inquiries over the past year have come up with incorrect results.'

I blinked. 'That's not very conclusive.'

'No. Precisely. If I were sure, I wouldn't be here talking to you.'

'I guess not.' I thought a bit. 'What sort of inquiries were they?'

'They were all syndicates. Inquiries into the suitability of people wanting to form syndicates to own horses. Making sure there weren't any undesirables sneaking into racing through the back door. Eddy gave all-clear reports on four proposed syndicates which do in fact all contain one or more people who would not be allowed through the gates.'

'How do you know?' I said. 'How did you find out?'

He made a face. 'I was interviewing someone last week in connection with a dope charge. He was loaded with spite against a group of people he said had let him down, and he crowed over me that those people all owned horses under false names. He told me the names, and I checked, and the four syndicates which contain them were all passed by Eddy.'

'I suppose,' I said slowly, 'they couldn't possibly be syndicates headed by Lord Friarly?'

He looked depressed. 'Yes, I'm afraid so. Lord Friarly mentioned to me earlier this afternoon that he'd asked you to take a look-see. Told me out of politeness. It just reinforced the idea I'd already had of asking you myself. But I want it kept quiet.'

'So does he,' I said reassuringly. 'Can you let me have Eddy's reports? Or copies of them? And the false and true names of the undesirables?'

He nodded. 'I'll see you get them.' He looked at his watch and stood up, the briskness returning to his manner like an accustomed coat. 'I don't need to tell you . . . But do be discreet.'

I joined him on his quick march to the door, where he left me at an even faster pace, sketching the merest wave of farewell. His backview vanished uprightly through the weighing room door, and I took myself out again to my car, reflecting that if I went on collecting jobs at the present rate I would need to call up the troops.

3

I telephoned the North London Comprehensive School and asked to speak to Chico Barnes.

'He's teaching judo,' a voice said repressively.

'His class usually ends about now.'

'Wait a minute.'

I waited, driving towards London with my right hand on the wheel and my left round the receiver and a spatter of rain on the windscreen. The car had been adapted for one-handed steering by the addition of a knob on the front face of the wheel's rim: very simple, very effective, and no objections from the police.

'Hello?'

Chico's voice, cheerful, full even in one single word of his general irreverent view of the world.

'Want a job?' I said.

'Yeah.' His grin travelled distinctly down the line. 'It's been too dead quiet this past week.'

'Can you go to the flat? I'll meet you there.'

28

'I've got an extra class. They lumbered me. Some other guy's evening class of stout ladies. He's ill. I don't blame him. Where are you phoning from?'

'The car. From Kempton to London. I'm calling in at Roehampton, at the limb centre, as it's on the way, but I could be outside your school in . . . say . . . an hour and a half. I'll pick you up. OK?'

'Sure,' he said. 'What are you going to the limb centre for?'

'To see Alan Stephenson.'

'He'll have gone home.'

'He said he'd be there, working late.'

'Your arm hurting you again?'

'No . . . Matter of screws and such.'

'Yeah,' he said. 'OK. See you.'

I put the phone down with the feeling of satisfaction that Chico nearly always engendered. There was no doubt that as a working companion I found him great: funny, inventive, persistent, and deceptively strong. Many a rogue had discovered too late that young slender Chico with his boyish grin could throw a twenty-stone man over his shoulder with the greatest ease.

When I first got to know him he was working, as I was, in the Radnor detective agency, where I had learned my new trade. At one point there had been a chance that I would become first a partner and eventually the owner of that agency, but although Radnor and I had come to an agreement, and had even changed the agency's name to Radnor-Halley, life had delivered an earthquake upheaval and decided things otherwise. It must have been only a day before the partnership agreements were ready to be signed, with finances arranged and the champagne approaching the ice, that Radnor himself sat down for a quiet snooze in his armchair at home, and never woke up.

Back from Canada, as if on stretched elastic, had immediately snapped an unsuspected nephew, brandishing a will in his favour and demanding his rights. He did not, he said forthrightly, want to sell half his inheritance to a one-handed ex-jockey, especially at the price agreed. He himself would be taking over and breathing new life into the whole works. He himself would be setting it all up in new modern offices, not the old crummy bomb-damaged joint in the Cromwell Road, and anyone who didn't like the transfer could vote with his feet.

Most of the old bunch had stayed on into the new order, but Chico had had a blazing row with the nephew and opted for the dole. Without much trouble he had then found the part-time job teaching judo, and the first time I'd asked for his help he'd joined up with enthusiasm. Since then I myself seemed to have become the most regularly employed investigator working in racing, and if Radnor's nephew didn't like it (and he was reputed to be furious) it was just too bad.

Chico bounced out through the swinging glass doors of the school with the lights behind him making a halo round his curly hair. Any resemblance to sainthood stopped precisely there, since the person under the curls was in no way long-suffering, god-fearing or chaste.

He slid into the car, gave me a wide grin, and said, 'There's a pub round the corner with a great set of bristols.'

Resignedly I pulled into the pub's car park, and followed him into the bar. The girl dispensing drinks was, as he'd said, nicely endowed, and moreover she greeted Chico with telling warmth. I listened to the flirting chit chat and paid for the drinks.

We sat on a bench by the wall, and Chico approached his pint with the thirst brought on by too much healthy exercise.

'Ah,' he said, putting down the tankard temporarily. 'That's better.' He eyed my glass. 'Is that straight orange juice?'

I nodded. 'Been drinking on and off all day.'

'Don't know how you bear it, all that high life and luxury.'

'Easily.'

'Yeah.' He finished the pint, went back for a refill and another close encounter with the girl, and finally retracked to the bench. 'Where do I go then, Sid? And what do I do?'

'Newmarket. Spot of pub-crawling.'

'Can't be bad.'

'You're looking for a head lad called Paddy Young. He's George Caspar's head lad. Find out where he drinks, and sort of drift into conversation.'

'Right.'

'We want to know the present whereabouts of three horses which used to be in his yard.'

'We do?'

'He shouldn't have any reason for not telling you, or at least, I don't think so.'

Chico eyed me. 'Why don't you ask George Caspar, right out? Be simpler, wouldn't it?'

'At the moment we don't want George Caspar to know we're asking questions about his horses.'

'Like that, is it?'

'I don't know, really.' I sighed. 'Anyway, the three horses are Bethesda, Gleaner, and Zingaloo.'

'OK. I'll go up there tomorrow. Shouldn't be too difficult. You want me to ring you?'

'Soon as you can.'

He glanced at me sideways. 'What did the limb man say?'

'Hallo, Sid, nice to see you.'

He made a resigned noise with his mouth. 'Might as well ask questions of a brick wall.'

'He said the ship wasn't leaking and the voyage could go on.'

'Better than nothing.'

'As you say.'

I went to Aynsford, as Charles had known I would, driving down on Saturday afternoon and feeling the apprehensive gloom deepen with every mile. For distraction I concentrated on Chico's news from Newmarket, telephoned through at lunchtime.

'I found him,' he said. 'He's a much-married man who has to take his pay packet home like a good boy on Friday evenings, but he sneaked out for a quick jar just now. The pub's nearly next door to the yard; very handy. Anyway, if you can understand what he says, and he's so Irish it's like talking to a foreigner, what it boils down to is that all three of those horses have gone to stud.'

'Did he know where?'

'Sure. Bethesda went to some place called Garvey's in Gloucestershire, and the other two are at a place just outside Newmarket, which Paddy Young called Traces, or at least I think that's what he said, although as I told you, he chews his words up something horrible.'

'Thrace,' I said. 'Henry Thrace.'

'Yeah? Well, maybe you can make sense of some other things he said, which were that Gleaner had a tritus and Zingaloo had the virus and Bruttersmit gave them both the tums down as quick as Concorde.'

'Gleaner had a what?'

'Tritus.'

I tried turning 'Gleaner had a tritus' into an Irish accent in my head and came up with Gleaner had arthritis, which sounded a lot more likely. I said to Chico, '. . . and Brothersmith gave them the thumbs down . . .'

'Yeah,' he said. 'You got it.'

'Where are you phoning from?'

'Box in the street.'

'There's a bit of boozing time left,' I said. 'Would you see if you can find out if this Brothersmith is George Caspar's vet, and if so, look him up in the phone book and bring back his address and number.'

'OK. Anything else?'

'No.' I paused. 'Chico, did Paddy Young give you any impression that there was anything odd in these three horses going wrong?'

'Can't say he did. He didn't seem to care much, one way or the other. I just asked him casual like where they'd gone, and he told me, and threw in the rest for good measure. Philosophical, you could say he was.'

'Right, then,' I said. 'Thanks.'

We disconnected, but he rang again an hour later to tell me that Brothersmith was indeed George Caspar's vet, and to give me his address.

'If that's all, then, Sid, there's a train leaving in half an hour, and I've a nice little dolly waiting for me round Wembley way who'll have her Saturday night ruined if I don't get back.'

The more I thought about Chico's report and Bobby Unwin's comments the less I believed in Rosemary's suspicions; but I'd promised her I would try, and try I still would, for a little while longer. For as long as it took me, anyway, to check up on Bethesda, Zingaloo and Gleaner, and talk to Brothersmith the vet.

Aynsford still looked its mellow stone self, but the daffodil-studded tranquillity applied to the exterior only. I stopped the car gently in front of the house and sat there wishing I didn't have to go in.

Charles, as if sensing that even then I might back off and drive away, came purposefully out of his front door and strode across the gravel. Watching for me, I thought. Waiting. Wanting me to come.

'Sid,' he said, opening my door and stooping down to smile. 'I knew you would come.'

'You hoped,' I said.

'All right.' The smile stayed in his eyes. 'Hoped. But I know you.'

I looked up at the front of the house, seeing only blank windows reflecting the greyish sky.

'Is she here?' I said.

He nodded. I turned away, went round to the back of the car, and lugged out my suitcase.

'Come on, then,' I said. 'Let's get it over.'

'She's upset,' he said, walking beside me. 'She needs your understanding.'

I glanced at him and said, 'Mm.' We finished the short journey in silence, and went through the door.

Jenny was standing there, in the hall.

I had never got used to the pang of seeing her on the rare occasions we had met since she left. I saw her as I had when I first loved her, a girl of not great classical beauty, but very pretty, with brown curling hair and a neat figure, and a way of holding her head high, like a bird on the alert. The old curving smile and the warmth in her eyes were gone, but I tended to expect them, with hopeless nostalgia.

'So you came,' she said. 'I said you wouldn't.'

I put down the suitcase and took the usual deep breath. 'Charles wanted me to,' I said. I walked the steps towards her, and, as always, we gave each other a brief kiss on the cheek. We had maintained the habit as the outward and public mark of a civilized divorce; but privately, I often thought, it was more like the ritual salute before a duel.

Charles shook his head impatiently at the lack of real affection, and walked ahead of us into the drawing room. He had tried in the past to keep us together, but the glue for any marriage had to come from the inside, and ours had dried to dust.

Jenny said, 'I don't want any lectures from you, Sid, about this beastly affair.'

'No.'

'You're not perfect yourself, even though you like to think so.'

32

'Give it a rest, Jenny,' I said.

She walked abruptly away into the drawing room, and I more slowly fol-lowed. She would use me, I thought, and discard me again, and because of Charles I would let her. I was surprised that I felt no tremendous desire to offer comfort. It seemed that irritation was still well in the ascendancy over compassion.

She and Charles were not alone. When I went in she had crossed the room to stand at the side of a tall blond man whom I'd met before; and beside Charles stood a stranger, a stocky young-old man whose austere eyes were disconcertingly surrounded by a rosy country face.

Charles said in his most ultra-civilized voice, 'You know Toby, don't you, Sid?' and Jenny's shield and supporter and I nodded to each other and gave the faint smiles of an acquaintanceship we would each have been happier without. 'And this, Sid, is my solicitor, Oliver Quayle. Gave up his golf to be here. Very good of him.'

'So you're Sid Halley,' the young-old man said, shaking hands. There was nothing in his voice either way, but his gaze slid down and sideways, seeking to see the half-hidden hand that he wouldn't have looked at if he hadn't known. It often happened that way. He brought his gaze back to my face and saw that I knew what he'd been doing. There was the smallest flicker in his lower eyelids, but no other remark. Judgement suspended, I thought, on either side.

Charles's mouth twitched, and he said smoothly, 'I warned you, Oliver. If you don't want him to read your thoughts, you mustn't move your eyes.'

'Yours don't move,' I said to him.

'I learned that lesson years ago.'

He made courteous sit-down motions with his hands, and the five of us sank into comfort and pale gold brocade.

'I've told Oliver,' Charles said, 'that if anyone can find this Nicholas Ashe person, you will.'

'Frightfully useful, don't you know,' drawled Toby, 'having a plumber in the family, when the pipes burst.'

It was a fraction short of offensive. I gave him the benefit of a doubt I didn't have, and asked nobody in particular whether the police wouldn't do the job more quickly.

'The trouble is,' Quayle said, 'that technically it is Jenny alone who is guilty of obtaining money by false pretences. The police have listened to her, of course, and the man in charge seems to be remarkably sympathetic, but . . .' He slowly shrugged the heavy shoulders in a way that skilfully com-bined sympathy and resignation, '. . . one feels they might choose to settle for the case they have.'

'But I say,' protested Toby, 'it was that Ashe's idea, all of it.'

'Can you prove it?' Quayle said.

'Jenny says so,' Toby said, as if that were proof enough.

Quayle shook his head. 'As I've told Charles, it would appear from all

33

documents that she signed that she did know the scheme was fraudulent. And ignorance, even if genuine, is always a poor, if not impossible defence.'

I said, 'If there's no evidence against him, what would you do, even if I did find him?'

Quayle looked my way attentively. 'I'm hoping that if you find him, you'll find evidence as well.'

Jenny sat up exceedingly straight and spoke in a voice sharp with perhaps anxiety but certainly anger.

'This is all rubbish, Sid. Why don't you say straight out that the job's beyond you?'

'I don't know if it is.'

'It's pathetic,' she said to Quayle, 'how he longs to prove he's clever, now he's disabled.'

The flicking sneer in her voice shocked Quayle and Charles into visible discomfort, and I thought dejectedly that this was what I'd caused in her, this compulsive need to hurt. I didn't just mind what she'd said, I minded bitterly that because of me she was not showing to Quayle the sunny-tempered person she would still be if I wasn't there.

'If I find Nicholas Ashe,' I said grimly, 'I'll give him to Jenny. Poor fellow.'

None of the men liked it. Quayle looked disillusioned, Toby showed he despised me, and Charles sorrowfully shook his head. Jenny alone, behind her anger, looked secretly pleased. She seldom managed nowadays to goad me into a reply to her insults, and counted it a victory that I'd done it and earned such general disapproval. My own silly fault. There was only one way not to let her see when her barbs went in, and that was to smile . . . and the matter in hand was not very funny.

I said, more moderately, 'There might be ways . . . if I can find him. At any rate, I'll do my best. If there's anything I can do . . . I'll do it.'

Jenny looked unplacated, and no one else said anything. I sighed internally. 'What did he look like?' I said.

After a pause Charles said, 'I saw him once only, for about thirty minutes, four months ago. I have a general impression, but that's all. Young, personable, dark haired, clean-shaven. Something too ingratiating in his manner to me. I would not have welcomed him as a junior officer aboard my ship.'

Jenny compressed her lips and looked away from him, but could not protest against this judgement. I felt the first faint stirrings of sympathy for her and tried to stamp on them: they would only make me more vulnerable, which was something I could do without.

I said to Toby, 'Did you meet him?'

'No,' he said loftily. 'Actually, I didn't.'

'Toby has been in Australia,' Charles said, explaining.

They all waited. It couldn't be shirked. I said directly to her, neutrally, 'Jenny?'

'He was *fun*,' she said vehemently, unexpectedly. 'My God, he was fun. And after you . . .' She stopped. Her hand swung round my way with bitter eyes. 'He was full of life and jokes. He made me laugh. He was terrific. He lit things up. It was like . . . it was like . . .' She suddenly faltered and stopped, and I knew what she was thinking, like us when we first met. Jenny, I thought desperately, don't say it, please don't.

Perhaps it was too much, even for her. How could people, I wondered for the ten thousandth useless time, how could people who had loved so dearly come to such a wilderness; and yet the change in us was irreversible, and neither of us would even search for a way back. It was impossible. The fire was out. Only a few live coals lurked in the ashes, searing unexpectedly at the incautious touch.

I swallowed. 'How tall was he?' I said.

'Taller than you.'

'Age?'

'Twenty-nine.'

The same age as Jenny. Two years younger than I. If he had told the truth, that was. A confidence trickster might lie about absolutely everything as a matter of prudence.

'Where did he stay, while he was . . . er . . . operating?'

Jenny looked unhelpful, and it was Charles who answered. 'He told Jenny he was staying with an aunt, but after he had gone, Oliver and I checked up. The aunt, unfortunately, proved to be a landlady who lets rooms to students in north Oxford. And in any case . . .' he cleared his throat, '. . . it seems that fairly soon he left the lodgings and moved into the flat Jenny is sharing with another girl.'

'He lived in your flat?' I said to Jenny.

'So what of it?' She was defiant. And something else . . .

'So when he left, did he leave anything behind?'

'No.'

'Nothing at all?'

'No.'

'Do you want him found?' I said.

To Charles and Quayle and Toby the answer to that question was an automatic yes, but Jenny didn't answer, and the blush that started at her throat rose fast to two bright spots on her cheekbones.

'He's done you great harm,' I said.

With stubbornness stiffening her neck, she said, 'Oliver says I won't go to prison.'

'Jenny!' I was exasperated. 'A conviction for fraud will affect your whole life in all sorts of horrible ways. I see that you liked him. Maybe you even loved him. But he's not just a naughty boy who pinched the jampot for a lark. He had callously arranged for you to be punished in his stead. *That's* the crime for which I'll catch him if I damned well can, even if you don't want me to.'

Charles protested vigorously, 'Sid, that's ridiculous. Of course she wants to see him punished. She agreed that you should try to find him. She wants you to, of course she does.'

I sighed and shrugged. 'She agreed, to please you. And because she doesn't think I'll succeed; and she's very likely right. But even *talk* of my succeeding is putting her in a turmoil and making her angry ... and it's by no means unknown for women to go on loving scoundrels who've ruined them.'

Jenny rose to her feet, stared at me blindly, and walked out of the room. Toby took a step after her and Charles too got to his feet, but I said with some force, 'Mr Quayle, please will you go after her and tell her the consequences if she's convicted. Tell her brutally, make her understand, make it shock.'

He had taken the decision and was on his way after her before I'd finished.

'It's hardly kind,' Charles said. 'We've been trying to spare her.'

'You can't expect Halley to show her any sympathy,' Toby said waspishly.

I eyed him. Not the brightest of men, but Jenny's choice of undemanding escort, the calm sea after the hurricane. A few months earlier she had been thinking of marrying him, but whether she would do it post-Ashe was to my mind doubtful. He gave me his usual lofty look of non-comprehension and decided Jenny needed him at once.

Charles watched his departing back and said, with a tired note of despair, 'I simply don't understand her. And it took you about ten minutes to see ... what I wouldn't have seen at all.' He looked at me gloomily. 'It was pointless, then, to try to reassure her, as I've been doing?'

'Oh, Charles, what a bloody muddle ... It won't have done any harm. It's just given her a way of excusing him ... Ashe ... and putting off the time when she'll have to admit to herself that she's made a shattering ... shaming ... mistake.'

The lines in his face had deepened with distress. He said sombrely, 'It's worse. Worse than I thought.'

'Sadder,' I said. 'Not worse.'

'Do you think you can find him?' he said. 'How on earth do you start?'

36

4

I started in the morning, having not seen Jenny again, as she'd driven off the previous evening with Toby at high speed to Oxford, leaving Charles and me to dine alone, a relief to us both; and they had returned late and not appeared for breakfast by the time I left.

I went to Jenny's flat in Oxford, following directions from Charles, and rang the door-bell. The lock, I thought, looking at it, would give me no trouble if there was no one in, but in fact, after my second ring, the door opened a few inches, on a chain.

'Louise McInnes?' I said, seeing an eye, some tangled fair hair, a bare foot and a slice of dark blue dressing gown.

'That's right.'

'Would you mind if I talked to you? I'm Jenny's ... er ... ex-husband. Her father asked me to see if I could help her.'

'You're Sid?' she said, sounding surprised. 'Sid Halley?'

'Yes.'

'Well ... wait a minute.' The door closed and stayed closed for a good long time. Finally it opened again, this time wide, and the whole girl was revealed. This time she wore jeans, a checked shirt, baggy blue sweater, and slippers. The hair was brushed, and there was lipstick: a gentle pink, unaggressive.

'Come in.'

I went in and closed the door behind me. Jenny's flat, as I would have guessed, was not constructed of plasterboard and held together with drawing pins. The general address was a large Victorian house in a prosperous side street, with a semi-circular driveway and parking room at the back. Jenny's section, reached by its own enclosed, latterly added staircase, was the whole of the spacious first floor. Bought, Charles had told me, with some of her divorce settlement. It was nice to see that on the whole my money had been well spent.

Switching on lights, the girl led the way into a large bow-fronted sitting room which still had its curtains drawn and the day before's clutter slipping haphazardly off tables and chairs. Newspapers, a coat, some kicked-off boots, coffee cups, an empty yoghurt carton in a fruit bowl, with spoon, some dying daffodils, a typewriter with its cover off, some scrunched-up pages that had missed the waste-paper basket.

Louise McInnes drew back the curtains, letting in the grey morning to dilute the electricity.

'I wasn't up,' she said unnecessarily.

'I'm sorry.'

The mess was the girl's. Jenny was always tidy, clearing up before bed. But the room itself was Jenny's. One or two pieces from Aynsford, and an overall similarity to the sitting room of our own house, the one we'd shared. Love might change, but taste endured. I felt a stranger, and at home.

'Want some coffee?' she said.

'Only if . . .'

'Sure. I'd have some anyway.'

'Can I help you?'

'If you like.'

She led the way through the hall and into a bare-looking kitchen. There was nothing precisely prickly in her manner, but all the same it was cool. Not surprising, really. What Jenny thought of me, she would say, and there wouldn't be much that was good.

'Like some toast?' She was busy producing a packet of white sliced bread and a jar of powdered coffee.

'Yes I would.'

'Then stick a couple of pieces in the toaster. Over there.'

I did as she said, while she ran some water into an electric kettle and dug into a cupboard for butter and marmalade. The butter was a half-used packet still in its torn greaseproof wrapping, the centre scooped out and the whole thing messy: exactly like my own butter packet in my own flat. Jenny had put butter into dishes automatically. I wondered if she did when she was alone.

'Milk and sugar?'

'No sugar.'

When the toast popped up she spread the slices with butter and marma-lade and put them on two plates. Boiling water went on to the brown powder in mugs, and milk followed straight from the bottle.

'You bring the coffee,' she said, 'and I'll take the toast.' She picked up the plates and out of the corner of her eye saw my left hand closing round one of the mugs. 'Look out,' she said urgently, 'that's hot.'

I gripped the mug carefully with the fingers that couldn't feel.

She blinked.

'One of the advantages,' I said, and picked up the other mug more gin-gerly by its handle.

She looked at my face, but said nothing: merely turned away and went back to the sitting room.

'I'd forgotten,' she said, as I put down the mugs on the space she had cleared for them on the low table in front of the sofa.

'False teeth are more common,' I said politely.

She came very near to a laugh, and although it ended up as a doubtful frown, the passing warmth was a glimpse of the true person living behind the slightly brusque façade. She scrunched into the toast and looked thoughtful, and after a chew and a swallow, she said, 'What can you do to help Jenny?'

'Try to find Nicholas Ashe.'

'Oh . . .'

There was another spontaneous flicker of smile, again quickly stifled by subsequent thought.

'You liked him?' I said.

She nodded ruefully. 'I'm afraid so. He is ... was ... such tremendous fun. Fantastic company. I find it terribly hard to believe he's just gone and left Jenny in this mess. I mean ... he lived here, here in this flat ... and we had so many laughs ... What he's done ... it's incredible.'

'Look,' I said, 'would you mind starting at the beginning and telling me all about it?'

'But hasn't Jenny ... ?'

'No.'

'I suppose,' she said slowly, 'that she wouldn't like admitting to you that he made such a fool of us.'

'How much,' I said, 'did she love him?'

'Love? What's love? I can't tell you. She was *in* love with him.' She licked her fingers. 'All fizzy. Bright and bubbly. Up in the clouds.'

'Have you been there? Up in the clouds?'

She looked at me straightly. 'Do you mean, do I know what it's like? Yes, I do. If you mean, was I in love with Nicky, then no I wasn't. He was fun, but he didn't turn me on like he did Jenny. And in any case, it was she who attracted him. Or at least ...' she finished doubtfully, '... it seemed like it.' She wagged her licked fingers. 'Would you give me that box of tissues that's just behind you?'

I gave her the box and watched as she wiped off the rest of the stickiness. She had fair eye-lashes and English rose skin, and a face that had left shyness behind. To soon for life to have printed unmistakable signposts; but there did seem, in her natural expression, to be little in the way of cynicism or intolerance. A practical girl, with sense.

'I don't really know where they met,' she said, 'except that it was somewhere here in Oxford. I came back here one day, and he was *here*, if you see what I mean? They were already ... well ... interested in each other.'

'Er,' I said, 'have you always shared this flat with Jenny?'

'More or less. We were at school together ... didn't you know? Well, we met one day and I told her I was going to be living in Oxford for two years while I wrote a thesis, and she said, had I anywhere to stay, because she'd seen this flat, but she'd like some company ... So I came. Like a shot. We've got on fine, on the whole.'

I looked at the typewriter and the signs of effort. 'Do you work here all the time?'

'Here or in the Sheldonian ... er, the library, that is ... or out doing other research. I pay rent to Jenny for my room ... and I don't know why I'm telling you all this.'

'It's very helpful.'

She got to her feet. 'It might be as well for you to see all the stuff. I've put it all in his room ... Nicky's room ... to get it out of sight. It's all too boringly painful, as a matter of fact.'

Again I followed her through the hall, and this time on further down the wide passage, which was recognizably the first-floor landing of the old house.

'That room,' she said, pointing at doors, 'is Jenny's. That's the bathroom. That's my room. And this one at the end was Nicky's.'

'When exactly did he go?' I said walking behind her.

'Exactly? Who knows? Some time on Wednesday. Two weeks last Wednesday.' She opened the white painted door and walked into the end room. 'He was here at breakfast, same as usual. I went off to the library, and Jenny caught the train to London to go shopping, and when we both got back, he was gone. Just gone. Everything. Jenny was terribly shocked. Wept all over the place. But of course, we didn't know then that he hadn't just left her, he'd cleared out with all the money as well.'

'How did you find out?'

'Jenny went to the bank on Friday to pay in the cheques and draw out some cash for postage, and they told her the account was closed.

I looked round the room. It had thick carpet, Georgian dressing chest, big comfort-promising bed, upholstered armchair, pretty, Jenny-like curtains, fresh white paint. Six large brown boxes of thick cardboard stood in a double stack in the biggest available space; and none of it looked as if it had ever been lived in.

I went over to the chest and pulled out a drawer. It was totally empty. I put my fingers inside and drew them along, and they came out without a speck of dust or grit.

Louise nodded. 'He had dusted. And hoovered, too. You could see the marks on the carpet. He cleaned the bathroom, as well. It was all sparkling. Jenny thought it was nice of him . . . until she found out just why he didn't want to leave any trace.'

'I should think it was symbolic,' I said absently.

'What do you mean?'

'Well . . . not so much that he was afraid of being traced through hair and fingerprints . . . but just that he wanted to feel that he'd wiped himself out of this place. So that he didn't feel he'd left anything of himself there. I mean . . . if you want to go back to a place, you subconsciously leave things there, you "forget" them. Well-known phenomenon. So if you subconsciously, as well as consciously, don't want to go back to a place, you may feel impelled to remove even your dust.' I stopped. 'Sorry. Didn't mean to bore you.'

'I'm not bored.'

I said matter-of-factly, 'Where did they sleep?'

'Here.' She looked carefully at my face and judged it safe to proceed. 'She used to come along here. Well . . . I couldn't help but know. Most nights. Not always.'

'He never went to her?'

'Funny thing, I never ever saw him go into her rom, even in the daytime. If he wanted her, he'd stand outside and call.'

'It figures.'

'More symbolism?' She went to the pile of boxes and opened the topmost. 'The stuff in here will tell you the whole story. I'll leave you to read it . . . I can't stand the sight of it. And anyway, I'd better clean the place up a bit, in case Jenny comes back.'

'You don't expect her, do you?'

She tilted her head slightly, hearing the faint alarm in my voice. 'Are you frightened of her?'

'Should I be?'

'She says you're a worm.' A hint of amusement softened the words.

'Yes, she would,' I said. 'And no, I'm not frightened of her. She just . . . distracts me.'

With sudden vehemence she said, 'Jenny's a super girl.' Genuine friendship, I thought. A statement of loyalties. The merest whiff of challenge. But Jenny, the super girl, was the one I'd married.

I said, 'Yes,' with inflection, and after a second or two she turned and went out of the room. With a sigh I started on the boxes, shifting them clumsily and being glad neither Jenny nor Louise was watching. They were large, and although one or two were not as heavy as the others, their proportions were all wrong for gripping electrically.

The top one contained two foot-deep stacks of office-size paper, white, good quality, and printed with what looked like a typewritten letter. At the top of each sheet there was an impressive array of headings, including, in the centre, an embossed and gilded coat of arms. I lifted out one of the letters, and began to understand how Jenny had fallen for the trick.

Research into Coronary Disability it said, in engraved lettering above the coat of arms, with, beneath it, the words *Registered Charity*. To the left of the gold embossing there was a list of patrons, mostly with titles, and to the right a list of the charity's employees, one of whom was listed as Jennifer Halley, Executive Assistant. Below her name, in small capital letters, was the address of the Oxford flat.

The letter bore no date and no salutation. It began about a third of the way down the paper, and said:

So many families nowadays have had sorrowful first-hand knowledge of the seriousness of coronary artery disease, which even where it does not kill can leave a man unable to continue with a full, strenuous working life.

Much work has already been done in the field of investigation into the causes and possible prevention of this scourge of modern man, but much more remains still to be done. Research funded by Government money being of necessity limited in today's financial climate, it is of the utmost importance that the public should be asked to support directly the essential programmes now in hand in privately run facilities.

We do know, however, that many people resent receiving straightforward fund-raising letters, however worthy the cause, so to aid 'Research into Coronary

Disability' we ask you to buy something, along the same principle as Christmas cards, the sale of which does so much good work in so many fields. Accordingly the Patrons, after much discussion, have decided to offer for sale a supply of exceptionally fine wax polish, which has been especially formulated for the care of antique furniture.

The wax is packed in quarter-kilo tins, and is of the quality used by expert restorers and museum curators. If you should wish to buy, we are offering the wax at five pounds a tin; and you may be sure that at least three-quarters of the revenue goes straight to Research.

The wax will be good for your furniture, your contribution will be good for the cause, and with your help there may soon be significant advances in the understanding and control of this killing disease.

If you should wish, please send a donation to the address printed above. (Cheques should be made out to Research into Coronary Disability.) You will receive a supply of wax immediately, and the gratitude of future heart patients everywhere.

Yours sincerely,
    Executive Assistant

I said 'Phew' to myself, and folded the letter and tucked it into my jacket. Sob stuff; the offer of something tangible in return; and the veiled hint that if you didn't cough up it could one day happen to you. And, according to Charles, the mixture had worked.

The second big box contained several thousand white envelopes, un-addressed. The third was half full of mostly handwritten letters on every conceivable type of writing paper; orders for wax, all saying, among other things, 'cheque enclosed'.

The fourth contained printed Compliments slips, saying that *Research into Coronary Disability* acknowledged the contribution with gratitude and had pleasure herewith in sending a supply of wax.

The fifth brown box, half empty, and the sixth, unopened and full, contained numbers of flat white boxes about six inches square by two inches deep. I lifted out a white box and looked inside. Contents, one flat round un-printed tin with a firmly screwed-on lid. The lid put up a fight, but I got it off in the end, and found underneath it a soft mid-brown mixture that certainly smelled of polish. I shut it up, returned the tin to its package, and left it out ready to take.

There seemed to be nothing else. I looked into every cranny in the room and down the sides of the armchair, but there wasn't as much as a pin.

I picked up the square white box and went back slowly and quietly towards the sitting room, opening the closed doors one by one, and looking at what they concealed. There had been two which Louise had not identified: one proved to be a linen cupboard, and the other a small unfurnished room containing suitcases and assorted junk.

Jenny's room was decisively feminine; pink and white, frothy with net and frills. Her scent lay lightly in the air, the violet scent of *Mille*. No use remembering the first bottle I'd given her, long ago in Paris. Too much time had passed. I shut the door on the fragrance and the memory and went into the bathroom. .

A white bathroom. Huge fluffy towels. Green carpet, green plants. Looking glass on two walls, light and bright. No visible toothbrushes: everything in cupboards, very tidy. Very Jenny. Roger & Gallet soap.

The snooping habit had ousted too many scruples. With hardly a hesitation I opened Louise's door and put my eyes round, trusting to luck she wouldn't come out into the hall and find me.

Organized mess, I thought. Heaps of papers, and books everywhere. Clothes on chairs. Unmade bed; not surprising, since I'd sprung her out of it.

A washbasin in a corner, no cap in the toothpaste, pair of tights hung to dry. An open box of chocolates. A haphazard scatter on the dressing chest. A tall vase with horsechestnut buds bursting. No smell at all. No long-term dirt, just surface clutter. The blue dressing gown on the floor. Basically the room was furnished much like Ashe's: and one could clearly see where Jenny ended and Louise began.

I pulled my head out and closed the door, undetected. Louise, in the sitting room, had been easily sidetracked in her tidying, and was sitting on the floor intently reading a book.

'Oh, hallo,' she said, looking up vaguely as if she had forgotten I was there. 'Have you finished?'

'There must be other papers,' I said. 'Letters, bills, cash books, that sort of thing.'

'The police took them.'

I sat on the sofa, facing her. 'Who called the police in?' I said. 'Was it Jenny?'

She wrinkled her forehead. 'No. Someone complained to them that the charity wasn't registered.'

'Who?'

'I don't know. Someone who received one of the letters, and checked up. Half those patrons on the letter-head don't exist, and the others didn't know their names were being used.'

I thought, and said, 'What made Ashe bolt just when he did?'

'We don't know. Maybe someone telephoned here to complain, as well. So he went while he could. He'd been gone for a week when the police turned up.'

I put the square white box on the coffee table. 'Where did the wax come from?' I said.

'Some firm or other. Jenny wrote to order it, and it was delivered here. Nicky knew where to get it.'

'Invoices?'

'The police took them.'

'These begging letters . . . who got them printed?'

43

She sighed. 'Jenny, of course. Nicky had some others, just like them, except that they had his name in the space where they put Jenny's. He explained that it was no use sending any more letters with his name and address on, as he'd moved. He was keen, you see, to keep on working for the cause . . .'

'You bet he was,' I said.

She was half-irritated. 'It's all very well to jeer, but you didn't meet him. You'd have believed him, same as we did.'

I left it. Maybe I would have. 'These letters,' I said. 'Who were they sent to?'

'Nicky had lists of names and addresses. Thousands of them.'

'Have you got them? The lists?'

She looked resigned. 'He took them with him.'

'What sort of people were on them?'

'The sort of people who would own antique furniture and cough up a fiver without missing it.'

'Did he say where he'd got them from?'

'Yes,' she said. 'From the charity's headquarters.'

'And who addressed the letters and sent them out?'

'Nicky typed the envelopes. Yes, don't ask, on my typewriter. He was very fast. He could do hundreds in a day. Jenny signed her name at the bottom of the letters, and I usually folded them and put them in the envelopes. She used to get writers' cramp doing it and Nicky would often help her.'

'Signing her name?'

'That's right. He copied her signature. He did it hundreds of times. You couldn't really tell the difference.'

I looked at her in silence.

'I know,' she said. 'Asking for trouble. But, you see, he made all that hard work with the letters seem such fun. Like a game. He was full of jokes. You don't understand. And then, when the cheques started rolling in, it was so obviously worth the effort.'

'Who sent off the wax?' I said gloomily.

'Nicky typed the addresses on labels. I used to help Jenny stick them on the boxes and seal the boxes with sticky tape, and take them to the post office.'

'Ashe never went?'

'Too busy typing. We used to wheel them round to the post office in those shopping bags on wheels.'

'And the cheques . . . I suppose Jenny herself paid them in?'

'That's right.'

'How long did all this go on?' I said.

'A couple of months, once the letters were printed and the wax had arrived.

'How much wax?'

'Oh we had stacks of it, all over the place. It came in those big brown boxes . . . sixty tins in each, ready packed. They practically filled the flat. Actually in the end Jenny wanted to order some more, as we were running very low, but Nicky said no, we'd finish what we had and take a breather before starting again.'

'He meant to stop anyway,' I said.

Reluctantly, she said, 'Yes.'

'How much money,' I said, 'did Jenny bank?'

She looked at me sombrely. 'In the region of ten thousand pounds. Maybe a bit more. Some people sent much more than a fiver. One or two sent a hundred, and didn't want the wax.'

'It's incredible.'

'The money just came pouring in. It still does, every day. But it goes direct to the police from the post office. They'll have a hell of a job sending it all back.'

'What about that box of letters in Ashe's room, saying "cheques enclosed"?'

'Those,' she said, 'are people whose money was banked, and who've been sent the wax.'

'Didn't the police want those letters?'

She shrugged. 'They didn't take them, anyway.'

'Do you mind if I do?'

'Help yourself . . .'

After I'd fetched them and dumped them in their box by the front door, I went back into the sitting room to ask her another question. Deep in the book again, she looked up without enthusiasm.

'How did Ashe get the money out of the bank?'

'He took a typewritten letter signed by Jenny saying she wanted to withdraw the balance so as to be able to give it to the charity in cash at its annual gala dinner, and also a cheque signed by Jenny for every penny.'

'But she didn't . . .'

'No. He did. But I've seen the letter and the cheque. The bank gave them to the police. You can't tell it isn't Jenny's writing. Even Jenny can't tell the difference.'

She got gracefully to her feet, leaving the book on the floor. 'Are you going?' she said hopefully. 'I've got so much to do. I'm way behind, because of Nicky.' She went past me into the hall, but when I followed her she delivered another chunk of dismay.

'The bank clerks can't remember Nicky. They pay out cash in thousands for wages every day, because there's so much industry in Oxford. They were used to Jenny in connection with that account, and it was ten days or more before the police asked questions. No one can remember Nicky there at all.'

'He's professional,' I said flatly.

'Every pointer to it, I'm afraid.' She opened the door while I bent down and awkwardly picked up the brown cardboard box, balancing the small white one on top.

'Thank you,' I said, 'for your help.'

'Let me carry that box downstairs.'

'I can do it,' I said.

She looked briefly into my eyes. 'I'm sure you can. You're too damned proud.' She took the box straight out of my arms and walked purposefully away. I followed her, feeling a fool, down the stairs and out on to the tarmac.

'Car?' she said.

'Round the back, but . . .'

As well talk to the tide. I went with her, weakly gestured to the Scimitar, and opened the boot. She dumped the boxes inside, and I shut them in.

'Thank you,' I said again. 'For everything.'

The faintest of smiles came back into her eyes.

'If you think of anything that could help Jenny,' I said, 'will you please let me know?'

'If you give me your address.'

I forked a card out of an inner pocket and gave it to her. 'It's on there.'

'All right.' She stood still for a moment with an expression I couldn't read. 'I'll tell you one thing,' she said. 'From what Jenny's said . . . you're not a bit what I expected.'

5

From Oxford I drove west to Gloucestershire and arrived at Garvey's stud farm at the respectable visiting hour of eleven-thirty, Sunday morning.

Tom Garvey, standing in his stable yard taking to his stud groom, came striding across as I braked to a halt.

'Sid Halley!' he said. 'What a surprise. What do you want?'

I grimaced through the open car window. 'Does everyone think I want something, when they see me?'

'Of course, lad. Best snooper in the business now, so they say. We hear things, you know, even us dim country bumpkins, we hear things.'

Smiling, I climbed out of the car and shook hands with a sixty-year-old near-rogue who was about as far from a dim country bumpkin as Cape Horn from Alaska. A big strong bull of a man, with unshakable confidence, a loud domineering voice, and the wily mind of a gypsy. His hand in mine was as hard as his business methods and as dry as his manner. Tough with men, gentle with horses. Year after year he prospered, and if I would have had every foal on the place exhaustively blood-typed before I believed its alleged breeding, I was probably in the minority.

'What are you after, then, Sid?' he said.

'I came to see a mare, Tom. One that you've got here. Just general interest.'

'Oh yes? Which one?'

'Bethesda.'

There was an abrupt change in his expression from half-amusement to no amusement at all. He narrowed his eyes and said brusquely, 'What about her?'

'Well . . . has she foaled, for instance?'

'She's dead.'

'Dead?'

'You heard, lad. She's dead. You'd better come in the house.'

He turned and scrunched away, and I followed. His house was old and dark and full of stale air. All the life of the place was outside, in fields and foaling boxes and the breeding shed. Inside, a heavy clock ticked loudly into silence, and there was no aroma of Sunday roast.

'In here.'

It was a cross between a dining room and an office: heavy old table and chairs at one end, filing cabinets and sagging armchairs at the other. No attempts at cosmetic decor to please the customers. Sales went on outside, on the hoof.

Tom perched against his desk and I on the arm of one of the chairs: not the sort of conversation for relaxing in comfort.

'Now then,' he said. 'Why are you asking about Bethesda?'

'I just wondered what had become of her.'

'Don't fence with me, lad. You don't drive all the way here out of general interest. What do you want to know for?'

'A client wants to know,' I said.

'What client?'

'If I were working for you,' I said, 'and you'd told me to keep quiet about it, would you expect me to tell?'

'No, lad. Guess I wouldn't. And I don't suppose there's much secret about Bethesda. She died foaling. The foal died with her. A colt, it would have been. Small, though.'

'I'm sorry,' I said.

He shrugged. 'It happens sometimes. Not often, mind. Her heart packed up.'

'Heart?'

'Aye. The foal was lying wrong, see, and the mare, she'd been straining longer than was good for her. We got the foal turned inside her once we found she was in trouble, but she just packed it in, sudden like. Nothing we could do. Middle of the night, of course, like it nearly always is.'

'Did you have a vet to her?'

47

'Aye, he was there, right enough. I called him when we found she'd started, because there was a chance it would be dicey. First foal, and the heart murmur, and all.'

I frowned slightly. 'Did she have a heart murmur when she came to you?'

'Of course she did, lad. That's why she stopped racing. You don't know much about her, do you?'

'No,' I said. 'Tell me.'

He shrugged. 'She came from George Caspar's yard, of course. Her owner wanted to breed from her on account of her two-year-old form, so we bred her to Timberley, which should have given us a sprinter, but there you are, best laid plans, and all that.'

'When did she die?'

'Month ago, maybe.'

'Well, thanks, Tom.' I stood up. 'Thanks for your time.'

He shoved himself off his desk. 'Bit of a tame turn-up for you, asking questions, isn't it? I can't square it with the old Sid Halley, all speed and guts over the fences.'

'Times change, Tom.'

'Aye, I suppose so. I'll bet you miss it, though, that roar from the stands when you'd come to the last and bloody well lift your horse over it.' His face echoed remembered excitements. 'By God, lad, that was a sight. Not a nerve in your body . . . don't know how you did it.'

I supposed it was generous of him, but I wished he would stop.

'Bit of bad luck, losing your hand. Still, with steeplechasing it's always something. Broken backs and such.' We began to walk to the door. 'If you go jump-racing you've got to accept the risks.'

'That's right,' I said.

We went outside and across to my car.

'You don't do too badly with that contraption, though, do you, lad? Drive a car and such.'

'It's fine.'

'Aye, lad.' He knew it wasn't. He wanted me to know he was sorry, and he'd done his best. I smiled at him, got into the car, sketched a thank-you salute, and drove away.

At Aynsford they were in the drawing room, drinking sherry before lunch: Charles, Toby and Jenny.

Charles gave me a glass of fino, Toby looked me up and down as if I'd come straight from a pig sty, and Jenny said she had been talking to Louise on the telephone.

'We thought you had run away. You left the flat two hours ago.'

'Sid doesn't run away,' Charles said, as if stating a fact.

'Limps, then,' Jenny said.

Toby sneered at me over his glass: the male in possession enjoying his

48

small gloat over the dispossessed. I wondered if he really understood the extent of Jenny's attachment to Nicholas Ashe, or if knowing, he didn't care.

I sipped the sherry: a thin dry taste, suitable to the occasion. Vinegar might have been better.

'Where did you buy all that polish from?' I said.

'I don't remember.' She spoke distinctly, spacing out the syllables, wilfully obstructive.

'Jenny!' Charles protested.

I sighed. 'Charles, the police have the invoices, which will have the name and address of the polish firm on them. Can you ask your friend Oliver Quayle to ask the police for the information, and send it to me.'

'Certainly,' he said.

'I cannot see,' Jenny said in the same sort of voice, 'that knowing who supplied the wax will make the slightest difference one way or the other.'

It appeared that Charles privately agreed with her. I didn't explain. There was a good chance, anyway, that they were right.

'Louise said you were prying for ages.'

'I liked her,' I said mildly.

Jenny's nose, as always, gave away her displeasure. 'She's out of your class, Sid,' she said.

'In what way?'

'Brains, darling.'

Charles said smoothly, 'More sherry, anyone?' and, decanter in hand, began refilling glasses. To me, he said, 'I believe Louise took a first at Cambridge in mathematics, I have played her at chess . . . you would beat her with ease.'

'A Grand Master,' Jenny said, 'can be obsessional and stupid and have a persecution complex.

Lunch came and went in the same sort of atmosphere, and afterwards I went upstairs to put my few things in my suitcase. While I was doing it Jenny came in to the room and stood watching me.

'You don't use that hand much,' she said.

I didn't answer.

'I don't know why you bother with it.'

'Stop it, Jenny.'

'If you'd done as I asked, and given up racing, you wouldn't have lost it.'

'Probably not.'

'You'd have a hand, not half an arm . . . not a stump.'

I threw my spongebag with too much force into the suitcase.

'Racing first. Always racing. Dedication and winning and glory. And me nowhere. It serves you right. We'd still have been married . . . you'd still have your hand . . . if you'd have given up your precious racing when I wanted you to. Being champion jockey meant more to you than I did.'

'We've said all this a dozen times,' I said.

'Now you've got nothing. Nothing at all. I hope you're satisfied.'

The battery charger stood on a chest of drawers, with two batteries in it. She pulled the plug out of the mains socket and threw the whole thing on the bed. The batteries fell out and lay on the bedspread haphazardly with the charger and its flex.

'It's disgusting,' she said, looking at it. 'It revolts me.'

'I've got used to it.' More or less, anyway.

'You don't seem to care.'

I said nothing. I cared, all right.

'Do you enjoy being crippled, Sid?'

Enjoy . . . Jesus Christ.

She walked to the door and left me looking down at the charger. I felt more than saw her pause there, and wondered numbly what else there was left that she could say.

Her voice reached me quite clearly across the room.

'Nicky has a knife in his sock.'

I turned my head fast. She looked both defiant and expectant. 'Is that true?' I asked.

'Sometimes.'

'Adolescent,' I said.

She was annoyed. 'And what's so mature about hurtling around on horses and knowing . . . *knowing* . . . that pain and broken bones are going to happen.'

'You never think they will.'

'And you're always wrong.'

'I don't do it any more.'

'But you would if you could.'

There was no answer to that, because we both knew it was true.

'And look at you,' Jenny said. 'When you have to stop racing, do you look around for a nice quiet job in stockbroking, which you know about, and start to lead a normal life? No, you damned well don't. You go straight into something which lands you up in fights and beatings and hectic scrambles. You can't live without danger, Sid. You're addicted. You may think you aren't, but it's like a drug. If you just imagine yourself working in an office, nine to five, and commuting like any sensible man, you'll see what I mean.'

I thought about it, silently.

'Exactly,' she said. 'In an office, you'd die.'

'And what's so safe about a knife in the sock?' I said. 'I was a jockey when we met. You knew what it entailed.'

'Not from the inside. Not all those terrible bruises, and no food and no drink, and no damned sex half the time.'

'Did he show you the knife, or did you just see it?'

'What does it matter?'

'Is he adolescent . . . or truly dangerous?'

'There you are,' she said. 'You'd prefer him dangerous.'

'Not for your sake.'

'Well . . . I saw it. In a little sheath, strapped to his leg. And he made a joke about it.'

'But you told me,' I said. 'So was it a warning?'

She seemed suddenly unsure and disconcerted, and after a moment or two simply frowned and walked away down the passage.

If it marked the first crack in her indulgence towards her precious Nicky, so much the better.

I picked Chico up on Tuesday morning and drove north to Newmarket. A windy day, bright, showery, rather cold.

'How did you get on with the wife, then?'

He had met her once and had described her as unforgettable, the overtones in his voice giving the word several meanings.

'She's in trouble,' I said.

'Pregnant?'

'There are other forms of trouble, you know.'

'Really?'

I told him about the fraud, and about Ashe, and his knife.

'Gone and landed herself in a whoopsy,' Chico said.

'Face down.'

'And for dusting her off, do we get a fee?'

I looked at him sideways.

'Yeah,' he said. 'I thought so. Working for nothing again, aren't we? Good job you're well-oiled, Sid, mate, when it comes to my wages. What is it this year? You made a fortune in anything since Christmas?'

'Silver, mostly. And cocoa. Bought and sold.'

'Cocoa?' He was incredulous.

'Beans,' I said. 'Chocolate.'

'Nutty bars?'

'No, not the nuts. They're risky.'

'I don't know how you find the time.'

'It takes as long as chatting up barmaids.'

'What do you want with all that money, anyway?'

'It's a habit,' I said. 'Like eating.'

Amicably we drew nearer to Newmarket, consulted the map, asked a couple of locals, and finally arrived at the incredibly well-kept stud farm of Henry Thrace.

'Sound out the lads,' I said, and Chico said 'Sure', and we stepped out of the car on to weedless gravel. I left him to it and went in search of Henry Thrace, who was reported by a cleaning lady at the front door of the house to be 'down there on the right, in his office'. Down there he was, in an armchair, fast asleep.

My arrival woke him, and he came alive with the instant awareness of people used to broken nights. A youngish man, very smooth, a world away from rough, tough, wily Tom Garvey. With Thrace, according to predigested opinion, breeding was strictly big business: handling the mares could be left to lower mortals. His first words, however, didn't match the image.

'Sorry. Been up half the night . . . Er, who are you, exactly? Do we have an appointment?'

'No.' I shook my head. 'I just hoped to see you. My name's Sid Halley.'

'Is it? Any relation to . . . Good Lord. You're him.'

'I'm him.'

'What can I do for you? Want some coffee?' He rubbed his eyes. 'Mrs Evans will get us some.'

'Don't bother, unless . . .'

'No. Fire away.' He looked at his watch. 'Ten minutes do? I've got a meeting in Newmarket.'

'It's very vague, really,' I said. 'I just came to inquire into the general health and so on of two of the stallions you've got here.'

'Oh. Which two?'

'Gleaner,' I said. 'And Zingaloo.'

We went through the business of why did I want to know, and why should he tell me, but finally, like Tom Garvey, he shrugged and said I might as well know.

'I suppose I shouldn't say it, but you wouldn't want to advise a client to buy shares in either of them,' he said, taking for granted this was really the purpose of my visit. 'They might have difficulty in covering their full quota of mares, both of them, although they're only four.'

'Why's that?'

'They've both got bad hearts. They get exhausted with too much exercise.'

'Both?'

'That's right. That's what stopped them racing as three-year-olds. And I reckon they've got worse since then.'

'Somebody mentioned Gleaner was lame,' I said.

Henry Thrace looked resigned. 'He's developed arthritis recently. You can't keep a damn thing to yourself in this town.' An alarm clock made a clamour on his desk. He reached over and switched it off. 'Time to go, I'm afraid.' He yawned. 'I hardly take my clothes off at this time of the year.' He took a battery razor out of his desk drawer, and attacked his beard. 'Is that everything then, Sid?'

'Yes,' I said. 'Thanks.'

Chico pulled the car door shut, and we drove away towards the town.

'Bad hearts,' he said.

'Bad hearts.'

'Proper epidemic, isn't it?'

'Let's ask Brothersmith, the vet.'

Chico read out the address, in Middleton Road.

'Yes, I know it. It was old Follett's place. He was our old vet, still alive when I was here.'

Chico grinned. 'Funny somehow to think of you being a snotty little apprentice with the head lad chasing you.'

'And chilblains.'

'Makes you seem almost human.'

I had spent five years in Newmarket, from sixteen to twenty-one. Learning to ride, learning to race, learning to live. My old guv'nor had been a good one, and because I saw every day his wife, his lifestyle, and his administrative ability, I'd slowly changed from a boy from the backstreets into something more cosmopolitan. He had shown me how to manage the money I'd begun earning in large quantities, and how not to be corrupted by it; and when he turned me loose I found he'd given me the status that went with having been taught in his stable. I'd been lucky in my guv'nor, and lucky to be for a long time at the top of the career I loved; and if one day the luck had run out it was too damned bad.

'Takes you back, does it?' Chico said.

'Yeah.'

We drove across the wide Heath and past the racecourse towards the town. There weren't many horses about: a late morning string, in the distance, going home. I swung the car round familiar corners and pulled up outside the vet's.

Mr Brothersmith was out.

If it was urgent, Mr Brothersmith could be found seeing to a horse in a stable along Bury Road. Otherwise he would be home to his lunch, probably, in half an hour. We said thank you, and sat in the car, and waited.

'We've got another job,' I said. 'Checking on syndicates.'

'I thought the Jockey Club always did it themselves.'

'Yes, they do. The job we've got is to check on the man from the Jockey Club who checks on the syndicates.'

Chico digested it. 'Tricky, that.'

'Without him knowing.'

'Oh yes?'

I nodded. 'Ex-Superintendent Eddy Keith.'

Chico's mouth fell open. 'You're joking.'

'No.'

'But he's the fuzz. The Jockey Club fuzz.'

I passed on Lucas Wainwright's doubts, and Chico said Lucas Wainwright must have got it wrong. The job, I pointed out mildly, was to find out whether he had or not.

'And how do we do that?'

'I don't know. What do you think?'

'It's you that's supposed to be the brains of this outfit.'

A muddy Range Rover came along Middleton Road and turned into Brothersmith's entrance. As one, Chico and I removed ourselves from the Scimitar, and went towards the tweed-jacketed man jumping down from his buggy.

53

'Mr Brothersmith?'

'Yes? What's the trouble?'

He was young and harassed, and kept looking over his shoulder, as if something was chasing him. Time, perhaps, I thought. Or lack of it.

'Could you spare us a few minutes?' I said. 'This is Chico Barnes, and I'm Sid Halley. It's just a few questions . . .'

His brain took in the name and his gaze switched immediately towards my hands, fastening finally on the left.

'Aren't you the man with the myoelectric prosthesis?'

'Er . . . yes.' I said.

'Come in, then. Can I look at it?'

He turned away and strode purposefully towards the side door of the house. I stood still and wished we were anywhere else.

'Come on, Sid,' Chico said, following him. He looked back and stopped. 'Give the man what he wants, Sid, and maybe he'll do the same for us.'

Payment in kind, I thought: and I didn't like the price. Unwillingly I followed Chico into what turned out to be Brothersmith's surgery.

He asked a lot of questions in a fairly clinical manner, and I answered him in impersonal tones learned from the limb centre.

'Can you rotate the wrist?' he said at length.

'Yes, a little.' I showed him. 'There's a sort of cup inside there which fits over the end of my arm, with another electrode to pick up the impulses for turning.'

I knew he wanted me to take the arm off and show him properly, but I wouldn't have done it, and perhaps he saw there was no point in asking.

'It fits very tightly over your elbow,' he said, delicately feeling round the gripping edges.

'So as not to fall off.'

He nodded intently. 'Is it easy to put on and remove?'

'Talcum powder,' I said economically.

Chico's mouth opened, and shut again as he caught my don't-say-it stare, and he didn't tell Brothersmith that removal was often a distinct bore.

'Thinking of fitting one to a horse?' Chico said.

Brothersmith raised his still-harassed face and answered him seriously. 'Technically it looks perfectly possible, but it's doubtful if one could train a horse to activate the electrodes, and it would be difficult to justify the expense.'

'It was only a joke,' Chico said faintly.

'Oh? Oh, I see. But it isn't unknown, you know, for a horse to have a false foot fitted. I was reading the other day about a successful prosthesis fitted to the fore-limb of a valuable broodmare. She was subsequently covered, and produced a live foal.'

'Ah,' Chico said. 'Now that's what we've come about. A broodmare. Only this one died.'

Brothersmith detached his attention reluctantly from false limbs and transferred it to horses with bad hearts.

54

'Bethesda,' I said, rolling down my sleeve and buttoning the cuff.

'Bethesda?' He wrinkled his forehead and turned the harassed look into one of anxiety. 'I'm sorry. I can't recall . . .'

'She was a filly with George Caspar,' I said. 'Beat everything as a two-year-old, and couldn't run at three because of a heart murmur. She was sent to stud, but her heart packed up when she was foaling.'

'Oh dear,' he said, adding sorrow to the anxiety. 'What a pity. But I say, I'm so sorry, but I treat so many horses, and I often don't know their names. Is there a question of insurance in this, or negligence, even? Because I assure you . . .'

'No,' I said reassuringly, 'nothing like that. Can you remember, then, treating Gleaner and Zingaloo?'

'Yes, of course. Those two. Wretched shame for George Caspar. So disappointing.'

'Tell us about them.'

'Nothing much to tell, really. Nothing out of the ordinary, except that they were both so good as two-year-olds. Probably that was the cause of their troubles, if the truth were told.'

'How do you mean?' I said.

His nervous tensions escaped in small jerks of his head as he brought forth some unflattering opinions. 'Well, one hesitates to say so, of course, to top trainers like Caspar, but it is all too easy to strain a two-year-old's heart, and if they are good two-year-olds they run in top races, and the pressure to win may be terrific, because of stud values and everything, and a jockey, riding strictly to orders, mind you, may press a game youngster so hard that although it wins it is also more or less ruined for the future.'

'Gleaner won the Doncaster Futurity in the mud,' I said thoughtfully. 'I saw it. It was a very hard race.'

'That's right,' Brothersmith said. 'I checked him thoroughly afterwards, though. The trouble didn't start at once. In fact, it didn't show at all, until he ran in the Guineas. He came in from that in a state of complete exhaustion. First of all we thought it was the virus but then after a few days we got this very irregular heart beat, and then it was obvious what was the matter.'

'What virus?' I said.

'Let's see . . . The evening of the Guineas he had a very slight fever, as if he were in for equine 'flu, or some such. But it didn't develop. So it wasn't that. It was his heart, all right. But we couldn't have foreseen it.'

'What percentage of horses develop bad hearts?' I said.

Some of the chronic anxiety state diminished as he moved confidently on to neutral ground.

'Perhaps ten per cent have irregular heart beats. It doesn't always mean anything. Owners don't like to buy horses which have them, but look at Night Nurse which won the Champion Hurdle, that had a heart murmur.'

'But how often do you get horses having to stop racing because of bad hearts?'

55

He shrugged. 'Perhaps two or three in a hundred.

George Caspar, I reflected, trained upwards of a hundred and thirty horses, year after year.

'On average,' I said, 'are George Caspar's horses more prone to bad hearts than any other trainer's?'

The anxiety state returned in full force. 'I don't know if I should answer that.'

'If it's "no",' I said, 'what's the hassle?'

'But your purpose in asking . . .'

'A client,' I said, lying with regrettable ease, 'wants to know if he should send George Caspar a sparkling yearling. He asked me to check on Gleaner and Zingaloo.'

'Oh, I see. Well, no, I don't suppose he has more. Nothing significant. Caspar's an excellent trainer, of course. If your client isn't too greedy when his horse is two, there shouldn't be any risk at all.'

'Thanks, then.' I stood up and shook hands with him. 'I suppose there's no heart trouble with Tri-Nitro?'

'None at all. Sound, through and through. His heart bangs away like a gong, loud and clear.'

6

'That's that, then,' Chico said over a pint and pie in the White Hart Hotel. 'End of case. Mrs Caspar's off her tiny rocker, and no one's been getting at George Caspar's youngsters except George Caspar himself.'

'She won't be pleased to hear it,' I said.

'Will you tell her?'

'Straight away. If she's convinced, she might calm down.'

So I telephoned to George Caspar's house, and asked for Rosemary, saying I was a Mr Barnes. She came on the line and said hallo in the questioning voice one uses to unknown callers.

'Mr . . . Barnes?'

'It's Sid Halley.'

The alarm came instantly. 'I can't talk to you.'

'Can you meet me, then?'

'Of course not. I've no reason for going to London.'

'I'm just down the road, in the town,' I said. 'I've things to tell you. And I don't honestly think there's any need for disguises and so on.'

'I'm not being seen with you in Newmarket.'

She agreed, however to drive out in her car, pick Chico up, and go where he directed: and Chico and I worked out a place on the map which looked a tranquillizing spot for paranoiacs. The churchyard at Barton Mills, eight miles towards Norwich.

We parked the cars side by side at the gate and Rosemary walked with me among the graves. She was wearing again the fawn raincoat and a scarf, but not this time, the false curls. The wind blew wisps of her own chestnut hair across her eyes, and she pulled them away impatiently: not with quite as much tension as when she had come to my flat, but still with more force than was needed.

I told her I had been to see Tom Garvey and Henry Thrace at their stud farms. I told her I had talked to Brothersmith; and I told her what they'd all said. She listened, and shook her head.

'The horses were nobbled,' she said obstinately. 'I'm sure they were.'

'How?'

'I don't know how.' Her voice rose sharply, the agitation showing in spasms of the muscles round her mouth. 'But I told you. I told you, they'll get at Tri-Nitro. A week today, it's the Guineas. You've got to keep him safe for a week.'

We walked along the path beside the quiet mounds and the grey weather-beaten headstones. The grass was mown, but there were no flowers, and no mourners. The dead there were long gone, long forgotten. Raw grief and tears now in the municipal plot outside the town; brown heaps of earth and brilliant wreaths and desolation in tidy rows.

'George has doubled the security on Tri-Nitro,' I said.

'I know that. Don't be stupid.'

I said reluctantly, 'In the normal course of events he'll be giving Tri-Nitro some strong work before the Guineas. Probably on Saturday morning.'

'I suppose so. What do you mean? Why do you ask?'

'Well . . .' I paused, wondering if indeed it would be sensible to suggest a way-out theory without testing it, and thinking that there was no way of testing it anyway.

'Go on,' she said sharply. 'What do you mean?'

'You could . . . er . . . make sure he takes all sorts of precautions when he gives Tri-Nitro that last gallop.' I paused. 'Inspect the saddle . . . that sort of thing.'

Rosemary said fiercely, 'What are you saying? Spell it out, for God's sake. Don't pussyfoot around it.'

'Lots of races have been lost because of too-hard training gallops too soon beforehand.'

'Of course,' she said impatiently. 'Everyone knows that. But George would never do it.'

'What if the saddle was packed with lead? What if a three-year-old was given a strong gallop carrying fifty pounds dead weight? And then ran under severe pressure a few days later in the Guineas? And strained his heart?'

'My God,' she said. 'My God.'

'I'm not saying that it did happen to Zingaloo and Gleaner, or anything like it. Only that it's a distant possibility. And if it's something like that . . . it must involve someone inside the stable.'

She had begun trembling again.

'You must go on,' she said. 'Please go on trying. I brought some money for you.' She plunged a hand into her raincoat pocket and brought out a smallish brown envelope. 'It's cash. I can't give you a cheque.'

'I haven't earned it,' I said.

'Yes, yes. Take it.' She was insistent, and finally I put it in my pocket, unopened.

'Let me consult George,' I said.

'No. He'd be furious. I'll do it . . . I mean, I'll warn him about the gallops. He thinks I'm crazy, but if I go on about it long enough he'll take notice.' She looked at her watch and her agitation increased. 'I'll have to go back now. I said I was going for a walk on the Heath. I never do that. I'll have to get back, or they'll be wondering.'

'Who'll be wondering?'

'George, of course.'

'Does he know where you are every minute of the day?'

We were retracing our steps with some speed towards the churchyard gates. Rosemary looked as if she would soon be running.

'We always talk. He asks where I've been. He's not suspicious . . . it's just a habit. We're always together. Well, you know what it's like in a racing household. Owners come at odd times. George likes me to be there.'

We reached the cars. She said goodbye uncertainly, and drove off homewards in a great hurry. Chico, waiting in the Scimitar, said, 'Quiet here, isn't it. Even the ghosts must find it boring.'

I got into the car and tossed Rosemary's envelope on to his lap. 'Count that,' I said, starting the engine. 'See how we're doing.'

He tore it open, pulled out a neat wad of expensive-coloured banknotes, and licked his fingers.

'Phew,' he said, coming to the end. 'She's bonkers.'

'She wants us to go on.'

'Then you know what this is, Sid,' he said, flicking the stack. 'Guilt money. To spur you on when you want to stop.'

'Well, it works.'

We spent some of Rosemary's incentive in staying overnight in Newmarket and going round the bars, Chico where the lads hung out and I with the trainers. It was Tuesday evening and very quiet everywhere. I heard nothing of any interest and drank more than enough whisky, and Chico came back with hiccups and not much else.

'Ever heard of Inky Poole?' he said.

'Is that a song?'

'No, it's a work jockey. What's a work jockey? Chico my son, a work jockey is a lad who rides work on the gallops.'

'You're drunk,' I said.

'Certainly not. What's a work jockey?'

'What you just said. Not much good in races but can gallop the best at home.'

'Inky Poole,' he said, 'is George Caspar's work jockey. Inky Poole rides Tri-Nitro his strong work at home on the gallops. Did you ask me to find out who rides Tri-Nitro's gallops?'

'Yes, I did,' I said. 'And you're drunk.'

'Inky Poole, Inky Poole,' he said.

'Did you talk to him?'

'Never met him. Bunch of the lads, they told me. George Caspar's work jockey, Inky Poole.'

Armed with raceglasses on a strap round my neck I walked along to Warren Hill at seven-thirty in the morning to watch the strings out at morning exercise. A long time, it seemed, since I'd been one of the tucked-up figures in sweaters and skull cap, with three horses to muck out and care for, and a bed in a hostel with rain-soaked breeches for ever drying on an airer in the kitchen. Frozen fingers and not enough baths, ears full of four-letter words and no chance of being alone.

I had enjoyed it all well enough, when I was sixteen, on account of the horses. Beautiful, marvellous creatures whose responses and instincts worked on a plane as different from humans' as water and oil, not mingling even where they touched. Insight into their senses and consciousness had been like an opening door, a foreign language glimpsed and half learned, full comprehension maddeningly baulked by not having the right sort of hearing or sense of smell, not sufficient skill in telepathy.

The feeling of oneness with horses I'd sometimes had in the heat of a race had been their gift to an inferior being; and maybe my passion for winning had been my gift to them. The urge to get to the front was born in them; all they needed was to be shown where and when to go. It could fairly be said that like most jump jockeys I had aided and abetted horses beyond the bounds of common sense.

The smell and sight of them on the Heath was like a sea breeze to a sailor. I filled my lungs and eyes, and felt content.

Each exercise string was accompanied and shepherded by its watchful trainer, some of them arriving in cars, some on horseback, some on foot. I collected a lot of 'Good morning, Sid's. Several smiling faces seemed genuinely pleased to see me; and some that weren't in a hurry stopped to talk.

'Sid!' exclaimed one I'd ridden on the Flat for in the years before my weight caught up with my height, 'Sid, we don't see you up here much these days.'

'My loss,' I said, smiling.

'Why don't you come and ride out for me? Next time you're here, give me a ring, and we'll fix it.'

'Do you mean it?'

'Of course I mean it. If you'd like to, that is.'

'I'd love it.'

'Right. That's great. Don't forget, now.' He wheeled away, waving, to shout to a lad earning his disfavour by slopping in the saddle like a disorganized jellyfish. 'How the bloody hell d'you expect your horse to pay attention if you don't?' The boy sat decently for all of twenty seconds. He'd go far, I thought, starting from Newmarket station.

Wednesday being a morning for full training gallops, there was the usual scattering of interested watchers: owners, pressmen, and assorted bookmakers' touts. Binoculars sprouted like an extra growth of eyes, and notes went down in private shorthand. Though the morning was cold the new season was warming up. There was a feeling overall of purpose, and the bustle of things happening. An industry flexing its muscles. Money, profit, and tax revenue making their proper circle under the wide Suffolk sky. I was still a part of it, even if not in the old way. And Jenny was right. I'd die in an office.

'Morning, Sid.'

I looked round. George Caspar, on a horse, his eyes on a distant string walking down the side of the Heath from his stable in Bury Road.

'Morning, George.'

'You staying up here?'

'Just for a night or two.'

'You should've let us know. We've always a bed. Give Rosemary a ring.' His eyes were on his string: the invitation a politeness, not meant to be accepted. Rosemary, I thought, would have fainted if she'd heard.

'Is Tri-Nitro in that lot?' I said.

'Yes, he is. Sixth from the front.' He looked round at the interested spectators. 'Have you seen Trevor Deansgate anywhere? He said he was coming up here this morning from London. Setting off early.'

'Haven't seen him.' I shook my head.

'He's got two in the string. He was coming to see them work.' He shrugged. 'He'll miss them if he isn't here soon.'

I smiled to myself. Some trainers might delay working the horses until the owners did arrive, but not George. Owners queued up for his favours and treasured his comments, and Trevor Deansgate for all his power was just one of a crowd. I lifted my raceglasses and watched while the string, forty strong, approached and began circling, waiting for their turn on the uphill gallop. The stable before George's had nearly finished, and George would be next.

The lad on Tri-Nitro wore a red scarf in the neck of his olive-green husky jacket. I lowered the glasses and kept my eye on him as he circled, and looked at his mount with the same curiosity as everyone else. A good-looking bay colt, well grown, with strong shoulders and a lot of heart room; but nothing about him to shout from the housetops that here was the wildly backed winter favourite for the Guineas and the Derby. If you hadn't known, you wouldn't have known, as they say.

'Do you mind photographs, George?' I said.

'Help yourself, Sid.'

'Thanks.'

I seldom went anywhere these days without a camera in my pocket. Six-teen millimetre, automatic light meter, all the expense in its lens. I brought it out and showed it to him, and he nodded. 'Take what you like.'

He shook up his patient hack and went away, across to his string, to begin the morning's business. The lad who rode a horse down from the stables wasn't necessarily the same one who rode it in fast work, and as usual there was a good deal of swapping around, to put the best lads up where it mat-tered. The boy with the red scarf dismounted from Tri-Nitro and held him, and presently a much older lad swung up on to his back.

I walked across to be close to the string, and took three or four photo-graphs of the wonder horse and a couple of closer shots of his rider.

'Inky Poole?' I said to him at one point, as he rode by six feet away.

'That's right,' he said. 'Mind your back. You're in the way.'

A right touch of surliness. If he hadn't seen me talking to George first, he would have objected to my being there at all. I wondered if his grudging against-the-world manner was the cause or the result of his not getting on as a jockey, and felt sympathy for him, on the whole.

George began detailing his lads in the small bunches that would go up the gallops together, and I walked back the fringes of things, to watch.

A car arrived very fast and pulled up with a jerk, alarming some horses alongside and sending them skittering, with the lads' voices rising high in alarm and protest.

Trevor Deansgate climbed out of his Jaguar and for good measure slammed the door. He was dressed in a city suit, in contrast to everyone else there, and looked ready for the boardroom. Black hair rigorously brushed, chin smoothly shaven, shoes polished like glass. Not the sort of man I would have sought as a friend, because I didn't on the whole like to sit at the feet of power, picking up crumbs of patronage with nervous laughter, but a force to be reckoned with on the racing scene.

Big scale bookmakers could be and often were a positive influence for good, a stance I thought sardonically that they had been pushed into, to sur-vive the lobby that knew that a Tote monopoly (and a less greedy tax climate) would put back into racing what bookmakers took out. Trevor Deansgate personified the new breed; urbane, a man of the world, seeking top company, becoming a name in the City, the sycophant of earls.

'Hallo,' he said, seeing me. 'I met you at Kempton . . . Do you know where George's horses are?'

'Right there,' I said, pointing. 'You're just in time.'

'Bloody traffic.'

He strode across the grass towards George, raceglasses swinging from his hand, and George said hallo briefly and apparently told him to watch the gallops with me, because he came straight back, heavy and confident, and stopped at my side.

'George says my two both go in the first bunch. He said you'd tell me how they're doing, insolent bugger. Got eyes, haven't I? He's going on up the hill.'

I nodded. Trainers often went up halfway and watched from there, the better to see their horses' action as they galloped past.

Four horses were wheeling into position at the starting point. Trevor Deansgate applied his binoculars, twisting them to focus. Navy suiting with faint red pinstripes. The well-kept hands, gold cuff links, onyx ring, as before.

'Which are yours?' I said.

'The two chestnuts. That one with the white socks is Pinafore. The other's nothing much.'

The nothing much had short cannon bones and a rounded rump. Might make a 'chaser one day, I thought. I liked the look of him better than the whippet-shaped Pinafore. They set off together up the gallop at George's signal, and the sprinting blood showed all the way to the top. Pinafore romped it and the nothing much lived up to his owner's assessment. Trevor Deansgate lowered his binoculars with a sigh.

'That's that, then. Are you coming to George's for breakfast?'

'No. Not today.'

He raised his glasses again and focussed them on the much nearer target of the circling string, and, from the angle, he was looking at the riders, not the horses. The search came to an end on Inky Poole: he lowered the glasses and followed Tri-Nitro with the naked eye.

'A week today,' I said.

'Looks a picture.'

I supposed that he, like all bookmakers, would be happy to see the hot favourite lose the Guineas, but there was nothing in his voice except admiration for a great horse. Tri-Nitro lined up in his turn and at a signal from George set off with two companions at a deceptively fast pace. Inky Poole, I was interested to see, sat as quiet as patience and rode with a skill worth ten times what he would be paid. Good work jockeys were undervalued. Bad ones could ruin a horse's mouth and temperament and whole career. It figured that for the stableful he'd got, George Caspar would employ only the best.

It was not the flat-out searching gallop they would hold on the following Saturday morning over a long smooth surface like the Limekilns. Up the incline of Warren Hill a fast canter was testing enough. Tri-Nitro took the whole thing without a hint of effort, and breasted the top as if he could go up there six times more without noticing.

Impressive, I thought. The Press, clearly agreeing, were scribbling in their notebooks. Trevor Deansgate looked thoughtful, as well he might, and George Caspar, coming down the hill and reining in near us, looked almost smugly satisfied. The Guineas, one felt, were in the bag.

After they had done their work the horses walked down the hill to join the still circling string where the work riders changed on to fresh mounts and set off again up to the top. Tri-Nitro got back his lad with the olive-green husky and the red scarf, and eventually the whole lot of them set off home.

'That's that, then,' George said. 'All set, Trevor? Breakfast?'

They nodded farewells to me and set off, one in the car, one on the horse. I had eyes mostly, however, for Inky Poole, who had been four times up the hill and was walking off a shade morosely to a parked car.

'Inky,' I said, coming up behind him, 'the gallop on Tri-Nitro . . . that was great.'

He looked at me sourly. 'I've nothing to say.'

'I'm not from the Press.'

'I know who you are. Saw you racing. Who hasn't?' Unfriendly: almost a sneer. 'What do you want?'

'How does Tri-Nitro compare with Gleaner, this time last year?'

He fished the car keys out of a zipper pocket in his anorak, and fitted one into the lock. What I could see of his face looked obstinately unhelpful.

'Did Gleaner, a week before the Guineas, give you the same sort of feel?' I said.

'I'm not talking to you.'

'How about Zingaloo?' I said. 'Or Bethesda?'

He opened his car door and slid down into the driving seat, taking out time to give me a hostile glare.

'Piss off,' he said. Slammed the door. Stabbed the ignition key into the dashboard and forcefully drove away.

Chico had arisen to breakfast but was sitting in the pub's dining room holding his head.

'Don't look so healthy,' he said when I joined him.

'Bacon and eggs,' I said. 'That's what I'll have. Or kippers, perhaps. And strawberry jam.'

He groaned.

'I'm going back to London,' I said. 'But would you mind staying here?' I brought the camera out of my pocket. 'Take the film out of that and get it developed. Overnight if possible. There's some pictures of Tri-Nitro and Inky Poole on there. We might find them helpful, you never know.'

'OK, then,' he said. 'But you'll have to ring up the Comprehensive and tell them that my black belt's at the cleaners.'

I laughed. 'There were some girls riding in George Caspar's string this morning,' I said. 'See what you can do.'

'That's beyond the call of duty.' But his eye seemed suddenly brighter. 'What am I asking?'

'Things like who saddles Tri-Nitro for exercise gallops, and what's the routine from now until next Wednesday, and whether anything nasty is stirring in the jungle.'

'What about you, then?'

'I'll be back Friday night,' I said. 'In time for the gallops on Saturday. They're bound to gallop Tri-Nitro on Saturday. A strong work-out, to bring him to a peak.'

'Do you really think anything dodgy's going on?' Chico said.

'A toss-up. I just don't know. I'd better ring Rosemary.'

I went through the Mr Barnes routine again and Rosemary came on the line sounding as agitated as ever.

'I can't talk. We've people here for breakfast.'

'Just listen, then,' I said. 'Try to persuade George to vary his routine, when he gallops Tri-Nitro on Saturday. Put up a different jockey, for instance. Not Inky Poole.'

'You don't think . . .' her voice was high, and broke off.

'I don't know at all,' I said. 'But if George changed everything about, there'd be less chance of skulduggery. Routine is the robber's best friend.'

'What? Oh yes. All right. I'll try. What about you?'

'I'll be out watching the gallop. After that, I'll stick around, until after the Guineas is safely over. But I wish you'd let me talk to George.'

'No. He'd be livid. I'll have to go now.' The receiver went down with a rattle which spoke of still unsteady hands, and I feared that George might be right about his wife being neurotic.

Charles and I met as usual at the Cavendish the following day, and sat in the upstairs bar's armchairs.

'You look happier,' he said, 'than I've seen you since . . .' he gestured to my arm, with his glass. 'Released in spirit. Not your usual stoical self.'

'I've been to Newmarket,' I said. 'Watched the gallops, yesterday morning.'

'I would have thought . . .' he stopped.

'That I'd be eaten by jealousy?' I said. 'So would I. But I enjoyed it.'

'Good.'

'I'm going up again tomorrow night and staying until after the Guineas next Wednesday.'

'And lunch, next Thursday?'

I smiled and bought him a large pink gin. 'I'll be back for that.'

In due course we ate scallops one-handedly in a wine and cheese sauce, and he gave me the news of Jenny.

'Oliver Quayle sent the address you asked for, for the polish.' He took a paper from his breast pocket and handed it over. 'Oliver is worried. He says

64

the police are actively pursuing their inquiries, and Jenny is almost certain to be charged.'

'When?'

'I don't know. Oliver doesn't know. Sometimes these things take weeks, but not always. And when they charge her, Oliver says, she will have to appear in a magistrates' court, and they are certain to refer the case to the Crown Court, as so much money is involved. They'll give her bail, of course.'

'Bail!'

'Oliver says she is unfortunately very likely to be convicted, but that if it is stressed that she acted as she did under the influence of Nicholas Ashe, she'll probably get some sympathy from the judge and a conditional discharge.'

'Even if he isn't found?'

'Yes. But of course if he *is* found, and charged, and found guilty, Jenny would with luck escape a conviction altogether.'

I took a deep breath that was half a sigh.

'Have to find him then, won't we?' I said.

'How?'

'Well ... I spent a lot of Monday, and all of this morning, looking through a box of letters. They came from the people who sent money, and ordered wax. Eighteen hundred of them, or thereabouts.'

'How do they help?'

'I've started sorting them into alphabetical order, and making a list.' He frowned sceptically, but I went on. 'The interesting thing is that all the surnames start with the letters L, M, N, and O. None from A to K, and none from P to Z.'

'I don't see ...'

'They might be part of a mailing list,' I said. 'Like for a catalogue. Or even for a charity. There must be thousands of mailing lists, but this one certainly did produce the required results, so it wasn't a mailing list for dog licence reminders, for example.'

'That seems reasonable,' he said drily.

'I thought I'd get all the names into order and then see if anyone, like Christie's or Sotheby's, say – because of the polish angle – has a mailing list which matches. A long shot, I know, but there's just a chance.'

'I could help you,' he said.

'It's a boring job.'

'She's my daughter.'

'All right then. I'd like it.'

I finished the scallops and sat back in my chair, and drank Charles's good cold white wine.

He said he would stay overnight in his club and come to my flat in the morning to help with the sorting, and I gave him a spare key to get in with, in case I should be out for a newspaper or cigarettes when he came. He lit a cigar and watched me through the smoke. 'What did Jenny say to you upstairs after lunch on Sunday?'

I looked at him briefly. 'Nothing much.'

'She was moody all day, afterwards. She even snapped at Toby.' He smiled. 'Toby protested, and Jenny said, "At least Sid didn't whine."' He paused. 'I gathered that she'd been giving you a particularly rough mauling, and was feeling guilty.'

'It wouldn't be guilt. With luck, it was misgivings about Ashe.'

'And not before time.'

From the Cavendish I went to the Portman Square headquarters of the Jockey Club, to keep an appointment made that morning on the telephone by Lucas Wainwright. Unofficial my task for him might be, but official enough for him to ask me to his office. Ex-Superintendent Eddy Keith, it transpired, had gone to Yorkshire to look into a positive doping test, and no one else was going to wonder much at my visit.

'I've got all the files for you,' Lucas said. 'Eddy's reports on the syndicates, and some notes on the rogues he OK'd.'

'I'll make a start then,' I said. 'Can I take them away, or do you want me to look at them here?'

'Here, if you would,' he said. 'I don't want to draw my secretary's attention to them by letting them out or getting them xeroxed, as she works for Eddy too, and I know she admires him. She would tell him. You'd better copy down what you need.'

'Right,' I said.

He gave me a table to one side of his room, and a comfortable chair, and a bright light, and for an hour or so I read and made notes. At his own desk he did some desultory pen-pushing and rustled a few papers, but in the end it was clear that it was only a pretence of being busy. He wasn't so much waiting for me to finish as generally uneasy.

I looked up from my writing. 'What's the matter?' I said.

'The . . . matter?'

'Something's troubling you.'

He hesitated. 'Have you done all you want?' he said, nodding at my work.

'Only about half,' I said. 'Can you give me another hour?'

'Yes, but . . . Look, I'll have to be fair with you. There's something you'll have to know.'

'What sort of thing?'

Lucas, who was normally urbane even when in a hurry, and whose naval habits of thought I understood from long practice with my Admiral father-in-law, was showing signs of embarrassment. The things that acutely embarrassed naval officers were collisions between warships and quaysides, ladies visiting the crew's mess desk with the crew present and at ease, and dishonourable conduct among gentlemen. It couldn't be the first two; so where were we with the third?

'I have not perhaps given you all the facts,' he said.

'Go on, then,'

'I did send someone else to check on two of the syndicates, some time ago. Six months ago.' He fiddled with some paperclips, no longer looking in my direction. 'Before Eddy checked them.'

'With what result?'

'Ah. Yes.' He cleared his throat. 'The man I sent – his name's Mason – we never received his report because he was attacked in the street before he could write it.'

Attacked in the street . . . 'What sort of attack?' I said. 'And who attacked him?'

He shook his head. 'Nobody knows who attacked him. He was found on the pavement by some passer-by, who called the police.'

'Well . . . have you asked him – Mason?' But I guessed at something of the answer, if not all of it.

'He's, er, never really recovered,' Lucas said regretfully. 'His head, it seemed, had been repeatedly kicked, as well as his body. There was a good deal of brain damage. He's still in an institution. He always will be. He's a vegetable . . . and he's blind.'

I bit the end of the pencil with which I'd been making notes. 'Was he robbed?' I said.

'His wallet was missing. But not his watch.' His face was worried.

'So it might have been a straightforward mugging?'

'Yes . . . except that the police treated it as intended homicide, because of the number and target of the boot marks.'

He sat back in his chair as if he'd got rid of an unwelcome burden. Honour among gentlemen . . . honour satisfied.

'All right,' I said. 'Which two syndicates was he checking?'

'The first two that you have there.'

'And do you think any of the people on them – the undesirables – are the sort to kick their way out of trouble?'

He said unhappily, 'They might be.'

'And am I,' I said carefully, 'investigating the possible corruption of Eddy Keith, or Mason's semi-murder?'

After a pause, he said, 'Perhaps both.'

There was a long silence. Finally I said, 'You do realize that by sending me notes at the races and meeting me in the tea-room and bringing me here, you haven't left much doubt that I'm working for you?'

'But it could be at anything.'

I said gloomily, 'Not when I turn up on the syndicates' doorsteps.'

'I'd quite understand,' he said, 'if, in view of what I've said, you wanted to . . . er . . .'

So would I, I thought. I would understand that I didn't want my head kicked in. But then what I'd told Jenny was true: one never thought it would happen. And you're always wrong, she'd say.

I sighed. 'You'd better tell me about Mason. Where he went, and who he saw. Anything you can think of.'

'It's practically nothing. He went off in the ordinary way and the next we heard was he'd been attacked. The police couldn't trace where he'd been, and all the syndicate people swore they'd never seen him. The case isn't closed, of course, but after six months it's got no sort of priority.'

We talked it over for a while, and I spent another hour after that writing notes. I left the Jockey Club premises at a quarter to six, to go back to the flat; and I didn't get there.

7

I went home in a taxi and paid it off outside the entrance to the flats, yet not exactly outside, because a dark car was squarely parked there on the double yellow lines, which was a towing-away place.

I scarcely looked at the car, which was my mistake, because as I reached it and turned away towards the entrance its nearside doors opened and spilled out the worst sort of trouble.

Two men in dark clothes grabbed me. One hit me dizzyingly on the head with something hard and the other flung what I later found was a kind of lasso of thick rope over my arms and chest and pulled it tight. They both bundled me into the back of the car where one of them for good measure tied a dark piece of cloth over my dazed half-shut eyes.

'Keys,' a voice said. 'Quick. No one saw us.'

I felt them fumbling in my pockets. There was a clink as they found what they were looking for. I began to come back into focus, so to speak, and to struggle, which was a reflex action but all the same another mistake.

The cloth over my eyes was reinforced by a sickly-smelling wad over my nose and mouth. Anaesthetic fumes made a nonsense of consciousness, and the last thing I though was that if I was going the way of Mason they hadn't wasted any time.

I was aware, first of all, that I was lying on straw.

Straw, as in a stable. Rustling when I tried to move. Hearing, as always, had returned first.

I had been concussed a few times over the years, in racing falls. I thought for a while that I must have come off a horse, though I couldn't remember which, or where I'd been riding.

Funny.

68

The unwelcome news came back with a rush. I had not been racing. I had one hand. I had been abducted in daylight from a London street. I was lying on my back on some straw, blindfolded, with a rope tied tight round my chest, above the elbows, fastening my upper arms against my body. I was lying on the knot. I didn't know why I was there . . . and had no great faith in the future.

Damn, damn, *damn*.

My feet were tethered to some immovable object. It was black dark, even round the edges of the blindfold. I sat up and tried to get some part of me disentangled; a lot of effort and no results.

Ages later there was a tramp of footsteps outside on a gritty surface, and the creak of a wooden door, and sudden light on the sides of my nose.

'Stop trying, Mr Halley,' a voice said. 'You won't undo those knots with one hand.'

I stopped trying. There was no point in going on.

'A spot of overkill,' he said, enjoying himself. 'Ropes *and* anaesthetic *and* blackjack *and* blindfold. Well, I did tell them of course, to be careful, and not to get within hitting distance of that tin arm. A villain I know has very nasty things to say about you hitting him with what he didn't expect.'

I knew the voice. Undertones of Manchester, overtones of all the way up the social ladder. The confidence of power.

Trevor Deansgate.

Last seen on the gallops at Newmarket, looking for Tri-Nitro in the string, and identifying him because he knew the work jockey, which most people didn't. Deansgate, going to George Caspar's for breakfast. Bookmaker Trevor Deansgate had been a question mark, a possibility, someone to be assessed, looked into. Something I would have done, and hadn't done yet.

'Take the blindfold off,' he said. 'I want him to see me.'

Fingers took their time over untying the tight piece of cloth. When it fell away, the light was temporarily dazzling; but the first thing I saw was the double barrel of a shotgun pointing my way.

'Guns too,' I said sourly.

It was a storage barn, not a stable. There was a stack of several tons of straw bales to my left, and on the right, a few yards away, a tractor. My feet were fastened to the trailer bar of a farm roller. The barn had a high roof, with beams; and one meagre electric light, which shone on Trevor Deansgate.

'You're too bloody clever for your own good,' he said. 'You know what they say? If Halley's after you, watch out. He'll sneak up on you when you think he doesn't know you exist, and they'll be slamming the cell doors on you before you've worked it out.'

I didn't say anything. What could one say? Especially sitting trussed up like a fool at the wrong end of a shotgun.

'Well, I'm not waiting for you, do you see?' he said. 'I know how bloody close you are to getting me nicked. Just laying your snares, weren't you? Just waiting for me to fall into your hands, like you've caught so many others.' He stopped and reconsidered what he'd said. 'Into your hand,' he said, 'and that fancy hook.'

He had a way of speaking to me that acknowledged mutual origins, that we'd both come a long way from where we'd started. It was not a matter of accent, but of manner. There was no need for social pretence. The message was raw, and between equals, and would be understood.

He was dressed, as before, in a City suit. Navy; chalk pin-stripe this time; Gucci tie. The well-manicured hands held the shotgun with the expertise of many a weekend on country estates. What did it matter, I thought, if the finger that pulled the trigger was clean and cared for. What did it matter if his shoes were polished . . . I looked at the silly details because I didn't want to think about death.

He stood for a while without speaking: simply watching. I sat without moving, as best I could, and thought about a nice safe job in a stockbroker's office.

'No bloody nerves, have you?' he said. 'None at all.'

I didn't answer.

The other two men were behind me to the right, out of my sight. I could hear their feet as they occasionally shuffled on the straw. Far too far away for me to reach.

I was wearing what I had put on for lunch with Charles. Grey trousers, socks, dark brown shoes; rope extra. Shirt, tie, and a recently bought blazer, quite expensive. What did that matter? If he killed me, Jenny would get the rest. I hadn't changed my will.

Trevor Deansgate switched his attention to the men behind me.

'Now listen,' he said, 'and don't snarl it up. Get these two pieces of rope and tie one to his left arm and one to the right. And watch out for any tricks.'

He lifted the gun a fraction until I could see down the barrels. If he shot from there, I thought, he would hit his chums. It didn't after all look like straight execution. The chums were busy tying bits of rope to both of my wrists.

'Not the left wrist, you stupid bugger,' Trevor Deansgate said. 'That one comes right off. Use your bloody head. Tie it high, above his elbow.'

The chum in question did as he said and pulled the knots tight, and almost casually picked up a stout metal bar, like a crowbar, standing there gripping it as if he thought that somehow I could liberate myself like Superman and still attack him.

Crowbar . . . Nasty shivers of apprehension suddenly crawled all over my scalp. There had been another villain, before, who had known where to hurt me most, the one who had hit my already useless left hand with a poker, and turned it from a ruin into a total loss. I had had regrets enough since, and all sorts of private agonies, but I hadn't realized, until that sickening moment, how much I valued what remained. The muscles that worked the electrodes,

70

they at least gave me the semblance of a working hand. If they were injured again I wouldn't have even that. As for the elbow itself . . . if he wanted to put me out of effective action for a long time, he had only to use that crowbar.

'You don't like that, do you, Mr Halley?' Trevor Deansgate said.

I turned my head back to him. His voice and face were suddenly full of a mixture of triumph and satisfaction, and what seemed like relief.

I said nothing.

'You're sweating,' he said.

He had another order for the chums. 'Untie that rope round his chest. And do it carefully. Hold on to the ropes on his arms.'

They untied the knot, and pulled the constricting rope away from round my chest. It didn't make much difference to my chances of escape. They were wildly exaggerating my ability in a fight.

'Lie down,' he said to me; and when I didn't at once comply, he said 'Push him down,' to the chums. One way or another, I ended on my back.

'I don't want to kill you,' he said. 'I could dump your body somewhere, but there would be too many questions. I can't risk it. But if I don't kill you, I've got to shut you up. Once and for all. Permanently.'

Short of killing me I didn't see how he could do it; and I was stupid.

'Pull his arm sideways, away from his body,' he said.

The pull on my left arm had a man's weight behind it and was stronger than I was. I rolled my head that way and tried not to beg, not to weep.

'Not that one, you bloody fool,' Trevor Deansgate said. 'The other one. The right one. Pull it out, to this side.'

The chum on my right used all his strength on the rope and hauled so that my arm finished straight out sideways, at right angles to my body, palm upwards.

Trevor Deansgate stepped towards me and lowered the gun until the black holes of the barrel were pointing straight at my stretched right wrist. Then he carefully lowered the barrel another inch, making direct contact on my skin, pressing down against the straw-covered floor. I could feel the metal rims hard across the bones and nerves and sinews. Across the bridge to a healthy hand.

I heard the click as he cocked the firing mechanism. One blast from a twelve bore would take off most of the arm.

A dizzy wave of faintness drenched all my limbs with sweat.

Whatever anyone said, I intimately knew about fear. Not fear of any horse, or of racing, or of falling, or of ordinary physical pain. But of humiliation and rejection and helplessness and failure . . . all of those.

All the fear I'd ever felt in all my life was as nothing compared with the liquifying, mind-shattering disintegration of that appalling minute. It broke me in pieces. Swamped me. Brought me down to a morass of terror, to a whimper in the soul. And instinctively, hopelessly, I tried not to let it show.

He watched motionlessly through uncountable intensifying silent seconds. Making me wait. Making it worse.

At length he took a deep breath and said, 'As you see, I could shoot off your hand. Nothing easier. But I'm probably not going to. Not today.' He paused. 'Are you listening?'

I nodded the merest fraction. My eyes were full of gun.

His voice came quietly, seriously, giving weight to every sentence. 'You can give me your assurance that you'll back off. You'll do nothing more which is directed against me, in any way, ever. You'll go to France tomorrow morning, and you'll stay there until after the Guineas. After that, you can do what you like. But if you break your assurance ... well you're easy to find. I'll find you, and I'll blow your right hand off. I mean it, and you'd better believe it. Some time or other. You'd never escape it. Do you understand?'

I nodded, as before. I could feel the gun as if it were hot. Don't let him, I thought. Dear God, don't let him.

'Give me your assurance. Say it.'

I swallowed painfully. Dredged up a voice. Low and hoarse. 'I give it.'

'You'll back off?'

'Yes.'

'You'll not come after me again, ever.'

'No.'

'You'll go to France and stay there until after the Guineas.'

'Yes.'

Another silence lengthened for what seemed a hundred years, while I stared beyond my undamaged wrist to the dark side of the moon.

He took the gun away, in the end. Broke it open. Removed the cartridges. I felt physically, almost uncontrollably, sick.

He knelt on his pin-striped knees beside me and looked closely at whatever defence I could put into an unmoving face and expressionless eyes. I could feel the treacherous sweat trickling down my cheek. He nodded, with grim satisfaction.

'I knew you couldn't face that. Not the other one as well. No one could. There's no need to kill you.'

He stood up again and stretched his body, as if relaxing a wound-up inner tension. Then he put his hands into various pockets, and produced things.

'Here are your keys. Your passport. Your cheque book. Credit cards.' He put them on a straw bale. To his chums, he said, 'Untie him, and drive him to the airport. To Heathrow.'

8

I flew to Paris and stayed right there where I landed, in an airport hotel, with no impetus or heart to go further. I stayed for six days, not leaving my room, spending most of the time by the window, watching the aeroplanes come and go.

I felt stunned. I felt ill. Disorientated and overthrown and severed from my own roots. Crushed into an abject state of mental misery, knowing that this time I really had run away.

It was easy to convince myself that logically I had had no choice but to give Deansgate his assurance, when he asked for it. If I hadn't, he would have killed me anyway. I could tell myself, as I continually did, that sticking to his instructions had merely been common sense: but the fact remained that when the chums decanted me at Heathrow they had driven off at once, and it had been of my own free will that I'd bought my ticket, waited in the departure lounge, and walked to the aircraft.

There had been no one there with guns to make me do it. Only the fact that as Deansgate had truly said, I couldn't face losing the other one. I couldn't face even the risk of it. The thought of it, like a conditioned response, brought out the sweat.

As the days passed, the feeling I had had of disintegration seemed not to fade but to deepen.

The automatic part of me still went on working: walking, talking, ordering coffee, going to the bathroom. In the part that mattered there was turmoil and anguish and a feeling that my whole self had been literally smashed in those few cataclysmic minutes on the straw.

Part of the trouble was that I knew my weaknesses too well. Knew that if I hadn't had so much pride it wouldn't have destroyed me so much to have lost it.

To have been forced to realize that my basic view of myself had been an illusion was proving a psychic upheaval like an earthquake, and perhaps it wasn't surprising that I felt I had, I really had, come to pieces.

I didn't know that I could face that, either.

I wished I could sleep properly, and get some peace.

When Wednesday came I thought of Newmarket and of all the brave hopes for the Guineas.

Thought of George Caspar, taking Tri-Nitro to the test, producing him proudly in peak condition and swearing to himself that this time nothing could go wrong. Thought of Rosemary, jangling with nerves, willing the horse to win and knowing it wouldn't. Thought of Trevor Deansgate, unsuspected, moving like a mole to vandalize, somehow, the best colt in the kingdom.

I could have stopped him, if I'd tried.

Wednesday for me was the worst day of all, the day I learned about despair and desolation and guilt.

On the sixth day, Thursday morning, I went down to the lobby and bought an English newspaper.

They had run the Two Thousand Guineas, as scheduled.

Tri-Nitro had started hot favourite at even money: and he had finished last.

I paid my bill and went to the airport. There were aeroplanes to everywhere, to escape in. The urge to escape was very strong. But wherever one went, one took oneself along. From oneself there was no escape. Wherever I went, in the end I would have to go back.

If I went back in my split-apart state I'd have to live all the time on two levels. I'd have to behave in the old way, which everyone would expect. Have to think and drive and talk and get on with life. Going back meant all that. It also meant doing all that, and proving to myself that I could do it, when I wasn't the same inside.

I thought that what I had lost might be worse than a hand. For a hand there were substitutes which could grip and look passable. But if the core of oneself had crumbled, how could one manage at all?

If I went back, I would have to try.

If I couldn't try, why go back?

It took me a long, lonely time to buy a ticket to Heathrow.

I landed at midday, made a brief telephone call to the Cavendish, to ask them to apologize to the Admiral because I couldn't keep our date, and took a taxi home.

Everything, in the lobby, on the stairs, and along the landing looking the same and yet completely different. It was I who was different. I put the key in the lock and turned it, and went into the flat.

I had expected it to be empty but before I'd even shut the door I heard a rustle in the sitting room, and then Chico's voice. 'Is that you, Admiral?'

I simply didn't answer. In a brief moment his head appeared, questioning, and after that, his whole self.

'About time too,' he said. He looked, on the whole, relieved to see me.

'I sent you a telegram.'

'Oh sure. I've got it here, propped on the shelf. *Leave Newmarket and go home stop shall be away for a few days will telephone.* What sort of telegram's that? Sent from Heathrow, early Friday. You been on holiday?'

'Yeah.'

I walked past him, into the sitting room. In there, it didn't look at all the same. There were files and papers everywhere, on every surface, with coffee-marked cups and saucers holding them down.

'You went away without the charger,' Chico said. 'You never do that, even overnight. The spare batteries are all here. You haven't been able to move that hand for six days.'

'Let's have some coffee.'

'You didn't take any clothes, or your razor.'

'I stayed in a hotel. They had throwaway razors, if you asked. What's all this mess?'

'The polish letters.'

'What?'

'You know. The polish letters. Your wife's spot of trouble.'

'Oh . . .'

I stared at it blankly.

'Look,' Chico said. 'Cheese on toast? I'm starving.'

'That would be nice.' It was unreal. It was all unreal.

He went into the kitchen and started banging about. I took the dead battery out of my arm and put in a charged one. The fingers opened and closed, like old times. I had missed them more than I would have imagined.

Chico brought the cheese on toast. He ate his, and I looked at mine. I'd better eat it, I thought, and didn't have the energy. There was the sound of the door of the flat being opened with a key, and after that, my father-in-law's voice from the hall.

'He didn't turn up at the Cavendish, but he did at least leave a message.' He came into the room from behind where I sat and saw Chico nodding his head in my direction.

'He's back,' Chico said. 'The boy himself.'

'Hallo, Charles,' I said.

He took a long slow look. Very controlled, very civilized. 'We have, you know, been worried.' It was a reproach.

'I'm sorry.'

'Where have you been?' he said.

I found I couldn't tell him. If I told him where, I would have to tell him why, and I shrank from why. I just didn't say anything at all.

Chico gave him a cheerful grin. 'Sid's got a bad attack of the brick walls.' He looked at his watch. 'Seeing that you're here, Admiral, I might as well get along and teach the little bleeders at the Comprehensive how to throw their grannies over their shoulders. And, Sid, before I go, there's about fifty messages on the phone pad. There's two new insurance investigations waiting to be done, and a guard job. Lucas Wainwright wants you, he's rung four times. And Rosemary Caspar has been screeching fit to blast the eardrums. It's all there, written down. See you, then. I'll come back here later.'

I almost asked him not to, but he'd gone.

'You've lost weight,' Charles said.

It wasn't surprising. I looked again at the toasted cheese and decided that coming back also had to include things like eating.

'Want some?' I said.

He eyed the congealing square. 'No thank you.'

Nor did I. I pushed it away. Sat and stared into space.

'What's happened to you?' he said.

'Nothing.'

'Last week you came into the Cavendish like a spring,' he said. 'Bursting with life. Eyes actually sparkling. And now look at you.'

'Well, don't,' I said. 'Don't look at me. How are you doing with the letters?'

'Sid . . .'

'Admiral.' I stood up restlessly, to escape his probing gaze. 'Leave me alone.'

He paused, considering, then said, 'You've been speculating in commodities, recently. Have you lost your money, is that it?'

I was surprised almost to the point of amusement.

'No,' I said.

He said, 'You went dead like this before, when you lost your career and my daughter. So what have you lost this time, if it isn't money? What could be as bad . . . or worse?'

I knew the answer. I'd learned it in Paris, in torment and shame. My whole mind formed the word *courage* with such violent intensity that I was afraid it would leap out of its own accord from my brain to his.

He showed no sign of receiving it. He was still waiting for a reply.

I swallowed. 'Six days,' I said neutrally. 'I've lost six days. Let's get on with tracing Nicholas Ashe.'

He shook his head in disapproval and frustration, but began to explain what he'd been doing.

'This thick pile is from people with names beginning with M. I've put them into strictly alphabetical order, and typed out a list. It seemed to me that we might get results from one letter only . . . are you paying attention?'

'Yes.'

'I took the list to Christie's and Sotheby's, as you suggested, and persuaded them to help. But the M section of their catalogue mailing list is not the same as this one. And I found that there may be difficulties with this matching, as so many envelopes are addressed nowadays by computers.'

'You've worked hard,' I said.

'Chico and I have been sitting here in shifts, answering your telephone, and trying to find out where you'd gone. Your car was still here, in the garage, and Chico said you would never have gone anywhere of your own accord without the battery charger for your arm.'

'Well . . . I did.'

'Sid . . .'

'No,' I said. 'What we need now is a list of periodicals and magazines dealing with antique furniture. We'll try those first with the M people.'

'It's an awfully big project,' Charles said doubtfully. 'And even if we do find it, what then? I mean, as the man at Christie's pointed out, even if we find whose mailing list was being used, where does it get us? The firm or magazine wouldn't be able to tell us which of the many people who had access to the list was Nicholas Ashe, particularly as he is almost certain not to have used that name if he had any dealings with them.'

'Mm,' I said. 'But there's a chance he's started operating again somewhere else, and is still using the same list. He took it with him, when he went. If we can find out whose list it is, we might go and call on some people who are on it, whose names start with A to K, and P to Z, and find out if they've received any of those begging letters recently. Because if they have, the letters will have that address on, to which the money is to be sent. And there, at that address, we might find Mr Ashe.'

Charles put his mouth into the shape of a whistle, but what came out was more like a sigh.

'You've come back with your brains intact, anyway,' he said.

Oh God, I thought, I'm making myself think to shut out the abyss. I'm in splinters . . . I'm never going to be right again. The analytical reasoning part of my mind might be marching straight on, but what had to be called the soul was sick and dying.

'And there's the polish,' I said. I still had in my pocket the paper he'd given me the week before. I took it out and put it on the table. 'If the idea of special polish is closely geared to the mailing list, then to get maximum results the polish is necessary. There can't be many private individuals ordering so much wax in unprinted tins packed in little white boxes. We could ask the polish firm to let us know if another lot is ordered. It's just faintly possible that Ashe will use the same firm again, even if not at once. He ought to see the danger . . . but he might be a fool.'

I turned away wearily. Thought about whisky. Went over and poured myself a large one.

'Drinking heavily, are you?' Charles said from behind me, in his most offensive drawl.

I shut my teeth hard, and said, 'No.' Apart from coffee and water, it was my first drink for a week.

'Your first alcoholic black-out, was it, these last few days?'

I left the glass untouched on the drinks tray and turned round. His eyes were at their coldest, as unkind as in the days when we'd first met.

'Don't be so bloody stupid,' I said.

He lifted his chin a fraction. 'A spark,' he said sarcastically. 'Still got your pride, I see.'

I compressed my lips and turned my back on him, and drank a lot of the scotch. After a bit I deliberately loosened a few tensed-up muscles, and said, 'You won't find out that way. I know you too well. You use insults as a lever, to sting people into opening up. You've done it to me in the past. But not this time.'

'If I find the right sting,' he said, 'I'll use it.'

'Do you want a drink?' I said.

'Since you ask, yes.'

We sat opposite each other in armchairs in unchanged companionship, and I thought vaguely of this and that and shied away from the crucifying bits.

'You know,' I said. 'We don't have to go trailing that mailing list around to see whose it is. All we do is ask the people themselves. Those . . .' I nodded towards the M stack. 'We just ask some of them what mailing lists they themselves are on. We'd only need to ask a few . . . the common denominator would be certain to turn up.'

When Charles had gone home to Aynsford I wandered aimlessly round the flat, tie off and in shirtsleeves, trying to be sensible. I told myself that nothing much had happened, only that Trevor Deansgate had used a lot of horrible threats to get me to stop doing something that I hadn't yet started. But I couldn't dodge the guilt. Once he'd revealed himself, once I knew he would do *something*, I could have stopped him, and I hadn't.

If he hadn't got me so effectively out of Newmarket I would very likely have still been prodding unproductively away, unsure even if there was anything to discover, right up to the moment in the Guineas when Tri-Nitro tottered in last. But I would also be up there now, I thought, certain and inquisitive; and because of his threat, I wasn't.

I could call my absence prudence, commonsense, the only possible course in the circumstances. I could rationalize and excuse. I could say I wouldn't have been doing anything that wasn't already being done by the Jockey Club. I came back, all the time, to the swingeing truth, that I wasn't there now because I was afraid to be.

Chico came back from his judo class and set to again to find out where I'd been; and for the same reasons I didn't tell him, even though I knew he wouldn't despise me as I despised myself.

'All right,' he said finally. 'You just keep it all bottled up and see where it gets you. Wherever you've been, it was bad. You've only got to look at you. It's not going to do you any good to shut it all up inside.'

Shutting it all up inside, however, was a lifelong habit, a defence learned in childhood, a wall against the world, impossible to change.

I raised at least half a smile. 'You setting up in Harley Street?'

'That's better,' he said. 'You missed all the fun, did you know? Tri-Nitro got stuffed after all in the Guineas yesterday, and they're turning George Caspar's yard inside out. It's all here, somewhere, in the *Sporting Life*. The Admiral brought it. Have you read it?'

I shook my head.

'Our Rosemary, she wasn't bonkers after all, was she? How do you think they managed it?'

'They?' I said.

'Whoever did it.'

'I don't know.'

'I went along to see the gallop on Saturday morning,' he said. 'Yeah, yeah, I know you sent the telegram about leaving, but I'd got a real little dolly lined up for a bit of the other on Friday night, so I stayed. One more night wasn't going to make any difference, and besides, she was George Caspar's typist.'

'She was . . .'

'Does the typing. Rides the horses sometimes. Into everything, she is, and talkative with it.'

The new scared Sid Halley didn't even want to listen.

'There was a right old rumpus all day Wednesday in George Caspar's house,' Chico said. 'It started at breakfast when that Inky Poole turned up and said Sid Halley had been asking questions that he, Inky Poole, didn't like.'

He paused for effect. I simply stared.

'Are you listening?' he said.

'Yes.'

'You got your stone face act on again.'

'Sorry.'

'Then Brothersmith the vet turned up and heard Inky Poole letting off, and he said funny, Sid Halley had been around him asking questions too. About bad hearts, he said. Same horses as Inky Poole was talking about. Bethesda, Gleaner and Zingaloo. And how was Tri-Nitro's heart, for good measure. My little dolly typist said you could've heard George Caspar blowing up all the way to Cambridge. He's really touchy about those horses.'

Trevor Deansgate, I thought coldly, had been at George Caspar's for breakfast, and had heard every word.

'Of course,' Chico said, 'some time later they checked the studs, Garvey's and Thrace's, and found you'd been there too. My dolly says your name is mud.'

I rubbed my hand over my face. 'Does your dolly know you were working with me?'

'Do us a favour. Of course not.'

'Did she say anything else?' What the hell am I asking for, I thought.

'Yeah. Well, she said Rosemary got on to George Caspar to change all the routine for the Saturday morning gallop, nagged him all day Thursday and all day Friday and George Caspar was climbing the walls. And at the yard they had so much security they were tripping over their own alarm bells.' He paused for breath. 'After that she didn't say much else on account of three martinis and time for tickle.'

I sat on the arm of the sofa and stared at the carpet.

'Next morning,' Chico said, 'I watched the gallop, like I said. Your photos came in very handy. Hundreds of ruddy horses . . . Someone told me which were Caspar's, and there was Inky Poole, scowling like in the pictures, so I just zeroed in on him and hung about. There was a lot of fuss when it came to Tri-Nitro. They took the saddle off and put a little one on, and Inky Poole rode on that.'

'It was Inky Poole, then, who rode Tri-Nitro, same as usual?'

'They looked just like your pictures,' Chico said. 'Can't swear to it more than that.'

I stared some more at the carpet.

'So what do we do next?' he said.

'Nothing . . . We give Rosemary her money back and draw a line.'

'But hey,' Chico said in protest. 'Someone got at the horse. You know they did.'

'Not our business, any more.'

I wished that he, too, would stop looking at me. I felt a distinct need to crawl into a hole and hide.

The doorbell rang with the long peal of a determined thumb. 'We're out,' I said; but Chico went and answered it.

Rosemary Caspar swept past him, through the hall and into the sitting room, advancing in the old fawn raincoat and a fulminating rage. No scarf, no false curls, and no loving kindness.

'So there you are,' she said forcefully. 'I knew you'd be here, skulking out of sight. You friend kept telling me when I telephoned that you weren't here, but I knew he was lying.'

'I wasn't here,' I said. As well try damming the St Lawrence with a twig.

'You weren't where I paid you to be, which was up in Newmarket. And I told you from the beginning that George wasn't to find out you were asking questions, and he did, and we've been having one God-awful bloody row ever since, and now Tri-Nitro has disgraced us unbearably and it's all your bloody fault.'

Chico raised his eyebrows comically. 'Sid didn't ride it . . . or train it.'

She glared at him with transferred hatred. 'And he didn't keep him safe, either.'

'Er, no,' Chico said. 'Granted.'

'As for you,' she said, swinging back to me. 'You're a useless bloody humbug. It's all rubbish, this detecting. Why don't you grow up and stop playing games? All you did was stir up trouble, and I want my money back.'

'Will a cheque do?' I said.

'You're not arguing, then?'

'No,' I said.

'Do you mean you admit that you failed?'

After a small pause, I said, 'Yes.'

'Oh.' She sounded as if I had unexpectedly deprived her of a good deal of what she had come to say, but while I wrote out a cheque for her she went on complaining sharply enough.

'All your ideas about changing the routine, they were useless. I've been on and on at George about security and taking care, and he says he couldn't have done any more, no one could, and he's in absolute despair – and I'd hoped, I'd really hoped, what a laugh, that somehow or other you would work a miracle, and that Tri-Nitro would win, because I was so sure, so sure . . . and I was right.'

I finished writing. 'Why were you always so sure?' I said.

'I don't know. I just *knew*. I've been afraid of it for weeks . . . otherwise I would not have been so desperate as to try you, in the first place. And I might as well not have bothered . . . it's caused so much trouble, and I can't bear it. I can't bear it. Yesterday was terrible. He should have won . . . I knew he wouldn't. I felt ill. I still feel ill.'

She was trembling again. The pain in her face was acute. So many hopes, so much work had gone into Tri-Nitro, such anxiety and such care. Winning races was to a trainer like a film to a film maker. If you got it right, they applauded: wrong, and they booed. And either way you'd poured your soul into it, and your thoughts and your skill and weeks of worry. I understood what the lost race meant to George, and Rosemary equally, because she cared so much.

'Rosemary . . .' I said, in useless sympathy.

'It's pointless Brothersmith saying he must have had an infection,' she said. 'He's always saying things like that. He's so wet, I can't stand him, always looking over his shoulder, I've never liked him. And it was his job anyway to check Tri-Nitro and he did, over and over, and there was nothing wrong with him, nothing. He went down to the post looking beautiful, and in the parade ring before that, there was nothing wrong, nothing. And then in the race, he just went backwards, and he finished . . . he came back . . . exhausted.' There was a glitter of tears for a moment, but she visibly willed them from overwhelming her.

'They've done dope tests, I suppose,' Chico said.

It angered her again. 'Dope tests! Of course they have. What do you expect? Blood tests, urine tests, saliva tests, dozens of bloody tests. They gave George duplicate samples, and that's why we're down here, he's trying to fix up with some private lab . . . but they won't be positive. It will be like before . . . absolutely nothing.'

I tore out the cheque and gave it to her, and she glanced at it blindly.

'I wish I'd never come here. My God, I wish I hadn't. You're only a jockey. I should have known better. I don't want to talk to you again. Don't talk to me at the races, do you understand.'

I nodded. I did understand. She turned abruptly to go away. 'And for God's sake don't speak to George, either.' She went alone out of the room, and out of the flat, and slammed the door.

Chico clicked his tongue and shrugged. 'You can't win them all,' he said. 'What could you do that her husband couldn't, not to mention a private police force and half a dozen guard dogs?' He was excusing me, and we both knew it.

I didn't answer.

'Sid?'

'I don't know that I'm going on with it,' I said. 'This sort of job.'

'You don't want to take any notice of what she said,' he protested. 'You can't give it up. You're too good at it. Look at the awful messes you've put right. Just because of one that's gone wrong . . .'

I stared hollowly at a lot of unseen things.

'You're a big boy now,' he said. And he was seven years younger than I, near enough. 'You want to cry on Daddy's shoulder?' He paused. 'Look, Sid mate, you've got to snap out of it. Whatever's happened it can't be as bad as when that horse sliced your hand up, nothing could. This is no time to die inside, we've got about five other jobs lined up. The insurance, and the guard job, and Lucas Wainwright's syndicates . . .'

'No,' I said. I felt leaden and useless. 'Not now, honestly, Chico.'

I got up and went into the bedroom. Shut the door. Went purposelessly to the window and looked out at the scenery of roofs and chimney pots, glistening in the beginnings of rain. The pots were still there, though the chimneys underneath were blocked off and the fires long dead. I felt at one with the chimney pots. When fires went out, one froze.

The door opened.

'Sid,' Chico said.

I said resignedly, 'Remind me to put a lock on that door.'

'You've got another visitor.'

'Tell him to go away.'

'It's a girl. Louise somebody.'

I rubbed my hand over my face and head and down to the back of my neck. Eased the muscles. Turned from the window.

'Louise McInnes?'

'That's right.'

'She shares the flat with Jenny,' I said.

'Oh, that one. Well then, Sid, if that's all for today I'll be off. And . . . er . . . be here tomorrow, won't you?'

'Yeah.'

He nodded. We left everything else unsaid. The amusement, mockery, friendship and stifled anxiety were all there in his face and his voice . . . Maybe he read the same in mine. At any rate he gave me a widening grin as he departed, and I went into the sitting room thinking that some debts couldn't be paid.

Louise was standing in the middle of things, looking around her in the way I had, in Jenny's flat. Through her eyes I saw my own room afresh: its irregular shape, high-ceilinged, not modern; and the tan leather sofa, the table with drinks by the window, the shelves with books, the prints framed and hung, and on the door, leaning against the wall, the big painting of racing horses which I'd somehow never bothered to hang up. There were coffee cups and glasses scattered about, and full ashtrays, and the piles of letters on the coffee table and everywhere else.

Louise herself looked different: the full production, not the Sunday morning tumble out of bed. A brown velvet jacket, a blazing white sweater, a soft mottled brown skirt with a wide leather belt round an untroubled waist. Fair hair washed and shining, rose petal make-up on the English rose skin. A detachment in the eyes which said that all this honey was not chiefly there for the attracting of bees.

'Mr Halley.'

'You could try Sid,' I said. 'You know me quite well, by proxy.'

Her smile reached halfway. 'Sid.'

'Louise.'

'Jenny says Sid is a plumber's mate's sort of name.'

'Very good people, plumbers' mates.'

'Did you know,' she said, looking away and continuing the visual tour of inspection, 'that in Arabic "Sid" means "lord"?'

'No, I didn't.'

'Well, it does.'

'You could tell Jenny,' I said.

Her gaze came back fast to my face. 'She gets to you, doesn't she?'

I smiled. 'Like some coffee? Or a drink?'

'Tea?'

'Sure.'

She came into the kitchen with me and watched me make it, and made no funny remarks about bionic hands, which was a nice change from most new acquaintances, who tended to be fascinated, and to say so, at length. Instead she looked around with inoffensive curiosity, and finally fastened her attention on the calendar which hung from the knob on the pine cupboard door. Photographs of horses, a Christmas hand-out from a bookmaking firm. She flipped up the pages, looking at the pictures of the future months, and stopped at December, where a horse and jockey jumping the Chair at Aintree were silhouetted spectacularly against the sky.

'That's good,' she said, and then, in surprise, reading the caption, 'That's *you*.'

'He's a good photographer.'

'Did you win that race?'

'Yes,' I said mildly. 'Do you take sugar?'

'No thanks.' She let the pages fall back. 'How odd to find oneself on a calendar.'

To me, it wasn't odd. How odd, I thought, to have seen one's picture in print so much that one scarcely noticed.

I carried the tray into the sitting room and put it on top of the letters on the coffee table. 'Sit down,' I said, and we sat.

'All these,' I said, nodding to them, 'are the letters which came with the cheques for the wax.'

She looked doubtful. 'Are they of any use?'

'I hope so,' I said, and explained about the mailing list.

'Good heavens.' She hesitated, 'Well, perhaps you won't need what I brought.' She picked up her brown leather handbag, and opened it. 'I didn't

83

come all this way specially,' she said. 'I've an aunt near here whom I visit. Anyway, I thought you might like to have this, as I was here, near your flat.'

She pulled out a paperback book. She could have posted it, I thought: but I was quite glad she hadn't.

'I was trying to put a bit of order into the chaos in my bedroom,' she said. 'I've a lot of books. They tend to pile up.'

I didn't tell her I'd seen them. 'Books do,' I said.

'Well, this was among them. It's Nicky's.'

She gave me the paperback. I glanced at the cover and put it down, in order to pour out the tea. *Navigation for Beginners*. I handed her the cup and saucer. 'Was he interested in navigation?'

'I've no idea. But I was. I borrowed it out of his room. I don't think he even knew I'd borrowed it. He had a box with some things in – like a tuck box that boys take to public school – and one day when I went into his room, the things were all on the chest of drawers, as if he was tidying. Anyway, he was out, and I borrowed the book . . . He wouldn't have minded, he was terribly easy-going . . . and I suppose I put it down in my room, and put something else on top, and just forgot it.'

'Did you read it?' I said.

'No. Never got round to it. It was weeks ago.'

I picked up the book and opened it. On the fly-leaf someone had written 'John Viking' in a firm legible signature in black felt-tip.

'I don't know,' Louise said, anticipating my question, 'whether that is Nicky's writing or not.'

'Does Jenny know?'

'She hasn't seen this. She's staying with Toby in Yorkshire.'

Jenny with Toby. Jenny with Ashe. For God's sake, I thought, what do you expect? She's gone, she's gone, she's not yours, you're divorced. And I hadn't been alone, not entirely.

'You look very tired,' Louise said doubtfully.

I was disconcerted. 'Of course not.' I turned the pages, letting them flick over from under my thumb. It was, as it promised to be, a book about navigation, sea and air, with line drawings and diagrams. Dead reckoning, sextants, magnetism and drift. Nothing of any note except a single line of letters and figures, written with the same black ink, on the inside of the back cover.

$$\text{Lift} = 22.024 \times V \times P \left(\frac{1}{T_1} - \frac{1}{T_2} \right)$$

I handed it over to Louise.

'Does this mean anything to you? Charles said you've a degree in mathematics.'

She frowned at it faintly. 'Nicky needed a calculator for two plus two.'

He had done all right at two plus ten thousand, I thought.

'Um,' she said. 'Lift equals 22.024 times volume times pressure, times . . . I should think this is something to do with temperature change. Not my subject, really. This is physics.'

'Something to do with navigation?' I said.

She concentrated. I watched the way her face grew taut while she did the internal scan. A fast brain, I thought, under the pretty hair.

'It's funny,' she said finally, 'but I think it's just possibly something to do with how much you can lift with a gas bag.'

'Airship?' I said, thinking.

'It depends what 22.024 is,' she said. 'That's a constant. Which means,' she added, 'it is special to whatever this equation is all about.'

'I'm better at what's likely to win the three-thirty.'

She looked at her watch. 'You're three hours too late.'

'It'll come round again tomorrow.'

She relaxed into the armchair, handing back the book. 'I don't suppose it will help,' she said, 'but you seemed to want anything of Nicky's.'

'It might help a lot. You never know.'

'But how?'

'It's John Viking's book. John Viking might know Nicky Ashe.'

'But . . . you don't know John Viking.'

'No,' I said, 'but he knows gas-bags. And I know someone who knows gas-bags. And I bet gas-bags are a small world, like racing.'

She looked at the heaps of letters, and then at the book. She said slowly, 'I guess you'll find him, one way or another.'

I looked away from her, and at nothing in particular.

'Jenny says you never give up.'

I smiled faintly. 'Her exact words?'

'No.' I felt her amusement. 'Obstinate, selfish, and determined to get his own way.'

'Not far off,' I tapped the book. 'Can I keep this?'

'Of course.'

'Thanks.'

We looked at each other as people do, especially if they're youngish and male and female, and sitting in a quiet flat at the end of an April day.

She read my expression and answered the unspoken thought. 'Some other time,' she said drily.

'How long will you be staying with Jenny?'

'Would that matter to you?' she said.

'Mm.'

'She says you're as hard as flint. She says steel's a pushover, beside you.'

I thought of terror and misery and self-loathing. I shook my head.

'What I see,' she said slowly, 'is a man who looks ill being polite to an unwanted visitor.'

'You're wanted,' I said. 'And I'm fine.'

She stood up, however, and I also, after her.

'I hope, I said, 'that you're fond of your aunt.'

'Devoted.'

She gave me a cool, half ironic smile in which there was also surprise. 'Goodbye . . . Sid.'

'Goodbye, Louise.'

When she'd gone I switched on a table light or two against the slow dusk, and poured a whisky, and looked at a pale bunch of sausages in the fridge and didn't cook them.

No one else would come, I thought. They had all in their way held off the shadows, particularly Louise. No one else real would come, but he would be with me, as he'd been in Paris . . . Trevor Deansgate. Inescapable. Reminding me inexorably of what I would rather forget.

After a while I stepped out of trousers and shirt and put on a short blue bathrobe, and took off the arm. It was one of the times when taking it off really hurt. It didn't seem to matter, after the rest.

I went back to the sitting room to do something about the clutter, but there was simply too much to bother with, so I stood looking at it, and held my weaker upper arm with my strong, whole, agile right hand, as I often did, for support, and I wondered which crippled one worse, amputation without or within.

Humiliation and rejection and helplessness and failure . . .

After all these years I would *not*, I thought wretchedly, I would damned well *not* be defeated by fear.

9

Lucas Wainwright telephoned the next morning while I was stacking cups in the dishwasher.

'Any progress?' he said, sounding very Commander-ish.

'I'm afraid,' I said regretfully, 'that I've lost all those notes. I'll have to do them again.'

'For heaven's sake.' He wasn't pleased. I didn't tell him that I'd lost the notes on account of being bashed on the head and dropping the large brown envelope that contained them in the gutter. 'Come right away, then. Eddy won't be in until this afternoon.'

Slowly, absentmindedly, I finished tidying up, while I thought about Lucas Wainwright, and what he could do for me, if he would. Then I sat at the table and wrote down what I wanted. Then I looked at what I'd written, and at my fingers holding the pen, and shivered. Then I folded the paper and put it in my pocket, and went to Portman Square deciding not to give it to Lucas, after all.

He had the files ready in his office, and I sat at the same table as before and re-copied all I needed.

'You won't let it drag on much longer, will you, Sid?'

'Full attention,' I said. 'Starting tomorrow. I'll go to Kent tomorrow afternoon.'

'Good.' He stood up as I put the new notes into a fresh envelope and waited for me to go, not through impatience with me particularly, but because he was that sort of man. Brisk. One task finished, get on with the next, don't hang about.

I hesitated cravenly and found myself speaking before I had consciously decided whether to or not. 'Commander. Do you remember that you said you might pay me for this job not with money, but with help, if I should want it?'

I got a reasonable smile and a postponement of the goodbyes.

'Of course I remember. You haven't done the job yet. What help?'

'Er . . . it's nothing much. Very little.' I took the paper out and handed it to him. Waited while he read the brief contents. Felt as if I had planted a landmine and would presently step on it.

'I don't see why not,' he said. 'If that's what you want. But are you on to something that we should know about?'

I gestured to the paper, 'You'll know about it as soon as I do, if you do that.' It wasn't a satisfactory answer, but he didn't press it. 'The only thing I beg of you, though, is that you won't mention my name at all. Don't say it was my idea, not to *anyone*. I . . . er . . . you might get me killed, Commander, and I'm not being funny.'

He looked from me to the paper and back again, and frowned. 'This doesn't look like a killing matter, Sid.'

'You never know what is until you're dead.'

He smiled. 'All right. I'll write the letter as from the Jockey Club, and I'll take you seriously about the death risk. Will that do?'

'It will indeed.'

We shook hands, and I left his office carrying the brown envelope, and at the Portman Square entrance, going out, I met Eddy Keith coming in. We both paused, as one does. I hoped he couldn't see the dismay in my face at his early return, or guess that I was perhaps carrying the seeds of his downfall.

'Eddy,' I said, smiling and feeling a traitor.

'Hello, Sid,' he said cheerfully, twinkling at me from above rounded cheeks. 'What are you doing here?' A good-natured normal inquiry. No suspicions. No tremor.

'Looking for crumbs,' I said.

He chuckled fatly. 'From what I hear, it's us picking up yours. Have us all out of work, you will, soon.'

'Not a chance.'

'Don't step on our toes, Sid.'

The smile was still there, the voice devoid of threat. The fuzzy hair, the big moustache, the big broad fleshy face still exuded good will: but the arctic had briefly come and gone in his eyes, and I was in no doubt that I'd received a serious warning off.

'Never, Eddy,' I said insincerely.

'See you, fella,' he said, preparing to go indoors, nodding, smiling widely, and giving me the usual hearty buffet on the shoulder. 'Take care.'

'You too, Eddy,' I said to his departing back: and under my breath, again, in a sort of sorrow, 'You too.'

I carried the notes safely back to the flat, and thought a bit, and telephoned to my man in gas-bags.

He said hallo and great to hear from you and how about a jar sometime, and no, he had never heard of anyone called John Viking. I read out the equation and asked if it meant anything to him, and he laughed and said it sounded like a formula for taking a hot air balloon to the moon.

'Thanks very much,' I said sarcastically.

'No, seriously, Sid. It's a calculation for maximum height. Try a balloonist. They're always after records . . . the highest, the furthest, that sort of thing.'

I asked if he knew any balloonists but he said sorry, no he didn't, he was only into airships, and we disconnected with another vague resolution to meet somewhere, sometime, one of these days. Idly, and certain it was useless, I leafed through the telephone directory, and there, incredibly, the words stood out bold and clear: The Hot Air Balloon Company, offices in London, number provided.

I got through. A pleasant male voice at the other end said that of course he knew John Viking, everyone in ballooning knew John Viking, he was a madman of the first order.

Madman?

John Viking, the voice explained, took risks which no sensible balloonist would dream of. If I wanted to talk to him, the voice said, I would undoubtedly find him at the balloon race on Monday afternoon.

Where was the balloon race on Monday afternoon?

Horse show, balloon race, swings and roundabouts, you name it, all part of the May Day holiday junketings at Highalane Park in Wiltshire. John Viking would be there. Sure to be.

I thanked the voice for his help and rang off, reflecting that I had forgotten about the May Day holiday. National holidays had always been work days for me, as for everyone in racing; providing the entertainment for the public's leisure. I tended not to notice them come and go.

Chico arrived with fish-and-chips for two in the sort of hygienic greaseproof wrappings which kept the steam in and made the chips go soggy.

'Did you know it's the May Day holiday on Monday?' I said.

'Running a judo tournament for the little bleeders, aren't I?'

He tipped the lunch on to two plates, and we ate it, mostly with fingers.

'You've come to life again, I see,' he said.

'It's temporary.'

'We'd better get some work done, then, while you're still with us.'

'The syndicates,' I said; and told him about the luckless Mason having been sent out on the same errand and having his brains kicked to destruction.

Chico shook salt on his chips. 'Have to be careful then, won't we?'

'Start this afternoon?'

'Sure.' He paused reflectively, licking his fingers. 'We're not getting paid for this, didn't you say?'

'Not directly.'

'Why don't we do these insurance inquiries, then? Nice quiet questions with a guaranteed fee.'

'I promised Lucas Wainwright I'd do the syndicates first.'

He shrugged. 'You're the boss. But that makes three in a row, counting your wife and Rosemary getting her cash back, that we've worked on for nothing.'

'We'll make up for it later.'

'You are going on, then?'

I didn't answer at once. Apart from not knowing whether I wanted to, I didn't know if I could. Over the past months Chico and I had tended to get somewhat battered by bully boys trying to stop us in our tracks. We didn't have the protection of being either in the Racecourse Security Service or the police. No one to defend us but ourselves. We had looked upon the bruises as part of the job, as racing falls had been to me, and bad judo falls to Chico. What if Trevor Deansgate had changed all that . . . Not just for one terrible week, but for much longer; for always?

'Sid,' Chico said sharply. 'Come back.'

I swallowed. 'Well . . . er . . . we'll do the syndicates. Then we'll see.' Then I'll know, I thought, I'll know inside me, one way or the other. If I couldn't walk into tigers' cages any more, we were done. One of us wasn't enough: it had to be both.

If I couldn't . . . I'd as soon be dead.

The first syndicate on Lucas's list had been formed by eight people, of whom three were registered owners, headed by Philip Friarly. Registered owners were those acceptable to the racing authorities, owners who paid their dues and kept the rules, were no trouble to anybody, and represented the source and mainspring of the whole industry.

Syndicates were a way of involving more people directly in racing, which was good for the sport, and dividing the training costs into smaller fractions, which was good for the owners. There were syndicates of millionaires, coal miners, groups of rock guitarists, the clientele of pubs. Anyone from Aunty Flo to the undertaker could join a syndicate, and all Eddy Keith should have done was check that everyone on the list was who they said they were.

'It's not the registered owners we're looking at,' I said. 'It's all the others.'

We were driving through Kent on our way to Tunbridge Wells. Ultra-respectable place, Tunbridge Wells. Resort of retired colonels and ladies who played bridge. Low on the national crime league. Hometown, all the same, of a certain Peter Rammileese, who was, so Lucas Wainwright's information had said, in fact the instigating member of all four of the doubtful syndicates, although his own name nowhere appeared.

'Mason,' I said, conversationally, 'was attacked and left for dead in the streets of Tunbridge Wells.'

'Now he tells me.'

'Chico,' I said. 'Do you want to turn back?'

'You got a premonition, or something?'

After a pause, I said 'No,' and drove a shade too fast round a sharpish bend.

'Look, Sid,' he said. 'We don't have to go to Tunbridge Wells. We're on a hiding to nothing, with this lark.'

'What do you think, then?'

He was silent.

'We do have to go,' I said.

'Yeah.'

'So we have to work out what it was that Mason asked, and not ask it.'

'This Rammileese,' Chico said. 'What's he like?'

'I haven't met him, myself, but I've heard of him. He's a farmer who's made a packet out of crooked dealings in horses. The Jockey Club won't have him as a registered owner, and most racecourses don't let him through the gates. He'll try to bribe anyone from the Senior Steward to the scrubbers, and where he can't bribe, he threatens.'

'Oh, jolly.'

'Two jockeys and a trainer, not so long ago, lost their licences for taking his bribes. One of the jockeys got the sack from his stable and he's so broke he's hanging around outside the racecourse gates begging for handouts.'

'Is that the one I saw you talking to, a while ago?'

'That's right.'

'And how much did you give him?'

'Never you mind.'

'You're a pushover, Sid.'

'A case of "but-for-the-grace-of-God",' I said.

'Oh, sure. I could see you taking bribes from a crooked horse dealer. Most likely thing on earth.'

'Anyway,' I said, 'what we're trying to find out is not whether Peter Rammileese is manipulating four racehorses, which he is, but whether Eddy Keith knows it, and is keeping quiet.'

'Right.' We sped deeper into rural Kent, and then he said, 'You know why we've had such good results, on the whole, since we've been together on this job?'

'Why, then?'

'It's because all the villains know you. I mean, they know you by sight, most of them. So when they see you poking around on their patch, they get the heebies, and start doing silly things like setting the heavies on us, and then we see them loud and clear, and what they're up to, which we wouldn't have done if they'd sat tight.'

I sighed and said 'I guess so,' and thought about Trevor Deansgate; thought and tried not to. Without any hands one couldn't drive a car . . . Just don't think about it, I told myself. Just keep your mind off it, it's a one way trip into jellyfish.

I swung round another corner too fast and collected a sideways look from Chico, but no comment.

'Look at the map,' I said. 'Do something useful.'

We found the house of Peter Rammileese without much trouble, and pulled into the yard of a small farm that looked as if the outskirts of Tunbridge Wells had rolled round it like a sea, leaving it isolated and incongruous. There was a large white farmhouse, three storeys high, and a modern wooden stable block, and a long, extra large barn. Nothing significantly prosperous about the place, but no nettles either.

No one about. I put the brake on as we rolled to a stop, and we got out of the car.

'Front door?' Chico said.

'Back door, for farms.'

We had taken only five or six steps in that direction, however, when a small boy ran into the yard from a doorway in the barn, and came over to us breathlessly.

'Did you bring the ambulance?'

His eyes looked past me, to my car, and his face puckered into agitation and disappointment. He was about seven, dressed in jodhpurs and T-shirt, and he had been crying.

'What's the matter?' I said.

'I rang for the ambulance . . . A long time ago.'

'We might help,' I said.

'It's Mum,' he said. 'She's lying in there, and she won't wake up.'

'Come on, you show us.'

He was a sturdy little boy, brown-haired and brown-eyed and very frightened. He ran towards the barn, and we followed without wasting time. Once through the door we could see that it wasn't an ordinary barn, but an indoor riding school, a totally enclosed area of about twenty metres wide by thirty-five long, lit by windows in the roof. The floor, wall to wall, was covered by a thick layer of tan-coloured wood chippings, springy and quiet for horses to work on.

There was a pony and a horse careering about; and, in danger from their hooves, a crumpled female figure lying on the ground.

Chico and I went over to her fast. She was young, on her side, face half downwards; unconscious, but not, I thought, deeply. Her breathing was shallow and her skin had whitened in a mottled fashion under her make-up, but the pulse in her wrist was strong and regular. The crash helmet which hadn't saved her lay several feet away on the floor.

'Go and ring again,' I said to Chico.

'Shouldn't we move her?'

'No . . . in case she's broken anything. You can do a lot of damage moving people too much when they're unconscious.'

'You should know.' He turned away and ran off towards the house.

'Is she all right?' the boy asked anxiously. 'Bingo started bucking and she fell off, and I think he kicked her head.'

'Bingo is the horse?'

'His saddle slipped,' he said: and Bingo, with the saddle down under his belly was still bucking and kicking like in a rodeo.

'What's your name?' I said.

'Mark.'

'Well, Mark, as far as I can see, your Mum is going to be all right, and you're a brave little boy.'

'I'm six,' he said, as if that wasn't so little.

The worst of the fright had died out of his eyes, now that he had help. I knelt on the ground beside his mother and smoothed the brown hair away from her forehead. She made a small moaning sound, and her eyelids fluttered. She was perceptibly nearer the surface, even in the short time we'd been there.

'I thought she was dying,' the boy said. 'We had a rabbit a little time ago . . . he panted and shut his eyes, and we couldn't wake him up again, and he died.'

'Your Mum will wake up again.'

'Are you sure?'

'Yes, Mark, I'm sure.'

He seemed deeply reassured, and told me readily that the pony was called Sooty, and was his own, and that his Dad was away until tomorrow morning, and there was only his Mum there, and him, and she'd been schooling Bingo because she was selling him to a girl for show-jumping.

Chico came back and said the ambulance was on its way. The boy, cheering up enormously, said we ought to catch the horses because they were cantering about and the reins were all loose, and if the saddles and bridles got broken his Dad would be bloody angry.

Both Chico and I laughed at the adult words, seriously spoken. While he and Mark stood guard over the patient, I caught the horses one by one, with the aid of a few horse-nuts which Mark produced from his pockets, and tied their reins to tethering rings in the walls. Bingo, once the agitating girths were undone and the saddle off, stood quietly enough, and Mark darted briefly away from his mother to give his own pony some brisk encouraging slaps and some more horse-nuts.

Chico said the emergency service had indeed had a call from a child fifteen minutes earlier, but he'd hung up before they could ask him where he lived.

'Don't tell him,' I said.

'You're a softie.'

'He's a brave little kid.'

'Not bad for a little bleeder. While you were catching the bucking bronco he told me his Dad gets bloody angry pretty often.' He looked down at the still unconscious girl. 'You really reckon she's OK, do you?'

'She'll come out of it. It's a matter of waiting.'

The ambulance came in due course, but Mark's anxiety reappeared, strongly, when the men loaded his mother into the van and prepared to depart. He wanted to go with her, and the men wouldn't take him on his own. She was stirring and mumbling, and it distressed him.

I said to Chico, 'Drive him to the hospital . . . Follow the ambulance. He needs to see her wide awake and speaking to him. I'll take a look round the house. His Dad's away until tomorrow.'

'Convenient,' he said sardonically. He collected Mark into the Scimitar, and drove away down the road, and I could see their heads talking to each other, through the rear window.

I went through the open back door with the confidence of the invited. Nothing difficult about entering a tiger's cage while the tiger was out.

It was an old house filled with brash new opulent furnishings, which I found overpowering. Lush loud carpets, huge stereo equipment, a lamp standard of a golden nymph and deep armchairs covered in black and khaki zigzags. Sitting and dining rooms shining and tidy, with no sign that a small boy lived there. Kitchen uncluttered, hygienic surfaces wiped clean. Study . . .

The positively aggressive tidiness of the study made me pause and consider. No horse trader that I'd ever come across had kept his books and papers in such neat rectangular stacks; and the ledgers themselves, when I opened them, contained up-to-the-minute entries.

I looked into drawers and filing cabinets, being extremely careful to leave everything squared up after me, but there was nothing there except the outward show of honesty. Not a single drawer or cupboard was locked. It was almost, I thought with cynicism, as if the whole thing was a stage dressing, orchestrated to confound any invasion of tax snoopers. The real records, if he kept any, were probably somewhere outside, in a biscuit tin, in a hole in the ground.

I went upstairs. Mark's room was unmistakable, but all the toys were in boxes, and all the clothes in drawers. There were three unoccupied bedrooms with the outlines of folded blankets showing under covers, and a suite of bedroom, dressing room and bathroom furnished with the same expense and tidiness as downstairs.

An oval dark red bath with taps like gilt dolphins. A huge bed with a bright brocade cover clashing with wall-to-wall jazz on the floor. No clutter on the curvaceous cream and gold dressing table, no brushes on any surface in the dressing room.

Mark's mum's clothes were fur and glitter and breeches and jackets. Mark's dad's clothes, thorn-proof tweeds, vicuna overcoat, a dozen or more suits, none of them hand-made, all seemingly bought because they were expensive. Handfuls of illicit cash, I thought, and nothing much to do with it. Peter Rammileese, it seemed was crooked by nature and not by necessity.

The same incredible tidiness extended through every drawer and every shelf, and even into the soiled linen basket, where a pair of pyjamas were neatly folded.

I went through the pockets of his suits, but he had left nothing at all in them. There were no pieces of paper of any sort anywhere in the dressing room.

Frustrated, I went up to the third floor, where there were six rooms, one containing a variety of empty suitcases, and the others, nothing at all.

No one, I thought on the way down again, lived so excessively carefully if they had nothing to hide; which was scarcely evidence to offer in court. The present life of the Rammileese family was an expensive vacuum, and of the past there was no sign at all. No souvenirs, no old books, not even any photographs except a recent one of Mark on his pony, taken outside the yard.

I was looking round the outbuildings when Chico came back. There were no animals except seven horses in the stable and the two in the covered school. No sign of farming in progress. No rosettes in the tack room, just a lot more tidiness and the smell of saddle-soap. I went out to meet Chico and asked what he had done with Mark.

'The nurses are stuffing him with jam butties and trying to ring his Dad. Mum is awake and talking. How did you get on? Do you want to drive?'

'No, you drive.' I sat in beside him. 'That house is the most suspicious case of no history I've ever seen.'

'Like that, eh?'

'Mm. And not a chance of finding any link with Eddy Keith.'

'Wasted journey, then,' he said.

'Lucky for Mark.'

'Yeah. Good little bleeder, that. Told me he's going to be a furniture moving man when he grows up.' Chico looked across at me and grinned. 'Seems he's moved house three times that he can remember.'

10

Chico and I spent most of Saturday separately traipsing around all the London addresses on the M list of wax names, and met at six o'clock, foot-sore and thirsty, at a pub we both knew in Fulham.

'We never ought to have done it on a Saturday, and a holiday weekend at that,' Chico said.

'No.' I agreed.

Chico watched the beer sliding mouth-wateringly into the glass. 'More than half of them were out.'

'Mine too. Nearly all.'

'And the ones that were in were watching the racing or the wrestling or groping their girl-friends, and didn't want to know.'

We carried his beer and my whisky over to a small table, drank deeply, and compared notes. Chico had finally pinned down four people, and I only two, but the results were there, all the same.

All six, whatever other mailing lists they had confessed to, had been in regular happy receipt of *Antiques for All*.

'That's it, then,' Chico said. 'Conclusive.' He leaned back against the wall, luxuriously relaxing. 'We can't do any more until Tuesday. Everything's shut.'

'Are you busy tomorrow?'

'Have a heart. The girl in Wembley.' He looked at his watch and swallowed the rest of the beer. 'And so long, Sid boy, or I'll be late. She doesn't like me sweaty.'

He grinned and departed, and I more slowly finished my drink and went home.

Wandered about. Changed the batteries. Ate some cornflakes. Got out the form books and looked up the syndicated horses. Highly variable form: races lost at short odds and won at long. All the signs of steady and expert fixing. I yawned. It went on all the time.

I pottered about some more, restlessly, sorely missing the peace that usually filled me in that place, when I was alone. Undressed, put on a bath-robe, pulled off the arm. Tried to watch the television: couldn't concentrate. Switched it off.

I usually pulled the arm off after I'd put the bathrobe on because that way I didn't have to look at the bit of me that remained below the left elbow. I could come to terms with the fact of it but still not really the sight, though it was neat enough and not horrific, as the messed up hand had been. I dare say it was senseless to be faintly repelled, but I was. I hated anyone except the limb man to see it; even Chico. I was ashamed of it, and that too was illogical. People without handicaps never understood that ashamed feeling, and nor had I, until that day soon after the original injury when I'd blushed crimson because I'd had to ask someone to cut up my food. There had been many times after that when I'd gone hungry rather than ask. Not having to ask, ever, since I'd had the electronic hand, had been a psychological release of soul-saving proportions.

The new hand had meant, too, a return to full normal human status. No one had treated me as an idiot, or with the pity which in the past had made me cringe. No one made allowances any more, or got themselves tongue-tied with trying not to say the wrong thing. The days of the useless deformity seemed in retrospect an unbearable nightmare. I was often quite grateful to the villain who had set me free.

With one hand, I was a self-sufficient man.

Without any . . .

Oh God, I thought. Don't think about it. *There is nothing either good or bad, but thinking makes it so.* Hamlet, however, didn't have the same problems.

I got through the night, and the next morning, and the afternoon, but at around six I gave up and got in the car, and drove to Aynsford.

If Jenny was there, I thought, easing up the back drive and stopping quietly in the yard outside the kitchen, I would just turn right round and go back to London, and at least the driving would have occupied the time. But no one seemed to be about, and I walked into the house from the side door which had a long passage into the house.

Charles was in the small sitting room that he called the wardroom, sitting alone, sorting out his much-loved collection of fishing flies.

He looked up. No surprise. No effusive welcome. No fuss. Yet I'd never gone there before without invitation.

'Hallo,' he said.

'Hallo.'

I stood there, and he looked at me, and waited.

'I wanted some company,' I said.

He squinted at a dry fly; 'Did you bring an overnight bag?'

I nodded.

He pointed to the drinks tray. 'Help yourself. And pour me a pink gin, will you? Ice in the kitchen.'

I fetched him his drink, and my own, and sat in an armchair.

'Come to tell me?' he said.

'No.'

He smiled. 'Supper then? And chess.'

We ate, and played two games. He won the first easily, and told me to pay attention. The second, after an hour and a half, was a draw. 'That's better,' he said.

The peace I hadn't been able to find on my own came slowly back with Charles, even though I knew it had more to do with the ease I felt with him personally, and the timelessness of his vast old house, than with a real re-solution of the destruction within. In any case, for the first time in ten days, I slept soundly for hours.

At breakfast we discussed the day ahead. He himself was going to the steeplechase meeting at Towcester, forty-five minutes northwards, to act as a Steward, an honorary job that he enjoyed. I told him about John Viking and the balloon race, and also about the visits to the M people, and *Antiques for All*, and he smiled with his own familiar mixture of satisfaction and amusement, as if I were some creation of his that was coming up to expectations. It was he who had originally driven me to become an investigator. Whenever I got anything right he took the credit for it himself.

'Did Mrs Cross tell you about the telephone call?' he said, buttering toast. Mrs Cross was his housekeeper, quiet, effective and kind.

'What telephone call?'

'Someone rang here about seven this morning, asking if you were here. Mrs Cross said you were asleep and could she take a message, but whoever it was said he would ring later.'

'Was it Chico? He might guess I'd come here, if he couldn't get me in the flat.'

'Mrs Cross said he didn't give a name.'

I shrugged and reached for the coffee pot. 'It can't have been urgent, or he'd have told her to wake me up.'

Charles smiled. 'Mrs Cross sleeps in curlers and face cream. She'd never have let you see her at seven o'clock in the morning, short of an earthquake. She thinks you're a lovely young man. She tells me so, every time you come.'

'For God's sakes.'

'Will you be back here, tonight?' he said.

'I don't know yet.'

He folded his napkin, looking down at it. 'I'm glad that you came, yesterday.'

I looked at him. 'Yeah,' I said. 'Well, you want me to say it, so I'll say it. And I mean it.' I paused a fraction, searching for the simplest words that would tell him what I felt for him. Found some. Said them. 'This is my home.'

He looked up quickly, and I smiled twistedly, mocking myself, mocking him, mocking the whole damned world.

Highalane Park was a stately home uneasily coming to terms with the plastic age. The house itself opened to the public like an agitated virgin only half a dozen times a year, but the parkland was always out for rent for game fairs and circuses, and things like the May Day jamboree.

They had made little enough effort on the roadside to attract the passing crowd. No bunting, no razzamatazz, no posters with print large enough to read at ten paces; everything slightly coy and apologetic. Considering all that, the numbers pouring on to the showground were impressive. I paid at the gate in my turn and bumped over some grass to park the car obediently in a row in the roped-off parking area. Other cars followed, neatly alongside.

There were a few people on horses cantering busily about in haphazard directions, but the roundabouts on the fairground to one side were silent and motionless, and there was no sight of any balloons.

I got out of the car and locked the door, and thought that one-thirty was probably too early for much in the way of action.

One can be so wrong.

A voice behind me said, 'Is this the man?'

I turned and found two people advancing into the small space between my car and the one next to it: a man I didn't know,, and a little boy, whom I did.

'Yes,' the boy said, pleased. 'Hallo.'

'Hallo, Mark,' I said. 'How's your Mum?'

'I told Dad about you coming.' He looked up at the man beside him.

'Did you now?' I thought his being at Highalane was only an extra-ordinary coincidence, but it wasn't.

'He described you,' the man said. 'That hand, and the way you could handle horses . . . I knew who he meant, right enough.' His face and voice were hard and wary, with a quality that I by now recognized on sight: guilty knowledge faced by trouble. 'I don't take kindly to you poking your nose around my place.'

'You were out,' I said mildly.

'Aye, I was out. And this nipper here, he left you there all alone.'

He was about forty, a wiry man with evil intentions stamped clearly all over him.

'I knew your car, too,' Mark said proudly. 'Dad says I'm clever.'

'Kids are observant,' his father said, with nasty relish.

'We waited for you to come out of a big house,' Mark said. 'And then we followed you all the way here.' He beamed, inviting me to enjoy the game. 'This is our car, next to yours.' He patted the maroon Daimler alongside.

The telephone call, I thought fleetingly. Not Chico. Peter Rammileese, checking around.

'Dad says,' Mark chatted on happily, 'that he'll take me to see those roundabouts while our friends take you for a ride in our car.'

His father looked down at him sharply, not having expected so much re-peated truth, but Mark, oblivious, was looking at a point behind my back.

I glanced round. Between the Scimitar and the Daimler stood two more people. Large unsmiling men from a muscular brotherhood. Brass knuckles and toecaps.

'Get into the car,' Rammileese said, nodding to his, not to mine. 'Rear door.'

Oh sure, I thought. Did he think I was mad? I stooped slightly as if to obey and then instead of opening the door scooped Mark up bodily, with my right arm, and ran.

Rammileese turned with a shout. Mark's face, next to mine, was astonished but laughing. I ran about twenty paces with him, and set him down in the path of his furiously advancing father, and then kept on going, away from the cars and towards the crowds in the centre part of the show-ground.

Bloody hell, I thought. Chico was right. These days we only had to twitch an eyelid for them to wheel out the heavies. It was getting too much.

It had been the sort of ambush that might have worked if Mark hadn't been there: one kidney punch and into the car before I'd got my breath. But they'd needed Mark, I supposed, to identify me, because although they knew me by name, they didn't by sight. They weren't going to catch me on the open showground, that was for sure, and when I went back to my car it would be with a load of protectors. Maybe, I thought hopefully, they would see it was useless, and just go away.

I reached the outskirts of the show-jumping arena, and looked back from over the head of a small girl sucking an ice-cream cornet. No one had called off the heavies. They were still doggedly in pursuit. I decided not to see what would happen if I simply stood my ground and requested the assorted families round about to save me from being frog-marched to oblivion and waking up with my head kicked in in the streets of Tunbridge Wells. The assorted families, with dogs and Grannies and prams and picnics, were more likely to dither with their mouths open and wonder what it had all been about, once it was over.

I went on, deeper into the show, circling the ring, bumping into children as I looked over my shoulder, and seeing the two men always behind me.

The arena itself was on my left, with show-jumping in progress inside, and ring-side cars encircling it outside. Behind the cars there was the broad grass walk-way along which I was going, and, on my right, the outer ring of the stalls one always gets at horse-shows. Tented shops selling saddlery, riding clothes, pictures, toys, hot dogs, fruit, more saddles, hardwear, tweeds, sheepskin slippers . . . an endless circle of small traders.

Among the tents, the vans: ice-cream vans, riding associations' caravans, a display of crafts, a fortune teller, a charity jumble shop, mobile cinema showing films of sheep dogs, a drop-sided juggernaut spilling out kitchen equipment in orange and yellow and green. Crowds along the fronts of all of them and no depth of shelter inside.

'Do you know where the balloons are?' I asked someone, and he pointed, and it was to a stall selling gas balloons of brilliant colours: children buying them and tying them to their wrists.

Not those, I thought. Surely not those. I didn't stop to explain, but asked again, further on.

'The balloon race? In the next field, I think, but it isn't time yet.'

'Thanks,' I said. The posters had announced a three o'clock start, but I'd have to talk to John Viking well before that, while he was willing to listen.

What was a balloon race, I wondered? Surely all balloons went at the same speed, the speed of the wind.

My trackers wouldn't give up. They weren't running, and nor was I. They just followed me steadily, as if locked on to a target by a radio beam; minds taking literally an order to stick to my heels. I'd have to get lost, I thought, and stay lost until after I'd found John Viking, and maybe then I'd go in search of helpful defences like show secretaries and first-aid ladies, and the single policeman out on the road directing traffic.

I was on the far side of the arena by that time, crossing the collecting ring area with children on ponies buzzing around like bees, looking strained as they went in to jump, and tearful or triumphant as they came out.

Past them, past the commentating box . . . 'Jane Smith had a clear round, the next to jump is Robin Daly on Traddles' . . . past the little private grandstand for the organizers and big-wigs – rows of empty folding seats – past an open-sided refreshment tent, full, and so back to the stalls.

I did a bit of dodging in and out of those, and round the backs, ducking under guy ropes and round dumps of cardboard boxes. From inside the depths of a stall hung thickly outside with riding jackets I watched the two of them go past, hurrying, looking about them, distinctly anxious.

They weren't like the two Trevor Deansgate had sent, I thought. His had been clumsier, smaller, and less professional. These two looked as if this sort of work was their daily bread; and for all the comparative safety of the show ground, where as a last resort I could get into the arena itself and scream for help, there was something daunting about them. Rent-a-thugs usually came at so much per hour. These two looked salaried, if not actually on the Board.

I left the riding jackets and dodged into the film about sheep dogs, which I dare say would have been riveting but for the shepherding going on outside, with me as the sheep.

I looked at my watch. After two o'clock. Too much time was passing. I had to try another sortie outside and find my way to the balloons.

I couldn't see them. I slithered among the crowd, asking for directions.

'Up at the end, mate,' a decisive man told me, pointing. 'Past the hot dogs, turn right, there's a gate in the fence. You can't miss it.'

I nodded my thanks and turned to go that way, and saw one of my trackers coming towards me, searching the stalls with his eyes and looking worried.

In a second he would see me . . . I looked around in a hurry and found I was outside the caravan of the fortune-teller. There was a curtain of plastic streamers, black and white, over the open doorway, and behind that a shadowy figure. I took four quick strides, brushed through the plastic strips, and stepped up into the van.

It was quieter inside and darker, with daylight filtering dimly through lace-hung windows. A Victorian sort of decor; mock oil lamps and chenille tablecloths. Outside, the tracker went past, giving the fortune-teller no more than a flickering glance. His attention lay ahead. He hadn't seen me come in.

The fortune-teller, however, had, and to her I represented business.

'Do you want your whole life, dear, the past and everything, or just the future?'

'Er . . .' I said. 'I don't really know. How long does it take?'

'A quarter of an hour, dear, for the whole thing.'

'Let's just have the future.'

I looked out of the window. A part of my future was searching among the ring-side cars, asking questions and getting a lot of shaken heads.

'Sit on the sofa beside me here, dear, and give me your left hand.'

'It'll have to be the right,' I said absently.

'No, dear.' Her voice was quite sharp. 'Always the left.'

Amused, I sat down and gave her the left. She felt it, and looked at it, and raised her eyes to mine. She was short and plump, dark-haired, middle-aged, and in no way remarkable.

'Well, dear,' she said after a pause, 'it will have to be the right, though I'm not used to it, and we may not get such good results.'

'I'll risk it,' I said; so we changed places on the sofa, and she held my right hand firmly in her two warm ones, and I watched the tracker move along the row of cars.

'You have suffered,' she said.

As she knew about my left hand, I didn't think much of that for a guess, and she seemed to sense it. She coughed apologetically.

'Do you mind if I use a crystal?' she said.

'Go ahead.'

I had vague visions of her peering into a large ball on a table, but she took a small one, the size of a tennis ball, and put it in the palm of my hand.

'You are a kind person,' she said. 'Gentle. People like you. People smile at you wherever you go.'

Outside, twenty yards away, the two heavies had met to consult. Not a smile, there, of any sort.

'You are respected by everyone.'

Regulation stuff, designed to please the customers.

Chico should hear it, I thought. Gentle, kind, respected . . . he'd laugh his head off.

She said doubtfully, 'I see a great many people, cheering and clapping. Shouting loudly, cheering you . . . does that mean anything to you, dear?'

I slowly turned my head. Her dark eyes watched me calmly.

'That's the past,' I said.

'It's recent,' she said. 'It's still there.'

I didn't believe it. I didn't believe in fortune-tellers. I wondered if she had seen me before, on a racecourse or talking on television. She must have.

She bent her head again over the crystal which she held on my hand, moving the glass gently over my skin.

'You have good health. You have vigour. You have great physical stamina . . . There is much to endure.'

Her voice broke off, and she raised her head a little, frowning. I had a strong impression that what she had said had surprised her.

After a pause, she said, 'I can't tell you any more.'

'Why not?'

'I'm not used to the right hand.'

'Tell me what you see,' I said.

She shook her head slightly and raised the calm dark eyes.

'You will live a long time.'

I glanced out through the plastic curtain. The trackers had moved off out of sight.

'How much do I owe you?' I said. She told me, and I paid her, and went quietly over to the doorway.

'Take care, dear,' she said. 'Be careful.'

I looked back. Her face was still calm, but her voice had been urgent. I didn't want to believe in the conviction that looked out of her eyes. She might have felt the disturbance of my present problem with the trackers, but no more than that. I pushed the curtain gently aside and stepped from the dim world of hovering horrors into the bright May sunlight, where they might in truth lie in wait.

II

There was no longer any need to ask where the balloons were. No one could miss them. They were beginning to rise like gaudy monstrous mushrooms, humped on the ground, spread all over an enormous area of grassland beyond the actual showground. I had thought vaguely that there would be two or three balloons, or at most six, but there must have been twenty.

Among a whole stream of people going the same way, I went down to the gate and through into the far field, and realized that I had absolutely under-estimated the task of finding John Viking.

There was a rope, for a start, and marshals telling the crowd to stand behind it. I ducked those obstacles at least, but found myself in a forest of half-inflated balloons, which billowed immensely all around and cut off any length of sight.

The first clump of people I came to see were busy with a pink and purple monster into whose mouth they were blowing air by means of a large engine-driven fan. The balloon was attached by four fine nylon ropes to the basket, which lay on its side, with a young man in a red crash helmet peering anxiously into its depth.

'Excuse me,' I said to a girl on the edge of the group. 'Do you know where I can find John Viking?'

'Sorry.'

The red crash helmet raised itself to reveal a pair of very blue eyes. 'He's here somewhere,' he said politely. 'Flies a Stormcloud balloon. Now would you mind getting the hell out, we're busy.'

I walked along the edge of things, trying to keep out of their way. Balloon races, it seemed, were a serious business and no occasion for light laughter and social chat. The intent faces leant over ropes and equipment, testing, checking, worriedly frowning. No balloons looked much like stormclouds. I risked another question.

'John Viking? That bloody idiot. Yes, he's here. Flies a Stormcloud.' He turned away, busy and anxious.

'What colour is it?' I said.

'Yellow and green. Look, go away, will you?'

There were balloons advertising whisky and marmalade and towns, and even insurance companies. Balloons in brilliant primary colours and pink-and-white pastels, balloons in the sunshine rising from the green grass in glorious jumbled rainbows. On an ordinary day, a scene of delight, but to me, trying to get round them to ask fruitlessly at the next clump gathered anxiously by its basket, a frustrating silky maze.

I circled a soft billowing black and white monster and went deeper into the centre. As if at a signal, there arose in a chorus from all around a series of deep-throated roars, caused by flames suddenly spurting from the large burners which were supported on frames above the baskets. The flames roared into the open mouths of the half-inflated balloons, heating and expanding the air already there and driving in more. The gleaming envelopes swelled and surged with quickening life, growing from mushrooms to toadstools, the tops rising slowly and magnificently towards the hazy blue sky.

'John Viking? Somewhere over there.' A girl swung her arm vaguely. 'But he'll be as busy as we are.'

As the balloons filled they began to heave off the ground and sway in great floating masses, bumping into each other, still billowing, still not full enough to live with the birds. Under each balloon the flames roared, scarlet and lusty, with the little clusters of helpers clinging to the baskets to prevent them escaping too soon.

With the balloons off the ground, I saw a yellow and green one quite easily; yellow and green in segments, like an orange, with a wide green band at the bottom. There was one man already in the basket, with about three people holding it down, and he, unlike everyone else in sight, wore not a crash helmet but a blue denim cap.

I ran in his direction, and even as I ran there was the sound of a starter's pistol. All around me the baskets were released, and began dragging and bumping over the ground; and a great cheer went up from the watching crowd.

I reached the bunch of people I was aiming for and put my hand on the basket.

'John Viking?'

No one listened. They were deep in a quarrel. A girl in a crash helmet, skiing jacket, jeans and boots stood on the ground, with the two helpers beside her looking glum and embarrassed.

'I'm not coming. You're a bloody madman.'

'Get in, get in dammit. The race has started.'

He was very tall, very thin, very agitated.

'I'm not coming.'

'You must.' He made a grab at her and held her wrist in a sinewy grip. It looked almost as if he were going to haul her wholesale into the basket, and she certainly believed it. She tugged and panted and screamed at him. 'Let go, John. Let go. I'm not coming.'

'Are you John Viking?' I said loudly.

He swung his head and kept hold of the girl.

'Yes, I am, what do you want? I'm starting this race as soon as my passenger gets in.'

'I'm not *going*,' she screamed.

I looked around. The other baskets were mostly airborne, sweeping gently across the area a foot or two above the surface, and rising in a smooth, glorious crowd. Every basket, I saw, carried two people.

'If you want a passenger,' I said. 'I'll come.'

He let go of the girl and looked me up and down.

'How much do you weigh?' And then, impatiently, as he saw the other balloons getting a head start, 'Oh, all right, get in. Get in.'

I gripped hold of a stay, and jumped, and wriggled, and ended standing inside a rather small hamper under a very large cloud of balloon.

'Leave go,' commanded the captain of this ship, and the helpers somewhat helplessly obeyed.

The basket momentarily stayed exactly where it was. Then John Viking reached above his head and flipped a lever which operated the burners, and there at close quarters, right above our heads, was the flame and the ear-filling roar.

The girl's face was still on a level with mine. 'He's mad,' she yelled. 'And you're crazy'

The basket moved away, bumped, and rose quite suddenly to a height of six feet. The girl ran after it and delivered a parting encouragement. 'And you haven't got a crash helmet.'

What I did have, though, was a marvellous escape route from two purposeful thugs, and a crash helmet at that moment seemed superfluous, particularly as my companion hadn't one either.

John Viking was staring about him in the remnants of fury, muttering under his breath, and operating the burner almost non-stop. His was the last balloon away. I looked down to where the applauding holiday crowd were watching the mass departure and a small boy darted suddenly from under the restraining rope, and ran into the now empty starting area, shouting and pointing. Pointing at John Viking's balloon, pointing excitedly at me.

My pal Mark, with his bright little eyes and his truthful tongue. My pal Mark, whom I'd liked to have strangled.

John Viking started cursing. I switched my attention from ground to air and saw that the reason for the resounding and imaginative obscenities floating to heaven was a belt of trees lying ahead which might prevent us going in the same direction. One balloon already lay in a tangle on the take-off side, and another, scarlet and purple, seemed set on a collision course.

John Viking yelled at me over the continuing roar of the burner, 'Hold on bloody tight with both hands. If the basket hits the tops of the trees we don't want to be spilled right out.'

The trees looked sixty feet high and a formidable obstacle, but most of the balloons had cleared them easily and were drifting away skywards, great bright pear-shaped fantasies hanging on the wind.

John Viking's basket closed with a rush towards the tree tops with the burner roaring over our heads like a demented dragon. The lift it should have provided seemed totally lacking.

'Turbulence,' John Viking shrieked. 'Bloody wind turbulence. Hold on. It's a long way down.'

Frightfully jolly, I thought, being tipped out of a hamper sixty feet from the ground without a crash helmet. I grinned at him, and he caught the expression and looked startled.

The basket hit the tree tops, and tipped on its side, tumbling me from the vertical to the horizontal with no trouble at all. I grabbed right-handed at whatever I could to stop myself falling right out, and I felt as much as saw that the majestically swelling envelope above us was carrying on with its journey regardless. It tugged the basket after it, crashing and bumping through the tops of the trees, flinging me about like a rag doll with at times most of my body hanging out in space. My host, made of sterner stuff, had one arm clamped like a vice round one of the metal struts which supported the burner, and the other twined into a black rubber strap. His legs were braced against the side of the basket, which was now the floor, and he changed his footholds as necessary, at one point planting one foot firmly on my stomach.

With a last sickening jolt and wrench the basket tore itself free, and we swung to and fro under the wobbling balloon like a pendulum. I was by this manoeuvre wedged into a disorganized heap in the bottom of the basket, but John Viking still stood rather splendidly on his feet.

There really wasn't much room, I thought, disentangling myself and straightening upwards. The basket, still swaying and shaking, was only four feet square, and reached no higher than one's waist. Along two opposite sides stood eight gas cylinders, four each side, fastened to the wickerwork with rubber straps. The oblong space left was big enough for two men to stand in, but not overgenerous even for that: about two feet by two feet per person.

John Viking gave the burner a rest at last, and into the sudden silence said forcefully, 'Why the hell didn't you hold on like I told you to? Don't you know you damned nearly fell out, and got me into trouble?'

'Sorry,' I said, amused. 'Is it usual to go on burning, when you're stuck on a tree?'

'It got us clear, didn't it?' he demanded.

'It sure did.'

'Don't complain, then. I didn't ask you to come.'

He was of about my own age; perhaps a year or two younger. His face under his blue denim yachting cap was craggy with a bone structure that might one day give him distinction, and his blue eyes shone with the brilliance of the true fanatic. John Viking the madman, I thought, and warmed to him.

'Check round the outsides, will you,' he said. 'See if anything's come adrift.'

It seemed he meant the outside of the basket, as he was himself looking outwards, over the edge. I discovered that on my side, too, there were bundles on the outside of the basket, either strapped to it tight, or swinging on ropes.

One short rope, attached to the basket, had nothing on the end of it. I pulled it up and showed it to him.

'Damnation,' he said explosively. 'Lost in the trees, I suppose. Plastic water container. Hope you're not thirsty.' He stretched up and gave the burner another long burst, and I listened in my mind to the echo of his Etonian drawl and totally understood why he was as he was.

'Do you have to finish first, to win a balloon race?' I said.

He looked surprised. 'Not this one. This is a two and a half hour race. The one who gets furthest in that time is the winner.' He frowned. 'Haven't you ever been in a balloon before?'

'No.'

'My God,' he said. 'What chance have I got?'

'None at all, if I hadn't come,' I said mildly.

'That's true.' He looked down from somewhere like six feet four. 'What's your name?'

'Sid,' I said.

He looked as if Sid wasn't exactly the sort of name his friends had, but faced the fact manfully.

'Why wouldn't your girl come with you?' I said.

'Who? Oh, you mean Popsy. She's not my girl. I don't really know her. She was going to come because my usual passenger broke his leg, silly bugger, when we made a bit of a rough landing last week. Popsy wanted to bring some ruddy big handbag. Wouldn't come without it, wouldn't be parted from it. I ask you! Where is the room for a handbag? And it was heavy, as well. Every pound counts. Carry a pound less, you can go a mile further.'

'Where do you expect to come down?' I said.

'It depends on the wind.' He looked up at the sky. 'We're going roughly north-east at the moment, but I'm going higher. There's a front forecast from the west, and I guess there'll be some pretty useful activity high up. We might make it to Brighton.'

'*Brighton.*' I had thought in terms of perhaps twenty miles, not a hundred. And he must be wrong, I thought: one couldn't go a hundred miles in a balloon in two and a half hours.

'If the wind's more from the north-west we might reach the Isle of Wight. Or France. Depends how much gas is left. We don't want to come down in the sea, not in this. Can you swim?'

I nodded. I supposed I still could: hadn't tried it one-handed. 'I'd rather not,' I said.

He laughed. 'Don't worry. The balloon's too darned expensive for me to want to sink it.'

Once free of the trees we had risen very fast, and now floated across country at a height from which cars on the roads looked like toys, though still recognizable as to size and colour.

Noises came up clearly. One could hear the cars' engines, and dogs barking, and an occasional human shout. People looked up and waved to us as we passed. A world removed, I thought. I was in a child's world, idyllically drifting with the wind, sloughing off the dreary earthbound millstones, free and rising and filled with intense delight.

John Viking flipped the lever and the flame roared, shooting up into the green-and-yellow cavern, a scarlet and gold tongue of dragon fire. The burn endured for twenty seconds and we rose perceptibly in the sudden ensuing silence.

'What gas do you use?' I said.

'Propane.'

He was looking over the side of the basket and around at the countryside, as if judging his position. 'Look, get the map out, will you. It's in the pouch thing, on your side. And for God's sake don't let it blow away.

I looked over the side, and found what he meant. A satchel-like object strapped on through the wickerwork, its outward-facing flap fastened shut with a buckle. I undid the buckle, looked inside, took a fair grip of the large folded map, and delivered it safely to the captain.

He was looking fixedly at my left hand, which I'd used as a sort of counterweight on the edge of the basket while I leaned over. I let it fall by my side, and his gaze swept upwards to my face.

'You're missing a hand,' he said incredulously.

'That's right.'

He waved his own two arms in a fierce gesture of frustration. 'How the *hell* am I going to win this race?'

I laughed.

He glanced at me. 'It's not damned funny.'

'Oh yes it is. And I like winning races . . . you won't lose it because of me.'

He frowned disgustedly. 'I suppose you can't be much more useless than Popsy,' he said. 'But at least they say she can read a map.' He unfolded the sheet I'd given him, which proved to be a map designed for the navigation of aircraft, its surface covered with a plastic film, for writing on. 'Look,' he said.

'We started from here.' He pointed. 'We're travelling roughly north-east. You take the map, and find out where we are.' He paused. 'Do you know the first bloody thing about using your watch as a compass, or about dead reckoning?'

I had a book about dead reckoning, which I hadn't read, in a pocket of the light cotton anorak I was wearing; and also, I thanked God, in another zippered compartment, a spare fully charged battery. 'Give me the map,' I said. 'And let's see.'

He handed it over with no confidence and started another burn. I worked out roughly where we should be, and looked over the side, and discovered straight away that the ground didn't look like the map. Where villages and roads were marked clearly on the map, they faded into the brown and green carpet of earth like patches of camouflage, the sunlight mottling them with shadows and dissolving them into ragged edges. The spread-out vistas all around looked all the same, defying me to recognize anything special, proving conclusively I was less use than Popsy.

Dammit, I thought. Start again.

We had set off at three o'clock, give a minute or two. We had been airborne for twelve minutes. On the ground the wind had been gentle and from the south, but we were now travelling slightly faster, and north-east. Say . . . fifteen knots. Twelve minutes at fifteen knots . . . about three nautical miles. I had been looking too far ahead. There should be, I thought, a river to cross; and in spite of gazing earnestly down I nearly missed it, because it was a firm blue line on the map and in reality a silvery reflecting thread that wound unobtrusively between a meadow and a wood. To the right of it, half hidden by a hill, lay a village, with beyond it, a railway line.

'We're there,' I said, pointing to the map.

He squinted at the print and searched the ground beneath us.

'Fair enough,' he said. 'So we are. Right. You keep the map. We might as well know where we are, all the way.'

He flipped the lever and gave it a long burn. The balloons ahead of us were also lower. We were definitely looking down on their tops. During the next patch of silence he consulted two instruments which were strapped on to the outside of the basket at his end, and grunted.

'What are those?' I said, nodding at the dials.

'Altimeter and rate-of-climb meter,' he said. 'We're at five thousand feet now, and rising at eight hundred feet a minute.'

'Rising?'

'Yeah.' He gave a sudden, wolfish grin in which I read unmistakably the fierce unholy glee of the mischievous child. 'That's why Popsy wouldn't come. Someone told her I would go high. She didn't want to.'

'How high?' I said.

'I don't mess about,' he said. 'When I race, I race to win. They all know I'll win. They don't like it. They think you should never take risks. They're all safety conscious these days and getting softer. Hah!' His scorn was absolute.

'In the old days, at the beginning of the century, when they had the Gordon Bennet races, they would fly for two days and do a thousand miles or more. But nowadays . . . safety bloody first.' He glared at me. 'And if I didn't have to have a passenger, I wouldn't. Passengers always argue and complain.'

He pulled a packet of cigarettes out of his pocket and lit one with a flick of a lighter. We were surrounded by cylinders of liquid gas. I thought about all the embargoes against naked flames near any sort of stored fuel, and kept my mouth shut.

The flock of balloons below us seemed to be veering away to the left; but then I realized that it was we who were going to the right. John Viking watched the changing direction with great satisfaction and started another long burn. We rose perceptibly faster, and the sun, instead of shining full on our backs, appeared on our starboard side.

In spite of the sunshine it was getting pretty cold. A look over the side showed the earth very far beneath, and one could now see a long way in all directions. I checked with the map, and kept an eye on where we were.

'What are you wearing?' he said.

'What you see, more or less.'

'Huh.'

During the burns, the flame over one's head was almost too hot, and there was always a certain amount of hot air escaping from the bottom of the balloon. There was no wind factor, as of course the balloon was travelling with the wind, at the wind's speed. It was sheer altitude that was making us cold.

'How high are we now?' I said.

He glanced at his instruments. 'Eleven thousand feet.'

'And still rising?'

He nodded. The other balloons, far below and to the left, were a cluster of distant bright blobs against the green earth.

'All that lot,' he said, 'will stay down at five thousand feet, because of staying under the airways.' He gave me a sideways look. 'You'll see on the map. The airways that the airlines use are marked, and so are the heights at which one is not allowed to fly through them.'

'And one is not allowed to fly through an airway at eleven thousand feet in a balloon?'

'Sid,' he said, grinning. 'You're not bad.'

He flicked the lever, and the burner roared, cutting off chat. I checked the ground against the map and nearly lost our position entirely, because we seemed suddenly to have travelled much faster, and quite definitely to the south-east. The other balloons, when I next looked, were out of sight.

In the next silence John Viking told me that the helpers of the other balloons would follow them on the ground, in cars, ready to retrieve them when they came down.

'What about you?' I asked. 'Do we have someone following?'

Did we indeed have Peter Rammileese following, complete with thugs, ready to pounce again at the further end? We were even, I thought fleetingly, doing him a favour with the general direction, taking him south-eastwards, home to Kent.

John Viking gave his wolfish smile, and said, 'No car on earth could keep up with us today.'

'Do you mean it?' I exclaimed.

He looked at the altimeter. 'Fifteen thousand feet,' he said. 'We'll stay at that. I got a forecast from the air boys for this trip. Fifty knot wind from two nine zero at fifteen thousand feet, that's what they said. You hang on, Sid, pal, and we'll get to Brighton.'

I thought about the two of us standing in a waist-high four-foot-square wicker basket, supported by terylene and hot air, fifteen thousand feet above the solid ground, travelling without any feeling of speed at fifty-seven miles an hour. Quite mad, I thought.

From the ground, we would be a black speck. On the ground, no car could keep up. I grinned back at John Viking with a satisfaction as great as his own, and he laughed aloud.

'Would you believe it?' he said. 'At last I've got someone up here who's not puking with fright.'

He lit another cigarette, and then he changed the supply line to the burner from one cylinder to the next. This involved switching off the empty tank, unscrewing the connecting nut, screwing it into the next cylinder, and switching on the new supply. There were two lines to the double burner, one for each set of four cylinders. He held the cigarette in his mouth throughout, and squinted through the smoke.

I had seen from the map that we were flying straight towards the airway which led in and out of Gatwick, where large aeroplanes thundered up and down not expecting to meet squashy balloons illegally in their path.

His appetite for taking risks was way out of my class. He made sitting on a horse over fences on the ground seem rather tame. Except, I thought with a jerk, that I no longer did it, I fooled around instead with men who threatened to shoot hands off . . . and I was safer up here with John Viking the madman, propane and cigarettes, mid-air collisions and all.

'Right,' he said. 'We just stay as we are for an hour and a half and let the wind take us. If you feel odd, it's lack of oxygen.' He took a pair of wool gloves from his pocket and put them on. 'Are you cold?'

'Yes, a bit.'

He grinned. 'I've got long johns under my jeans, and two sweaters under my anorak. You'll just have to freeze.'

'Thanks very much.' I stood on the map and put my real hand deep into the pocket of my cotton anorak and he said at least the false hand couldn't get frostbite.

He operated the burner and looked at his watch and the ground and the altimeter, and seemed pleased with the way things were. Then he looked at me in slight puzzlement and I knew he was wondering, now that there was time, how I happened to be where I was.

'I came to Highalane Park to see you,' I said. 'I mean, you, John Viking, particularly.'

He looked startled. 'Do you read minds?'

'All the time.' I pulled my hand out of one pocket and dipped into another, and brought out the paperback on navigation. 'I came to ask you about this. It's got your name on the flyleaf.'

He frowned at it, and opened the front cover. 'Good Lord. I wondered where this had got to. How did you have it?'

'Did you lend it to anyone?'

'I don't think so.'

'Um . . .' I said. 'If I describe someone to you, will you say if you know him?'

'Fire away.'

'A man of about twenty-eight,' I said. 'Dark hair, good looks, full of fun and jokes, easy-going, likes girls, great company, has a habit of carrying a knife strapped to his leg under his sock, and is very likely a crook.'

'Oh yes,' he said, nodding. 'He's my cousin.'

12

His cousin, Norris Abbott. What had he done this time, he demanded, and I asked, what had he done before?

'A trail of bouncing cheques that his mother paid for.'

Where did he live, I asked. John Viking didn't know. He saw him only when Norris turned up occasionally on his doorstep, usually broke and looking for free meals.

'A laugh a minute for a day or two. Then he's gone.'

'Where does his mother live?'

'She's dead. He's alone now. No parents, or brothers or sisters. No relatives except me.' He peered at me, frowning. 'Why do you ask all this?'

'A girl I know wants to find him.' I shrugged. 'It's nothing much.'

He lost interest at once and flicked the lever for another burn. 'We use twice the fuel up here as near the ground,' he said afterwards. 'That's why I brought so much. That's how some nosey parker told Popsy I was planning to go high, and through the airways.'

By my reckoning the airway was not that far off.

'Won't you get into trouble?' I said.

The wolf grin came and went. 'They've got to see us, first. We won't show up on radar. We're too small for the equipment they use. With a bit of luck, we'll sneak across and no one will be any the wiser.'

I picked up the map and studied it. At fifteen thousand feet we would be illegal from when we entered controlled airspace until we landed, all but the last two hundred feet. The airway over Brighton began at a thousand feet above sea level and the hills to the north were eight hundred feet high. Did John Viking know all that? Yes, he did.

When we had been flying for one hour and fifty minutes he made a fuel line change from cylinder to cylinder that resulted in a thin jet of liquid gas spurting out from the connection like water out of a badly joined hose. The jet shot across the corner of the basket and hit a patch of wickerwork about six inches below the top rail.

John Viking was smoking at the time.

Liquid propane began trickling down the inside of the basket in a stream. John Viking cursed and fiddled with the faulty connection, bending over it; and his glowing cigarette ignited the gas.

There was no ultimate and final explosion. The jet burnt as jets do, and directed its flame in an organized manner at the patch of basket it was hitting. John Viking threw his cigarette over the side and snatched off his denim cap, and beat at the burning basket with great flailing motions of his arm, while I managed to stifle the jet at source by turning off the main switch on the cylinder.

When the flames and smoke and cursing died down, we had a hole six inches in diameter right through the basket, but no other damage.

'Baskets don't burn easily,' he said calmly, as if nothing had happened. 'Never known one burn much more than this.' He inspected his cap, which was scorched into black-edged lace, and gave me a maniacal four seconds from the bright blue eyes. 'You can't put out a fire with a crash helmet,' he said.

I laughed quite a lot.

It was the altitude, I thought, which was making me giggle.

'Want some chocolate?' he said.

There were no signposts in the sky to tell us when we crossed the boundary of the airway. We saw an aeroplane or two some way off, but nothing near us. No one came buzzing around to direct us downward. We simply sailed straight on, blowing across the sky as fast as a train.

At ten past five he said it was time to go down, because if we didn't touch ground by five-thirty exactly he would be disqualified, and he didn't want that; he wanted to win. Winning was what it was all about.

'How would anyone know exactly when we touched down?' I said.

He gave me a pitying look and gently directed his toe at a small box strapped to the floor beside one of the corner cylinders.

'In here is a barograph, all stuck about with pompous red seals. The judges seal it, before the start. It shows variations in air pressure. Highly sensitive. All our journey shows up like a row of peaks. When you're on the ground, the trace is flat and steady. It tells the judges just when you took off and when you landed. Right?'

'Right.'

'OK. Down we go, then.'

He reached up and untied a red cord which was knotted to the burner frame, and pulled it. 'It opens a panel at the top of the balloon,' he said. 'Lets the hot air out.'

His idea of descent was all of a piece. The altimeter unwound like a broken clock and the rate-of-climb meter was pointing to a thousand feet a minute, downwards. He seemed to be quite unaffected, but it made me queasy and hurt my ear drums. Swallowing made things a bit better, but not much. I concentrated, as an antidote, on checking with the map to see where we were going.

The Channel lay like a broad grey carpet to our right, and it was incredible but, whichever way I looked at it, it seemed that we were on a collision course with Beachy Head.

'Yeah,' John Viking casually confirmed. 'Guess we'll try not to get blown off those cliffs. Might be better to land on the beach further on . . .' He checked his watch. 'Ten minutes to go. We're still at six thousand feet . . . that's all right . . . might be the edge of the sea . . .'

'Not the sea,' I said positively.

'Why not? We might have to.'

'Well,' I said, 'this . . .' I lifted my left arm. 'Inside this hand-shaped plastic there's actually a lot of fine engineering. Strong pincers inside the thumb and first two fingers. A lot of fine precision gears and transistors and printed electrical circuits. Dunking it in the sea would be like dunking a radio. A total ruin. And it would cost me two thousand quid to get a new one.'

He was astonished. 'You're joking.'

'No.'

'Better keep you dry, then. And anyway, now we're down here, I don't think we'll get as far south as Beachy Head. Probably further east.' He paused and looked at my left hand doubtfully. 'It'll be a rough landing. The fuel's cold from being so high . . . the burner doesn't function well on cold fuel. It takes time to heat enough air to give us a softer touch-down.'

A softer touch-down took time . . . too much time.

'Win the race,' I said.

His face lit into sheer happiness. 'Right,' he said decisively. 'What's that town just ahead?'

I studied the map. 'Eastbourne.'

He looked at his watch. 'Five minutes.' He looked at the altimeter and at Eastbourne, upon which we were rapidly descending. 'Two thousand feet. Bit dicey, hitting the roofs. There isn't much wind down here, is there . . . But if I burn, we might not get down in time. No, no burn.'

A thousand feet a minute, I reckoned, was eleven or twelve miles an hour. I had been used for years to hitting the ground at more than twice that speed . . . though not in a basket, and not when the ground might turn out to be fully inhabited by brick walls.

We were travelling sideways over the town, with houses below us. Descent was very fast. 'Three minutes,' he said.

The sea lay ahead again, fringing the far side of the town, and for a moment it looked as if it was there we would have to come down after all. John Viking, however, knew better.

'Hang on,' he said. 'This is it.'

He hauled strongly on the red cord he held, which led upwards into the balloon. Somewhere above, the vent for the hot air widened dramatically, the lifting power of the balloon fell away, and the solid edge of Eastbourne came up with a rush.

We scraped the eaves of grey slate roofs, made a sharp diagonal descent over a road and a patch of grass, and smashed down on a broad concrete walk twenty yards from the waves.

'Don't get out. Don't get out,' he yelled. The basket tipped on its side and began to slither along the concrete, dragged by the still half-inflated silken mass. 'Without our weight, it could still fly away.'

As I was again wedged among the cylinders, it was superfluous advice. The basket rocked and tumbled a few more times and I with it, and John Viking cursed and hauled at his red cord and finally let out enough air for us to be still.

He looked at his watch, and his blue eyes blazed with triumph.

'We've made it. Five twenty-nine. That was a bloody good race. The best ever. What are you doing next Saturday?'

I went back to Aynsford by train, which took forever, with Charles picking me up from Oxford station not far short of midnight.

'You went on the balloon race,' he repeated disbelievingly. 'Did you enjoy it?'

'Very much.'

'And your car's still at Highalane Park?'

'It can stay there until the morning,' I yawned. 'Nicholas Ashe now has a name, by the way. He's someone called Norris Abbott. Same initials, silly man.'

'Will you tell the police?'

'See if we can find him, first.'

He glanced at me sideways. 'Jenny came back this evening, after you'd telephoned.'

'Oh no.'

'I didn't know she was going to.'

I supposed I believed him. I hoped she would have gone to bed before I arrived, but she hadn't. She was sitting on the gold brocade sofa in the drawing room, looking belligerent.

'I don't like you coming here so much,' she said.

A knife to the heart of things from my pretty wife.

Charles said smoothly, 'Sid is welcome here always.'

'Discarded husbands should have more pride than to fawn on their fathers-in-law, who put up with it because they're sorry for them.'

'You're jealous,' I said, surprised.

She stood up fast, as angry as I'd ever seen her.

'How dare you?' she said. 'He always takes your side. He thinks you're bloody marvellous. He doesn't know you like I do, all your stubborn little ways and your meanness and thinking you're always *right*.'

'I'm going to bed,' I said.

'And you're a coward as well,' she said furiously. 'Running away from a few straight truths.'

'Good night, Charles,' I said. 'Good night, Jenny. Sleep well, my love, and pleasant dreams.'

'You . . .' she said. 'You . . . I hate you, Sid.'

I went out of the drawing room without fuss and upstairs to the bedroom I thought of as mine; the one I always slept in nowadays at Aynsford.

You don't have to hate me, Jenny, I thought miserably; I hate myself.

Charles drove me to Wiltshire in the morning to collect my car, which still stood where I'd left it, though surrounded now by acres of empty grass. There was no Peter Rammileese in sight, and no thugs waiting in ambush. All clear for an uneventful return to London.

'Sid,' Charles said, as I unlocked the car door. 'Don't pay any attention to Jenny.'

'No.'

'Come to Aynsford whenever you want.'

I nodded.

'I mean it, Sid.'

'Yeah.'

'Damn Jenny,' he said explosively.

'Oh no. She's unhappy. She . . .' I paused. 'I guess she needs comforting. A shoulder to cry on, and all that.'

He said austerely, 'I don't care for tears.'

'No,' I sighed and got into the car, waved goodbye, and drove over the bumpy grass to the gate. The help that Jenny needed, she wouldn't take from me; and her father didn't know how to give it. Just another of life's bloody muddles, another irony in the general mess.

I drove into the city and around a few small circles, and ended up in the publishing offices of *Antiques for All*, which proved to be only one of a number of specialist magazines put out by a newspaper company. To the *Antiques* editor, a fair-haired earnest young man in heavy-framed specs, I explained both the position and the need.

'Our mailing list?' he said doubtfully. 'Mailing lists are strictly private, you know.'

I explained all over again, and threw in a lot of pathos. My wife behind bars if I didn't find the con man, that sort of thing.

Oh very well,' he said. 'But it will be stored in a computer. You'll have to wait for a print-out.'

I waited patiently, and received in the end a stack of paper setting out fifty-three thousand names and addresses, give or take a few dead ones.

'And we want it back,' he said severely. 'Unmarked and complete.'

'How did Norris Abbott get hold of it?' I asked.

He didn't know, and neither the name nor the description of Abbott/Ashe brought any glimmer of recognition.

'How about a copy of the magazine, for good measure?'

I got that too, and disappeared before he could regret all his generosity. Back in the car, I telephoned Chico and got him to come to the flat. Meet me outside, I said. Carry my bag upstairs and earn your salary.

He was there when I pulled up at a vacant parking meter and we went upstairs together. The flat was empty, and quiet, and safe.

'A lot of leg work, my son,' I said, taking the mailing list out of the package I had transported it in, and putting it on the table. 'All your own.'

He eyed it unenthusiastically. 'And what about you?'

'Chester races,' I said. 'One of the syndicate horses runs there tomorrow. Meet me back here Thursday morning, ten o'clock. OK?'

'Yeah.' He thought. 'Suppose our Nicky hasn't got himself organized yet, and sends out his begging letters next week, after we've drawn a blank?'

'Mm . . . Better take some sticky labels with this address on, and ask them to send the letters here, if they get them.'

'We'll be lucky.'

'You never know. No one likes being conned.'

'May as well get started, then.' He picked up the folder containing the magazine and mailing list, and looked ready to leave.

'Chico . . . Stay until I've repacked my bag. I think I'll start northwards right now. Stay until I go.'

He was puzzled. 'If you like, but what for?'

'Er . . .'

'Come on, Sid. Out with it.'

'Peter Rammileese and a couple of guys came looking for me yesterday at Highalane Park. So I'd just like you around, while I'm here.'

'What sort of guys?' he said suspiciously.

I nodded. 'Those sort. Hard eyes and boots.'

'Guys who kick people half to death in Tunbridge Wells?'

'Maybe,' I said.

'You dodged them, I see.'

'In a balloon.' I told him about the race while I put some things in a suitcase. He laughed at the story but afterwards came quite seriously back to business.

'Those guys of yours don't sound like your ordinary run-of-the-mill rent-a-thug,' he said. 'Here, let me fold that jacket, you'll turn up at Chester all creased.' He took my packing out of my hands and did it for me, quickly and neatly. 'Got all the spare batteries? There's one in the bathroom.' I fetched it. 'Look, Sid, I don't like these syndicates.' He snapped the locks shut and carried the case into the hall. 'Let's tell Lucas Wainwright we're not doing them.'

'And who tells Peter Rammileese?'

'We do. We ring him up and tell him.'

'You do it,' I said. 'Right now.'

We stood and looked at each other. Then he shrugged and picked up the suitcase. 'Got everything?' he said. 'Raincoat?' We went down to the car and stowed my case in the boot. 'Look, Sid, you just take care, will you? I don't like hospital visiting, you know that.'

'Don't lose that mailing list,' I said. 'Or the editor of *Antiques* will be cross.'

I booked unmolested into a motel and spent the evening watching television, and the following afternoon arrived without trouble at Chester races.

All the usual crowd were there, standing around, making the usual conversations. It was my first time on a racecourse since the dreary week in Paris, and it seemed to me when I walked in that the change in me must be clearly visible. But no one, of course, noticed the blistering sense of shame I felt at the sight of George Caspar outside the weighing room, or treated me any differently from usual. It was I alone who knew I didn't deserve the smiles and the welcome. I was a fraud. I shrank inside. I hadn't known I would feel so bad.

The trainer from Newmarket who had offered me a ride with his string was there, and repeated his offer.

'Sid, do come. Come this Friday, stay the night with us, and ride work on Saturday morning.'

There wasn't much, I reflected, that anyone could give me that I'd rather accept: and besides, Peter Rammileese and his merry men would have a job finding me there.

'Martin . . . Yes, I'd love to.'

'Great.' He seemed pleased. 'Come for evening stables, Friday night.'

He went on into the weighing room, and I wondered if he would have asked me if he'd known how I'd spent Guineas day.

Bobby Unwin buttonholed me with inquisitive eyes. 'Where have you been?' he said. 'I didn't see you at the Guineas.'

'I didn't go.'

'I thought you'd be bound to, after all your interest in Tri-Nitro.'

'No.'

'I reckon you had the smell of something going on, there, Sid. All that interest in the Caspars, and about Gleaner and Zingaloo. Come clean, now, what do you know?'

'Nothing, Bobby.'

'I don't believe you.' He gave me a hard unforgiving stare and steered his beaky nose towards more fruitful copy in the shape of a top trainer enduring a losing streak. I would have trouble persuading him, I thought, if I should ever ask for his help again.

Rosemary Caspar, walking with a woman friend to whom she was chatting, almost bumped into me before either of us was aware of the other being there. The look in her eyes made Bobby Unwin seem loving.

'Go away,' she said violently. 'Why are you here?'

The woman friend looked very surprised. I stepped out of the way without saying a word, which surprised her still further. Rosemary impatiently twitched her onwards, and I heard her voice rising, 'But surely, Rosemary, that was Sid Halley . . .'

My face felt stiff. It's too bloody much, I thought. I couldn't have made their horse win if I'd stayed. *I couldn't* . . . but I might have. I would always think I might have, if I'd tried. If I hadn't been scared out of my mind.

'Hallo Sid,' a voice said at my side. 'Lovely day, isn't it?'

'Oh, lovely.'

Philip Friarly smiled and watched Rosemary's retreating back. 'She's been snapping at everyone since that disaster last week. Poor Rosemary. Takes things so much to heart.'

'You can't blame her,' I said. 'She said it would happen, and no one believed her.'

'Did she tell you?' he said curiously.

I nodded.

'Ah,' he said, in understanding. 'Galling for you.'

I took a deep loosening breath and made myself concentrate on something different.

'That horse of yours, today,' I said. 'Are you just giving it a sharpener, running it here on the Flat?'

'Yes,' he said briefly. 'And if you ask me how it will run, I'll have to tell you that it depends on who's giving the orders, and who's taking them.'

'That's cynical.'

'Have you found out anything for me?'

'Not very much. It's why I came here.' I paused. 'Do you know the name and address of the person who formed your syndicates?'

'Not offhand,' he said. 'I didn't deal with him myself, do you see? The syndicates were already well advanced when I was asked to join. The horses had already been bought, and most of the shares were sold.'

'They used you,' I said. 'Used your name. A respectable front.'

He nodded unhappily. 'I'm afraid so.'

'Do you know Peter Rammileese?'

'Who?' He shook his head. 'Never heard of him.'

'He buys and sells horses,' I said. 'Lucas Wainwright thinks it was he who formed your syndicates, and he who is operating them, and he's bad news to the Jockey Club and barred from most racecourses.

'Oh dear.' He sounded distressed. 'If Lucas is looking into them . . . What do you think I should do, Sid?'

'From your own point of view,' I said, 'I think you should sell your shares, or dissolve the syndicates entirely, and get your name out of them as fast as possible.'

'All right, I will. And Sid . . . next time I'm tempted, I'll get you to check on the other people in the syndicate. The Security section are supposed to have done these, and look at them!'

'Who's riding your horse today?' I said.

'Larry Server.'

He waited for an opinion, but I didn't give it. Larry Server was middle ability, middle employed, rode mostly on the Flat and sometimes over hurdles, and was to my mind in the market for unlawful bargains.

'Who chooses the jockey?' I said. 'Larry Server doesn't ride all that often for your horse's trainer.'

'I don't know,' he said doubtfully. 'I leave all that to the trainer, of course.'

I made a small grimace.

'Don't you approve?' he said.

'If you like,' I said, 'I'll give you a list of jockeys for your jumpers that you can at least trust to be trying to win. Can't guarantee their ability, but you can't have everything.'

'Now who's a cynic?' He smiled, and said with patent and piercing regret, 'I wish you were still riding them, Sid.'

'Yeah.' I said it with a smile, but he saw the flicker I hadn't managed to keep out of my eyes.

With a compassion I definitely didn't want, he said, 'I'm so sorry.'

'It was great while it lasted,' I said lightly. 'That's all that matters.'

He shook his head, annoyed with himself for his clumsiness.

'Look,' I said, 'if you were *glad* I'm not still riding them I'd feel a whole lot worse.'

'We had some grand times, didn't we? Some exceptional days.'

'Yes, we did.'

There could be an understanding between an owner and a jockey, I thought, that was intensely intimate. In the small area where their lives touched, where the speed and the winning were all that mattered, there could be a privately shared joy, like a secret, that endured like cement. I hadn't felt it often, nor with many of the people I had ridden for, but with Philip Friarly, nearly always.

A man detached himself from another group near us, and came towards us with a smiling face.

'Philip. Sid. Nice to see you.'

We made the polite noises back, but with genuine pleasure, as Sir Thomas Ullaston, the reigning Senior Steward, head of the Jockey Club, head, more or less, of the whole racing industry, was a sensible man and a fair and open-minded administrator. A little severe at times, some thought, but it wasn't a job for a soft man. In the short time since he'd been put in charge of things there had been some good new rules and a clearing out of injustices, and he was as decisive as his predecessor had been weak.

'How's it going, Sid?' he said. 'Caught any good crooks lately?'

'Not lately,' I said ruefully.

He smiled to Philip Friarly, 'Our Sid's putting the Security section's nose out of joint, did you know? I had Eddy Keith along in my office on Monday complaining that we give Sid too free a hand, and asking that we shouldn't let him operate on the racecourse.'

'Eddy Keith?' I said.

'Don't look so shocked, Sid,' Sir Thomas said teasingly. 'I told him that racing owed you a great deal, starting with the saving of Seabury racecourse itself and going right on from there, and that in no way would the Jockey Club ever interfere with you, unless you did something absolutely diabolical, which on past form I can't see you doing.'

'Thank you,' I said faintly.

'And you may take it,' he said firmly, 'that that is the official Jockey Club view, as well as my own.'

'Why,' I said slowly, 'does Eddy Keith want me stopped?'

He shrugged. 'Something about access to the Jockey Club files. Apparently you saw some, and he resented it. I told him he'd have to live with it, because I was certainly not in any way going to put restraints on what I consider a positive force for good in racing.'

I felt grindingly undeserving of all that, but he gave me no time to protest.

'Why don't both of you come upstairs for a drink and a sandwich? Come along, Sid, Philip . . .' He turned, gesturing us to follow, leading the way.

We went up those stairs marked 'Private' which on most racecourses lead to the civilized luxuries of the Stewards' box, and into a carpeted glass-fronted room looking out to the white-railed track. There were several groups of people there already, and a manservant handing around drinks on a tray.

'I expect you know most people,' Sir Thomas said, hospitably making introductions. 'Madelaine, my dear . . .' to his wife, '. . . do you know Lord Friarly, and Sid Halley?' We shook her hand. 'And oh yes, Sid,' he said, touching my arm to bring me around face to face with another of his guests . . .

'Have you met Trevor Deansgate?'

13

We stared at each other, probably equally stunned.

I thought of how he had last seen me, on my back in the straw barn, spilling my guts out with fear. He'll see it still in my face, I thought. He knows what he's made of me. I can't just stand here without moving a muscle . . . and yet I must.

My head seemed to be floating somewhere above the rest of my body, and an awful lot of awfulness got condensed into four seconds.

'Do you know each other?' Sir Thomas said, slightly puzzled.

Trevor Deansgate said. 'Yes. We've met.'

There was at least no sneer either in his eyes or his voice. If it hadn't been impossible, I would have thought that what he looked was *wary*.

'Drink, Sid?' said Sir Thomas; and I found the man with the tray at my elbow. I took a tumbler with whisky-coloured contents and tried to stop my fingers trembling.

Sir Thomas said conversationally, 'I've just been telling Sid how much the Jockey Club appreciates his successes, and it seems to have silenced him completely.'

Neither Trevor Deansgate nor I said anything. Sir Thomas raised his eyebrows a fraction and tried again. 'Well, Sid, tell us a good thing for the big race.'

I dragged my scattered wits back into at least a pretence of life going uneventfully on.

'Oh . . . Winetaster, I should think.'

My voice sounded strained to me, but Sir Thomas seemed not to notice. Trevor Deansgate looked down to the glass in his own well-manicured hand and swivelled the ice cubes round in the golden liquid. Another of the guests spoke to Sir Thomas, and he turned away, and Trevor Deansgate's gaze came immediately back to my face filled with naked savage threat. His voice, quick and hard, spoke straight from the primitive underbelly, the world of violence and vengeance and no pity at all.

'If you break your assurance, I'll do what I said.'

He held my eyes until he was sure I had received the message, and then he too turned away, and I could see the heavy muscles of his shoulders bunching formidably inside his coat.

'Sid,' Philip Friarly said, appearing once more at my side. 'Lady Ullaston wants to know . . . I say, are you feeling all right?'

I nodded a bit faintly.

'My dear chap, you look frightfully pale.'

'I . . . er . . .' I took a vague grip on things. 'What did you say?'

'Lady Ullaston wants to know . . .' He went on at some length, and I listened and answered with a feeling of complete unreality. One could literally be torn apart in spirit while standing with a glass in one's hand making social chit chat to the Senior Steward's lady. I couldn't remember, five minutes later, a word that was said. I couldn't feel my feet on the carpet. I'm a mess, I thought.

The afternoon went on. Winetaster got beaten in the big race by a glossy dark filly called Mrs Hillman, and in the race after that Larry Server took Philip Friarly's syndicate horse to the back of the field, and stayed there. Nothing improved internally, and after the fifth I decided it was pointless staying any longer, since I couldn't even effectively think.

Outside the gate there was the usual gaggle of chauffeurs leaning against cars, waiting for their employers; and also, with them, one of the jump jockey's whose licence had been lost through taking bribes from Rammileese.

I nodded to him, as I passed. 'Jacksy.'

'Sid.'

I walked on to the car, and unlocked it, and slung my raceglasses on to the back seat. Got in. Started the engine. Paused for a bit, and reversed all the way back to the gate.

'Jacksy?' I said. 'Get in. I'm buying.'

'Buying what?' He came over and opened the passenger door, and sat in beside me. I fished my wallet out of my rear trouser pocket and tossed it into his lap.

'Take all the money,' I said. I drove forward through the car park and out through the distant gate on to the public road.

'But you dropped me quite a lot, not long ago,' he said.

I gave him a fleeting sideways smile. 'Yeah. Well . . . this is for services about to be rendered.'

He counted the notes. 'All of it?' he said doubtfully.

'I want to know about Peter Rammileese.'

'Oh no.' He made as if to open the door, but the car by then was going too fast.

'Jacksy,' I said, 'no one's listening but me, and I'm not telling anyone else. Just say how much he paid you and what for, and anything else you can think of.'

He was silent for a bit. Then he said, 'It's more than my life's worth, Sid. There's a whisper out that he's brought two pros down from Glasgow for a special job and anyone who gets in his way just now is liable to be stamped on.'

'Have you seen these pros?' I said, thinking that I had.

'No. It just come through on the grapevine, like.'

'Does the grapevine know what the special job is?'

He shook his head.

'Anything to do with syndicates?'

'Be your age, Sid. Everything to do with Rammileese is always to do with syndicates. He runs about twenty. Maybe more.'

Twenty, I thought, frowning. I said, 'What's his rate for the job of doing a Larry Server, like today?'

'Sid,' he protested.

'How does he get someone like Larry Server on to a horse he wouldn't normally ride?'

'He asks the trainers nicely, with a fistful of dollars.'

'He bribes the *trainers*?'

'It doesn't take much, sometimes.' He looked thoughtful for a while. 'Don't you quote me, but there were races run last autumn where Rammi-leese was behind every horse in the field. He just carved them up as he liked.'

'It's impossible,' I said.

'No. All that dry weather we had, remember? Fields of four, five or six runners, sometimes, because the ground was so hard? I know of three races for sure when all the runners were his. The poor sodding bookies didn't know what had hit them.'

Jacksy counted the money again. 'Do you know how much you've got here?' he said.

'Just about.'

I glanced at him briefly. He was twenty-five, an ex-apprentice grown too heavy for the Flat and known to resent it. Jump jockeys on the whole earned less than the Flat boys, and there were the bruises besides, and it wasn't everyone who like me found steeplechasing double the fun. Jacksy didn't; but he could ride pretty well, and I'd raced alongside him often enough to know he wouldn't put you over the rails for nothing at all. For a consideration, yes, but for nothing, no.

The money was troubling him. For ten or twenty he would have lied to me easily: but we had a host of shared memories of changing rooms and horses and wet days and mud and falls and trudging back over sodden turf in paper-thin racing boots, and it isn't so easy, if you're not a real villain, to rob someone you know as well as that.

'Funny,' he said, 'you taking to this detecting lark.'

'Riotous.'

'No, straight up. I mean, you don't come after the lads for little things.'

'No,' I agreed. Little things like taking bribes. My business, on the whole, was with the people who offered them.

'I kept all the newspapers,' he said. 'After that trial.'

I shook my head resignedly. Too many people in the racing world had kept those papers, and the trial had been a trial for me in more ways than one. Defence counsel had revelled in deeply embarrassing the victim; and the prisoner, charged with causing grievous bodily harm with intent, contrary to section 18 of the Offences Against the Person Act 1861 (or in other words, bopping an ex-jockey's left hand with a poker), had been rewarded by four years in clink. It would be difficult to say who had enjoyed the proceedings less, the one in the witness box or the one in the dock.

Jacksy kept up his disconnected remarks, which I gathered were a form of time-filling while he sorted himself out underneath.

'I'll get my licence back for next season,' he said.

'Great.'

'Seabury's a good track. I'll be riding there in August. All the lads think it's fine the course is still going, even if . . .' He glanced at my hand. 'Well . . . you couldn't race with it anyway, could you, as it was?'

'Jacksy,' I said, exasperated. 'Will you or won't you?'

He flipped through the notes again, and folded them, and put them in his pocket.

'Yes. All right. Here's your wallet.'

'Put it in the glove box.'

He did that, and looked out of the window. 'Where are we going?' he said.

'Anywhere you like.'

'I got a lift to Chester. He'll have gone without me by now. Can you take me south, like, and I'll hitch the rest.'

So I drove towards London, and Jacksy talked.

'Rammileese gave me ten times the regular fee, for riding a loser. Now listen, Sid, you swear this won't get back to him?'

'Not through me.'

'Yeah. Well, I suppose I do trust you.'

'Get on, then.'

'He buys quite good horses. Horses that can win. Then he syndicates them. I reckon sometimes he makes five hundred per cent profit on them, for a start. He bought one I knew of for six thousand and sold ten shares at three thousand each. He's got two pals who are OK registered owners, and he puts one of them in each syndicate, and they swing it so some fancy figurehead takes a share, so the whole thing looks right.'

'Who are the two pals?'

He gulped a lot, but told me. One name meant nothing, but the other had appeared on all of Philip Friarly's syndicates.

'Right,' I said. 'On you go.'

'The horses get trained by anyone who can turn them out looking nice for double the usual training fees and no questions asked. Then Rammileese works out what races they're going to run in, and they're all running way below their real class, see, so that when he says go, by Christ you're on a flyer.' He grinned. 'Twenty times the riding fee, for a winner.'

It sounded a lot more than it was.

'How often did you ride for him?'

'One or two, most weeks.'

'Will you do it again, when you get your licence back?'

He turned in his seat until his back was against the car's door and spent a long time studying the half he could see of my face. His silence itself was an answer, but when we had travelled fully three miles he sighed deeply and said, finally, 'Yes.'

As an act of trust, that was remarkable.

'Tell me about the horses,' I said, and he did, at some length. The names of some of them were a great surprise, and the careers of all of them as straightforward as Nicholas Ashe.

'Tell me how you got your licence suspended,' I said.

He had been riding for one of the amenable trainers, he said, only the trainer hadn't had an amenable wife. 'She had a bit of a spite on, so she shopped him with the Jockey Club. Wrote to Thomas Ullaston personally, I ask you. Of course, the whole bleeding lot of Stewards believed her, and suspended the lot of us, me, him, and the other jock who rides for him, poor sod, who never got a penny from Rammileese and wouldn't know a backhander if it smacked him in the face.'

'How come,' I said casually, 'that no one in the Jockey Club has found out about all these syndicates and done something positive about Rammileese?'

'Good question.'

I glanced at him, hearing the doubt in his voice and seeing the frown. 'Go on,' I said.

'Yeah . . . This is strictly a whisper, see, not even a rumour hardly, just something I heard . . .' He paused, then he said, 'I don't reckon it's true.'

'Try me.'

'One of the bookies . . . I was waiting about outside the gates at Kempton, see, and these two bookies came out, and one was saying that the bloke in the Security Service would smooth it over if the price was right.' He stopped again, and went on, 'One of the lads said I'd never have got suspended if that bitch of a trainer's wife had sent her letter to the Security Service and not to the big white chief himself.'

'Which of the lads said that?'

'Yeah. Well, I can't remember. And don't look like that, Sid, I really can't. It was months ago. I mean, I didn't even think about it until I heard the bookies at Kempton. I don't reckon there could be anyone that bent in the Security Service, do you? I mean, not in the Jockey Club.'

His faith was touching, I thought, considering his present troubles, but in days gone by I would have thought he was right. Once plant the doubt, though, and one could see there were a lot of dirty misdeeds that Eddy Keith might have ignored in return for a tax-free gain. He had passed the four Friarly syndicates: and he might have done all of the twenty or more. He might even have put Rammileese's two pals on the respectable owners' list, knowing they weren't. Somehow or other, I would have to find out.

'Sid,' Jacksy said. 'Don't you get me in bad with the brass. I'm not repeating what I just told you, not to no stewards.'

'I won't say you told me,' I assured him. 'Do you know those two bookies at Kempton?'

'Not a chance. I mean, I don't even know they were bookies. They just looked like them. I mean, I thought "bookies" when I saw them.'

So strong an impression was probably right, but not of much help; and Jacksy, altogether, had run dry. I dropped him where he wanted, at the outskirts of Watford, and the last thing he said was that if I was going after Rammileese to keep him, Jacksy, strictly out of it, like I'd promised.

I stayed in a hotel in London instead of the flat, and felt overcautious. Chico, however, when I telephoned, said it made sense. Breakfast, I suggested, and he said he'd be there.

He came, but without much hooray. He had trudged around all day visiting the people on the mailing list, but no one had received a begging letter from Ashe within the last month.

'Tell you what, though,' he said. 'People beginning with A and B and right down to K have had wax in the past, so it'll be the Ps and Rs that get done next time, which narrows the leg-work.'

'Great,' I said, meaning it.

'I left sticky labels everywhere with your address on, and some of them said they'd let us know, if it came. But whether they'll bother . . .'

'It would only take one,' I said.

'That's true.'

'Feel like a spot of breaking and entering?'

'Don't see why not.' He started on a huge order of scrambled eggs and sausages. 'Where and what for?'

'Er . . .' I said. 'This morning you do a recce. This evening, after office hours but before it gets dark, we drift along to Portman Square.'

Chico stopped chewing in mid-mouthful, and then carefully swallowed before saying, 'By Portman Square, do you mean the Jockey Club?'

'That's right.'

'Haven't you noticed they let you in the front door?'

'I want a quiet look-see that they don't know about.'

He shrugged. 'All right then. Meet you back here after the recce?'

I nodded. 'The Admiral's coming here for lunch. He went down to the wax factory yesterday.'

'That should put a shine in his eyes.'

'Oh very funny.'

While he finished the eggs and attacked the toast I told him most of what Jacksy had said about the syndicates, and also about rumours of kickbacks in high places.

'And that's what we're looking for? Turning out Eddy Keith's office to see what he didn't do when he should've?'

'You got it. Sir Thomas Ullaston – Senior Steward – says Eddy was along complaining to him about me seeing the files, and Lucas Wainwright can't let me see them without Eddy's secretary knowing, and she's loyal to Eddy. So if I want to look, it has to be quiet.' And would breaking into the Jockey Club, I wondered, be considered 'absolutely diabolical' if I were found out?

'OK,' he said. 'I got the judo today, don't forget.'

'The little bleeders,' I said, 'are welcome.'

Charles came at twelve, sniffing the air of the unfamiliar surroundings like an unsettled dog.

'I got your message from Mrs Cross,' he said. 'But why here? Why not the Cavendish, as usual?'

'There's someone I don't want to meet,' I said. 'He won't look for me here. Pink gin?'

'A double.'

I ordered the drinks. He said, 'Is that what it was, for those six days? Evasive action?'

I didn't reply.

He looked at me quizzically. 'I see it still hurts you, whatever it was.'

'Leave it, Charles.'

He sighed and lit a cigar, sucking in smoke and eyeing me through the flame of the match. 'So who don't you want to meet?'

'A man called Peter Rammileese. If anyone asks, you don't know where I am.'

'I seldom do.' He smoked with enjoyment, filling his lungs and inspecting the burning ash as if it were precious. 'Going off in balloons . . .'

I smiled. 'I got offered the post of regular co-pilot to a madman.'

'It doesn't surprise me,' he said drily.

'How did you get on with the wax?'

He wouldn't tell me until after the drinks had come, and then he wasted a lot of time asking why I was drinking Perrier water and not whisky.

'To keep a clear head for burglary,' I said truthfully, which he half believed and half didn't.

'The wax is made,' he said finally, 'in a sort of cottage industry flourishing next to a plant which processes honey.'

'Beeswax!' I said incredulously.

He nodded. 'Beeswax, paraffin wax, and turpentine, that's what's in that polish.' He smoked luxuriously, taking his time. 'A charming woman there was most obliging. We spent a long time going back over the order books. People seldom ordered as much at a time as Jenny had done, and very few stipulated that the tins should be packed in white boxes for posting.' His eyes gleamed over the cigar. 'Three people, all in the last year, to be exact.'

'Three . . . Do you think . . . it was Nicholas Ashe, three times?'

'Always about the same amount,' he said, enjoying himself. 'Different names and addresses, of course.'

'Which you did bring away with you?'

'Which I did.' He pulled a folded paper out of an inner pocket. 'There you are.'

'Got him,' I said, with intense satisfaction. 'He's a fool.'

'There was a policeman there on the same errand,' Charles said. 'He came just after I'd written out those names. It seems they really are looking for Ashe, themselves.'

'Good. Er . . . did you tell them about the mailing list?'

'No, I didn't.' He squinted at his glass, holding it up to the light, as if one pink gin were not the same as the next and he wanted to memorize the colour. 'I would like it to be you who finds him first.'

'Hm.' I thought about that. 'If you think Jenny will be grateful, you'll be disappointed.'

'But you'll have got her off the hook.'

'She would prefer it to be the police.' She might even be nicer to me, I thought, if she was sure I had failed: and it wasn't the sort of niceness I would want.

Chico telephoned during the afternoon.

'What are you doing in your bedroom at this time of day?' he demanded.

'Watching Chester races on television.'

'Stands to reason,' he said resignedly. 'Well, look, I've done the recce, and we can get in all right, but you'll have to be through the main doors before four o'clock. I've scrubbed the little bleeders. Look, this is what you do. You go in through the front door, right, as if you'd got pukka business. Now, in the hall there's two lifts. One that goes to a couple of businesses that are on the first and second floors, and as far as the third, which is all Jockey Club, as you know.'

'Yes,' I said.

'When all the little workers and Stewards and such have gone home, they leave that lift at the third floor, with its doors open, so no one can use it. There's a night porter, but after he's seen to the lift he doesn't do any rounds, he just stays downstairs. And oh yes, when he's fixed the lift he goes down your actual stairs, locking a door across the stairway at each landing, which makes three in all. Got it?'

'Yes.'

'Right. Now there's another lift which goes to the top four floors of the building, and up there there's eight flats, two on each floor, with people living in them. And between those floors and the Jockey Club below, there's only one door locked across the stairway.'

'I'm with you,' I said.

'Right. Now I reckon the porter in the hall, or whatever you call him, he might just know you by sight, so he'd think it odd if you came after the offices were closed. So you'd better get there before and go up in the lift to the flats, go right up to the top, and I'll meet you there. It's OK, there's a sort of seat by a window, read a book or something.'

'I'll see you,' I said.

I went in a taxi, armed with a plausible reason for my visit if I should meet anyone I knew in the hall: but in fact I saw no one, and stepped into the lift to the flats without any trouble. At the top, as Chico had said, there was a bench by a window, where I sat and thought unproductively for over an hour. No one came or went from either of the two flats. No one came up in the lift. The first time its doors opened, it brought Chico.

Chico was dressed in white overalls and carried a bag of tools. I gave him a sardonic head-to-foot inspection.

'Well, you got to look the part,' he said defensively. 'I came here like this earlier, and when I left I told the chap I'd be back with spare parts. He just nodded when I walked in just now. When we go, I'll keep him talking while you gumshoe out.'

'If it's the same chap.'

'He goes off at eight. We better be finished by then.'

'Was the Jockey Club lift still working?' I said.

'Yeah.'

'Is the stairway door above the Jockey Club locked?'

'Yeah.'

'Let's go down there, then, so we can hear when the porter brings the lift up and leaves it.'

He nodded. We went through the door beside the lift, into the stair well, which was utilitarian, not plushy, and lit by electric lights, and just inside there dumped the clinking bag of tools. Four floors down we came to the locked door, and stood there, waiting.

The door was flat, made of some filling covered on the side on which we stood by a sheet of silvery metal. The keyhole proclaimed a mortice lock set into the depth of the door, the sort of barrier which took Chico about three minutes, usually, to negotiate.

As usual on these excursions, we had brought gloves. I thought back to one of the first times, when Chico had said, 'One good thing about that hand of yours, it can't leave any dabs.' I wore a glove over it anyway, as being a lot less noticeable if we were ever casually seen where we shouldn't be.

I had never got entirely used to breaking in, not to the point of not feeling my heart beat faster or my breath go shallow. Chico, for all his longer experience at the same game, gave himself away always by smoothing out the laughter lines round his eyes as the skin tautened over his cheekbones. We stood there waiting, the physical signs of stress with us, knowing the risks.

We heard the lift come up and stop. Held our breaths to see if it would go down again, but it didn't. Instead, we were electrified by the noise of someone unlocking the door we were standing behind. I caught a flash of Chico's alarmed eyes as he leapt away from the lock and joined me on the hinge side, our backs pressed hard against the wall.

The door opened until it was touching my chest. The porter coughed and sniffed on the other side of the barrier, looking, I thought, up the stairs, checking that all was as it should be.

The door swung shut again, and the key clicked in the lock. I let a long-held breath out in a slow soundless whistle, and Chico gave me the sickly grin that came from semi-released tension.

We felt the faint thud through the fabric of the building as the door on the floor below us was shut and locked. Chico raised his eyebrows and I nodded, and he applied his bunch of lock pickers to the problem. There was a faint scraping noise as he sorted his way into the mechanism, and then the application of some muscle, and finally his clearing look of satisfaction as the metal tongue retracted into the door.

We went through, taking the keys but leaving the door unlocked, and found ourselves in the familiar headquarters of British racing. Acres of carpet, comfortable chairs, polished wood furniture, and the scent of extinct cigars.

The Security Section had its own corridor of smaller workadays offices, and down there without difficulty we eased into Eddy Keith's.

None of the internal doors seemed to be locked, and I supposed there was in fact little to steal, bar electric typewriters and other such trifles. Eddy Keith's filing cabinets all slid open easily, and so did the drawers in his desk.

In the strong evening sunlight we sat and read the reports on the extra syndicates that Jacksy had told me of. Eleven horses whose names I had written down, when he'd gone, so as not to forget them. Eleven syndicates apparently checked and accepted by Eddy, with Rammileese's two registered-owner pals appearing inexorably on all of them: and as with the previous four, headed by Philip Friarly, there was nothing in the files themselves to prove anything one way or the other. They were carefully, meticulously presented, openly ready for inspection.

There was one odd thing: the four Friarly files were all missing.

We looked through the desk. Eddy kept in it a few personal objects: a battery razor, indigestion tablets, a comb, and about sixteen packs of book matches, all from gambling clubs. Otherwise there was simple stationery, pens, a pocket calculator and a desk diary. His engagements, past and future, were merely down as the race meetings he was due to attend.

I looked at my watch. Seven forty-five. Chico nodded and began putting the files back neatly into their drawers. Frustrating, I thought. An absolute blank.

When we were ready to go I took a quick look into a filing cabinet marked 'Personal' which contained slim factual files about everyone presently employed by the Jockey Club, and everyone receiving its pensions. I looked for a file marked 'Mason', but someone had taken that, too.

'Coming?' Chico said.

I nodded regretfully. We left Eddy's office as we'd found it and went back to the door of the stairway. Nothing stirred. The headquarters of British racing lay wide open to intruders, who were having to go empty away.

14

On Friday afternoon, depressed on many accounts, I drove comparatively slowly to Newmarket.

The day itself was hot, the weather reportedly stoking up to the sort of intense heatwave one could get in May, promising a glorious summer that seldom materialized. I drove in shirtsleeves with the window open, and decided to go to Hawaii and lie on the beach for a while, like a thousand years.

Martin England was out in his stable yard when I got there, also in shirtsleeves and wiping his forehead with a handkerchief.

'Sid!' he said, seeming truly pleased. 'Great. I'm just starting evening stables. You couldn't have timed it better.'

We walked round the boxes together in the usual ritual, the trainer visiting every horse and checking its health, the guest admiring and complimenting and keeping his tongue off the flaws. Martin's horses were middling to good, like himself, like the majority of trainers, the sort that provided the bulk of all racing, and of all jockeys' incomes.

'A long time since you rode for me,' he said, catching my thought.

'Ten years or more.'

'What do you weigh, now, Sid?'

'About ten stone, stripped.' Thinner, in fact, than when I'd stopped racing.

'Pretty fit, are you?'

'Same as usual,' I said. 'I suppose.'

He nodded and we went from the fillies' side of the yard to the colts. He had a good lot of two-year-olds, it seemed to me, and he was pleased when I said so.

'This is Flotilla,' he said, going to the next box. 'He's three. He runs in the Dante at York next Wednesday, and if that's OK he'll go for the Derby.'

'He looks well,' I said.

Martin gave a carrot to his hope of glory. There was pride in his kind, fiftyish face, not for himself but for the shining coat and quiet eye and waiting muscles of the splendid four-legged creature. I ran my hand down the glossy neck, and patted the dark bay shoulder, and felt the slender, rock-hard forelegs.

'He's in great shape,' I said. 'Should do you proud.'

He nodded with the thoroughly normal hint of anxiety showing under the pride, and we continued down the line, patting and discussing, and feeling content. Perhaps this was what I really needed, I thought: forty horses and hard work and routine. Planning and administering and paperwork. Pleasure enough in preparing a winner, sadness enough in seeing one lose. A busy, satisfying, out-of-doors lifestyle, a businessman on the back of a horse.

I thought of what Chico and I had been doing for months. Chasing villains, big and small. Wiping up a few messy bits of the racing industry. Getting knocked about, now and then. Taking our wits into minefields and fooling with people with shotguns.

It would be no public disgrace if I gave it up and decided to train. A much more normal life for an ex-jockey, everyone would think. A sensible, orderly decision, looking forward to middle and old age. I alone ... and Trevor Deansgate ... would know why I'd done it. I could live for a long time, knowing it.

I didn't want to.

In the morning at seven-thirty I went down to the yard in jodhpurs and boots and a pull-on jersey shirt. Early as it was, the air was warm, and with the sounds and bustle and smell of the stables all around my spirits rose from bedrock and hovered at somewhere about knee level.

Martin, standing with a list in his hand, shouted good morning, and I went down to join him to see what he'd given me to ride. There was a five-year-old, up to my weight, that he'd think just the job.

Flotilla's lad was leading him out of his box, and I watched him admiringly as I turned towards Martin.

'Go on, then,' he said. There was amusement in his face, enjoyment in his eyes.

'What?' I said.

'Ride Flotilla.'

I swung towards the horse, totally surprised. His best horse, his Derby hope, and I out of practice and with one hand.

'Don't you want to?' he said. 'He'd've been yours ten years ago as of right. And my jockey's gone to Ireland to race at the Curragh. It's either you or one of my lads, and to be honest, I'd rather have you.'

I didn't argue. One doesn't turn down a chunk of heaven. I thought he was a bit mad, but if that was what he wanted, so did I. He gave me a leg-up, and I pulled the stirrup leathers to my own length, and felt like an exile coming home.

'Do you want a helmet?' he said, looking around vaguely as if expecting one to materialize out of the tarmac.

'Not for this.'

He nodded. 'You never have.' And he himself was wearing his usual checked cloth cap, in spite of the heat. I had always preferred riding bareheaded except in races: something to do with liking the feel of lightness and moving air.

'What about a whip?' he said.

He knew that I'd always carried one automatically, because a jockey's whip was a great aid to keeping a horse balanced and running straight: a tap down on the shoulder did the trick, and one pulled the stick through from hand to hand, as required. I looked at the two hands in front of me. I thought that if I took a whip and fumbled, I might drop it: and I needed above all to be efficient.

I shook my head. 'Not today.'

'Right, then,' he said. 'Let's be off.'

With me in its midst the string pulled out of the yard and went right through Newmarket town on the horse-walks along the back roads, out to the wide sweeping Limekilns gallops to the north. Martin, himself riding the quiet five-year-old, pulled up there beside me.

'Give him a sharpish warm-up canter for three furlongs, and then take him a mile up the trial ground, upsides with Gulliver. It's Flotilla's last work-out before the Dante, so make it a good one. OK?'

'Yes,' I said.

'Wait until I get up there,' he pointed, 'to watch.'

'Yep.'

He rode away happily towards a vantage point more than half a mile distant, from where he could see the whole gallop. I wound the left hand rein round my plastic fingers and longed to be able to feel the pull from the horse's mouth. It would be easy to be clumsy, to upset the lie of the bit and the whole balance of the horse, if I got the tension wrong. In my right hand, the reins felt alive, carrying messages, telling Flotilla, and Flotilla telling me, where we were going, and how, and how fast. A private language, shared, understood.

Let me not make a mess of it, I thought. Let me just be able to do what I'd done thousands of times in the past, let the old skill be there, one hand or no. I could lose him the Dante and the Derby and any other race you cared to mention, if I got it really wrong.

The boy on Gulliver circled with me, waiting for the moment, answering my casual remarks in monosyllables and grunts. I wondered if he was the one who would have ridden Flotilla if I hadn't been there, and asked him, and he said, grumpily, yes. Too bad, I thought. Your turn will come.

Up the gallop, Martin waved. The boy on Gulliver kicked his mount into a fast pace at once, not waiting to start evenly together. You little sod, I thought. You do what you damned well like, but I'm going to take Flotilla along at the right speeds for the occasion and distance, and to hell with your tantrums.

It was absolutely great, going up there. It suddenly came right, as natural as if there had been no interval and no missing limb. I threaded the left rein through bad and good hands alike and felt the vibrations from both sides of the bit, and if it wasn't the most perfect style ever seen on the Heath, it at least got the job done.

Flotilla swept over the turf in a balanced working gallop and came upsides with Gulliver effortlessly. I stayed beside the other horse then for most of the way, but as Flotilla was easily the better I took him on from six furlongs and finished the mile at a good pace that was still short of strain. He was fit, I

133

thought, pulling him back to a canter. He would do well in the Dante. He'd given me a good feel.

I said so to Martin, when I rejoined him, walking back. He was pleased, and laughed. 'You can still ride, can't you? You looked just the same.'

I sighed internally. I had been let back for a brief moment into the life I'd lost, but I wasn't just the same. I might have managed one working gallop without making an ass of myself, but it wasn't the Gold Cup at Cheltenham.

'Thanks,' I said, 'for a terrific morning.'

We walked back through the town to his stable and to breakfast, and afterwards I went with him in his Land Rover to see his second lot work on the racecourse side. When we got back from that we sat in his office and drank coffee and talked for a bit, and with some regret I said it was time I was going.

The telephone rang. Martin answered it, and held out the receiver to me. 'It's for you, Sid.'

I thought it would be Chico, but it wasn't. It was, surprisingly, Henry Thrace, calling from his stud farm just outside the town.

'My girl assistant says she saw you riding work on the Heath,' he said. 'I didn't really believe her, but she was sure. Your head, without a helmet, unmistakable. With Martin England's horses, she said, so I rang on the off-chance.'

'What can I do for you?' I said.

'Actually it's the other way round,' he said. 'Or at least, I think so. I had a letter from the Jockey Club earlier this week, all very official and everything, asking me to let them know at once if Gleaner or Zingaloo died, and not to get rid of the carcass. Well, when I got that letter I rang Lucas Wainwright, who signed it, to ask what the hell it was all about, and he said it was really *you* who wanted to know if either of those horses died. He was telling me that in confidence, he said.'

My mouth went as dry as vinegar.

'Are you still there?'

'Yes,' I said.

'Then I'd better tell you that Gleaner has, in fact, just died.'

'When?' I said, feeling stupid. 'Er . . . how?' My heart rate had gone up to at least double. Talk about over-reacting, I thought, and felt the fear stab through like toothache.

'A mare he was due to cover came into use, so we put him to her,' he said, 'this morning. An hour ago, maybe. He was sweating a lot, in this heat. It's hot in the breeding shed, with the sun on it. Anyway, he served her and got down all right, and then he just staggered and fell and died almost at once.'

I unstuck my tongue. 'Where is he now?'

'Still in the breeding shed. We're not using it again this morning so I've left him there. I've tried to ring the Jockey Club, but it's Saturday and Lucas Wainwright isn't there, and anyway, as my girl said that you yourself were actually here in Newmarket . . .'

'Yes,' I said. I took a shaky breath. 'A post-mortem. You would agree, wouldn't you?'

'Essential, I'd say. Insurance, and all that.'

'I'll try and get Ken Armadale,' I said. 'From the Equine Research Establishment. I know him . . . Would he do you?'

'Couldn't be better.'

'I'll ring you back.'

'Right,' he said, and disconnected.

I stood there with Martin's telephone in my hand and looked into far dark spaces. It's too soon, I thought. Much too soon.

'What's the matter?' Martin said.

'A horse I've been inquiring about has died.' . . . Oh God Almighty . . . 'Can I use your phone?' I said.

'Help yourself.'

Ken Armadale said he was gardening and would much rather cut up a dead horse. I'll pick you up, I said, and he said he'd be waiting. My hand, I saw remotely, was actually shaking.

I rang back to Henry Thrace, to confirm. Thanked Martin for his tremendous hospitality. Put my suitcase and myself in the car, and picked up Ken Armadale from his large modern house on the southern edge of Newmarket.

'What am I looking for?' he said.

'Heart, I think.'

He nodded. He was a strong dark-haired research vet in his middle thirties, a man I'd dealt with on similar jaunts before, to the extent that I felt easy with him and trusted him, and as far as I could tell he felt the same about me. A professional friendship, extending to a drink in a pub but not to Christmas cards, the sort of relationship that remained unchanged and could be taken up and put down as need arose.

'Anything special?' he said.

'Yes . . . but I don't know what.'

'That's cryptic.'

'Let's see what you find.'

Gleaner, I thought. If there were three horses I should definitely be doing nothing about, they were Gleaner and Zingaloo and Tri-Nitro. I wished I hadn't asked Lucas Wainwright to write those letters, one to Henry Thrace, the other to George Caspar. If those horses died, let me know . . . but not so soon, so appallingly soon.

I drove into Henry Thrace's stud farm and pulled up with a jerk. He came out of his house to meet us, and we walked across to the breeding shed. As with most such structures, its walls swept up to a height of ten feet, unbroken except for double entrance doors. Above that there was a row of windows, and above those, a roof. Very like Peter Rammileese's covered riding school, I thought, only smaller.

The day, which was hot outside, was very much hotter inside. The dead horse lay where he had fallen on the tan-covered floor, a sad brown hump with milky grey eyes.

'I rang the knackers,' Ken said. 'They'll be here pretty soon.'

Henry Thrace nodded. It was impossible to do the post-mortem where the horse lay, as the smell of blood would linger for days and upset any other horse that came in there. We waited for not very long until the lorry arrived with its winch, and when the horse was loaded, we followed it down to the knackers' yard where Newmarket's casualties were cut up for dog food. A small hygienic place; very clean.

Ken Armadale opened the bag he had brought and handed me a washable nylon boiler suit, like his own, to cover trousers and shirt. The horse lay in a square room with whitewashed walls and a concrete floor. In the floor, runnels and a drain. Ken turned on a tap so that water ran out of the hose beside the horse, and pulled on a pair of long rubber gloves.

'All set?' he said.

I nodded, and he made the first long incision. The smell, as on past occasions, was what I liked least about the next ten minutes, but Ken seemed not to notice it as he checked methodically through the contents. When the chest cavity had been opened he removed its whole heart-lung mass and carried it over to the table which stood under the single window.

'This is odd,' he said, after a pause.

'What is?'

'Take a look.'

I went over beside him and looked where he was pointing, but I hadn't his knowledge behind my eyes, and all I saw was a blood-covered lump of tissue with tough-looking ridges of gristle in it.

'His heart?' I said.

'That's right. Look at these valves . . .' He turned his head to me, frowning. 'He died of something horses don't get.' He thought it over. 'It's a great pity we couldn't have had a blood sample before he died.'

'There's another horse at Henry Thrace's with the same thing,' I said. 'You can get your blood sample from him.'

He straightened up from bending over the heart, and stared at me.

'Sid,' he said. 'You'd better tell me what's up. And outside, don't you think, in some fresh air.'

We went out, and it was a great deal better. He stood listening, with blood all over his gloves and down the front of his overalls, while I wrestled with the horrors in the back of my mind and spoke with flat lack of emotion from the front.

'There are . . . or were . . . four of them,' I said. 'Four that I know of. They were all top star horses, favourites all winter for the Guineas and the Derby. That class. The very top. They all came from the same stable. They all went out to race in Guineas week looking marvellous. They all started hot favourites, and they all totally flopped. They all suffered from a mild virus infection at about that time, but it didn't develop. They all were subsequently found to have heart murmurs.'

Ken frowned heavily. 'Go on.'

'There was Bethesda, who ran in the One Thousand Guineas two years ago. She went to stud, and she died of heart failure this spring, while she was foaling.'

Ken took a deep breath.

'There's this one,' I said, pointing. 'Gleaner. He was favourite for the Guineas last year. He then got a really bad heart, and also arthritis. The other horse at Henry Thrace's, Zingaloo, he went out fit to a race and afterwards could hardly stand from exhaustion.'

Ken nodded. 'And which is the fourth one?'

I looked up at the sky. Blue and clear. I'm killing myself, I thought. I looked back at him and said, 'Tri-Nitro.'

'Sid!' He was shocked. 'Only ten days ago.'

'So what is it?' I said. 'What's the matter with them?'

'I'd have to do some tests to be certain,' he said. 'But the symptoms you've described are typical, and those heart valves are unmistakable. That horse died from swine erysipelas, which is a disease you get only in pigs.'

Ken said, 'We need to keep that heart for evidence.'

'Yes,' I said.

Dear God . . .

'Get one of those bags, will you?' he said. 'Hold it open.' He put the heart inside. 'We'd better go along to the Research Centre, later. I've been thinking . . . I know I've got some reference papers there about erysipelas in horses. We could look them up, if you like.'

'Yes,' I said.

He peeled off his blood-spattered overalls. 'Heat and exertion,' he said. 'That's what did for this fellow. A deadly combination, with a heart in that state. He might have lived for years, otherwise.'

Ironic, I thought bitterly.

He packed everything away, and we went back to Henry Thrace. A blood sample from Zingaloo? No problem, he said.

Ken took enough blood to float a battleship, it seemed to me, but what was a litre to a horse which had gallons. We accepted reviving Scotches from Henry with gratitude, and afterwards took our trophies to the Equine Research Establishment along the Bury Road.

Ken's office was a small extension to a large laboratory, where he took the bag containing Gleaner's heart over to the sink and told me he was washing out the remaining blood.

'Now come and look,' he said.

This time I could see exactly what he meant. Along all the edges of the valves there were small knobbly growths, like baby cauliflowers, creamy white.

'That's vegetation,' he said. 'It prevents the valves from closing. Makes the heart as efficient as a leaking pump.'

'I can see it would.'

137

'I'll put this in the fridge, then we'll look through those veterinary journals for that paper.'

I sat on a hard chair in his utilitarian office while he searched for what he wanted. I looked at my fingers. Curled and uncurled them. This can't be happening, I thought. It's only three days since I saw Trevor Deansgate at Chester. *If you break your assurance, I'll do what I said.*

'Here it is,' Ken exclaimed, flattening a paper open. 'Shall I read you the relevant bits?'

I nodded.

'Swine erysipelas – in 1938 – occurred in a horse, with vegetative endocarditis – the chronic form of the illness in pigs.' He looked up. 'That's those cauliflower growths. Right?'

'Yes.'

He read again from the paper. 'During 1944 a mutant strain of erysipelas rhusiopathiae appeared suddenly in a laboratory specializing in antisera production and produced acute endocarditis in the serum horses.'

'Translate,' I said.

He smiled. 'They used to use horses for producing vaccines. You inject the horse with pig disease, wait until it develops antibodies, draw off blood, and extract the serum. The serum, injected into healthy pigs, prevents them getting the disease. Same process as for all human vaccinations, smallpox and so on. Standard procedure.'

'OK,' I said. 'Go on.'

'What happened was that instead of growing antibodies as usual, the horses themselves got the disease.'

'How could that happen?'

'It doesn't say, here. You'd have to ask the pharmaceutical firm concerned, which I see is the Tierson vaccine lab along at Cambridge. They'd tell you, I should think, if you asked. I know someone there, if you want an introduction.'

'It's a long time ago,' I said.

'My dear fellow, germs don't die. They can live like time-bombs, waiting for some fool to take stupid liberties. Some of these labs keep virulent strains around for decades. You'd be surprised.'

He looked down again at the paper, and said, 'You'd better read these next paragraphs yourself. They look pretty straightforward.' He pushed the journal across to me, and I read the page where he pointed.

1 24–48 hours after intra-muscular injection of the pure culture, inflammation of one or more of the heart valves commences. At this time, apart from a slight rise in temperature and occasional palpitations, no other symptoms are seen unless the horse is subjected to severe exertion, when auricular fibrillation or interference with the blood supply to the lungs occurs; both occasion severe distress which only resolves after 2–3 hours' rest.

2 Between the second and the sixth day pyrexia (temperature rise) increases and white cell count of the blood increases and the horse is listless and off food. This could easily be loosely diagnosed as 'the virus'. However, examination by stethoscope reveals a progressively increasing heart murmur. After about ten days the temperature returns to normal and, unless subjected to more than walk or trot, the horse may appear to have recovered. The murmur is still present and it then becomes necessary to retire the horse from fast work since this induces respiratory distress.

3 Over the next few months vegetations grow on the heart valves, and arthritis in some joints, particularly of the limbs, may or may not appear. The condition is permanent and progressive and death may occur suddenly following exertion or during very hot weather, sometimes years after the original infection.

I looked up. 'That's it, exactly, isn't it,' I said.

'Bang on the nose.'

I said slowly, 'Intra-muscular injection of the pure culture could absolutely not have occurred accidentally.'

'Absolutely not,' he agreed.

I said, 'George Caspar had his yard sewn up so tight this year with alarm bells and guards and dogs that no one could have got within screaming distance of Tri-Nitro with a syringeful of live germs.'

He smiled, 'You wouldn't need a syringeful. Come into the lab, and I'll show you.'

I followed him, and we fetched up beside one of the cupboards with sliding doors that lined the whole of the wall. He opened the cupboard and pulled out a box, which proved to contain a large number of smallish plastic envelopes.

He tore open one of the envelopes and tipped the contents on to his hand: a hypodermic needle attached to a plastic capsule only the size of a pea. The whole thing looked like a tiny dart with a small round balloon at one end, about as long, altogether, as one's little finger.

He picked up the capsule and squeezed it. 'Dip that into liquid, you draw up half a teaspoonful. You don't need that much pure culture to produce a disease.'

'You could hold that in your hand, out of sight,' I said.

He nodded. 'Just slap the horse with it. Done in a flash. I use these sometimes for horses that shy away from a syringe.' He showed me how, holding the capsule between thumb and index finger, so that the sharp end pointed down from his palm. 'Shove the needle in and squeeze,' he said.

'Could you spare me one of these?'

'Sure,' he said, giving me an envelope. 'Anything you like.'

I put it in my pocket. Dear God in heaven.

Ken said slowly, 'You know, we might just be able to do something about Tri-Nitro.'

'How do you mean?'

He pondered, looking at the large bottle of Zingaloo's blood, which stood on the draining board beside the sink.

'We might find an antibiotic which would cure the disease.'

'Isn't it too late?' I said.

'Too late for Zingaloo. But I don't think those vegetations would start growing at once. If Tri-Nitro was infected . . . say . . .'

'Say two weeks ago today, after his final working gallop.'

He looked at me with amusement. 'Say two weeks ago, then. His heart will be in trouble, but the vegetation won't have started. If he gets the right antibiotic soon, he might make a full recovery.'

'Do you mean . . . back to normal?'

'Don't see why not.'

'What are you waiting for?' I said.

15

I spent most of Sunday beside the sea, driving north-east from Newmarket to the wide deserted coast of Norfolk. Just for somewhere to go, something to do, to pass the time.

Even though the sun shone, the wind off the North Sea was keeping the beaches almost empty; small groups were huddled into the shelter of flimsy canvas screens, and a few intrepid children built castles.

I sat in the sun in a hollow in a sand dune which was covered with coarse tufts of grass, and watched the waves come and go. I walked along the shore, kicking the worm casts. I stood looking out to sea, holding up my left upper arm for support, aware of the weight of the machinery lower down, which was not so very heavy, but always there.

I had often felt released and restored by lonely places, but not on that day. The demons came with me. The cost of pride . . . the price of safety. If you didn't expect so much of yourself, Charles had said once, you'd give yourself an easier time. It hadn't really made sense. One was as one was. Or at least, one was as one was until someone came along and broke you all up.

If you sneezed on the Limekilns, they said in Newmarket, it was heard two miles away on the racecourse. The news of my attendance at Gleaner's post-mortem would be given to George Caspar within a day. Trevor Deansgate would hear of it: he was sure to.

I could still go away, I thought. It wasn't too late. Travel. Wander by other seas, under other skies. I could go away and keep very quiet. I could still escape from the terror he induced in me. I could still . . . run away.

I left the coast and drove numbly to Cambridge. Stayed in the University Arms Hotel and, in the morning, went along to Tierson Pharmaceuticals Vaccine Laboratories. I asked for, and got, a Mr Livingston, who was maybe sixty and greyishly thin. He made small nibbling movements with his mouth when he spoke. He looks a dried-up old cuss, Ken Armadale had said, but he's got a mind like a monkey.

'Mr Halley, is it?' Livingston said, shaking hands in the entrance hall. 'Mr Armadale has been on the phone to me, explaining what you want. I think I can help you, yes I do indeed. Come along, come along, this way.'

He walked in small steps before me, looking back frequently to make sure I was following. It seemed to be a precaution born of losing people, because the place was a labyrinth of glass-walled passages with laboratories and gardens apparently intermixed at random.

'The place just grew,' he said, when I remarked on it. 'But here we are.' He led the way into a large laboratory which looked through glass walls into the passage on one side, and a garden on another, and straight into another lab on the third.

'This is the experimental section,' he said, his gestures embracing both rooms. 'Most of the laboratories just manufacture the vaccines commercially, but in here we potter about inventing new ones.'

'And resurrecting old ones?' I said.

He looked at me sharply. 'Certainly not. I believe you came for information, not to accuse us of carelessness.'

'Sorry,' I said placatingly. 'That's quite right.'

'Well then. Ask your question.'

'Er, yes. How did the serum horses you were using in the nineteen forties get swine erysipelas?'

'Ah,' he said. 'Pertinent. Brief. To the point. We published a paper about it, didn't we? Before my time, of course. But I've heard about it. Yes. Well, it's possible. It's possible. It happened. But it shouldn't have done. Sheer carelessness, do you see? I hate carelessness. Hate it.'

Just as well, I thought. In his line of business, carelessness might be fatal.

'Do you know anything about the production of erysipelas antiserum?' he said.

'You could write it on a thumbnail.'

'Ah,' he said. 'Then I'll explain as to a child. Will that do?'

'Nicely,' I said.

He gave me another sharp glance in which there was this time amusement.

141

'You inject live erysipelas germs into a horse. Are you with me? I am talking about the past, now, when they did use horses. We haven't used horses since the early 1950s, and nor have Burroughs Wellcome, and Bayer in Germany. The past, do you see?'

'Yes,' I said.

'The horse's blood produces antibodies to fight the germ, but the horse does not develop the disease, because it is a disease pigs get and horses don't.'

'A child,' I assured him, 'would understand.'

'Very well. Now sometimes the standard strain of erysipelas becomes weakened, and in order to make it virulent again we pass it through pigeons.'

'Pigeons?' I said, very politely.

He raised his eyebrows. 'Customary practice. Pass a weak strain through pigeons to recover virulence.'

'Oh, of course,' I said.

He pounced on the satire in my voice. 'Mr Halley,' he said severely. 'Do you want to know all this or don't you?'

'Yes, please,' I said meekly.

'Very well, then. The virulent strain was removed from the pigeons and subcultured on to blood agar plates.' He broke off, looking at the blankness of my ignorance. 'Let me put it this way. The live virulent germs were transferred from the pigeons on to dishes containing blood, where they then multiplied, thus producing a useful quantity for injecting into the serum horses.'

'That's fine,' I said. 'I do understand.'

'All right.' He nodded. 'Now the blood on the dishes was bull's blood. Bovine blood.'

'Yes,' I said.

'But owing to someone's stupid carelessness, the blood agar plates were prepared one day with horse blood. This produced a mutant strain of the disease.' He paused. 'Mutants are changes which occur suddenly and for no apparent reason throughout nature.'

'Yes,' I said again.

'No one realized what had happened,' he said. 'Until the mutant strain was injected into the serum horses and they all got erysipelas. The mutant strain proved remarkably constant. The incubation period was always 24–48 hours after inoculation, and endocarditis . . . that is, inflammation of the heart valves . . . was always the result.'

A youngish man in a white coat, unbuttoned down the front, came into the room next door, and I watched him vaguely as he began pottering about.

'What became of this mutant strain?' I said.

Livingston nibbled a good deal with the lips, but finally said, 'We would have kept some, I dare say, as a curiosity. But of course it would be weakened by now, and to restore it to full virulence, one would have to . . .'

'Yeah,' I said. 'Pass it through pigeons.'

He didn't think it was funny. 'Quite so,' he said.

'And all this passing through pigeons and subculture on agar plates, how much skill does this take?'

He blinked. 'I could do it, of course.'

I couldn't. Any injections I'd handled had come in neat little ampoules, packed in boxes.

The man in the next room was opening cupboards, looking for something.

I said, 'Would there be any of this mutant strain anywhere else in the world, besides here? I mean, did this laboratory send any of it out to anywhere else?'

The lips pursed and the eyebrows went up. 'I've no idea,' he said. He looked through the glass and gestured towards the man in the next room. 'You could ask Barry Shummuck. He would know. Mutant strains are his speciality.'

He pronounced 'Shummuck' to rhyme with 'hummock'. I know the name, I thought. I . . . *oh my God.*

The shock of it fizzed through my brain and left me half breathless. I knew someone too well whose real name was Shummuck.

I swallowed and felt shivery. 'Tell me more about your Mr Shummuck,' I said.

Livingston was a natural chatterer and saw no harm in it. He shrugged. 'He came up the hard way. Still talks like it. He used to have a terrible chip on his shoulder. The world owed him a living, that sort of thing. Shades of student demos. He's settled down recently. He's good at his job.'

'You don't care for him?' I said.

Livingston was startled. 'I didn't say that.'

He had, plainly, in his face and in his voice. I said only, 'What sort of accent?'

'Northern. I don't know exactly. What does it matter?'

Barry Shummuck looked like no one I knew. I said slowly, hesitantly, 'Do you know if he has . . . a brother?'

Livingston's face showed surprise. 'Yes, he has. Funny thing, he's a bookmaker.' He pondered. 'Some name like Terry. Not Terry . . . Trevor, that's it. They come here together sometimes, the two of them . . . thick as thieves.'

Barry Shummuck gave up his search and moved towards the door.

'Would you like to meet him?' Mr Livingston said.

Speechlessly, I shook my head. The last thing I wanted, in a building full of virulent germs which he knew how to handle and I didn't, was to be introduced to the brother of Trevor Deansgate.

Shummuck went through the other door and into the glass-walled corridor, and turned in our direction.

Oh no, I thought.

He walked purposefully along and pushed open the door of the lab we were in. Head and shoulders leaned forward.

'Morning, Mr Livingston,' he said. 'Have you seen my box of transparencies, anywhere?'

The basic voice was the same, self-confident and slightly abrasive. Manchester accent, much stronger. I held my left arm out of sight half behind my back and willed him to go away.

'No,' said Mr Livingston, with just a shade of pleasure. 'But Barry, can you spare . . .'

Livingston and I were standing in front of a work bench which held various empty glass jars and a row of clamps. I turned leftwards, with my arm still hidden, and clumsily, with my right hand, knocked over a clamp and two glass jars.

More clatter than breakage. Livingston gave a quick nibble of surprised annoyance, and righted the rolling jars. I gripped the clamp, which was metal and heavy, and would have to do.

I turned back towards the door.

The door was shutting. The backview of Barry Shummuck was striding away along the corridor, the front edges of his white coat flapping.

I let a shuddering breath out through my nose and carefully put the clamp back at the end of the row.'

'He's gone,' Mr Livingston said. 'What a pity.'

I drove back to Newmarket, to the Equine Research Establishment and Ken Armadale.

I wondered how long it would take chatty Mr Livingston to tell Barry Shummuck of the visit of a man called Halley who wanted to know about a pig disease in horses.

I felt faintly, and continuously sick.

'It's been made resistant to all ordinary antibiotics,' Ken said. 'A real neat little job.'

'How do you mean?'

'If any old antibiotic would kill it, you couldn't be sure the horse wouldn't be given a shot as soon as he had a temperature, and never develop the disease.'

I sighed. 'So how do they make it resistant?'

'Feed it tiny doses of antibiotic until it becomes immune.'

'All this is technically difficult, isn't it?'

'Yes, fairly.'

'Have you ever heard of Barry Shummuck?'

He frowned. 'No, I don't think so.'

The craven inner voice told me urgently to shut up, to escape, to fly to safety . . . to Australia . . . to a desert.

'Do you have a cassette recorder here?' I said.

'Yes. I use it for making notes while I'm operating.' He went out and

fetched it and set it up for me on his desk, loaded with a new tape. 'Just talk,'
he said. 'It has a built-in microphone.'

'Stay and listen,' I said. 'I want . . . a witness.'

He regarded me slowly. 'You look so strained . . . It's no gentle game, is it,
what you do?'

'Not always.'

I switched on the recorder, and for introduction spoke my name, the
place, and the date. Then I switched off again and sat looking at the fingers I
needed for pressing the buttons.

'What is it, Sid?' Ken said.

I glanced at him and down again. 'Nothing.'

I had got to do it, I thought. I had absolutely got to. I was never in any
way going to be whole again, if I didn't.

If I had to choose, and it seemed to me that I did have to choose, I would
settle for wholeness of mind, and put up with what it cost. Perhaps I could
deal with physical fear. Perhaps I could deal with anything that happened to
my body, and even with helplessness. What I could not forever deal with . . .
and I saw it finally with clarity and certainty . . . was despising myself.

I pressed the 'play' and 'record' buttons together, and irrevocably broke
my assurance to Trevor Deansgate.

16

I telephoned Chico at lunchtime and told him what I'd found out about
Rosemary's horses.

'What it amounts to,' I said, 'is that those four horses had bad hearts
because they'd been given a pig disease. There's a lot of complicated info
about how it was done, but that's now the Steward's headache.'

'Pig disease?' Chico said disbelievingly.

'Yeah. That big bookmaker Trevor Deansgate has a brother who works in
a place that produces vaccines for inoculating people against smallpox and
diphtheria and so on, and they cooked up a plan to squirt pig germs into
those red-hot favourites.'

'Which duly lost,' Chico said. 'While the bookmaker raked in the lolly.'

'Right,' I said.

It felt very odd to put Trevor Deansgate's scheme into casual words and to
be talking about him as if he were just one of our customary puzzles.

'How did you find out?' Chico said.

'Gleaner died at Henry Thrace's, and the pig disease turned up at the post-mortem. When I went to the vaccine lab I saw a man called Shummuck who deals in odd germs, and I remembered that Shummuck was Trevor Deansgate's real name. And Trevor Deansgate is very thick with George Caspar . . . and all the affected horses, that we know of, have come from George Caspar's stable.'

'Circumstantial, isn't it?' Chico said.

'A bit, yes. But the Security Service can take it from there.'

'Eddy Keith?' he said sceptically.

'He can't hush this one up, don't you worry.'

'Have you told Rosemary?'

'Not yet.'

'Bit of a laugh,' Chico said.

'Mm.'

'Well, Sid mate,' he said. 'This is results day all round. We got a fix on Nicky Ashe.'

Nicky Ashe with a knife in his sock. A pushover, compared with . . . compared with . . .

'Hey,' Chico's voice said aggrievedly through the receiver. 'Aren't you pleased?'

'Yes, of course. What sort of fix?'

'He's been sending out some of those damn fool letters. I went to your place this morning, just to see, like, and there were two great envelopes there with our sticky labels on.'

'Great,' I said.

'I opened them. They'd both been sent to us by people whose names started with P. All that leg work paid off.'

'So we've got the begging letter?'

'We sure have. It's exactly the same as the ones your wife had, except for the address to send the money to, of course. Got a pencil?'

'Yeah.'

He read the address, which was in Clifton, Bristol. I looked at it thoughtfully. I could either give it straight to the police, or I could check it first myself. Checking it, in one certain way, had persuasive attractions.

'Chico,' I said. 'Ring Jenny's flat in Oxford and ask for Louise McInnes. Ask her to ring me here at the Rutland Hotel in Newmarket.'

'Scared of your missus, are you?'

'Will you do it?'

'Oh sure.' He laughed, and rang off. When the bell rang again, however, it was not Louise at the other end, but still Chico.

'She's left the flat,' he said. 'Your wife gave me her new number.' He read it out. 'Anything else?'

'Can you bring your cassette player to the Jockey Club, Portman Square, tomorrow afternoon at, say, four o'clock?'

146

'Like last time?'

'No,' I said. 'Front door, all the way.'

Louise, to my relief, answered her telephone. When I told her what I wanted, she was incredulous.

'You've actually *found* him?'

'Well,' I said. 'Probably. Will you come, then, and identify him?'

'Yes.' No hesitation. 'Where and when?'

'Some place in Bristol.' I paused, and said diffidently, 'I'm in Newmarket now. I could pick you up in Oxford this afternoon, and we could go straight on. We might spot him this evening . . . or tomorrow morning.'

There was a silence at the other end. Then she said, 'I've moved out of Jenny's flat.'

'Yes.'

Another silence, and then her voice, quiet, and committed.

'All right.'

She was waiting for me in Oxford, and she had brought an overnight bag.

'Hallo,' I said, getting out of the car.

'Hallo.'

We looked at each other. I kissed her cheek. She smiled with what I had to believe was enjoyment, and slung her case in the boot beside mine.

'You can always retreat,' I said.

'So can you.'

We sat in the car, however, and I drove to Bristol feeling contented and carefree. Trevor Deansgate wouldn't yet have started looking for me, and Peter Rammileese and his boys hadn't been in sight for a week, and no one except Chico knew where I was going. The shadowy future, I thought, was not going to spoil the satisfactory present. I decided not even to think of it, and for most of the time, I didn't.

We went first to the country house hotel which someone had once told me of, high on the cliffs overlooking the Avon gorge, and geared to rich-American-tourist comfort.

'We'll never get in here,' Louise said, eyeing the opulence.

'I telephoned.'

'How organized! One room or two?'

'One.'

She smiled as if that suited her well, and we were shown into a large wood-panelled room with stretches of carpet, antique polished furniture, and a huge fourposter bed decked with American-style white muslin frills.

'My God,' Louise said. 'And I expected a motel.'

'I didn't know about the fourposter,' I said a little weakly.

'Wow,' she said, laughing. 'This is more *fun*.'

We parked the suitcases and freshened up in the modern bathroom tucked discreetly behind the panelling, and went back to the car: and Louise smiled to herself all the way to the new address of Nicholas Ashe.

It was a prosperous-looking house in a prosperous-looking street. A solid five-or-six-bedroomed affair, mellowed and white-painted and uninformative in the early evening sun.

I stopped the car on the same side of the road, pretty close, at a place from where we could see both the front door and the gate into the driveway. Nicky, Louise had said on the way down, often used to go out for a walk at about seven o'clock, after a hard day's typing. Maybe he would again, if he was there.

Maybe he wouldn't.

We had the car's windows open because of the warm air. I lit a cigarette, and the smoke floated in a quiet curl through lack of wind. Very peaceful, I thought, waiting there.

'Where do you come from?' Louise said.

I blew a smoke ring. 'I'm the posthumous illegitimate son of a twenty-year-old window cleaner who fell off his ladder just before his wedding.'

She laughed. 'Very elegantly put.'

'And you?'

'The legitimate daughter of the manager of a glass factory and a magistrate, both alive and living in Essex.'

We consulted about brothers and sisters, of which I had none and she had two, one of each. About education, of which I'd had some and she a lot. About life in general, of which she'd seen a little, and I a bit more.

An hour passed in the quiet street. A few birds sang. Sporadic cars drove by. Men came home from work and turned into the driveways. Distant doors slammed. No one moved in the house we were watching.

'You're patient,' Louise said.

'I spend hours doing this, sometimes.'

'Pretty unexciting.'

I looked at her clear intelligent eyes. 'Not this evening.'

Seven o'clock came and went; and Nicky didn't.

'How long will we stay?'

'Until dark.'

'I'm hungry.'

Half an hour drifted by. I learned that she liked curry and paella and hated rhubarb. I learned that the thesis she was writing was giving her hell.

'I'm so far behind schedule,' she said, 'and . . . oh my goodness, *there he is.*'

Her eyes had opened very wide. I looked where she looked, and saw Nicholas Ashe.

Coming not from the front door, but from the side of the house. My age, or a bit younger. Taller, but of my own thin build. My colouring. Dark hair, slightly curly. Dark eyes. Narrow jaw. All the same.

He looked sufficiently like me for it to be a shock, but was nevertheless quite different. I took my baby camera out of my trouser pocket and pulled it open with my teeth as usual, and took his picture.

When he reached the gate he paused and looked back, and a woman ran after him calling, 'Ned, Ned, wait for me.'

'Ned!' Louise said, sliding down in her seat. 'If he comes this way, won't he see me?'

'Not if I kiss you.'

'Well, do it,' she said.

I took, however, another photograph.

The woman looked older, about forty; slim, pleasant, excited. She tucked her arm into his and looked up at his eyes, her own clearly, even from twenty feet away, full of adoration. He looked down and laughed delightfully, then he kissed her forehead and swung her round in a little circle on to the pavement, and put his arm round her waist, and walked towards us with vivid gaiety and a bounce in his step.

I risked one more photograph from the shadows of the car, and leaned across and kissed Louise with enthusiasm.

Their footsteps went past. Abreast of us they must have seen us, or at least my back, for they both suddenly giggled lightheartedly, lovers sharing their secret with lovers. They almost paused, then went on, their steps growing softer until they had gone.

I sat up reluctantly.

Louise said 'Whew!' but whether it was the result of the kiss, or the proximity of Ashe, I wasn't quite sure.

'He's just the same,' she said.

'Casanova himself,' I said drily.

She glanced at me swiftly and I guessed she was wondering whether I was jealous of his success with Jenny, but in fact I was wondering whether Jenny had been attracted to him because he resembled me, or whether she had been attracted to me in the first place, and also to him, because we matched some internal picture she had of a sexually interesting male. I was more disturbed than I liked by the physical appearance of Nicholas Ashe.

'Well,' I said, 'that's that. Let's find some dinner.'

I drove back to the hotel, and we went upstairs before we ate, Louise saying she wanted to change out of the blouse and skirt she had worn all day.

I took the battery charger out of my suitcase and plugged it in: took a spent battery from my pocket, and rolled up my shirtsleeve and snapped out the one from my arm, and put them both in the charger. Then I took a charged battery from my suitcase and inserted it in the empty socket in the arm. And Louise watched.

I said, 'Are you . . . revolted?'

'No, of course not.'

I pulled my sleeve down and buttoned the cuff.

'How long does a battery last?' she said.

'Six hours, if I use it a lot. About eight, usually.'

She merely nodded, as if people with electric arms were as normal a people with blue eyes. We went down to dinner and ate sole and afterwards strawberries, and if they'd tasted of seaweed I wouldn't have cared. It wasn't only because of Louise, but also because since that morning I had stopped tearing myself apart, and had slowly been growing back towards peace. I could feel it happening, and it was marvellous.

We sat side by side on a sofa in the hotel lounge, drinking small cups of coffee.

'Of course,' she said, 'now that we have seen Nicky, we don't really need to stay until tomorrow.'

'Are you thinking of leaving?' I said.

'About as much as you are.'

'Who is seducing whom?' I said.

'Mm,' she said, smiling. 'This whole thing is so unexpected.'

She looked calmly at my left hand, which rested on the sofa between us. I couldn't tell what she was thinking, but I said on impulse, 'Touch it.'

She looked up at me quickly. 'What?'

'Touch it. Feel it.'

She tentatively moved her right hand until her fingers were touching the tough, lifeless plastic skin. There was no drawing back, no flicker of revulsion in her face.

'It's metal, inside there,' I said. 'Gears and levers and electric circuits. Press harder, and you'll feel them.'

She did as I said, and I saw her surprise as she discovered the shape of the inner realities.

'There's a switch inside there too,' I said. 'You can't see it from the outside, but it's just below the thumb. One can switch the hand off, if one wants.'

'Why would you want to?'

'Very useful for carrying things, like a briefcase. You shut the fingers round the handle, and switch the current off, and the hand just stays shut without you having to do it all yourself.'

I put my right hand over and pushed the switch off and on, to show her.

'It's like the push-through switch on a table lamp,' I said. 'Feel it. Push it.'

She fumbled a bit because it wasn't all that easy to find if one didn't know, but in the end pushed it both ways, off and on. Nothing in her expression but concentration.

She felt some sort of tension relax in me, and looked up, accusingly.

'You were testing me,' she said.

I smiled. 'I suppose so.'

'You're a pig.'

I felt an unaccustomed uprush of mischief. 'As a matter of fact,' I said, holding my left hand in my right, 'if I unscrew it firmly round this way several times the whole hand will come right off at the wrist.'

'Don't do it,' she said, horrified.

I laughed with absolute enjoyment. I wouldn't have thought I would ever feel that way about that hand.

'Why does it come right off?' she said.

'Oh . . . servicing. Stuff like that.'

'You look so different,' she said.

I nodded. She was right. I said, 'Let's go to bed.'

'What a world of surprises,' she said, a good while later. 'Almost the last thing I would have expected you to be as a lover is gentle.'

'Too gentle?'

'No. I liked it.'

We lay in the dark, drowsily. She herself had been warmly receptive and generous, and had made it for me an intense sunburst of pleasure. It was a shame, I thought hazily, that the act of sex had got so cluttered up with taboos and techniques and therapists and sin and voyeurs and the whole commercial ballyhoo. Two people fitting together in the old design should be a private matter, and if you didn't expect too much, you'd get on better. One was as one was. Even if a girl wanted it, I could never have put on a pretence of being a rough, aggressive bull of a lover, because, I thought sardonically, I would have laughed at myself in the middle. And it had been all right, I thought, as it was.

'Louise,' I said.

No reply.

I shifted a little deeper for comfort, and drifted, like her, to sleep.

A while later, awake early as usual, I watched the daylight strengthen on her sleeping face. The fair hair lay tangled round her head in the way I had seen it first, and her skin looked soft and fresh. When she woke, even before she opened her eyes, she was smiling.

'Good morning,' I said.

'Morning.'

She moved towards me in the big bed, the white muslin frills on the canopy overhead surrounding us like a frame.

'Like sleeping in clouds,' she said.

She came up against the hard shell of my left arm, and blinked from the awareness of it.

'You don't sleep in this when you're alone, do you?' she said.

'No.'

'Take it off, then.'

I said with a smile, 'No.'

She gave me a long considering inspection.

'Jenny's right about you being like flint,' she said.

'Well, I'm not.'

'She told me that at the exact moment some chap was smashing up your arm you were calmly working out how to defeat him.'

I made a face.

'Is it true?' she said.

'In a way.'

'Jenny said . . .'

'To be honest,' I said, 'I'd rather talk about you.'

'I'm not interesting.'

'That's a right come-on, that is,' I said.

'What are you waiting for, then?'

'I do so like your retreating maidenly blushes.'

I touched her lightly on her breast and it seemed to do for her what it did for me. Instant arousal, mutually pleasing.

'Clouds,' she said contentedly. 'What do you think of when you're doing it?'

'Sex?'

She nodded.

'I feel. It isn't thought.'

'Sometimes I see roses . . . on trellises . . . scarlet and pink and gold. Sometimes spiky stars. This time it will be white frilly muslin clouds.'

I asked her, after.

'No. All bright sunlight. Quite blinding.'

The sunlight, in truth, had flooded into the room, making the whole white canopy translucent and shimmering.

'Why didn't you want the curtains drawn, last night?' she said. 'Don't you like the dark?'

'I don't like sleeping when my enemies are up and about.'

I said it without thinking. The actual truth of it followed after, like a freezing shower.

'Like an animal,' she said, and then, 'What's the matter?'

Remember me, I thought, as I am. And I said, 'Like some breakfast?'

We went back to Oxford. I took the film to be developed, and we had lunch at *Les Quat' Saisons*, where the delectable pâté de turbot and the superb quenelle de brochet soufflée kept the shadows at bay a while longer. With the coffee, though, came the unavoidable minute.

'I have to be in London at four o'clock,' I said.

Louise said, 'When are you going to the police about Nicky?'

'I'll come back here on Thursday, day after tomorrow, to pick up the photos. I'll do it then.' I reflected. 'Give that lady in Bristol two more happy days.'

'Poor thing.'

'Will I see you, Thursday?' I said.

'Unless you're blind.'

Chico was propping up the Portman Square building with a look of resignation, as if he'd been there for hours. He shifted his shoulder off the stonework at my on-foot approach and said 'Took your time, didn't you?'

'The car park was full.'

From one hand he dangled the black cassette recorder we used occasionally, and he was otherwise wearing jeans and a sports shirt and no jacket. The hot weather, far from vanishing, had settled in on an almost stationary high pressure system, and I was also in shirtsleeves, though with a tie on, and a jacket over my arm. On the third floor all the windows were open, the street noises coming up sharply, and Sir Thomas Ullaston, sitting behind his big desk, had dealt with the day in pale blue shirting with white stripes.

'Come in, Sid,' he said, seeing me appear in his open doorway. 'I've been waiting for you.'

'I'm sorry I'm late,' I said, shaking hands. 'This is Chico Barnes, who works with me.'

He shook Chico's hand. 'Right,' he said. 'Now you're here, we'll get Lucas Wainwright and the others along.' He pressed an intercom button and spoke to his secretary. 'And bring some more chairs, would you?'

The office slowly filled up with more people than I'd expected, but all of whom I knew at least to talk to. The top administrative brass in full force, about six of them, all urbane worldly men, the people who really ran racing. Chico looked at them slightly nervously as if at an alien breed, and seemed to be relieved when a table was provided for him to put the recorder on. He sat with the table between himself and the room, like a barrier. I fished into my jacket for the cassette I'd brought, and gave it to him.

Lucas Wainwright came with Eddy Keith on his heels: Eddy was looking coldly out of the genial face; big bluff Eddy whose warmth for me was slowly dying.

'Well, Sid,' Sir Thomas said. 'Here we all are. Now, on the telephone yesterday you told me you had discovered how Tri-Nitro had been nobbled for the Guineas, and as you see . . . we are all very interested.' He smiled. 'So fire away.'

I made my own manner match theirs: calm and dispassionate, as if Trevor Deansgate's threat wasn't anywhere in my mind, instead of continually flashing through it like stabs.

'I've . . . er . . . put it all on to tape,' I said. 'You'll hear two voices. The other is Ken Armadale, from the Equine Research. I asked him to clarify the veterinary details, which are his province, not mine.'

The well-brushed heads nodded. Eddy Keith merely stared. I glanced at Chico, who pressed the start button, and my own voice, disembodied, spoke loudly into a wholly attentive silence.

'This is Sid Halley, at the Equine Research Establishment, on Monday, May fourteenth . . .'

I listened to the flat sentences, spelling it out. The identical symptoms in four horses, the lost races, the bad hearts. My request, via Lucas Wainwright, to be informed if any of the three still alive should die. The post-mortem on Gleaner, with Ken Armadale repeating in greater detail my own simpler account. His voice explaining, again after me, how horses had come to be infected by a disease of pigs. His voice saying, 'I found active live germs in the lesions on Gleaner's heart valves, and also in the blood taken from Zingaloo . . .' and my voice continuing, 'A mutant strain of the disease was produced at the Tierson Vaccine Laboratory at Cambridge in the following manner . . .'

It wasn't the easiest of procedures to understand, but I watched the faces and saw that they did, particularly by the time Ken Armadale had gone through it all again, confirming what I'd said.

'As to motive and opportunity,' my voice said, 'we come to a man called Trevor Deansgate . . .'

Sir Thomas's head snapped back from its forward, listening posture, and he stared at me bleakly from across the room. Remembering, no doubt, that he had entertained Trevor Deansgate in the Stewards' box at Chester. Remembering perhaps that he had brought me and Trevor Deansgate there face to face.

Among the other listeners the name had created an almost equal stir. All of them either knew him or knew of him: the big up-and-coming influence among the bookmakers, the powerful man shouldering his way into top-rank social acceptance. They knew Trevor Deansgate, and their faces were shocked.

'The real name of Trevor Deansgate is Trevor Shummuck,' my voice said. 'There is a research worker at the vaccine laboratory called Barry Shummuck, who is his brother. The two brothers, on friendly terms, have been seen together at the laboratories on several occasions . . .'

Oh God, I thought. My voice went on, and I listened in snatches. I've really done it. There's no going back.

'. . . This is the laboratory where the mutant strain originally arose . . . unlikely after all this time for there to be any of it anywhere else . . .

'Trevor Deansgate owns a horse which George Caspar trains. Trevor Deansgate is on good terms with Caspar . . . watches the morning gallops and goes to breakfast. Trevor Deansgate stood to make a fortune if he knew in advance that the over-winter favourites for the Guineas and the Derby couldn't win. Trevor Deansgate had the means – the disease; the motive – money; and the opportunity – entry into Caspar's well-guarded stable. It would seem, therefore, that there are grounds for investigating his activities further.'

My voice stopped, and after a minute or two Chico switched off the recorder. Looking slightly dazed himself, he ejected the cassette and laid it carefully on the table.

'It's incredible,' Sir Thomas said, but not as if he didn't believe it. 'What do you think, Lucas?'

Lucas Wainwright cleared his throat. 'I think we should congratulate Sid on an exceptional piece of work.'

Except for Eddy Keith, they agreed with him and did so, to my embarrassment, and I thought it generous of him to have said it all, considering the Security themselves had done negative dope tests and left it at that. But then the Security, I reflected, hadn't had Rosemary Caspar visiting them in false curls and hysteria: and they hadn't had the benefit of Trevor Deansgate revealing himself to them as a villain before they even positively suspected him, threatening vile things if they didn't leave him alone.

As Chico had said, our successes had stirred up the enemy to the point where they were likely to clobber us before we knew why.

Eddy Keith sat with his head very still, watching me. I looked back at him, probably with much the same deceptively blank outer expression. Whatever he was thinking, I couldn't read. What I thought about was breaking into his office, and if he could read that he was clairvoyant.

Sir Thomas and the administrators, consulting among themselves, raised their heads to listen when Lucas Wainwright asked a question.

'Do you really think, Sid, that Deansgate infected those horses himself?' He seemed to think it unlikely. 'Surely he couldn't produce a syringe anywhere near any of those horses, let alone all four.'

'I did think,' I said, 'that it might have been someone else . . . like a work jockey, or even a vet . . .' Inky Poole and Brothersmith, I thought, would have had me for slander if they could have heard. '. . . But there's a way almost anyone could do it.'

I dipped again into my jacket and produced the packet containing the needle attached to the pea-sized bladder. I gave the packet to Sir Thomas, who opened it, tipping the contents on to his desk.

They all looked. Understood. Were convinced.

'He'd be more likely to do it himself if he could,' I said. 'He wouldn't want to risk anyone else knowing, and perhaps having a hold over him.'

'It amazes me,' Sir Thomas said with apparent genuineness, 'how you work these things out, Sid.'

'But I . . .'

'Yes,' he said, smiling. 'We all know what you're going to say. At heart you're still a jockey.'

There seemed to be a long pause. Then I said. 'Sir, you're wrong. This . . .' I pointed to the cassette, 'is what I am now. And from now on.'

His face sobered into a long frowning look in which it seemed that he was reassessing his whole view of me, as so many others had recently done. It was to him, as to Rosemary, that I still appeared as a jockey, but to myself, no longer. When he spoke again his voice was an octave lower, and thoughtful.

'We've taken you too lightly.' He paused. 'I did mean what I said to you at Chester about being a positive force for good in racing, but I also see that I thought of it as something of an unexpected joke.' He shook his head slowly. 'I'm sorry.'

Lucas Wainwright said briskly, 'It's been increasingly clear what Sid has become.' He was tired of the subject and waiting as usual to spur on to the next thing. 'Do you have any plans, Sid, as to what to do next?'

'Talk to the Caspars,' I said. 'I thought I might drive up there tomorrow.'

'Good idea,' Lucas said. 'You won't mind if I come? It's a matter for the Security Service now, of course.'

'And for the police, in due course,' said Sir Thomas, with a touch of gloom. He saw all public prosecutions for racing-based crimes as sources of disgrace to the whole industry, and was inclined to let people get away with things, if prosecuting them would involve a damaging scandal. I tended to agree with him, to the point of doing the same myself, but only if privately one could fix it so that the offence wouldn't be repeated.

'If you're coming, Commander,' I said to Lucas Wainwright, 'perhaps you could make an appointment with them. They may be going to York. I was simply going to turn up at Newmarket early and trust to luck, but you won't want to do that.'

'Definitely not,' he said crisply. 'I'll telephone straight away.'

He bustled off to his own office, and I put the cassette into its small plastic box and handed it to Sir Thomas.

'I put it on tape because it's complicated, and you might want to hear it again.'

'You're so right, Sid,' said one of the administrators, ruefully. 'All that about pigeons . . .!'

Lucas Wainwright came back. 'The Caspars are at York, but went by air-taxi and are returning tonight. George Caspar wants to see his horses work, in the morning, before flying back to York. I told his secretary chap that it was of the utmost importance I see Caspar, so we're due there at eleven. Suit you, Sid?'

'Yes, fine.'

'Pick me up here, then, at nine?'

I nodded. 'OK.'

'I'll be in my office, checking the mail.'

Eddy Keith gave me a final blank stare and without a word removed himself from the room.

Sir Thomas and all the administrators shook my hand and also Chico's; and going down in the lift Chico said, 'They'll be kissing you next.'

'It won't last.'

We walked back to where I had left the Scimitar, which was where I shouldn't have. There was a parking ticket under the wiper blade. There would be.

'Are you going back to the flat?' Chico said, folding himself into the passenger's seat.

'No.'

'You still think those boot men . . .'

'Trevor Deansgate,' I said.

Chico's face melted into half-mocking comprehension.

'Afraid he'll duff you up?'

'He'll know by now . . . from his brother,' I shivered internally from a strong flash of the persistent horrors.

'Yeah, I suppose so.' It didn't worry him. 'Look, I brought that begging letter for you . . .'

He dug into a trouser pocket and produced a much-folded and slightly grubby sheet of paper. I eyed it disgustedly, reading it through. Exactly the same as the ones Jenny had sent, except signed with a flourish 'Elizabeth More', and headed with the Clifton address.

'Do you realize they may have to produce this filthy bit of paper in court?'

'Been in my pocket, hasn't it?' he said defensively.

'What else've you got in there? Potting compost?'

He took the letter from me and put it in the glove box, and let down the window.

'Hot, isn't it?'

'Mm.'

I wound down my side window, and started the car, and drove him back to his place in Finchley Road.

'I'll stay in the same hotel,' I said. 'And look . . . come to Newmarket with me tomorrow.'

'Sure, if you want. What for?'

I shrugged, making light of it. 'Bodyguard.'

He was surprised. He said wonderingly, 'You can't really be afraid of him . . . this Deansgate . . . are you?'

I shifted in my seat a bit, and sighed.

'I guess so,' I said.

17

I talked to Ken Armadale in the early evening. He wanted to know how my session with the Jockey Club had gone, but more than that he sounded smugly self-satisfied, and not without reason.

'That erysipelas strain has been made immune to practically every antibiotic in the book,' he said. 'Very thorough. But I reckon there's an obscure little bunch he won't have bothered with, because no one would think of pumping them into horses. Rare, they are, and expensive. All the signs I have here are that they would work. Anyway, I've tracked some down.'

'Great,' I said. 'Where?'

'In London, at one of the teaching hospitals. I've talked with the pharmacist there, and he's promised to pack some in a box and leave it at the reception desk for you to collect. It will have Halley on it.'

'Ken, you're terrific.'

'I've had to mortgage my soul, to get it.

I picked up the parcel in the morning and arrived at Portman Square to find Chico again waiting on the doorstep. Lucas Wainwright came down from his office and said he would drive us in his car, if we liked, and I thought of all the touring around I'd been doing for the past fortnight, and accepted gratefully. We left the Scimitar in the car park which had been full the day before, a temporary open-air affair in a cleared building site and set off to Newmarket in a large, air-conditioned Mercedes.

'It's too darned hot,' Lucas said, switching on the refrigeration. 'Wrong time of year.'

He had come tidily dressed in a suit, which Chico and I hadn't: jeans and sports shirts and not a jacket between us.

'Nice car, this,' Chico said admiringly.

'You used to have a Merc, Sid, didn't you?' Lucas said.

I said yes, and we talked about cars half the way to Suffolk. Lucas drove well but as impatiently as he did everything else. A pepper and salt man, I thought, sitting beside him. Brown and grey speckled hair, brownish grey eyes, with flecks in the iris. Brown and grey checked shirt, with nondescript tie. Pepper and salt in his manner, in his speech patterns, in all his behaviour.

He said, as in the end he was bound to, 'How are you getting on with the syndicates?'

Chico, sitting in the back seat, made a noise between a laugh and a snort.

'Er . . .' I said. 'Pity you asked, really.'

'Like that, is it?' Lucas said, frowning.

'Well,' I said. 'There is very clearly something going on, but we haven't come up with much more than rumour and hearsay.' I paused. 'Any chance of us collecting expenses?'

He was grimly amused. 'I suppose I could put it under the heading of general assistance to the Jockey Club. Can't see the administrators quibbling, after yesterday.'

Chico gave me a thumbs up sign from behind Lucas's head, and I thought I would pile it on a bit while the climate was favourable, and recover what I'd paid to Jacksy.

'Do you want us to go on trying?' I said.

'Definitely.' He nodded positively. 'Very much so.'

We reached Newmarket in good time and came to a smooth halt in George Caspar's well-tended driveway.

There were no other cars there; certainly not Trevor Deansgate's Jaguar. On that day he should be in the normal course of things at York, attending to his bookmaking business. I had no faith that he was.

George, expecting Lucas, was not at all pleased to see me, and Rosemary, coming downstairs and spotting me in the hall, charged across the parquet and rugs with shrill disapproval.

'Get out,' she said. 'How dare you come here?'

Two spots of colour flamed in her cheeks, and she looked almost as if she was going to try to throw me out bodily.

'No, no, I say,' Lucas Wainwright said, writhing as usual with naval embarrassment in the face of immodest female behaviour. 'George, make your wife *listen* to what we've come to tell you.'

Rosemary was persuaded, with a ramrod stiff back, to perch on a chair in her elegant drawing room, while Chico and I sat lazily in armchairs, and Lucas Wainwright did the talking, this time, about pig disease and bad hearts.

The Caspars listened in growing bewilderment and dismay, and when Lucas mentioned 'Trevor Deansgate' George stood up and began striding about in agitation.

'It isn't possible,' he said. 'Not Trevor. He's a friend.'

'Did you let him near Tri-Nitro, after that last training gallop?' I said.

George's face gave the answer.

'Sunday morning,' Rosemary said, in a hard cold voice. 'He came on the Sunday. He often does. He and George walked round the yard.' She paused. 'Trevor likes slapping horses. Slaps their rumps. Some people do that. Some people pat necks. Some people pull ears. Trevor slaps rumps.'

Lucas said, 'In due course, George, you'll have to give evidence in court.'

'I'm going to look a damned fool, aren't I?' he said sourly. 'Filling my yard with guards and taking Deansgate in myself.'

Rosemary looked at me stonily, unforgiving.

'I told you they were being nobbled. I told you. You didn't believe me.'

Lucas looked surprised. 'But I thought you understood, Mrs Caspar. Sid did believe you. It was Sid who did all this investigating, not the Jockey Club.'

Her mouth opened, and stayed open, speechlessly.

'Look,' I said awkwardly. 'I've brought you a present. Ken Armadale along at the Equine Research has done a lot of work for you, and he thinks Tri-Nitro can be cured, by a course of some rather rare antibiotics. I've brought them with me from London.'

I stood up and took the box to Rosemary: put it into her hands, and kissed her cheek.

'I'm sorry, Rosemary love, that it wasn't in time for the Guineas. Maybe the Derby . . . but anyway the Irish Derby and the Diamond Stakes, and the Arc de Triomphe. Tri-Nitro will be fine for those.'

Rosemary Caspar, that tough lady, burst into tears.

We didn't get back to London until nearly five, owing to Lucas insisting on going to see Ken Armadale and Henry Thrace himself, face to face. The Director of Security to the Jockey Club was busy making everything official.

He was visibly relieved when Ken absolved the people who'd done blood tests on the horses after their disaster races.

'The germ makes straight for the heart valves, and in the acute stage you'd never find it loose in the blood, even if you were thinking of illness and not merely looking for dope. It's only later, sometimes, that it gets freed into the blood, as it had in Zingaloo, when we took that sample.'

'Do you mean,' Lucas demanded, 'that if you did a blood test on Tri-Nitro at this minute you couldn't prove he had the disease?'

Ken said, 'You would only find antibodies.'

Lucas wasn't happy. 'Then how can we prove in court that he has got it?'

'Well,' Ken said, 'you could do an erysipelas antibody count today and another in a week's time. There would be a sharp rise in the number present, which would prove the horse must have the disease, because he's fighting it.'

Lucas shook his head mournfully. 'Juries won't like this.'

'Stick to Gleaner,' I said, and Ken agreed.

At one point Lucas disappeared into the Jockey Club rooms in the High Street and Chico and I drank in the White Hart and felt hot.

I changed the batteries. Routine. The day crawled.

'Let's go to Spain,' I said.

'Spain?'

'Anywhere.'

'I could just fancy a senorita.'

'You're disgusting.'

'Look who's talking.'

We reordered and drank and still felt hot.

'How much do you reckon we'll get?' Chico said.

'More or less what we ask.'

George Caspar had promised, if Tri-Nitro recovered, that the horse's owner would give us the earth.

'A fee will do,' I said drily.

Chico said, 'What will you ask, then?'

'I don't know. Perhaps five per cent of his prize money.'

'He couldn't complain.'

We set off southwards, finally, in the cooling car, and listened on the radio to the Dante Stakes at York.

Flotilla, to my intense pleasure, won it.

Chico, in the back seat, went to sleep. Lucas drive as impatiently as on the way up: and I sat and thought of Rosemary and Trevor Deansgate, and Nicholas Ashe, and Trevor Deansgate, and Louise, and Trevor Deansgate.

Stab. Stab. '*I'll do what I said.*'

Lucas dropped us at the entrance to the car park where I'd left the Scimitar. It would be like a furnace inside, I thought, sitting there all day in the sun. Chico and I walked over to it across the uneven stone-strewn ground.

Chico yawned.

A bath, I thought. A long drink. Dinner. Find a hotel room again . . . not the flat.

There was a Land Rover with a two-horse trailer parked beside my car. Odd, I thought idly, to see them in central London. Chico, still yawning, walked between the trailer and my car to wait for me to unlock the doors.

'It'll be baking,' I said, fishing down into my pocket for the keys, and looking downwards into the car.

Chico made a choking sort of noise. I looked up, and thought confusedly how fast, how very fast a slightly boring hot afternoon could turn to stone cold disaster.

A large man stood in the space between the trailer and my car with his left arm clamped around Chico, who was facing me. The man was more or less supporting Chico's weight, because Chico's head lolled forward.

In his right hand the man held a small pear-shaped black truncheon.

The second man was letting down the ramp at the rear of the trailer.

I had no difficulty in recognizing them. The last time I'd seen them I'd been with a fortune teller who hadn't liked my chances.

'Get in the trailer, laddie,' the one holding Chico said to me. 'The right-hand stall, laddie. Nice and quick. Otherwise I'll give your friend another tap or two. On the eyes, laddie. Or the base of the brain.'

Chico, on the far side of the Scimitar, mumbled vaguely and moved his head. The big man raised his truncheon and produced another short burst of uncompromising Scottish accent.

'Get in the trailer,' he said. 'Go right in, to the back.'

Seething with fury, I walked round the back of my car and up the ramp into the trailer. The right-hand stall, as he'd said. To the back. The second man stood carefully out of hitting distance, and there was no one else in the car park.

I found I was still holding my car keys, and put them back automatically into my pocket. Keys, handkerchief, money . . . and in the left-hand pocket, only a discharged battery. No weapon of any sort. A knife in the sock, I thought. I should have learned from Nicholas Ashe.

The man holding Chico came round to the back of the trailer and half dragged, half carried Chico into the left-hand stall.

'You make a noise, laddie,' he said, putting his head round to my side of the central partition, 'and I'll hit your friend here. On the eyes, laddie, and your friend won't have much face to speak of. Get it?'

I thought of Mason in Tunbridge Wells. A vegetable, and blind.

I said nothing at all.

'I'm travelling in here with your friend, all the way,' he said. 'Just remember that, laddie.'

The second man closed the ramp, shutting out the sunlight, creating instant night. Where many trailers were open at the top at the back, this one was not.

Numb, I suppose, is how I felt.

The engine of the Land Rover started, and the trailer moved, backing out of the parking slot. The motion was enough to rock me against the trailer's side, enough to show I wasn't going very far standing up.

My eyes slowly adjusted to a darkness which wasn't totally black owing to various points where the ramp fitted less closely than others against the back of the trailer. In the end I could see clearly, as if it mattered, the variations that had been done to turn an ordinary trailer into an escape-proof transport. The extra piece at the back, closing the gap usually left open for air, and the extra piece inside, lengthways, raising the central partition from head height to the roof.

Basically, it was still a box built to withstand the weight and kicks of horses. I sat helplessly on the floor, which was bare of everything except muddy dust, and thought absolutely murderous thoughts.

After all that unpredictable travelling around I had agreed to go with Lucas and had stupidly left my car in plain vulnerable view all day. They must have picked me up at the Jockey Club, I thought. Either yesterday, or this morning. Yesterday, I thought, there had been no room in the car park, and I'd left my car in the street and got a ticket . . .

I hadn't been to my flat. I hadn't been back to Aynsford. I hadn't been to the Cavendish, or to any routine place.

I had, in the end, gone to the Jockey Club.

I sat and cursed and thought about Trevor Deansgate.

The journey lasted for well over an hour: a hot, jolting depressing time which I spent mostly in consciously not wondering what lay at the end of it. After a while I could hear Chico talking, through the partition, though not the words. The flat, heavy, Glaswegian voice made shorter replies, rumbling like thunder.

A couple of pros from Glasgow, Jacksy had said. The one in with Chico, I thought, was certainly that. Not an average bashing mindless thug, but a hard man with brain power; and so much the worse.

Eventually the jolting stopped, and there were noises of the trailer being unhitched from the coupling: the Land Rover drove away, and in the sudden quiet I could hear Chico plainly.

'What's happening?' he said, and sounded still groggy.

'You'll find out soon enough, laddie.'

'Where's Sid?' he said.

'Be quiet, laddie.'

There was no sound of a blow, but Chico was quiet.

The man who had raised the ramp came and lowered it, and six-thirty, Wednesday evening, flooded into the trailer.

'Out,' he said.

He was backing away from the trailer as I got to my feet, and he held a pitchfork at the ready, the sharp tines pointing my way.

From deep in the trailer I looked out and saw where we were. The trailer itself, disconnected from the Land Rover, was inside a building, and the building was the indoor riding school on Peter Rammileese's farm.

Timber-lined walls, windows in the roof, open because of the heat. No way that anyone could see in, casually, from outside.

'Out,' he said again, jerking the fork.

'Do what he says, laddie,' said the threatening voice of the man with Chico. 'At once.'

I did what he said.

Walked down the ramp on to the quiet tan-coloured riding-school floor.

'Over there.' He jerked the fork. 'Against the wall.' His voice was rougher, the accent stronger, than the man with Chico. For sheer bullying power, there wasn't much to choose.

I walked, feeling that my feet didn't belong to me.

'Back to the wall. Face this way.'

I turned with my shoulders lightly touching the wood.

Behind the man with the pitchfork, standing where from in the trailer I hadn't been able to see him, was Peter Rammileese. His face bore a nasty mixture of satisfaction, sneer, and anticipation, quite unlike the careful intentness of the two Scots. He had driven the Land Rover, I supposed; out of my sight.

The man with Chico brought Chico to the top of the ramp and held him there. Chico half stood and half lay against him, smiling slightly and hopelessly disorganized.

'Hallo, Sid,' he said.

The man holding him lifted the hand holding the truncheon, and spoke to me.

'Now listen, laddie. You stand quite still. Don't move. I'll finish your friend so quick you won't see it happen, if you move. Get it?'

I made no response of any kind, but after a moment he nodded sharply to the one with the pitchfork.

He came towards me slowly; warily. Showing me the prongs.

I looked at Chico. At the truncheon. At damage I couldn't risk.

I stood . . . quite still.

The man with the pitchfork raised it from pointing at my stomach to pointing at my heart, and from there, still higher. Slowly, carefully, one step at a time, he came forward until one of the prongs brushed my throat.

'Stand still,' said the man with Chico, warningly.

I stood.

The prongs of the pitchfork slid past my neck, one each side, below my chin, until they came to rest on the wooden surface behind me. Pushing my head back. Pinning me by the neck against the wall, unharmed. Better than through the skin, I thought dimly, but hardly a ball for one's self respect.

When he'd got the fork aligned as he wanted it, he gave the handle a strong thrusting jerk, digging the sharp tines into the wood. After that he put his weight into pushing against the handle, so that I shouldn't dislodge what he'd done, and get myself free. I had seldom felt more futile or more foolish.

The man holding Chico moved suddenly as if relaxed, carrying Chico bodily down the ramp and giving him a rough over-balancing shove at the bottom. As weak as a rag doll, Chico sprawled on the soft wood shavings, and the man strode over to me to feel for himself the force being applied in keeping me where I was.

He nodded to his partner. 'And you keep your mind on your business,' he said to him. 'Never mind yon other laddie. I'll see to him.'

I looked at their faces, remembering them for ever.

The hard callous lines of cheekbone and mouth. The cold eyes, observant and unfeeling. The black hair and pale skins. The set of a small head on a thick neck, the ears flat. The heavy shape of a jaw blue with beard. Late thirties, I guessed. Both much alike, and both giving forth at great magnitude the methodical brutality of the experienced mercenary.

Peter Rammileese, approaching, seemed in comparison a matter of sponge. Despite his chums' disapproval he too put a hand on the pitchfork handle and tried to give it a shake. It seemed to surprise him that he couldn't.

He said to me, 'You'll keep your snotty nose out, after this.'

I didn't bother to answer. Behind them, Chico got to his feet, and for one surging moment I thought that he'd been fooling them a bit with the concussed act, and was awake and on the point of some effective judo.

It was only a moment. The kick he aimed at the man who had been holding him wouldn't have knocked over a house of cards. In sick and helpless fury I watched the truncheon land again on Chico's head, sending him down on to his knees, deepening the haze in his brain.

The man with the pitchfork was doing what he'd been told and concentrating on keeping up the pressure on the handle. I tugged and wrenched at it with desperation to get free, and altogether failed, and the big man with Chico unfastened his belt.

I saw with incredulity that what he'd worn round his waist was not a leather strap but a length of chain, thin and supple, like the stuff in grandfather clocks. At one end he had fixed some sort of handle, which he grasped; and he swung his arm so that the free end fizzed through the air and wrapped itself around Chico.

Chico's head snapped up and his eyes and mouth opened with astonishment, as if the new pain had cleared away the mists like a flamethrower. The man swung his arm again and the chain landed on Chico, and I could hear myself shouting, 'Bastards, bloody bastards . . .' and it made no different at all.

Chico swayed to his feet and took some stumbling steps to get away, and the man followed him, hitting him all over with unvarying ferocity, taking a pride in his work.

I yelled incoherently . . . unconnected words, screaming at him to stop . . . feeling anger and grief and an agony of responsibility. If I hadn't taken Chico to Newmarket . . . if I hadn't been afraid of Trevor Deansgate . . . it

164

was because of my fear that Chico was there . . . on that day . . . God . . . Bastard. Stop it . . . Stop . . . Wrenched at the pitchfork and couldn't get free.

Chico lurched and stumbled and finally crawled in a wandering circle round the riding school, and ended lying on his stomach not far away from me. The thin cotton of his shirt twitched when the chain landed, and I saw dotted red streaks of blood in the fabric here and there.

Chico . . . God . . .

It wasn't until he lay entirely still that the torment stopped. The man stood over him, looking down judiciously, holding his chain in a relaxed grasp.

Peter Rammileese looked if anything disconcerted and scared, and it was he who had got us there, he who had arranged it.

The man holding the pitchfork stopped looking at me for the first time and switched his attention to where Chico lay. It was only a partial shift of his balance, but it made all the difference to the pressure on my neck. I wrenched at the handle with a force he wasn't ready for, and finally got myself away and off the wall: and it wasn't the man with Chico I sprang at in bloodlusting rage, but Peter Rammileese himself, who was nearer.

I hit him on the side of the face with all my strength, and I hit him with my hard left arm, two thousand quid's worth of delicate technology packed into a built-in club.

He screeched and raised his arms round his head, and I said 'Bastard' with savage intensity and hit him again, on the ribs.

The man with Chico turned his attentions to me, and I discovered, as Chico had, that one's first feeling was of astonishment. The sting was incredible: and after the lacerating impact, a continuing fire.

I turned on the man in a rage I wouldn't have thought I could feel, and it was he who backed away from me.

I caught the next swing of his chain on my unfeeling arm. The free end wrapped itself round the forearm, and I tugged with such fierceness that he lost his grip on the handle. It swung down towards me, a stitched piece of leather; and if there had been just the two of us I would have avenged Chico and fought our way out of there, because there was nothing about cold blood in the way I went for him.

I grasped the leather handle, and as the supple links unwound and fell off my arm I swung the chain in a circle above my head and hit him an almighty crack around the shoulders. From his wide opening eyes and the outraged Scottish roar I guessed that he was learning for the first time what he had inflicted on others.

The man with the pitchfork at that point brought up the reserves, and although I might perhaps have managed one, it was hopeless against two.

He came charging straight at me with the wicked prongs and although I dodged them like a bullfighter the first man grabbed my right arm with both of his, intent on getting his chain back.

I swung round towards him in a sort of leap, and with the inside of my metal wrist hit him so hard on the ear and side of the head that the jolt shuddered up through my elbow and upper arm into my shoulder.

For a brief second I saw into his eyes at very close quarters: saw the measure of a hard fighting man, and knew he wasn't going to sit on the ramp of the trailer and wail, as Peter Rammileese was doing.

The crash on the head all the same loosened his grasp enough for me to wrench myself free, and I lunged away from him, still clutching his chain, and turned to look for the pitchfork. The pitchfork man, however, had thrown the fork away and was unfastening his own belt. I jumped towards him while he had both his hands at his waist and delivered to him too the realities of their chosen warfare.

In the half-second in which both of the Scots were frozen with shock I turned and ran for the door, where, somewhere outside, there had to be people and safety and help.

Running on wood shavings felt like running through treacle, and although I got to the door I didn't get through it, because it was a large affair like a chunk of wall which pushed to one side on rollers, and it was fastened shut by a bolt which let down into the floor.

The pitchfork man reached me there before I even got the bolt up, and I found that his belt wasn't leather either, nor grandfather clock innards, but more like the chain for tethering guard dogs. Less sting. More thud.

I still had the stinger, and I swung round low from trying to undo the bolt and wrapped it round his legs. He grunted and rushed at me, and I found the other man right at my back, both of them clutching, and unfortunately I did them no more damage after that, though not for want of trying.

He got his chain back because he was stronger than I was and banged my hand against the wall to loosen my grasp, the other one holding on to me at the same time, and I thought well I'm damned well not going to make it easy for you and you'll have to work for what you want: and I ran round the place, and made them run, round the trailer, and round by the walls and down again to the door at the end.

I picked up the pitchfork and for a while held them off, and threw it at one of them, and missed; and because one can convert pain into many other things so as not to feel it, I felt little except rage and fury and anger, and concentrated on those feelings to make them a shield.

I ended as Chico had done, stumbling and swaying and crawling and finally lying motionless on the soft floor. Not so far from the door . . . but a long way from help.

They'll stop now I'm still, I thought: they'll stop in a minute: and they did.

18

I lay with my face in the wood shavings and listened to them panting as they stood over me, both of them taking great gulps of breath after their exertions.

Peter Rammileese apparently came across to them, because I heard his voice from quite close, loaded with spite, mumbling and indistinct.

'Kill him,' he said. 'Don't stop there. Kill him.'

'Kill *him*?' said the man who'd been with Chico. 'Are you crazy?' He coughed, dragging in air. 'Yon laddie . .'

'He's broken my jaw.'

'Kill him yourself then. We're not doing it.'

'Why not? He's cut your ear half off.'

'Grow up, mon.' He coughed again. 'We'd be grassed inside five minutes. We've been down here too long. Too many people've seen us. And this laddie, he's won money for every punter in Scotland. We'd be inside in a week.'

'I want you to kill him,' Peter Rammileese said, insisting.

'You're not paying,' said the Scot, flatly, still breathing heavily. 'We've done what was ordered, and that's that. We'll go into your house now for a beer, and after dark we'll dump these two, as arranged, and then we're finished. And we'll go straight up north tonight, we've been down here too long.'

They went away, and rolled the door open, and stepped out. I heard their feet on the gritty yard, and the door closing, and the metal grate of the outside bolt, which was to keep horses in, and would do for men.

I moved my head a bit to get my nose clear of the shavings, and looked idly at the colour of them too close to my eyes, and simply lay where I was, feeling shapeless, feeling pulped, and stupid, and defeated.

Jelly. A living jelly. Red. On fire. Burning, in a furnace.

There was a lot of romantic rubbish written about fainting from pain, I thought. One absolutely tended not to, because there was no provision for it in nature. The mechanics were missing. There were no fail-safe cut-offs on sensory nerves: they went right on passing the message for as long as the message was there to pass. No other system had evolved, because through millennia it had been unnecessary. It was only man, the most savage of animals, who inflicted pain for its own sake on his fellows.

I thought: I did manage it once, for a short time, after very much too long. I thought: this isn't as bad as that, so I'm going to stay here awake, so I may as well find something to think about. If one couldn't stop the message passing, one could distract the receptors from paying much attention, as in acupuncture; and over the years I'd had a lot of practice.

I thought about a night I'd spent once where I could see a hospital clock. To distract myself from a high state of awfulness I'd spent the time counting.

If I shut my eyes and counted for five minutes, five minutes would be gone: and every time I opened my eyes to check, it was only four minutes; and it had been a very long night. I could do better than that, nowadays.

I thought about John Viking in his balloon, and imagined him scudding across the sky, his blue eyes blazing with the glee of breaking safety regulations like bubbles. I thought about Flotilla on the gallops at Newmarket, and winning the Dante Stakes at York. I thought about races I'd ridden in, and won, and lost; and I thought about Louise, a good deal about Louise and fourposter beds.

Afterwards I reckoned that Chico and I had lain there without moving for over an hour, though I hadn't any clear idea of it at the time. The first sharp intrusion of the uncomfortable present was the noise of the bolt clicking open on the outside of the door, and the grinding noise as the door itself rolled partially open. They were going to dump us, they'd said, after dark; but it wasn't yet dark.

Footsteps made no sound on that soft surface, so that the first thing I heard was a voice.

'Are you asleep?'

'No,' I said.

I shifted my head back a bit and saw little Mark squatting there on his heels, in his pyjamas, studying me with six-year-old concern. Beyond him, the door, open enough to let his small body through. On the other side of the door, out in the yard, the Land Rover.

'Go and see if my friend's awake,' I said.

'OK.'

He straightened his legs and went over to Chico, and I'd got myself up from flat to kneeling by the time he returned with his report.

'He's asleep,' he said, looking at me anxiously. 'Your face is all wet. Are you hot?'

'Does your Dad know you're down here?' I said.

'No he doesn't. I had to go to bed early, but I heard a lot of shouting. I was frightened, I think.'

'Where's your Dad now?' I said.

'He's in the sitting room with those friends. He's hurt his face and he's bloody angry.'

I practically smiled. 'Anything else?'

'Mum was saying what did he expect, and they were all having drinks.' He thought a bit. 'One of his friends said his eardrum was burst.'

'If I were you,' I said, 'I'd go straight back to bed and not let them catch you out here. Otherwise your Dad might be bloody angry with you too, and that wouldn't be much fun, I shouldn't think.'

He shook his head.

'Good night, then,' I said.

'Good night.'

'And leave the door open,' I said. 'I'll shut it.'

'All right.'

He gave me a trusting and slightly conspiratorial smile, and crept out of the doorway to sneak back to bed.

I got to my feet and staggered around a bit, and made it to the door.

The Land Rover stood there about ten feet away. If the keys were in it, I thought, why wait to be dumped? Ten steps. Leant against the grey-green bodywork, and looked through the glass.

Keys. In the ignition.

I went back into the riding school and over to Chico, and knelt beside him because it was a lot less demanding than bending.

'Come on,' I said. 'Wake up. Time to go.'

He groaned.

'Chico, you've got to walk. I can't carry you.'

He opened his eyes. Still confused, I thought, but a great deal better.

'Get up,' I said urgently. 'We can get out, if you'll try.'

'Sid . . .'

'Yeah,' I said. 'Come on.'

'Go away. I can't.'

'Yes, you damned well can. You just say, "Sod the buggers," and it comes easy.'

It came harder than I'd thought, but I half lugged him to his feet, and put my arm round his waist, and we meandered waveringly to the door like a pair of drunken lovers.

Through the door, and across to the Land Rover. No furious yells of discovery from the house: and as the sitting room was at the far end of it, with a bit of luck they wouldn't even hear the engine start.

I shovelled Chico on to the front seat and shut the door quietly, and went round to the driving side.

Land Rovers, I thought disgustedly, were made for left-handed people. All the controls, except the indicators, were on that side: and whether it was because I myself was weak, or the battery was flat, or I'd damaged the machinery by using it as a club, the fingers of my left hand would scarcely move.

I swore to myself and did everything with my right hand, which meant twisting, which would have hurt if I hadn't been in such a hurry.

Started the engine. Released the brake. Shoved the gear lever into first. Did the rest thankfully with my feet, and set off. Not the smoothest start ever, but enough. The Land Rover rolled to the gate, and I turned out in the opposite direction from London, thinking instinctively that if they found we'd gone and chased after us, it would be towards London that they would go in pursuit.

The 'sod the buggers' mentality lasted me well for two or three miles and through some dicey one-handed gear changing, but suffered a severe setback when I looked at the petrol gauge and found it pointing to nearly empty.

The question of where we were going had to be sorted out, and immediately: and before I'd decided, we came round a bend and found in front of us a large garage, still open, with attendants by the pumps. Hardly believing it, I swerved untidily into the forecourt, and came to a jerking halt by the two-star.

Money in right-hand pocket, along with car keys and a handkerchief. I pulled all of them out in a handful and separated the crumpled notes. Opened the window beside me. Gave the attendant who appeared the money and said I'd have that much petrol.

He was young, a school-kid, and he looked at me curiously.

'You all right?'

'It's hot,' I said, and wiped my face with the handkerchief. Some wood shavings fell out of my hair. I must indeed have looked odd.

The boy merely nodded, however, and stuck the petrol nozzle into the Land Rover's filling place, which was right beside the driver's door. He looked across me to Chico, who was half lying on the front seats with his eyes open.

'What's wrong with him, then?'

'Drunk,' I said.

He looked as if he thought we both were, but he simply finished the filling, and replaced the cap, and turned away to attend to the next customer. I went again through the tedious business of starting right-handedly, and pulled out on to the road. After a mile I turned off the main road into a side road, and went round a bend or two, and stopped.

'What's happening?' Chico said.

I looked at his still wuzzy eyes. Decide where to go, I thought. Decide for Chico. For myself, I already knew. I'd decided when I found I could drive without hitting things, and at the garage which had turned up so luckily, and when I'd had enough money for the petrol, and when I hadn't asked the boy to get us help in the shape of policemen and doctors.

Hospitals and bureaucracy and questions and being prodded about; all the things I most hated. I wasn't going near any of them, unless I had to for Chico.

'Where did we go, today?' I said.

After a while he said, 'Newmarket.'

'What's twice eight?'

Pause. 'Sixteen.'

I sat in a weak sort of gratitude for his returning wits, waiting for strength to go on. The impetus which had got me into the Land Rover and as far as that spot had ebbed away and left room for a return of fire and jelly. Power would come back, I thought, if I waited. Stamina and energy always came in cycles, so that what one couldn't do one minute, one could the next.

'I'm burning,' Chico said.

'Mm.'

'That was too much.'

I didn't answer. He moved on the seat and tried to sit upright, and I saw the full awareness flood into his face. He shut his eyes tight and said *Jesus*, and after a while he looked at me through slits, and said, 'You too?'

'Mm.'

The long hot day was drawing to dusk. If I didn't get started I thought vaguely, I wouldn't get anywhere.

The chief practical difficulty was that driving a Land Rover with one hand was risky, if not downright dangerous, as I had to leave go of the steering wheel and lean to the left every time I changed gear: and the answer to that was to get the left-hand fingers to grip the knob just once, and tightly, so that I could switch off the current, and the hand would stay there on the gear lever, unmoving, until further notice.

I did that. Then I switched on the side-lights, and the head-lights, dipped. Then the engine. I'd give anything for a drink, I thought, and set off on the long drive home.

'Where are we going?' Chico said.

'To the Admiral's.'

I had taken the southern route round Sevenoaks and Kingston and Coln-brook, and there was the M4 motorway stretch to do, and the cross at Maidenhead to the M40 motorway just north of Marlow, and then round the north Oxford ring road and the last leg to Aynsford.

Land Rovers weren't built for comfort and jolted the passengers at the best of times. Chico groaned now and then, and cursed, and said he wasn't getting into a mess like that again, ever. I stopped twice briefly on the way from weakness and general misery, but there wasn't much traffic, and we rolled into Charles's drive in three and a half hours, not too bad for the course.

I switched the Land Rover off and my left hand on, and couldn't get the fingers to move. That was all it needed, I thought despairingly, the final humiliation of that bloody evening, if I had to detach myself from the socket end and leave the electric part of me stuck to the gears. Why, *why*, couldn't I have two hands, like everyone else.

'Don't struggle,' Chico said, 'and you'll do it easy.'

I gave a cough that was somewhere between a laugh and a sob, and the fingers opened a fraction, and the hand fell off the knob.

'Told you,' he said.

I laid my right arm across the steering wheel and put my head down on that, and felt spent and depressed . . . and punished. And someone, some-how, had got to raise the strength to go in to tell Charles we were there.

He solved that himself by coming out to us in his dressing gown, the light streaming out behind him from his open front door. The first I knew, he was standing by the window of the Land Rover, looking in.

'Sid?' he said incredulously. 'Is it you?'

I dragged my head off the steering wheel and opened my eyes, and said, 'Yeah.'

'It's after midnight,' he said.

I got a smile at least into my voice. 'You said I could come any time.'

An hour later, Chico was upstairs in bed and I sat sideways on the gold sofa, shoes off, feet up, as I often did.

Charles came into the drawing room and said the doctor had finished with Chico and was ready for me, and I said no thanks very much and tell him to go home.

'He'll give you some knock-out stuff, like Chico.'

'Yes, and that's exactly what I don't want, and I hope he was careful about Chico's concussion, with those drugs.'

'You told him yourself about six times, when he came.' He paused. 'He's waiting for you.'

'I mean it, Charles,' I said. 'I want to think. I want just to sit here and think, so would you please say goodbye to the doctor and go to bed.'

'No,' he said. 'You can't.'

'I certainly can. In fact, I have to, while I still feel . . .' I stopped. While I still feel *flayed*, I thought: but one couldn't say that.

'It's not sensible.'

'No. The whole thing isn't sensible. That's the point. So go away and let me work it out.'

I had noticed before that sometimes when the body was injured the mind cleared sharply and worked for a while with acute perception. It was a time to use, if one wanted to; not to waste.

'Have you seen Chico's skin?' he said.

'Often,' I said flippantly.

'Is yours in the same state?'

'I haven't looked.'

'You're exasperating.'

'Yeah,' I said. 'Go to bed.'

When he'd gone I sat there deliberately and vividly remembering in mind and body the biting horror I'd worked so hard to blank out.

It had been too much, as Chico said.

Too much.

Why?

Charles came downstairs again at six o'clock, in his dressing gown, and with his most impassive expression.

'You're still there, then,' he said.

'Yuh.'

'Coffee?'

'Tea,' I said.

He went and made it, and brought two big steaming mugs, naval fashion. He put mine on the table which stood along the back of the sofa, and sat with his in an armchair. The empty-looking eyes were switched steadily my way.

'Well?' he said.

I rubbed my forehead. 'When you look at me,' I said, hesitatingly. 'Usually, I mean. Not now. When you look at me, what do you see?'

'You know what I see.'

'Do you see a lot of fears and self-doubts, and feelings of shame and uselessness and inadequacy?'

'Of course not.' He seemed to find the question amusing, and then sipped the scalding tea, and said more seriously, 'You never show feelings like that.'

'No one does,' I said. 'Everyone has an outside and an inside, and the two can be quite different.'

'Is that just a general observation?'

'No.' I picked up the mug of tea, and blew across the steaming surface. 'To myself, I'm a jumble of uncertainty and fear and stupidity. And to others . . . well, what happened to Chico and me last evening was because of the way others see us.' I took a tentative taste. As always when Charles made it, the tea was strong enough to rasp the fur off your tongue. I quite liked it, sometimes. I said, 'We've been lucky, since we started this investigating thing. In other words, the jobs we've done have been comparatively easy, and we've been getting a reputation for being successful, and the reputation has been getting bigger than the reality.'

'Which is, of course,' Charles said drily, 'that you're a pair of dim-witted layabouts.'

'You know what I mean.'

'Yes, I do. Tom Ullaston rang me here yesterday morning, to arrange about stewards for Epsom, he said, but I gathered it was mostly to tell me what he thought about you, which was, roughly speaking, that if you had still been a jockey it would be a pity.'

'It would be great,' I said sighing.

'So someone lammed into you and Chico yesterday to stop you chalking up another success?'

'Not exactly,' I said.

I told him what I had spent the night sorting out; and his tea got cold.

When I'd finished he sat for quite a while in silence, simply staring at me in best give-away-nothing manner.

Then he said, 'It sounds as if yesterday evening was . . . terrible.'

'Well, yes, it was.'

More silence. Then, 'So what next?'

'I was wondering,' I said diffidently, 'if you'd do one or two jobs for me today, because I . . . er . . .'

'Of course,' he said. 'What?'

'It's your day for London. Thursday. So could you bear to drive the Land Rover up instead of the Rolls, and swap it for my car?'

'If you like,' he said, not looking enchanted.

'The battery charger's in it, in my suitcase,' I said.

'Of course I'll go.'

'Before that, in Oxford, could you pick up some photographs? They're of Nicholas Ashe.'

'Sid!'

I nodded. 'We found him. There's a letter in my car, too, with his new address on. A begging letter, same as before.'

He shook his head at the foolishness of Nicholas Ashe. 'Any more jobs?'

'Two. I'm afraid. The first's in London, and easy. But as for the other . . . Would you go to Tunbridge Wells?'

When I told him why, he said he would, even thought it meant cancelling his afternoon's board-meeting.

'And would you lend me your camera, because mine's in the car . . . and a clean shirt?'

'In that order?'

'Yes, please.'

Wishing I didn't have to move for a couple of thousand years I slowly unstuck myself from the sofa some time later and went upstairs, with Charles's camera, to see Chico.

He was lying on his side, his eyes dull and staring vaguely into space, the effect of the drugs wearing off. Sore enough to protest wearily when I told him what I wanted to photograph.

'Sod off.'

'Think about barmaids.'

I peeled back the blanket and sheet covering him and took pictures of the visible damage, front and back. Of the invisible damage there was no measure. I put the covers back again.

'Sorry,' I said.

He didn't answer, and I wondered whether I was really apologizing for disturbing him at that moment or more basically for having tangled his life in mine, with such dire results. A hiding to nothing was what he'd said we were on with those syndicates, and he'd been right.

I took the camera out on to the landing and gave it to Charles.

'Ask for blown-up prints by tomorrow morning,' I said.

'Tell him it's for a police case.'

'But you said no police . . .' Charles said.

'Yes, but if he thinks it's already for the police, he won't go trotting round to them when he sees what he's printing.'

'I suppose it's never occurred to you,' Charles said, handing over a clean shirt, 'that it's your view of you that's wrong, and Thomas Ullaston's that's right?'

I telephoned to Louise and told her I couldn't make it, that day, after all.

Something's come up, I said, in the classic evasive excuse, and she answered with the disillusion it merited.

'Never mind, then.'

'I do mind, actually,' I said. 'So how about a week tomorrow? What are you doing after that for a few days?'

'Days?'

'And nights.'

Her voice cheered up considerably. 'Research for a thesis.'

'What subject?'

'Clouds and roses and stars, their variations and frequency in the life of your average liberated female.'

'Oh Louise,' I said. 'I'll . . . er . . . help you all I can.'

She laughed and hung up, and I went along to my room and took off my dusty, stained, sweaty shirt. Looked at my reflection briefly in the mirror and got no joy from it. Put on Charles's smooth sea island cotton and lay on the bed. I lay on one side, like Chico, and felt what Chico felt; and at one point or other, went to sleep.

In the evening I went down and sat on the sofa, as before, to wait for Charles, but the first person who came was Jenny.

She walked in, saw me, and was immediately annoyed. Then she took a second look, and said, 'Oh no, not again.'

I said merely, 'Hallo.'

'What is it this time? Ribs, again?'

'Nothing.'

'I know you too well.' She sat at the other end of the sofa, beyond my feet. 'What are you doing here?'

'Waiting for your father.'

She looked at me moodily. 'I'm going to sell that flat in Oxford,' she said.

'Are you?'

'I don't like it any more. Louise McInnes has left, and it reminds me too much of Nicky . . .'

After a pause I said, 'Do I remind you of Nicky?'

With a flash of surprise she said, 'Of course not.' And then, more slowly, 'But he . . .' she stopped.

'I saw him,' I said. 'Three days ago, in Bristol. And he looks like me, a bit.'

She was stunned, and speechless.

'Didn't you realize?' I said.

She shook her head.

'You were trying to go back,' I said. 'To what we had, at the beginning.'

'It's not true.' But her voice said that she saw it was. She had even told me so, more or less, the evening I'd come to Aynsford to start finding Ashe.

'Where will you live?' I said.

'What do you care?'

I supposed I would always care, to some extent, which was my problem, not hers.

'How did you find him?' she said.

'He's a fool.'

She didn't like that. The look of enmity showed where her instinctive preference still lay.'

'He's living with another girl,' I said.

She stood up furiously, and I remembered a bit late that I really didn't want her to touch me.

'Are you telling me that to be beastly?' she demanded.

'I'm telling you so you'll get him out of your system before he goes on trial and to jail. You're going to be damned unhappy if you don't.'

'I hate you,' she said.

'That's not hate, that's injured pride.'

'How dare you!'

'Jenny,' I said. 'I'll tell you plainly, I'd do a lot for you. I've loved you a long time, and I do care what happens to you. It's no good finding Ashe and getting him convicted of fraud instead of you, if you don't wake up and see him for what he is. I want to make you angry with him. For your own sake.'

'You won't manage it,' she said fiercely.

'Go away,' I said.

'What?'

'Go away. I'm tired.'

She stood there looking as much bewildered as annoyed, and at that moment Charles came back.

'Hallo,' he said, taking a disapproving look at the general atmosphere. 'Hallo, Jenny.'

She went over and kissed his cheek, from long habit.

'Has Sid told you he's found your friend Ashe?' he said.

'He couldn't wait.'

Charles was carrying a large brown envelope. He opened it, pulled out the contents, and handed them to me: the three photographs of Ashe, which had come out well, and the new begging letter.

Jenny took two jerky strides and looked down at the uppermost photograph.

'Her name is Elizabeth More,' I said slowly. 'His real name is Norris Abbott. She calls him Ned.'

The picture, the third one I'd taken, showed them laughing and entwined, looking into each other's eyes, the happiness in their faces sharply in focus.

Silently, I gave Jenny the letter. She opened it and looked at the signature at the bottom, and went very pale. I felt sorry for her, but she wouldn't have wanted me to say so.

She swallowed, and handed the letter to her father.

'All right,' she said after a pause. 'All right. Give it to the police.'

She sat down again on the sofa with a sort of emotional exhaustion slackening her limbs and curving her spine. Her eyes turned my way.

'Do you want me to thank you?' she said.

I shook my head.

'I suppose one day I will.'

'There's no need.'

With a flash of anger she said, 'You're doing it again.'

'Doing what?'

'Making me feel guilty. I know I'm pretty beastly to you sometimes. Because you make me feel guilty, and I want to get back at you for that.'

'Guilty for what?' I said.

'For leaving you. For our marriage going wrong.'

'But it wasn't your fault,' I protested.

'No, it was yours. Your selfishness, your pigheadedness. Your bloody determination to win. You'll do anything to win. You always have to win. You're so hard. Hard on yourself. Ruthless to yourself. I couldn't live with it. No one could live with it. Girls want men who'll come to them for comfort. Who say, I need you, help me, comfort me, kiss away my troubles. But you . . . you can't do that. You always build a wall and deal with your own troubles in silence, like you're doing now. And don't tell me you aren't hurt because I've seen it in you too often, and you can't disguise the way you hold your head, and this time it's very bad, I can see it. But you'd never say, would you, Jenny, hold me, help me, I want to cry?'

She stopped, and in the following silence made a sad little gesture with her hand.

'You see?' she said. 'You can't say it, can you?'

After another long pause I said, 'No.'

'Well,' she said. 'I need a husband who's not so rigidly in control of himself. I want someone who's not afraid of emotion, someone uninhibited, someone weaker. I can't live in the sort of purgatory you make of life for yourself. I want someone who can break down. I want . . . an ordinary man.'

She got up from the sofa and bent over and kissed my forehead.

'It's taken me a long time to see all that,' she said. 'And to say it. But I'm glad I have.' She turned to her father. 'Tell Mr Quayle I'm cured of Nicky, and I won't be obstructive from now on. I think I'll go back to the flat now. I feel a lot better.'

She went with Charles towards the door, and then paused and looked back, and said, 'Goodbye, Sid.'

'Goodbye,' I said: and I wanted to say Jenny, hold me, help me, I want to cry: but I couldn't.

19

Charles drove himself and me to London the following day in the Rolls with me still in a fairly droopy state and Charles saying we should put it off until Monday.

'No,' I said.

'But even for you this is daunting ... and you're dreading it.'

Dread, I thought, was something I felt for Trevor Deansgate, who wasn't going to hold off just because I had other troubles. Dread was too strong a word for the purpose of the present journey; and reluctance too weak. Aversion, perhaps.

'It's better done today,' I said.

He didn't argue. He knew I was right, otherwise he wouldn't have been persuaded to drive me.

He dropped me at the door of the Jockey Club in Portman Square, and went and parked the car, and walked back again. I waited for him downstairs, and we went up in the lift together: he in his City suit, and I in trousers and a clean shirt, but no tie and no jacket. The weather was still hot. A whole week of it, we'd had, and it seemed that everyone except me was bronzed and healthy.

There was a looking glass in the lift. My face stared out of it, greyish and hollow-eyed, with a red streak of a healing cut slanting across near the hairline on my forehead, and a blackish bruise on the side of my jaw. Apart from that I looked calmer, less damaged and more normal than I felt, which was a relief. If I concentrated, I should be able to keep it that way.

We went straight to Sir Thomas Ullaston's office, where he was waiting for us. Shook hands, and all that.

To me he said, 'Your father-in-law told me on the telephone yesterday, that you have something disturbing to tell me. He wouldn't say what it was.'

'No, not on the telephone,' I agreed.

'Sit down, then. Charles ... Sid ...' He offered chairs, and himself perched on the edge of his big desk. 'Very important, Charles said. So here I am, as requested. Fire away.'

'It's about syndicates,' I said. I began to tell him what I'd told Charles, but after a few minutes he stopped me.

'No. Look, Sid, this is not going to end here simply between me and you, is it? So I think we must have some of the others in, to hear what you're saying.'

I would have preferred him not to, but he summoned the whole heavy mob; the Controller of the Secretariat, the Head of Administration, the Secretary to the Stewards, the Licensing Officer, who dealt with the registration of owners, and the Head of Rules Department, whose province was disciplinary action. They came into the room and filled up the chairs, and for the second time in four days turned their serious civilized faces my way, to listen to the outcome of an investigation.

It was because of Tuesday, I thought, that they would listen to me now. Trevor Deansgate had given me an authority I wouldn't otherwise have had, in that company, in that room.

I said, 'I was asked by Lord Friarly, whom I used to ride for, to look into four syndicates, which he headed. The horses were running in his colours, and he wasn't happy about how they were doing. That wasn't surprising, as their starting prices were going up and down like yoyos, with results to match. Lord Friarly felt he was being used as a front for some right wicked goings on, and he didn't like it.'

I paused, knowing I was using a light form of words because the next bit was going to fall like lead.

'On the same day, at Kempton, Commander Wainwright asked me to look into the same four syndicates, which I must say had been manipulated so thoroughly that it was a wonder they weren't a public scandal already.'

The smooth faces registered surprise. Sid Halley was not the natural person for Commander Wainwright to ask to look into syndicates, which were the normal business of the Security Section.

'Lucas Wainwright told me that all four syndicates had been vetted and OK'd by Eddy Keith, and he asked me to find out if there was any unwelcome significance in that.'

For all that I put it at its least dramatic, the response from the cohorts was of considerable shock. Racing might suffer from its attraction for knaves and rogues, as it always had, but corruption within the headquarters itself? Never.

I said, 'I came here to Portman Square to make notes about the syndicates, which I took from Eddy Keith's files, without his knowledge. I wrote the notes in Lucas's office, and he told me about a man he'd sent out on the same errand as myself, six months ago. That man, Mason, had been attacked, and dumped in the streets of Tunbridge Wells, with appalling head injuries, caused by kicks. He was a vegetable, and blind. Lucas told me also that the man who had formed the syndicates, and who had been doing the manipulating, was a Peter Rammileese, who lived at Tunbridge Wells.'

The faces were all frowningly intent.

'After that I ... er ... went away for a week, and I also lost the notes, so I had to come back here and do them again, and Eddy Keith discovered I'd been seeing his files, and complained to you, Sir Thomas, if you remember?'

'That's right. I told him not to fuss.'

There were a few smiles all around, and a general loosening of tension. Inside me, a wilting fatigue.

'Go on, Sid,' Sir Thomas said.

Go on, I thought. I wished I felt less weak, less shaky, less continuously sore. Had to go on, now I'd started. Get on with it. Go on.

I said, 'Well, Chico Barnes, who was here with me on Tuesday ...' They nodded. 'Chico and I, we went down to Tunbridge Wells, to see Peter Rammileese. He was away, as it happened. His wife and little son were there, but the wife had fallen off a horse and Chico went to the hospital with her, taking the little boy, which left me, and an open house. So I . . . er . . . looked around.'

Their faces said 'Tut tut', but none of their voices.

'I looked for any possible direct tie-in with Eddy, but actually the whole place was abnormally tidy and looked suspiciously prepared for any searches any tax men might make.'

They smiled slightly.

'Lucas warned me at the beginning that as what I was doing was unofficial, I couldn't be paid, but that he'd give me help instead, if I needed it. So I asked him to help me with the business of Trevor Deansgate, and he did.'

'In what way, Sid?'

'I asked him to write to Henry Thrace, to make sure that the Jockey Club would hear at once if Gleaner died, or Zingaloo, and to tell me, so that I could get a really thorough post-mortem done.'

They all nodded. They remembered.

'And then,' I said, 'I found Peter Rammileese on my heels with two very large men who looked just the sort to kick people's heads in and leave them blinded in Tunbridge Wells.'

No smiles.

'I dodged them that time, and I spent the next week rolling around England in unpredictable directions so that no one could really have known where to find me, and during that time, when I was chiefly learning about Gleaner and heart valves and so on, I was also told that the two big men had been imported especially from Scotland for some particular job with Peter Rammileese's syndicates. There was also some rumour of someone high up in the Security Service who would fix things for crooks, if properly paid.'

They were shocked again.

'Who told you that, Sid?' Sir Thomas asked.

'Someone reliable,' I said, thinking that maybe they wouldn't think a suspended jockey like Jacksy as reliable as I did.

'Go on.'

'I wasn't really making much progress with those syndicates, but Peter Rammileese apparently thought so, because he and his two men laid an ambush for Chico and me, the day before yesterday.'

Sir Thomas reflected. 'I thought that was the day you were going to Newmarket with Lucas to see the Caspars. The day after you were here telling us about Trevor Deansgate.'

'Yes, we did go to Newmarket. And I made the mistake of leaving my car in plain view near here all day. The two men were waiting beside it when we got back. And . . . er . . . Chico and I got abducted, and where we landed up was at Peter Rammileese's place at Tunbridge Wells.'

Sir Thomas frowned. The others listened to the unemotional relating of what they must have realized had been a fairly violent occurrence with a calm understanding that such things could happen.

There had seldom been, I thought, a more silently attentive audience.

I said, 'They gave Chico and me a pretty rough time, but we did get out of there, owing to Peter Rammileese's little boy opening a door for us by chance, and we didn't end up in Tunbridge Wells streets, we got to my father-in-law's house near Oxford.'

They all looked at Charles, who nodded.

I took a deep breath. 'At about that point,' I said, 'I . . . er . . . began to see things the other way round.'

'How do you mean, Sid?'

'Until then, I thought the two Scotsmen were supposed to be preventing us from finding what we were looking for, in those syndicates.'

They nodded. Of course.

'But supposing it was exactly the reverse . . . Supposing I'd been pointed at those syndicates in order to be led to the ambush. Suppose the ambush itself was the whole aim of the exercise.'

Silence.

I had come to the hard bit, and needed the reserves I didn't have, of staying power, of will. I was aware of Charles sitting steadfastly beside me, trying to give me his strength.

I could feel myself shaking. I kept my voice flat and cold, saying the things I didn't like saying, that had to be said.

'I was shown an enemy, who was Peter Rammileese. I was given a reason for being beaten up, which was the syndicates. I was fed the expectation of it, through the man Mason. I was being given a background to what was going to happen; a background I would accept.'

Total silence and blank, uncomprehending expressions.

I said, 'If someone had savagely attacked me out of the blue, I wouldn't have been satisfied until I had found out who and why. So I thought, supposing someone wanted to attack me, but it was imperative that I didn't find out who or why. If I was given a false who, and a false why, I would believe in those, and not look any further.'

One or two very slight nods.

'I did believe in that who and that why for a while,' I said. 'But the attack, when it came, seemed out of all proportion . . . and from something one of our attackers said I gathered it was not Peter Rammileese himself who was paying them, but someone else.'

Silence.

'So, after we had reached the Admiral's house, I began thinking, and I thought, if the attack itself was the point, and it was not Peter Rammileese who had arranged it, then who had? Once I saw it that way, there was only one possible who. The person who had laid the trail for me to follow.'

The faces began to go stiff.

I said, 'It was Lucas himself who set us up.'

They broke up into loud, jumbled, collective protest, moving in their chairs with embarrassment, not meeting my eye, not wanting to look at someone who was so mistaken, so deluded, so pitiably ridiculous.

'No, Sid, really,' Sir Thomas said. 'We've a great regard for you . . .' The others looked as if the great regard was now definitely past tense, '. . . but you can't say things like that.'

'As a matter of fact,' I said slowly, 'I would much rather have stayed away and not said it. I won't tell you any more, if you don't want to hear it.' I rubbed my fingers over my forehead from sheer lack of inner energy, and Charles half made, and then stopped himself making, a protective gesture of support.

Sir Thomas looked at Charles and then at me, and whatever he saw was enough to calm him from incredulity to puzzlement.

'All right,' he said soberly, 'we'll listen.'

The others all looked as if they didn't want to, but if the Senior Steward was willing, it was enough.

I said, with deep weariness and no satisfaction, 'To understand the *why* part, it's necessary to look at what's been happening during the past months. During the time Chico and I have been doing . . . what we have. As you yourself said, Sir Thomas, we've been successful. Lucky . . . tackling pretty easy problems . . . but mostly sorting them out. To the extent that a few villains have tried to stop us dead as soon as we've appeared on the skyline.'

The disbelief still showed like snow in July, but at least they seemed to understand that too much success invited retaliation. The uncomfortable shiftings in the chairs grew gradually still.

'We've been prepared for it, more or less,' I said. 'In some cases it's even been useful, because it's shown us we're nearing the sensitive spot . . . But what we usually get is a couple of rent-a-thug bullies in or out of funny masks, giving us a warning bash or two and telling us to lay off. Which advice,' I added wryly, 'we have never taken.'

They had all begun looking at me again, even if sideways.

'So then people begin to stop thinking of me as a jockey, and gradually see that what Chico and I are doing isn't really the joke it seemed at first. And we get what you might call the Jockey Club Seal of Approval, and all of a sudden, to the really big crooks, we appear as a continuing, permanent menace.'

'Do you have proof of that, Sid?' Sir Thomas said.

Proof . . . Short of getting Trevor Deansgate in there to repeat his threat before witnesses, I had no proof. I said, 'I've had threats . . . only threats, before this.'

A pause. No one said anything, so I went on.

'I understand on good authority,' I said, with faint amusement, 'that there would be some reluctance to solve things by actually killing us, as people who had won money in the past on my winners would rise up in wrath and grass on the murderers.'

Some tentative half-smiles amid general dislike of such melodrama.

'Anyway, such a murder would tend to bring in its trail precisely the investigation it was designed to prevent.'

They were happier with that.

'So the next best thing is an ultimate deterrent. One that would so sicken Chico and me that we'd go and sell brushes instead. Something to stop us investigating anything else, ever again.'

It seemed all of a sudden as if they did understand what I was saying. The earlier, serious attention came right back. I thought it might be safe to mention Lucas again, and when I did there was none of the former vigorous reaction.

'If you could just imagine for a moment that there *is* someone in the Security Service who can be bribed, and that it is the Director himself, would you, if you were Lucas, be entirely pleased to see an independent investigator making progress in what had been exclusively your territory? Would you, if you were such a man, be pleased to see Sid Halley right here in the Jockey Club being congratulated by the Senior Steward and being given carte blanche to operate wherever he liked throughout racing?'

They stared.

'Would you, perhaps, be afraid that one of these days Sid Halley would stumble across something you couldn't afford for him to find out? And might you not, at that point, decide to remove the danger of it once and for all? Like putting weedkiller on a nettle, before it stings you.'

Charles cleared his throat. 'A pre-emptive strike,' he said smoothly, 'might appeal to a retired Commander.'

They remembered he had been an Admiral, and looked thoughtful.

'Lucas is only a man,' I said. 'The title of Director of Security sounds pretty grand, but the Security Service isn't that big, is it? I mean, there are only about thirty people in it full time, aren't there, over the whole country?'

They nodded.

'I don't suppose the pay is a fortune. One hears about bent policemen from time to time, who've taken bribes from crooks. Well . . . Lucas is constantly in contact with people who might say, for instance, how about a quiet thousand in readies, Commander, to smother my little bit of trouble?'

The faces were shocked.

'It does happen, you know,' I said mildly. 'Backhanders are a flourishing industry. I agree that you wouldn't want the head of racing security to be shutting his eyes to skulduggery, but it's more a breach of trust than anything aggressively wicked.'

What he'd done to Chico and me was indeed aggressively wicked, but that wasn't the point I wanted to make.

'What I'm saying,' I said, 'is that in the wider context of the everyday immoral world, Lucas's dishonesty is no great shakes.'

They looked doubtful, but that was better than negative shakes of the head. If they could be persuaded to think of Lucas as a smallish-scale sinner they would believe more easily that he'd done what he had.

'If you start from the idea of a deterrent,' I said. 'You see everything from the other side.' I stopped. The inner exhaustion didn't. I'd like to sleep for a week, I thought.

'Go on, Sid.'

'Well . . .'

I sighed. 'Lucas had to take the slight risk of pointing me at something he was involved in, because he needed a background he could control. He must have been badly shocked when Lord Friarly said he'd asked me to look into those syndicates, but if he had already toyed with the idea of getting rid of me, I'd guess he saw at that point how to do it.'

One or two of the heads nodded sharply in comprehension.

'Lucas must have been sure that a little surface digging wouldn't get me anywhere near him – which it didn't – but he minimized the risk by specifically directing my attention to Eddy Keith. It was safe to set me investigating Eddy's involvement with the shady side of the syndicates, because of course he wasn't involved. I could look for ever, and find nothing.' I paused. 'I don't think I was supposed to have much time to find out anything at all. I think that catching us took much longer than was intended in the original plan.'

Catching us . . . catching me. They'd have taken me alone, but both had been better for them . . . and far worse for me . . .

'Took much longer? How do you mean?' Sir Thomas said.

Concentrate, I thought. Get on with it.

'From Lucas's point of view, I was very slow,' I said. 'I was working on the Gleaner thing, and I didn't do anything at all about the syndicates for a week after he asked me. Then directly I'd been told about Peter Rammileese and Mason, and could have been expected to go down to Tunbridge Wells, I went away somewhere else entirely, for another week; during which time Lucas rang Chico four times to ask him where I was.'

Silent attention, as before.

'When I came back, I'd lost the notes, so I did them again in Lucas's office, and I told him Chico and I would go down to Peter Rammileese's place the following day, Saturday. I think it's likely that if we had done so the . . . er . . . deterring . . . would have been done then, but in fact we went the same afternoon that I'd been talking to Lucas, on the Friday, and Peter Rammileese wasn't there.'

Weren't they all thirsty, I wondered? Where was the coffee? My mouth was dry and a good deal of me hurt.

'It was on that Friday morning that I asked Lucas to write to Henry Thrace. I also asked him – entreated him, really – not to mention my name at all in connection with Gleaner, as it might get me killed.'

A lot of frowns awaited an explanation.

'Well . . . Trevor Deansgate had warned me in those sort of terms to stop investigating those horses.'

Sir Thomas managed to raise his eyebrows and imply a frown at one and the same time.

'Are those the threats you mentioned before?' he said.

'Yes, and he repeated them when you . . . er . . . introduced us, in your box at Chester.'

'Good God.'

'I wanted to get the investigation of Gleaner done by the Jockey Club so that Trevor Deansgate wouldn't know it had anything to do with me.'

'You did take those threats seriously,' Sir Thomas said thoughtfully.

I swallowed. 'They were . . . seriously given.'

'I see,' said Sir Thomas, although he didn't. 'Go on.'

'I didn't actually tell Lucas about the threats themselves,' I said. 'I just begged him not to tie me in with Gleaner. And within days, he had told Henry Thrace that it was I, not the Jockey Club, who really wanted to know if Gleaner died. At the time I reckoned that he had just been careless or forgetful, but now I think he did it on purpose. Anything which might get me killed was to him a bonus, even if he didn't see how it could do.'

They looked doubtful. Doubts were possible.

'So then Peter Rammileese – or Lucas – traced me to my father-in-law's house, and on the Monday Peter Rammileese and the two Scots followed me from there to a horse show, where they had a shot at abduction, which didn't come off. After that I kept out of their way for eight more days, which must have frustrated them no end.'

The faces waited attentively.

'During that time I learned that Peter Rammileese was manipulating not four, but nearer twenty syndicates, bribing trainers and jockeys wholesale. It was then also that I learned about the bribable top man in the Security Service who was turning a blind eye to the goings on, and I regret to say I thought it must be Eddy Keith.'

'I suppose,' Sir Thomas said, 'that that was understandable.'

'So, anyway, on Tuesday Chico and I came here, and Lucas at last knew where I was. He asked to come to Newmarket with us on Wednesday, and he took us there in his own super four-litre air-conditioned highly expensive Mercedes, and although he's usually so keen to get on with the next thing, he wasted hours doing nothing in Newmarket, during which time I now think he was in fact arranging and waiting for the ambush to be properly set up, so that this time there should be no mistakes. Then he drove us to where the Scots were waiting for us, and we walked straight into it. The Scots did the special job they had been imported for, which was deterring Chico and me, and I heard one of them tell Peter Rammileese that now that they had done what was ordered they were going north straight away, they'd been in the south too long.'

Sir Thomas was looking slightly strained.

'Is that all, Sid?'

'No. There's the matter of Mason.'

Charles stirred beside me, uncrossing and recrossing his legs.

'I asked my father-in-law to go to Tunbridge Wells yesterday, to ask about Mason.'

Charles said, in his most impressive drawl, 'Sid asked me to see if Mason existed. I saw the police fellows in Tunbridge Wells. Very helpful, all of them. No one called Mason, or anything else for that matter, has ever been found near to death and blinded in their streets, ever.'

'Lucas told me about Mason's case in great detail,' I said. 'He was very convincing, and of course I believed him. But have any of you ever heard of anyone called Mason who was employed by the Security Service, that was so badly injured?'

They silently, bleakly, shook their heads. I didn't tell them that I'd finally had doubts about Mason because there was no file for him in 'Personnel'. Even in a good cause, our breaking and entering wouldn't please them.

A certain amount of gloom had settled on their faces, but there were also questions they wanted to ask. Sir Thomas put their doubts into words.

'There's one obvious flaw in your reverse view of things, Sid, and that is that this deterrent . . . hasn't deterred you.'

After a pause I said, 'I don't know that it hasn't. Neither Chico nor I could go on, if it meant . . . if we thought . . . anything like that would happen again.'

'Like exactly what, Sid?'

I didn't reply. I could feel Charles glancing my way in his best noncommittal manner, and it was he, eventually, who got quietly to his feet, and walked across the room, and gave Sir Thomas the envelope which contained the pictures of Chico.

'It was a chain,' I said matter-of-factly.

They passed the photographs round in silence. I didn't particularly look to see what they were thinking, I was just hoping they wouldn't ask what I knew they would: and Sir Thomas said it baldly. 'Was this done to you as well?'

I reluctantly nodded.

'Will you take your shirt off, then, Sid?'

'Look,' I said. 'What does it matter? I'm not laying any charges of assault or grievous bodily harm, or anything like that. There's going to be no police, no court case, nothing. I've been through all that once, as you know, and I'm not, absolutely not, doing it again. This time there's to be no noise. All that's necessary is to tell Lucas I know what's been happening, and if you think it right, to get him to resign. There's nothing to be gained by anything else. You don't want any public scandal. It would be harmful to racing as a whole.'

'Yes, but . . .'

'There's Peter Rammileese,' I said. 'Perhaps Eddy Keith might really sort out those syndicates, now. It would only get Rammileese deeper in if he boasted that he'd bribed Lucas, so I shouldn't think he would. I doubt if he'd talk about Chico and me, either.'

Except perhaps, I thought sardonically, to complain that I'd hit him very hard.

'What about the two men from Glasgow?' Sir Thomas said. 'Are they just to get away with it?'

'I'd rather that than go to court again as a victim,' I said. I half smiled. 'You might say that the business over my hand successfully deterred me from that sort of thing for the rest of my life.'

A certain amount of urbane relief crept into both the faces and the general proceedings.

'However,' Sir Thomas said. 'The resignation of the Director of Security cannot be undertaken lightly. We must judge for ourselves whether or not what you have said is justified. The photographs of Mr Barnes aren't enough. So please . . . take off your shirt.'

Bugger it, I thought. I didn't want to. And from the distaste in their faces, they didn't want to see. I hated the whole damn thing. Hated what had happened to us. Detested it. I wished I hadn't come to Portman Square.

'Sid,' Sir Thomas said seriously. 'You must.'

I undid the buttons and stood up and slid the shirt off. The only pink bit of me was the plastic arm, the rest being mottled black with dark red crisscrossed streaks. It looked, by that time, with all the bruising coming out, a lot worse than it felt. It looked, as I knew, appalling. It also looked, on that day, the worst it would. It was because of that that I'd insisted on going to Portman Square on that day. I hadn't wanted to show them the damage, yet I'd known they would insist, and I would have to: and if I had to, that day was the most convincing. The human mind was deviously ambivalent, when it wanted to defeat its enemies.

In a week or so, most of the marks would have gone, and I doubted whether there would be a single permanent external scar. It had all been quite precisely a matter of outraging the sensitive nerves of the skin, transient, leaving no trace. With such a complete lack of lasting visible damage, the Scots would know that even if they were brought to trial, they would get off lightly. For a hand, all too visible, the sentence had been four years. The going rate for a few days' surface discomfort was probably three months. In long robbery-with-violence sentences it was always the robbery that stretched the time, not the violence.

'Turn round,' Sir Thomas said.

I turned round, and after a while I turned back. No one said anything. Charles looked at his most unruffled. Sir Thomas stood up and walked over to me, and inspected the scenery more closely. Then he picked up my shirt from the chair, and held it for me to put on again.

I said 'Thank you,' and did up the buttons. Pushed the tails untidily into the top of my trousers. Sat down.

It seemed quite a long time before Sir Thomas lifted the inter-office telephone and said to his secretary, 'Would you ask Commander Wainwright to come here, please?'

If the administrators still had any doubts, Lucas himself dispelled them. He walked briskly and unsuspectingly into a roomful of silence, and when he saw me sitting there he stopped moving suddenly, as if his brain had given up transmitting to his muscles.

The blood drained from his face, leaving the grey-brown eyes staring from a barren landscape. I had an idea that I must have looked like that to Trevor Deansgate, in the Stewards' box at Chester. I thought that quite likely, at that moment, Lucas couldn't feel his feet on to the carpet.

'Lucas,' Sir Thomas said, pointing to a chair, 'sit down.'

Lucas fumbled his way into the chair with his gaze still fixedly on me, as if he couldn't believe I was there, as if by staring hard enough he could make me vanish.

Sir Thomas cleared his throat. 'Lucas, Sid Halley, here, has been telling us certain things which require explanation.'

Lucas was hardly listening. Lucas said to me, 'You can't be here.'

'Why not?' I said.

They waited for Lucas to answer, but he didn't.

Sir Thomas said eventually, 'Sid has made serious charges. I'll put them before you, Lucas, and you can answer as you will.'

He repeated more or less everything I'd told them, without emphasis and without mistake. The judicial mind, I thought, taking the heat out of things, reducing passion to probabilities. Lucas appeared to be listening, but he looked at me all the time.

'So you see,' Sir Thomas said finally, 'we are waiting for you to deny – or admit – that Sid's theories are true.'

Lucas turned his head away from me and looked vaguely round the room.

'It's all rubbish, of course,' he said.

'Carry on,' said Sir Thomas.

'He's making it all up.' He was thinking again, fast. The briskness in some measure returned to his manner. 'I certainly didn't tell him to investigate any syndicates. I certainly didn't tell him I had doubts about Eddy. I never talked to him about this imaginary Mason. He's invented it all.'

'With what purpose?' I said.

'How should I know?'

'I didn't invent coming here twice to copy down notes of the syndicates,' I said. 'I didn't invent Eddy complaining because I'd seen those files. I didn't invent you telephoning Chico at my flat four times. I didn't invent you dropping us at the car park. I didn't invent Peter Rammileese, who might be persuaded to . . . er . . . talk. I could also find those two Scots, if I tried.'

'How?' he said.

I'd ask young Mark, I thought. He would have learnt a lot about the friends in all that time: little Mark and his accurate ears.

I said, 'Don't you mean, I invented the Scots?'

He glared at me.

'I could also,' I said slowly, 'start looking for the real reasons behind all this. Trace the rumours of corruption to their source. Find out who, besides Peter Rammileese, is keeping you in Mercedes.'

Lucas Wainwright was silent. I didn't know that I could do all I'd said, but he wouldn't want to bet I couldn't. If he hadn't thought me capable he'd have seen no need to get rid of me in the first place. It was his own judgement I was invoking, not mine.

'Would you be prepared for that, Lucas?' Sir Thomas said.

Lucas stared my way some more, and didn't answer.

'On the other hand,' I said, 'I think if you resigned, it would be the end of it.'

He turned his head away from me and stared at the Senior Steward instead.

Sir Thomas nodded. 'That's all, Lucas. Just your resignation, now, in writing. If we had that, I would see no reason to proceed any further.'

It was the easiest let-off anyone could have had, but to Lucas, at that moment, it must have seemed bad enough. His face looked strained and pale, and there were tremors round his mouth.

Sir Thomas produced from his desk a sheet of paper, and from his pocket a gold ball-point pen.

'Sit here, Lucas.'

He rose and gestured to Lucas to sit by the desk.

Commander Wainwright walked over with stiff legs and shakily sat where he'd been told. He wrote a few words, which I read later. *I resign from the post of Director of Security to the Jockey Club. Lucas Wainwright.*

He looked around at the sober faces, at the people who had known him well, and trusted him, and had worked with him every day. He hadn't said a word, since he'd come into the office, of defence or appeal. I thought: how odd it must be for them all, facing such a shattering readjustment.

He stood up, the pepper and salt man, and walked towards the door.

As he came to where I sat he paused and looked at me blankly, as if not understanding.

'What does it take,' he said, 'to stop you?'

I didn't answer.

What it took rested casually on my knee. Four strong fingers, and a thumb, and independence.

20

Charles drove us back to Aynsford.

'You'll get a bellyful of courtrooms anyway,' he said. 'With Nicholas Ashe, and Trevor Deansgate.'

'It's not so bad just being an ordinary witness.'

'You've done it a good few times, now.'

'Yes,' I said.

'What will Lucas Wainwright do after this, I wonder.'

'God knows.'

Charles glanced at me. 'Don't you feel the slightest desire to gloat?'

'Gloat?' I was astounded.

'Over the fallen enemy.'

'Oh yes?' I said. 'And in your war at sea, what did you do when you saw an enemy drowning? Gloat? Push him under?'

'Take him prisoner,' Charles said.

After a bit I said, 'His life from now on will be prison enough.'

Charles smiled his secret smile, and ten minutes further on he said, 'And do you forgive him, as well?'

'Don't ask such difficult questions.'

Love thine enemy. Forgive. Forget. I was no sort of Christian, I thought. I could manage not to hate Lucas himself. I didn't think I could forgive: and I would never forget.

We rolled on to Aynsford, where Mrs Cross, carrying a tray upstairs to her private sitting room, told me that Chico was up, and feeling better, and in the kitchen. I went along there and found him sitting alone at the table, looking at a mug of tea.

'Hallo,' I said.

'Hallo.'

There was no need, with him, to pretend anything. I filled a mug from the pot and sat opposite him.

'Bloody awful,' he said. 'Wasn't it?'

'Yeah.'

'And I was dazed, like.'

'Mm.'

'You weren't. Made it worse.'

We sat for a while without talking. There was a sort of stark dullness in his eyes, and none of it, any longer, was concussion.

'Do you reckon,' he said, 'they let your head alone, for that?'

'Don't know.'

'They could've.'

I nodded. We drank the tea, bit by bit.

'What did they say, today?' he said. 'The brass.'

'They listened. Lucas resigned. End of story.'

'Not for us.'

'No.'

I moved stiffly on the chair.

'What'll we do?' he said.

'Have to see.'

'I couldn't . . .' He stopped. He looked tired and sore, and dispirited.

'No,' I said. 'Nor could I.'

'Sid . . . I reckon . . . I've had enough.'

'What, then?'

'Teach judo.'

And I could make a living, I suppose, from equities, commodities, insurance, and capital gains. Some sort of living . . . not much of a life.

In depression we finished the tea, feeling battered and weak and sorry for ourselves. I couldn't go on if he didn't, I thought. He'd made the job seem worthwhile. His naturalness, his good nature, his cheerfulness: I needed them around me. In many ways I couldn't function without him. In many ways, I wouldn't bother to function, if I didn't have him to consider.

After a while I said, 'You'd be bored.'

'What, with Wembley and not hurting, and the little bleeders?'

I rubbed my forehead, where the stray cut itched.

'Anyway,' he said, 'it was you, last week, who was going to give up.'

'Well . . . I don't like being . . .' I stopped.

'Beaten,' he said.

I took my hand away and looked at his eyes. There was the same thing there that had suddenly been in his voice. An awareness of the two meanings of the word. A glimmer of sardonic amusement. Life on its way back.

'Yeah.' I smiled twistedly. 'I don't like being beaten. Never did.'

'Sod the buggers, then?' he said.

I nodded. 'Sod 'em.'

'All right.'

We went on sitting there, but it was a lot better, after that.

Three days later, on Monday evening, we went back to London, and Chico, humouring the fears he didn't take seriously, came with me to the flat.

The hot weather had gone back to normal, or in other words, warm-front drizzle. Road surfaces were slippery with the oily patina left by hot dry tyres, and in West London every front garden was soggy with roses. Two weeks to the Derby . . . and perhaps Tri-Nitro would run in it, if the infection cleared up. He was fit enough, apart from that.

The flat was empty and quiet.

'Told you,' Chico said, dumping my suitcase in the bedroom. 'Want me to look in the cupboards?'

'As you're here.'

He raised his eyebrows to heaven and did an inch by inch search.

'Only spiders,' he said. 'They've caught all the flies.'

We went down to where I'd parked at the front and I drove him to his place.

'Friday,' I said. 'I'm going away for a few days.'

'Oh yes? Dirty weekend?'

'You never know. I'll call you, when I get back.'

'Just the nice gentle crooks from now on, right?'

'Throw all the big ones back,' I said.

He grinned, waved, and went in, and I drove away with lights going on everywhere in the dusk. Back at the flats I went round to the lock-up garages to leave the car in the one I rented there, out of sight.

Unlocked the roll-up door, and pushed it high. Switched the light on. Drove the car in. Got out. Locked the car door. Put the keys in my pocket.

'Sid Halley,' a voice said.

A voice. *His* voice.

Trevor Deansgate.

I stood facing the door I'd just locked, as still as stone.

'Sid Halley.'

I had known it would happen, I supposed. Sometime, somewhere, like he'd said. He had made a serious threat. He had expected to be believed. I had believed him.

Oh God, I thought. It's too soon. It's always too soon. Let him not see the terror I feel. Let him not know. Dear God . . . give me courage.

I turned slowly towards him.

He stood a step inside the garage, in the light, the thin drizzle like a dark grey-silver sheet behind him.

He held the shotgun, with the barrels pointing my way.

I had a brick wall on my left and another behind me, and the car on my right; and there were never many people about at the back of the flats, by the garages. If anyone came, they'd hardly dawdle around, in the rain.

'I've been waiting for you,' he said.

He was dressed, as ever, in city pinstripes. He brought, as always, the aura of power.

With eyes and gun facing unwaveringly my way, he stretched up behind him quickly with his left hand and found the bottom edge of the roll-up door. He gave it a sharp downward tug, and it rolled down nearly to the ground behind him, closing us in. Both hands, clean, manicured, surrounded by white cuffs, were back on the gun.

'I've been waiting for you, on and off, for days. Since last Thursday.'

I didn't say anything.

'Last Thursday two policemen came to see me. George Caspar telephoned. The Jockey Club warned me they were going to take proceedings. My solicitor told me I'd lose my bookmaking licence. I would be warned off from racing, and might well go to jail. Since last Thursday, I've been waiting for you.'

His voice, as before, was a threat in itself, heavy with the raw realities of the urban jungle.

'The police have been to the lab. My brother is losing his job. His career. He worked hard for it.'

'Let's all cry,' I said. 'You both gambled. You've lost. Too bloody bad.'

His eyes narrowed and the gun barrels moved an inch or two as his body reacted.

'I came here to do what I said I would.'

Gambled ... lost ... so had I.

'I've been waiting in my car around these flats,' he said. 'I knew you'd come back, some time or other. I knew you would. All I had to do was wait. I've spent most of my time here, since last Thursday, waiting for you. So tonight you came back ... with that friend. But I wanted you on your own ... I went on waiting. And you came back. I knew you'd come, in the end.'

I said nothing.

'I came here to do what I promised. To blow your hand off.' He paused. 'Why don't you beg me not to? Why don't you go down on your bloody knees and beg me not to?'

I didn't answer. Didn't move.

He gave a short laugh that had no mirth in it at all. 'It didn't stop you, did it, that threat? Not for long. I thought it would. I thought no one could risk losing both their hands. Not just to get me busted. Not for something small, like that. You're a bloody fool, you are.'

I agreed with him on the whole. I was also trembling inside, and concerned that he shouldn't see it.

'You don't turn a hair, do you?' he said.

He's playing with me, I thought. He must know I'm frightened. No one could possibly, in those circumstances, not be frightened to death. He's making me sweat ... wanting me to beg him ... and I'm not ... *not* ... going to.

'I came here to do it,' he said. 'I've been sitting here for days, thinking about it. Thinking of you with no hands ... with just stumps ... two plastic hooks.'

Sod you, I thought.

'Today,' he said, 'I started thinking about myself. I shoot off Sid Halley's right hand, and what happens to me?' He stared at me with increased intensity. 'I get the satisfaction of fixing you, making you a proper cripple instead of half a one. I get revenge ... hideous delightful revenge. And what else do I get? I get ten years, perhaps. You can get life for GBH, if it's bad enough. Both hands ... that might be bad enough. That's what I've been sitting here today thinking. And I've been thinking of the feeling there'd be against me in the slammer, for shooting your other hand off. Yours, of all people. I'd be better off killing you. That's what I thought.'

I thought numbly that I wasn't so sure either that I wouldn't rather be dead.

'This evening,' he said, 'after you'd come back for ten minutes, and gone away again. I thought of rotting away in jail year after year wishing I'd had the bloody sense to leave you alone. I reckoned it wasn't worth years in jail, just to know I'd fixed you. Fixed you alive, or fixed you dead. So I decided, just before you came back, not to do that, but just to get you down on the ground squealing for me not to. I'd have my revenge that way. I'd remind you of it, all your life. I'd tell people I'd had you crawling. Make them snigger.'

Jesus, I thought.

'I'd forgotten,' he said, 'what you're like. You've no bloody nerves. But I'm not going to shoot you. Like I said, it's not worth it.'

He turned abruptly, and stooped, putting one hand under the garage door. Heaved; rolled it upwards and open.

The warm drizzle in the dark outside fell like shoals of silver minnows. The gentle air came softly into the garage.

He stood there for a moment, brooding, holding his gun: and then he gave me back what in the straw-barn he'd taken away.

'Isn't there *anything*,' he said bitterly, 'that you're afraid of?'

Trial Run

MOSCOW

KEY

1. HIPPODROME
2. LENIN STADIUM (OLYMPIC ATHLETICS)
3. UNIVERSITY
4. INTOURIST HOTEL
5. NATIONAL HOTEL
6. BOLSHOI THEATRE
7. LENIN MUSEUM
8. GUM (DEPARTMENT STORE)
9. LUBIANKA
10. BRITISH EMBASSY
11. KREMLIN
12. ARAGVI RESTAURANT
13. FIFTIETH ANNIVERSARY SQUARE
14. RED SQUARE
15. ST BASIL'S CATHEDRAL
16. DERZHINSKY SQUARE
17. LOOK-OUT POINT
18. COMMERCIAL SECTION

0 MILES   1

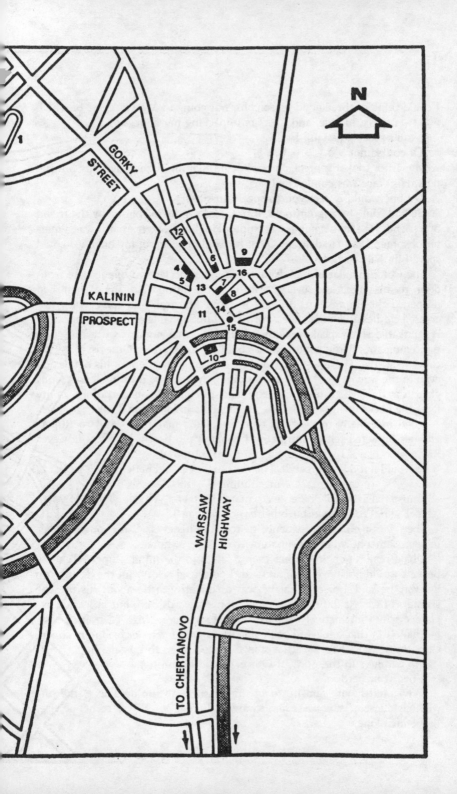

I

I could think of three good reasons for not going to Moscow, one of which was twenty-six, blonde, and upstairs unpacking her suitcase.

'I can't speak Russian,' I said.

'Of course not.'

My visitor took a genteel sip of pink gin, sighing slightly over my obtuseness. His voice was condescending.

'No one would expect you to speak Russian.'

He had come by appointment, introduced on the telephone by the friend of a friend. He said his name was Rupert Hughes-Beckett; that it was a matter of some . . . ah . . . delicacy. That he would be glad of my help, if I could spare him half an hour.

The word 'mandarin' had drifted into my mind when I opened the front door to his ring, and every gesture, every intonation since then had deepened the impression. A man of about fifty, tall and spare, with uncreased clothes and quiet shoes. An aura of unflappable civilized composure. A cultivated voice speaking without much lip movement, as if a muscular tightening round the mouth area could in itself prevent the issue of incautious words. There was control, too, in every movement of his hands and even in the way he used his eyes, rationing their forays into small courteous glances at my background between longer disciplined concentrations on my face, the backs of his own hands, or the glass holding his drink.

I had met many men of his type, and liked many, too, but to Rupert Hughes-Beckett I felt an antipathy I couldn't pin down. Its effect however was all too plain: I wished to say no to his proposals.

'It would not take a great deal of your time,' he said patiently. 'A week . . . two weeks, we calculate, at a maximum.'

I mustered a careful politeness to match his own. 'Why don't you go yourself?' I said. 'You would have better access than I.'

The faintest hint of impatience twitched in his eyes. 'It is thought better to send someone who is intimate with . . . ah . . . horses.'

Ribald replies got no further than a laugh in the mind. Rupert Hughes-Beckett would not have been amused. I perceived also, from the disapproving way he said 'horses', that he was as unenthusiastic about his present errand as I was. It did nothing to warm me towards him, but at least it explained why I instinctively disliked him. He had done his well-trained best, but hadn't in that one word been able to disguise his inner feeling of superciliousness: and I had met that stance far too often to mistake it.

'No cavaliers in the Foreign Office?' I said flippantly.

'I beg your pardon?'

'Why me?' I said: and heard in the question all the despair of the unwillingly chosen. Why *me*? I don't want it. Take it away. Pick someone else. Leave me alone.

'I gather it was felt you should be approached because you have . . . ah . . . *status*,' he said, and smiled faintly as if deprecating such an extravagant statement. 'And, of course,' he added, 'the time.'

A right kick in the guts, I thought; and kept my face flat and still. Then I took off my glasses and squinted at them against the light, as if trying to see if they were clean, and then put them back on again. It was a delaying tactic I had used all my life, most often unconsciously, to give myself a space for thought: a habit that had started when I was about six and a schoolmaster asked me in an arithmetic lesson what I had done with the multiplicand.

I had pulled off my owl-like silver rims and stared at his suddenly fuzzy outline while I thought wild panicky thoughts. What on earth was a multiplicand?

'I haven't seen it, sir. It wasn't me, sir.'

His sardonic laugh had stayed with me down the years. I had exchanged the silver rims for gold, and then for plastic, and finally for tortoiseshell, but I still took them off when I couldn't answer.

'I've got a cough,' I said. 'And it is November.'

The frivolousness of this excuse was measured by a deepening silence and a gradual reverential bowing of the Hughes-Beckett head over the crystal tumbler.

'I'm afraid that the answer is no,' I said.

He raised his head and gave me a calm civil inspection. 'There will be some disappointment,' he said. 'I might almost go as far as to say . . . ah . . . dismay.'

'Flatter someone else,' I said.

'It was felt that *you* . . .' He left the words unfinished, hanging in the air.

'Who felt?' I asked. 'Who, exactly, felt?'

He shook his head gently, put down the emptied glass, and rose to his feet.

'I will convey your reply.'

'And regrets,' I said.

'Very well, Mr Drew.'

'I wouldn't have been successful,' I said. 'I'm not an investigator. I'm a farmer.'

He gave me a sort of sideways down-the-nose look where a less inhibited man would have said, 'Come off it.'

I walked with him into the hall, helped him on with his coat, opened the front door, and watched him walk bareheaded through the icy dark to his waiting chauffeur-driven Daimler. He gave me, by way of farewell, merely a five-second full-frontal view of his bland expression through the window. Then the big car crunched away on the gravel towards the gate, and I coughed in the cold air and went back inside.

Emma was walking down the oval sweep of Regency staircase in her Friday evening come-for-the-weekend clothes: jeans, cotton check shirt, baggy sweater and cowboy boots. I wondered fleetingly whether, if the house stood for as long again, the girls of the twenty-second century would look as incongruous against those gracefully curving walls.

'Fish fingers and the telly, then?' she said.

'More or less.'

'You've got bronchitis again.'

'It isn't catching.'

She reached the bottom of the stairs and made without pause towards the kitchen. It always took a while with her for the brittle stresses of the week to drop away, and I was used to the jerky arrivals and the spiky brush-offs of the first few hours. I no longer tried to greet her with warmth. She wouldn't be kissed much before ten, nor loved before midnight, and she wouldn't relax until Saturday tea-time. Sunday we would slop around in easy contentment, and at six on Monday morning she would be gone.

Lady Emma Louders-Allen-Croft, daughter, sister and aunt of dukes, was 'into', as she would say, 'the working girl ethos'. She was employed full-time, no favours, in a bustling London department store, where, despite her search for social abasement, she had recently been promoted to bed linen buyer on the second floor. Emma, blessed with organizational skills above the average, was troubled about her rise, a screw-up one could trace back directly to her own schooling, where she, in an expensive boarding-school for highborn young ladies, had been taught in fierily left-wing sociology lessons that brains were elitist and that manual work was the noble path to heaven.

Her search for immolation, which had led to exhausting years of serving at tables in cafés as well as behind the counters in shops, seemed to be as strong as ever. She would in no way have starved without employment, but might quite likely have gone to drink or pot.

I believed, and she knew I did, that someone with her abilities and restless drive should have taken a proper training, or at least gone to university, and contributed more than a pair of hands; but I had learned not to talk about it, as it was one of the many no-man's-lands which led to shrieks and sulks.

'Why the hell do you both with that mixed-up kook?' my step-brother frequently asked. Because, as I never told him, a shot of undiluted life-force every couple of weekends was better for the heart than his monotonous daily jogging.

Emma was looking into the refrigerator, the light shining out of it on to her fine-boned face and thick platinum hair. Her eye-brows were so pale as to be invisible without pencil, and her lashes the same without mascara. Sometimes she made up her eyes like sunbursts; sometimes, like that evening, she let nature take its course. It depended on the tide of ideas.

'Haven't you any yoghurt?' she demanded.

I sighed. A flood of health foods was not my favourite. 'Nor wheatgerm either,' I said.

'Kelp,' she said firmly.

'What?'

'Seaweed. Compressed into tablets. Very good for you.'

'I'm sure.'

'Apple cider vinegar. Honey. Organically grown vegetables.'

'Are we off avocados and hearts of palm?'

She pulled out a chunk of Dutch cheese and scowled at it. 'They're imported. We should limit imports. We need a siege economy.'

'No more caviar?'

'Caviar is immoral.'

'Would it be immoral if it was plentiful and cheap?'

'Stop arguing. What did your visitor want? Are these crème caramels for supper?'

'Yes, they are,' I said. 'He wanted me to go to Moscow.'

She straightened up and glared at me. 'That's not very funny.'

'A month ago you said crème caramels were food for angels.'

'Don't be stupid.'

'He said he wanted me to go to Moscow. On an errand, not to embrace the Marxist-Leninist philosophy.'

She slowly shut the refrigerator door.

'What sort of errand?'

'He wanted me to look for somebody. But I'm not going.'

'Who?'

'He didn't say.' I turned away from her. 'Come and have a drink in the sitting-room. There's a fire in there.'

She followed me back through the hall and folded herself into a large armchair with a glass of white wine.

'How are the pigs, geese, and mangold-wurzels?'

'Coming along nicely,' I said.

I had no pigs, geese, or, indeed, mangold-wurzels. I had a lot of beef cattle, three square miles of Warwickshire, and all the modern problems of the food producer. I had grown used to measuring yield in tonnes per hectare but was still unconvinced by government policies which paid me sometimes *not* to grow certain crops, and threatened to prosecute me if I did.

'And the horses?' Emma said.

'Ah well . . .'

I stretched out lazily in my chair and watched the light from the table lamp fall on her silvery head, and decided it was really high time I stopped wincing over the thought that I would be riding in no more races.

'I suppose I'll sell the horses,' I said.

'There's still hunting.'

'It's not the same. And these are not hunters. They're race-horses. They should be on a track.'

'You've trained them all these years . . . why don't you just get someone else to ride them?'

'I only trained them because I was riding them. I don't want to do it for anyone else.'

She frowned. 'I can't imagine you without horses.'

'Well,' I said, 'nor can I.'

'It's a bloody shame.'

'I thought you subscribed to the "we know what's best for you and you'll damn well put up with it" school of thought.'

'People have to be protected from themselves,' she said.

'Why?'

She stared. 'Of course they do.'

'Safety precautions are a growth industry,' I said with some bitterness. 'Masses of restrictive legislation to stop people taking everyday risks . . . and accidents go right on happening, and we have terrorists besides.'

'You're still in a right tizz, aren't you?'

'Yes.'

'I thought you'd got over it.'

'The first fury may have worn off,' I said. 'The resentment will last for ever.'

I had been lucky in my racing, lucky in my horses, and steeplechasing had taken me, as it had so many others, to soul-filling heights and depths of passion and fear and triumphant exaltation. Left to myself I would in that autumn have been busily racing at every opportunity and fixing my sights as usual on the big amateur events in the spring; for, while I hadn't the world's toughest physique when it came to chest infections, to which I was as maddeningly prone as cars to rust, I was still, at thirty-two, as muscularly strong as I would ever be. But someone, somewhere, had recently dreamed up the nannying concept that people should no longer be allowed to ride in jump races *wearing glasses*.

Of course a lot of people thought it daft for anyone to race in glasses anyway, and I daresay they were right: but although I'd broken a few frames and suffered a few superficial cuts from them, I'd never damaged my actual eyes. And they were *my eyes*, God dammit.

There were restrictions now on contact lenses, though not a total ban: but although I had tried and persevered to the point of perpetual inflammation, my eyes and contacts remained incompatible. So if I couldn't wear contacts, I could no longer race. So goodbye to twelve years' fun. Goodbye to endeavour, to speed, to mind-blowing exhilaration. Too bad, too bad about your misery, it's all for your own good.

The weekend drifted along on its normal course. A drive round the farm on Saturday morning, visit to the local Stratford-upon-Avon races in the afternoon, dinner with friends in the evening. Sunday morning, getting up late, we sprawled in the sitting-room with logs on the fire, newspapers around like snow, and the prospect of toasted ham sandwiches for lunch. Two satisfactory nights had been passed, with another, one hoped, ahead. Emma was at her softest, and we were as near to a married state as we were ever likely to get.

Into this domestic calm drove Hughes-Beckett in his Daimler. The wheels crunched on the gravel: I stood up to see who had arrived, and Emma also. We watched the chauffeur and a man sitting beside him get out of the car and open the two rear doors. From one stepped Hughes-Beckett, looking apprehensively up the façade of the house, and from the other . . .

Emma's eyes widened. 'My god . . . isn't that . . . ?'

'Yes, it is.'

She swept a wild look round the cosy untidy room. 'You can't bring them in here.'

'No. The drawing-room.'

'But . . . did you know they were coming?'

'Of course not.'

'Good heavens.'

We watched the two visitors stroll the few steps towards the front door. Talk about not taking no for an answer, I thought. This was wheeling up the big guns with a vengeance.

'Well, go on,' said Emma. 'See what they want.'

'I know what they want. You sit here by the fire and do the crossword while I think of ways of telling them they can't have it.'

I went to the front door and opened it.

'Randall,' said the Prince, holding out his hand to be shaken. 'Well, at least you're at home. Can we come in?'

'Of course, sir.'

Hughes-Beckett followed him over the threshold with an expression compounded of humiliation and triumph: he might not have been able to persuade me himself, but he was going to take joy in seeing me capitulate to someone else.

I led them into the blue and gold formal drawing-room where at least the radiators were functioning even if there was no welcoming fire.

'Now, Randall,' said the Prince. 'Please go to Moscow.'

'Can I offer your Royal Highness a drink?' I said.

'No, you can't. Now, Randall, sit down and listen, and stop beating about the bush.'

The cousin of the monarch parked his backside firmly on a silk-covered Regency sofa and waved Hughes-Beckett and me towards adjoining chairs. He was of my generation, though a year or two older, and we had met countless times over the years because of our common pleasure in horses. His taste had taken him more to hounds and to polo than racing, although we had galloped alongside in several point-to-points. He was strong-minded and direct, and could be bracing to the point of bossiness, and I had also seen his tears over the broken-necked body of his favourite hunter.

We had met from time to time on indoor social occasions, but we were not close private personal friends, and before that day he had not been to my house, nor I to his.

'My wife's brother,' he said. 'Johnny Farringford. You know him, don't you?'

'We've met,' I said. 'I don't really know him.'

'He wants to ride in the next Olympics. In Moscow.'

'Yes, sir. So Mr Hughes-Beckett said.'

'In the Three-Day-Event.'

'Yes.'

'Well, Randall, there's this problem ... what you might call, a *question-mark* ... We can't let him go to Russia unless it's cleared up. We simply can't ... or at least, I simply *won't* ... have him going there if the whole thing is going to blow up in our faces. I am not, positively not, going to let him go if there is any chance of an ... *incident* ... which would be in a way embarrassing to ... er ... other members of my family. Or to the British nation as a whole.' He cleared his throat. 'Now I know Johnny is not in line to the throne or anything like that, but he is after all an earl and my brother-in-law, and as far as the Press of the world is concerned, that's fair game.'

'But, sir,' I said, protesting mildly. 'The Olympics are still some way off. I know Lord Farringford is good, but he might not be selected, and then there would be no problem at all.'

The Prince shook his head. 'If the problem isn't dealt with, however good Johnny is, even if he's the best we've got, he will not be selected.'

I looked at him speculatively. 'You would prevent it?'

'Yes, I should.' His voice was positive. 'It would no doubt cause a great deal of friction in my own home, as both Johnny and my wife have set their hearts on his getting a place in the team. He has a real chance, too, I admit. He won several Events during the summer and he's been working hard at improving his dressage to international standards. I don't want to stand in his way ... In fact, that's why I'm here, asking you to be a good chap and find out what, if anything, there is to make it risky for him to go to Russia.'

'Sir,' I said. 'Why me? Why not the diplomats?'

'They've passed the buck. They think, and I must say I agree, that a private individual is the best bet. If there is ... anything ... we don't want it in official records.'

I said nothing, but my disinclination must have been obvious.

'Look,' the Prince said, 'we've known each other a long time. You've twice the brains I have, and I trust you. I'm damned sorry about your eyesight, and all that, but you've got a lot of empty time to fill now, and if your agent can run your estate like clockwork while you chunter round Cheltenham and Aintree, he can do it while you go to Moscow.'

I said, 'I suppose you didn't get the no-glasses rule passed just so that I'd have time to go on your errand?'

He listened to the bitterness in my voice, and chuckled in his throat. 'Most likely it was all the other amateurs, who wanted you out of their day-light.'

'A couple have already sworn it wasn't.'

'Will you go, then?' he said.

I looked at my hands and bit my fingernails and took my glasses off and put them on again.

'I know you don't want to,' he said. 'But I don't know who else to ask.'

'Sir ... well ... can we leave it until the spring? I mean ... you might think of someone better ...'

'It's got to be now, Randall. Right this minute, in fact. We've got the chance of buying one of the top young German horses, a real cracker, for Johnny. We ... that is, his trustees ... I suppose I should explain ... His money is in trust until he is twenty-five, which is still three years ahead, and although of course he has a generous living allowance, a big item like an Olympic-type horse needs to come out of the capital. Anyway, we will be happy to buy this horse, and we have an option on it, but they are pressing for a reply. We must say yes or no by Christmas. It is too expensive except for an all-out attempt at the Olympics, and we are damned lucky to have been given the few weeks' option. They've got other buyers practically queueing for it.'

I stood up restlessly, went to the window, and looked out at the cold November sky. Winter in Moscow, chasing someone's possible indiscretion, maybe digging up a lot of private dirt, was an absolutely revolting prospect.

'Please, Randall,' said the Prince. 'Please go. Just give it a try.'

Emma was standing by the sitting-room window watching the Daimler roll away down the drive. She glanced assessingly at my face.

'I see he suckered you,' she said.

'I'm still fighting a rearguard action.'

'You haven't a chance.'

She walked across the panelled room and sat on the long stool in front of the fire, stretching out her hands to the warmth. 'It's too ingrained in you. Service to the sovereign, and all that. Grandfather an equerry, aunt a lady-in-waiting. Stacks like them in your family for generations back. What hope have you got? When a Prince says jump, all your ancestors' genes spring to attention and salute.'

2

The Prince lived in a modest house only a shade larger than my own, but a hundred years older, and he opened his door to me himself, although he did have living-in staff, which I did not. But then, he also had a wife, three children, and, apparently, six dogs. A dalmatian and a whippet oozed between his legs and the doorposts and bowled over to give me a good sniffing as I climbed out of my Mercedes, with a yapping collection of terriers cantering along in their wake.

'Kick 'em out of your way,' advised the Prince loudly, waiting on his doorstep. 'Get *down*, Fingers, you spotted oaf.'

The dalmatian paid little attention, but I reached the door unchewed. Shook the Prince's hand. Made the small bow. Followed him across the rugs of his pillared hall into an ample sort of study. Leather-bound books in tidy rows lined two of the walls, with windows, doors, portraits and fireplace leaving small surrounds of pale green emulsion on the others. On his big cluttered desk stood ranks of photographs in silver frames, and in one corner a huge white cyclamen in a copper bowl drooped its pale heads in the greyish light.

I knew, and the Prince knew I knew, that his act in opening his door to me himself was a very unusual token of appreciation. He really must have been quite extraordinarily relieved, I thought, that I had agreed to take even the partial step I had: and I wondered a bit uneasily about the size of the pitfalls which he knew would lie ahead.

'Good of you, Randall,' he said, waving me to a black leather armchair. 'Did you have a good drive? We'll rustle up some coffee in a minute . . .'

He sat in a comfortable swivel chair beside his desk and kept up the flow of courteous chatter. Johnny Farringford, he said, had promised to be there by ten-thirty: he took a quick look at his watch and no doubt found it was roughly fifteen minutes after that already. It was good of me to come, he said again. It was probably better, he said, that I shouldn't be tied in too closely with Johnny at this stage, so it was perhaps wiser we should meet at the Prince's house, and not at Johnny's, if I saw what he meant.

He was strongly built, fairly tall, brown-haired, blue-eyed, with the easy good looks of youth beginning to firm into the settled character of coming middle age. The eyebrows were bushier than five years earlier, the nose more pronounced, and the neck a little thicker. Time was turning him from an athlete into a figurehead, and giving me unwanted insights into mortality on a Monday morning.

Another quick look at his watch, this time accompanied by a frown. I thought hopefully that perhaps the precious Johnny wouldn't turn up at all, and I could go contentedly back home and forget the whole thing.

The two tall windows of the study looked out to the sweep of drive in front of the house, in the same way as those of my own sitting-room. Perhaps the Prince, too, found it useful to have early warning of people calling: time to dodge, if he wanted.

My Mercedes was clearly in view on the wide expanse of raked gravel, standing alone, bluish-grey and quiet. While I idly watched, a white Rover suddenly travelled like an arrow across the uncluttered area, making straight for my car's back. As if in horrorstruck inevitable slow-motion I waited helplessly for the crash.

There was a noise like the emptying of ten metal dustbins into a pulverizing plant, followed by the uninterrupted blowing of the horn, as the unconscious driver of the Rover slumped over the steering wheel.

'Christ!' said the Prince, appalled and leaping to his feet. 'Johnny!'

'My car!' I said, involuntarily betraying my regrettable priorities.

The Prince was fortunately already on his way to the study door, and I followed on his heels across the hall, bursting into the fresh air after him at a run.

The reverberating crunch and the wailing horn had brought an assortment of horrified faces to the windows and to the fringe of the scene, but it was the Prince and I who reached the tangle first.

The front of the Rover had half mounted the back of my car in a sort of monstrous mechanical mating, so that the Rover's wheels were slightly off the ground. The whole arrangement looked most precarious, and an assaulting smell of petrol brought one face to face with possibilities.

'Get him out,' said the Prince urgently, tugging at the handle of the driver's door. 'God . . .'

The door had buckled under the impact, and was wedged shut. I raced round to the far side, and tried the passenger door. Same thing. If he'd tried, Johnny Farringford couldn't have hit my Mercedes any straighter.

The rear doors were locked. The hatchback also. The horn blew on, urgent and disturbing.

'Jesus,' shouted the Prince frantically. 'Get him out.'

I climbed up on to the concertina'd mess between the two vehicles and slithered through the space where the windscreen had been, carrying with me a shower of crumbling glass. Knelt on the passenger seat, and hauled the unconscious man off the horn button. The sudden quiet was a blessing, but there was nothing reassuring about Johnny Farringford's face.

I didn't wait to look beneath the blood. I stretched across behind him, supporting his lolling head, and pulled up the locking catch on the offside rear door. The Prince worked at it feverishly from the outside, but it took a contortionist manoeuvre from me and a fierce stamp from my heel to spring it open: the thought of sparks from the scraping metal was a vivid horror, as I could now hear, as well as scarcely breathe from, the flood of escaping petrol.

It didn't make it any better that it was the petrol from my own car, or that I'd filled the capacious tank that very morning.

The Prince put his head and shoulders into the Rover and thrust his wrists under his brother-in-law's armpits. I squirmed back into the buckled front space and disengaged the flopping feet from the clutter of clutch, brake and accelerator pedals. The Prince heaved with his considerable strength and I lifted the lower part of the inert body as best I could, and, between us, we shifted him over the back of his seat and out through the rear door. I let go of his legs as the Prince tugged him backwards, and he flopped out free on to the gravel like a calf from a cow.

God help him, I thought, if we've made any broken bones worse by our rough handling, but anything on the whole was better than incineration. I scrambled along Johnny Farringford's escape route with no signs of calm unhurried nonchalance.

Assistance had arrived in a houseman's coat and in gardening clothes, and the victim was carried more carefully from then on.

'Take him away from the car,' the Prince was saying to them while turning back towards me. 'The petrol . . . Randall, get out, man.'

Superfluous advice. I'd never felt so slow, so awkward, so over-equipped with knees and elbows and ankle joints.

Whether the balance of one vehicle on the other was in any case unstable, or whether my far from delicate movements rocked it over the brink, the effect was the same: the Rover began to move while I was still inside it.

I could hear the Prince's voice, rising with apprehension, 'Randall . . .'

I got one foot out free: began to put my weight on it, and the Rover shifted further. I stumbled, hung on to the door frame, and pulled myself out by force of arms. Landed sideways on hip and elbow, sprawling and ungainly.

I rolled and put my feet where they ought to be, with my hands on the ground like a runner, to get a bit of purchase. Behind me the Rover's heavy weight crunched backwards and tore itself off my Mercedes with metal screeching violently on metal, but I dare say it was some form of electrical short-circuiting which let go with a shower of sparks like a hundred cigarette lighters in chorus.

The explosion threw the two cars apart and left both of them burning like mini infernos. There was a hissing noise in the air as the expanding vapour flashed into a second's flame, and a positive roaring gust of hot wind, which helped me onwards.

'Your hair's on fire,' observed the Prince, as I reached him.

I rubbed a hand over it, and so it was. Rubbed with both hands rather wildly, and put the conflagration out.

'Thanks,' I said.

'Not at all.'

He grinned at me in an un-Princely and most human fashion. 'And your glasses, I see, haven't shifted an inch.'

A doctor and a private ambulance arrived in due course for Johnny Farringford, but long before that he had woken up and looked around him in bewilderment. He was lying, by that time, on the long comfortable sofa in the family sitting-room, attended by the Princess, his sister, who was taking things matter-of-factly and mopping his wounds with impressive efficiency.

'What happened?' Farringford said, opening dazed eyes.

Bit by bit they told him: he had driven his car across a space as big as a tennis court, straight into the back of my Mercedes. Nothing else in sight.

'Randall Drew,' added the Prince, making the introduction.

'Oh.'

'Damn silly thing to do,' said the Princess disparagingly, but in her concerned face I read the lifelong protectiveness of older sister to little brother.

'I don't . . . remember.'

He looked at the red stains on the swabs which were piling up on a tray beside him, at the blood dripping from a cut on one finger, and appeared to be going to be sick.

'He used to pass out at the sight of blood,' said his sister. 'A good job he's grown out of it.'

Johnny Farringford's injuries had resolved themselves into numerous cuts to the face but no obviously broken bones. However, he winced every time he moved, pressing his arm across his waist as if to hold himself together, which spoke to me rather reminiscently of cracked ribs.

He was a willowy, fairly tall young man with a great deal of crinkly reddish hair extending into tufty bits of beard down the outer sides of the jaw. His nose looked thin and sharp, and an out-of-door tan sat oddly on his skin over the pallor of shock.

'Creeping . . . shit,' he said suddenly.

'It could have been worse,' said the Prince, dubiously.

'No . . . ' Farringford said. 'They hit me.'

'Who did?' The Prince mopped a bleeding cut and clearly thought the remark was the rambling of concussion.

'Those men . . . I . . . ' He broke off and focused his dazed eyes with great deliberation on the Prince's face, as if the act of keeping his glance steady was also helping to reorganize his thoughts.

'I drove here . . . after. I felt . . . I was sweating. I remember turning in through the gates . . . and seeing the house . . .'

'Which men?' said the Prince.

'The ones you sent . . . about the horse.'

'I didn't send any men.'

Farringford blinked slowly and re-established the concentrating stare.

'They came . . . to the stable. Just when I was thinking . . . time to come here . . . see this fellow . . . someone . . . you want me to . . .'

The Prince nodded. 'That's right. Randall Drew, here.'

'Yeah . . . well . . . Higgins had got my car out . . . the Rover . . . said I wanted the Porsche but something about new tyres . . . so I just went into the yard . . . to see if Groucho's legs OK . . . which Lakeland said they were, but wanted to look myself, you know . . . So there they were, saying could they have a word . . . you'd sent them. I said I was in a hurry . . . got into the Rover . . . they just crowded in after me . . . punched me . . . one of them drove down the road, past the village . . . then they stopped . . . and the sods knocked me about . . . gave them as good as I got . . . but two to one . . . no good, you know.'

'They robbed you?' the Prince said. 'We'll have to consider the police.' He looked worried. Police meant publicity, and unfavourable publicity was anathema to the Prince.

'No . . .' Farringford closed his eyes. 'They said . . . to keep away . . . from Alyosha.'

'They *what*?' The Prince jerked as if he too had been hit.

'That's right . . . knew you wouldn't like it . . .'

'What else did they say.'

'Nothing. Bloody ironic . . . ' said Farringford rather faintly. 'It's you . . . who wants Alyosha . . . found . . . Far as I'm concerned . . . whole thing can stay . . . buried.'

'Just rest,' said the Princess anxiously, wiping red oozing drops from his grazed forehead. 'Don't talk any more, Johnny, there's a lamb.' She looked up at the two of us, standing at the sofa's foot. 'What will you do about the cars?'

The Prince stared morosely at the two burnt-out wrecks and at five empty extinguishers which lay around like scarlet torpedoes. An acrid smell in the November air was all that was left of the thick column of smoke and flame which had risen higher than the rooftops. The firemen, still in the shape of houseman and gardener, stood in the background, looking smugly at their handiwork and waiting for the next gripping instalment.

'Do you suppose he fainted?' said the Prince.

'It sounds like it, sir,' I said. 'He said he was sweating. Not much fun being beaten up like that.'

'And he never could stand the sight of blood.'

The Prince traced with his eye the path the Rover would have taken with an unconscious driver had not my car been parked slap in the way.

'He'd've crashed into one of those beeches,' said the Prince. 'And his foot was on the accelerator . . .'

Across the lawn a double row of stately, mature trees stretched away from the house, thick with criss-crossing branches, and bare except for a last dusting of dried brown leaves. They had been planted, one would guess, as a break against the north-east winds, in an age when sculpture of the land was designed to delight the eye of future generations, and their sturdy trunks would have stopped a tank, let alone a Rover. They were lucky, I thought, to have survived where so many had fallen to drought, fungus and gales.

'I'm glad he didn't hit the beeches,' said the Prince, and left me unsure whether it was for Johnny's sake or theirs. 'Sorry about your car, of course. I hope it was insured, and all that? Better just tell the insurers it was a parking accident. Keep it simple. Cars get written off so easily, these days. You don't want to claim against Johnny, or anything like that, do you?'

I shook my head reassuringly. The Prince smiled faintly with relief and relaxed several notches.

'We don't want the place crawling with Press, do you see? Telephoto lenses . . . Any sniff of this and they'd be down here in droves.'

'But too late for the action,' I said.

He looked at me in alarm. 'You won't say anything about us hauling Johnny out, will you? Not to anyone. I don't want the Press getting hold of a story like that. It really doesn't do.'

'Would you mind people knowing you would take a slight risk to rescue your wife's brother, sir?'

'Yes, I should,' he said positively. 'Don't you say a word, there's a good chap.' He cast a glance at my singed hair. 'And not so much of the "slight", come to that.' He put his head on one side. 'We could say you did it yourself, if you like.'

'No, sir, I don't like.'

'Didn't think you would. You wouldn't want them crawling all over you with their notebooks any more than I should.'

He turned away and with a movement of his hand that was more a suggestion than a command, he called over the hovering gardener.

'What do we do about all this, Bob?' he said.

The gardener was knowledgeable about breakdown trucks and suitable garages, and said he would fix it. His manner with the Prince was comfortable and spoke of long-term mutual respect, which would have irritated the anti-royalists no end.

'Don't know what I'd do without Bob,' confirmed the Prince as he walked back towards the house. 'If I ring up shops or garages and say who I am they either don't believe it and say yes, they're the Queen of Sheba, or else they're so fussed they don't listen properly and get everything wrong. Bob will get those cars shifted without any trouble, but if I tried to arrange it myself the first people to arrive would be the reporters.'

He stopped on the doorstep and looked back at the skeleton of what had been my favourite vehicle.

'We'll have to fix you a car to get home in,' he said. 'Lend you one,'

'Sir,' I said. 'Who or what is Alyosha?'

'Ha!' he said explosively, his head turning to me sharply, his eyes suddenly shining. 'That's the first bit of interest you've shown without me actually forcing you into it.'

'I did say I would see what I could do.'

'Meaning to do as precious little as possible.'

'Well, I . . .'

'And looking as if you'd been offered rotting fish.'

'Er . . . ' I said. 'Well . . . what about Alyosha?'

'That's just the *point*,' the Prince said. 'We don't *know* about Alyosha. That's just what I want you to find *out*.'

Johnny Farringford got himself out of hospital and back home pretty fast, and I drove over to see him three days after the accident.

'Sorry about your car,' he said, looking at the Range-Rover in which I had arrived. 'Bit of a buggers' muddle, what?'

He was slightly nervous, and still pale. The numerous facial cuts were healing with the quick crusts of youth and looked unlikely to leave permanent scars; and he moved as if the soreness still in his body was after all more a matter of muscle than bone. Nothing, I thought a shade ruefully, that would stop him training hard for the Olympics.

'Come in,' he said. 'Coffee, and all that.'

He led the way into a thatched cottage and we stepped straight into a room that deserved a magazine article on traditional country living. Stone flagged floors, good rugs, heavy supporting beams, inglenook fire-place, exposed old bricks, and masses of sagging sofas and chairs in faded chintzy covers.

'This place isn't mine,' he said, sensing my inspection. 'It's rented. I'll get the coffee.'

He headed towards a door at the far end, and I slowly followed. The kitchen, where he was pouring boiling water into a filter pot, was as modern as money could make it.

'Sugar? Milk?' he said. 'Would you rather have tea?'

'Milk, please. Coffee's fine.'

He carried the loaded tray back into the living-room and put it on a low table in front of the fire-place. Logs were stacked there ready on a heap of old dead ash, but the fire, like the cottage itself, was cold. I coughed a couple of times and drank the hot liquid gratefully, warmed inside if not out.

'How are you feeling now?' I asked.

'Oh . . . all right.'

'Still shaken, I should imagine.'

He shivered. 'I understand I'm lucky to be alive. Good of you to dig me out, and all that.'

'It was your brother-in-law, as much as me.'

'Beyond the call of duty, one might say.'

He fidgeted with the sugar bowl and his spoon, making small movements for their own sake.

'Tell me about Alyosha,' I said.

He flicked a quick glance at my face and looked away, leaving me the certainty that what he mainly felt at that moment was depression.

'There's nothing to tell,' he said tiredly. 'Alyosha is just a name which cropped up in the summer. One of the German team died at Burghley in September, and someone said it was because of Alyosha who came from Moscow. Of course, there were enquiries and so on, but I never heard the results because I wasn't directly involved, do you see?'

'But . . . indirectly?' I suggested.

He gave me another quick glance and a faint smile.

'I knew him quite well. The German chap. One does, do you see? One meets all the same people everywhere, at every international event.'

'Yes,' I said.

'Well . . . I went out with him one evening, to a club in London. I was

214

stupid, I admit it, but I thought it was just a gambling club. He played back-gammon, as I do. I had taken him to my club a few days earlier, you know, so I thought he was just repaying my, er, hospitality.'

'But it wasn't just a gambling club?' I said, prompting him as he lapsed into gloomy silence.

'No.' He sighed. 'It was full of, well . . . transvestites.' His depression in-creased. 'I didn't realize, at first. No one would have done. They all *looked* like women. Attractive. Pretty, even, some of them. We were shown to a table. It was dark. And there was this girl, in the spotlight, doing a striptease, taking off a lot of cloudy gold scarf things. She was beautiful . . . dark-skinned, but not black . . . marvellous dark eyes . . . the most stunning little breasts. She undressed right down to the skin and then did a sort of dance with a bright pink feathery boa thing . . . it was brilliant, really. One would see her backview totally naked, but when she turned round there was always the boa falling in the . . . er . . . strategic place. When it was over, and I was applauding, Hans leant across grinning like a monkey and said into my ear, that she was a boy.' He grimaced. 'I felt a complete fool. I mean . . . one doesn't mind seeing performances like that if one *knows*. But to be taken in . . .'

'Embarrassing,' I said, agreeing.

'I laughed if off,' he said. 'I mean, one has to, doesn't one? And there was a sort of weird fascination, of course. Hans said he had seen the boy in a nightclub in West Berlin, and he had thought it might amuse me. He seemed to be enjoying my discomfiture. Thought it a huge joke. I had to pre-tend to take it well, do you see, because he was my host, but to be honest, I thought it a bit *off*.'

A spot of dented pride, I thought.

'The Event started two days after that,' he said, 'and Hans died the day after, after the cross-country.'

'How?' I asked. 'How did he die?'

'Heart attack.'

I was surprised. 'Wasn't he a bit young?'

'Yes,' Johnny said. 'Only thirty-six. Makes one think, doesn't it?'

'And then what happened?' I said.

'Oh . . . nothing, really. Nothing one could put one's finger on. But there were these rumours flying about, and I expect I was the last to hear them, that there was something *queer* about Hans, and about me as well. That we were, in fact, gay, if you see what I mean? And that a certain Alyosha from Moscow was jealous and had made a fuss with Hans, and because of it all he had a heart attack. And there was a *message*, do you see, that if I ever went to Moscow, Alyosha would be waiting.'

'What sort of message? I mean, in what form was it delivered?' I said.

He looked frustrated. 'But that's just it, the message itself was only a rumour. Everyone seemed to know it. I was told it by several people. I just don't know who started it.'

'Did you take it seriously?' I asked.

'No, of course I didn't. It's all rubbish. No one would have the slightest reason to be jealous of me when it came to Hans Kramer. In fact, you know, I more or less avoided him after that evening, as much as one could do without being positively boorish, do you see?'

I put my empty cup on the tray and wished I had worn a second sweater. Johnny himself seemed totally impervious to cold.

'But your brother-in-law,' I said, 'takes it very seriously indeed.'

He made a face. 'He's paranoid about the Press. Haven't you noticed?'

'He certainly doesn't seem to like them.'

'They *persecuted* him when he was trying to keep them off the scent of his romance with my sister. I thought it a bit of a laugh, really, but I suppose it wasn't to him. And then there was a lot of brouhaha, if you remember, because a fortnight after the engagement our mama upped and scarpered with her hairdresser.'

'I'd forgotten that,' I said.

'Just before I went to Eton,' Johnny said. 'It slightly deflated my confidence, do you see, at a point when a fellow needs all he can get.' He spoke flippantly, but the echo of a desperate hurt was clearly there. 'So they couldn't get married for months, and when they did, the papers raked up my mama's sex-life practically every day. And any time there's any real news story about any of us, up it pops again. Which is why HRH has this *thing*.'

'I can see,' I said soberly, 'why he wouldn't want you mixed up in a murky scandal at the Olympics with the eyes of the gossip columns swivelling your way like searchlights. Particularly with transvestite overtones.'

The Prince's alarm, indeed, seemed to me now to be entirely justified, but Johnny disagreed.

'There can't be any scandal, because there *isn't* any,' he said. 'The whole thing is absolutely stupid.'

'I think that's what your brother-in-law wants to prove, and the Foreign Office also, because anyone going to Russia is vulnerable, but anyone with a reputation for homosexual behaviour is a positive political risk, as it is still very much against the law there. They do want you to take part in the Olympics. They're trying to get me to investigate the rumours entirely for your sake.'

He compressed his mouth obstinately. 'But there isn't any need.'

'What about the men?' I said.

'What men?'

'The men who attacked you and warned you off Alyosha.'

'Oh.' He looked blank. 'Well . . . I should think it's obvious that whoever Alyosha is, she doesn't want any investigation any more than I do. It will probably do her a lot of *harm* . . . did you think of that?'

He stood up restlessly, picked up the tray, and carried it out to the kitchen. He rattled the cups out there for a bit and when he came back showed no inclination to sit down again.

'Come out and see the horses,' he said.

'Tell me about the men first,' I said persuasively.

'What about them?'

He put a foot on a pile of logs beside the fire and fiddled unnecessarily with the fire tongs.

'Were they English?'

He looked up in surprise. 'Well, I suppose so.'

'You heard them speak. What sort of accents did they have?'

'Ordinary. I mean . . . well, you know . . . ordinary working-class accents.'

'But they differ,' I said. He shook his head, but all accents differed, to my mind, to an infinitely variable degree.

'Well,' I said, 'were they Irish? Scots? Geordies? London? Birmingham? Liverpool? West Country? All those are easy.'

'London, then,' he said.

'Not foreign? Not Russian, for example?'

'No.' He seemed to see the point for the first time. 'They had a rough, sloppy way of speaking, swallowing all the consonants. Southern England. London or the South-East, I should think, or Berkshire.'

'The accent you hear around here, every day?'

'I suppose so, yes. Anyway, I didn't notice anything special about it.'

'What did they look like?'

'They were both big.' He arranged the fire irons finally in a tidy row and straightened to his full height. 'Taller than I am. They were just men. Nothing remarkable. No beards or limps or scars down the cheek. I'm awfully sorry to be so useless, but honestly I don't think I'd know them again if I passed them in the street.'

'But you would,' I guessed, 'if they walked into this room.'

'You mean I'd *feel* it was them?'

'I mean I expect you remember more than you think, and if your memory were jogged it would all come rushing back.'

He looked doubtful, but he said, 'If I do see them again, I'll certainly let you know.'

'They might of course return with another, er, warning,' I said thoughtfully. 'If you can't persuade your brother-in-law to drop the whole affair.'

'Christ, do you think so?' He swung his thin beaky nose towards the door as if expecting instant attack. 'You do say the most bloody comforting things, don't you?'

'The crude deterrent,' I said.

'What?'

'Biff bang.'

'Oh . . . yes.'

'Cheap and often effective,' I said.

'Yes, well. I mean . . . so what?'

'So who was it meant to deter? You, me, or your brother-in-law?'

He gave me a slow look behind which the alternatives seemed to be being inspected for the first time.

'See what you mean,' he said. 'But it's too subtle for me by half. Come out and see the horses. Now those I do understand. Even if they kill you, there's no malice.'

He shed a good deal of his nervousness and most of his depression as we walked the fifty yards across the country road to the stables. Horses were his natural element, and being among them obviously gave him comfort and confidence. I wondered whether his half-controlled jitters with me were simply because I was human, and not because of my errand.

The stable yard was a small quadrangle of elderly wooden boxes round an area of impacted clay and gravel. There were clipped patches of grass, a straggling tree, and empty tubs for flowers. Green paint, nearing the end of its life. A feeling that weeds would grow in the spring.

'When I inherit the lolly, I'll buy a better yard,' Johnny said, uncannily picking up my thoughts again. 'This is rented. Trustees, do you see.'

'It's a friendly place,' I said mildly.

'Unsuitable.'

The trustees however had put the money where it mattered, which was in four legs, head and tail. Although it was then the comparative rest period of their annual cycle, the five resident horses looked well-muscled and fit. For the most part bred by thoroughbred stallions out of hunter mares, they had looks as well as performance, and Johnny told me the history of each with a decisive and far from casual pride. I saw come alive in him for the first time the single-minded, driving fanaticism which had to be there: the essential fuel for Olympic fire.

Even the crinkly hair seemed to crisp into tighter curls, though I dare say this was due to the dampness in the air. But there was nothing climatic about the zeal in the eye, the tautness of the jaw, or the intensity of his manner. Enthusiasm of that order was bound to be infectious. I found myself responding to it easily, and understood why everyone was so anxious to make his Russian journey possible.

'I've an outside chance for the British team with this fellow,' he said, briskly slapping the rounded quarters of a long-backed chestnut, and reeling off the fullest list of successes. 'But he's not top world class. I know that. I need something better. The German horse. I've seen him. I really covet that horse.' He let out his breath abruptly and gave a small laugh, as if hearing his own obsession and wanting to disguise it. 'I do go on a bit.'

The self-deprecation in his voice showed nowhere in his healing face.

'I want a Gold,' he said.

3

My packing for Moscow consisted, in order of priority, of an army of defences for dicky lungs, mostly on a be-prepared-and-it-won't-happen basis; a thick woolly scarf; a spare pair of glasses; a couple of paperbacks and a camera.

Emma surveyed my medicine box with a mixture of amusement and horror.

'You're a hypochondriac,' she said.

'Stop poking around. Everything in there is tidy.'

'Oh, sure. What are these?' She lifted a small plastic pill bottle and shook it.

'Ventolin tablets. Put them down.'

She opened the cap instead and shook one on to her palm.

'Pink and tiny. What do they do?'

'Help one breathe.'

'And these?' She picked up a small cylindrical tin and read the yellow label. 'Intal spincaps?'

'Help one breathe.'

'And this? And this?' She picked them out and laid them in a row. 'And these?'

'Ditto, ditto, ditto.'

'And a syringe, for God's sake. Why a syringe?'

'Last resort. If a shot of adrenalin doesn't work, one sends for the undertaker.'

'Are you serious?'

'No,' I said; but the truth was probably yes. I had never actually found out.

'What a fuss over a little cough.' She looked at the fearsome array of life-support systems with all the superiority of the naturally healthy.

'Gloomsville,' I agreed. 'And put them all back.'

She humoured me by replacing them with excessive care.

'You know,' she said, 'surely all these things are for asthma, not bronchitis.'

'When I get bronchitis, I get asthma.'

'And vice versa?'

I shook my head. 'How about hopping into bed?'

'At half-past four on a Sunday afternoon with an invalid?'

'It's been done before.'

'So it has,' she agreed: and it was done again, with not a cough or a wheeze to be heard.

Rupert Hughes-Beckett, in his London office, the next morning, handed me an air ticket, a visa, a hotel reservation, and a sheet of names and addresses. Not enough.

'How about my answers?' I said.

'I'm afraid . . . ah . . . they are not yet available.'

'Why not?'

'The enquiries are still . . . ah . . . in hand.'

He was not meeting my eyes. He was finding the backs of his own hands as fascinating as he had in my sitting-room. He must know every freckle, I thought. Every wrinkle and every vein.

'Do you mean you haven't even started?' I said incredulously. 'My letter must have reached you by last Tuesday at the latest. Six days ago.'

'With your visa photographs, yes. You must understand there are . . . ah . . . *problems* in obtaining a visa at such short notice.'

I said, 'What is the point of a visa if I don't have the information? And couldn't you have got both at once?'

'We thought . . . ah . . . the *telex*. At the Embassy. We can send you the answers as they reach us.'

'And I trot around there every five minutes to see if the carrier pigeon has fluttered into the loft?'

He smiled austerely, a minuscule movement of the severely controlled lips.

'You can telephone,' he said. 'The number is on that paper.' He leaned back a little in his five-star office chair and looked earnestly at his hand to see if the knuckle-to-wrist scenery had changed at all in the last half minute. 'We did of course have a word with the doctor who attended Hans Kramer.'

'Well?' I prompted, as he seemed to have stopped there.

'He was the doctor in attendance at the Three-Day-Event. He was seeing a girl with a broken collar-bone when someone came to tell him that one of the Germans had collapsed. He left the girl almost immediately, but by the time he reached him, Kramer was already dead. He tried heart massage, he says, and a suitable injection, and mouth-to-mough resuscitation, but all to no avail. The body was . . . ah . . . cyanosed, and the cause of death was . . . ah . . . cardiac arrest.'

'Or in other words, heart attack.'

'Ah . . . yes. There was an autopsy, of course. Natural causes. So sad in someone so young.'

None of this present caper would have been necessary, I thought moodily, if Hans Kramer had not been so inconsiderate as to drop in his tracks. There was nothing like death for spawning and perpetuating myths, and it looked certain the Alyosha crop had circulated simply because Kramer hadn't been around to deny them.

'The names and addresses of the rest of the German team?' I said.

'To follow.'

'And the names and addresses of the members of the Russian team which came over for the International Horse Trials at Burghley?'

'To follow.'

'And of the Russian observers?'

'To follow.'

I stared at him. The most hopeful lead I'd unearthed in several telephone calls to people in the Event world had been the frequent reference to 'the Russian observers': three men who in a semi-official capacity had attended a number of horse trials during the past season, not just the International Event for which their team had been entered. The reasons for their presence had been described variously as 'spying', 'seeing how Events should be run', 'nicking our best horses', and 'assessing the standard they had to reach to make the West look stupid at the Olympics'.

I said to Hughes-Beckett, 'The Prince told me you had agreed to do some of the spadework.'

'We will,' he said. 'But on the scene of international politics your errand is of limited importance. My office has been working this week on matters on greater urgency than ... ah ... horses.'

The same faint undisguisable contempt coloured his voice and pinched his nostrils.

'Do you expect me to succeed in this task?' I said.

He studied the back of his hand and didn't answer.

'Do you *wish* me to succeed?'

He lifted his gaze to my face as if it were a two-ton weight.

'I would be grateful if you would bear in mind that clearing the way for Lord Farringford to be able to be considered for the Olympics, always supposing that he or his horse should prove to be good enough, is not something for which we would willingly sacrifice any ... ah ... bargaining positions with the Soviet Union. We would in particular not wish to find ourselves in the position of having to tender an *apology*.'

'It's a wonder you asked me to go,' I said.

'The Prince wished it.'

'And he leaned on you?'

Hughes-Beckett folded his mouth primly. 'It is not a totally unreasonable request. If we altogether disapproved of your errand we would not have helped in any way.'

'All right,' I said, rising to my feet and stowing the various papers into pockets. 'I take it that you would like me to go, which will prove you are not obstructive, and to ask a few harmless questions, and get some inconclusive answers, and for the Prince not to buy the German horse, and for Johnny Farringford not to be picked for the team, and for no one to make waves?'

He regarded me with all the world-weariness of a senior civil servant, saying nothing but meaning yes.

'We have reserved a room for you for two weeks,' he said. 'But of course you can return earlier if you wish.'

'Thanks.'

'And if you read that sheet of paper, you will find we have given you one or two ... ah ... contacts, who may be helpful.'

I glanced at the short list, which was headed by the British Embassy, Naberezhnaya Morisa Teresa 12.

'One of those lower down is a man concerned with training the Soviet team for the Olympic Three-Day-Event.'

'Well,' I said, pleasantly surprised, 'that's better.'

He said with faint smugness, 'We have not been entirely idle, as you supposed.' He cleared his throat. 'The last name on the list is that of a student at Moscow University. He is English, and is there on an exchange visit for one year. He speaks Russian, of course. We have written to him to tell him you will be coming. He will be helpful if you need an interpreter, but we ask that nothing you do will prejudice his ... ah ... continued acceptance for the rest of the academic year.'

'And he is more important than horses?'

Hughes-Beckett achieved a remote and frosty smile. 'Most things are,' he said.

The ticket he had provided found me the next day sitting comfortably in the first class on an Aeroflot flight which arrived at six in the evening, local time. Most of my fellow-travellers in the privileged cabin were black: Cubans, I idly wondered? But then, in a shifting world, they could be from anywhere: today's ally, tomorrow's exterminee. They wore superbly-tailored suits with white shirts and elegant ties, and were met at the doors of the aeroplane on landing by extra-long limousines. Those of less note went through normal immigration procedures, but without, in my case, any great delay. The customs men waved me through as if uninterested, though on the next bench they seemed to be taking apart a man of much my age. Every scrap of paper was being read, every pocket emptied, and the lining of the suitcase closely examined. The object of these attentions bore them stolidly, without expression. No protest, no indignation, nor, as far as I could see, any apprehension. As I went on my way, one of the officers picked up a pair of underpants and carefully felt his way round the waistband.

I was thinking purposefully of taxis, but it transpired that I, too, had been provided with a reception committee. A girl in a brown coat and a fawn knitted hat approached me tentatively, and said, 'Mr Drew?'

She saw from my reaction that she had the right man. She said, 'My name is Natasha. I am from Intourist. We will be looking after you during your stay here. We have a car to take you to your hotel.' She turned towards a slightly older woman standing a pace or two away. 'This is my colleague, Anna.'

'How kind of you to take so much trouble,' I said politely. 'How did you know me?'

Natasha glanced matter-of-factly at a paper in her hand. 'Englishman, thirty-two years old, dark wavy hair, glasses with mottled brown frames, no moustache or beard, good clothes.'

'The car is outside,' Anna said. I thought that that wasn't totally surprising, as cars usually were, at airports.

Anna was short, stocky, and soberly clad in a grey coat with a darker grey woolly hat. There was something forbidding in her face, a stiffness which continued downwards through the forward-thrusting abdomen to the functional toes of her boots. Her manner was welcoming enough, but would continue to be, I reckoned, only as long as I behaved as she thought I should.

'Do you have a hat?' Natasha said, solicitously. 'It is cold outside. You should have a fur hat.'

I had already had a taste of the climate in the scamper from aircraft to bus, and from bus to airport door. Most of the passengers seemed to have sprouted headgear on the flight and had emerged in black fur with ear-flaps, but I was huddled only into my fluffy scarf.

'You lose much body-heat through the head,' said Natasha seriously. 'Tomorrow you must buy a hat.'

'Very well,' I said.

She had splendid dark eyebrows and creamy white skin, and wore smooth pale pink lipstick. A touch of humour would have put the missing sparkle into her brown eyes, but then a touch of humour in the Soviets would have transformed the world.

'You have not been to Moscow before?'

'No,' I said.

There was a group of four large men in dark overcoats standing by the exit doors. They were turned inwards towards each other as if in conversation, but their eyes were directed outwards, and none of them was talking. Natasha and Anna walked past them as if they were wallpaper.

'Who asked you to meet me?' I asked curiously.

'Our Intourist office,' Natasha said.

'But . . . who asked *them*?'

Both girls gave me a blank look and no answer, leaving me to gather that they didn't know, and that it was something they would not expect to know.

The car, which had a driver who spoke no English, travelled down straight wide empty roads towards the city, with wet snowflakes whirling thinly away in the headlights. The road surfaces were clear, but lumpy grey-white banks lined the verges. I shivered in my overcoat from aversion more than discomfort: it was warm enough in the car.

'It is not cold for the end of November,' Natasha said. 'Today it has been above freezing all day. Usually by now the snow has come for the winter, but instead we have had rain.'

The bus stops, I saw, had been built to deal with life below zero. They were enclosed in glass, and brightly lit inside; and in a few there were groups of inward-facing men, three, not four, who might or might not be there to catch a bus.

'If you wish,' Anna said, 'tomorrow you can make a conducted tour of the city by coach, and the next day there is a visit to the Exhibition of Economic Achievements.'

'We will do our best for tickets for the ballet and the opera,' said Natasha, nodding hopefully.

'There are always many English people in your hotel visiting Moscow on package holidays,' Anna said, 'and it will be possible for you to join them in a conducted tour of the Kremlin or other places of interest.'

I looked from one to the other and came to the conclusion that they were genuinely trying to be helpful.

'Thank you,' I said, 'but mostly I shall be visiting friends.'

'If you tell us where you want to go,' Natasha said earnestly, 'we will arrange it.'

My room at the Intourist Hotel was spacious enough for one person, with a bed along one side wall and a sofa along the other, but the same sized area with twin beds, glimpsed through briefly opened doors, must have been pretty cramped for two. I also had a wide shelf along the whole wall under the window, with a telephone and a table lamp on it; a chair, a built-in wardrobe, and a bathroom. Brown carpet, reddish patterned curtains, dark green sofa and bedcover. An ordinary, functional, adequate hotel room which could as well have been in Sydney, Los Angeles or Manchester for all its national flavour.

I unpacked my sparse belongings and looked at my watch. 'We have arranged your dinner for eight o'clock,' Anna had said. 'Please come to the restaurant then. I will be there to help you plan what you want to do tomorrow.' The nursemaiding care would have to be discouraged, I thought, but, as it was no part of my brief to cause immediate dismay, I decided to go along meekly. A short duty-free reviver, however, seemed a good idea.

I poured scotch into a toothmug and sat on the sofa to drink it; and the telephone rang.

'Is that Randall Drew?'

'Yes,' I said.

'Come to the bar of the National Hotel at nine o'clock,' said the voice. 'Leave your hotel, turn right, turn right at the street corner. The National Hotel will be on your right. Enter, leave your coat, climb the stairs, turn right. The bar is along the passage a short way, on the left. Nine o'clock. I'll see you, Mr Drew.'

The line clicked dead before I could say, 'Who are you?'

I went on drinking the scotch. The only way to find out was to go.

After a while I took out the paper Hughes-Beckett had given me, and because the telephone seemed to be connected directly to an outside line, I dialled the number of the English student at the Russian university. A Russian voice answered, saying I knew not what.

'Stephen Luce,' I said distinctly. 'Please may I speak to Stephen Luce?'

The Russian voice said an English word, 'Wait,' and I waited. Three minutes later, by what seemed to me a minor miracle, a fresh English voice said, 'Yes? Who is it?'

'My name is Randall Drew,' I said. 'I . . .'

'Oh yes,' he interrupted. 'Where are you calling from?'

'My room at the Intourist Hotel.'

'What's your number? The telephone number, on the dial.'

I read it out.

'Right,' he said. 'I'd better meet you tomorrow. Twelve o'clock suit you? My lunch hour. In Red Square, in front of St Basil's Cathedral. OK?'

'Er, yes,' I said.

'Fine,' he said. 'Have to go now. Bye.' And he rang off.

It had to be catching, I thought. Something in the Moscow air. I dialled the number of the man concerned with training the Soviet team, and again a Russian voice answered. I asked in English for Mr Kropotkin, but this time without luck. After a couple of short silences at the other end, as I repeated my request, there was a burst of agitated incomprehensible speech, followed by a sharp decisive click.

I had better fortune with the British Embassy, and found myself talking to the cultural attaché.

'Sure,' he said in Etonian tones, 'we know all about you. Care to come for a drink tomorrow evening? Six o'clock suit you?'

'Perfectly,' I said. 'I . . .'

'Where are you calling from?' he said.

'My room at the Intourist Hotel.' I gave him the telephone number, unasked.

'Splendid,' he said. 'Look forward to seeing you.'

Again the swift click. I finished the scotch and considered the shape of my telephone calls. My naïvety, I reflected, must, to the old hands in the city, have been frightening.

Anna waited, hovering, in the dining-room, and came forward as I appeared. Unwrapped, she wore a green wool suit with rows of bronze-coloured beads, and would have fitted unremarkably into the London business scene. Her hair, with a few greys among the prevailing browns, was clean and well shaped, and she had the poise of one accustomed to plan and advise.

'You can sit here,' she said, indicating a stretch of tables beside a long row of windows. 'There are some English people sitting here, on a tour.'

'Thank you.'

'Now,' she said, 'tomorrow . . .'

'Tomorrow,' I said pleasantly, 'I thought I would walk around Red Square and the Kremlin, and perhaps GUM. I have a map and a guide book, and I'm sure I won't get lost.'

'But we can add you on to one of the guided tours,' she said persuasively. 'There is a special two-hour tour of the Kremlin, with a visit to the Armoury.'

'I'd honestly rather not. I'm not a great one for museums and so on.'

She looked disapproving, but after another fruitless try, she told me that my lunch would be ready at one-thirty, when the Kremlin party returned. 'Then at two-thirty there is the bus tour of the city.'

'Yes,' I said. 'That will be fine.'

I saw as well as sensed the release of tension within her. Visitors who went their own way were clearly a problem, though I did not yet understand why. My semi-compliance, anyway, had temporarily earned me qualified good marks, and she said, as if promising sweeties to a child, that Bolshoi tickets for the opera were almost a certainty.

The tables, each set for four, began to fill up. A middle-aged couple from Lancashire joined me with enquiring smiles, closely followed by the man who had been picked clean by the customs officers. We all exchanged the sort of platitudes that strangers thrust together by chance use to demonstrate non-aggression, and the Lancashire lady commented on the extent of the airport search.

'We had to wait ever such a long time on the bus before you came out,' she said.

The unasked question floated in the air. The object of her curiosity, who was uniformed in jeans, jersey and longish hair, spooned sour cream into his borsch and took his time over replying.

'They took me off and searched me down to my skin,' he said finally, enjoying the sensationalism.

The Lancashire lady said 'ooh' in mock terror and was flatteringly impressed. 'What were they looking for?'

He shrugged. 'Don't know. There was nothing to find. I just let them get on with it, and in the end they said I could go.'

His name, he said, was Frank Jones. He taught in a school in Essex and it was his third trip to Russia. A great country, he said. The Lancashire couple regarded him doubtfully, and we all shaped up to some greyish meat of undiscernible origin. The ice-cream coming later was better, but one would not, I thought, have made the journey for the gastronomic delights.

Duty done, I set off to the National Hotel in overcoat and woolly scarf, with sleet stinging my face and wetting my hair and a sharp wind invading every crevice. Pavements and roadway glistened with a wetness that was not yet ice, but the quality of the cold was all the same piercing, and I could feel it deep down inside my lungs. All it would take to abort the whole mission, I thought, would be a conclusive bout of bronchitis, and for a tempting minute I felt like opening my arms to the chill: but anything on the whole was probably better than coughing and spitting and looking at hotel bedroom walls.

The bar of the National Hotel was a matter of shady opulence, like an unmodernized Edwardian pub or a small London club gone slightly to seed. There were rugs on the floor, three long tables with eight or ten chairs round each, and a few separate small tables for three or four. Most of the chairs were occupied and there was a two-deep row in front of the bar which stretched across one end of the room. The voices around me spoke English, German, French and a lot of other tongues, but there was no one enquiring of every newcomer whether he was Randall Drew, newly-arrived from England.

After an unaccosted few minutes I turned to the bar and in due course got myself a whisky. It was by then nine-fifteen. I drank for a while standing up, and then, when one of the small tables became free, sitting down; but I drank altogether alone. At nine thirty-five I bought a second drink, and at nine-fifty I reckoned that if all my investigating were to be as successful I wouldn't need bronchitis.

At two minutes to ten I looked at my watch and drained my glass, and a man detached himself from the row of drinkers at the bar and put two fresh tumblers on the table.

'Randall Drew?' he said, pulling up an empty chair and sitting down. 'Sorry to keep you waiting, sport.'

He had been there, I remembered, as long as I had; standing by the bar, exchanging words now and then with his neighbours and the barman, or looking down into his glass in the way of habitual pubbers, as if expecting to see the wisdom of the ages written in alcohol and water.

'Why did you,' I asked, 'keep me waiting?'

The only reply I got was a grunt and an expressionless look from a pair of hard grey eyes. He pushed one of the tumblers my way and said it was my tipple, he thought. He was solid and in his forties, and wore his dark double-breasted jacket open, so that it flapped about him and hung forward when he moved. He had flatly-combed black hair going a little thin on top, and a neck like a vigorous tree trunk.

'You want to be careful in Moscow,' he said.

'Mm,' I said. 'Do you have a name?'

'Herrick. Malcolm Herrick.' He paused, but I'd never heard of him. 'Moscow correspondent of the *Watch*.'

'How do you do,' I said politely, but neither of us offered a hand.

'This is no kids' playground, sport,' he said. 'I'm telling you for your own good.'

'Kind,' I murmured.

'You're here to ask damnfool questions about that four-letter Farring-ford.'

'Why four-letter?' I asked.

'I don't like him,' he said flatly. 'But that's neither here nor there. I've asked all the questions there are to ask about that shit, and there's damn all to find out. And if there'd been a smell there, I'd've found it. There's no one like an old newshound, sport, if there's any dirt to be dug up about noble earls.'

Even his voice gave an impression of hard muscle. I wouldn't have liked to have him knock on my door, I thought, if I were caught in a newsworthy tragedy: he would be about as compassionate as a tornado.

'How come you've been looking?' I asked. 'And how did you know I was here, and on what errand, and staying at the Intourist? And how did you manage to telephone me within an hour of my arrival?'

He gave me another flat, hard, expressionless stare.

'We do want to know a lot, don't we, sport?' He took a mouthful of his drink. 'Little birds round at the Embassy. What else?'

'Go on,' I said, as he seemed to have stopped.

'Can't reveal sources,' he said automatically. 'But I'll tell you sport, this is no new story. It's weeks since I did my bloodhound bit, and the Embassy staff have also put out their own feelers, and if you ask me they even set one of their Intelligence bods on to it on the quiet, on account of the queries that were popping up everywhere. It all turned out to be one big yawn. It's bloody silly sending you out here as well. Some fanatic in London doesn't seem to want to take "no story" for an answer, and "no story" is all the story there is.'

I took off my glasses and squinted at them against the light, and after a while put them on again.

'Well,' I said mildly, 'it's nice of you to bother to tell me all that, but I can't really go home straight away without *trying*, can I? I mean, they are paying my fare and expenses, and so on. But I wonder,' I went on tentatively, 'if perhaps you could tell me who you saw, so that I wouldn't duplicate a whole lot of wasteful legwork.'

'Christ, sport,' he exploded, 'you really do want your hand held, don't you?' He narrowed his eyes and compressed a firm mouth, and considered it. 'All right. There were three Russian observers in England last summer going round these damnfool horse trials. Officials from some minor committee set up here to arrange details of the equestrian events at the Games. I spoke to all three of them along at that vast Olympic committee centre they've got on Gorky Street, opposite the Red Army Museum. They had all seen Farringford riding at all the horse trials they had been to, but there was absolutely no link at all between Farringford and anything to do with Russia. *Niet, niet* and *niet*. Unanimous opinion.'

'Oh well,' I said resignedly, 'what about the Russian team which went to the international trials that were held at Burghley?'

'Those riders are unavailable, sport. You try interviewing a brick wall. The official reply that was given to the Embassy was that the Russian team had no contact with Farringford, minimum contact with any British civilians, and in any case did not speak English.'

I thought it over. 'And did you come across anything to do with a girl called Alyosha?'

He choked over his drink at the name, but it was apparently mirth, and his laugh held a definite hint of sneer.

'Alyosha, sport, is not a girl, for a start. Alyosha is a man's name. A diminutive. Like Dickie for Richard. Alyosha is a familiar version of Alexei.'

'Oh . . .'

'And if you fell for all that guff about the German who died having a boy friend from Moscow, you can forget it. Over here they still throw you in jug for it. There are as many homosexuals here as warts on a billiard ball.'

'And the rest of the German team? Did you reach them too, to ask questions?'

'The diplomats did. None of the Krauts knew a thing.'

'How many Alyoshas in Moscow?' I said.

'How many Dickies in London? The two cities are roughly the same size.'

'Have another drink?' I said.

He rose to his feet with the nearest he'd come to a smile, but the brief show of teeth raised no echoing glimmer in the eyes.

'I'll get them,' he said. 'You give me the cash.'

I gave him a fiver, which did the trick nicely with change to spare. Only Western foreign currency, the barman had told me, was acceptable in that bar. Roubles and Eastern bloc equivalents were no good. The bar was for non-Curtain visitors, who were to hand over as big a contribution to the tourist trade as possible, all in francs, marks, dollars and yen. The change came back meticulously, and correctly, in the currency in which one had paid.

Malcolm Herrick loosened up a little over the second drink and told me a bit about working in Moscow.

'There used to be dozens of British correspondents here, but most of the papers have called them back. Only five or six of us left now, except for the news agency guys. Reuters, and so on. The fact is, if anything big breaks in Moscow it's the outside world that hears about it first, and we get it fed back to us on the world news service on the radio. We might as well not be here for all the inside info we get for ourselves.'

'Do you yourself speak Russian?' I said.

'I do not. The Russians don't like Russian speakers working here.'

'Why ever not?' I said, surprised.

He looked at me pityingly. 'The system over here is to keep foreigners away from the Russians and Russians away from foreigners. Foreigners who work here full time have to live in compounds, with Russian guards on the gates. All the journalists, diplomats and news agency people live in compounds. We even have our offices there. No need to go out, sport. The news comes in, courtesy of telex.'

He seemed to be more cynical than bitter. I wondered what sort of stories he wrote for the *Watch*, which was a newspaper more famous for its emotional crusades than its accuracy. It was also a paper I seldom read, as its racing columnist knew more about orchids than good things for Ascot.

We finished the drinks and stood up to depart.

'Thank you for your help,' I said. 'If I think of anything else, can I give you a ring? Are you in the phone book?'

He gave me a final flat grey stare in which there was a quality of dour triumph. I was not going to succeed where he had failed, his manner said, so I might as well retire at once.

'There's no telephone directory in Moscow,' he said.

My turn to stare.

'If you want to know a number,' he said, 'you have to ask Directory Enquiries. You probably have to tell them why you want the number, and if they don't approve of you knowing it, they won't give it to you.'

He pulled a spiral-bound reporters' notebook out of his pocket and wrote down his number, ripping off the page and handing it to me.

'And use a public telephone, sport. Not the one in your room.'

I scurried the two hundred yards back to the Intourist in heavier sleet which was turning to snow. I collected my keys, went up in the lift, and said 'good evening' in English to the plump lady who sat at a desk from which she could keep an eye on the corridor to the bedrooms. Anyone coming from the lifts to the rooms had to pass her. She gave me a stolid inspection and said what I supposed to be 'goodnight' in Russian.

My room was on the eighth floor, looking from the front of the hotel down to Gorky Street. I drew the curtains and switched on the reading lamp.

There was something indefinably different in the way my belongings lay tidily around it. I pulled open a drawer or two, and felt my skin contract in a primeval ripple down my back and legs.

While I had been out, someone had searched my room.

4

I lay in bed with the lamp on and looked at the ceiling, and wondered why I should feel so disturbed. I was not one of those spies in or out of the cold who was entirely at home with people ferreting through their belongings, and probably felt deprived if they didn't. I had read and enjoyed all the books, and had hoisted in some of the jargon: mole, sleeper, spook, *et al*. But as for that world affecting me personally: that was as unexpected as a scorpion on the breakfast toast.

Yet I was in Moscow to ask questions. Perhaps that made me a legitimate target for irregular attention. And of course the most immediate questions remained unanswered, and so far unanswerable.

Who, exactly, had done the searching? And why?

There had been nothing of significance for anyone to find. The paper with potentially useful names and addresses had been in my pocket. I had concealed in my luggage no guns, no codes, no tiny technology, no anti-Soviet propaganda. I had been told it was illegal to import bibles and crucifixes into Russia, and had not done so. I had brought no forbidden books, no pornography, and no newspapers. No drugs . . .

Drugs . . .

I fairly bounded out of bed and yanked open the drawer in which I'd stored my box of assorted air freight. Heaved a considerable sigh of relief, once the lid was open, to see the pills and inhalers and syringe and adrenalin ampoules all more or less in the positions Emma had given them. I couldn't for certain tell whether or not they had been inspected, but at least nothing was missing. A hypochondriac Emma might well call me, but the sad fact remained that at certain dire times the contents of that box were all that held off the Hereafter. The fates that had given me wealth had been niggardly on health: a silver spoon that bent easily. Even at my age, if one was prone to chest troubles, insurance premiums were loaded. If one's father and grandfather had both died young for lack of salbutamol or beclomethasone dipropionate, or sundry other later miracles, one discovered that actuaries' hearts were as hard as flint.

In between times, and to be fair there were far more in between times than troubles, I was as bursting with health and vigour as any other poor slob living in the damp, cold, misty, bronchitic climate of the British Isles.

I shut the box and replaced it in the drawer: climbed back into bed, switched out the light, and took off my glasses, folding them neatly to hand for the morning. How soon, I wondered, could I decently make use of my return ticket.

Red Square looked greyish brown, with snowflakes blowing energetically across it in a fiendish wind. I stood in front of St Basil's Cathedral taking photographs in light dim enough to develop them by, wondering if even the deep intense red of the huge brick walls of the Kremlin would make a mark on the emulsion. The vast slush-covered expanse, where sometimes the self-aggrandizing parades beat hell out of the road surface for newsreels, was on that day trodden only by miserable-looking groups of tourists, shepherded in straggling crocodiles to and from a group of buses parked nearby.

The Cathedral itself was small, a cluster of brilliantly coloured and encrusted onion-shaped domes on stalks of different height, like a fantasy castle out of Disney. Snow lay on the onions now, dimming the blues and greens and golds that sparkled on the picture postcards, but I stood there wondering how a nation which had produced a building of such joyous, magnificent imagination could have come to its latter-day greyness.

'Ivan the Great commissioned that cathedral,' said a voice behind my right shoulder. 'When it was finished he was overwhelmed with its beauty; and he put out the eyes of his architect, so that he should not design anything more splendid for anyone else.'

I turned slowly round. A shortish young man stood there, wearing a dark blue overcoat, a black fur hat, and an unexpectant expression on a round face.

Round brown eyes full of bright intelligence, alive in a way that Russians faces were not. A person, I judged, whose still soft outlines of youth hid a mind already sharply adult. I'd had a bit of the same trouble myself at the same age, ten years or so ago.

'Are you Stephen Luce?' I said.

A smile flickered and disappeared. 'That's right.'

'I would rather not have known about the architect.'

'Why?'

'I don't like horror movies.'

'Life is a horror movie,' he said. 'Do you want to see Lenin's tomb?' He half turned away and pointed an arm to the middle distance, where a queue were waiting outside a large box-like building halfway along the Kremlin wall. 'The Cathedral isn't a church now, it's some sort of store. You can go into the Tomb, though.'

'No, thank you.'

He moved off, however, in that direction, and I went with him.

'Over there,' he said, pointing to one side of the Tomb, 'is a small bust of Stalin, on a short pillar. It has recently appeared there, without any ceremony. You may think this is of no great note, but in point of fact it is very interesting. At one time Stalin was with Lenin in the Tomb. Revered, and all that. Then there was a spot of revisionism, and Stalin was the ultra *persona non grata*, so they took him out of the Tomb and put up a small statue outside, instead. Then they did a spot more revisionism, and removed even the statue, leaving nothing but a curt plaque in the ground where it had been. But now we have a new statue, back on the same spot. This one is not the old proud glare of world domination, but a downward-looking, pensive, low-profile sort of thing. Fascinating, don't you think?'

'What are you reading at the University?' I said.

'Russian history.'

I looked from the rebirth of Stalin to the dead cathedral. 'Tyrants come and go,' I said. 'Tyranny is constant.'

'Some things are best said in the open air.'

I looked at him straightly. 'How much will you help me?' I asked.

'Why don't you take some photographs?' he said. 'Behave like a tourist.'

'No one thinks I'm a tourist, unless having one's room searched is par for the packages.'

'Oh gee,' he said quaintly. 'In that case, let's just walk.'

At tourist pace we left Red Square and went towards the river. I huddled inside my coat and pulled my scarf up over my ears to meet the fur hat I had bought that morning, following Natasha's instructions.

'Why don't you untie the ear-flaps?' Stephen Luce said, untying a black tape bow on top of his own head. 'Much warmer.' He pulled the formerly folded-up flaps down over his ears, and let the black tape ties dangle free. 'Don't tie the tapes under your chin,' he said, 'or they'll think you're a pouff.'

I pulled the flaps down and let the tapes flutter in the wind, as he did.

'What do you want me to do?' he said.

'Come with me to see some men about some horses.'

'When?'

'Mornings are best, for horse people.'

He took a minute over replying, then said doubtfully, 'I suppose I could cut tomorrow's lecture, just for once.'

How like Hughes-Beckett, I thought sardonically, to equip me with an interpreter whose time was measured in lunch hours and missed lectures. I glanced at the round, troubled face in its frame of black fur, and more or less decided then and there that my whole mission was impossible.

'Do you know Rupert Hughes-Beckett?' I said.

'Never heard of him.'

I sighed. 'Who was it who wrote to you, asking you to help me?'

'The Foreign Office. A man called Spencer. I know *him*. They are sponsoring me, sort of, you see. Through college. The idea being that eventually I'll work for them. Though I might not, in the end. It's all a bit suffocating, that diplomatic waxworks.'

We reached the approach to the bridge over the river, and Stephen threw out an arm in another of his generous gestures.

'Over there is the British Embassy,' he said, pointing.

I couldn't see much for snow. I took off my glasses, dried them as best I could on a handkerchief, and enjoyed for a minute or two a clearer look at the world.

'Turn off right at the far side of the bridge,' Stephen said. 'Go down the steps to the other road running beneath it, along beside the river, and the Embassy's that pale yellow building along there, giving a good imitation of Buckingham Palace.'

I told him I was going for a drink with the cultural attaché and he said the best of British luck, and not to miss seeing the Ambassador's loo, it had the best view of the Kremlin in the whole of Moscow.

'I say,' he said, as we went on over the bridge, 'do you mind telling me what you're actually here for?'

'Didn't they say?'

'No. Only to interpret, if necessary.'

I shook my head in frustration. 'Chasing a will-o'-the-wisp. Looking for a rumour called Alyosha. Some say he doesn't exist and others that he doesn't want to be found. All I have to do is find him, see who he is and what he is, and decide whether he poses any sort of threat to a chap who wants to ride in the Olympics. And since you asked, I will now bore your ears off by telling you the whole story.'

He listened with concentration and his ears remained in place. When I'd finished he was walking with a springier step.

'Count me in, then,' he said. 'And hang the lectures. I'll borrow someone else's notes.' We turned at the end of the bridge to go back, and between the snowflakes I saw his dark brown eyes shining with humorous life. 'I thought you were here just fact-finding for the Games. In a general way, and semi-official. This is more fun.'

'I haven't thought so,' I said.

He laughed. 'Ve have vays of making you sit up and enjoy yourself.'

'Ve had better have vays of keeping it all very discreet.'

'Oh sure. Do you want the benefit of the immense experience of a lifetime of living in Moscow?'

'Whose?' I said.

'Mine, of course. I've been here eleven weeks. Lifetimes are comparative.'

'Fire away,' I said.

'Never do anything unusual. Never turn up when you're not expected, and always turn up if you are.'

I said, 'That doesn't sound very extraordinary.'

I received a bright amused shot from the brown eyes. 'Some English people touring here by car decided to go to a different town for a night from the one they had originally booked. Just an impulse. They were fined for it.'

'*Fined?*' I was amazed.

'Yes. Can you imagine a foreign tourist being fined in England because he went to Manchester instead of Birmingham? Can you imagine an English hotel doing anything but shrug if he didn't turn up? But everything here is regulated. There are masses of people just standing around watching other people, and they all report what they seem, because that's their job. They are employed to watch. There's no unemployment here. Instead of handing a bloke dole money and letting him spend it in civilized ways like soccer and gambling and pubs, they give him a job watching. Two birds with one stone, and all that.'

'Standing in groups at airports and in bus shelters, and dotted around outside hotels?'

He grinned. 'So right. Those guys in bus stops are there to stop all foreign-registered cars going out of Moscow, to check their destinations and visas, because all foreigners need a visa to go more than thirty kilometres from the centre. Sometimes they stop Russian cars, but not often. Anyway, there's a joke here that you always see at least three Russians together when they've any regular contact with foreigners. One alone might be tempted, two might conspire, but if there are three, one will always inform.'

'Cynical.'

'And practical. What did you say you'd do today? I take it you have In-tourist girls looking after you?'

'Natasha and Anna,' I said. 'I told them I'd be in the hotel to lunch and go on a bus tour of the city afterwards.'

'Then you'd better do it,' he said judiciously. 'I'm not sure they don't get into trouble if they lose their charge, so to speak.'

I paused at the centre of the bridge to look over the parapet at the iron grey water. Snow speckled everything and filled the air like torn tissue-paper. To the right along the river bank stretched the long red beautiful walls of the Kremlin, with golden towers at intervals and vistas of golden onion domes inside. A walled city, a fortress, with defunct churches and active government offices and the daily tread of millions of tourists. To the left, on the opposite bank, the British Embassy.

'Better move on,' Stephen said. 'Two men standing still on a bridge in the snow . . . that's suspicious.'

'I don't believe it.'

'You'd be surprised.'

We walked on, however, and went back up the incline to Red Square.

'Job number one,' I said. 'Will you make a call for me?'

I showed him the Olympic team trainer's name and number, and we stopped at a glass-walled telephone box. Telephone calls, it appeared, were cheap. Stephen brushed away my offered rouble and produced a two-kopek coin.

'What shall I say?' he asked.

'Say I'd like to see him tomorrow morning. Say I was very impressed with the Russian team at the International Horse Trials and would like to congratulate him and ask his advice. Say I'm frightfully important in the horse world. Lay it on a bit. He doesn't know me.' I gave him some well-known Eventing names. 'Say I'm a colleague of theirs.'

'Are you?' he said, dialling the number.

'I know them,' I said. 'That's why I was sent. Because I know the horse people.'

Someone answered at the other end, and Stephen launched into what was to me a vague jumble of noises. A softer-sounding language than I had for some reason expected. Pleasing.

He talked for quite some time, and listened, and talked, and listened, and talked, and finally rang off.

'Success,' he said. 'Eleven o'clock. Outside the stables, round the far side of the racecourse.'

'The Hippodrome,' I said.

'That's right.' His eyes gleamed. 'The Olympic horses exercise there on the track.'

'Fantastic,' I said, astounded. 'Bloody incredible.'

'And you were wrong about one thing,' Stephen said. 'He did know who you are. He said you went to ride in a race called the Pardubice in Czechoslovakia, and he saw you finish third. He seemed in point of fact to be quite pleased to be going to meet you.'

'Nice of him,' I said modestly.

Stephen spoilt it. 'Russians love a chance of talking to people from the outside. They see so few, that they love it.'

We agreed that he should meet me outside the hotel the following morning, and his cheerfulness was catching.

'When you go on that bus tour,' he said as we parted, 'you'll stop in Derzhinsky Square. With a statue of Derzhinsky on a tall column. There's a big store for children there. What the guide won't tell you, though, is that the building next to it, across the street, is the Lubianka.'

There were taxis waiting outside the hotel but none of the drivers spoke English, and either they didn't understand the words 'British Embassy', or the address written in English script, or they understood but refused to take me there. In any case, I got a chorus of shaken heads, so in the end I walked. It was still snowing, but wetly, and what lay on the ground was slush. After a mile and a half of it my feet were soaking and icy and my mood deepening from cross to vile.

Following Stephen's instructions, I found the steps at the far side of the bridge and descended to the lower level, walking along there with dark heavy buildings on my left and the chest-high river wall on the right. When I at length reached the gateway of the Embassy a Russian soldier stepped out of a sentry box and barred my way.

An odd argument then took place in which neither protagonist could understand a word the other said. I pointed vigorously at my watch, and to the Embassy door, and said, 'I am English,' several times very loudly, and got even crosser. The Russian finally, dubiously, stood back a pace and let me through into the short driveway. The huge front door of the Embassy itself was opened, with a lot less fuss, by a dark blue uniform with gilt buttons and braids.

Inside, the hall and stairs and visible doorways were rich with the glossy wood and glass and plaster mouldings of more elegant ages. There was also a large leather-topped desk behind which sat a one-man reception committee, and, standing near him, a tall languid man with noble bones and greying hair combed carefully backwards.

The dark blue uniform offered to relieve me of my coat and hat, and the man at the desk asked if he could help me.

'The cultural attaché?' I said. 'I've an appointment.'

The grey-haired man moved gently like a lily in the wind and said the cultural attaché happened to be himself. He extended a limp hand and a medium smile, and I responded with the merest shade more warmth to both. He murmured platitudes about the weather and air travel while he made some internal judgements about me, but it appeared that I had passed his private tests because he suddenly changed mental gears and asked with some charm whether I would care to see over the Embassy itself before we went to his office for a drink. His office, he explained, was in a separate building.

We climbed the stairs and made a tour of the reception rooms, and duly inspected the loo with the best view of the Kremlin. The cultural attaché, who had identified himself as Oliver Waterman, kept up a genial informed chatter as if he showed visitors round this route every day of the week: which, on reflection, perhaps he did. We ended, after a short windy outside walk, in a more modern-looking first-floor suite of carpeted book-lined offices, where he wasted no time in pouring hefty drinks.

'Don't know what we can do for you,' he said, settling deep into a leather armchair, and waving me to one similar. 'This Farringford business seems to be a fuss over nothing.'

'You hope,' I said.

He smiled thinly. 'True. But there's no fire without smoke, and we haven't had even a whiff.'

'Did you yourself interview the three Russian observers?' I asked.

'Er,' he said, clearing his throat and looking concerned. 'Which observers would those be?'

Resignedly I explained. His expression cleared gradually as if a responsibility had been taken from him.

'But, you see,' he said pleasantly, 'we in the Embassy would not speak to them ourselves. We approached our opposite numbers for relevant information, and were informed that no one knew anything of any significance.'

'You couldn't have spoken to those men face to face in their own homes?'

He shook his head. 'It is actively discouraged, if not positively forbidden, for private contacts to take place.'

'Forbidden by them, or by us?'

'Bit of both. But by us, definitely.'

'So you never really get to know the Russian people, even though you live here?'

He shook his head without any visible regret. 'There is always a risk, in unofficial contacts.'

'So xenophobia works both ways?' I said.

He uncrossed his legs and recrossed them left over right. 'Fear of foreigners is older than the conscious mind,' he said, smiling as if he had said it often before. 'But, now, about your enquiries . . .'

The telephone at his elbow interrupted him. He picked up the receiver in a leisurely fashion after the third ring, and said merely, 'Yes?'

A slight frown creased his high smooth forehead. 'Very well, bring him round.' He replaced the receiver and continued with his former sentence. 'About your enquiries, we can offer you telex facilities, if you need them, and if you'll give me your room's telephone number I can ring you if any messages arrive for you.'

'I gave you the number,' I said.

'Oh, did you?' He looked vague. 'I'd better take it again, my dear chap.'

I repeated the number from memory, and he wrote it on a notepad.

'Let me see to your glass,' he said, splashing away with a lavish hand. 'And then perhaps you might meet one or two of my colleagues.'

There were the noises of people arriving downstairs. Oliver Waterman stood up and brushed his smooth hair back with the insides of both wrists; a gesture of preparing himself, I reckoned, more than any need for grooming.

There was one loud intrusive voice rising above a chorus of two others, one male, one female, and as they came up the stairs I found myself putting a name to it. With no sense of surprise I watched Malcolm Herrick advance through the doorway.

'Evening, Oliver,' he said confidently, and then, seeing me, 'Well, sport, if it isn't our sleuth. Made any progress?'

From a fleeting glance at Oliver Waterman's face I gathered that his re-action to Malcolm Herrick was much like mine. It was impossible not to attend to what Herrick said because of the physical force of his speech, the result no doubt of years of journalistic necessity; but there was no visible warmth behind the sociable words, and possibly even a little malice.

'Drink, Malcolm?' Oliver suggested, with true diplomatic civility.

'Couldn't be better.'

Oliver Waterman, bottle and glass in hand, made introducing motions be-tween me and the other newcomers. 'Randall Drew ... Polly Paget, Ian Young. They work here with me in this department.'

Polly Paget was a sensible-looking lady in flat shoes, past girlhood but not quite middle-aged, wearing her hair short and her cardigan long. She gave Oliver Waterman a small straightforward smile and accepted her drink before Herrick, as of right. He himself looked as if he thought attaché's assis-tants should be served after him.

If I hadn't been told Ian Young's name or heard him speak, I would have taken him for a Russian. I looked at him curiously, realizing how familiar I had already become with the skin texture and stillness of expression of the Moscow population. Ian Young had the same white heavyish face in which nothing discernible was going on. His voice, when he spoke, which at that time was very little, was unremarkably English.

Malcolm Herrick effortlessly dominated what conversation there was, tell-ing Oliver Waterman, it seemed to me, just what he should do about a particularly boring row which had just broken out over a forthcoming visit of a prestigious orchestra.

When Polly Paget offered a suggestion, Herrick interrupted without listening and squashed her. Oliver Waterman said, 'Well, perhaps, yes, you may be right,' at intervals, while not looking Herrick in the eye except in the briefest of flashes, a sure sign of boredom or dislike. Ian Young sat looking at Herrick with an unnerving lack of response, by which Herrick was not in the least unnerved: and I drank my drink and thought of the wet walk back.

All possible juice extracted from the music scandal, Herrick switched his attention back to me.

'Well, then, sport, how's it going?'

'Slow to stop,' I said.

He nodded. 'Told you so. Too bad. That whole ground's been raked fine and there's not a pebble to be found. Wish there was. I need a decent story.'

'Or indecent, for preference,' Polly Paget said. Herrick ignored her.

'Did you talk to the chef d'équipe?' I said.

'Who?' said Oliver Waterman. I saw from Herrick's face that he hadn't, but also that he wasn't going to admit it unless forced to: and even then, I guessed, he would pooh-pooh the necessity.

I said to Oliver Waterman, 'Mr Kropotkin. The man who oversees the training of the horses and riders for the horse trials. The non-playing cap-tain, so to speak. I was given his name by Rupert Hughes-Beckett.'

'So you'll be seeing him?' Waterman said.

'Yes, tomorrow morning. He seems to be all that's left.'

Ian Young stirred. 'I talked with him,' he said.

Every head turned his way. Thirty-five or so, I thought. Thick-set, brown-haired, wearing a crumpled grey suit and a blue and white striped shirt with the points of the collar curling up like a dried sandwich. He raised his eyebrows and pursed his mouth, which for him was an excessive change of expression.

'In the course of the discreet preliminary enquiries required by the Foreign Office, I too was given his name. I talked with him pretty exhaustively. He knows nothing about any scandal to do with Farringford. A complete dead end.'

'There you are then,' Waterman said, shrugging. 'As I said before, there's no fire. Not a spark.'

'Mm,' I said. 'It would be best that way. But there is a spark. Or there was, in England.' And I told them about Johnny Farringford being beaten up by two men who warned him to stay away from Alyosha.

Their faces showed differing levels of dismay and disbelief.

'But my dear chap,' said Oliver Waterman, recovering his former certainty, 'surely that means that this Alyosha, whoever he is, is absolutely determined not to be dropped into any sort of mess? So surely that makes it all the safer for Farringford to come to the Olympics?'

'Except,' I said apologetically, 'that of course Farringford was also told in the summer that if he came to Moscow, Alyosha would be waiting to extract revenge for the stresses which gave Hans Kramer a heart attack.'

There was a short thoughtful silence.

'People change their minds,' said Polly Paget at length, judiciously. 'Maybe in the summer, when Kramer died, this Alyosha sounded off a bit hysterically, and now, on reflection, the last thing he wants is to be involved.'

Herrick shook his head impatiently, but it seemed to me the most sensible solution yet advanced.

'I really hope you're right,' I said. 'The only trouble will be proving it. And the only way to prove it, as it always has been, is for me to find Alyosha, and talk to him, and get from him his own positive assurance that he means Farringford no harm.'

Polly Paget nodded. Oliver Waterman looked mildly despairing; and Malcolm Herrick unmirthfully laughed.

'Good luck to you, then, sport,' he said. 'You'll be here till Doomsday. I tell you, I've looked for this bloody Alyosha, and he doesn't exist.'

I sighed a little and looked at Ian Young. 'And you?' I said.

'I've looked too,' he said. 'There isn't a trace.'

There seemed little else to say. The party broke up, and I asked Waterman if he could telephone for a taxi.

'My dear chap,' he said regretfully. 'They won't come here. They don't like to be contaminated by stopping outside the British Embassy. You can probably catch an empty one on the main road, if you walk along to the bridge.'

We shook hands at his outer door, and, again swathed in overcoat and fur hat, I set off towards the guarded gate. It had stopped snowing at last, which improved the prospects slightly. Ian Young, however, called out after me and offered a lift in his car, which I gratefully agreed to. He sat stolidly behind his steering-wheel, dealing with darkness, falling snow and road-obscuring slush as if emotion had never been invented.

'Malcolm Herrick,' he said, still dead-pan, 'is a pain in the arse.'

He turned left out of the gate, and drove along beside the river.

'And you're stuck with him,' I said.

His silence was assent. 'He's a persistent burrower,' he said. 'Gets a story if it's there.'

'You're telling me to go home and forget it?'

'No,' he said, turning more corners. 'But don't stir up the Russians. They take fright very easily. When they're frightened they attack. People of great endurance, full of courage. But easily alarmed. Don't forget.'

'Very well,' I said.

'You have a man called Frank Jones sitting at your table at the hotel,' he said.

I glanced at him. His face was dead calm.

'Yes,' I said.

'Did you know he was in the KGB?'

I copied his impassiveness. I said, 'Did you know that you are going a very long way round to my hotel?'

He actually reacted: even went so far as to smile. 'How did you know?'

'Went on a bus tour. Studied the maps.'

'And does Frank Jones sit with you always?'

'So far,' I said, nodding. 'And a middle-aged couple from Lancashire. We sat together by chance at dinner yesterday, our first night here, and you know how it is, people tend to return to the same table. So yes, the same four of us have sat together today at breakfast and lunch. What makes you think he is in the KGB? He's as English as they come, and he was thoroughly searched at the airport on the way in.'

'Searched so that you could see, I suppose?'

'Yes,' I said, thinking. 'Everyone on the plane could see.'

'Cover,' he said. 'There's no mistake. He's not sitting at your table by accident. He came with you from England and he'll no doubt go back with you. Has he searched your room yet?'

I said nothing. Ian Young very faintly smiled again.

'I see he has,' he said. 'What did he find?'

'Clothes and cough mixture.'

'No Russian addresses or phone numbers?'

'I had them in my pocket,' I said. 'Such as they are.'

'Frank Jones,' he said, driving round back streets, 'has a Russian grandmother, who has spoken the language to him all his life. She married a

240

British sailor, but her sympathies were all with the October Revolution. She recruited Frank in the cradle.'

'But if he is KGB,' I said, 'why do you let him ... operate?'

'Better the devil you know.' We swung into yet another deserted street. 'Every time he comes back we are alerted by our passport control people back home. They send a complete passenger list of the flight he comes on, because he always travels with his business. So we scan it. We get someone out pronto to the airport to see where he goes. We follow. Tut tut. We see him book into the Intourist. We drift into the dining-room. If it's safe, he also *sits* with his business. We see he's with you. We know all about you. We relax. We wish Frank well. We certainly don't want to disturb him. If his masters discovered we knew all about him, next time they'd send someone else. And then where would we be? When Frank comes, we know to pay attention. Worth his weight in roubles, Frank is, to us.'

We went slowly and quietly down a dark road. Snow fell and melted wetly as it touched the ground.

'What is he likely to do?' I said.

'About you? Report where you go, who you see, what you eat and how many times you crap before breakfast.'

'Sod,' I said.

'And don't ditch him unless you have to, and if you have to, for God's sake make it look accidental.'

I said doubtfully, 'I've had no practice at this sort of thing.'

'Obvious. You didn't notice him follow you from your hotel.'

'Did he?' I said, alarmed.

'He was walking up and down the Naberezhnaya waiting for you to come out. He saw you drive out with me. He'll go back to the Intourist and wait for you there.'

The lights from the dashboard shone dimly on his big impassive face. The economy of muscle movement extended, I had noticed, throughout his body. His head turned little upon his neck: his hands remained in one position on the steering-wheel. He didn't shift in his seat, or drum with his fingers. In his heavy raincoat, thick leather gloves, and fur hat with the ear-flaps up, he looked every inch a Russian.

'What is your job here?' I said.

'Cultural assistant.' His voice gave away as little as his face. Ask silly questions, I thought.

He slowed the car still further and switched off the headlights, and, with the engine barely audible, swung into a cobbled courtyard, and stopped. Put on the handbrake. Half turned in his seat to face me.

'You'll be a few minutes late for dinner,' he said.

5

He seemed to be in no hurry to explain. We sat in complete darkness listening to the irregular ticking of metal as the engine cooled to zero in the Moscow night. In time, as my eyes adjusted, I could see dark high buildings on each side, and some iron railings ahead, with bushes behind them.

'Where are we?' I said.

He didn't answer.

'Look . . . ' I said.

He interrupted. 'When we get out of the car, do not talk. Follow me, but say nothing. There are always people standing in the shadows . . . if they hear you speak English, they will be suspicious. They'll report our visit.'

He opened the car door and stood up outside. He seemed to take it for granted that I should trust him, and I saw no particular reason not to. I stood up after him and closed the door quietly, as he had done, and followed where he led.

We walked towards the railings, which proved to contain a gate. Ian Young opened it with a click of iron, and it swung on unoiled hinges with desolate little squeaks, falling shut behind us with a positive clink. Beyond it, a curving path led away between straggly bare-branched bushes, the dim light showing that in this forlorn public garden the snow lay greyly unmelted, covering everything thinly, like years of undisturbed dust.

There were a few seats beside the path, and glimpses of flat areas which might in summer be grass; but in late November the melancholy of such places could seep into the soul like fungus.

Ian Young walked purposefully onward, neither hurrying nor moving with caution: a man on a normal errand, not arousing suspicion.

At the far side of the garden we reached more railings and another gate. Again the opening click, the squeaks, the closing clink. Ian Young turned without pause to the right and set off along the slushy pavement.

In silence, I followed.

Lights from windows overhead revealed us to be in a residential road of large old buildings with alleys and small courtyards in between. Into one of these yards, cobbled and dark, Ian Young abruptly turned.

Again I went with him, unspeaking.

Scaffolding climbed the sides of the buildings there, and heaps of rubble cluttered the ground. We picked our way over broken bricks and metal tubing and scattered planks, going, as far as I could see, nowhere.

There was, however, a destination. To reach it, we had to step through the scaffolding and over an open ditch which looked like the preliminary earthworks of new drains: and on the far side of the mud and slush there was a heavy wooden door in a dark archway. Ian Young pushed the door, which seemed to have no fastening, and it opened with the easy grind of constant use.

Inside, out of the wind, there was a dimmish light in a bare grey entrance. Gritty concrete underfoot, no paint, no decoration of any kind on the greyish concrete walls. There was a flight of concrete steps leading upwards, and, beside them, a small lift in an ancient-looking cage.

Ian Young pulled open the outer and inner folding metal gates of the lift, and we stepped inside. He closed the gates, pushed the fourth floor button, and forbade me, with his eye, to utter a word.

We emerged from the lift on to a bare landing; wooden-floored, not concrete. There were two closed doors, wooden, long ago varnished, one at each end of the rectangular space. Ian Young stepped to the left, and pressed the button of a bell.

The hallway was very quiet. One could not hear the sound of ringing when he pushed the button, as he did again, in a short-short-long rhythm. There were no voices murmuring behind the doors. No feet on the stairs. No feeling of nearby warmth and life. The lobby to limbo, I thought fancifully; and the door quietly opened.

A tall woman stood there, looking out with the lack of expression which I by now regarded as normal. She peered at Ian Young, and then, more lingeringly, at me. Her eyes travelled back again, enquiringly.

Ian Young nodded.

The woman stepped to one side, tacitly inviting us in. Ian Young went steadfastly over the threshold, and it was far too late for me to decide that on the other side of the door was where I had no wish to be. It swung shut behind me, and the woman slid a bolt.

Still no one spoke. Ian Young took off his coat and hat, and gestured for me to do the same. The woman hung them carefully on pegs in a row that already accommodated a good many similar garments.

She put a hand on Ian Young's arm and led the way along the passage of what seemed to be a private flat. Another closed wooden door was opened, and we went into a moderately-sized living-room.

There were five men there, standing up. Five pairs of eyes focused steadily on my face, five blank expressions covering who knew what thoughts.

They were all dressed tidily and much alike in shirts, jackets, trousers and indoor shoes, but they varied greatly in age and build. One of them, the slimmest, of about my own age, held himself rigid, as if facing an ordeal. The others were simply wary, standing like wild deer scenting the wind.

A man of about fifty, grey-haired and wearing glasses, stepped forward to greet Ian Young and give him a token hug.

He talked to him in Russian, and introduced him to the other four men in a mumble of long names I couldn't begin to catch. They nodded to him, each in turn. A little of the tension went out of the proceedings and small movements occurred in the herd.

'Evgeny Sergeevich,' Ian Young said. 'This is Randall Drew.'

The fiftyish man slowly extended his hand, which I shook. He was neither welcoming nor hostile, and in no hurry to commit himself either way. More dignity than power, I thought: and he was inspecting me with intensity, as if wishing to peer into my soul. He saw instead, I supposed, merely a thinnish, grey-eyed, dark-haired man in glasses, giving his own impression of a stone wall.

To me, Ian Young at last spoke. 'This is out host, Evgeny Sergeevich Titov. And our hostess, his wife, Olga Ivanovna.' He made a small semi-formal bow to the woman who had let us in. She gave him a steady look, and it seemed to me that the firmness of her features came from iron reserves within.

'Good evening,' I said, and she replied seriously in English, 'Good evening.'

The rigid young man, still tautly strung, said something urgently in Russian.

Ian Young turned to me. 'He is asking if we were followed. You can answer. Were we followed?'

'No,' I said.

'Why don't you think so?'

'No one followed us through the garden. The gates make an unmistakable noise. No one came through them after us.'

Ian Young turned away from me and spoke to the group in Russian. They listened to him with their eyes on me, and when he had finished they stirred, and began to move apart from each other, and to sit down. Only the rigid one remained standing, ready for flight.

'I have told them they can trust you,' Ian Young said. 'If I am wrong, I will kill you.'

His eyes were cool and steady, looking unwaveringly into mine. I listened to his words, which in other contexts would have been unbelievable and embarrassing, and I saw that he quite simply meant what he said.

'Very well,' I said.

A flicker of something I couldn't read moved in his mind.

'Please sit down,' Olga Ivanovna said, indicating a deep chair with arms on the far side of the room. 'Please sit down there.' She spoke the English words with a strong Russian accent, but that she knew any English at all put me to shame.

I walked across and sat where she pointed, knowing that they had discussed and planned that I should be placed there, from where I couldn't escape unless they chose to let me go. The deep chair embraced me softly like a bolstered prison. I looked up and found Ian Young near me, looking down. I half closed my eyes, and faintly smiled.

'What do you expect?' he said.

'To learn why we are here.'

'You are not afraid.' Half a statement, half a question.

'No,' I said. 'They are.'

He glanced swiftly at the six Russians and then looked back, with concentration, at me.

'You are not the usual run of bloody fool,' he said.

The rigid young man, still also on his feet, said something impatiently to Ian Young. He nodded, looked from me to the rigid man and back again, took a visible breath, and entrusted me with a lot of dangerous knowledge.

'This is Boris Dmitrevich Telyatnikov,' he said.

The rigid young man raised his chin as if the name itself were an honour.

Ian Young said, 'Boris Dmitrevich rode in the Russian team at the International Horse Trials in England in September.'

It was a piece of information which had me starting automatically to my feet, but even the beginnings of the springing motion reawoke the alarm in all the watchers. Boris Dmitrevich took an actual step backwards.

I relaxed into the chair and looked as mild as possible, and the atmosphere of precarious trust crept gingerly back.

'Please tell him,' I said, 'that I am absolutely delighted to meet him.'

The same could obviously not be said for Boris Dmitrevich Telyatnikov, but I was there from their choice, not my own. I reckoned if they hadn't wanted to see me pretty badly, they wouldn't have put themselves at what they clearly felt was considerable risk.

Olga Ivanovna brought a hard wooden chair and placed it facing me, about four feet away. She then fetched another and placed it near me, at right angles. Ian Young took this seat next to me, and Boris Dmitrevich the one opposite.

While this was going on, I took a look round the room, which had bookshelves over much of the wall space and cupboards over the rest. The single large window was obscured by solid wooden cream-painted shutters, fastened by a flat metal bar through slots. The floor was of bare wooden boards, dark stained, unpolished and clean. Furniture consisted of a table, an old sofa covered with a rug, several hard chairs, and the one deep comfortable one in which I sat. All the furniture, except for the two chairs repositioned for Boris Dmitrevich and Ian Young, was ranged round the walls against the bookshelves and cupboards, leaving the centre free. There were no softeners: no curtain, cushions, or indoor plants. Nothing extravagant, frivolous, or wasteful. Everything of ancient and sensible worth, giving an overall impression of shabbiness stemming from long use but not underlying poverty. A room belonging to people who chose to have it that way, not who could not afford anything different.

Ian Young carried on a short conversation with Boris Dmitrevich in impenetrable Russian, and then did a spot of translation, looking more worried than I liked.

'Boris wants to warn us,' he said, 'that what you are dealing with is not some tomfool scandal but something to do with killing people.'

'With *what*?'

He nodded. 'That's what he said.' He turned his head back to Boris, and they talked some more. It appeared, from the expressions all around me, that what Boris was saying was no news to anyone except Ian Young and myself.

Boris was built like a true horseman, of middle height, with strong shoulders and well-coordinated movements. He was good-looking, with straight black hair and ears very flat to his head. He spoke earnestly to Ian Young, his dark eyes flicking my way every few seconds as if to check that he could still risk my hearing what he had to tell.

'Boris says,' Ian Young said, the shock showing, 'that the German, Hans Kramer, was murdered.'

'No,' I said confidently. 'There was an autopsy. Natural causes.'

Ian shook his head. 'Boris says that someone has found a way of causing people to drop down dead from heart attacks. He says that the death of Hans Kramer was . . .' he turned back briefly to Boris to consult, and then back to me, ' . . . the death of Hans Kramer was a sort of demonstration.'

It seemed ridiculous. 'A demonstration of what?'

A longer chat ensued. Ian Young shook his head and argued. Boris began to make fierce chopping motions with his hands, and spots of colour appeared on his cheeks. I gathered that his information had at this point entered the realms of guesswork, and that Ian Young didn't believe what was being said. Time to take a pull back to the facts.

'Look,' I said, interrupting the agitated flow. 'Let's start at the beginning. I'll ask some questions, and you get me the answers. OK?'

'Yes,' Ian Young said, subsiding. 'Carry on.'

'Ask him how he travelled to England, and where he went, and where he stayed, and how his team fared in the finals.'

'But,' he said, puzzled, 'what has that to do with Hans Kramer?'

'Not much,' I said. 'But I know how the Russians travelled and where they stayed and how they fared, and I just want to do my own private bit of checking that Boris is who he says he is; and also if he talks about unloaded things like that he will calm down and we can then get the beliefs without the passion.'

He blinked. 'My God,' he said.

'Ask him.'

'Yes.' He turned to Boris and delivered the question.

Boris answered patiently that they travelled by motor horse box across Europe to The Hague, and from there by sea to England, still with the horse boxes, and drove on to Burghley, where they stayed in quarters especially reserved for them.

'How many horses, and how many men?' I said.

Boris said six horses, and stumbled over the number of people. I suggested that this was because the Russians had paid for only seven 'human' tickets but had actually taken ten or more men . . . Make it a joke, I said to Ian Young: not an insult.

He made it enough of a joke for Boris and everyone else almost to laugh, which handily released much tension all round and steadied the temperature.

'They want to know how you know,' Ian said.

'The shipping agent told me. Tickets were bought for six riders and a chef d'équipe, but three or four grooms travelled among the legs of the horses. The shipping agents were amused, not angry.'

Ian relayed the answer and got another round of appreciative noises in the throat. Boris gave a more detailed account of the Russian team's performance in the trials than I had memorized, and by the end I had no doubt that he was genuine. He had also recovered his temper and lost his rigidity, and I reckoned we might go carefully back to the minefield.

'Right,' I said. 'Now ask him if he knew Hans Kramer personally. If he ever spoke to him face to face, and if so in what language.'

The question at once stiffened up the sinews, but the reply looked only moderately nervous.

Ian Young translated. 'Yes, he did talk to Hans Kramer. They spoke German, though Boris says he knows only a little German. He had met Hans Kramer before, when they both rode in the same trials, and they were friendly together.'

'Ask him what they talked about,' I said.

The answer came easily, predictably, with shrugs. 'Horses. The trials. The Olympics. The weather.'

'Anything else?'

'No.'

'Anything to do with backgammon, gambling clubs, homosexuals or transvestites?'

I saw by the collective indrawn breaths of disapproval round about that if Boris had been discussing such things he had better not say so. His own positive negative, however, looked real enough.

'Does he know Johnny Farringford?' I said.

It appeared that Boris knew who Johnny was, and had seen him ride, but had not spoken to him.

'Did he see Hans Kramer and Johnny Farringford together?'

Boris had not noticed one way or the other.

'Was he there on the spot when Hans Kramer died?'

Boris's unemotional response told me the answer before Ian translated.

'No, he wasn't. He had finished his cross-country section before Hans Kramer set out. He saw Hans Kramer being *weighed* . . . is that right?' Ian Young looked doubtful.

'Yes,' I said. 'The horses have to carry minimum weights, to make it a fairer test. There is a weighing machine on the course, to weigh the riders with their saddles just before they set off, and also as soon as they come back. The same as in riding.'

Boris, it appeared, had had to wait while Hans Kramer was weighed out, before himself weighing in. He had wished Hans Kramer good luck. *'Alles Gute.'* The irony of it lugubriously pleased the listening friends.

'Please ask Boris why he thinks Hans Kramer was murdered.' I said the words deliberately flatly, and Ian Young relayed them the same way, but they reproduced in Boris the old high alarm.

'Did he hear anyone say so?' I asked decisively, to cut off the emotion.
'Yes.'
'Who said so?'
Boris did not know the man who said so.
'Did he say it to Boris face to face?'
No. Boris had overheard it.
I could see why Ian Young had doubted the whole story.
'Ask in what language this man spoke.'
In Russian, Boris said, but he was not a Russian.
'Does he mean that the man spoke Russian with a foreign accent?'
That was right.
'What accent?' I said patiently. 'From what country?'
Boris didn't know.
'Where was Boris when he overheard this man?'
It seemed a pretty harmless question to me, but it brought an abrupt intense stillness into the room.
Evgeny Sergeevich Titov finally stirred and said something lengthily to Ian.
'They want you to understand that Boris should not have been where he was. That if he tells you, you will hold his future in your power.'
'I see,' I said.
There was a pause.
Ian said, 'I think they're waiting for you to swear you will never reveal where he was.'
'Perhaps he had better just tell me what he heard,' I said.
There was a brief consultation among all of them, but they must have decided before I came that I would have to know.
Evgeny Sergeevich did the talking. Boris, he said, had been on a train, going to London. It was absolutely against orders. If he had been discovered, he would have been sent home immediately in disgrace. He would never be considered for the Olympic team, and he might even have faced imprisonment, as he was carrying letters and other papers to Russians who had defected to the West. The papers were not political, Evgeny said earnestly, but just personal messages and photographs from the defectors' families still in Russia, and a few small writings for publication in literary magazines. Not State secrets, but highly illegal. There would have been much trouble for many people, not just for Boris, if he had been stopped and searched. So that when he heard someone speaking Russian on the train he had been very frightened, and his first urgent priority had been to keep out of sight himself, not to see who had been speaking. He had crept out of the carriage he was in, and walked forward as far as he could through the train. When it reached London, he left it fast, and was met by friends at the barrier.
'I understand all that,' I said, when Ian Young finished translating. 'Tell them I won't tell.'
Encouraged, Boris came to the nub.

'There were two men,' Ian Young relayed. 'Because of the noise of the train, Boris could only hear one of them.'

'Right. Go on.'

Boris spoke into a breath-held attentive silence. Ian Young listened with his former scepticism once again showing.

'He says,' he said, 'that he overheard a man say, "It was a perfect demonstration. You could kill half the Olympic riders the same way, if that's what you want. But it will cost you." Then the other man said something inaudible, and the voice Boris could hear said, "I have another client." The other man spoke, and then the man Boris could hear said, "Kramer took ninety seconds."'

Bloody hell, I thought. Shimmering scarlet *hell.*

Boris crept away at that point, Ian said. Boris was too worried about being discovered himself for the meaning of what he had heard to sink in. And in any case it was not until the next day that he learned of Kramer's death. When he did hear, he was shattered. Before that, he had thought the ninety seconds was something to do with timing on the Event course.

'Ask him to repeat what he heard the man say,' I said.

The exchanges took place.

'Did Boris use exactly the same words as the first time?' I said.

'Yes, exactly.'

'But you don't believe him?'

'He half heard something perfectly innocent and the rest's imagination.'

'But he believes it,' I said. 'He got angry when you argued. He certainly believes that's what he heard.'

I thought it over, all too aware of seven pairs of eyes directed unwaveringly at my face.

'Please ask Mr Titov,' I said, 'why he has persuaded Boris to tell us all this. I might guess, but I would like him to confirm it.'

Evgeny, sitting on a wooden chair in front of a bookcase, answered with responsibility visibly bowing his shoulders. Lines ridged his forehead. His eyes were sombre.

Ian said, 'He has been very worried since Boris came home from England and told him what he had heard. There was the possibility that Boris was mistaken, and also the possibility that he was not. If he did really hear what he thought he heard, there might be another murder at the Olympics. Or more than one. As a good Russian, Evgeny was anxious that nothing should harm his country in the eyes of the world. It wouldn't do for competitors to be murdered on Russian soil. A way had to be found of warning someone who could get an investigation made, but Evgeny knew no one in England or Germany to write to, even if you could entrust such a letter to the mail. He couldn't explain how he had come by such knowledge, because Boris's whole life would be spoiled, and yet he couldn't see anyone believing the story without Boris's own testimony, so he was up a creek without a paddle.'

'Or words to that effect?'

'You got it.'

'Ask if they know anyone called Alyosha who is even remotely concerned with the Russian team, or the trials, or the Olympics, or Hans Kramer, or anything.'

There was a general unhurried discussion, and the answer was no.

'Is Boris related to Evgeny?' I said.

The question was asked and answered.

'No. Boris just values Evgeny's advice . . . Evgeny consulted the others.'

I looked thoughtfully at Ian. His face, as always, gave away as much as a slab of granite, and I found it disconcerting to have no clue at all to what he was thinking.

'You yourself knew Mr Titov before this evening, didn't you?' I said. 'And you'd been here before?'

'Yes, two or three times. Olga Ivanovna works in Cultural Relations, and she's a good friend. But I have to be careful. I'm not allowed to be here.'

'Complicated,' I agreed.

'Evgeny rang me this afternoon and said you were in Moscow, and would I bring you here this evening. I said I would if I could, after you'd been to the Embassy.'

The speed of communications had me gasping. 'Just how did Evgeny know I was in Moscow?'

'Nikolai Alexandrovich happened to tell Boris . . .'

'*Who?*'

'Nikolai Alexandrovich Kropotkin. The chef d'équipe. You have an appointment with him tomorrow morning.'

'For Christ's sake . . .'

'Kropotkin told Boris, Boris told Evgeny, Evgeny rang me, and I had heard from Oliver Waterman that you would be round for a drink.'

'So simple,' I said, shaking my head. 'And if Evgeny knew you, why didn't he tell you all this weeks ago?'

Ian Young gave me a cool stare and relayed the question.

'Evgeny says it was because Boris wouldn't talk to me.'

'Well, go on,' I said, as he stopped. 'Why did Boris decide he *would* talk to *me?*'

Ian shrugged, and asked, and translated Boris's reply.

'Because you are a rider. A man who knows horses. Boris trusts you because you are a comrade.'

6

The lifts at the Intourist Hotel did not stop at the lower of the two restaurant floors, which was where the English tourists ate. One could either walk up one storey from the lobby, or stop the lift at the floor above and walk down. I did that, after parking my coat in my room, and walked down the shallow treads of the broad circular staircase, where, through the handrail, I could see the faces in the dining-room before they looked up and saw me.

Natasha was on her feet, consulting her watch and looking worried. The Lancashire Wilkinsons were drinking coffee, unaffected: and if I read anxiety and anger into the fidgets of Frank Jones it was probably only because I guessed they were there.

'Evening,' I said, reaching the bottom. 'Am I too late? Is there anything left?'

Natasha sped across with visible relief. 'We thought you were lost.'

I gave her a full and ingenuous story about a friend driving me up to the University to look down on the lights of the city by night. The Wilkinsons listened with interest, and Frank with slowly evaporating tenseness, as they all, like me, had been up at the semi-official look-out spot in the afternoon on the bus tour; and I almost convinced myself. 'Afraid we were a bit longer than I expected,' I said apologetically.

The Wilkinsons and Frank stayed for company while I ate, and kept up a thoroughly touristy flow of chat. I looked at Frank with a great deal more interest than before, trying to see behind the mask, and failing to do so. Outwardly he was still a raw-boned twenty-eight or so with an undercombed generosity of reddish-brown curls and the pits and scars of long-term acne. His views were still diluted Marx and his manner still based on the belief in his own superiority to the bulk of mankind.

There were four courses to the evening meal, and the only choice was eat it or don't. The meat looked identical to the tasteless rubber of the evening before, and when it arrived I stared at it gloomily.

'Aren't you going to eat that?' Frank demanded, pointing fiercely at my plate.

'Are you still hungry? Would you care for it?' I said.

'Do you mean it?' He took me at my word, slid the plate in front of him, and set to, proving that both his appetite and molars were a lot stronger than mine.

'Did you know,' he said with his mouth full, giving us a by now accustomed lecture, 'that in this country rents are very low, and electricity and transport and telephone calls are cheap. And when I say cheap, I mean cheap.'

Mrs Wilkinson, who had twice the life of Mister, sighed with envy over so perfect a world.

'But then,' I said, 'if you're a retired welder from Novosibirsk, you can't go on a package tour of London, just for a bit of interest.'

'There, Dad,' Mrs Wilkinson said. 'That's true.'

Frank chewed on the meat and made no comment.

'Isn't it term time?' I said to him innocently.

He took his time getting to swallowing-point while he thought of the answer. He was between jobs, he said. Left one school back in July, starting at another in January.

'What do you teach?' I said.

He was vague. 'You know. This and that. Bit of everything. Junior school, of course.'

Mrs Wilkinson told him that her nephew, who had ingrowing toenails, had always wanted to be a teacher. Frank opened his mouth and then decided not to ask what ingrowing toenails had to do with it, and I smothered my laughter in ice-cream and blackcurrant jam.

I was glad to laugh. I needed something to laugh about. The intensity and fear that had vibrated among the Russians in Evgeny Titov's flat remained with me as a sort of hovering claustrophobic depression. Even leaving the place had had to be carefully managed. It would never have done, I gathered, for so many people to have left at once. Evgeny and Olga had pressed Ian Young and me to stay for a further ten minutes after Boris had gone, so that if anyone were watching, we should not be connected.

'Is it always like this?' I had asked Ian Young, and he had said prosaically, 'Pretty much.'

Evgeny, having shifted the burden of his knowledge squarely on to me, had shaken hadns gravely in farewell, clasping my hands in both of his. He had done his best, I supposed. He had passed on the flaming torch, and if now the Olympics were scorched by it, it would be my fault, not his.

Olga had seen us out with the same prudence as she had let us in. We picked our way through the scaffolding – 'old apartment building being renovated' Ian explained in the car later – and walked back through the garden. There were still only two sets of black footprints in the snow on the path – our own from the outward journey; and no one came after us through the gates. Two dark silent figures, we eased our way into the car, and the noise of the engine starting seemed suddenly too loud for safety. To have to live like that, constantly wary, seemed to me dreadful. Yet the Russians and even Ian Young considered it normal: and perhaps that was most dreadful of all.

'What are you going to do?' Ian asked, driving back towards the city centre. 'About this story of Boris's?'

'Ask around,' I said vaguely. 'What are you?'

'Nothing. It's just his overheated imagination.'

I didn't altogether agree with him, but I didn't argue.

'And I'd be glad if you'd do me a favour, my old son.'

'What's that?' I said, internally amused.

'Don't mention Evgeny or his apartment to anyone from the Embassy. Don't mention our visit. I like our good Oliver to be able to put his hand on his heart among the natives and swear he has no knowledge of any of his staff making private visits to Russian homes.'

'All right.'

He turned into a wide, well-lit, dual-carriageway which at eight-thirty held as much traffic as four in the morning back home.

'And don't get them into trouble,' he said. 'Evgeny and Boris.'

'Or you'll kill me.'

'Yeah ... ' He laughed awkwardly. 'Well ... it sounds stupid, out here.'

I didn't ask if he really meant it. It was a question to which there was no answer, and I hadn't any intention of putting him to the test.

With the image of Ian Young in my mind I glanced across the table at Frank Jones: the one who looked Russian and walked carefully on the wrong side of the regulations, and the other who looked English and harmless and could throw you to the spikes.

Natasha brought her marvellous eyebrows to the table and drew up a chair. She wore a neat pink wool dress, which went with the lipstick and displayed curves where they looked best. Her voice had a small disarming lisp, and she was achieving a slightly anxious smile.

'Tomorrow,' she said, 'the Exhibition of Economic Achievements...'

'Tomorrow,' I said, providing my best giving-no-offence expression, 'I'm going to see some horses. I'm sure the exhibition is great, but I'm much better at horses, and I have this absolutely wonderful chance to see some of your very best, your really top horses, and ones that are being trained for the Olympics, and that will be such a treat for me that I simply can't miss it.'

The floweriness more or less did the trick, and it was Frank who asked, with natural-looking interest, where the horses were that I was going to see.

'At the racecourse,' I said. 'They are stabled near there, I believe.'

I saw no point in not telling him. It would have looked odd if I hadn't, and in any case he could have found out by following.

Stephen Luce appeared promptly at ten the following morning outside the hotel, his round cheerful face the brightest thing under the grey Moscow sky. I made the passage from hot air to cold through the double entrance to join him, passing at least six men standing around doing nothing.

'Metro and bus to the Hippodrome,' Stephen said. 'I've looked up the stops.'

'Taxi,' I said firmly.

'But taxis are expensive, and the metro's cheap.'

'And the far side of the Hippodrome could be two miles' walk from the front entrance.'

We took a taxi. Pale greeny-grey saloon, with a meter. Stephen carefully explained where we wanted to go, but the driver had to stop and ask twice when we reached the area. Passengers, it appeared, very seldom asked to be driven to the back of the racecourse. I resisted two attempts to decant us with vague assurances that the place we wanted was 'just down there', and finally with a scowl or two and some muttering under the breath we drove right into the stable area, with the track itself lying a hundred yards ahead.

'You're very persistent,' Stephen said, as I counted out the fare.

'I don't like wet feet.'

The air temperature must have been about one degree centigrade and the humidity ninety-five per cent: a damp icy near-drizzle. The slushy snow lay around sullenly melting, lying in puddles on the packed clay surface in the centre of the stable roadways, banked up in ruts along the edges.

To left and right a double row of lengthy stable blocks stretched away, built of concrete on the barn principle, with the horses totally enclosed, and not sticking their heads out into the open air. Ahead the stable area led directly out through a wide gap on to the railed racing circuit, which was of the grey sticky consistency of dirt tracks the world over.

In the distance, over on the far side, one could see the line of stands, grey and lifeless at that time of day. All around us, where the morning action lay, horses and men trudged about their business and paid no attention to us at all.

'It's staggering,' Stephen said, looking around. 'You practically can't get into anywhere in the Soviet Union without talking your way past some sort of guard, and we just drove straight in here.'

'People who work with horses are anti-bureaucratic.'

'Are you?' he said.

'Every inch. Stick to essentials, and make your own decisions.'

'And to hell with committees?'

'The question nowadays is whether it's possible.' I watched some horses without saddles being led on their way from a stable block out towards the track, their feet plopping splashily in the wet. 'You know something? These are not racehorses.'

'It's a racecourse,' he said, as if I were crazy.

'They're trotters.'

'What do you mean?'

'Trotting races. The driver sits on a little chariot thing called a sulky, and the horse pulls it along at a fast trot. Like that,' I added pointing, as a horse and sulky came into view on the track.

It wheeled up speedily to the entrance of the stables, and there the handlers unfastened the harness which held the shafts of the sulky, and led the horse away. The sulky was harnessed to the next horse to be exercised, and the driver took up the reins and got on with his job.

'Don't you think we ought to look for Mr Kropotkin?' Stephen suggested.

'Not really. We're still a few minutes early. If we just stand here, maybe he will come and find us.'

Stephen looked as if life were full surprises but not altogether bad ones, and several more horses slopped past. The stable hands leading them all seemed to be small weatherbeaten men with unshaven chins and layers of uncoordinated clothes. None of them wore gloves. None of them even looked our way, but shambled on with stolid unsmiling faces.

A new and larger string of horses appeared, coming not from one of the stable blocks, but across the road we had arrived by, and in through the unguarded, ungated entrance. Instead of being led, these were ridden; and the riders were neatly dressed in jodhpurs and quilted jackets. On their heads they wore not leather caps but crash helmets, with the chin-straps meticulously fastened.

'What are those?' Stephen said, as they approached.

'They're not thoroughbreds . . . not racehorses. I should think those might be the eventers.'

'How can you tell they're not racehorses?'

'Thicker bones,' I said. 'The more solid shape of the head. And more hair round the fetlocks.'

Stephen said 'Oh' as if he wasn't much wiser, and we noticed that behind the horses walked a purposeful man in a dark overcoat and a fur hat. His gaze had fallen upon us, and he changed course ten degrees to starboard and came our way.

Stephen went a step to meet him.

'Nikolai Alexandrovich Kropotkin?' he said.

'Da,' said the newcomer. 'That is so.'

His voice was as deep as chocolate and the Russian intonation very pronounced. He looked at me closely. 'And you are Randall Drew,' he said, carefully stressing each word separately.

'Mr Kropotkin, I am very pleased to meet you,' I said.

He clasped my outstretched hand and gave it a good pump with both of his own.

'Randall Drew. Pardubice. You are three.'

'Third,' I said, nodding.

Words failed him in English and he rumbled away in his own language.

'He is saying,' Stephen said, his eyes grinning, 'that you are a great horseman with a bold heart and hands of silk, and he is honoured to see you here.'

Mr Kropotkin broke off the exaggerations to shake hands in a perfunctory way with Stephen, giving him the fast head-to-toe inspection of a horseman for a horse. He said something to him abruptly which Stephen said afterwards was 'Do you ride?' and on receiving a negative treated him henceforth merely as a translating machine, not as a valued friend.

'Please tell Mr Kropotkin that the Russian team rode with great courage and skill at the International Trials, and the fitness of his horses here today does his management great credit.'

Mr Kropotkin's appreciation of the compliments showed in a general aura of pleased complacency. He was a big man of about sixty, carrying a good deal of excess weight but still light on his feet. A heavy greying moustache overhung his upper lip, and he had a habit of smoothing the outer edges downwards with his forefinger and thumb.

'You watch horses,' he said, his way with English putting the words half way between a command and an invitation. I would be pleased to, I said, and we walked forward on to the track.

His five charges were circling there, waiting for the instructions which he gave decisively but briefly in his rolling bass. The riders stopped circling and divided into two groups.

'Horses canter,' Kropotkin said, sweeping out an arm. 'Round.'

'Yes,' I said.

He and I stood side by side in the manner of horse-watchers the world over and eyed the training exercises. There was a lot of muscle, I thought, and all five had good free-flowing actions; but it was impossible to tell how good each was at Eventing, because speed alone had little to do with it.

Kropotkin launched into several sentences and waited impatiently for Stephen to translate.

'These are a few of the Olympic possibles. It is too soon to decide yet. There are other horses in the south, where it is warmer. All the flat race-horses from the track have gone south to the Caucasus for the winter. Some horses are training there for the Olympics also, but he will have them back in Moscow next summer.'

'Tell him I am very interested.'

Kropotkin received the news with what I took to be satisfaction. He too had the inexpressive face and unsmiling eyes which were the Moscow norm. Mobility of features, I supposed, was something one did or didn't learn in childhood from the faces all round; and the fact that they didn't show, didn't conclusively prove that admiration and contempt and hate and glee weren't going on inside. It had become, I dared say, imprudent to show them. The unmoving countenance was the first law of survival.

The horses came back from circling the mile-long track without a flutter of the nostril. The riders dismounted and spoke to Kropotkin with respect. They didn't look to me like Olympic material either on horseback or on their feet: nothing of the self-confident presence of Boris: but I asked all the same.

'*Niet*,' Kropotkin said. 'Misha is young. Is good.'

He pointed at a boy of about nineteen who was, like the others, leading his horse round in a circle under Kropotkin's stony gaze. Kropotkin added more in Russian, and Stephen translated.

'He says they are all grooms, but he is teaching Misha, because he is brave and has good hands and can get horses to jump.'

A dark green horse box drove in through the stable area behind us, its engine making an untuned clatter which stirred up the horses. Kropotkin stolidly watched while it made a bad job of reversing down between the two rows of stable blocks, its old-fashioned wooden sides rattling from the vibration of the engine. The noise abated slightly once it was out of sight on the other side of a concrete barn, and when Kropotkin could once again make himself heard, he said a good deal to Stephen.

'Mr Kropotkin says,' Stephen said, 'that Misha went to the International

Trials in September as a groom, and perhaps you would like to talk to him also. Mr Kropotkin said that when a man from the British Embassy came to ask him some questions about Lord Farringford and Hans Kramer, he said he knew nothing, and that was true. But he has remembered since then that Misha does know something about Hans Kramer, but not Lord Farringford, and he arranged for Misha to be riding this morning in case you should wish to see him.'

'Yes,' I said. 'Thank you very much indeed.'

Kropotkin made a small inclination of the head, and addressed himself to the riders.

'He's telling them to lead the horses back to the stable, and to be careful crossing the road outside. He's telling Misha to stay behind.'

Kropotkin turned back to me and stroked his moustache. 'Horse of Misha is good. Go to Olympics,' he said.

I looked at Misha's charge with interest, though there was no way in which it stood out from the others. A hardy chestnut with a white blaze down its nose, and two white socks: a rough coat, which would be normal at that time of year, and a kind eye.

'Good,' Kropotkin said, slapping its rump.

'He looks bold and tough,' I said. Stephen translated and Kropotkin did not demur.

The four other horses were led away, and Kropotkin introduced Misha formally but without flourish.

'Mikhail Alexeevich Tarevsky,' he said, and to the boy added what was clearly an instruction to answer whatever I asked.

'*Da*, Nikolai Alexandrovich,' he said.

I thought there were better places for conducting interviews than in near-freezing semi-drizzle on an open dirt track, but neither Kropotkin nor Misha seemed aware of the weather, and the fact that Stephen and I were shifting from one cold foot to the other evoked no offers of our adjourning to a warm office.

'In England,' said the boy, 'I learn little English.'

His voice and manner were serious, and his accent a great deal lighter than Kropotkin's. His eyes, unexpectedly blue in his weather-tanned face, looked full of unguarded intelligence. I smiled at him involuntarily, but he only stared gravely back.

'Please tell me what you know of Hans Kramer,' I said.

Kropotkin instantly rumbled something positive, and Stephen said, 'He wishes Misha to speak in Russian, so that he may hear. He wishes me to translate what you ask.'

'OK,' I said. 'Ask Misha what he knows of Kramer. And for God's sake let's get on. I'm congealing.'

Misha stod beside his horse, pulling the reins over the chestnut's head to hold them more easily below the mouth for leading, and stroking his neck from time to time to soothe him. I couldn't see that it was doing any good for an Olympic-type horse to stand around getting chilled so soon after exercise, but it wasn't my problem. The chestnut, certainly, didn't seem to mind.

Stephen said, 'Mikhail Alexeevich – that is, Misha – says that he was near Hans Kramer when he died.'

It was amazing how suddenly I no longer felt the cold.

'How near?'

The answer was lengthy. Stephen listened and translated.

'Misha says he was holding the horse of one of the Russian team who was being weighed – is that right? – and Hans Kramer was there. He had just finished the cross-country, and had done well, and people were there round him, congratulating him. Misha was half watching, and half watching for the rider of the horse.'

'I understand,' I said. 'Go on.'

Misha talked. Stephen said, 'Hans Kramer staggered and fell to the ground. He fell not far from Misha; about three metres. An English girl went to help him and someone else ran off to fetch the doctor. Hans Kramer looked very ill. He could not breathe properly. But he was trying to say something. Trying to tell the English girl something. He was lying flat on the ground. He could hardly breathe. He was saying words as loudly as he could. Like trying to shout.'

Misha waited until Stephen had finished, clearly understanding what Stephen was saying and punctuating the translation with nods.

'Hans Kramer was saying these words in German?' I said.

'Da,' said Misha, but Kropotkin interrupted, wanting to be told the question. He made an assenting gesture with his hand to allow Misha to proceed.

'And does Misha speak German?'

Misha, it appeared, had learned German in school, and had been with the team's horses to East Germany, and knew enough to make himself understood.

'All right,' I said. 'What did Hans Kramer say?'

Misha said the words in German, and then in Russian, and one word flared out of both like a beacon.

Alyosha.

Stephen lit up strongly with excitement, and I thought there was probably a good deal to be said for a face that gave nothing away. His enthusiasm seemed to bother Kropotkin, who made uneasy movements as if on the point of retreat.

'Cool it,' I said to Stephen flatly. 'You're frightening the birds.'

He gave me a quick surprised look, but dampened his manner immediately.

'Hans Kramer said,' he reported in a quiet voice, '"I am dying. It is Alyosha. Moscow." And then he said, "God help me." And then he died.'

'How did he die?' I said.

Misha, via Stephen, said that he turned blue, and seemed to stop breathing, and then there was a sort of small jolt right through his body, and someone said it was his heart stopping; it was a heart attack. The doctor came, and agreed it was a heart attack. He tried to bring Hans Kramer back to life, but it was useless.

The four of us stood in the Russian drizzle thinking about the death of a German in England on a sunny September day.

'Ask him what else he remembers,' I said.

Misha shrugged. 'The English girl and some of the people near had understood what Hans Kramer had said. The English girl was saying to other people that he had said he was dying because of Alyosha who came from Moscow, and other people were agreeing. It was very sad. Then the Russian rider came back from being weighed, and Misha had to attend to him and the horse, and he saw from a little way off that the ambulance people came with a stretcher. They put Hans Kramer on the stretcher and put a rug right over him and over his face, and carried him off.'

'Um,' I said, thinking. 'Ask him again what Hans Kramer said.'

Hans Kramer had said, 'I am dying. It is Alyosha. Moscow. God help me.' He had not had time to say any more, although Misha thought he had been trying to.

'Is Misha sure that Hans Kramer did not say "I am dying because of Alyosha from Moscow"?'

Misha, it seemed, was positive. There had been no 'because', and no 'from'. Only, 'I am dying. It is Alyosha. Moscow. God help me.' Misha remembered very clearly, he said, because Alyosha was his own father's name.

'Is it really?' I said, interested.

Misha said that he himself was Mikhail Alexeevich Tarevsky. Mikhail, son of Alexei. And Alyosha was the affectionate form of Alexei. Misha was certain Hans Kramer had said, 'It is Alyosha. *Es ist* Alyosha.'

I looked unseeingly over the sodden racecourse.

'Ask Misha,' I said slowly, 'if he can describe any of the people who were with Kramer before he staggered and fell down. Ask if he remembers if any of them was carrying anything, or doing anything, which did not fit in to the normal scene. Ask if anyone gave Kramer anything to eat or drink.'

Stephen stared. 'But it was a heart attack.'

'There might have been,' I said mildly, 'contributive factors. A shock. An argument. An accidental blow. An allergy. A sting from a wasp.'

'Oh, I see.' He asked the alarming question as if they were indeed harmless. Misha answered straightforwardly, taking them the same way.

'Misha says,' Stephen reported, 'that he did not know any of the people round Hans Kramer, except that he had seen them at the trials that day and the day before. The Russians are not allowed to mix with the other grooms and competitors, so he had not spoken to them. He himself had seen nothing which could have given anybody a heart attack, but of course he had not been watching closely. But he couldn't remember any argument, or blow, or wasp. He couldn't remember for certain whether Hans Kramer had eaten or drunk anything, but he didn't think so.'

'Well,' I said, pondering, 'was there anyone there who Misha considers could have been Alyosha?'

The answer to that was that he didn't really think so, because when Hans Kramer was saying that name he was not saying it *to* anyone, except perhaps to the English girl, but *she* couldn't have been Alyosha, because it was a man's name.

The cold was creeping back. If Misha knew any more, I didn't know how to unlock it.

I said, 'Please thank Misha for his very intelligent help, and tell Mr Kropotkin how much I value his assistance in letting me speak to Misha in this way.'

The compliments were received as due, and Kropotkin, Stephen and I began to walk off the track, back towards the main stable area and the road beyond. Misha, leading the horse, followed a few paces behind us.

As we passed the opening between the two rows of stable blocks, the green wooden horse box, whose engine had been grumbling away in the background all the while we had been talking, suddenly revved up into a shattering roar.

Misha's horse reared with fright, and Misha cried out. Automatically I turned back to help him. Misha, facing me, was tugging downwards on the reins, with the chestnut rearing yet again above him, and the horse's bunched quarters were, so to speak, staring me in the face.

As I came towards him, Misha's gaze slid over me and fastened on something behind my back. His eyes opened wide in fear. He yelled something to me in Russian, and then he simply dropped the reins and ran.

7

From a purely reflex action I grabbed the reins which he had left dangling on the ground and at the same time glanced back over my shoulder.

The time to death looked like three seconds.

The towering top of the green horse box blotted out the sky. The engine accelerated to a scream. I could remember the pattern of the radiator grill for ever after. Six tons unladen weight, I thought. One had time, I found, for the most useless thoughts. Thoughts could be measured in fizzing ten-thousandths of a second. Action took a little longer.

I grabbed the horse's mane with my left hand and the front of the saddle with my right, and half-jumped, half-hauled myself on to his back.

The horse was terrified already by the noise and the proximity of the horse box, but horses don't altogether understand about the necessity of removing themselves pronto from under the wheels of thundering juggernauts. Frightened horses, on the whole, are more apt to run *into* the paths of vehicles, than away.

Horses, on the other hand, are immensely receptive of human emotions, especially when the human is on their back, and scared out of his wits. The chestnut unerringly got the unadulterated message of fear, and bolted.

From a standing start a fit horse can beat most cars over a hundred yards, but the horse box was a long way from standing. The chestnut's blast-off kept him merely a few yards ahead of the crushing green killer roaring on our heels.

If the horse had had the right sort of sense he would have darted away to left or right down some narrow cranny where the horse box couldn't follow. Instead, he galloped ahead in a straight true line, making disaster easy.

It was of only moderate help that I was still grasping a section of rein. Owing to the fact of Misha having taken the reins over the horse's head to lead him, they were not now neatly to hand, with each rein leading tidily to its own side of the bit: they were both on the left side and came from below the horse's mouth. Since horses are normally steered by pulling the bit upwards against the mouth's sensitive corners, any urgent instructions had little chance of getting through. There were also the difficulties that my feet were not in the stirrups, I was wearing a heavy overcoat, and my fur hat was tipping forward over my spectacles. The chestnut took his own line and burst out on to the open spaces of the track.

He swerved instinctively to the right, which was the way he always trained, and his quarters thrust him onwards with the vigour of a full-blown stampede. His hurtling feet set up clouds of spray behind us, and it was while I was wondering how long he could keep up the pace and hoping it was for ever, that I first thought that perhaps the sound of the motor had diminished.

Too good to be true, I thought. On the straight and level, a horse box could go faster than a horse; perhaps it was in overdrive and simply made less noise that way.

I risked a look over my shoulder, and my spirits were up as swiftly as a helium balloon. The horse box had given up the chase. It was turning on the track, and going back the way it had come.

'Glory be', I thought, and 'Allelujah', and 'Oh noble beast'; jumbled thanks to the horse and his putative maker.

There was still the problem of getting the noble beast to stop. Panic had infected him easily. Non-panic was not getting through.

My hat fell completely off. Speed drove cold air through my hair, and stung my ears. The drizzle misted my glasses. Heavy double-breasted close-buttoned overcoats were definitely bad news on bolters. Flapping trousers never reassured any horse. I thought that if I didn't do something about the pedals and steering I could very well ignominiously fall off: and what would Mr Kropotkin have to say if I let his Olympic horse go loose?

Little by little, a vestige of control returned to the proceedings. It was after all a mile-long, left-hand circuit, and the one way I had a chance of influencing our direction was to the left. Constant pressure on the reins pulled the chestnut's head all the time towards the inner rails, and, once I'd managed to put my feet in the stirrups, pressure from my right knee did the same. Some soothing exhortations like 'Whoa there, boy, whoa there you old beauty' also seemed to help; even if the words were English, the tone and intention were identical.

Somewhere on the home stretch in front of the stands the steam went out of the flight, and in a few strides after that, he was walking. I patted his neck and made further conversation, and after a bit, he stood still.

This time, unlike after his training canter, he showed great signs of exertion, taking in breaths in gusts through his nostrils, and heaving out his ribs to inflate his lungs. I brushed the wet off my glasses, and undid a couple of buttons on my coat.

'There you are, then, chum,' I said. 'You're a good old boy, my old fellow,' and patted his neck some more.

He shifted only a little while I cautiously leaned far forward to his ears, and put my arms right round under his chin, and brought the reins back over his head. It seemed to me that he was almost relieved to have his headgear returned to its normal riding configuration, because he trotted off along the track again at my signal with all the sweetness of a horse well-schooled in dressage.

Kropotkin had come a little way out to meet us, but no man walked far on that sticky dirt from choice, and he was back by the stable entrance when the chestnut and I completed the circuit.

Kropotkin showed considerable emotion, which was not surprisingly all for his horse. After I had dismounted and handed the reins to a stunned-looking Misha, he rumbled away in basso profundo, anxiously feeling each leg and standing back to assess the overall damage. Finally he spoke at some length to Stephen, and waved an arm in a gesture which was neither anger nor apology, but perhaps somewhere between the two.

'Mr Kropotkin says,' Stephen relayed, 'that he doesn't know what the horse box was doing here today. It is one of the horse boxes which take the Olympic horses, when they travel. Mr Kropotkin had not ordered a box to come to the track. They are always parked beside the stables he is in charge of, across the road. He is sure that none of the drivers would drive so badly in a stable area. He cannot understand how you and the horse came to be in the way when the horse box prepared to leave the stables.' Stephen's eyebrows were rising. 'I say,' he said dubiously, 'you weren't in its way. The bloody thing drove straight at you.'

'Never mind,' I said. 'Tell Mr Kropotkin that I quite understand what he is saying. Tell him I regret having stood in the way of the horse box. Tell him that I am glad the horse is unharmed, and that I see no reason why I should need to mention the morning's happenings to any other person.'

Stephen stared. 'You learn fast.'

'Tell him what I said.'

Stephen obliged. Kropotkin's manner lost so much tension that I only then realized quite the extent of his anxiety. He even went so far as to produce a definite lightening of the features: almost a smile. He also said something about which Stephen seemed less doubtful.

'He says you ride like a Cossack. Is that a compliment?'

'Near enough.'

Kropotkin spoke again, and Stephen translated.

'Mr Kropotkin says he will give you any further help he can, if you ask.'

'Thank you very much,' I said.

'Friend,' the deep voice said in its slow heavy English. 'You ride good.'

I pushed my glasses hard against the bridge of my nose and thought murderous thoughts about the people who had stopped me racing.

Stephen and I trudged about half a mile to where Kropotkin had said there was a taxi rank.

'I thought you'd be one for rushing off to the police,' Stephen said.

'No.' I picked some of the dirt off my fur hat, which someone had retrieved. 'Not this trip.'

'Not this country,' he said. 'If you complain to the fuzz here, you as likely as not surface in clink.'

I gave up cleanliness in favour of a warm head. 'Hughes-Beckett would have a fit.'

'All the same,' Stephen said, 'whatever Kropotkin may say, that horse box was trying to kill you.'

'Or Misha. Or the horse,' I said, untying the ear-flaps.

'Do you really believe that?'

'Did you see the driver?' I asked.

Yes and no. He had one of those balaclava things on under a fur hat with the ear-flaps down. Everything covered except his eyes.'

'He took a hell of a risk,' I said thoughtfully. 'But then, he darned near succeeded.'

'You take it incredibly calmly,' Stephen said.

'Would you prefer screaming hysterics?'

'I guess not.'

'There's a taxi.' I waved, and the green-grey saloon swerved our way and slowed. We piled aboard.

'I've never seen anyone jump on a horse like you did,' Stephen said, as we set off to the Intourist. 'One second on the ground, the next, galloping.'

'You never know what you can do until Nemesis breathes down your neck.'

'You look,' Stephen said, 'like one of those useless la-di-dahs in the tele-ads, and you perform . . . ' Words failed him.

'Yeah,' I said. 'Depressing, isn't it?'

He laughed. 'And by the way . . . Misha gave me a telephone number.' He put a hand in a pocket and brought out a crumpled scrap of paper. 'He gave it to me while Kropotkin was chasing after you on the track. He says he wants to tell you something without Kropotkin knowing.'

'Does the taxi driver speak English?' I asked.

Stephen looked only faintly and transiently alarmed. 'They never do,' he said. 'You could tell them they stink like untreated sewage and they wouldn't turn a hair. Just try it.'

I tried it.

The taxi driver didn't turn a hair.

On the principle of turning up where and when expected, I arrived on time for lunch in the Intourist dining-room. The soup and the blinis were all right, and the ice-cream with blackcurrant jam was fine, but the meat with its attendant teaspoonfuls of chopped carrot, chopped lettuce, and inch-long chips went across the table to Frank.

'You'll fade away,' said Mrs Wilkinson, without too much concern. 'Don't you like meat?'

'I grow it,' I said. 'Beef, that is. On a farm. So I suppose I get too fussy over stuff like this.'

Mrs Wilkinson looked at me doubtfully. 'I would never have guessed you worked on a farm.'

'Er . . . well, I do. But it's my own . . . passed down from my father.'

'Can you milk a cow?' Frank said, with a hint of challenge.

'Yes,' I said mildly. 'Milk. Plough. The lot.'

He gave me a sharp look from over my chips, but in fact I spoke the truth. I had started learning the practical side of farming from about the age of two, and had emerged from agricultural college twenty years later with the technology. Since then, under Government sponsorship, I'd done some work on the interacting chemistry of land and food, and had set aside some experimental acres for research. After racing, this work had been my chief interest . . . and from now on, I supposed, my only one.

Mrs Wilkinson said disapprovingly, 'You don't keep calves in those nasty crate things, do you?'

'No, I don't.'

'I never do like to think of all the poor animals being killed, when I buy the weekend chops.'

'How were the Economic Achievements?'

'We saw a space capsule.' She launched into a grudgingly admiring out-line of the exhibition. 'Pity we don't have one in England,' she said.

'Exhibition like that, I mean. Permanent. Blowing our own trumpet for a change, like.'

'Did you go?' I asked Frank.

'No.' He shook his head, munching. 'Been before, of course.'

He didn't say where he had been instead. I hadn't noticed him following Stephen and me, but he might have done. If he had, what had he seen?

'Tomorrow we're going to Zagorsk,' Mrs Wilkinson said.

'Where's that?' I asked, watching Frank chew and learning nothing from his face.

'A lot of churches, I think,' she said vaguely. 'We're going in a bus, with visas, because it's out of Moscow.'

I glanced at her as she sat beside me, divining a note of disappointment in her voice. She was a short woman, solid, late fifties, with the well-intentioned face of the bulk of the English population. As equally typical shrewdness lived inside and poked its nose out occasionally in tellingly direct remarks. The more I saw of Mrs Wilkinson, the more I saw to respect.

Opposite her, next to Frank, Mr Wilkinson ate his lunch and as usual said nothing. I had gathered he had come on the trip to please his wife, and would as soon be at home with a pint and Manchester United.

'Quite a few people are going to the Bolshoi this evening, to the ballet,' said Mrs Wilkinson a little wistfully. 'But Dad doesn't like that sort of thing, do you, Dad?'

Dad shook his head.

Mrs Wilkinson said in a lower voice to me, confidingly, 'He doesn't like those things the men wear. Those tights. You know showing all the muscles of their behinds . . . and those things in front.'

'Cod-pieces,' I said, straight faced.

'What?' She looked embarrassed, as if I'd used too strong a swear-word for her shock-threshold.

'That's what they're called. Those things which disguise the outlines of nature.'

'Oh.' She was relieved. 'It would be much nicer if they wore *tunics*, that's what I think. Then they wouldn't be so *obvious*. And you could concentrate on the dancing.'

Mr Wilkinson muttered something which might or might not have been 'Poncing about', and filled his mouth with ice-cream.

Mrs Wilkinson looked as if she'd heard that before, and instead said to me, 'Did you see your horses?'

Frank's concentration on food skipped a beat.

'They were great,' I said, and enlarged for two minutes on the turn-out and the training exercise. There was nothing else in Frank's reaction to say he knew I was giving an incomplete account, but then I supposed if there had been, he would have been bad at his job.

Natasha drifted up purposefully to complicate my life.

'We have been lucky,' she said earnestly. 'We have a ticket for you in a box at the Bolshoi tomorrow evening, for the opera.'

I caught Mr Wilkinson's eye, with its message of sardonic sympathy, as I started feebly to thank her.

'It is *The Queen of Spades*,' Natasha said firmly.

'Er ... ' I said.

'Everyone enjoys the opera at the Bolshoi,' she said. 'There is no better opera in the world.'

'How splendid,' I said. 'I will look forward to it.'

She began to look approvingly and I seized the moment to say I would be going out with friends for the evening, and not to expect me in for dinner. She tried very delicately to lead me into saying exactly where I was going, but as at that moment I didn't actually know, except that it was anywhere for some decent grub, she was out of luck.

'And this afternoon ... ' I said, forestalling her, 'the Lenin museum.'

She brightened a good deal. At last, she was no doubt thinking, I was behaving as a good tourist should.

'Mind if I tag along?' Frank said, shovelling in the last of my lunch. His face looked utterly guileless, and I understood the full beauty of his method of working. If following a person might raise their suspicions, tag along in full sight.

'Pleasure,' I said. 'Meet you in the lobby, in half an hour,' and I vanished as soon as he'd started his specially ordered double portion of ice-cream. It would take a good deal to shift him before he had finished it.

I made fast tracks out of the hotel and along to the main Post Office, which was conveniently nearby.

Telephoned to the Embassy. Reached Oliver Waterman.

'This is Randall Drew,' I said.

'Where are you calling from?' he said, interrupting.

'The Post Office.'

'Ah. Right. Carry on, then.'

'Have there been any telex messages for me, from Hughes-Beckett, or anyone in London?'

'Ah, yes,' he said vaguely. 'There was something, I think, my dear chap. Hang on ...' He put the receiver down and I could hear searching sounds and consulting voices. 'Here we are,' he said, coming back. 'Got a pencil?'

'Yes,' I said patiently.

'Yuri Ivanovich Chulitsky.'

'Please spell it,' I said.

He did so.

'Got it,' I said. 'Go on.'

'There isn't any more.'

'Is that the whole of the message?' I asked incredulously.

His voice sounded dubious. 'The whole message, as received by us from the telex people, is "inform Randall Drew Yuri Ivanovich Chulitsky", and then there are a few numbers, and that's all.'

'Numbers?'

'Could be a telephone number, perhaps. Anyway, here they are: 180-19-16. Got that?'

I read them back, to check.

'That's right, my dear chap. How's it going?'

'Fair,' I said. 'Can you send a telex for me, if I give you the message?'

'Ah,' he said. 'I think I should warn you that there's a spot of trouble brewing on the international scene, and the telex is pretty busy. They told us pretty shirtily just now not to bother them with unessentials like music. Unessentials, I ask you. Anyway, my dear chap, if you want to be sure your message gets off, I should take it along there yourself.'

'Take it where?' I said.

'Oh yes, I was forgetting you wouldn't know. The telex machine is not here in the Embassy, but along with the Commercial section in Kutuzovsky Prospect. That's the continuation of Kalinin Prospect. Do you have a map?'

'I'll find it,' I said.

'Tell them I sent you. They can check with me, if they want. And I should stand over them, my dear chap. Make yourself a bit of a nuisance, so they send it to get rid of you.'

'I'll take your advice,' I said, smiling to myself.

'The British Club is along there in Kutuzovsky Prospect,' he said languidly. 'Full of temporary exiles, wallowing in nostalgia. Sad little place. I don't go there much.'

'If any more messages come for me,' I said, 'please would you ring me at the Intourist Hotel?'

'Certainly,' he said civilly. 'Do give me your number.'

I stifled the urge to tell him I'd given it to him twice already. I repeated it again, and wondered whether, by the time I left, he would find his office scattered with small pieces of paper all bearing the same number, which he would peer at with willowy bewilderment while smoothing back his greywinged hair.

I rang off and debated whether or not to lose Frank there and then, and make tracks for the telex: but the message would keep for an hour or two and wasn't worth the stirring up of trouble. I hurried back to the Intourist, went upstairs, came downstairs, and strolled out of the lift to find Frank waiting.

'Oh there you are,' he said. 'Thought I'd missed you.'

'Off we go, then,' I said fatuously, and we walked out of the hotel, down into the long pedestrian tunnel which led under The Fiftieth Anniversary of the October Revolution Square and up into a cobbled street with the red walls of the Kremlin away to the right.

On the underground way he gave me his thoughts on Comrade Lenin, who was, according to Frank, the only genius of the twentieth century.

'Born, of course, in the nineteenth,' I said.

'He bought freedom to the masses,' Frank declared reverently.

'Freedom to do what?' I said.

Frank ignored me. Somewhere under the wet and woolly sociological guff which he ladled so unstintingly over the Wilkinsons and me, there had to be a hard-core card-carrying fully-indoctrinated communist. I looked at Frank's angular, pitted face framed in a long striped college scarf, and thought he was marvellous: he was giving a faultless performance as a poorly-educated left-wing encumbrance of the National Union of Teachers, so convincing that it was hard to believe he was acting.

It flickered across my mind that perhaps Ian Young was wrong, and Frank was not KGB after all: but then if Ian was what I thought, he would be right. If Frank were not KGB, why should Ian say he was?

I wondered how many lies I had been told since I had arrived in Moscow: and how many more I had yet to hear.

Frank more or less genuflected on the threshold of the Lenin museum, and we went inside to have our ears bent about the clothes, desk, car and so on that the liberator of the masses had personally used. And this was the face, I thought, looking at the prim little bearded visage reproduced without stint on paintings and posters and booklets and cards, who had launched a million murders and left his disciples bloodily empire-building round the world. This was the visionary who had unleashed the holocausts: the man who had meant to do good.

I looked at my watch and told Frank I'd had enough of the place; I needed some fresh air. He ignored the implied insult and followed me out, simply saying that he had visited the museum every time he'd been to Moscow and never tired of it. Easy enough to believe that that, at least, was true.

Stephen, back from lunch and an unmissable tutorial, was waiting, as arranged, outside. He had arranged, that is, to meet only me. Frank was surplus to requirements.

I introduced them without explanations. 'Frank Jones . . . Stephen Luce;' and they disliked each other at once.

Had they been dogs, there would have been some unfriendly sniffing and a menacing show of teeth: as it was, their noses actually wrinkled. I wondered whether Stephen's instinctive response was to the real Frank, or to the cover Frank: to an individual or to a type.

Frank, I supposed, merely guessed that any friend of mine was no friend of his; and if Ian were right about him following me, he had certainly seen Stephen before.

Neither of them wanted to say anything to the other.

'Well, Frank,' I said cheerfully, hiding my amusement, 'thank you for your company. I'm off now with Stephen for the rest of the day. See you at breakfast, I guess.'

'You bet.'

We turned away, but after a step or two Stephen glanced back, frowning. I looked where he did: Frank's back view, walking off.

'Haven't I seen him before?' Stephen said.

'Where?'

'Couldn't say. Yesterday morning, up here in the Square, maybe.'

We were walking along the side of Red Square, towards the GUM department store.

'He's staying at the Intourist,' I said.

Stephen nodded, dismissing it. 'Where to?' he said.

'Phone box.'

We found one and inserted the two kopeks, but there was no answer from the number Misha had given us. Tried again, this time for Yuri Ivanovich Chulitsky. Same result.

'Telex in Kutuzovsky Prospect,' I said. 'Where do we get a taxi?'

'The metro is cheap. Only five kopeks, however far you go.'

He couldn't understand why I should want to spend money when I didn't have to: incredulity halfway to exasperation filled his eyes and voice. I gave in with a shrug and we went by metro, with me battling as usual against the claustrophobic feeling I always got from hurtling through mole-runs far underground. The cathedral-like stations of the Moscow metro seemed to have been built to the greater glory of technology (down with churches) but on the achingly long and boring escalators I found myself quite missing London's vulgar advertisements for bras. Ritzy, jazzy, noisy, dirty, uninhibited old London, greedy and gutsy and grabbing at life. Gold coaches and white horses along the Mall instead of tanks, and garbage collectors on strike.

'Do the dustbin men ever strike here?' I said to Stephen.

'Strikes? Don't be silly. Strikes are not allowed in Russia.'

We finally resurfaced, and after a good deal of asking and walking, arrived at the Commercial section, which was guarded as before by a soldier. Again we talked our way in, and, by following Oliver Waterman's advice and making a nuisance of myself, I persuaded the inmates to telex my message, which was: REQUEST DETAILS OF LIFE AND BACKGROUND OF HANS KRAMER. ALSO WHEREABOUTS OF HIS BODY. ALSO NAME AND TELEPHONE NUMBER OF THE PATHOLOGIST WHO DID THE AUTOPSY.

'Don't expect an answer,' I was told brusquely. 'There's all hell breaking loose in some place in Africa which is choc-a-bloc with Soviet guns and so-called advisers. The telex is steaming. The diplomats have priority. You'll be way down the list.'

'Thanks very much,' I said, and we trudged our way back to the pavement outside.

'Now what?' Stephen said.

'Try those numbers again.'

We found a glass-walled box nearby and put the kopeks in the slot. No answer, as before.

'Probably not home from work yet,' Stephen said.

I nodded. At four in the afternoon the daylight was fading fast to dusk, the lighted windows shining brighter with every minute.

'What do you want to do now?' Stephen said.

'I don't know.'

'Like to come up to the University, then? We're not all that far away, actually. Nearer than to your hotel.'

'No hope of anything to eat, there, I suppose?' I said.

He looked surprised. 'Yes, if you like. There's a sort of supermarket for students in the basement, and kitchens upstairs. We can buy something and eat in my room, if you like.' He seemed doubtful. 'It won't be as good as the Intourist Hotel, though.'

'I'll risk it.'

'I'll ring up and say you're coming,' he said, turning back to the telephone box.

'Can't we just go?'

He shook his head. 'In Russia, everything has to be arranged first. If it is arranged, it is OK. If it's not arranged, it's irregular, suspicious, or subversive, and what's more, you won't get in.' He fished around for another two-kopek piece and put it to good use.

Coming out of the telephone box and saying my visit was fixed, he began planning a route via the metro, but I was no longer listening. Two men were walking towards us, talking intently. From thinking there was something familiar about one of them I progressed by a series of mental jumps to realizing that I knew them both.

They were Ian Young and Malcolm Herrick.

8

They were, if anything, more surprised to see me.

'Randall!' Ian said. 'What are you doing here?'

'If it isn't the sleuth!' Malcolm Herrick's English voice boomed confidently into Kutuzovsky Prospect, scorning discretion. 'Found Alyosha yet, sport?'

'Afraid not,' I said. 'This is Stephen Luce. A friend. English.'

'Malcolm Herrick,' said the Moscow correspondent of the *Watch*, introducing himself, shaking hands, and waiting for a reaction. None came. He must have been used to it. 'Moscow correspondent of the *Watch*,' he said.

'Great stuff,' said Stephen vaguely, obviously not having read a word from the Herrick pen.

'Are you going to the British Club?' Ian asked. 'We're just on our way there.'

His watchful eyes waited for a reply. There were some replies I saw no harm in giving, and this was one.

'I came to send a telex,' I said. 'Oliver's suggestion.'

'The snake,' Herrick said unexpectedly, narrowing his eyes. 'He usually gives messages for the telex to the guy in the hall.'

'And the guy in the hall relays them to you?' I said.

'Sources, sources, sport.' He tapped the side of his nose.

Ian was unmoved. 'If an answer comes,' he said to me, 'I'll see that you get it.'

'I'd be grateful.'

'Where are you going now, sport?' Malcolm said, loud and direct as always.

'To the University, with Stephen, for tea.'

'Tea!' He made a face. 'Look, why don't we meet later for a decent meal? All of us,' he added expansively, including Ian and Stephen. 'The Aragvi do you, Ian?'

Ian, who had not reacted visibly to the original suggestion, seemed to find favour with the choice of place, and nodded silently. Malcolm started giving me directions, but Stephen said he knew the way.

'Great then,' Malcolm said. 'Eight-thirty. Don't be late.'

The faint drizzle which had persisted all day seemed to be intensifying into sleet. It put, anyway, an effective damper on further conversation in the street, and by common consent we split up and went our own ways.

'Who is the man who looks Russian?' Stephen asked, ducking his head down and sideways to avoid the stinging drops. 'The one imitating the Sphinx.'

'Let's get that taxi,' I said, waving to a grey-green car coming with the green light shining for availability in its windscreen.

'Expensive,' he protested automatically, slithering into the back seat beside me. 'Ve vill have to cure this disgusting bourgeois habit.' He had a rich way of imitating a Russian accent while sardonically putting forward the Russian point of view. 'Vorkers of the Vorld unite . . . and go on the metro.'

'Caviar is immoral,' I said drily.

'Caviar is not bourgeois. Caviar is for everyone who can scrape up a fortune in roubles.' He considered me, relapsing into ordinary English, 'Why did you say caviar is immoral? It's not like you.'

'Not my idea. A friend's.'

'Girl?'

I nodded.

'Aha,' he said. 'I diagnose a rich middle-class socialist rebelling against mummy.'

'Not far out,' I said, a touch sadly.

He peered anxiously at my face. 'I haven't offended you?'

'No.'

I got him to ask the taxi driver to stop by a telephone kiosk, and to wait while we tried our numbers again. There was still no answer from Misha, but the second number was answered at the first ring. Stephen, holding the receiver, made a brief thumbs up sign to me, and spoke. Listened, spoke again, and handed the receiver to me. 'It is Yuri Ivanovich Chulitsky himself. He says he speaks English.'

I took the instrument. 'Mr Chulitsky?' I said.

'Yes.'

'I am an Englishman visiting Moscow,' I said. 'My name is Randall Drew. I have been given your name and telephone number by the British Embassy. I wonder if I could talk with you?'

There was a longish pause. Then the voice at the other end, calm and with an accent that was a carbon copy of Stephen's imitation, said, 'Upon what subject?'

Owing to the meagreness of the telex bearing his name, I couldn't entirely answer. I said hopefully, 'Horses?'

'Horses.' He sounded unenthusiastic. 'Always horses. I do not know horses. I am architect.'

'Er,' I said. 'Have you already talked about horses to another Englishman?'

A pause. Then the voice, measured and still calm. 'That is so. In Moscow, yes. And in England, yes. Many times.'

Bits of light began to dawn. 'You were at the International Horse Trials? At Burghley, in September?'

The pause. Then, 'At many horse trials. September . . . and August.'

Bingo, I thought. One of the observers.

'Mr Chulitsky,' I said, persuasively, 'please may I meet you? I've been talking to Nikolai Alexandrovich Kropotkin, and if you want to check up on me, I think he will tell you it would be all right for you to talk to me.'

A very long pause. Then he said, 'Are you writing for newspaper?'

'No,' I said.

'I telephone Nikolai Alexandrovich,' he said. 'I find his number.'

'I have it here,' I said, and read it out slowly.

'You telephone again. One hour.'

The receiver went down at his end with a decisive crash, and Stephen and I went back to the taxi.

Stephen said, 'When we get up to my room, don't say anything you don't want overheard. Or not until I tell you it's OK.'

'Are you serious?'

'I'm a foreigner. I live in the section of the University reserved for foreign students. Every room in Moscow which is used by foreigners should be considered bugged until proved different.'

The University building, of vast blocks of narrow windows punctuated by soaring fluted towers, like an immense grey stone blancmange, looked from its hill to the river and the city centre beyond: and on the far bank lay, spread out, the Lenin stadium, where the Olympic athletes were scheduled to run and jump and throw things.

'How will they manage with the whole city full of foreigners?' I said.

'Apartheid will prevail.' The Russian accent made it a wicked joke. 'Segregation will be ruthlessly maintained.'

'Why did you come to Russia,' I said, 'feeling as you do?'

He gave me a quick bright glance. 'I love the place and hate the regime, the same as everyone else. And nowhere's a prison when you can get out.'

The taxi shed us at the gate, and we walked to the foreign students' entrance, a door dwarfed by the sheer height of the adjoining walls. Inside, coming down to human scale, there was a dumpy middle-aged woman behind a desk. She looked at Stephen with a lack of reaction which meant she knew him, and then at me; and she was out of her seat and barring my way with the speed of a rattlesnake.

Stephen spoke to her in Russian. She dourly shook her head. Together they consulted a list on her desk; and with severe looks she let me through.

'Dragons like that guard doorways all over Russia,' Stephen said. 'The only way past is to be expected. Short of slaying them, of course.'

We went for a long walk which ended one floor down in a help-yourself foodshop. All the packages were unfamiliar, and owing to the Cyrillic alphabet, which made restaurants look like 'РЕСТОРАН' to Western eyes, I couldn't even guess at the contents. Stephen went round unerringly, choosing what later turned out to be crisp-sided cream cakes and ending with a bottle of milk.

A girl stood at the cash desk before us, paying for her groceries. A pretty girl, with light-brown hair curling on to her shoulders, and the sort of waist Victorian young ladies swooned over. When Stephen greeted her, she turned her head and gave him a flashing smile with a fair view of excellent teeth. The smile, I saw, of at least good friends.

Stephen introduced her as Gudrun, and the unpretty lady behind the cash register pointed to her packages and clearly told her to pick them up and go.

The girl picked up her bottle of milk, and the bottom fell out of it. Milk cascaded on to the floor. Gudrun stood looking bewildered with the whole-looking bottle still in her hand and milk stains all over her legs.

I watched the pantomime that followed. Stephen was saying she should have another bottle. The unpretty lady shook her head and pointed to the cash register. Everyone engaged in battle, and the unpretty lady won.

'She made her *buy* another bottle,' said Stephen, disgusted, as we set off on another interior tramp.

'So I gathered.'

'They make the bottles like tubes here, and just stick a disc in for the bottoms. Anyway,' he finished cheerfully, 'she's coming along to my room for a cup of tea.'

Gudrun was West German, from Bonn. She filled and illuminated

273

Stephen's tiny cell, which was eight feet long by six across, and contained a bed, a table covered with books, a chair, and a glass-fronted bookcase. On the bare wooden floor there was one small imitation Brussels rug, and at the tall narrow window, skimpy green curtains.

'The Ritz,' I said ironically.

'I'm lucky,' Stephen said, taking three mugs from the bookcase and making a space for them on the table. 'A lot of the Russian students are two to a room this size.'

If you had two beds in here you couldn't open the door,' I said.

Gudrun nodded. 'They stand the beds up against the wall in the daytime.'

'No protest marches?' I said. 'No demos for better conditions?'

'They are not allowed,' Gudrun said seriously. 'Anyone who tried would lose his place.'

She spoke English perfectly, with hardly a trace of accent. Her Russian, Stephen said, was just as good. His own German was passable, his French excellent. I sighed, internally, for a skill I'd never acquired.

Stephen went off to make the tea.

'Don't come,' he said. 'The kitchen is filthy. About twenty of us share it, and we're all supposed to clean it, so nobody does.'

Gudrun sat on the bed and asked me how I was enjoying Moscow, and I sat on the chair and said fine. I asked her how she was enjoying her course, and she said fine.

'If the Russians are so keen to keep foreigners at arm's length,' I said, 'why do they allow foreign students in the University?'

She glanced involuntarily round the walls, a revealing glimpse into the way they all lived. The walls had ears; literally.

'We are exchange students,' she said. 'For Stephen, there is a Russian student in London. For me a Russian student in Bonn. Those students are dedicated communists.'

'Spreading the gospel and recruiting?'

She nodded a shade unhappily, again glancing at the walls and not liking my frankness. I went back to harmless chit chat, and Stephen presently arrived to distribute the goodies, which, for me at least, nicely filled an aching void.

'Show you something,' he said, stuffing the last of the cake into his mouth and shifting along to the end of the bed, on which he was sitting. 'A little trick.'

He picked up what I saw was a tape-recorder, and switched it on. Then with a theatrical flourish he stood up and pressed it against the wall beside my head.

Nothing happened. He removed it and pressed it to another spot. Again nothing. He took it away, and put it delicately against a spot above his bed. From the tape-recorder came a high-pitched whine.

'Abracadabra,' he said, taking the tape-recorder down and switching it off. 'From ordinary walls, you get nothing. From a live mike inside a wall, you get feedback.'

'Do they know?' I said.

'Of course they do. Like to borrow it?' He pointed to the recorder.

'Very much.'

'Then I'll dash to get a chit to take it out.'

'A chit?'

'Yes. You can't just walk out of here carrying things. They say it's to stop people stealing, but it's just the usual phobia about knowing what goes on.'

I glanced at the wall behind his head. Stephen laughed. 'If you *don't* complain about the whole bloody repressive Soviet system they suspect you're putting on an act.'

In the corridor, from the telephone installed for the students, I called Yuri Ivanovich Chulitsky. The telephone was safe, Stephen said. The only telephones which were tapped were those in the houses of known dissidents: and Yuri Chulitsky would be anything but a dissident, if he had been sent to England as an observer.

He answered at once.

'I talk with Nikolai Alexandrovich,' he said. 'I meet you tomorrow.'

'Thank you very much.'

'I drive car. I come outside National Hotel, ten o'clock, tomorrow morning. Is right?'

'Is right,' I said.

'Ten o'clock.' Down went the receiver with the same crash, before I could ask him how I would know him or his car. I supposed that when I saw him, I would know.

Stephen tried the other number. The bell rang hollowly at the far end, and after ten rings we prepared to give up. Then the ringing stopped and there was suddenly a breathless voice on the line.

'It's Misha,' Stephen said.

'You talk to him. It's easier.'

Stephen listened. 'He wants to see you again, and it must be tonight. He says he is going to Rostov tomorrow with two horses. The snow is coming, and the horses are going south. Nikolai Alexandrovich – that is, Mr Kropotkin – is going next week. It was decided today.'

'All right,' I said. 'When and where?'

Stephen asked, and was told. He wrote it down, and the directions took some time.

'Well,' he said, slowing replacing the receiver and looking at what he had written, 'it is miles out of the centre. I think it must be an apartment block. He says he will wait outside, and when you arrive, don't speak English until he says it's OK.'

'Aren't you coming?'

'You don't really need me. Misha does speak some English.' He handed me the address, written in Russian script. 'Show that to a taxi driver. He'll find it. And I'll meet you later, at the Aragvi.'

I looked beyond him to the open door of his room. Gudrun half-sat, half-lay, on the bed, her long legs sprawled in invitation.

I hesitated, but finally I said, 'I wish you could come. Someone did try to kill Misha or me this morning. I expect you'll laugh, but if I'm going off into the wilds to meet him, I would feel safer with a back-up system.'

He didn't laugh. He said goodbye to Gudrun, and came. He also said, 'Ve have vays of postponing our pleasures until tomorrow,' and made a joke of it: and I thought that for plain good nature he would be hard to beat.

'It's very difficult to think of a good meeting place, if you're an ordinary Russian and you want to talk to a foreigner,' Stephen said. 'There are no pubs in Russia. No discreet little cafés. And there are always watchers, with tongues. You'd have to be pretty solid with the hierarchy to be seen any-where public with a foreigner.'

We flagged a passing taxi, again without much of a wait.

'No shortage of these,' I said, climbing in. Then, as Stephen's mouth opened, I interrupted. 'Don't say it. Taxis are dear, the metro's cheap.'

'And the taxi charges have practically doubled recently.'

'Ask the driver to go via the Intourist Hotel, so that I can drop off the re-corder.'

'Right.'

We sped down the Komsomolsky Prospect and I looked two or three times out of the back window. A medium-sized black car followed us faith-fully, but we were on a main road where that was likely to happen anyway.

'When we get to the Intourist,' I said, 'I will get out and say goodnight to you unmistakably. I'll then go into the hotel, and you and the taxi will drive off, and go round the corner, and wait for me outside the National Hotel en-trance. I'll dump the tape-recorder, and come and meet you there.'

Stephen looked out of the rear window.

'Seriously,' he said. 'Do you think you're being followed?'

'Seriously,' I said. 'Most of the time.'

'But . . . who by?'

'Would you believe, the KGB?'

For all his guided tour to the prying state, he was staggered. 'What makes you think so?'

'The Sphinx told me.'

It reduced him to silence. Ve have vays of making you stop talking, I thought facetiously. We arrived in due course at the Intourist, and went through the act.

I spent some time on the pavement talking to Stephen through the taxi window, and then bade him goodnight in ringing tones, and waved a fare-well as I went through the double glass entrance; overdoing it, no doubt. I collected my key from the desk, removed hat and coat, and went up in the lift. Then I parked the tape-recorder in my room, and without hurrying, so as not to alert the old biddy sitting watchfully at her desk by the lifts, walked back, still carrying outdoor clothes, and descended to the ground floor.

There were several routes from the lifts to the front door, as it was a very large hotel: I took the most roundabout, putting on hat and coat on the way, and wafted at an ordinary pace out again on to the pavement. No doubt the watchers there took general note, but no one broke away to bob in my wake.

I stopped at the corner and glanced back. No one seemed to be peeling off to look in non-existent shop windows. I walked on, thinking that if the followers were determined as well as professional, my amateur attempts at evasion would have been useless. But they would have had no reason to suppose I knew they were there, or that I would try to duck them, as I had given no signs so far of wanting to; so perhaps they might think I was still somewhere inside the hotel.

The taxi driver was agitated and grumbling at having had to wait a long time where he was not supposed to. Stephen greeted my arrival with signs of relief, and we set off again with a jerk.

'Your friend Frank went into the hotel just after you,' Stephen said. 'Did you see him?'

'No,' I said tranquilly.

He didn't pursue it. 'The driver says the temperature is dropping. It has been warm for November, he says.'

'It's December, today.'

'He says it will snow.'

We motored a good way northwards, and then north-east, through the wide well-lit mostly empty streets. When the roads became narrower I said, 'Ask the driver to stop for a moment.'

'What now?' Stephen said.

'See if we've a tail.'

No car stopped behind us, however, and when we went on, we found no stationary car waiting ahead. I asked Stephen to get the driver to circle a fairly large block. The driver, thoroughly disillusioned by these junketings, began muttering under his breath.

'Get him to drop us before we reach the address,' I said. 'We don't want him undoing the good work by reporting our exact destination.'

A large tip on top of the big fare cured most of the driver's grumbles, but wouldn't, I guessed, keep his mouth shut. He sped off back to the brighter lights as if glad to be rid of us. But no black cars, or any others, passed or stopped. As far as we could tell, we were on our own.

We stood in an area which was being developed. On each side, end on to the road, were ranks of newly-built apartment blocks, all about forty feet thick and nine storeys high, clad in grey-white pebbledash and stretching away into the darkness with ranks of windows front and back.

'Standard issue housing,' Stephen said. 'Egg boxes for the masses. Six square metres of floorspace per person; the maximum regulation allowance.'

We walked along the slushy pavement, the only people in sight. The block we were currently passing was unfinished, with its walls in place but empty holes for windows. The one after that, although still uninhabited, had glass.

The one after that looked furnished, and the one after that had residents. It proved also to be where we were going.

A last look at the street showed no one taking the slightest notice of us. We wheeled into the broad space between the two blocks and discovered from the numbers that the entrance we wanted was the second door along. We went towards it without haste, and stopped a few spaces short.

We waited. A minute ticked past, and another. No Misha. With every lungful the wet freezing air chilled from the inside out. If we had travelled all this way for nothing, I thought, I would be less than amused.

A voice spoke softly, from behind us.

'Come.'

9

We turned, startled. We hadn't heard him, but there he stood in his leather coat and his leather cap, young and neat. He made a small beckoning movement with his head, and turned on his heel. We followed him out into the street, along the pavement, and round into the space between the next two blocks. He made steadily for one of the entrances, and in silence we traipsed in his footsteps.

Inside, the brightly lit and warm hall smelled of new paint. There were two lifts, both not working, and a flight of stairs. Misha addressed himself to the stairs. We followed.

On the landing above there were four doors, all closed. Misha continued up the stairs. On the next landing, four identical doors, again all closed. Misha went on climbing. On the fourth floor, we stopped for breath.

Between the fifth and sixth floors we came across two young men struggling to carry upwards an electric cooker. They had ropes and protective wadding around it, and leather straps with carrying handles to help them, but they were both sweating and panting from exertion. They stopped work, with the cooker poised precariously half on and half off a step, to let us pass. Misha said something which sounded consoling, and on we went at a slower and slower pace.

It had to be the ninth floor, I thought. Or the roof.

The ninth floor. Misha produced a key, unlocked one of the uninformative doors, and led us in.

The apartment consisted of kitchen, bathroom, and two meagre rooms, and was almost unfurnished. There were some rather gloomy green tiles in the kitchen, and nothing much else; certainly no cooker. The bare necessities in the bathroom. Bare floors, bare windows and bare walls in the two rooms, with two wooden chairs and a table in one of them, and the frame of a bed in the other. But, like everywhere indoors in Moscow, it was warm.

Misha closed the door behind us, and we took off our hats and coats. Misha swept an arm around, embracing the flat, and Stephen translated what he said.

'It is his sister's flat. When the flats are ready, the people on the list draw lots for them. His sister and her husband drew the ninth floor, and she hates it and is very depressed. They have a baby. Until the lifts are working she will have to carry the baby and her shopping up nine floors all the time. The cooker for the flat is provided, but it has to be carried up, like we saw the others doing. All the furniture has to be carried up, by friends.'

'Why don't the lifts work?' I said.

Misha said (via Stephen) that it was because the caretaker said the interiors of the lifts would be damaged if people used them for taking up cookers and furniture, so the lifts would not be switched on until all the flats were furnished and occupied. It seemed monstrous, but it was quite true.

'Why don't they put an extra, temporary, lining inside the lifts, and remove it later?' I said.

Misha shrugged. It was impossible to argue, he said. The caretaker would not listen, and he was in control. He gestured to us to sit on the chairs, and he himself perched half on and half off the table. He was thin but strong, fit rather than under-nourished. The vivid blue eyes in the tanned face looked at us with more friendliness than in the morning and reinforced my belief in his brains.

'Thank you for coming,' he said. 'Tomorrow, I go. I speak again.'

'Tell Stephen in Russian,' I said. 'It will be easier for you. And you can say more.'

He nodded a shade regretfully, but saw the sense of it. He spoke in bursts, waiting for Stephen to catch up, and again nodding as he heard his intentions put into English.

'Later, after we had gone,' Stephen translated, 'Nikolai Alexandrovich, Mr Kropotkin, had more visitors; your friend the English journalist, Malcolm Herrick, and someone who sounds like the Sphinx. They came together. Mr Kropotkin got Misha to repeat to them what he had just told us. Misha thinks that Mr Kropotkin knew the Sphinx quite well . . .'

'His name is Ian,' I said. 'And yes, they had talked together before.'

'Mr Kropotkin thinks you need help,' Stephen went on. 'He sent Misha to fetch his little book with telephone numbers, and he telephoned to several people to ask if they knew anything about Alyosha, and if they did, to tell him, and he would tell you. Boris Dmitrevich Telyatnikov, who is one of the possible Olympic riders, came in the afternoon to see the horses, and Mr

Kropotkin asked him also. Boris said he didn't know anything about Alyosha, but Misha thinks Boris was worried.'

'Yes,' I said. 'Carry on.'

'Practically everyone in Moscow who has anything to do with the Olympic equestrian games now seems to be looking for Alyosha.'

'My God,' I said.

Misha looked a little anxious. 'Nikolai Alexandrovich help,' he said. 'You save horse. Nikolai Alexandrovich help.'

'It is kind of him,' I said dazedly.

Stephen listened, and reported. 'The Sphinx . . . Ian . . . told Mr Kropotkin that once you had found Alyosha and talked to him, you could go home. Mr Kropotkin said, "Then we will find Alyosha for him. He saved our best horse. Nothing is too much."'

'My God,' I said again.

'According to what Mr Kropotkin told everybody, the horse swung unexpectedly in front of the horse box as it approached. The driver had no time to swerve, but you rescued the horse.'

'Is that what Misha thinks?' I said.

'Niet.' Misha understood and was positive. 'Driver go . . . boom.' He smashed his fist unmistakably into his hand.

'Did you know him?' I asked.

'Niet. No see.'

It was the horse box, Misha told Stephen, in which he and the chestnut and another horse were to travel the next day to Rostov. When he had led the chestnut back to its stable, the horse box had been parked in its usual place. Mr Kropotkin had felt the engine, to make sure it was that horse box which we had seen, and yes, the engine was warm. No one could be found who had driven it. Mr K's view of things was that the driver was ashamed of his carelessness and afraid of being disciplined.

'Well,' Stephen said, standing up, and straightening his spine, 'thank you for telling us.'

Misha hopped off the table and waved him back to his chair, talking earnestly.

'That is not why he asked us to come here,' Stephen relayed.

'No,' I said. 'He gave you his phone number before all this happened.'

'Never miss a trick, do you?'

'I don't really know,' I said.

'That figures.'

'I speak to German,' Misha said.

'What?' I looked at him with quickened interest. 'Do you mean you spoke to Hans Kramer?'

Misha regretfully did not. Misha told Stephen that he had become friends with the boy who had looked after Hans Kramer's horse. He had been unable to tell us that in the morning, because of course it was forbidden to talk to the foreigners and he had disobeyed orders.

'Yes,' I said resignedly. 'Go on.'

It appeared that the two young men had formed a pleasant habit of re-tiring to a disused hay-loft to talk and smoke cigarettes. Smoking in the stables was forbidden also. Misha had enjoyed both talk and smoke, because they were forbidden.

Misha's blue eyes were brightly alive, full of pleasure at his own daring, and totally unsophisticated.

'What did you talk about?' I prompted.

Horses, of course. And Hans Kramer. The German boy disliked Kramer, who was, Stephen translated succinctly, a bastard.

'In what way?'

Misha talked. Stephen translated. 'Kramer was apparently OK with horses, but he liked to play nasty little jokes on people.'

'Yes, I was told of one,' I said, thinking of Johnny and the pink-boa girl-boy. 'Go on.'

'He was also a thief.'

I showed disbelief. Misha nodded vigorously, not just with his head, but from halfway up his back.

'Misha says,' Stephen went on, 'that Kramer stole a case from the veterin-ary surgeon's car when he called to see the horses of the British team, before the trials began.'

'A case containing drugs?' I said.

'*Da*,' Misha said. 'Drug.'

'People are always stealing cases from doctors and vets,' I said. 'You'd think they would chain them up like bicycles, not leave them around in cars. Well . . . so was Kramer an addict?'

I felt doubtful as I said it, because heavy drug addiction and international-standard riding didn't seem to be happy bedfellows. Misha, however, didn't know. The German boy had told him there was a fuss when the vet dis-covered his loss, but Kramer had hidden the case.

'How did the German boy know?'

'He found it somewhere in the stable, hidden in Kramer's kit. Four days later, when Kramer died, the German boy took the case to the hay-loft, and he and Misha shared out the contents.'

'For God's sake,' I said.

'It sounds to me,' said Stephen, speaking frankly after another long tale from Misha, 'that the German boy took the case itself and all the saleable items like barbiturates, and gave Misha the rubbish. Not surprising, really. Our Misha is a proper little innocent at large.'

'What did he do with his share?'

Stephen consulted. 'Brought it back to Moscow with some other stuff . . . souvenirs of the trip, that's all. To remind him of the happy talks in the hay-loft.'

I stared vacantly at the double-glazed window, seeing in my mind not an uncurtained black square, but an old-world cottage in England.

Johnny Farringford, I thought, had not wanted to be thought to be connected too much with Kramer. He had not wanted me to see or find Alyosha; had wanted the rumours forgotten, and had denied there was any scandal to hush up. Suppose, I thought bleakly, that the Alyosha business was after all unimportant, and the thing Johnny desperately did not want uncovered, was nothing to do with unorthodox sex but all to do with drugs.

'Has Misha still got the stuff he brought back?' I said.

Misha had.

'Would you let me see it?' I asked him.

Misha was not unwilling, but said he would be going away first thing in the morning.

'Is it important?' Stephen said.

'Only in a negative sort of way.' I sighed. 'If Kramer had the case for four days before he died, he probably took out of it what he wanted. Then the German boy took his share ... whatever Misha still has, it is not what Kramer wanted ... which might tell us something. Besides barbiturates, vets usually carry other things. Pethidine, for example. It's a painkiller, but I believe it is so addictive for humans that you can get hooked by using it a few times. And Butazolidin ... and steroids ...'

'Got you,' Stephen said, and spoke to Misha. Between them they had a long chat which ended in evident agreement.

'Misha says his souvenirs are at his mother's flat, but he himself has a room with the other grooms, near the stable. He has to be back there soon, and tomorrow morning he goes. He can't get to his mother's. But he will telephone, and ask his sister, who lives at home until she moves into this place, to bring the stuff to you tomorrow morning. But she cannot come to the hotel, as it would not do to be seen talking to foreigners, so she will meet you inside the main entrance of GUM. She will wear a red woollen hat with a white pompom, which Misha gave her last week for her birthday, and a long red scarf. She speaks some English, because she learned it in school.'

'Great,' I said. 'Could she make it fairly early? I have to meet Chulitsky outside the National Hotel at ten.'

Misha said he thought she could get there by half-past nine, and on that we agreed.

I thanked Misha for all his trouble and kindness in giving us this information. I enthusiastically shook his hand.

'Is good,' he said, looking pleased. 'You save horse. Nikolai Alexandrovich say help. I help.'

We arrived outside the Aragvi restaurant ten minutes late because of an absence of taxis in the far-flung suburb, and a scarcity of buses. The metro, we had discovered, came to an end three miles short of the flat. Misha travelled towards the city centre with us, but apart, not looking at us, not speaking. He left us on the train, when he reached his interchange station, without a flicker of a farewell, his face as stolid as the others ranged about.

'Don't tell Malcolm Herrick what Misha has just told us,' I said, as we hurried the last hundred yards on foot. 'He's a newspaperman. My brief is to hush up what I can, not get it printed in the *Watch*; and we'd get Misha into trouble.'

'Silent as the sepulchre,' Stephen promised, in a voice which spoke of teaching grandmothers something about eggs.

The Aragvi turned out to be less than half a mile from the Intourist Hotel: up Gorky Street, and turn right at the traffic lights. Malcolm and Ian were waiting a short distance short of it and Malcolm grumbled, quietly for him, that we had kept them waiting in the cold.

There was a short queue outside the restaurant, shivering.

'Follow me, and don't talk until we are inside,' Malcolm said. He by-passed the queue and opened the firmly-shut door. The by now familiar argument took place, and finally, grudgingly, we were let in.

'I booked,' Malcolm said as we peeled off our coats. 'I come here often. You'd never think it.'

The place was full, and somewhere there was some music. We were led to the one vacant table and a bottle of vodka materialized within five seconds.

'Of the two decent restaurants in Moscow,' Malcolm said, 'I like this the better.'

'Two?' I said.

'That's right. What do you want to eat?' He peered into the large menu. 'The food is Georgian. It is a Georgian restaurant. Most of the customers are from Georgia.'

'For Georgia, USSR, read Texas, USA,' Ian said.

The menu was written exclusively in Russian, and while the other three chose from it, I used my eyes instead on the customers. There were three men at the next table, and beyond them, sitting with their backs to the wall, two more. Very few women. The faces, I realized, were livelier, and varied. The two men over by the wall, for instance, were not Moscow types: they had sallower skins, fierce dark eyes, black curling hair. They ate with concentration, intent on their food.

The three men at the table next to ours were on the other hand intent on their drink. Not much tablecloth showed between full bottles, empty bottles, full and empty glasses. The men, one huge, one medium, one small, were diving into vast tulip-shaped glasses of champagne.

Malcolm looked up from the menu and followed my gaze. 'Georgians,' he said. 'Born with hollow legs.' I watched with fascination while the gold liquid disappeared like beer. The eyes of the smallest were faintly glazed. The huge one looked as sober as his grey flannel suit; and there were three empty vodka bottles on the table.

Ian, Malcolm and Stephen all ordered expertly, and I told Stephen just to double his for me. The food when it came was strange and spicy, and light years away from the grey chunks down the road. The huge man at the next table roared at the waiter, who hurried to bring a second bottle of champagne.

'Well, how's it going, sport?' Malcolm said, forking some chicken in bean sauce into his mouth.

'The smallest one's legs are full.' I said.

'What?' He looked round at the three men. 'No, I meant the Sherlock Holmes bit. What've you come up with so far?'

'The German who died at Burghley called on Alyosha with his dying breath,' I said. 'And that's about all.'

'And anyway, you knew that,' said Stephen.

I kicked him under the table. He gave me a sharp enquiring look and then realized that except for Misha we wouldn't have been aware that they knew. Neither Malcolm nor Ian commented, however. The four of us ate thoughtfully.

'Not much in that, is there, sport?' Malcolm said.

'Alyosha must exist,' I said. 'Alyosha. Moscow.' I sighed. 'I'll have to go on looking.'

'What'll you do next?' Ian said.

I took off my glasses, and squinted at them, and polished some non-existent smears with my handkerchief.

'Er,' I said.

'How bad are your eyes, sport?' Malcolm said, interrupting. 'Let's look through your windows.'

Short of breaking the frames, I couldn't have prevented him. He took the glasses firmly out of my hand and placed them on his own nose.

To me, his face, and all the others in the place, looked a distorted blur. Colours told me roughly where hair, eyes and clothes were, but outlines had vanished.

'Christ,' Malcolm said. 'You must have corkscrew vision.'

'Astigmatism,' I said.

'And some.'

They all had a go at looking at the world through my eyes, and then handed them back. Everything became nicely sharp again.

'In both eyes?' Ian said.

I nodded. 'And both different. Frightfully handy.'

The small man at the next table was propping his head up with his champagne glass and seemed to be going to sleep. The friends kept up a steady intake and ignored him. The huge one roared at the waiter again and held up three fingers, and with my mouth open I watched three more bottles of vodka arrive at the table.

Coffee was brought for us, but I was glued to the scene in front. The small man's head, still balanced on the glass of champagne, sank lower and lower. The glass came to rest on the table, and the hand holding it dropped away, and the little man sat there with his head on the glass, fast asleep.

'Georgians,' said Malcolm, glancing at them, as if that explained everything.

The huge man paid the bill and stood up, rising to a good seven feet tall.

He tucked the three full bottles of vodka under one arm and the sleeping friend under the other, and made the stateliest of exits.

'Bloody marvellous,' I said.

The waiter who had served them came and spoke to us, watching the departure with respect.

Malcolm said, 'The waiter says they started with a whole bottle of vodka each. Then they had two more bottles of vodka between them. Five in all. Then the two bottles of champagne. No one but Georgians could do that.'

I said mildly, 'I thought you didn't speak Russian.'

He gave me a startled glance and a short burst of the flat hard stare of the first evening.

'Yeah, sport. I remember. I told you I don't speak Russian ... Well, I don't. That doesn't mean I don't know it. It means I don't let the Russkies in general cotton on. Right, sport?'

'Right,' I agreed.

'It's not in your file,' Ian said, conversationally.

'Dead right. The Russkies have my file too, don't forget. I learned the lingo in private from twelve long-playing records and some text books, and you just forget that piece of information pronto.'

'Never misses a trick,' Stephen said.

'Who doesn't?'

'Our friend Randall.'

Ian regarded me with slightly narrowed eyes, and Malcolm called for the bill.

The two sallow men from over by the wall had gone in the wake of the Georgians, and the place was emptying fast. We collected our coats and hats and shuddered out into the saturated air. It seemed colder to me than ever. The other three made off for the metro, and I risked a fine by crossing Gorky Street above ground instead of tunnelling under. After eleven at night there were even fewer cars than usual to mow one down, and not another pedestrian in sight, let alone a policeman.

The Intourist Hotel lay in the distance, down the slight hill, with its large canopy stretching out over the pavement. I turned up my coat collar, wondering, for about the tenth time, why most of the centre of the canopy was an intentional rectangular hole, like a skylight without glass, open to every drop of rain or snow which cared to fall. As a shelter for people arriving and departing the canopy was a non-starter. Of as much practical use as a bath with no plug.

A mind floating along in neutral is in rotten shape for battle. A black car rolled quietly down the road beside me and came to a halt ten paces ahead. The driver got out of the car, and the front passenger door opened. The front passenger stood up on to the pavement, and as I approached, he sprang at me.

The surprise was absolute. His hand snaked out towards my spectacles, and I hit it violently aside as one would a wasp. When it came to saving my sight, my reflexes were always instantaneous: but for the rest, I was unbalanced.

He crowded after me across the pavement to pin me against the unyielding stone of the flanking building. His friend hustled to help. There was a fierce brutal strength in their manner, and there was also no doubt that, whatever they intended next, their first target was still my eyes.

One wouldn't actually choose to fight while wearing a thick overcoat and a fur hat, even if the opposition were similarly handicapped. To fight, however, seemed imperative.

I kicked the storming passenger very viciously on the knee, and when his head came forward I grabbed hold of the woolly balaclava he wore under his hat and swung him round so that his head hit the wall.

The driver arrived like a whirlwind and grabbed my arm, his other hand again aiming at my glasses. I ducked. His fingers sank only into fur. My hat, dislodged, fell off. I let go with a kick at him which connected but not very effectively, and I also opened my mouth and started shouting.

I shouted 'Ya-ya-ya-ya-ya' at the top of my voice, roaring into the empty street, which had no traffic noise to drown the decibels.

They hadn't expected such a racket. I felt the impetus slacken in them fractionally, and I tore myself out of their grasp and ran. Ran downhill, towards the Intourist. Ran with all the power I could bring to every muscle. Ran like the Olympics.

I heard one of the car doors slam. Heard the car coming behind me. Went on running.

There was life and waiting taxis and people outside the Intourist. There were also the watchers, earning their keep. I wondered fleetingly if watchers ever went to the help of people running away from other people in black cars, and supposed not.

Not in Moscow.

I didn't bother to yell for their help. I simply ran. And I made it. Just.

The men in the car must have decided it was too near the Intourist for them to make another attack, especially as I was now running flat out and not walking along with woolly thoughts. In any case, after it had passed me, the car didn't stop, but accelerated away past the hotel, and turned right at the end of the street, and went out of sight.

I slowed to a fast walk for the last hundred yards, heart thumping madly and chest heaving to take in vast lungfuls of cold wet air. I was nothing like as fit, I thought grimly, as I would have been in any other autumn, when I'd been racing.

I covered the last few yards at ordinary walking pace, and attracted no more eyes than usual when I went in through the big double airlock-type glass entrance. The warmth inside seemed suddenly cloying, stoking up the sweat of exertion: I peeled off my coat and collected my room key, and thought that nothing on earth would persuade me to go back up Gorky Street to retrieve my hat.

My room looked calm and sane, as if to reassure me that hotel guests could not be frighteningly attacked in one of the main streets of the city.

It could happen in Piccadilly, I thought. It could happen in Park Avenue and the Champs Elysées and the Via Veneto. What was so different about Gorky Street?

I threw my coat and room key on to the bed, poured a large reviver from the duty free scotch, and sank on to the sofa to drink it.

Two attacks in one day. Too bloody much.

The first had been a definite attempt to cripple or kill. The second had been – perhaps – an attempt at abduction. Without glasses, I would have been a pushover. They could have got me into the car. And after the drive . . . what destination?

Did the Prince expect me to stick to the task until I was dead? Probably not, I thought; but then the Prince hadn't known what he was sending me into.

More than anything, I'd been lucky. I could be lucky again. Failing that, I had better be careful. My heart gradually steadied. My breath quickened to normal. I drank the scotch, and felt better.

After a while I put down my glass and picked up the tape-recorder. Switched it on. Started methodically beside the window, and made slow comprehensive sweeps of the walls. Top to bottom. Every inch.

There was no whine.

I switched the recorder off and put it down. No whine was inconclusive. It didn't mean no listening probe embedded into the plaster, it meant no listening probe switched on.

I went slowly to bed and lay awake in the dark, thinking about the driver and the passenger in the black car. Apart from general awareness of their age, twenty-three, and height, five-nine, they had left me with three clear impressions. The first was that they knew about my eyesight. The second, that the savage quality I had sensed in their attack was a measure of the ferocity in their minds. And third, that they were not Russian.

They had not spoken, so their voices had given me no clue. They had worn only the sober garb of the Russian man-in-the-street. Their faces had been three-quarters covered, with the result that I had seen only their eyes, and even those, very briefly.

So why did I think . . . ? I pulled the duvet over my shoulders and turned comfortably on to one side. The Russians, I thought drowsily, didn't behave like that unless they were KGB, and if the KGB had wanted to arrest me they would not have done it in that way, and they would not have failed. Other Russians were tamed by deterrents like labour camps, psychiatric hospitals, and the death sentence. Frank's voice drifted back to me from breakfast. 'There are no muggings in Russia. The crime rate is very low indeed. There are practically no murders.'

'Repression is always the outcome of revolution,' I said.

'Are you sure you've got it the right way round?' Mrs Wilkinson asked me, looking puzzled.

'People don't actually like being purged of their lazy and libertine old ways,' I said. 'So you have to force their mouths open, to give them the medicine. Revolutionaries everywhere are by nature aggressive, oppressive, and repressive. It's they who have the power-over-others complex. All for your own good of course.'

I got no rise out of Frank. He merely repeated that in a perfect socialist state like Russia there was no need for crime. The State supplied all needs, and gave to the people whatever it was good for them to have.

Sixty years or so on from the October Revolution (now confusingly celebrated in November owing to the up-dating of the calendar) its wind-sown seeds were germinating their bloody crops around the world, but way back where it all started the second and third generation were not given to acts of private violence.

The eyes looking out of the balaclavas had burned with a hunger for a harvest yet to come: sixty years younger than the blank dull look of a people for whom everything was provided.

10

Frank followed me to GUM the following morning.

When I had gone in through the main door without once looking back, I stood still in the shadows, and watched, and presently he appeared, hurrying a little.

At breakfast, upon Natasha's insistent enquiry, I had said I was going to see some more horse people, but before that I was going to GUM to buy a new hat, as I had lost my last one.

The tiniest frown crossed Frank's face, and he looked at me with a shade of speculation. I remembered that when he had followed me into the hotel the evening before, after I had ostensibly said goodnight to Stephen, I had been wearing the hat. How careful one had to be, I thought, over the most innocent remarks.

'Where did you lose your hat?' he said, showing only friendly interest.

'Must have dropped it in the foyer or the lift,' I said easily, 'I don't really know.'

Natasha suggested I ask at the desk. I would, I said; and did. One learned. If not fast enough, one learned in the end.

I turned away from GUM's main door while Frank was still a little way off, and saw the red woollen hat with a white pompom immediately. Below the hat there were two blue-grey eyes in an elfin face, and straight hair in escaping wisps. She looked too young and slight to be married and a mother, and I could see why nine storeys up with no lifts was a crying disaster.

'Elena?' I said, tentatively.

She nodded a fraction, and turned to walk purposefully away. I followed a few paces behind. For talking to a foreigner she would have to pick her own moment, and it suited me well for it to be out of Frank's sight.

She wore a grey coat with a red scarf falling jauntily over her shoulder, and carried a string bag with a paper-wrapped parcel inside it. I shortened the distance between us and said so that she could hear, 'I want to buy a hat.' She gave no sign of understanding, but when she stopped it was, in fact, outside a shop selling hats.

The inside of GUM was not a department store along Western lines but like those in the Far East; a huge collection of small shops all under one roof. A covered market, two storeys high, with intersecting alleys and a glassed roof far above. Drips of melted snow fell through the cracks in the heavens and made small puddles underfoot.

I bought the hat. Elena waited outside in the alley displaying no interest in me, and set off again when I came out. I looked carefully around for Frank, but couldn't see him. Shoppers blocked every long perspective; and it worked both ways. If I couldn't see him, very likely he couldn't see me.

Elena squeezed through a long queue of stolid people and stopped outside a shop selling folk arts and crafts. She transferred the string bag to my hand with the smallest of movements and no ceremony whatsoever. Her gaze was directed towards the goods in the window, not at me.

'Misha say give you this.' Her accent was light and pretty, but I gathered from the disapproval in her tone that she was on this errand strictly for her brother's sake, and not for mine.

I thanked her for coming.

'Please not bring trouble for him.'

'I promise I won't,' I said.

She nodded briefly, glancing quickly at my face, and away.

'You go now, please,' she said. 'I queue.'

'What is the queue for?'

'Boots. Warm boots, for winter.'

I looked at the queue, which stretched a good way along one of the ground-floor alleys, and up a staircase, and along the gallery above, and away out of sight. It hadn't moved a step forward in five minutes.

'But it will take you all day,' I said.

'Yes. I need boots. When boots come in shop, everyone comes to buy. It is normal. In England, the peasants have no boots. In Soviet Union, we are fortunate.'

She walked away without any more farewell than her brother had given on the metro, and attached herself to the end of the patient line. The only thing that I could think of that England's bootless peasantry would so willingly queue all day for would be Cup Final tickets.

A glance into the tissue-wrapped parcel revealed that what Misha had sent, or what Elena had bought, was a painted wooden doll.

Frank picked me up somewhere between GUM and the pedestrian tunnel under Fiftieth Anniversary et cetera Square. I caught a glimpse of him behind me underground: a split second of unruly curls and college scarf bobbing along in the crowd. If I hadn't been looking, I wouldn't have noticed.

It was already after ten. I lengthened my stride and finished the journey fairly fast, surfacing on the north side of the square and veering left towards the National Hotel.

Parked just beyond the entrance was a small bright yellow car, with, inside it, a large Russian in a high state of fuss.

'Seven minutes late,' he said. 'For seven minutes I sit here illegally. Get in, get in, do not apologize.'

I eased in beside him and he shot off with a crash of gears and a fine disregard for other traffic.

'You have been to GUM,' he said accusingly. 'And therefore you are late.'

I followed the direction of his gaze and began to feel less bewildered by his clairvoyance: he was looking at the printed tissue-paper inside the string bag which Elena had given me. How cautious of her, I thought, to have brought Misha's sovenirs in a wrapping to suit the rendezvous, in a bag any foreign tourist could acquire. A bag, too, I thought contentedly, that friend Frank would not query. The secret of survival in Russia was to be unremarkable.

Yuri Ivanovich Chulitsky revealed himself, during the time I spent with him, as a highly intelligent man with a guilt-ridden love of luxury and a repressed sense of humour. The wrong man for the regime, I thought, but striving to live honourably within its framework. In a country where an out-of-line opinion was a treachery, even if unspoken, he was an unwilling mental traitor. Not to believe what one believes one should believe is a spiritual torment as old as doctrine, and Yuri Chulitsky, I grew to understand, suffered from it dismally.

Physically he was about forty, plumply unfit, with pouches already under his eyes, and a habit of raising the centre of his upper lip to reveal the incisors beneath. He spoke always with deliberation, forming the words carefully and precisely, but that might have been only the effect of using English, and, as on the telephone, he gave the impression that every utterance was double-checked internally before being allowed to escape.

'Cigarette?' he said, offering a packet.

'No . . . thank you.'

'I smoke,' he said, flicking a lighter one-handed with the dexterity of long practice. 'You smoke?'

'Cigars, sometimes.'

He grunted. The fingers on his left hand, resting on the steering-wheel with the cigarette stuck between them, were tanned yellowish brown, but otherwise his fingers were white and flexible, with spatulate tips and short well-tended nails.

'I go see Olympic building,' he said. 'You come?'

'Sure,' I said.

'At Chertanovo.'

'Where?'

'Place for equestrian games. I am architect. I design buildings at Chertanovo.' He pronounced design like dess-in, but his meaning was clear. 'I go today see progress. You understand?'

'Every word,' I said.

'Good. I see in England how equestrian games go. I see need for sort buildings ... ' He stopped and shook his head in frustration.

'You went to see what sort of things happened during international equestrian games, so that you would know what buildings would be needed, and how they should best be designed for dealing with the needs and numbers of the Olympics.'

He smiled lop-sidedly. 'Is right. I go also Montreal. Is not good. Moscow games, we build good.'

The leisurely one-way system in central Moscow meant, it seemed to me, mile-long detours to return to where one started, but facing the other way. Yuri Chulitsky swung his bright little conveyance round the corners without taking his foot noticeably off the accelerator, the bulk of his body making the car's skin seem not much more than a metal overcoat.

At one point, arriving at a junction with a main road, we were stopped dead by a policeman. Yuri Chulitsky shrugged a trifle and switched off the engine.

'What's the matter?' I said.

The main road had, I saw, been totally cleared of traffic. Nothing moved on it. Chulitsky said something under his breath, so I asked again, 'What's the matter? Has there been an accident?'

'No,' he said. 'See lines in road?'

'Do you mean those white ones?'

There were two parallel white lines painted down the centre of the main road, with a space of about six feet between them. I had noticed them on many of the widest streets, but thought of them vaguely as some sort of no-man's-land between the two-way lines of traffic.

'White lines go to Kremlin,' Chulitsky said. 'Politburo people drive to Kremlin in white lines. Every people's car stop.'

I sat and watched. After three or four minutes a long black car appeared, driving fairly fast in lonely state up the centre of the road, between the white lines.

'Chaika,' Chulitsky said, as the limousine slid lengthily past, showing curtains drawn across the rear windows. 'Is official car. Chaika, in English, is seagull.'

He started his engine, and presently the policeman stepped out of the middle of the side road and waved us on our way.

'Was that the Chairman?' I asked.

'No. Many politburo peoples go in Chaika on white lines. All people's cars always stop.'

Democratic, I thought.

The small yellow car sped south of the city, along what he told me was the road to Warsaw, but which to my eyes was plainly labelled M4.

He said, 'Nikolai Alexandrovich Kropotkin say tell you what you ask. You ask. I tell.'

'I'm looking for someone called Alyosha.'

'Alyosha? Many people called Alyosha. Nikolai Alexandrovich say find Alyosha for Randall Drew. Who is this Alyosha?'

'That's the problem,' I said. 'I don't know, and I haven't been able to find out. No one seems to know who he is.' I paused. 'Did you meet Hans Kramer in England?'

'*Da*. German. He die.'

'That's right. Well . . . he knew Alyosha. The autopsy said Kramer died of a heart attack, but people near him when he died thought he was saying that Alyosha had caused him to have a heart attack. Er . . . have I said that clearly enough?'

'Yes. Is clear. About Alyosha, I cannot help.'

I supposed I would have been surprised if he had said anything different.

'You have been asked before, about Alyosha?' I said.

'Please?'

'An Englishman came to see you at the Olympic committee building. He saw you and the two colleagues who went with you to England.'

'Is right,' he agreed gruffly. 'Is writing for newspaper.'

'Malcolm Herrick.'

'*Da*.'

'You all said you knew nothing at all about anything.'

A long pause; then he said, 'Herrick is foreigner. Comrades not say things to Herrick.'

He relapsed into silence, and we drove steadily along the Warsaw highway, leaving the city centre behind and making for another lot of egg-box suburbs. Some light powdery snow began to fall, and Yuri switched on the windscreen wipers.

'Today, tomorrow, it snow. This snow not melt. Stay all winter.'

'Do you like the winter?' I said.

'No. Winter is bad for building. Today is last day is possible see progress of buildings at Chertanovo. So I go now.'

I said I would be most interested in the buildings, if he felt like showing me round. He laughed in a small deep throaty rumble, but offered no explanation.

I asked him if he had personally known Hans Kramer, but he had spoken to him only about buildings. 'Well . . . Johnny Farringford?' I asked.

'Johnny ... Farringford. Are you saying *Lord* Farringford? Is a man with red hairs? Ride in British team?'

'That's the one,' I said.

'I see him many times. Many places. I talk with him. I ask him about buildings. He is no good about buildings. I ask other peoples. Other peoples is more good.' He stopped, obviously unimpressed by the planning ability of earls, and we drove four or five miles while he seemed to be thinking deeply about anything except my mission: but finally, as if coming to a difficult decision, he said, 'Is not good Lord Farringford come to Olympics.'

I held my breath. Damped down every quick and excited question. Managed in the end to say without even a quaver, 'Why?'

He had relapsed however into further dep thought.

'Tell me,' I said, without pressure.

'It is for my country good if he come. It is for your country not good. If I tell you, I speak against the good for my country. It is difficult for me.'

'Yes,' I said.

After a long way he turned abruptly off the M4 to the right, along a lesser, but still dual-carriageway road. There was, as usual, very little traffic, and without much ado he swung round in a U turn across the central reservation to face the way we had come. He pulled in by the roadside and stopped with a jerk.

On our left the road was lined as far as the eye could see with rows of apartment buildings, greyish white. On our right there was a large flat snow-sprinkled space bordered on the far side by a stretch of black-looking forest of spindly young trees packed tightly together. On the side near the road there was a wire fence, and between the fence and the road itself, a wide ditch full of white half-melted slush.

'Is there,' Yuri said, pointing into this far from promising landscape with a gleam of relaxed humour, 'equestrian games.'

'Ye gods,' I said.

We got out of the car into the bitter air. I looked away down the road in the direction we had originally been travelling. There were tall concrete lamp standards, electricity pylons, dense black forest on the left, white unending impersonal apartment blocks on the right, a grey double road with no traffic, and, at the side, wet white snow. Over it all softly fell the powdery forerunners of the winter freeze. It was silent and ugly and as desolate as a desert.

'In summer,' Yuri said, 'forest is green. Is beautiful place for equestrian games. Is grass. Everything beautiful.'

'I'll take your word for it,' I said.

Further along, on the side of the road where we had stopped, there were two large hoardings, one bearing a long announcement about the Olympics, and the other sporting a big picture of the stadium as it was one day going to be. The stands looked most ingenious, shaped like a Z, with the top and bottom ranks of the seats facing one way, and the centre rank facing the other. Events, it appeared, would take place on both sides of the stands.

Yuri gestured to me to return to the car, and he drove us through a gate in the wire, on to the site itself. There were a few men there driving mechanical earth-movers, though how they knew what they were moving was a mystery to me, as the whole place looked a sea of jumbled mud with pools of icy slush amid the usual broken white blanket of half-melted snow.

Yuri reached into the space behind my seat and brought forth a huge pair of thigh-high gumboots. These he put on by planting them firmly outside the opened car door, removing his walking shoes, wrapping his trousers round his legs, and sinking his feet into the depths as he stood up.

'I talk to men,' he said. 'You wait.'

Superfluous advice, I thought. Yuri unfastened his ear-flaps against the chill wind and talked to his men, trudging about and making sweeping gestures with his arms. After a fair while he returned and reversed the gumboot process, tucking the now wet and muddy objects in behind his own driving seat.

'Is good,' he said, lifting the centre of his lip and giving me a gleam of teeth. 'We finish foundations. In spring, when snow melt, we build quickly. Stadium,' he pointed. 'Stables.' He pointed again. 'Restaurants, buildings for riders, buildings for officials, buildings for television. There,' he waved an arm at a huge slightly undulating area bordered by forest, 'is cross-country for trials, like Badminton and Burghley. In summer, is beautiful.'

'Will everyone who wants to come to the Games get visas?' I said.

'*Da*. All people have visas.'

'It isn't always like that.' I said neutrally, and he replied in the same level tone. 'For Olympics, all people have visas. Stay in hotels. Is good.'

'What about the Press?' I said. 'And the television people?'

'We build Press building for foreign Press. Also television building for foreign television peoples, near Moscow television building. Use same . . . ' He described a transmitting mast with his hands. 'Foreign peoples go only in these buildings. In England, we ask Press people about Press buildings. We see what Press peoples need. We ask many Press people. We ask Herrick.'

'Herrick?' I said. 'Did you ask him in England, or in Moscow?'

'In England. He help us. He come to Burghley. We see him with Lord Farringford. So we ask him. We ask many peoples about buildings. We ask Hans Kramer about buildings. He was . . . ' Words failed him but gestures did not. Hans Kramer, I gathered, had given the Russian observers a decisively rude brush-off.

He tied up the ear-flaps of his hat without taking it off. I spent the time scanning the road for anything that looked like a following car, but saw nothing of note. A bus passed, its tyres making a swishing noise on the slushy tarmac. I thought that the low level of traffic on most roads would make a following car conspicuous: but on the other hand there seemed to be very little variety in make, so that one car tended to look exactly like the next. Difficult to spot a tail. Easy, however, to follow a bright yellow box on wheels.

'What sort of car is this?' I said.

'Zhiguli,' he said. 'Is my car.' He seemed proud of it. 'Not many peoples have car. I am architect, have car.'

'Is it expensive?' I asked.

'Car expensive. Petrol cheap. Driving examination, very difficult.'

He finished the bow on his hat, checked that his boots were inside, slammed the door, and backed briskly out on to the road.

'How is everyone going to get here?' I said. 'Competitors and spectators.'

'We build metro. New station.' He thought. 'Metro on top of ground, not deep. New metro for Chertanovo peoples. Many new buildings here. Chertanovo is new place. I show you.'

We set off back towards the Warsaw highway, but before we reached it he turned off to the right, and drove up another wide road where apartment blocks were springing up like mushrooms. All whitish grey; all nine storeys high, marching away into the distance.

'In Soviet all people have house,' Yuri said. 'Rent is cheap. In England, expensive.' He shot me an amused look as if challenging me to argue with his simplistic statement. In a country where everything was owned by the state, there was no point in charging high rents. To enable people to pay high rents, or high prices for electricity, transport and telephones, for that matter, it would be necessary to pay higher wages. Yuri Chulitsky knew it as well as I did. I would have to be careful, I told myself, not to underestimate the subtlety of his thoughts because of the limitations of the English they were expressed in.

'Can I make a trade with you?' I said. 'A bargain? One piece of information in exchange for another?'

For that I got a quick, sharp, piercing glance, but all he said was, 'Car need petrol.' He pulled off the road into a station with pumps, and removed himself from the car to talk to the attendant.

I found myself taking off my glasses and polishing the already clean lenses. The playing-for-time gesture, which was not at that moment needed. I wondered if it had been intuitively sparked off by Yuri's purchase of petrol, which seemed hardly urgent as the tank was well over half full, according to the gauge.

While I watched, the needle crept round to full. Yuri paid and returned to the car, and we set off back towards the city centre.

'What information you exchange?' he said.

'I don't have it all yet.'

A muscle twitched beside his mouth. 'You diplomat?' he said.

'A patriot. Like you.'

'You tell me information.'

I told him a great deal. I told him what had really happened at the Hippodrome, not Kropotkin's watered-down version, and I told him of the attack in Gorky Street. I also told him, though without names or places or details, the gist of what Boris Telyatnikov had overheard, and the inferences one could draw from it. He listened, as any faithful Russian would, with a growing sense of dismay. When I stopped, he drove a good way without speaking, and in the end his comment was oblique.

'You want lunch?' he said.

II

He took me to what he called the Architects' Circle and in the big basement restaurant there, gave me food I hadn't believed existed in Moscow. Prime smoked salmon, delicious ham off the bone, tender red beef. An apple and some grapes. Vodka to toss off for starters, followed by excellent red wine. Good strong coffee at the end. He himself ate and drank with as much enjoyment as I did.

'Marvellous,' I said appreciatively. 'Superb.'

Yuri leaned back at last and lit a cigarette, and told me that every profession had its Circle. There was a Writers' Circle, for instance, to which all Soviet writers belonged. If they did not belong to the Circle, they did not get published. They could of course be expelled from the Circle, if it was considered that what they wrote was not suitable. Yuri's manner dared me to suggest that he didn't entirely agree with this system.

'What about architects?' I asked mildly.

Architects, I gathered, had to be politically sound, if they wished to be members of the Architects' Circle. Naturally, if one did not belong to the circle, one was not allotted anything to design.

Naturally.

I drank my coffee and made no remark. Yuri watched me, and smiled with a touch of melancholy.

'I give information,' he said, 'about Lord Farringford.'

'Thank you.'

'You are clever man.' He sighed and shrugged resignedly, and kept his side of the bargain. 'Lord Farringford is foolish man. With Hans Kramer, he go bad places. Sex places.' Distaste showed in his face, and the top lip lifted even further off the incisors. 'In London, is disgusting pictures. In the street. All people can see. Disgusting.' He searched for a word. 'Dirty.'

'Yes,' I said.

'Lord Farringford and Hans Kramer go into these places. Three, four times.

'Are you sure it was more than once?' I said attentively.

'Sure. We see. We . . . follow.' The confession came out on a downward inflection, drifting off into silence, as if he hadn't quite said what he had.

Wow, I thought: and what I said, without any emphasis of any sort, was, 'Why did you follow?'

He struggled a great deal with his conscience, but he told me what I was sure was the truth.

'Comrade with me, he look in England and in many country for foolish peoples. When foolish peoples come to Soviet Union, comrade use . . . make . . .'

'Your comrade makes use of them through their liking for pornography?'

He blew out a sharp breath.

'And if Farringford comes to the Olympics, your comrade will make use of him?'

Silence.

'What use could Farringford be? He isn't a diplomat . . .' I stopped, thought, and went on more slowly. 'Do you mean,' I said, 'that in return for not . . . embarrassing the British people, for not exposing a scandalous misdemeanour into which your comrade has lured him, your comrade will demand some concession from the British government?'

'Say again,' he said.

I said it again, more forthrightly. 'Your comrade traps Farringford into a dirty mess. Your comrade says to the British government, give me what I want, or I publish the mess.'

He didn't directly admit it. 'The comrades of my comrade,' he said.

'Yes,' I agreed. 'Those comrades.'

'Farringford is rich man,' Yuri said. 'For rich man, comrade feel . . . ' He didn't know the word, but his meaning was unmistakable, and it was contempt.

'For all rich men?' I said.

'Of course. Rich man bad. Poor man good.' He spoke with utter conviction and no suggestion of cynicism, stating, I supposed, one of humanity's most fundamental beliefs. Camels through eyes of needles, and all that. Rich men never got to heaven, and serve them right. Which left absolutely no hope of eternal bliss for Randall Drew, who had an unequal share of this world's goods . . . If I warned Johnny Farringford, I wondered, putting a stop to my dribbling thoughts, would it be enough? Or would it really be wiser for him to stay at home?

'Yuri,' I said, 'how about another bargain?'

'Explain.'

'If I learn more here, I will exchange it for a promise that your comrade will not try to trap Farringford, if he comes to the Olympics.'

He stared. 'You ask things impossible.'

'A promise in writing,' I said.

'Is impossible. Comrade with me . . . impossible.'

297

'Yeah . . . Well, it was just a thought.' I reflected. 'Then if I learn more, I would exchange it for information about Alyosha.'

Yuri studied the tablecloth and I studied Yuri.

'I cannot help,' he said.

He stubbed out his cigarette and raised his eyes to meet mine. I was aware of a fierce intensity of thought going on behind the steady gaze, but upon what subject I couldn't guess.

'I take you,' he said finally, 'to Intourist Hotel.'

He dropped me in fact round the corner outside the National, where he had picked me up, implying, though not saying, that there was no sense in engaging the attention of the watchers unnecessarily.

It was by that time growing dark, as for various reasons our lunch had been delayed in arrival and leisurely in the eating, not least because of a wedding party going on in the next room. The bride had worn a long white dress and a minuscule veil. Did they get married in church? I asked. Of course not, Yuri said: it was not allowed. Pagan rituals, it seemed, had survived the rise and fall of Christianity.

The powdery snowfall of the morning had thickened into a determined regularity, but by no means into a raging blizzard. The wind, in fact, had dropped, but so had the temperature, and there was a threatening bite to the cold. I walked the short distance from one hotel to the other among a crowd of hurrying pedestrians and no men in black cars attempted to pick me off.

I arrived at the Intourist entrance at the same time as the Wilkinsons and their package tour, fresh back from the coach trip to Zagorsk.

'It was quite interesting,' said Mrs Wilkinson gamely, pushing through into the suddenly crowded foyer. 'I couldn't hear the guide very well, and it seemed wrong somehow, guided tours going in through churches, when there were people in there praying. Did you know that they don't have any chairs in Russian churches? No pews. Everyone has to stand all the time. My feet are fair killing me. There's a lot of snow out in the country. Dad slept most of the way, didn't you, Dad?'

Dad morosely nodded.

Mrs Wilkinson, along with nearly everyone else on the bus tour, carried a white plastic bag with a green and orange swirly pattern on it.

'There was a tourist shop there. You know, foreign currency shop. I bought ever such a pretty matroshka.'

'What's a matroshka?' I said, waiting beside her at the desk, to collect our room keys.

'One of these,' she said, fishing into the white plastic depths and tearing off some tissue-paper. 'These dolls.'

She produced with a small flourish an almost identical double of the fat brightly-coloured wooden doll I too carried in the string bag dangling from my left hand.

'I think matroshka means little mother,' she said. 'Anyway, you know, they pull apart and there's another smaller one inside, and you go right down to a tiny one in the middle. There are nine inside here. I'm going to give it to my grandchildren.' She beamed with simple pleasure, and I beamed right back. If only all the world, I thought regretfully, were as wholesome and as harmless as the Wilkinsons.

Wholesome and harmless did, I supposed, describe the outward appearance of my tidy room upstairs, but this time, when I swept the walls with the tape-recorder, I heard the whine. High-pitched, assaulting the ear, and originating from a spot about five feet up from the floor, and about midway along the bed. I switched off the recorder and wondered who, if anyone, was listening.

The matroshka doll which Elena had handed me proved, on a closer look, to be a well-worn specimen with paint scratched off all over her pink-cheeked face and bright blue dress and yellow apron. In shape she was a very large elongated egg, slightly smaller round the head than lower down, and flat at the bottom, in order to stand. In all, about ten inches high and rotund in circumference.

Pull apart she should, Mrs Wilkinson had said, and pull apart she did, across the middle, though either the two halves were a naturally tight fit, or else Misha or Elena had used some sort of glue. I tugged and wrenched, and the little mother finally gave birth with a reluctant jerk and scattered her close-packed secrets all over the sofa.

I collected Misha's souvenirs of England and laid them out on the dressing-table shelf; a row of valueless bits and pieces brought home by an unsophisticated young rider.

Easily the largest in size was the official programme of the International Event, printed in English but with the results and winners written in, in several places, in Russian script. The programme had been rolled to fit into the mastroshka doll, and lay in an opening tube with the pages curling.

There were two picture postcards, unused, with views of London. A brown envelope containing a small bunch of wilted grass. An empty packet of Players cigarettes. A small metal ashtray with a horse's head painted on the front, and 'Made in England' stamped into the back. A flat tin of mentholated cough pastilles. Several pieces of paper and small cards with writing on, and, finally, the things which had come from the vet's stolen case.

Stephen had been right in thinking that Misha's share had not been very much, and I wondered what in fact he had made of it, with all the wording on the labels being in English.

There were four flat two by two inch sachets of a powder called Equipalazone, each sachet containing one gram of phenylbutazone B Vet C, otherwise known succinctly in the horse world as 'bute'.

I had used the drug countless times myself, in ten years of training my own horses, as it was the tops at reducing inflammation and pain in strained and injured legs. In Eventing and show jumping one could give it to the horses up to the minute they performed, but in British racing, though not in some other countries, it had to be out of the system before the 'off'. Bute might be the subject of controversy and dope tests, but it was also about as easy to get hold of as aspirins, and one did not have to get it through a vet. The amount that Misha had brought home was roughly a single day's dose.

There was next a small plastic tub of sulphanilamide powder, which was useful for putting on wounds, to dry and heal them: and a sample-sized round tin of gamma benzine hexachloride, which, as far as I could remember, was anti-louse powder. There was a small, much folded advertisement leaflet extolling a cure for ringworm; and that was all.

No barbiturates. No pethidine. No steroids. Either Kramer, or the German lad, had cleaned out the lot.

Well, I thought, as I began to pack everything back into the doll; so much for that. I went through everything again, more thoroughly, just to make sure. Opened up the sample-sized tin of louse powder, which contained louse powder, and the small plastic tub of sulphanilamide powder, which contained sulphanilamide powder. Or at least I supposed they did. If the two white powders were actually LSD or heroin, I wasn't sure that I would know.

The Equipalazone sachets were foil-packed, straight from the manufacturers, and hadn't been tampered with. I stuffed them back into the doll.

There was nothing lodged between the leaves of the programme. I shook it; nothing fell out. The writings on the pieces of card and paper were some in Russian and some in German, and I laid these aside for a translation from Stephen. The empty cigarette packet contained no cigarettes, or anything else, and the small tin of cough lozenges contained . . . er . . . no cough lozenges. The tin of cough lozenges contained another piece of paper, much handled and wrinkled, and three very small glass phials in a bed of cotton wool.

The phials were of the same size and shape as those I had for adrenalin: tiny glass capsules less than two inches in length, with a much-narrowed neck a third of the way along, which snapped off, so that one could put a hypodermic needle through the resulting opening, and down into the liquid, to draw it up. Each phial in the tin contained one millilitre of colourless liquid, enough for one human-sized injection. Half a teaspoonful. Not enough, to my mind, for a horse.

I held one of the phials up in the light, to see the printing on it, but as usual with such baby ampoules it was difficult to see the lettering. Not adrenalin. As far as I could make out, it said 0.4 mg naloxone, which was spectacularly unhelpful, as I'd never heard of the stuff. I unfolded the piece of paper, and that was no better, as whatever was written there was written in Russian script. I put the paper back in the tin and closed it, and set it aside with the other mysteries for Stephen to look at.

Stephen himself had planned to spend the day between lectures and Gudrun, but had said he would be near the telephone from four o'clock onwards, if I should want him. It frankly didn't seem worthwhile for me to traipse up to the University, or for him to come down, to decipher Misha's bits of paper, without first seeing if it could be done by wires; so I rang him.

'How's it going?' he said.

'The walls are whining.'

'Oh cripes.'

'Anyway,' I said, 'if I spell some German words out to you, can you tell me what they mean?'

'If you think it's wise.'

'Stop me if you don't think so,' I said.

'OK.'

'Right. Here goes with the first.' I read out, letter by letter, as far as I could judge, the three lines of German handwriting on one of the cards.

Stephen was laughing by the end. 'It says "With all good wishes for today and the future, Volker Springer." That's a man's name.'

'Good God.'

I looked at the other cards more attentively, and saw something I had entirely missed. At the bottom of one of them, signed with a flourish, was a name I knew.

I read out that card too, letter by letter.

'It says,' Stephen said, '"Best memories of a very good time in England. Your friend . . ." Your friend who?'

'Hans Kramer,' I said.

'Bull's eye.' Stephen's voice crackled in my ear. 'Are those by any chance Misha's souvenirs?'

'Yes.'

'Autographs, no less. Anything else?'

'One or two things in Russian. They'll have to wait until tomorrow morning.'

'I'll be with you at ten, then. Gudrun sends her love.'

I put the receiver down, and almost immediately the bell rang again. A female English voice, calm, cultured, and on the verge of boredom.

'Is that Randall Drew?'

'Yes,' I said.

'Polly Paget here,' she said. 'Cultural attaché's office, at the Embassy.'

'How nice to speak to you.'

I had a vivid picture of her; short hair, long cardigan, flat shoes and common sense.

'A telex has just come for you. Ian Young asked me to phone and tell you, in case you were waiting for it.'

'Yes, please,' I said. 'Could you read it to me?'

'Actually, it is complicated, and very long. It really would be better, I think, if you came to collect it. It would take a good half hour for me to dictate it while you write it down, and to be honest I don't want to waste the time. I've a lot still to do, and it's Friday evening, and we're shutting down soon for the weekend.'

'Is Ian there?' I asked.

'No, he left a few minutes ago. And Oliver is out on official business.

There's just me holding the fort. If you want your message before Monday, I'm afraid it means coming to get it.'

'How does it start?'

With an audible sigh and a rustle of paper, she began, 'Hans Wilhelm Kramer, born July 3rd, 1941, in Dusseldorf, Germany, only child of Heinrich Johannes Kramer, industrialist . . .'

'Yes, all right,' I said, interrupting. 'I'll come. How long will you be there?' I had visions of uncooperative taxis, of having to walk.

'An hour or so. If you're definitely coming, I'll wait for you.'

'You're on,' I said. 'Warm the scotch.'

Having grown a little wilier I engaged a taxi to drive me to the far side of the bridge, pointing to a street map to show where I meant. The road over the bridge, I had found, extended into the Warsaw highway and was the road we had taken to Chertanovo. In another couple of days I would have Moscow's geography in my head for ever.

I paid off the driver and stepped out into the falling snow, which had increased to the point of flakes as big as rose petals and as clinging as love. They settled on my sleeve as I shut the taxi's door, and on my shoulders, and on every flat surface within sight. I found I had stupidly forgotten my gloves. I thrust my hands in my pockets, and turned down the steps to the lower road, to turn there along to the Embassy.

It had seemed to me that I was unfollowed and safe; but I was wrong. The tigers were waiting under the bridge.

They had learned a few lessons from the abortive mission in Gorky Street.

For a start, they had chosen a less public place. The only sanctuary within running distance was now not the big bustling well-lit mouth of the Intourist Hotel, but the heavily-closed front door of the Embassy, with an obstructive guard outside at the gate.

They had learned that my reflexes weren't the slowest on record, and also that I had no inhibitions about kicking them back.

There were still only two of them, but this time they were armed. Not with guns, but with riot sticks. Nasty hard things like baseball bats, swinging from a loop of leather round the wrist.

The first I knew of it was when one chunk of timber connected shatteringly with the side of my head. The fur ear-flaps perhaps saved my skull from being cracked right open, but I reeled dizzily, bewildered, not realizing what had happened, spinning under the weight of the blow.

I had a second's clear view of them, like a snapshot. Two figures in the streetlights against the dark shadows under the bridge. The snow falling more sparsely in the bridge's shelter. The arms raised, with the heavy truncheons swinging.

They were the same men: no doubt of it. The same brutal quality, the same quick ferocity, the same unmerciful eyes looking out of the same bala-clavas. The same message that human rights were a laugh.

I stumbled, and my hat fell off, and I tried to protect myself with my arms, but it wasn't much good. There's a limit to the damage even a riot stick can do through thick layers of jacket and overcoat, so that to an extent the onslaught was disorientating more than lethal, but bash numbers three or four by-passed my feeble barriers and knocked off my glasses. I stretched for them, tried to catch them, got hit on the hand, and lost them entirely in the falling snow.

It seemed to be all they were waiting for. The battering stopped, and they grabbed me instead. I kicked and punched at targets I could no longer pro-perly see, and did too little damage to stop the rot.

It felt as though they were trying to lift me up, and for a fraction of time I couldn't think why. Then I remembered where we were. On the road beside the river . . . which flowed along uncaringly on the other side of the breast-high wall.

Desperation kept me struggling when there was absolutely no reasonable hope.

I had seen the Moscow River from several bridges, and everywhere its banks were the same. Not sloping grassy affairs shading gently into the water, but grey perpendicular walls rising straight from the river bed to about eight feet above the surface of the water. They looked like defences against flooding more than tourist attractions: designed to keep everything between them from getting out.

I clung grimly to whatever I could reach. I tore at their faces. At their hands. I raised from one of them a grunt and from the other a muttered word in a language I didn't recognize.

I didn't rationally think that anyone would come along the road and beat them off. I fought only because while I was still on the road I was alive, but if I hit the water I would be as good as dead. Instinct and anger, and nothing else.

It was hopeless, really. They had me off my feet, and I was being bundled over. I carried on with the limpet act. I pulled the knitted balaclava clean off one of them, but whatever he might have feared, I still couldn't have sworn to a positive identification. One of the streetlights was shining full on his face and I saw him as if he'd been drawn by Picasso.

In my racing days I had kept my glasses anchored by a double headstrap of elastic, a handy gadget now gathering dust with my five-pound saddle. It had never crossed my mind that it might mean the difference between life or death in Moscow.

They pushed and shoved, and more and more of my weight was trans-ferred over the wall. It all seemed both agonizingly fast and painfully endless: a few seconds of physical flurry that stretched in my mind like eternity.

I was hanging on to the parapet and life with one hand, the rest of me dangling over the water.

They swung, as I had time to realize, one of the riot sticks. There was an excruciating slam on my fingers. I stopped being able to use them, and dropped off the wall like a leech detached.

12

Winter had already penetrated the Moscow River. I went down under the surface, and the sudden incredible cold was the sort of numbing punching shock which Arctic Ocean bathers don't survive.

I kicked my way up into the air, but I knew in my heart that the battle was lost. I felt weak and half-blind, and it was dark, and thickly snowing. The temperature made me breathless, and my right hand had no feeling. My clothes got heavier as they saturated. Soon they would drag me under. The current carried me down river, under the bridge and out the other side, away from the Embassy; and even while I tried to shout for help I thought that the only people who would hear me would be the two who wouldn't give it.

The yell, in any case, turned into a mouthful of icy water; and that seemed the final reality.

Lethargy began slowing my attempts to swim and dulling my brain. Resolution ebbed away. Coherent thought was ending. I was anaesthetized by cold: a lump of already mindless matter with all other bodily systems freezing fast to a halt, sinking without will or means to struggle.

I began, in fact, to die.

I dimly heard a voice calling.

'Randall . . . Randall . . .'

A bright light shone on my face.

'Randall, this way. Hold on . . .'

I couldn't hold on. My legs had given their last feeble kick. The only direction left was downwards into a deep numbing death.

Something fluffy fell on my face. Fluffier and of more substance than snow. I was past using a hand to grab it, past even thinking that I should. But somewhere in the last vestiges of consciousness an instinct must still have been working, because I opened my mouth to whatever had fallen across it, and bit it.

I held a lot of soft stuff between my teeth. There was a tug on it, as if something was pulling. I gripped it tighter.

Another tug. My head, which had been almost under water, came up again a few inches.

A sluggish thought crept back along the old mental pathways. If I held on to the line I might be pulled out on to the bank, like a fish.

I should hold on, I vaguely thought, with more than my teeth.

Hands.

There was a problem about hands.

Couldn't feel them.

'Randall, hold on. There's a ladder along here.'

I heard the words, and they sounded silly. How could I climb a ladder when I couldn't feel my hands?

All the same, I was awake enough to know that I had been given one last tiny chance, and I clenched my jaws over the soft lifeline with a grip that only total blackout might loosen.

The line pulled me against the wall.

'Hold on,' yelled the voice. 'It's along here. Not far. Just hold on.'

I was bumping along the wall. Not far might be too far. Not far was as far as the sun.

'Here it is,' shouted the voice. 'Can you see it? Just beside you. I'll shine the torch on it. There. Grab hold, can't you?'

Grab hold. Of what?

I lay there like a log.

'Jesus Christ,' said the voice. The light came on my face again, and then went off. I heard sounds coming nearer, coming down the river side of the wall.

'Give me your hands.'

I couldn't.

I felt someone lift up my right arm, pulling it by the sleeve out of the water.

'Jesus Christ,' he said again; and dropped it back.

He pulled my left arm out.

'Hold on with that,' he commanded, and I felt him trying to curl my fingers round some sort of horizontal bar.

'Look,' he said. 'You've got to climb out of the bloody river. You're bloody nearly dead, do you know that? You've been in there too bloody long. And if you don't get out within a minute, bloody nothing will save you. Do you hear that? For Christ's sake . . . *climb*.'

I couldn't see what I was supposed to climb, even if I had the strength. I felt him put my right arm up again out of the water, and I thought he was trying to thread my right hand behind the horizontal bar until I had the bar against my wrist.

'Put your feet on one of the steps under the water,' he said. 'Feel for them. The ladder goes down a long way.'

I began vaguely to understand. Tried to lodge a foot on an underwater horizontal bar, and by some miracle found one. He felt the faint support to my weight.

'Right. The bars are only a foot apart. I'll put your left hand up to the next one. And whatever you do, don't let your right hand slip out.'

I dredged up the last remnants of refrigerated strength and pushed, and rose twelve inches up the wall.

'That's right,' said the voice above me, sounding heartily relieved. 'Now keep bloody going, and don't fall off.'

I kept bloody going and I didn't fall off, though it seemed like Mount Everest and the Matterhorn rolled into one. At some point when half of me was out of the water I opened my mouth and let the fluffy but now sodden thing fall out: and there was an exclamation from above and presently the line was tied round my left wrist instead.

He went up the ladder above me, still cursing, still instructing, still yelling at me to hurry up.

Step by slow step, we ascended. When I reached the top he was standing on the far side, grabbing hold of me to roll me over on to the flat solid land. My legs buckled helplessly as they touched down, and I ended in a dripping heap on the snow-covered ground.

'Take your coat and jacket off,' he commanded. 'Don't you realize cold kills as fast as bloody bullets?'

I could crookedly see him in the streetlights, but it was his voice I at last conclusively recognized, though I supposed that at some point up the wall I had sub-consciously known.

'Frank,' I said.

'Yes. Get on with it. Look, let me unbutton this.' His fingers were strong and quick. 'Take them off.' He tugged fiercely and stripped off the clinging wet sleeves. 'Shirt too.' He ripped it off, so that the snow fell on to my bare skin. 'Now put this on.' He guided my arms into something dry and warm, and he buttoned up the front.

'Right,' he said. 'Now you'll bloody well have to walk back to the bridge. It's only about a hundred yards. Get up, Randall, and *come on.*'

There was a sharp edge to his voice, and it struck me that it was because he too was feeling cold, because whatever it was that was sheltering me had come off him. I stumbled along with him on rubbery knees and kept wanting to laugh weakly at the irony of things in general. Didn't have enough breath, however, for such frivolities.

When I nearly walked into a lamp post he said irritably, 'Can't you see?'

'Lost my g-glasses,' I said.

'Do you mean,' he said incredulously, 'that you can't even see a bloody big lamp standard without them?'

'Not . . . reliably.'

'Jesus Christ.'

Inside his coat my whole body was shuddering, chilled deep into the realms of hypothermia. Although they were apparently functioning, my legs didn't feel as if they belonged to me, and there was still a pervading wuzziness in the thinking department.

We arrived at a flight of steps and toiled upwards to the main road. A black car rolled up and stopped beside us with amazing promptness. Frank threw my wet coats into the back of the car and shovelled me in after them. He himself sat in the front, instructing the driver briefly in Russian, with the result that we went round the by now familiar and lengthy one-way system and arrived in due course outside the Intourist Hotel.

Frank took my coats and escorted me through the front doors into the embrace of the central heating. He collected my room key without asking me the number. Shovelled me into the lift, pressed the button for the eighth floor, and saw me to my door. He fitted the key, and turned it, and steered me inside.

'What are you going to do, if you can't see?' he said.

'G . . . got a s . . . spare pair.'

'Where?'

'T . . . top drawer.'

'Sit down,' he said, practically pushing me on to the sofa; and only the tiniest push was necessary. I heard him opening the drawer, and presently he put the reserves into my hands. I fumbled them on to my nose and again the world took on its proper shape.

He was looking at me with unexpected concern, his face firm and intelligent: but even while I watched the hawk-like quality dissolved, and the features slackened into the mediocrity we saw at meals.

He was wearing, I saw, only a sweater over his shirt, and, wound round his neck, his long striped college scarf. My life-line.

I said, 'I'd b . . . better give you your coat,' and tried to undo the buttons. The fingers of my right hand seemed both feeble and painful, so I did them with the left.

'You'd better have a hot bath,' he said diffidently. No decision, no swearing, no immense effectiveness in sight.

'Yes,' I said. 'Thanks.'

His eyes flickered. 'Lucky I happened along.'

'Luckiest thing in my life.'

'I was just out for a walk,' he said. 'I saw you get out of a taxi ahead and go down those steps. Then I heard a shout and a splash, and I thought it couldn't possibly be you, of course, but anyway I thought I'd better see. So I went down after you, and luckily I had my torch with me, and well . . . there you are.'

He had omitted to ask how I could have fallen accidentally over a breast-high wall.

I said obligingly, 'It's all a bit of a blank, actually,' and it undoubtedly pleased him.

He helped me out of his coat and into my dressing-gown.

'Will you be all right, then?' he said.

'Fine.'

He seemed to want to go, and I made no move to stop him. He picked up his torch and his hat, from where they were lying on the sofa, and his coat, and, murmuring something about me getting the hotel to dry my clothes, he extricated himself from what must have been to him a slightly embarrassing proximity.

I felt very odd indeed. Hot and cold at the same time, and a little light-headed. I took off the rest of my clammy clothes and left them in a damp heap on the bathroom floor.

The fingers on my right hand were in dead trouble. They hadn't bled much because of their immersion in ice-water, but there were nasty tears in the skin of three of them from nails to knuckles, and no strength anywhere at all.

I looked at my watch, but it had stopped.

I really had to get a grip on things, I thought. I really had to start functioning. It was imperative.

I went over to the telephone and dialled the number of the University, foreign students department. Stephen was fetched, sounding amiable.

'Something else?' he said.

'What time is it? My watch has stopped.'

'You didn't ring just to ask me that? It's five-past-six, actually.'

Five-past-six . . . it seemed incredible. It was only three-quarters of an hour since I had set off to the Embassy. Seemed more like three-quarters of a century.

'Look,' I said. 'Will you do me a great favour? Will you go . . .' I stopped. A wave of malaise travelled dizzily around my outraged nervous system. My breath came out in a weird groaning cough.

Stephen said slowly, 'Are you all right?'

'No,' I said. 'Look . . . will you go to the British Embassy, and pick up a telex which is waiting there for me, and bring it to the Intourist? I wouldn't ask, but . . . if I don't get it tonight I can't have it until Monday . . . and be careful . . . because we have rough friends . . . At the Embassy, ask for Polly Paget in the cultural attaché's office.'

'Have the rough friends had another go with a horse box?' he said anxiously. 'Is that why you can't go yourself?'

'Sort of.'

'All right,' he said. 'I'm on my way.'

I put the receiver back in its cradle and wasted a few minutes feeling sorry for myself. Then I decided to ring Polly Paget, and couldn't remember the number.

The number was on a sheet of paper in my wallet. My wallet was or had been in the inside pocket of my jacket. My jacket was wet, and in the bathroom, where Frank had put it. I screwed up the energy, and went to look.

One wallet, still in the pocket, but, not surprisingly, comprehensively

damp. I fished out and unfolded the list of telephone numbers and was relieved to see‹ they could still be read.

Polly Paget sounded annoyed that I had not even started out.

'I've finished my jobs,' she said crossly. 'I want to leave now.'

'A friend is coming instead of me,' I said. 'Stephen Luce. He'll be there
soon. Please do wait.'

'Oh very well.'

'And could you give me Ian Young's phone number? Where he lives, I
mean.'

'Hang on.' She went away, and came back, and read out the number.
'That's his flat here in the Embassy grounds. As far as I know, he'll be home
most of the weekend. Like all of us. Nothing much ever happens in
Moscow.'

Lady, I thought, you're a hundred per cent wrong.

Stephen came, and brought Gudrun.

I had spent the interval putting on dry pants, trousers and socks, and lying
on the bed. I disregarded Frank's advice about hot baths, on the Ophelia
principle that I'd had too much of water already. It would be just too
damned silly to pass out and drown surrounded by white tiles.

Stephen's cheerful grin faded rapidly.

'You look like death. Whatever's happened?'

'Did you bring the telex?'

'Yes, we did. Reams of it. Sit down before you fall down.'

Gudrun folded her elegant slimness on to the sofa and Stephen dispensed
my scotch into toothmugs. I went back to sitting on the bed, and pointed to
the sensitive spot on the wall. Stephen nodding, picked up the tape recorder,
switched it on, and applied it to the plaster.

No whine.

'Off duty,' he said. 'So tell us what's happened.'

I shook my head slightly. 'A dust-up.' I didn't particularly want to include
Gudrun. 'Let's just say . . . I'm still here.'

'And ve have vays of not making a fuss?'

I more or less smiled. 'Reasons.'

'They'd better be good. Anyway, here's your hot news from home.' He
pulled an envelope out of his pocket and threw it to me. I made the mistake
of trying to catch it naturally with my right hand, and dropped it.

'You've hurt your fingers,' Gudrun said, showing concern.

'Squashed them a bit.' I took the telex message out of the envelope and, as
reported, there was reams of it: Hughes-Beckett busy proving, I thought sardonically, that my poor opinion of his staff work was unjustified.

'While I read all this,' I said. 'Would you cast your peepers over that stuff
there?' I pointed to the cough-lozenge tin and Misha's pieces of paper.
'Translate them for me, would you?'

They picked up the little bunch of papers and shuffled through them,
murmuring. I read the first section of the telex, which dealt exhaustively

with Hans Kramer's life history, and included far more details than I'd expected or asked for. He had won prizes on ponies from the age of three. He had been to eight different schools. He appeared to have been ill on and off during his teens and twenties, as there were several references to doctors and clinics, but he seemed to have grown out of it at about twenty-eight. His earlier interest in horses had from that time intensified, and he had begun to win horse trials at top level. For two years, until his death, he had travelled extensively on the international scene, sometimes as an individual, and sometimes as part of the West German team.

Then came a paragraph headed 'CHARACTER ASSESSMENT', which uninhibitedly spoke ill of the dead. 'TOLERATED BUT NOT MUCH LIKED BY FELLOW MEMBERS OF EVENT TEAM. UNUSUAL PERSONALITY, COLD, UNABLE TO MAKE FRIENDS. ATTRACTED BY PORNOGRAPHY, HETERO AND HOMO, BUT HAD NO KNOWN SEXUAL RELATIONSHIP OF ANY LENGTH. LATENT VIOLENCE SUSPECTED, BUT BEHAVIOUR IN GENERAL SELF-CONTROLLED.'

Then a bald, brief statement. 'BODY RETURNED TO PARENTS, STILL LIVING IN DUSSELDORF. BODY CREMATED.'

There was a good deal more to read on other subjects, but I looked up from the typed sheets to see how Stephen and Gudrun were doing.

'What've you got?' I said.

'Four autographs of Germans. A list in Russian of brushes and things to do with looking after horses. Another list in Russian of times and places, which I should think refer to the horse trials, as they say things like "cross-country start two-forty remember weight-cloth". Both of those must have been written by Misha, because there is also a sort of diary, in which he lists what he did for his horses, and what feed he gave them, and so on, and that's all.'

'What about the paper in the cough-lozenge tin?' I said.

'Ah. Yes. Well. To be frantically honest, we can't be much help with that.'

'Why not?'

'It doesn't make sense.' He raised his eyebrows at me comically. 'Or do ve have vays of sorting out gibberish?'

'You never know.'

'Well, right then. We are of the opinion that the letters on the paper probably say the same thing twice over, once in Russian and once in German. But they aren't ordinary words in either language, and they're all strung together anyway, without a break.'

'Could you write them in English?'

'Anything to oblige.'

He picked up the envelope which had contained the telex and wrote a long series of letters, one by one.

'There are some letters which come near the end, which do make an actual English word . . .' He finished writing, and handed me the envelope. 'There you are. Crystal as mud.'

I read: Etorphinehydrochloride245mgacepromazinemaleatelomgchloro-cresolol-dimethylsulphoxide9oantagonistnaloxone.

'Does it mean anything?' Stephen said. 'A chemical formula?'

'God knows.' My brains felt like scrambled eggs. 'Maybe it's what's in these ampoules: they're stamped with something about naloxone.'

Stephen held one of the baby phials up to the light, to read the lettering. 'So they are. Massive chemical name for a minute little product.' He put the phial back in the tin, and the original paper on top of it. 'There you are, then. That's the lot.' He closed the tin and put it down. 'What a dingy-looking matroshka.' He picked up the doll. 'Where did you get it?'

'It contains the rest of Misha's souvenirs.'

'Does it? Can I look?'

He had almost as much difficulty in pulling it apart as I had had the first time, and everything scattered in a shower out of it, as before. Stephen and Gudrun crawled about on the floor, picking up the pieces.

'Hm,' he said, reading the veterinary labels. 'More of the same gobbledegook. Anything of any use?'

'Not unless you have bed bugs.'

He put everything back in the doll, and also the tin and the autographs.

'Do you want me to take this out to Elena's new flat some time, after she's settled in?' he said.

'That would be great, if you have the time.'

'Better to give Misha his bits back again.'

'Yes.'

Stephen looked at me closely. 'Gudrun and I are on our way out to supper with some friends, and I think you'd better come with us.' I opened my mouth to say I didn't feel like it and he gave me no chance to get the words out. 'Gudrun, be a lamb and go and wait for us in those armchairs by the lifts, while I get our friend here into some clothes and do his buttons up.' He waved at my non-functioning fingers. 'Go on, Gudrun, love, we won't be long.'

Good-temperedly, she departed, long-legged and liberal.

'Right then,' Stephen said, as the door shut behind her. 'How bad is your hand? Come on, do come with us. You can't just sit there all evening looking dazed.'

I remembered dimly that I was supposed to be going to the opera. Natasha's earnest ticket to fantasy seemed as irrelevant as dust: yet if I stayed alone in my room I should feel worse than I did already, and if I slept there would be visions of death in balaclavas . . . and hotel bedrooms were not in themselves fortresses.

Frank had not mentioned seeing my attackers, and very likely when he ran to the rescue they had kept out of his sight. But that didn't mean that they hadn't hung around for a bit . . . and they might know that he had fished me out.

'Randall!' Stephen said sharply.

'Sorry . . . ' I coughed convulsively, and shivered. 'Wouldn't your friends mind, if I came?'

'Of course not.' He slid open the wardrobe door and pulled out my spare jacket. 'Where's your coat . . . and hat?'

'Shirt first,' I said. 'That checked one . . .'

I stood up stiffly and took off the dressing-gown. There were beginnings of bruise marks on my arms, where the riot sticks had landed, but otherwise, I was glad to see, my skin had returned from an interesting pale turquoise to its more normal faded tan. Stephen helped me speechlessly to the point where he went into the bathroom for something and came out looking incredulous.

'All your clothes are wet!'

'Er, yes. I got shoved in the river.'

He pointed to my hand. 'With that sort of shove?'

'I fear so.'

He opened and closed his mouth like a goldfish. 'Do you realize that the temperature tonight has dropped way below zero?'

'You don't say.'

'And the Moscow River will freeze to solid ice any day now?'

'Too late.'

'Are you delirious?'

'Shouldn't be surprised.' I struggled into a couple of sweaters, and felt lousy. 'Look,' I said weakly, 'I don't think I can manage the friends . . . but I also don't want to stay in this room. Would there be any chance, do you think, of me booking into a different hotel?'

'Not the faintest. An absolute non-starter. No other hotel would be allowed to take you without a fortnight's advance booking and a lot of paperwork, and probably not even then.' He looked around. 'What's wrong with this room, though? It looks fine to me.'

I rubbed my hands over my forehead, which was sweating. The two sweaters, I thought, were aptly named.

I said, 'Three times in two days, someone's tried to kill me. I'm here through luck . . . but I've a feeling the luck's running out. I just don't want to . . . to stand up in the butts.'

'*Three* times?'

I told him about Gorky Street. 'All I want is a safe place to sleep.' I pondered. 'I think I'll ring Ian Young . . . he might help.'

I dialled the number Polly Paget had given me for Ian's flat in the Embassy grounds. The bell rang and rang there, but the Sphinx was out on the town.

'Damn,' I said, with feeling, putting down the receiver.

Stephen's brown eyes were full of troubled thought. 'We could slip you into the University,' he said. 'But my bed's so narrow.'

'Lend me the floor.'

'You're serious?'

'Mm.'

'Well . . . all right.' He looked at his watch. 'It's too late to get you in through the proper channels, so to speak. They'll have knocked off for the day . . . We'll have to work the three card trick.'

He took his student pass out of his pocket and gave it to me.

'Show it to the dragon when you go in, and keep on going, straight up the stairs. They don't know all the students by sight, and she won't know you aren't me. Just go on up to my rom. OK?'

I took the pass and stowed it in a pocket in my jacket. 'How will you get in, though?' I said.

'I'll ring a friend who has a room in the block,' he said. 'He'll collect my pass from you, and bring it out to me, when Gudrun and I get back.'

He held my jacket for me to put on, and then picked up the sheets of telex and folded them back into the envelope. I put the envelope in my jacket and thought about black cars.

'I'd awfully like to make sure I'm not followed,' I said.

Stephen raised his eyes to heaven. 'All in the service,' he said. 'What do you want me to do?'

What we did, in the event, was for me to travel in one taxi to the University Prospect, the tourist stopping place for the view down over the stadium to the city, and for him and Gudrun to follow in another. We all got out of the cars there in the thickly falling snow and exchanged vehicles.

'I'll swear nothing followed you,' Stephen said. 'If anyone did, they used about six different cars, in relays.'

'Thanks a lot.'

'Any time.'

He told the taxi driver where to take me, and disappeared with Gudrun into the night.

13

The dragon on the door was arguing with someone else when I went in. I shoved Stephen's pass under her nose closely enough for her to see that it *was* a pass, and kept it moving. Her eyes hardly slid my way as her tongue lashed into some unfortunate offender, and I went on up the stairs as if I lived there.

Stephen's cell-like room felt a proper sanctuary. I struggled out of my jacket and one sweater and collapsed gratefully on to his bed.

For quite a long time I simply lay there, waiting for what one might call the life force to flow back. What with illness and the inevitable knocks of life on the land, not to mention the crunches involved in jump racing, I was fairly experienced in the way one's body dealt with misfortunes. I was accustomed to the lassitude that damped it down while it put itself to rights, and to the way that this would eventually lift it into a new feeling of vigour. I knew that the fierce soreness of my fingers would get worse for at least another twelve hours, and would then get better. I'd been concussed enough times to know that the sponginess in my mind would go away slowly, like fog clearing, leaving only an externally tender area of bruised scalp.

All that, in fact, would be the way of it if I gave it rest and time: but rest and time were two commodities I was likely to lack. Better to make the most of what I had. Better, I dared say, to sleep: but one factor I was not used to, and had never had to deal with before, was keeping me thoroughly awake. The sharp threat of death.

There wouldn't be any more lucky escapes. The fourth close encounter would be the last. For if my attackers had learned one thing conclusively during the past two days, it must have been that it was necessary to kill at once, and fast. No fooling around with horse boxes, kidnappings, or icy rivers. Next time . . . if there was a next time . . . I should be dead before I realized what had happened. It was enough, I thought, to send one scurrying to the airport . . . to leave the battle to be fought by someone else.

After a while I sat up and took the long telex out of my pocket.

Read again the pages about Hans Kramer.

Eight schools. Doctors, hospitals, and clinics. Ill-health, like mine. And, like me, success on ponies, and on horses. Like me, a spot of foreign travel to equestrian events: I to the awesome Pardubice in Czechoslovakia and the Maryland Hunt Cup over fixed timber fences in America, and he to top-rank horse trials around Europe: Italy, France, Holland and England.

Died at Burghley in September of a heart attack, aged thirty-six. Body shipped home, and cremated.

End of story.

I took off my glasses and tiredly rubbed my eyes. If there was anything useful to be gleaned from all the unasked detail it was totally invisible to my current mental sight.

I tried to clear my mind by shaking it, which was about as useful as stirring old port with a teaspoon. Bits of sediment clogged my thoughts and little green spots slid around behind my eyes.

I read the rest of the telex twice and by the end had taken in hardly a word.

Start again.

YURI CHULITSKY, ARCHITECT, PHONE NUMBER SUPPLIED EARLIER BUT NOW REPEATED . . . ONE OF THE RUSSIAN OBSERVERS IN ENGLAND DURING AUGUST AND SEPTEMBER LAST. FORMERLY WENT TO OLYMPICS AT MONTREAL. ADVISER ON BUILDINGS NECESSARY FOR EQUESTRIAN GAMES AT MOSCOW.

Yes, I knew all that.

IGOR NAUMOVICH TELYATIN, COORDINATOR OF BROADCASTING. NO TELE-
PHONE NUMBER AVAILABLE. RUSSIAN OBSERVER, IN ENGLAND DURING
AUGUST AND SEPTEMBER. HIS BELIEF; TO LEARN THE BEST GENERAL POSI-
TIONING FOR TV COVERAGE; TO SEE WHAT OTHER FACILITIES WERE
ESSENTIAL AND WHICH MERELY DESIRABLE; TO SEE HOW BEST TO GIVE THE
WORLD A GOOD VIEW OF SOVIET SHOWMANSHIP AND EFFICIENCY.
SERGEI ANDREEVICH GORSHKOV. NO TELEPHONE NUMBER AVAILABLE.
RUSSIAN OBSERVER, STATED TO BE STUDYING CROWD CONTROL AT BIG
EQUESTRIAN EVENTS, WHERE THE MOBILITY OF SPECTATORS WAS A PROBLEM.
RELIABLY REPORTED TO BE A FULL COLONEL OF KGB, AN EXTREME HARD-
LINER, WITH A DEEP CONTEMPT FOR WESTERN STANDARDS. SINCE HIS VISIT,
INFORMATION HAS COME TO HAND THAT HE HAS IN THE PAST ATTEMPTED TO
COMPROMISE MEMBERS OF THE EMBASSY STAFF, AND THEIR VISITORS,
FAMILY, AND FRIENDS, STRONGLY ADVISE AGAINST CONTACT.

I put the sheets down. Hughes-Beckett, if it was indeed he who had sent the
telex, which was unsigned and had no indication of origin, was up to his old
tricks of seeming to help while encouraging failure. Flooding me with use-
less-looking information while warning me away from the one who really
might pose a threat to Johnny Farringford.

Hughes-Beckett, I thought a shade irritably, had not the slightest idea of
what was actually going on.

To be fair to him, how could he know if I didn't tell him?

The mechanics of telling him were not that easy. Anything sent from the
Embassy via the telex ran the gauntlet of Malcolm Herrick's inside informer:
and since Malcolm had learned of Oliver telling me to send a message
directly from Kutuzovsky Prospect, he had probably made his arrangements
there as well. The one place I did not want my adventures turning up was on
the front page of the *Watch*.

There was the telephone, to which someone at either end might listen.
There was the mail, which was slow, and might be intercepted.

There was Ian, who, if I read it right, probably had his own secure hot-line
to the ears back home, but might not have the authority to lend it to any odd
private citizen who applied.

In the back of my mind, also, there hovered an undefined question mark
about the soundness of Ian as an ally.

Stephen's friend duly came to collect Stephen's pass, at shortly after eleven:
and Stephen and Gudrun returned, full of bonhomie and onions.

'Onions!' Gudrun said. 'Back in the shops today after four months without them. No eggs, of course. It's always something.'

'Want some tea?' Stephen suggested, and went to make it.

There floated about both of them the glow of an evening well spent, and perversely their warmth depressed my already low spirits to sinking point; like Scrooge at Christmas.

'What you need,' Stephen said, coming back and making an accurate diagnosis with a glance, 'is half a pint of vodka and some good news.'

'Supply them,' I said.

'Have a biscuit.'

He unearthed a packet from the recesses of the bookcase and cleared a space on the table for the mugs. Then, seeming to be struck by a thought, he began rigging up a contraption of drawing-pins and string, and upon the string he threaded his bedside alarm clock, so that it hung there loudly ticking on the wall. It was only towards the end of this seemingly senseless procedure that I remembered that that exact spot was the lair of the bug.

'Better interference than nothing, if they're listening,' he said cheerfully. 'And they get a right earful when the alarm goes off.'

The tea probably did more good than the unavailable vodka. A certain amount of comfort began to creep along the nerves.

'All visitors have to be gone by ten-thirty,' Stephen nonchalantly said.

'Will they check?'

'I've never known it.'

Halfway down the mug a modicum of order returned to my thoughts. Very welcome: like a friend much missed.

'Gudrun,' I said lazily, 'would you cast your peepers over something for me?'

'Sorry?'

I put down the mug and picked up the telex, and she noticed the up-to-date state of the hand I hadn't used.

'Oh!' she said. 'That must really hurt.'

Stephen looked from my fingers to my face. 'Are they broken?' he said.

'Can't tell.'

I could scarcely move them, which proved nothing one way or the other. They had swelled like sausages, and gone dark, and it was a fair certainty the nails would go black, if they didn't actually come off. It was no worse, really, than if one had been galloped on by a horse, and injuries of that order had been all in the day's work. I smiled lop-sidedly at their horrified faces and handed Gudrun the telex.

'Would you read all the stuff about Hans Kramer, and see if it means anything to you which it doesn't to me? He was German, and you are a German, and you might see a significance I've missed.'

'All right.' She looked doubtful, but compliantly read right to the end.

'What strikes you?' I said.

She shook her head. 'Nothing very much.'

'He went to eight different schools,' I said. 'Would that be usual?'

'No.' She frowned. 'Not unless his family moved a lot.'

'His father was and is a big industrialist in Dusseldorf.'

She read through the schools again, and finally said, 'I think one of these places specializes in children who are ... different. Perhaps they have troubles with epilepsy, or perhaps they are ...' She made tumbling motions with her hands, at a loss for the word.

'Mixed-up?'

'That's right. But they also take people who have a special talent and need special schooling. Like athletes. Perhaps Hans Kramer went there because he was exceptionally good at riding.'

'Or because seven other schools slung him out?'

'Perhaps, yes.'

'What about the doctors and hospitals?'

She read through the list again and her mouth negatively pursed, and finally shook her head.

'Would they be, for instance,' I said, 'anything to do with orthopaedics?'

'Bones and things?'

'Yes.'

Her eyes went back to the list, but the no's had it.

'Anything to do with heart troubles? Are any of those people or places specialists in chest surgery?'

'I honestly don't know.'

I thought. 'Well,' I said, 'anything to do with psychiatry?'

'I'm awfully sorry, but I don't know much about ...' Her eyes widened suddenly and she looked rather wildly down at the list. 'Oh my goodness ...'

'What is it?'

'The Heidelberg University clinic.'

'What about it?'

'Don't you know?' She saw from my face that I didn't. 'Hans Kramer attended it, it says here, for about three months in nineteen seventy.'

'Yes,' I said. 'Why is that important?'

'Nineteen seventy ... There was a doctor called Wolfgang Huber working there. He was supposed to be great at straightening out ... mixed-up ... children from rich families. Not *little* children ... teenagers and young adults, our age. People who were violently rebellious against their parents.'

'He seems to have managed it all right with Hans Kramer, then,' I said. 'Because isn't that clinic the last on the list?'

'Yes,' Gudrun said. 'But you don't understand.'

'Tell me.'

She could hardly frame the sentences, so intense were her thoughts.

'Dr Huber taught them that to cure themselves they had to destroy the system which was making them feel the way they did. He told them they would have to destroy the world of their parents ... He called it terrorism therapy.'

'My God.'

'And ... and ... ' Gudrun practically gasped for breath. 'I don't know what effect it had on Hans Kramer ... but ... Dr Huber was deliberately teaching his patients ... to follow in the footsteps of Andreas Baader and Ulrike Meinhof.'

Time, as they say, stood still.

'You've seen a ghost,' Stephen said.

'I've seen a pattern . . . and a plan.'

The teachings of Dr Wolfgang Huber, I supposed, had been a sort of extreme extension of the theories behind the communist revolution. Destroy the corrupt capitalist system and you will emerge into a clean healthy society run by the workers. A seductive, idealistic dream which seemed always to appeal most to intellectuals of the middle class, who had both the brains and the means to pursue it.

Even in the hands of visionaries the doctrine had led to widespread killing. People like Dr Huber, however, had preached their gospel not to reasoning adults, but to already disturbed youth, and the result in widening ripples had been the Baader-Meinhof followers, the Palestinian Black September, the Irish Republican Army, the Argentinian ERP and the Japanese Red Army, with endless virulent offshoots among small groups like Croatians, South Moluccans, and Basques.

The place most free from terrorism was the land which still encouraged and nurtured it, the land where the seedling had raised its attractive head.

At the Munich Olympics, the world had awakened in a state of shock to the existence of the growing crop.

Eight years later, at the Moscow Olympics, someone was planning to carry the fruit home.

14

Stephen lent me his bed and went to share Gudrun's, which seemed to please them both well, and was certainly all right by me. Foreign students were positively encouraged to lie together, he said sardonically, so that they didn't go out and pursue the natives.

I shivered a good deal, and at the same time felt feverish, which boded ill.

I didn't sleep much, though that didn't matter. My hand throbbed like a pile-driver but my head was clear, and I much preferred it that way round. I spent most of the time thinking and wondering and guessing, and coming back to the problem of the next day. I had somehow got to take some positive steps towards staying permanently alive.

In the morning Stephen fetched some tea, lent me his razor, and bounced cheerfully off to a student breakfast.

He returned with some things like empty hamburger buns from the basement supermarket, and found me studying the long string of letters on the envelope which had held the telex.

'Deciphering the chemical junk?' he said.

'Trying.'

'How's it coming?'

'I don't know enough,' I said. 'Look ... when all this was written in Russian and German, was it *translated*? I mean ... are you sure that this is what was meant?'

'It wasn't translated,' Stephen said. 'It was those letters in that order, but written in formal German script ... the sort you see in books. The Russian script version was more or less phonetically the same, but there are more letters in the Russian alphabet, so we adjusted the Russian letters to be the equivalent of the German ... was that all right?'

'Yes,' I said. 'You see here where it reads "antagonist"?'

'Uh huh.'

'Was that word translated into Russian or German? Or were the letters a n t a et cetera written in German script?'

'It wasn't translated, as such, because antagonist is much the same word in all three languages.'

'Thanks.'

'Is that of any help?'

'Yes, in a way,' I said.

'You amaze me.'

We buttered and shared the hamburger buns and drank some more tea, and I coughed on and off with an ominous hollowness.

After that I cadged a sheet of paper and wrote the long row of letters into sensible words, adding a few reasonable-looking decimal points. The revised effort read:

    etorphine hydrochloride 2.45 mg
    acepromazine maleate 1.0 mg
    chlorocresol 0.1 –
    dimethyl sulphoxide 90
    antagonist naloxone.

Stephen looked over my shoulder. 'That, of course,' he said, 'makes a world of difference.'

'Um,' I said thoughtfully. 'Would you do me a favour?'

'Fire away.'

'Lend me an empty tape for your recorder, and another one with music on it. Or rather, two empty tapes, if you have them.'

'Is that all?' He sounded disappointed.

'That's for starters.'

He rustled around and produced three tapes in plastic boxes.

'They've all got music on,' he said. 'But you can record on top, if you like.'
'Great.' I hesitated, because what I wanted him to do besides sounded melodramatic; but facts had to be faced. I folded the list of chemicals in half and gave it to him. 'Would you mind keeping that?' I made my voice as matter-of-fact as possible. 'Keep it until after I've got home. I'll send you a postcard to say it's OK to tear it up.'

He looked puzzled. 'I don't see . . .'

'If I don't get home, or you don't get a postcard from me, will you send it to Hughes-Beckett at the Foreign Office. I've put the address on the back. Tell him that Hans Kramer had it, and ask him to show it to a vet.'

'A *vet*?'

'That's right.'

'Yes, but . . .' He realized exactly what I'd said. 'If you don't get home . . .'

'Yeah . . . well . . . fourth time unlucky, and all that.'

'For heaven's sake.'

'Do you have lectures on Saturdays?' I said.

His eyebrows vanished upwards under his hair. 'Is that a general invitation to put my head in the trap alongside yours?'

'Probably just to make phone calls and tell taxis where to go.'

He gave an exaggerated shrug and a large gesture of surrender, and put on an expression of 've have vays of not believing a vord you say'. 'What first?'

'Ring Mr Kropotkin,' I said. 'And if he's in, ask if I can come to see him this morning.'

Kropotkin, it seemed, was not only in but anxious. 'He says he's been trying to get you at the hotel. He says to arrive at ten o'clock, and we can find him inside the first stable block on the left, on the racecourse.

'Fine . . . ' I blew a cooling breath on to my hot, swollen fingers. 'I think I'll also try Ian Young.'

Ian Young was back on British soil and seemed to take a while to realize who he was talking to. He was feeling fragile, and no one, he said eventually, with a mixture of misery and admiration, could drink like the Russians; and please would I not talk so loudly.

Sorry, I said, pianissimo. Could he please tell me how best to make a telephone call to England. Try from the main Post Office just round the corner from my hotel, he said. Ask for the International operator. He was discouraging, however, about my prospects.

'Sometimes you can get through in ten minutes, but it's usually more like two hours, and with the new flap going on this morning you'll be lucky if you get through at all.'

'Newer than the dust-up in Africa?' I said.

'Oh sure. Some high-up guy has defected. In Birmingham, of all places. Shock, horror, drama, and all that. Is it important?'

'I want to ring my vet . . . about my horses,' I said. 'Could I get through from the Embassy?'

'I doubt if you'd do any better. There's no one like the Russians for blank obstruction. Brick wall specialists, the Russians.' He yawned. 'Did you get you telex last night?'

'Yes, thanks.'

'Make the most of it, I should.' He yawned again. 'Do you feel like swilling the hair of the dog with me? Round about noon?'

'Don't see why not.'

'Good . . . Go past Oliver's office, and past the tennis court . . . and my flat's in the row at the back of the grounds, second door from the left.' He put down the receiver with all the gentleness of the badly hungover.

The snow had temporarily stopped, though the sky was a threatening oily yellow-grey and the air cold enough to freeze the nose's mucus lining in its tracks. I started coughing and gasping for breath before we'd gone a hundred steps, and Stephen thought it extraordinary.

'What's the matter?' he said, his own lungs chugging easily away like an electric bellows.

'Taxi . . .'

We caught one without much difficulty, and immediately, within its comparative warmth and with the help of the pocket bronchidilator inhaler I kept in my pocket like loose change, my chest stopped its infuriating heaving.

'Are you always like this when it's cold?' Stephen said.

'It depends. The river didn't help.'

He looked mildly anxious. 'You caught a chill? Come to think . . . it's not surprising.'

We stopped twice on the way. The first time, to buy two bottles of vodka; one to give to Kropotkin and one to keep. The second time to buy me yet another hat to top off my assorted clothing, which now consisted, from the skin outwards, of a singlet, shirt, two sweaters, jacket, and Stephen's spare coat, which was a size too small and left my forearms sticking out like an orphan.

The main roads had already been cleared of the overnight snow, but the Hippodrome itself was white. There were horses there all the same, exercising on the track, and even one or two trotters pulling sulkies. We paid off the taxi practically at the stable door, and went inside to enquire of Kropotkin.

He was waiting for us in a small dark office used by one of the trainers of the trotters. There were heaps of tyres everywhere, which seemed stunningly incongruous in a stable until one remembered the sulkies' wheels, and apart from that only a desk with a great deal of scattered paperwork, and a chair, and large numbers of photographs pinned to the walls.

Nikolai Alexandrovich cordially grasped my hastily offered left hand and pumped it up and down with both of his own.

'Friend,' he said, the heavy bass voice reverberating in the small space. 'Good friend.'

He accepted the gift of vodka as the courtesy it represented. Then he set the chair ceremoniously for me to sit on, and himself lodged comfortably with his backside half on the desk. Stephen, it seemed, could stand on his own two feet; and, via Stephen, Kropotkin and I exchanged further suitable opening compliments.

We arrived in due course at the meat inside the pastry.

'Mr Kropotkin says,' Stephen said, 'that he asked everyone in the world of horses to give any help they could in the matter of Alyosha.'

I expressed my warmest appreciations and felt the faintest quickening of the pulse.

'No one, however,' Stephen continued, 'knows who Alyosha is. No one knows anything about him.'

My pulse returned to normal with depressing speed.

'Kind of him to try,' I said, sighing slightly.

Kropotkin stroked his moustache downwards with his thumb and forefinger and then set off again into a deep rumble.

Stephen did a dead-pan translation although with more interest in his eyes.

'Mr Kropotkin says that although no one knows who Alyosha is, someone has sent him a piece of paper with the name Alyosha on it, and the piece of paper originally came from England.'

It hardly sounded the ultimate solution, but definitely better than nothing.

'May I see it?' I said.

It appeared, though, that Nikolai Alexandrovich was not to be rushed. Bread and butter first; sweeties after.

'Mr Kropotkin says,' Stephen translated, 'that you should understand one or two things about the Soviet system.' His eyebrows went upwards and his nostrils twitched with the effort of keeping a straight face. 'He says it is not always possible for Soviet citizens to speak with total freedom.'

'Tell him I've noticed. Er . . . tell him I understand.'

Kropotkin looked at me broodingly and stroked his moustache.

'He would like it,' Stephen said, relaying the next wedge of rumble, 'if you could use everything you have learned here at the Hippodrome without explaining where you heard it.'

'Give him my most solemn assurance,' I said sincerely, and I think Kropotkin was probably convinced more by my tone than the actual words. After a suitable pause, he continued.

'Mr Kropotkin says,' Stephen faithfully reported, 'that he doesn't know who sent him the paper. It was delivered to his flat by hand yesterday evening, with a brief note of explanation, and a hope that it would be handed on to you.'

'Does he sound as if he really doesn't know who sent it, or do you think he's just not telling?'

'Impossible to know,' Stephen said.

Nikolai Alexandrovich showed signs at last of producing the goods. With great deliberation he drew a large black wallet from an inside pocket and opened it wide. His blunt fingers carefully sank into a deep section at the back, and he slowly drew out a white envelope. He accompanied the hand-over ceremony with a small speech.

'He says,' Stephen said, 'that to himself this paper does not seem to be of much significance. He wishes it were. He would like it to be of some use to you, because of his earnest desire to express his thanks for your speed in saving the Olympic horse.'

'Tell him that if it should turn out to be a significant paper, I will always remember and appreciate the trouble he has taken to help.'

Kropotkin received the compliment graciously, and slowly parted with the envelope. I took it from him at the same unhurried pace, and drew out the two smallish sheets of paper which were to be found inside.

They were fastened to each other with a small paper-clip. The top one, white, and unremarkable, bore a short paragraph written in Russian.

The lower, also white but torn from a notebook and ruled with faint blue lines, was chiefly covered with a variety of geometric doodles, done in pencil. Near the top there were two words: *For Alyosha*, and about an inch lower down, surrounded by doodled stars, *J. Farringford*. Underneath that, one below the other, as in a list, were the words Americans, Germans, French, and below that a row of question-marks. That seemed to be more or less all, though near the bottom of the page, in their own individual doodled boxes, were four sets of letters and numbers, which were DEP PET, 1855, K's C, and 1950.

On top of all the scribbles, across the whole page from top to bottom, there was the wide flowing S-shaped scrawl of someone crossing out what they had written.

I turned the small page over. The reverse side bore about fifteen lines of what must have been handwriting, written in ballpoint, but this had been meticulously scribbled over, line by line, also in ballpoint but in a slightly different colour.

Kropotkin was watching me expectantly. I said, 'I am very pleased. This is most interesting.' He understood the words, and looked heavily satisfied.

The business at that point seemed to be over, and after a few more compliments on both sides we stepped from the office into the central corridor of the stable block. Kropotkin invited me to see the horses, and we walked side by side along to where each side of the corridor was lined with loose boxes.

Stephen made choking noises behind me as he reached them, which I guessed was because of the smell. My own nose twitched a bit over the unusually piercing stink of ammonia, but the trotters seemed none the worse for it. They would be racing that evening, Kropotkin said, because the snow was not yet too deep. Stephen manfully translated to the end, but gulped at the eventual fresh air as if it were a fountain in the desert.

There were still several horses exercising on the track, and to my eyes they came from lower down the equine class system than racehorses or eventers.

'All the riding clubs are here,' Kropotkin explained through Stephen. 'All stables for horses in Moscow are in this district, and all exercising is done at the Hippodrome. All the horses are owned by the State. The best horses go for racing and breeding, and the Olympics; then the clubs share what is left. Most horses stay in Moscow all winter, because they are very hardy. And I wonder,' added Stephen on his own account, 'what it smells like in these barns come March!'

Kropotkin said a solemn goodbye at the still unattended main entrance. He was a great old guy, I thought, and through him and Misha I had learned a good deal.

'Friend,' I said. 'I wish you well.'

He pumped my hand with emotion in both of his, and then gave me the accolade of a hug.

'My God,' said Stephen as we walked away. 'Talk about schmaltzy sob-stuff . . . '

'A little sentiment does no harm.'

'Ah . . . but did it do any good?'

I handed him the envelope and coughed all the way to the taxi rank.

'To Nikolai Alexandrovich, by hand,' said Stephen, reading the envelope. 'So whoever sent it, knew Kropotkin fairly well. You'd only use that form of someone's name . . . the patronymic Alexandrovich without the last name Kropotkin . . . if you knew him.'

'It would be more surprising if they *didn't* know each other.'

'I guess so.' He picked out the two small clipped-together pages. 'This paragraph on the front says, "*Note paper*" . . . sort of jotting paper, that is . . . "*used at International Horse Trials. Please give it to Randall Drew.*"'

'Is that all?'

'That's the lot.'

He peered at the second page, and I waved uninhibitedly at a taxi cruising with its windscreen light on. Once more on our way, Stephen handed back the treasure trove.

'Not much cop,' he said. 'A case of the lion straining to produce a gnat.'

The taxi driver spoke into my thoughtful silence.

'He wants to know where we're going,' Stephen said.

'Back to the hotel.'

We stopped however on the way at a shop he identified as a chemist. The Russian letters on the shop-front, when approximated into English, read Apotek. Apothecary . . . what else? I went inside with him, seeking dampeners for the troubles in fingers and chest, but ended only with the equivalent of aspirins. For his own purchase, he leaned across a counter and spoke low to the ear of a buxom battleaxe.

She replied very loudly, and all the nearby customers turned to stare at him. His face was a scarlet study of embarrassment, but all the same he stood his ground and brought the transaction to the desired conclusion.

'What did she say?' I asked, as we left.

'She said "This foreigner wants . . . preservativy . . ." And don't bloody laugh.'

My chuckle anyway ended in a cough. 'Preservativy being contraceptives?'

'Gudrun insists.'

'I should darned well think so.'

At the hotel we went straight through the foyer to the lifts, as I had taken my room key with me to the University so as not to advertise my absence to the reception desk.

Up to the eighth floor, past the watchful lady at the desk, and along the corridor . . . and the door of my room was open.

Cleaners?

Not cleaners. The person who was standing inside was Frank.

He had his back to the door and was over by the dressing shelf under the window, head bent, looking down at something in his hands.

'Hello, Frank,' I said.

He turned round quickly, looking very startled: and what he was holding was the matroshka. Intact, I saw, with all her secrets still inside. His fingers were still tight with the effort of trying to open her.

'Er . . .' he said. 'You didn't come to breakfast. I . . . er . . . came to see if you were all right. After last night. I mean, falling in the river . . .'

Not bad, I thought, as a spot of thinking on the feet.

'I went to the Hippodrome to see the horses work,' I said, playing the game that anyone could play if they had a lying tongue.

Frank relaxed his grip and put the painted doll slowly down on the shelf, giving his best weak-schoolteacher laugh.

'Right on, then,' he said. 'Natasha was worried about you not coming to breakfast. Shall I tell her you'll be in for lunch?'

Lunch . . . the prosaically normal in the middle of a minefield.

'Why not?' I said. 'And I'll have a guest.'

Frank looked at Stephen with sustained dislike, and took himself off; and I descended a bit feebly on to the sofa.

'Let's have a drink,' I said.

'Scotch or vodka?' He pulled the morning's newly-bought bottle out of his overcoat pocket and stood it on the shelf.

'Scotch.'

I took two of the Apotek's pills with it, without noticeable results.

Looked at my watch, now miraculously ticking again despite immersion. Eleven-thirty. Picked up the telephone.

'Ian?' I said. 'How's the hangover?'

From the sound of it, on the mend. The hair of the dog had bitten an hour ago, no doubt. I said I couldn't make it after all before lunch, and how about him tottering along to my room at the hotel at about six?

Totter, he said, might just about describe it, by then: but he would come.

Stephen was sweeping the walls with the tape-recorder, trying to find the tender spot. I pointed to it, but again there was no whine. And then, just as he was about to give up, the whine suddenly began.

'Switched on, by God,' he said under his breath.

'Let's have some music.'

He pulled the three tapes from his obliging overcoat and slotted in an energetic rendering of *Prince Igor*.

'What next?'

'I brought some paperbacks . . . which would you like?'

'And you?' he said, looking at the titles.

'Drink and think.'

So the bug listened for an hour to Stephen turning the pages of *The Small Back Room* against the urgencies of Borodin, and I listened inside my head to everything I'd been told, both in England and Moscow, and tried to see a path through the maze.

Lunch seemed unreal.

The Wilkinsons were there, and Frank was there. Frank hadn't told the Wilkinsons he'd saved my life the evening before, and behaved throughout as if nothing of the sort had ever happened. What he thought of my silence on the subject was a mystery.

Natasha and Anna tried by a mixture of scolding and persuasion to make me promise to stop disappearing without telling them where I was going and I helpfully said I would do my best, without meaning a word of it.

Frank ate my meat.

Mrs Wilkinson talked. 'We've always voted Labour, Dad and me, but isn't it funny, in England it's always the far left people who want more and more immigrants, but here, where it's about as far left as you can get, there aren't any. You don't see black people walking around in Moscow, do you?'

Frank took no notice.

'It just strikes me as funny, that's all,' Mrs Wilkinson said. 'Still, I don't suppose there's much of a queue in India for wanting to live in Moscow, come to think.'

Mr Wilkinson muttered to his small-sized chips, 'They've got more sense.' He wouldn't say much else for the rest of the day.

Frank came to life with a routine damnation of the anti-black policies of the National Front.

Mrs Wilkinson gave me a comical look of bewilderment and despair at never being able to get through to Frank.

'Front,' I said mildly, 'is an overworked word. A cliché. We have Fronts for this and Fronts for that . . . One should always ask what . . . if anything . . . is *behind* a Front.'

It was again ice-cream with blackcurrant jam. I quite liked it.

Stephen ate like Frank and told me afterwards that the Intourist Hotel food was high class luxury compared with the students' grub.

Apart from all that, which seemed to be going on in a separate life, I was more positively hearing the voices of Boris and Evgeny, and Ian, and Malcolm, and Oliver, and Kropotkin, and Misha and Yuri Chulitsky, and

Gudrun and the Prince and Hughes-Beckett and Johnny Farringford . . . and the dead voice of Hans Kramer: I could hear them all clearly.

But where, oh where, was Alyosha?

15

Upstairs in my room Stephen balanced the chair on my bed; my suitcase on the chair, and the tape-recorder on the suitcase: and switched on. The whine came forth, alive and healthy.

He switched off the 'record' button and pressed the 'play', and the listeners got a close earful of a tape of Stravinsky which seemed to be suffering from wow if not flutter.

I spent the time pondering the pieces of paper Kropotkin had given me; the back as much as the front.

'You don't happen to have any blue glass handy, I suppose?' I said. 'Of a certain particular shade?'

'Blue *glass*?'

'Yes . . . a blue filter. You see all this handwriting which has been scribbled out? It was written in a darker colour of blue than the scribble . . . you can see the dark loops underneath.'

'Well . . . so what?'

'So if you looked at the page through some blue glass which was the same colour as the lighter scribble, you might be able to see the darker blue writing. The colour of the glass, so to speak, would cancel out the colour of the scribble, and you could read what was left.'

'For crying out loud . . .' he said. 'I suppose you could. And where would that get you?'

'I might guess who sent this to Kropotkin, but I'd like to be certain.'

'But it could be *anybody*.'

I shook my head. 'I'll show you something.'

I opened the drawer which contained my private pharmacy and brought out the folded piece of paper which lay beneath it. Opening it, and smoothing out the crease, I laid it on the dressing shelf, and put Kropotkin's paper beside it.

'They're the same!' Stephen said.

'That's right. Torn from the same type of notebook: white paper, faint blue lines, spiral binding.'

The two notebook pages lay side by side with their ragged torn-off fringes at the top. On one, 'For Alyosha', 'J. Farringford', and all the rest. And on the other, the name Malcolm Herrick, and a telephone number.

'He gave that to me the first night I was in Moscow,' I said. 'In the bar of the National Hotel.'

'Yes ... but ... Those notebooks are universal. You can buy them everywhere. Students ... typists ... Aren't they especially printed to take shorthand?'

'And constantly used by newspaper reporters,' I said. 'Who have a great habit of crossing out pages when they've finished with them. I've seen them over and over, at the races, talking to me maybe when I've won a race. They flick over the pages to find a fresh one ... they go all through the pad one way, and then they turn it over and start on the backs. And to save themselves looking through endless pages afterwards to find just the bits they want, they put a scribble or a cross over the whole page when they've finished with it ... just like this one, which we got from Kropotkin.'

I turned over the sheet Malcolm had given me with his telephone number on, and there, on the back, were some notes about a visiting puppet theatre, sprawlingly crossed through with a wide flowing S.

'*Malcolm*,' said Stephen, looking bewildered. 'Why should Malcolm send this to Kropotkin?'

'I shouldn't think he did. Maybe he just gave it to whoever did that writing on the back.'

'But why should he?' Stephen said frustratedly. 'And what does it matter? It's all *crazy*.'

'It's unlikely that he'll remember who he gave an odd piece of paper to nearly three months ago,' I said. 'But I think ... we might ask him.'

I dialled the number on the paper, and he was at home. His big voice positively crackled through the receiver.

'Where've you been, sport? Been trying to reach you. Moscow at weekends is like Epsom when they're racing at Ascot.'

'Out to the Hippodrome,' I said obligingly.

'Zat so? How's it going? Found Alyosha yet?'

'Not yet.'

'Told you it was a bum steer, sport. I looked. I told you. If I couldn't find a story, there is no story. Right?'

'You're an old hand, and I'm not,' I said. 'But Kropotkin at the Hippodrome has called on all the horse people in Moscow to work on it. So we've an army of allies.'

He grunted, not sounding very pleased. 'Has the army come up with anything?'

'Only with something pretty small, so far. In fact,' I said, half making a joke of it, 'a page which looks as if it came from one of your notebooks.'

'A what?'

'Page ... with the name Alyosha on it. And Johnny Farringford's name, ringed with stars. And a lot of doodling. I'm sure you wouldn't remember writing it. But the thing is . . . do you remember lending or giving a piece of scrap paper to anyone at Burghley who could now be here in Moscow?'

'Christ, sport, you ask damn silly questions.'

'Yeah . . . ' I said, coughing on a sigh. 'Um . . . if you're dead bored, care to come to the Intourist Hotel for a drink in my room, around six? I'm going out for a bit, but I'll be back by then.'

'Sure,' he said easily. 'Bloody good idea. Saturday night's made for drinking. What's the room number?'

I told him and he said fine, and disconnected. I put the receiver down slowly and reflected that I'd done some silly things in my time but that that probably topped the lot.

'I thought you didn't much like him,' Stephen said.

I made a face and shrugged. 'Maybe I owe him for the dinner in the Aragvi.'

I sat on the sofa and gingerly explored my right-hand fingers with those of the left. The worst of the soreness was beginning to wear off, and I could bend and unbend them a bit. It seemed probable that a couple of bones were cracked, though one often couldn't tell for sure without X-rays. I supposed I should count myself lucky they weren't splintered.

'When do you doodle?' I said.

'Doodle?'

'Like that.' I nodded towards the page of Malcolm's notebook.

'Oh . . . during lectures, mostly. I do zigzags, and triangles, not boxes, stars and question-marks. Any time when I'm listening with a pencil in my hand, I suppose. On the telephone, for instance. Or listening to the radio.'

'Mm . . . Well . . . ' I stopped unsuccessfully doctoring my fingers and got through on the telephone to the International operator. Calls to England, I was told, would entail a long delay. How long was a long delay? Calls to England were not at present being connected. Did that mean hours or days? The International operator couldn't or wouldn't say. Frustratedly, I stood up. 'Let's go out.'

'Where to?'

'Anywhere. Round and round Moscow in a taxi.'

'Out of thugs' reach?'

'Sometimes,' I said with mock disparagement, 'you're quite bright.'

We took with us the matroshka in its string bag, and also (in my pocket along with the telex) the two pages from Malcolm's notebook, on the basis that as these four treasures were the only tangible results of my efforts, they should not be carelessly left around to be pinched by Frank or anyone else who could open my bedroom door.

Even though he'd stopped saying it was cheaper on the metro, Stephen boggled a bit at the expense of that afternoon. The Prince was paying, I said, dealing out roubles in hefty instalments at half-hour intervals to a taxi driver who thought I was mad. Stephen suggested the University, for which in the morning he had got me a visitor's pass in order to avoid the juggling of the day before: but for some reason I always thought best on wheels, and had planned many a campaign while driving continually up and down on a tractor. There was something about a moving background that triggered shifts of mind, and left new ideas standing sharp and clear where they hadn't existed before. I was an outdoor man, after all.

We saw a lot of Moscow, old parts and new. Old elegance and new functionalism, historically at odds but united in the silent white freezing slide into hibernation. Thick white caps on the golden domes. Shops with more space than goods. Huge advertisements saying 'Glory to the Communist Party' over the rooftops. On me the cumulative effect was a powerful pervading melancholy, a sadness for so great a city entangled in such suffocating bureaucracy, such denial of liberty, such a need to look over its shoulder before it spoke.

When darkness closed in we stopped once, to buy a couple of glasses and some reinforcements in the booze line, and a souvenir for me to take home to Emma: and I chose a bright new matroshka with all its little matroshkas nestling inside, because it seemed to me that what I had been doing in Moscow had been in effect like opening that sort of doll. When one pulled off one layer, there was another layer underneath. Remove that, and another layer revealed. Under that, another: and under that, another. And, in the centre, not a tiny wooden mama with rosy cheeks, but a germinating seed of terror.

When we finally returned to my room it looked uninvaded, undisturbed.

Perhaps we could have stayed there safely; but wasted precautions were never to be regretted. 'If only' were the saddest words in the language.

The tape-recorder still stood silently on its precarious tower, and, when Stephen pressed the 'record' button, it told us mutely that the listeners slept.

It was five to six. We left the recorder switched on, and went along to the armchairs by the lifts to await the guests.

Ian came first, by no means drunk but slightly rocking. It made no difference to his face, which was as white, calm and expressionless as ever, or to his speech, which had no fuzzy edges. He told us with great lucidity that on Friday evenings and Saturdays, when there was no flap on, he embraced the great Russian leisure-time activity with the fervour of the converted. And where, he asked, did I keep the bottle?

We retracked down the corridor to my room. Ian chose vodka and had tossed off his first before I had finished pouring Stephen's. I refilled his glass, and got myself some scotch.

Without visible emotion he regarded the tape-recorder.

'If you play that up there much, my old son,' he said, 'you'll want to look around for a sticky stranger. If they think you've got something to hide, they'll plant another car.'

Stephen silently reached for the recorder and took it on a thorough journey round the room. Ian watched, absentmindedly downed his drink, and poured himself a replacement with an almost steady hand.

The search results were fortunately nil. Back on its perch, still no whine. Stephen left the recorder there on sentry duty, and he and Ian sat down on the sofa.

Ian spent five minutes describing the extreme boredom of the diplomatic life as lived by the British in Moscow, and left me fervently wishing he were stone cold sober.

Malcolm arrived like a gale blowing in from the desert, hard, noisy and dry.

'Extra,' he said boisterously, picking up the vodka bottle and reading the label. 'The Rolls-Royce of the domestic distilleries. I see you cotton on to the best pretty damn quick, sport.'

'Stephen's choice,' I said. 'Help yourself.'

For him too, it appeared, Saturday night was to-hell-with-inhibitions night. He poured and tossed back in one draught enough to put an abstainer asleep for a month. 'You didn't tell me it was a party, sport,' he said.

'Only the four of us.'

'Could have brought a bottle.'

At the present rate of consumption, we might need it. Stephen was looking as if that sort of party was low in his list of favourite hobbies, and I guessed that he was only staying out of a vague sense of not leaving the sinking ship before the rats.

'What've you got, then, sport?' Malcolm said, with half a toothmugful in his grasp. 'What's all this about a page from my notebook?'

I fished it out of my pocket and gave it to him. He buried his nose in his glass and looked at the small page sideways, over the rim. Some loose drops of vodka trickled down his chin.

'Christ, sport,' he said, removing the glass and wiping himself up with the back of his hand, 'it's just a lot of doodles.' He turned it over. 'What's all this writing?'

'I don't know.'

He looked at his watch and seemed to be coming to a fast decision. A fresh gulp brought him near to the bottom of the glass, and he put it down on the dressing shelf with a snap.

'Look, mate, got to run.' He folded the page of notebook and began to put it in his jacket pocket.

'I'd like to keep that for a bit,' I said mildly. 'If you wouldn't mind.'

'What on earth for?' He tucked it firmly away out of sight.

'To see if I can decipher the writing on the other side.'

'But what's the point?'

'I'd just like to know who you gave it to in England . . . to see what he wrote on it.'

Malcolm still hesitated. Ian clawed his way to his feet and helped himself to Extra.

'Oh give it to him, Malcolm,' he said irritably. 'What the hell does it matter?'

Malcolm collected observant stares from three pairs of eyes and reluctantly put his hand in his pocket.

'It won't do you any bloody good, sport.' His voice was sharp with the beginnings of malice.

'All the same,' I said, taking back the note and stowing it away, 'it's interesting, don't you think? You wrote that page at Burghley . . . but you didn't tell me you were at that meeting. I was surprised that you didn't mention being there. I was surprised you *were* there, actually.'

'So what? I went to write it up.'

'For the *Watch*? I thought you were a foreign correspondent, not a sportswriter.'

'Look, sport,' he said, the muscles setting like rock in his solid neck. 'Just what is the point of all this crap?'

'The point is,' I said, 'that you know . . . you've known all along . . . what I came here to find out, and you've been trying all along to make sure I ended up in a fog . . . if not in a mortuary.'

Stephen and Ian had their mouths open.

'Ball,' Malcolm said.

'Can you drive a horse box?'

His only reply was a stare of intense animosity reinforced by some sort of inner decision.

'Dinner at the Aragvi,' I said. 'Your invitation, your dinner. There were two men there, sitting near us. They in my sight . . . I in theirs. Face to face, for a couple of hours. After that, they would always know me again. You took my glasses away . . . and everyone could see I was lost without them. When we left the restaurant I was attacked in Gorky Street . . . by two men who tried first to knock my glasses off, and then to bundle me into a car. They wore balaclavas, but I saw their dark un-Russian eyes very clearly. And I asked myself . . . who knew that I would be walking alone down Gorky Street at precisely that moment?'

'This is a load of horse shit. Look, sport, you'll end in a psychiatric hospital at the wrong end of a needle if you go on like this.'

Malcolm was deeply angry but his basic confidence was unshaken. He was still certain that I would not hit the absolute bull's-eye.

'The telex,' I said. 'And your little informer. I've no doubt that when a very long telex came for me, you were told. So I set off to the Embassy by the shortest route, and on the way I was jumped on by the same two men, who were *waiting for me*. That time I was saved only by a sort of ironic miracle . . . but when I got my senses back I asked myself, who could possibly have known I would make that journey?'

'Half of Moscow,' Malcolm said roughly.

'I knew,' Ian said, sounding studiedly impartial.

'Of course,' Malcolm said forcefully. 'And Ian knew we were dining at the

Aragvi. And Ian knew you were going to see Kropotkin at the Hippodrome, because you told us both in Oliver's office . . . So why the hell aren't you accusing Ian of all this? You're off your bloody rocker, sport, and I'll have you for slander if you don't back down and apologize this immediate bloody instant.' He looked at his watch again and revised this ultimatum. 'I'm not staying here to listen to any more of this bloody junk.'

'Ian helped me. You just told me to go home,' I said.

'All for your own bloody good.'

'It isn't enough,' Ian said uneasily. 'Randall . . . all this might be *possible*, but you've surely got it all wrong.'

'I haven't got to prove anything to any court of law,' I said. 'All I do have to do is to let Malcolm know what I think. That's enough. If a prying neighbour knew you were planning to rob a bank, you'd be a fool to go on with the plan. So call me a prying neighbour . . . but what Malcolm was planning was far worse than robbing banks.'

'What, then?' Ian said.

'Killing people at the Olympics.'

Malcolm's reaction went a long way to convincing Ian and Stephen. The shock turned his skin as white as the walls, leaving odd blotchy patches of broken thread veins on cheeks and nose. He literally lost his breath: his mouth opened, and no sound came out. There was sick disbelief in his eyes; and this time I really had chopped into the self-confidence with a lethal axe.

'So you may never get to court,' I told him. 'But if any of the Olympic riders die the same way Hans Kramer died, the world will know where to look.'

He was, in effect, stunned: almost as if losing consciousness on his feet. The room was still, with a silent intensity you could almost touch. Ian and Stephen and I all watched him almost without breathing: and at this impossibly fraught moment, someone knocked briskly on the door.

It was Ian's bad luck that it was he who moved first and went to open it.

Malcolm's friends attacked with their usual brutal speed, bursting in through the opening door like bulls and hitting out at whatever stood in their way. The sheer animal fury swept into the room like an emotional volcano, and the half-concealing balaclavas only seemed to intensify the horrendous impact.

The swinging riot stick wielded by the one in front crunched solidly into Ian's head. He fell without a sound and lay unmoving by the bathroom door.

The one behind kicked shut the door to the corridor and strode forward purposefully, holding a small screw-topped glass jar. On his hands, he wore rubber gloves. In the little jar, a pale golden liquid, like champagne.

Everything happened exceedingly fast.

Malcolm came to life with wide-staring eyes and shouted, 'Alyosha.' Then he said, 'No, no.' Then, as he saw the riot stick swinging at Stephen he said, 'No, no, that one,' and pointed at me.

I leapt on to the bed and picked up the tape-recorder, and threw it at the man who was attacking Stephen. It hit him in the face and hurt him, and he turned my way even more murderously than before.

The man with the little jar unscrewed its cap.

'That one,' Malcolm screamed, pointing at me. 'That one.'

The man with the jar stared with appalling ferocity at Malcolm, and drew back his arm.

Malcolm screamed.

Screamed.

'No. No. No.'

I picked up the chair and lashed out at the man with the jar, but the one with the riot stick stood in the way.

The man with the jar threw the contents into Malcolm's face. Malcolm gave a high wailing cry like a seagull.

I crashed the chair down again and hit the wrist of the jar-carrier with a blow like chopping wood. He dropped the jar and jerked with agony. I jumped off the sofa and laid into both of them with the chair with a fury fed by theirs, and Stephen picked up one of the vodka bottles and slammed it at one of the eye-slits of the balaclavas.

I had never in my life felt such a rage. I hated those men. Shook with hate. I swung the chair not to preserve my life, but to smash theirs. Sheer primitive blood-lusting vengeful hatred, not only for what they were doing in this city and this room, but for all their counterparts round the world. For all the helpless hostages, for all the ransom victims, I was bashing back.

It may have been reprehensible and uncivilized, but it was certainly effective. Stephen smashed his bottle against the wall and crowded into them with the broken ends thrusting forward sharply, and I simply belted them with chair and feet and fury, and we beat them back into the narrow passage by the bathroom, where Ian still lay unmoving.

With what looked like a joint and instantaneous decision they suddenly turned their backs on us, dragged open the door to the corridor and fled.

I turned back into the room, panting.

'After them,' Stephen said, gasping.

'No . . . come back . . . ' I heaved for breath. 'Shut the door . . . Got to see to Malcolm.'

'Malcolm . . .?'

'Dying,' I said. 'Ninety seconds . . . Jesus Christ.'

Malcolm had collapsed, half on the floor, half on the bed, and was whimpering.

'Open the matroshka,' I said urgently. 'Misha's matroshka. Quick. Quick . . . Get that tin with the naloxone.'

I yanked open the drawer which contained my breathing things and snatched out the plastic box. My fingers wouldn't work properly. Serve him bloody right, I thought violently, if I couldn't save his life because they'd smashed my hand when he tried to have me killed.

334

Couldn't tear the strong plastic cover off the hypodermic syringe. Hurry. For God's sake hurry . . . Did it with my teeth.

'This?' Stephen said, holding out the cough-lozenge tin. I opened it and put in on the dressing shelf.

'Yes . . . Get his trousers down.'

Ninety seconds. Jesus Christ.

My hands were trembling.

Malcolm was gasping audibly for air.

'He's turning blue,' Stephen said with horror.

The needle was packed inside the syringe. I got it out and fitted it in place.

'He's hardly breathing,' Stephen said. 'And he's unconscious.'

I snapped the neck of one of the ampoules of naloxone. Stood it with shaking hands upright on the shelf. Mustn't . . . mustn't knock it over. Needed two good hands, two hands working properly and not shaking.

I picked up the syring in my right hand and the ampoule in my left. I was right-handed . . . I couldn't do it at all the other way round, though I would have done, if I could. Lowered the needle into the precious teaspoonful of liquid. Hauled up the plunger of the syringe, sucking it in. My fingers hurt. So what, so what. Ninety seconds . . . all but gone.

I turned to Malcolm. Stephen had pulled the trousers down to expose a bit of rump. I shoved the needle into the muscle, and pressed the plunger: and God, I thought, could do the rest.

We lifted him on to the bed, which was no mean task, taking off his jacket and tie and ripping open the front of his shirt. His colour and breathing were still dreadful, but no worse. He was conscious again, and terrified, and said, 'Bastards,' between his teeth.

Along by the bathroom Ian began groaning. Stephen went over to him, and found him rapidly regaining consciousness and trying to rise to his feet. He helped him up and supported him, and got him as far as the sofa.

The little glass jar lay near the sofa on the carpet, and Stephen almost automatically bent down to pick it up.

'Don't touch it,' I said, my voice going high with alarm. 'Don't touch it, Stephen. It'll kill you.'

'But it's empty.'

'I doubt it,' I said. 'And I think a few drops would be enough.' I picked up the fallen chair and planted it over the jar. 'That'll have to do for now . . . Don't let Ian touch it.'

I turned back to Malcolm. His breathing seemed to be slightly stronger, but not by much.

'How do we get a doctor?' I said.

Stephen gave me a despairing look which I interpreted as dismay at getting ourselves enmeshed in any form of Soviet officialdom, but he picked up the telephone and dialled through to the reception desk.

'Tell them the doctor should bring naloxone.'

He repeated the request twice and spelled it out once, but looked troubled as he replaced the receiver. 'She said she would call a doctor, but about the naloxone . . . she said the doctor would know what to bring. Unhelpful. Obstructive. The more you insist, the more they just stick their toes in.'

'Randall . . .'

Malcolm's lusty voice came out as a weak croak.

'Yes?' I bent over him, to hear better.

'Get . . . the . . . bastards.'

I took a deep breath. 'Why did they throw the stuff at you, and not at me?'

He seemed to hear and understand, but he didn't answer. Sweat stood out suddenly in great beads all over his face, and he began gasping again for air.

I filled the syringe from the second ampoule of naloxone, and pushed the needle into his haunch. The reaction came again, sluggish but definite, taking the laboured edge off the breathing but leaving him in a dangerous state of exhaustion.

'The bastards . . . said . . . I . . . robbed them.'

'How do you mean?'

'I sold them . . . the stuff. They said . . . it wasn't worth . . . the money.'

'How much did they pay you?' I said.

'Fifty . . . thousand . . .'

'Pounds?'

'Christ . . . sport . . . of course. They said . . . this afternoon . . . I'd robbed . . . them. I told them . . . to come here . . . finish you . . . too clever . . . by half. Didn't know Ian . . . would . . . be here.'

I reflected that when he had found Ian and Stephen with me he had attempted to leave and intercept his friends before they reached my rom. No one could tell whether the outcome would have been much different if he'd succeeded. The friends were about as predictable as forked lightning.

I took a toothmug to the bathroom, half filled it with water, and brought it back to hold to Malcolm's mouth. It did little more than wet his lips, but that seemed to be all he wanted.

Looked at my watch. It was two minutes since I'd given him the second injection: four since the first. It seemed a lifetime.

Ian was recovering fast and beginning to ask questions. It was extraordinary, I thought, that no one at all had heard the fracas and come running. No one had heard . . . or reacted . . . to Malcolm's scream, and I would have thought they would have heard Malcolm's scream in the Kremlin. When the bugs were switched off, the walls were deaf.

Malcolm went into another sudden and devastating collapse. I grimly filled the syringe from the last ampoule and injected the teaspoonful into his muscles.

There was no more naloxone: no safety margin for any of us.

336

16

The upswing came again. He breathed a little more positively and regained consciousness, although his skin was still greyish blue and his pupils remained pinpoints.

'I feel . . . dizzy,' he said.

I gave him a few sips of water and said casually, 'Was it you or your friends who poured the stuff on Hans Kramer?'

'Christ, sport . . . not me. I'm no killer . . .'

'What about the horse box?'

'Only meant . . . to hurt you . . . frighten . . . send you home.' He took another sip. 'Reckoned you wouldn't stay . . .'

'But your friends weren't fooling,' I said. 'Not in Gorky Street, and not by the river.'

'They said . . . not safe . . . with Kropotkin helping . . . you might . . . find out . . . things.'

'Mm,' I said. 'And that was after you told them that I knew what Hans Kramer had said when he was dying?'

'Bloody boy . . . Misha . . .'

'Was this deadly liquid your idea, or Hans Kramer's?' I said.

'I learned of it . . . by chance. Got Hans . . . to steal it.' He achieved a faint sneer. 'Stupid bastard . . . conned him . . . he did it for nothing . . . for his ideals . . .'

'He went to the Heidelberg Clinic,' I said.

'Christ . . . ' Even in his cooperative state, he was unpleasantly surprised. 'In the telex . . . didn't think you'd spot that, but it was . . . risky. They wanted to prevent . . . you from seeing it.'

'So why did they kill Hans? Why Hans, who had helped you?'

He was tiring visibly. His voice was faint, and his breathing was still slow and shallow.

'Cover . . . all . . . tracks . . .'

Ian stood up restlessly and came over to the bed. It was the first close view he'd had of Malcolm since the attack, and the shock penetrated the inscrutability of his face.

'Look, Randall,' he said, horrified, 'leave all these questions until he's better. Whatever he's done, it will keep.'

He had no idea, I thought, of the sort of thing we were dealing with, and it was hardly the moment to tell him.

I gave Malcolm some more water, and because of Ian's intervention he began to reflect and regret that he had so willingly answered. Reactivated hostility sharpened visibly in his pin-point eyes, and when I took the glass from his lips his whole face settled into the old stubborn mould.

'What are their names?' I said. 'And their nationality?'

'Sod off . . .'

'Randall!' Ian protested. 'Not yet.'

'One of them is Alyosha,' Stephen said, steering a careful path round the chair, and crossing to join us. 'Didn't you hear? Malcolm called one of them Alyosha.'

There was almost a laugh from the bed. A large sardonic sneer twisted his mouth. His voice, although almost a whisper, came out loaded with spite.

'Alyosha, sport,' he said, 'will kill you yet.'

Stephen looked at him incredulously. 'But your *friends* tried to kill you . . . It's Randall who saved you.'

'Balls.'

'He's confused,' I said. 'Just leave it.'

'Christ . . . ' Malcolm said. 'I feel sick.'

Stephen looked rapidly around for a suitable receptacle, but there wasn't one, and it wasn't needed.

Malcolm's shallow breathing perceptibly lessened. I picked up his wrist, and could feel no pulse. His eyes slowly closed.

'Do something,' Ian said urgently.

'We can try artificial respiration,' I said. 'But not mouth to mouth.'

'Why not?'

'That stuff was thrown at his face . . . You can't trust it.'

'Do you mean he's dying?' Stephen said. 'After all?'

Ian energetically began pulling Malcolm's arms up and backwards in the old method of artificial respiration, refusing to let him go without having done everything possible.

Malcolm's neck and hands and bare chest turned from bluish grey to dark indigo. Only his face stayed pale.

Ian persevered, hauling the rib cage up and down, trying to get air into the lungs mechanically. Stephen and I watched in silence for what seemed a very long time.

I didn't try to stop him. Stopping had to be his own decision. And I suppose some quality in Malcolm's total lack of response finally convinced him, because he reluctantly laid the arms down to rest, and turned to us a blank and Sphinx-like face.

'He's dead,' he said flatly.

'Yes.'

There was a long pause while no one could quite bring themselves to say what was in all of our minds, but Ian at length put it into words.

'The doctor's on his way. What do we tell him?'

'Heart attack?' I suggested.

The others nodded.

'Let's tidy up, then,' I said, looking round at the aftermath of battle. 'What we desperately need is some rubber gloves.'

The small glass jar still lay on its side under the guarding chair. I reckoned it would have to be shovelled somehow into a toothmug, and was looking around for a suitable long spoon for supping with the devil when Stephen brought out his packet from the chemist.

'What about these?' he said. 'They supposed to be impermeable.'

On any other occasion we'd have laughed too much to make it possible. Instead, I quite seriously dressed the thumb and fingers of my left hand in preservativy, keeping them in place with an elastic band round my knuckles.

Stephen had protested that as they were his preservativy, it should be he who used them, especially as I was proposing a left-handed operation. Shut up, I said, and let's get on. It was my job, I thought. It was where the buck stopped. A matter of the beginning and the end of responsibility.

He removed the chair. I knelt on the floor, and, summoning up an act of faith in the baggy and improvised rubber glove, picked up the little jar and stood it upright in the toothglass.

My mouth, to be honest, was dry.

The jar had looked more or less empty when it lay on its side, but this had been deceptive. There was now clearly about a dessertspoonful of pale golden liquid lying in the bottom. Pale gold . . . a pretty shade of death.

'The cap of the jar must be somewhere,' I said. 'But don't touch it.'

Ian found it under the sofa. He shifted the end of the sofa, and I picked up the small screw-top and put it in the glass alongside the jar.

'What will you do with it?' Stephen said, looking at the remnants with understandable awe.

'Dilute it.'

I took the toothmug into the bathroom and stood it in the centre of the bath. Then I put in the plug, and turned on the taps. The water poured in in a tumbling cascade and the level quite soon rose to cover the glass. The little jar floated out like a bathtime toy, still holding its fearsome cargo. I pushed it, with my covered fingertips, into the depths.

Turned off the taps. Stirred the jar around in the water briskly with the handle of my toothbrush, and then pulled out the plug to let the water run away. When it had gone, the washed jar, the cap, and the toothglass lay in harmless wet heaps on the clear white enamel. I picked them out of the bath and put them into the wash basin, and immersed them once again, to make doubly certain.

Then I stripped off the preservativy and flushed them appropriately down the loo: and took a great deep breath of relief.

In the room Stephen and Ian had straightened and restored everything to order. The syringe and the empty ampoules were out of sight. The matroshka stood with her two halves joined. The broken bottle and its scattered fragments had vanished. The chair stood quietly by the dressing shelf. The tape recorder stood upon it harmlessly. My suitcase was back in the wardrobe. All tidy. All calm. All innocent.

And Malcolm . . . Malcolm lay in his permanent silence with his trousers up and fastened, and his shirt buttoned to near the top. His jacket and tie lay on the sofa, but folded neatly, not in the heap into which we'd thrown them. Malcolm dead looked a deal more peaceful than Malcolm dying.

The Russian doctor came with an expressionless face and unemotionally began to roll out the red tape. Stephen and Ian gathered that he took a poor view of foreigners who keeled over on Saturday evenings when all services were at a low ebb.

We drifted around as we were told, waiting mostly in the chairs by the lifts and not speaking much. The stumpy lady at the desk came and went several times, and Stephen asked her if she found her work boring.

She said stolidly that nothing much ever happened, but her job was her job. Stephen translated question and answer, and we nodded sympathetically and guessed she'd been away from her desk when Malcolm's friends called.

The doctor was unsuspicious. In England, Hans Kramer's death had been adjudged a heart attack even after an autopsy, and with luck it would happen again. The doctor had not mentioned having been asked to bring naloxone, and it appeared that the reception desk had not, in fact, passed on Stephen's request: fortunately, as it turned out.

Ian developed a thundering headache from the effects of vodka and concussion and sat moaning gently with his eyes shut.

Stephen bit a couple of fingernails.

I coughed.

There were a good many unsmiling faces coming and going, some of which finally said we could return to my room, for Stephen and Ian to retrieve their hats and coats, and me to pack to remove to another room in the hotel.

Ian groaned off home at that point, but Stephen helped to carry my belongings up in the lift to the fifteenth floor. The new room was identical in lay-out; slightly different in colour: and there was no stiff shape lying under a white sheet on the bed.

Stephen cast his gaze round the walls and put two fingers to his mouth. I nodded. It didn't seem worthwhile fiddling about with the tape-recorder. We made one or two suitable and shocked remarks about heart attacks, just in case, and left it at that.

I had found that in his fast tidying he had rolled all the broken glass and ampoules and the syringe in my dressing-gown and stowed it in the suitcase. We had judged it sensible, in discussion while walking along the corridor, to get rid of them altogether, so we put them all in the outermost shell of the new matroshka, leaving a smaller little mother beaming upon the shelf. We put the rubbish-filled doll into the string bag, and picked up the tape-recorder, and very quietly let ourselves out of the room.

The lady at the fifteenth floor desk gave us an uninterested stare. We smiled at her as we waited for the lifts, but smiling back wasn't her habit.

Made it to the ground floor. No trouble. Strolled unhurriedly around the longer route to the door, unaccosted. Walked outside under the watching eyes, which did nothing more than watch.

Climbed into a taxi. Travelled trustfully, and arrived safely at the University.

There was nowhere private to suffer from reaction. Stephen and I were both shaking after we'd taken off our hats and coats in his room, and we felt a great compulsive need to talk. I had seldom found anything so difficult as making asinine conversation with a mind stuffed with the evening's horrors, but the recorder has proved definitely again that we were not alone. The un-released tension made us both uncomfortable to the point of not being able to meet each other's eyes. In the end he said a shade violently that he would brew tea and empty the matroshka into the students' communal rubbish bin: and I went into the passage and made a long telephone call to Yuri Chu-litsky.

17

Yuri picked me up in the wan December light of nine o'clock on a Sunday morning from outside the National Hotel.

There had been a fresh fall of snow during the night, and the roads had not yet been cleared, so that everything lay like Malcolm under a white shroud, and my spirits were as low as the air temperature.

The bright yellow car zoomed up like a golden cube, and I slid into the passenger seat beside him, coughing violently.

'You have illness?' he said, letting in the clutch as if cogs were made of titanium.

Death warmed up, I thought: but it wasn't the best of similes.

'You say,' Yuri said, 'you want very important comrade.' The familiar accent rose above the engine noise. The bags under his eyes looked heavier and there was a slumped quality in his body. The upper lip rose convulsively two or three times, giving me the gleams of teeth. He lit a cigarette, one-handed, expertly, dragging the smoke urgently into his lungs. There was a fine dampness on his forehead.

He had come dressed, as I had, in his neatest and most formal suit, with clean shirt, and tie. He was nervous, I thought: which made two of us.

'I get Major-General,' he said. 'Is very high comrade.'

I was impressed. I had asked him for a comrade of sufficient rank to be able to make decisions: although from what I'd known before and seen since I'd arrived, it had seemed that there was no one at all of that stature. The Soviet method seemed to be 'action only after consultation', or 'until the committee's met, just keep saying *Niet*'. No official would make a decision on his own, for fear of it being wrong.

'Where are we going?' I said.

'Architects' Circle.'

So even the Major-General wasn't sure enough to meet me upon official ground.

'He say,' Yuri said, 'you call him Major-General. He not say his name.'

'Very well.'

We drove a little without speaking. I coughed a bit and thought of the night gone past, much of which I had spent writing. It had been a laborious process physically, as I couldn't hold the pen properly. In the heat of battle I'd picked up a chair and gripped it hard to cut and thrust; but the anaesthesia of hot blood was definitely missing in the cold hours after midnight. In the morning, when he had returned from Gudrun, I had given Stephen the explanatory sheets to read, while I put the telex, the formula, and the two pages of Malcolm's notebook into a large envelope.

He had read to the end, and looked at me speechlessly.

I smiled lop-sidedly. 'Ve have vays of taking out insurance.'

I put the hand-written sheets into the envelope, and addressed it to the Prince, which raised his mobile eyebrows another notch. Then I looked at the walls and by common consent we went out and strolled down the passage.

'If the comrades should be so inhospitable as to cast me in the clink,' I said, 'you just beetle round to the Embassy tomorrow morning and insist on seeing Oliver Waterman personally. Tell him the mountains will fall on his head if he doesn't send that envelope off pronto in the diplomatic bag.'

Stephen said, I know of a letter which was supposed to come to Moscow by diplomatic bag but ended up in Ulan Bator.'

'So helpful.'

'They say the Lubianka goes down seven floors underground.'

'Thanks very much.'

'Don't go,' he said.

'Come to lunch in the Intourist Hotel,' I said. 'They have pretty good ice-cream.'

Yuri drove round a white corner at speed and corrected the resultant skid with a practised flick.

'Yuri,' I said, 'did you deliver a page of Malcolm's notebook to Mr Kropotkin?'

The ash fell off his cigarette. His upper lip did a positive jig.

'I thought it must be you,' I said. 'You said you talked to him at Burghley, about buildings. If one could disentangle the writing on the back of that piece of paper with the help of blue filters, would it be notes about buildings?'

He was silent.

'I'll not speak of it,' I said diffidently. 'But I would like to know.'

There was another of the long familiar pauses, and in the end he said, 'I think paper not help,' as if it excused his action in delivering it.

'It helped very much.'

He moved his head in a way that I took to mean satisfaction, though I guessed that he still felt uneasy about allying himself with a foreigner. I wondered how I would feel if I were helping a Russian investigator and was not sure that anything he discovered might not be to the detriment of my own country. It made Yuri's dilemma most human, most understandable. And he was another, I thought, to whom I must do no harm.

Even at that hour on that day, there was a dragon on guard inside the door: short, dumpy, female, and stolid. She showed no pleasure at all in letting us through.

We shed our coats and hats. Everywhere in reception areas in Moscow there were acres of rails and hangers, and to every acre, a man in charge. We took our numbered discs and went through into the lofty ground-floor hall. Hall as in large meeting area, not as in entrance passage.

I had seen it two days earlier, passing through to the restaurant. Yellowish parquet floor, lightweight metal and plastic armchairs, and upright boards in loose groups, which divided the space like random screens. Pinned upon these with colour-headed drawing pins were large matt-surfaced blown-up photographs of recent architectural activity.

Yuri led the way round one set of screens and arrived at an open central spot.

There were three of the light armchairs grouped round a low table there; and on one of the chairs, a man.

He stood up as we approached.

He was of about my own height. Solid of body. Immensely well groomed. Dark hair sprinkled with grey, smoothly brushed back. About fifty, perhaps. Chin freshly shaven, everything immaculate. He wore understated spectacles and an elegantly cut business suit. The impression of power was instant and lasting.

'Major-General,' Yuri said deferentially, 'this is Randall Drew.'

We exchanged a few preliminary courtesies. He spoke perfect English with only the ghost of an accent; and his voice was markedly urbane. Rupert Hughes-Beckett, Soviet version, I thought.

'I would have asked you to come to my office,' he said, 'except that on Sundays it is not fully staffed, and perhaps here also we will be less interrupted.'

He waved me to one of the chairs, and sat down again himself. Yuri delicately hovered. The Major-General suggested pleasantly, in English, that he should go and organize some coffee, and wait for it to be made.

He watched Yuri's obediently departing backview, and then turned to me.

'Please begin,' he said.

'I was sent to Moscow,' I said for openers, 'by the British Foreign Office, and by the Prince.' I gave the Prince his full title, because I guessed that even to a good son of the revolution the fact that I was on an errand for the monarch's cousin might pull some weight.

The Major-General gave me a placid stare from uninformative grey eyes. 'Please continue.'

'My brief was to find out if John Farringford ... Lord Farringford, the Prince's brother-in-law ... would be likely to be involved in a damaging scandal if he should come to ride in the Olympic Equestrian Games. There was some mention of a certain Alyosha. I was to find and interview this Alyosha, and see how the land lay ... Er ... am I making myself clear?'

'Perfectly,' he said courteously. 'Please go on.'

'John Farringford had indiscreetly visited several rather perverted sexual entertainments in London with a German rider, Hans Kramer. This German subsequently died at the International Horse Trials, and people near him said that in his last few breaths he distinctly said, "It is Alyosha".' I paused. 'For some reason that I cannot understand, a rumour arose that if Farringford came to Moscow, Alyosha would be waiting. The implication was clear that Alyosha would cause trouble. It was this rumour which led the Prince to ask me to look into things.'

'I follow,' he said slowly.

'Well ... I came,' I said. A couple of coughs convulsively squeezed my chest. There was a well-known slow fever stoking up in there, but for that day at least it would be manageable. The next day, and the next and next, would be a matter of luck. I girded up at least the mental loins.

I said, 'I found I was not investigating a minor muckheap, but something a great deal different. I asked to see you today because what I discovered was a terrorist plot to disrupt the Olympic Games.'

He was not surprised, and Yuri, of course, must have told him that much in order to persuade him to meet me. Not surprised, but unconvinced.

'Not in the Soviet Socialist Republics,' he said with flat disavowal. 'We have no terrorists here. Terrorists would not come here.'

'I'm afraid they have.'

'It is impossible.'

I said, 'If you encourage a plague, you must expect to catch it.'

His reaction to this unwise statement was an ominous stiffening of the spine and a raising of the chin, but at least we advanced into a territory in which he was prepared to face the possibility of pus on his own doorstep.

'I am telling you this so that you can avert a disaster in your capital,' I said neutrally. 'If you don't wish to hear me, I'll leave now.'

I didn't move, however, and nor did he.

After a pause he said, 'Please proceed.'

'The terrorists aren't Russians, I'll grant you that,' I said. 'And so far as I know, you only have two here at present. But I think they live here all the time ... and no doubt at the Games they would be reinforced.'

'Who are they?'

344

I took off my glasses, and squinted at them, and put them on again.

'If you keep a check on every foreigner who lives here in your city,' I said, 'you should seek out two men of between twenty and thirty years old, one of whom has today a badly bruised or broken wrist, and the other a damaged face. They may in addition have other bruises and cuts. They have sallow skins, dark eyes, and dark curling hair. I could if necessary identify them.'

'Their names?'

I shook my head. 'I don't know.'

'And what could they hope to achieve?' he said, as if the whole idea was ridiculous. 'It would be impossible for them to take hostages in this country.'

'I don't think they mean to,' I said. 'The trouble with taking hostages is that it involves so much time. Time while the demands are delivered and discussed. Time, which means feeding the captors and the hostages, and sewage, and absolutely mundane things like that. The longer it goes on, the less chance there is of success. And the world has grown tired of these threats, and a great deal tougher. It's no longer seen as sense to release imprisoned terrorists to save innocent lives, when the released terrorists simply go out and kill a different lot of innocents. And I agree with you that a mass kidnapping here would be smartly stepped on by your comrades. But these men didn't mean to kidnap, they meant to kill.'

He showed no emotion at all. 'And how would they do this? And how would it help them?'

'Suppose,' I said, 'that they killed, for instance, Lord Farringford. Suppose they then said, if such and such a demand of ours is not met, a member of the French riding team will die, and a member of the Germans, and a member of the Americans. Or all the American team. Suppose they moved terrorism to a different level, where the hostages had no chance at all. No one would know who the hostages were until they were dead, and the supply of potential hostages would be the number of people at the Games.'

He briefly thought it over and was not convinced.

'The theory is possible,' he said. 'But there is no suitable weapon. The murderers would quickly be caught.'

'Their weapon is a liquid,' I said. 'A spoonful per person would be enough. It doesn't have to be drunk. It is deadly if it's just poured on the skin. And that's what makes the equestrian part of the Games so vulnerable, because it is there that the performers and the spectators mingle most freely.'

A longer pause. I couldn't tell what he was thinking. I took a breath to go on, but he interrupted.

'Such liquids are extremely top secret and are kept in places of the utmost security,' he said. 'Are your supposed terrorists going to break into highly-guarded laboratories to steal it?' The urbanity in his voice said that he thought this unlikely.

I pulled out of my pocket a copy I had made of the formula, and handed it to him.

'That liquid is neither top secret nor difficult to obtain,' I said. 'And it kills within ninety seconds. One of my supposed terrorists could tip a spoonful on to your bare hand without you thinking anything of it, and he'd be lost in the crowd before you could say you felt ill.'

He unfolded the paper with the slightest of frowns, and read the list of words.

'What is it?' he said. 'I am no chemist.'

'Etorphine,' I said. 'That, I think, is a morphine derivative. Etorphine, ace-promazine and chlorocresol, those first three ingredients, would be an anaesthetic. I am absolutely certain, though I haven't been able to check it in Moscow, as I could at home, that they make up a particularly useful anaesthetic for use on animals.'

'Anaesthetic?' he said dubiously.

'It anaesthetizes horses and farm animals,' I said. 'But it is fatal for humans, in the tiniest amounts.'

'Why should anyone wish to use such a dangerous anaesthetic?' he said.

'Because it is the best for the animals,' I said. 'I've seen it used twice. Once on one of my horses, and once on a bull. Both animals recovered quickly, with none of the complications we used to get.'

'You've seen it . . .'

'Yes. And each time, the vet prepared a syringe of a neutralizing agent for use on himself, if he should be so unfortunate as to scratch himself with the needle of the syringeful of anaesthetic. He filled the neutralizing syringe before he even touched the phial with the anaesthetic, and he wore rubber gloves. He told me that the excellence of the anaesthetic for the animal's welfare was worth the precautions.'

'But is this . . . rare?'

I shook my head. 'More or less routine.'

'You said . . .' He thought briefly. 'You said "scratch himself". Does that mean this mixture would have to enter through a cut . . . a break in the skin? But you said it would be enough just to pour it . . .'

'Yes,' I said. 'Well . . . most liquids don't penetrate the skin, and that doesn't either. Normally all a vet does have to worry about is getting it into him through a cut or a scratch, except that if they do get a drop on them accidentally, even if there's no cut involved, they sluice it off again with a bucket or so of water.'

'Did your vet have the water ready also?'

'He did indeed.'

'Please go on,' he said.

'If you look at the formula again,' I said, 'you'll see that the next ingredient is dimethyl sulphoxide, and I actually do know what that is, because I've used it myself countless times on my horses.'

'Another sort of anaesthetic?'

'No. One uses it on sprains, bruises, sore shins . . . on practically everything. It's a general purpose embrocation.'

'But . . .'

'Well,' I said. 'Its chief property is that it's a liquid which *does* penetrate the skin. It carries its active ingredients through to the tissues beneath.'

He gave me a grave comprehending stare.

I nodded. 'So if one mixes the embrocation with the anaesthetic, it will go clean through the skin into the blood stream.'

He took a visibly deep breath, and said, 'What happens exactly if this mixture invades the body?'

'Depressed breathing and cardiac arrest,' I said. 'Very quick. It looks like a heart attack.'

He looked pensively down at the paper.

'What does this last line mean?' he said. 'Antagonist naloxone.'

'An antagonist is a drug which works against another drug.'

'So naloxine is . . . an antidote?'

'I don't think it's the stuff they give animals to bring them back to consciousness,' I said. 'I think it's what the vet prepares as a precaution for himself.'

'Do you mean . . . you have to give the animal a second injection? The anaesthetic does not simply wear off?'

'I don't know if it would in the end,' I said. 'But it's always reversed as soon as possible, as far as I know.'

'So naloxone is for humans.'

'Even terrorists wouldn't handle the stuff without protecting themselves,' I said. 'And I think,' I went on tentatively, 'that the amount of naloxone needed would depend on the amount of liquid one had absorbed. With animals, you see, the vet uses equal quantities of anaesthetic and reviving agent. And sometimes a further injection of reviver is needed.'

For Malcolm, I thought, it had simply been a matter of quantities. Too much killing liquid: not enough naloxone. His bad luck.

'All right,' the Major-General said, tucking the formula away into an inner pocket. 'Now please will you tell me what led you to these conclusions.'

I coughed because I couldn't help it, and took off my glasses and put them on again because the outcome of telling him might be not what I hoped.

'It started,' I said, 'at the International Horse Trials which were held in England in September. At that event, a British journalist, Malcolm Herrick, who worked here in Moscow as a correspondent for the *Watch*, persuaded Hans Kramer to steal a vet's case of drugs when the vet came to attend some of the horses. Malcolm Herrick received the anaesthetic from Kramer. He then mixed it with the embrocation, which is easy to come by. And he then sold it to the terrorists for fifty thousand pounds.'

'For *what*?' The Major-General showed the first sign of uncontrolled surprise.

'Yes . . . It was not a matter of ideology, but of hard cash. Someone, after all, sells weapons to the terrorists. They don't actually manufacture their

347

own guns. Fifty thousand, you are no doubt thinking, was a great deal too much for an easily accessible commodity. The thing was, of course, that Herrick didn't tell them what it was. I dare say he made out that it was, in fact, one of your top secret things from maximum security laboratories. Anyway, they paid for it, but not without a demonstration . . . A sort of trial run.'

I waited for the Major-General to comment, but nothing came.

'They used a little of it on Hans Kramer,' I said. 'Herrick no doubt suggested he should be the test victim because if he was dead he couldn't tell anyone he had given the stuff to Herrick.'

'Given . . . ? Didn't he *sell* it to Herrick?'

'No. Kramer sympathized with terrorists. He did it for the cause.'

The Major-General slightly compressed his lips.

'Go on.'

'Kramer's death was adjudged a heart attack. Herrick returned to Moscow, and so did the two terrorists. I think this may mean that he knew them here . . . met them here, perhaps . . . and that *because* he knew them, he thought up the scheme to sell them a compound he had at one time heard of by chance. And that is where everything would have stood until the Olympics; a nice little time-bomb ticking away in the dark. Except that people started asking questions about Alyosha.'

'At which point you came to Moscow.'

I nodded. Coughed. Wished the coffee would come. Swallowed with a dry mouth, and continued with the dicey bits.

'Since then, Herrick has tried to persuade me to go home, both with words and trying to knock me over with a motor horse box. The two terrorists have also had a go, and I'm only still here because I've been lucky. But sometime yesterday they discovered that they'd paid a great deal of money for a very cheap product, and they became extremely angry.'

I took a much needed deep breath. 'Herrick had told them to come to my room at the Intourist Hotel and finish me off properly. I think he meant them to do it by mechanical means . . . bashing my head in, and so forth. But when they came, they brought a good deal of the liquid in a small jar, perhaps all they had, and whether they meant any of it for me or not, they threw nearly all of it at Herrick.'

His mouth slowly opened and shut again.

I ploughed on. 'I had two friends with me, besides Herrick. We fought off the terrorists, which is why one of them has a damaged wrist and the other a damaged face, as well as other minor injuries, and they ran away.'

'Malcolm Herrick . . . is dead?'

'We called a doctor,' I said. 'The doctor believes it was a heart attack. Unless someone does an extremely thorough autopsy, that's how it will stand.'

The very faintest of smiles crossed his pale face. He rubbed a hand slowly round his jawline, and watched me with assessing eyes.

'How have you learned all this?' he said.

'I've listened.'

'To Russian people? Or all to foreigners?'

'Everyone who has spoken to me has been concerned that Russia should not be shamed by terrorism at the Games.'

'You speak like a diplomat,' he said.

The chin-rubbing went on for a bit. Then he said, 'And Alyosha. Did you in the end find this Alyosha?'

'Mm,' I said. 'Hans Kramer and Malcolm Herrick both said "Alyosha" in horror before they died. They both knew what they were dying of . . . and I think they had given it that name. A sort of code name, so that they could talk of it conveniently. I couldn't find Alyosha, because Alyosha is not a person. It's the liquid. Alyosha is the way of death.'

18

Yuri Chulitsky drove me back to the Intourist and actually dropped me outside the door. He shook my left hand emotionally, and gave me several pats on the shoulder. And then, with a great air of having a burden well shed, he drove away.

He had been visibly pleased when the Major-General had shaken his hand on parting, and on the way back to the hotel he had stopped the car abruptly by the kerb and put the handbrake on with a jerk.

'He said is good I ask him to meet you,' he said. 'Was correct decision.'

'Great,' I said, and meant it.

'Now, I keep bargain.'

I looked at him in surprise.

'You help my country. I tell you about Alyosha.'

I was puzzled. 'Tell me what?'

'I tell peoples, many peoples, is not good Lord Farringford come to Moscow. I say, in Moscow, Alyosha is waiting. Alyosha is not good peoples.'

'You told people . . . people in England?'

'*Da.* Peoples tell me, Hans Kramer die, it is Alyosha, Hans Kramer is bad man, is friend of Lord Farringford. Is bad Lord Farringford come to Moscow. So I say to peoples . . . Alyosha is bad peoples. Alyosha is trouble if Lord Farringford come.'

I shook my head slowly in amazement.

'But why, Yuri? Why didn't you want Lord Farringford to come to Moscow?'

He took a long time to answer. The longest pause of all. The lip went up and down six times. He lit a cigarette and took several deep drags. And at last he gave birth to his treason.

'Is not good . . . comrades use Lord Farringford . . . not good we follow him . . . use him in bad things . . . I feel shame for comrades who do this. I feel shame . . . for my country.'

Stephen and Ian were both sitting in the foyer, waiting and looking glum.

'My God,' Stephen said, seeing me standing before them. 'They've let you go!' His face lit into instant good spirits. 'Where are the handcuffs?'

'Being debated, I should think.'

There was still nowhere private to talk, since we couldn't trust my new room, so we simply transferred to the end of the line of seats along the foyer wall, and fell silent if anyone came close.

'What's happening?' Ian said.

'With luck, nothing much. I don't think they'll want to advertise terrorist activity in Moscow, not if they can help it. From your knowledge of this place, would you think the comrades would hush up a murder? Would they be allowed to? I had to tell the big noise that Malcolm was bumped off.'

Ian said, 'Easier here than anywhere else, my old son. If it suits them to say our pal died of a heart attack, they'll say it.'

'Let's hope it suits,' I said fervently.

'Look,' Ian said, 'Stephen has told me all you wrote last night. You must think me a poor dumb cluck not to have put all this together myself. But when I looked into it, I got nowhere.'

'But then I had the password,' I said, slightly smiling.

'Alyosha?' he said, puzzled.

'No . . . Horse.'

'The brotherhood of the saddle,' Stephen said sardonically. 'It opens the most private doors all around the world.'

'And don't you scoff,' I said. 'Because you're right.'

'There's just one thing we want to know,' Ian said, his calm unchanging face showing no sign of the previous day's ravages. 'And that is, why were you so utterly certain that Malcolm was at the heart of things? I mean . . . it was all so circumstantial . . . but you were quite sure.'

'Um . . . ' I said. 'It was nothing conclusive in itself. It was really just one more circumstance . . . and there were already so many. It was the page from his notebook, which Yuri Chulitsky sent to Kropotkin. You remember what it looked like? All doodles. So when do you doodle? When you're listening, or waiting. When you're waiting for an answer on the telephone. If you remember, near the bottom of the page there were some letters and numbers, DEP PET 1855 and K's C 1950. Well . . . they meant nothing much to me at first sight, but yesterday afternoon while we were rolling around Moscow, I thought . . . suppose Malcolm doodled because he was *waiting* for those numbers . . . and then we passed a metro station and I thought of trains . . .

And there it damn well was, staring me in the face. DEP PET 1855 meant Depart Peterborough 18.55 hours, and K's C 1950 meant arrive King's Cross at 19.50. He had been ringing up the time-table enquiries to find out.'

'But what's so blinding about that?' Stephen said.

'Peterborough is the main line station for Burghley.'

'So,' Ian said slowly, seeing the point, 'when Boris overheard what he did on the train from Burghley to London, he was listening to Malcolm . . . who was selling his goods to his friends.'

'It seemed possible,' I said. 'In fact, it seemed extremely likely. And on that same sheet of paper, probably while still waiting for the time-table people to answer, because they take ages sometimes, Malcolm pencilled in Johnny Farringford as a star possibility for Alyosha. I don't know how well he knew Johnny, but he didn't like him. He referred to him as a shit.'

'But why on earth should he give such an incriminating piece of paper to anyone else?' Stephen said. 'He was really stupid.'

I shook my head. 'It was only by the merest chance that it reached me and meant anything. To him, it was only a doodle. He scrawled over it. It was just a piece of rubbish to be thrown away . . . or given to someone who wanted some scrap paper for making notes.'

'How's your cough?' Stephen said.

'Bloody awful. Let's have some lunch.'

Because there were three of us, we sat at a different table, the next one along from the Wilkinsons and Frank.

Ian eyed Frank benignly and asked me quietly if the *status* in that area was still *quo*.

'Does he know I know?' I said. 'No, he doesn't. Does he know you know? Who can tell?'

'Does he know I know you know they know she knows you know?' Stephen said.

Mrs Wilkinson leaned across the gap. 'Are you going home on Tuesday, like us?' she said. 'Dad and I won't be sorry to be back, will we, Dad?'

Dad looked as if he couldn't wait.

'I hope so,' I said.

Natasha brought the soaring eyebrows and a fixed smile and said I hadn't kept my promise to tell her where I was going.

Nothing, it seemed, had changed; except that it was Stephen who ate my meat.

After lunch the three of us went up to my room for Ian and Stephen to collect the coats and hats they had left there just before, and while we were debating when next to telephone and next to meet, there was a sharp knock on the door.

'Christ, not again,' Ian said, instinctively putting a hand to his bruised head.

351

I went to the door and said, 'Who is it?'

No reply.

Stephen came and said, 'Who is it?' in Russian.

There was this time an answer, but to Stephen it seemed unwelcome. 'He said the Major-General sent him.'

I let down the drawbridge. Outside in the corridor stood two large men with stolid faces, flat uniformed caps, and long great-coats. From the look on Stephen's face, I guessed that the posse had come for the outlaw.

One of them handed me a stuck-down envelope addressed to Randall Drew. Inside there was an extremely brief hand-written note, saying simply, 'Accompany my officers', and below that, 'Major-General'.

Stephen, looking round-eyed and a little pale, said, 'I'll wait here. We'll both wait here.'

'No ... You'd better go. I'll telephone.'

'If you don't,' he said, 'first thing in the morning, I take the goods to Oliver Waterman. Is that right?'

'Uhuh.'

I pulled hat and coat from the wardrobe and put them on. The two large unsmiling men unsmilingly waited. We all walked along in a cluster of five, and went down in the lift without saying very much.

During our process through the foyer there was a certain amount of drawing aside of skirts, and several frightened glances. The bulk and intent of my two escorts was unmistakable. No one wanted to be involved in my disaster.

They had come in a large black official car, with a uniformed driver. They gestured to me to sit in the back. I had a parting view of Ian and Stephen's strained-looking faces as they stood side by side on the pavement, and then the car set off and made unerringly for Derzhinsky Square.

The long façade of the Lubianka loomed along one side of it, looking like a friendly insurance-company building if one didn't know better. The car, however, swept past its huge sides and pulled up in front of the big building next door, which was pale blue with white painted scrolls, and would on any other day have looked rather pretty.

My escorts opened the car door for me to get out, and walked beside me into the building. Inside, Lubianka or not, it was clearly no jolly children's home. We marched at a sturdy pace down wide institutional corridors, and came to a halt outside an unmarked door. One of my escorts knocked, opened the door, and stood aside for me to go in. With a dry mouth and galloping pulse, I went.

It was a comfortable, old-fashioned office, with a lot of dark polished wood and glass-fronted cupboards. A desk. A table. Three or four chairs. And by the window, holding back a dark curtain to look out at the snowy street, the Major-General.

He turned, and walked towards me, and held out his hand. I was so relieved that I automatically gave him my right one in return, and tried not to wince when he grasped it. I wondered if he knew he'd just given me one of the most shaking half hours of my life.

'Come,' he said. 'I have something to show you.'

He led me through a second door in the back wall of the office, into a narrower secondary corridor. After a few yards we came to a door which opened on to a staircase, leading down. We descended to the next floor, and went along another, grittier corridor.

We stopped at a totally smooth metal door. The Major-General pressed a button in the wall beside it, and the door swung open. He went into the room in front of me, and beckoned to me to follow.

I stepped into a square, bare room, brightly lit.

There were two armed policemen standing guard in there, and two other men, sitting on stools, with their arms fastened behind their backs.

If I was surprised to see them, it was nothing to their reaction on seeing me. One of them spat, and the other said something which seemed to shake even the KGB.

'These are the men?' the Major-General said.

'Yes.'

I looked into the faces remembered from the Aragvi restaurant. Into the eyes remembered from Gorky Street and under the bridge. Into the souls that had killed Hans Kramer and Malcolm Herrick.

One seemed slightly older, and had a drooping moustache. His lips were a little retracted, showing a gleam of teeth clenched in a travesty of a grin; and even in this place he exuded a bitter hostility.

The other had taut skin over sharp bones, and the large eye-sockets of so many fanatics. Across the eyebrow and down the side of his face there was a scarlet cut, and there was a split swelling on his lower lip.

'Which of them killed Herrick?' said the Major-General.

'The one with the moustache.'

'He says his wrist is broken,' the Major-General remarked conversationally. 'They were waiting at the airport. We had no trouble finding them. They speak very little English, by the way.'

'Who are they?' I said.

'They are journalists.' He sounded surprised at this discovery. 'Tarek Zanetti,' pointing to the man with the moustache, 'and Mehmet Sarai, with the cut.'

Their names meant nothing to me, even if they were the ones they were born with, which might be doubtful.

'They have been living in the same compound as Herrick,' the Major-General said. 'He could have seen them easily every day.'

'Do they belong to something like the Red Brigades?' I asked.

'Something new, we think,' he said. 'A breakaway group. But we have yet to make more than the most preliminary interrogation. Immediately they arrived here, I sent for you. However, I will show you something. When we searched the bags they were attempting to leave with, we found this.' He took a letter out of his pocket, and gave it to me. I unfolded it, but it was typewritten in a language I didn't know even by sight.

I shook my head and began to hand it back.

'Read lower down.'

I did as he said, and came across the familiar words, etorphine . . . acepro-
mazine . . . chlorocresol . . . dimethyl sulphoxide.

'It's a copy of a report from a chemical company,' he said, 'sending an
analysis asked for by your friend with the moustache. It seems to have been
delivered to him yesterday.'

'So they wanted to find out what they'd bought.'

'It would seem so.' He took back the letter and restored it to his pocket.
'That is all,' he said. 'Your positive identification of these men was required,
but nothing more. You are at liberty to go back to England when you wish.'
He hesitated slightly, then continued, 'It is believed that you will be discreet.'

'I will,' I said, and hesitated in my turn. 'But . . . these two will have colleagues . . . and that liquid does exist.'

'It may be necessary,' he said heavily, 'to search every spectator at the entrances.'

'There's a quicker way.'

'What is that?'

'It will be summer . . . Watch for anyone wearing gloves. If they have rubber gloves underneath, arrest them.'

He gazed at me from behind his glasses and rubbed his chin, and slowly
said, 'I see why they sent you.'

'And gallons of naloxone at every turn . . .'

'We will work out many precautions.'

I looked across for the last time at the naked hate-filled faces of international terrorism, and thought about alienation and the destructive steps
which led there.

The intensifying to anger of the natural scorn of youth for the mess their
elders had made of the world. The desire to punish violently the objects of
scorn. The death of love for parents. The permanent sneer for all forms of
authority. The frustration of not being able to scourge the despised majority.
And after that, the deeper, malignant distortions . . . The self-delusion that
one's feelings of inadequacy were the fault of society, and that it was necessary to destroy society in order to feel adequate. The infliction of pain and
fear, to feed the hungry ego. The total surrender of reason to raw emotion,
in the illusion of being moved by a sort of divine rage. The choice of an un-
attainable end, so that the violent means could go on and on. The addictive
orgasm of the act of laying waste.

'What are you thinking?' the Major-General said.

'That they are self-indulgent.' I turned away from them with a sense of release. 'It is easier to smash than to build.'

'They are pigs,' he said, with disdain.

'What will you do with them?'

But that was one question he had no intention of answering directly. He
simply said, with polished blandness, 'Their newspapers must find other
writers.'

The *Watch*, I thought, would be facing the same problem: and an old irrelevant piece of information floated to the surface.

'Ulrike Meinhof was a journalist,' I said.

19

The flight home was met at Heathrow at four in the afternoon by one of Hughes-Beckett's minions, who whisked me off to what he called a debriefing and I called a bloody nuisance.

I coughed my way into the mandarin's office and protested. I got an insincere apology and a small glass of sherry, when the only thing to bring me back to animation was a quadruple scotch.

'Can't it wait until tomorrow?' I said, feeling feverish.

'The Prince wants you to meet him at Fontwell Park races in the morning.'

'I thought of staying in bed.'

'What's wrong with your arm?' he said, disregarding this frivolous statement and eyeing Stephen and Gudrun's farewell attempt at a restful sling for the journey.

'Fingers got hammered. But not sickled.' I must be lightheaded, I thought. Lightheaded from the upsurge of relief at being back where liberty still poked up a few persistent tendrils. Lightheaded at the sight of people smiling in the street. At Christmas trees, and bright lights and cornucopias of shops. One could spurn the affluent society and seek the simple life if one wanted to: the luxury lay in being able to choose.

Hughes-Beckett eased himself in his comfortable office chair and studied the back of his hand.

'And how . . . ah . . . did it go?' he said.

I told him more or less exactly what I had told the Major-General. He stopped looking at his hands and came to mental life in a very positive and alert way, quite different from his habitual air of boredom.

I talked and coughed, and coughed and talked, and he gave me another and slightly larger sherry.

'So there you are,' I said finally. 'As far as I could tell there will be a great deal of hush over the whole scene. And as for Johnny Farringford . . . well, I got no definite assurances, but I doubt if after this the comrades would consider him a suitable prospect. So from that point of view I think it would be safe for him to go . . . but it's of course up to you and the Prince.'

I stood up. I really felt most unwell. Nothing new, however. The story of my life.

He came with me all the way to the front door and saw me off in an official car, which represented a radical rethink on his part of the usefulness of horses.

I found that meeting the Prince at Fontwell Park races involved lunch with him, the Princess, Johnny Farringford, the Chairman of the racecourse, sundry Stewards and assorted ladies, all in the glass-walled corner box at the top of the stands, looking down over the green turf.

There was a lot of champagne and civilized chat, which on other days would have pleased me well enough: but the shadows of Moscow still sat close at my shoulder, and I thought of the fear of Boris and Evgeny and the doubts and caution of Yuri and Misha and Kropotkin. I should be glad to hear in time from Ian and Stephen that none of them had come to harm.

I had spent a toss-and-turn night in a hotel and hired a car and driver to take me to the races. Practically every remedy in the plastic box had been pressed into service, to only moderate avail. It was a bore to drag around with lungs filled up like sumps and every breath an effort, but I'd ridden in races in that state once or twice in my foolish life, so why fret at some gentle spectating. Bits of lines of the Scottish ballad of the dying Lord Randall, with whom I'd identified heavily as a child, ran from long habit in my mind, more as a sort of background music than organized thought, but now with an added new meaning . . .

. . . make my bed soon,
For I'm weary wi' hunting, and fain would lie doon.

'Randall,' the Prince said, 'we must talk.'

We talked in short snatches through the afternoon, standing alone on the Stewards' balcony between the races, using the times when everyone else went down to look at the horses in the parade ring.

Make my bed soon . . .

'There were two plots involving Johnny,' I said.

'*Two?*'

'Mm . . . Being who he is, he's a natural target. He always will be. It's something that needs to be faced.'

I told him bit by bit about the terrorists, and about the identity of Alyosha. It all shocked him a great deal more deeply than it had those two wily gamesplayers, Hughes-Beckett and the Major-General.

'Dreadful. Dreadful,' he said.

'There was also,' I said eventually, 'some question of the KGB setting him up.'

'How do you mean?'

I explained about the pornography.

'Johnny?' The Prince looked surprised and most displeased. 'The bloody fool . . . doesn't he realize that is just what the Press are always looking for?'

'If he was warned, sir . . .'

'Warned?' He looked grim. 'You can safely leave that to me.'

I'd like to be a fly on the wall, I thought.

A memory struck him. 'But look here, Randall,' he said. 'What about those two men who attacked Johnny on the day he came to my house? The day he crashed into your car. Where did they come from? Were they . . . the terrorists?'

'No . . . Um . . . as a matter of fact . . . they didn't exist.'

He gave me a right Royal stare. 'Are you meaning to say that Johnny was *lying*?'

Yes. I was. I said, however, more temperately, 'I think he invented them, certainly.'

'But he couldn't have done! He was badly beaten up.'

I shook my head. 'He was injured from crashing into my car.'

'There you are, Randall,' the Prince said with exasperation. 'He only crashed because he was already hurt.'

'Er . . .' I said. 'I think, sir, that he crashed because he fainted at the sight of blood. I think . . . he cut his finger to make it bleed . . . to put some blood on his face to back up his story of being attacked . . . and when he got to the front of your house he simply passed out. He had his foot on the accelerator, and his car kept on going.'

'You can't be right!'

'You could ask him, sir.'

Make my bed soon . . .

'But why, Randall? Why ever should he invent such a story?'

'He passionately wants to go to the Olympics. He didn't want people poking into his relationship with Hans Kramer, which was a little less innocent than he would have us believe, but not really so terrible. I would guess he was afraid all the same that if you found out you might not buy him the new horse . . . so he invented two men and a beating up to persuade you not to send me to look for Alyosha. I quite believe that Johnny himself knew of no scandal, but he didn't know what I might find out about Hans. He didn't want me to look, that was all.'

'But,' he said, looking bewildered, 'it had the opposite effect. After that I was more sure than ever that the rumours must be looked into.'

I watched Johnny and the Princess weaving their way through the crowds returning to the stands for the next race, his crisp red curls gleaming like copper in the December air.

I sighed. 'He's a great rider, sir.'

The Prince slid me a sideways glance. 'We all do dumb things from time to time, Randall. Is that it?'

'Yes, sir.'

. . . and fain would lie doon.

'Why are you so sure they weren't your terrorists?'

'Because from Johnny's account they weren't at all the same sort of people. Johnny said they spoke English and were ordinary British men . . . which the terrorists were not.'

Johnny and the Princess climbed the steps and came up on to the balcony. The Princess was untroubled, but Johnny had been uncomfortable with me all day.

I said mildly, 'Johnny, how well did you know Malcolm Herrick?'

'Who?'

'Herrick. Journalist. Wrote for the *Watch*.'

'Oh, him.' Johnny's face said it was an unwelcome memory. 'He was at Burghley. Always hanging around Hans. Fr . . . Hans Kramer.' He hesitated, shrugged, and went on. 'I didn't like the fellow. Why? What's he done? He called me "sport" all the time. Can't say I liked it, what? I told him to piss off. Haven't seen him since.

It seemed a bit much to put a man at the top of the death list for saying piss off, but Malcolm had done it. 'Sport' and 'piss off' . . . next stop, Alyosha.

For I'm weary wi' hunting, and fain . . .

'Cards on the table, Johnny,' the Prince said. 'Were you beaten up by those two chaps, or weren't you?'

The Farringford expression went through a lot of motions in very quick time. He started to nod and say yes, and then switched his gaze suddenly to my face. Correctly read my scepticism; realized I had told the Prince; changed his plea instantaneously to guilty, and finished with a sheepish little-boy grin.

The Prince compressed his lips and shook his head. 'Grow up, Johnny,' he said.

Emma came for the weekend, two days later, silver and brittle and a-jangle with tensions.

'How boring of you to be in bed,' she said. 'I'm lousy at mopping fevered brows.'

She moved restlessly round the room, getting rid of electric energy in purposeless fidgeting.

'You're wheezing like an old granny,' she said. 'And spitting . . . That's a really disgusting disease.'

'I thought you liked facing life's nitty-gritties.'

'Why did you want me to come?' she said, rearranging the brushes on my dressing chest. 'You usually tell me to stay away, when you're ill.'

'I wanted your company.'

'Oh.' She seemed disconcerted, gave me a quick sharp glance like a startled bird, and went out of the room. Friday night, I thought ruefully, was too soon for truth.

She returned in an hour, bringing a tray; bringing supper. Soup, bread, fruit, cheese, and a bottle of wine.

'They seemed to be lying around,' she said defensively, 'so I thought I might as well lug them up here.'

'Great.'

We ate in reasonable peace, and she asked about Moscow.

'You might like it there,' I said, peeling a tangerine. 'Mind you, over there the life you choose to lead here wouldn't be an act of rebellion, but a necessity forced upon you.'

'I hate you sometimes.'

'If you ever get tired of your shop,' I said, 'I could give you another job here.'

'What as?'

'Domestic servant. Nanny. Cook. Laundry-maid. General all-purpose dogsbody. Farmhand. Wife.'

'It wouldn't work.'

I looked at the shining fall of platinum hair and at the finality in the delicate well-loved determined face. The patterns of youth couldn't be changed. One became a rebel, a romantic, a puritan, a bigot, a hypocrite, a saint, a crusader, a terrorist ... One became it young and stayed it forever. She could never return to the well-off, well-ordered country life she had kicked her way out of. She would revisit it uneasily for weekends as long as I pleased her, but one Monday morning she would drive off and not come back.

I might regret, might feel lost and lonely without her, but she was depressingly right.

As a long-term prospect, it wouldn't work.

In the New Year edition of the *Horse and Hound* I read that the Germans had sold one of their best young horses to Lord Farringford, who would be training it in the hope of being considered for the Olympic Games.

Twice Shy

Part One

Jonathan

I

I told the boys to stay quiet while I went to fetch my gun.

It usually worked. For the five minutes that it took me to get to the locker in the common-room and to return to the classroom, thirty fourteen-year-old semi-repressed hooligans cold be counted on to be held in a state of fragile good behaviour, restrained only by the promise of a lesson they'd actually looked forward to. Physics in general they took to be unacceptably hard mental labour, but what happened when a gun spat out a bullet . . . that was *interesting*.

Jenkins delayed me for a moment in the common-room: Jenkins with his sour expression and bad-tempered moustache, telling me I could teach momentum more clearly with chalk on a blackboard, and that an actual firearm was on my part simply self-indulgent dramatics.

'No doubt you're right,' I said blandly, edging round him.

He gave me his usual look of frustrated spite. He hated my policy of always agreeing with him, which was, of course, why I did it.

'Excuse me,' I said, retreating, 'Four A are waiting.'

Four A, however, weren't waiting in the hoped-for state of gently simmering excitement. They were, instead, in collective giggles fast approaching mild hysteria.

'Look,' I said flatly, sensing the atmosphere with one foot through the door, 'steady down, or you'll copy notes . . .'

This direst of threats had no result. The giggles couldn't be stifled. The eyes of the class darted between me and my gun and the blackboard, which was still out of my sight behind the open door, and upon every young face there was the most gleeful anticipation.

'OK,' I said, closing the door, 'so what have you writ-'

I stopped.

They hadn't written anything.

One of the boys stood there, in front of the blackboard, straight and still: Paul Arcady, the wit of the class. He stood straight and still because, balanced on his head, there was an apple.

The giggles all around me exploded into laughter, and I couldn't myself keep a straight face.

'Can you shoot it off, sir?'

The voices rose above a general hubbub.

'William Tell could, sir.'

'Shall we call an ambulance, sir, just in case?'

'How long will it take a bullet to get through Paul's skull, sir?'

'Very funny,' I said repressively, but indeed it *was* very funny, and they knew it. But if I laughed too much I'd lose control of them, and control of such a volatile mass was always precarious.

'Very clever, Paul,' I said. 'Go and sit down.'

He was satisfied. He'd produced his effect perfectly. He took the apple off his head with a natural elegance and returned in good order to his place, accepting as his due the admiring jokes and the envious catcalls.

'Right then,' I said, planting myself firmly where he had stood, 'by the end of this lesson you'll all know how long it would take for a bullet travelling at a certain speed to cross a certain distance . . .'

The gun I had taken to the lesson had been a simple air-gun, but I told them also how a rifle worked, and why in each case a bullet or a pellet came out fast. I let them handle the smooth metal: the first time many of them had seen an actual gun, even an air-gun, at close quarters. I explained how bullets were made, and how they differed from the pellets I had with me. How loading mechanisms worked. How the grooves inside a rifle barrel rotated the bullet, to send it out spinning. I told them about air friction, and heat.

They listened with concentration and asked the questions they always did.

'Can you tell us how a bomb works, sir?'

'One day,' I said.

'A nuclear bomb?'

'One day.'

'A hydrogen . . . cobalt . . . neutron bomb?'

'One day.'

They never asked how radio waves crossed the ether, which was to me a greater mystery. They asked about destruction, not creation; about power, not symmetry. The seed of violence born in every male child looked out of every face, and I knew how they were thinking, because I'd been there myself. Why else had I spent countless hours at their age practising with a .22 cadet rifle on a range, improving my skill until I could hit a target the size of a thumbnail at fifty yards, nine times out of ten. A strange, pointless, sublimated skill, which I never intended to use on any living creature, but had never since lost.

'Is it true, sir,' one of them said, 'that you won an Olympic medal for rifle shooting?'

'No, it isn't.'

'What, then, sir?'

'I want you all to consider the speed of a bullet compared to the speed of other objects you are all familiar with. Now, do you think that you could be flying along in an aeroplane, and look out of the window, and see a bullet keeping pace with you, appearing to be standing still just outside the window?'

The lesson wound on. They would remember it all their lives, because of the gun. Without the gun, whatever Jenkins might think, it would have faded into the general dust they shook from their shoes every afternoon at four o'clock. Teaching, it often seemed to me, was as much a matter of image-jerking as of imparting actual information. The facts dressed up in jokes were the ones they got right in exam.

I liked teaching. Specifically I liked teaching physics, a subject I suppose I embraced with passion and joy, knowing full well that most people shied away in horror. Physics was only the science of the unseen world, as geography was of the seen. Physics was the science of all the tremendously powerful invisibilities – of magnetism, electricity, gravity, light, sound, cosmic rays ... Physics was the science of the mysteries of the universe. How could *anyone* think it dull?

I had been for three years head of the physics department of the East Middlesex Comprehensive, with four masters and two technicians within my domain. My future, from my present age of thirty-three, looked like a possible deputy head-mastership, most likely with a move involved, and even perhaps a headship, though if I hadn't achieved that by forty I could forget it. Headmasters got younger every year; mostly, cynics suggested, because the younger the man they appointed, the more the authorities could boss him about.

I was, all in all, contented with my job and hopeful of my prospects. It was only at home that things weren't so good.

Four A learned about momentum and Arcady ate his apple when he thought I wasn't looking. My peripheral vision after ten years of teaching was, however, so acute that at times they thought I could literally see out of the back of my head. It did no harm: it made control easier.

'Don't drop the core on the floor, Paul,' I said mildly. It was one thing to let him eat the apple – he deserved it – but quite another to let him think I hadn't seen. Keeping a grip on the monsters was a perpetual psychological game, but also priority number one. I'd seen stronger men than myself reduced to nervous breakdowns by the hunting-pack instincts of children.

When the end-of-lesson bell rang, they did me the ultimate courtesy of letting me finish what I was saying before erupting into the going-home stampede. It was, after all, the last lesson on Friday – and God be thanked for weekends.

I made my way slowly round the four physics laboratories and the two equipment rooms, checking that everything was in order. The two technicians, Louisa and David, were dismantling and putting away all apparatus not needed on Monday, picking Five E's efforts at radio-circuitry to pieces and returning the batteries, clips, bases and transistors to the countless racks and drawers in the equipment rooms.

'Shooting anyone special?' Louisa said, eyeing the gun which I was carrying with me.

'Didn't want to leave it unattended.'

'Is it loaded?' Her voice sounded almost hopeful. By late Friday, she was always in the state in which one never asked her for an extra favour: not, that is, unless one was willing to endure a weepy ten minutes of 'you don't realize how much this job entails', which, on most occasions, I wasn't. Louisa's tantrums, I reckoned, were based on her belief that life had cheated her, finding her at forty as a sort of store-keeper (efficient, meticulous and helpful) but not a Great Scientist. 'If I'd gone to college ...' she would say, leaving the strong impression that if she had, Einstein would have been relegated. I dealt with Louisa by retreating at the warning signs of trouble, which was maybe weak, but I had to live with her professionally, and bouts of sullenness made her slow.

'My list for Monday!' I said, handing it to her.

She glanced disparagingly down it. 'Martin has ordered the oscilloscopes for third period.'

'See what you can manage,' I said.

'Can you make do with only two?'

I said I supposed so, smiled, hoped it would keep fine for her gardening, and left for home.

I drove slowly with the leaden feeling of resignation clamping down, as it always did on the return journey. Between Sarah and me there was no joy left; no springing love. Eight years of marriage, and nothing to feel but a growing boredom.

We had been unable to have children. Sarah had hoped for them, longed for them, pined for them. We'd been to every conceivable specialist and Sarah had had countless injections and pills and two operations. My own disappointment was bearable, though none the less deep. Hers had proved intractable and finally disabling in that she had gone into a state of permanent depression from which it seemed nothing could rescue her.

We'd been told by encouraging therapists that many childless marriages were highly successful, husband and wife forging exceptionally strong bonds through their misfortune, but with us it had worked in reverse. Where once there had been passion there was now politeness; where plans and laughter, now a grinding hopelessness; where tears and heartbreak, silence.

I hadn't been enough for her, without babies. I'd been forced to face the fact that to her motherhood mattered most, that marriage had been but the pathway, that many a man would have done. I wondered unhappily from time to time how soon she would have divorced me had it been I who had proved infertile: and it was profitless also to guess that we would have been contented enough for ever if she herself had been fulfilled.

I dare say it was a marriage like many another. We never quarrelled. Seldom argued. Neither of us any longer cared enough for that; and as a total, prolonged way of life it was infinitely dispiriting.

It was a homecoming like thousands of others. I parked outside the closed garage doors and let myself into the house with arms full of air-gun and exercise books. Sarah, home as usual from her part-time job as a dentist's receptionist, sat on the sofa in the sitting-room reading a magazine.

'Hallo,' I said.

'Hallo. Good day?'

'Not bad.'

She hadn't looked up from her pages. I hadn't kissed her. Perhaps for both of us it was better than total loneliness, but not much.

'There's ham for supper,' she said. 'And coleslaw. That all right?'

'Fine.'

She went on reading; a slim fair-haired girl, still arrestingly pretty but now with a settled resentful expression. I was used to it, but in flashes suffered unbearable nostalgia for the laughing eagerness of the early days. I wondered sometimes if she noticed that the fun had gone out of me, too, although I could sometimes feel it still bubbling along inside, deeply buried.

On that particular evening I made an effort (as I did more and more rarely) to jog us out of our dimness.

'Look, let's just dump everything and go out to dinner. Maybe to Florestan's, where there's dancing.'

She didn't look up. 'Don't be silly.'

'Let's just go.'

'I don't want to.' A pause. 'I'd rather watch television.' She turned a page, and added with indifference, 'And we can't afford Florestan's prices.'

'We could, if you'd enjoy it.'

'No, I wouldn't.'

'Well,' I sighed, 'I'll make a start on the books, then.'

She nodded faintly. 'Supper at seven.'

'All right.'

I turned to go.

'There's a letter for you from William,' she said with boredom in her voice. 'I put it upstairs.'

'Oh? Well, thanks.'

She went on reading, and I took my stuff up to the third and smallest of our three bedrooms, which I used as a sort of study-cum-office. The estate agent who had shown us the house had brightly described the room as 'just right for the nursery', and had nearly lost himself the sale. I'd annexed the place for myself and made it as masculine as possible, but I was aware that for Sarah the spirit of unborn children still hovered there. She rarely went in. It was slightly unusual that she should have put the letter from my brother on my desk.

It said:

Dear Jonathan,

Please can I have thirty pounds? It's for going to the farm at half-term. I wrote to Mrs Porter, and she'll have me. She says her rates have gone up because of inflation. It can't be for what I eat, as she mostly gives me bread and honey. (No complaints.) Also actually I need some money for riding, in case they won't let me earn any more rides at the stables by mucking out, they were a bit funny about it last time, something to do with the law and exploiting juveniles, I ask you. Roll on sixteen. Anyway, if you could make it fifty quid it would be fine. If I can earn my riding, I'll send the extra twenty back, because if you don't want your heavy dough lifted at this high-class nick you have to have it embedded in concrete. Half-term is a week on Friday, early this term, so could you send it pronto?

Did you notice that Clinker did win the Wrap-Up 'chase at Stratford? If you don't want me to be a jockey, how about a tipster?

Hope you are well. And Sarah.

William.

P.S. Can you come for sports day, or for Blah-Blah day? I've got a prize for two plus two, you'll be astounded to hear.

Blah-Blah day was Speech Day at which the school prizes were handed out. I'd missed every one of William's for one reason or another. I would go this time, I thought. Even William might sometimes feel lonely with no one close to him ever to see him collect his prizes, which he did with some monotony.

William went to public school thanks to a rich godfather who had left him a lot of money on trust 'for his education and vocational training, and good luck to the little brat'. William's trustees regularly paid his fees to the school and maintenance for clothes and etceteras to me, and I passed on cash to William as required. It was an arrangement which worked excellently on many counts, not least that it meant that William didn't have to live with Sarah and me. Her husband's noisy and independent-minded brother was not the child she wanted.

William spent his holidays on farms, and Sarah occasionally said that it was most unfair that William should have more money than I had and that William had been spoiled rotten from the day my mother had discovered she was pregnant again at the age of forty-six. Sarah and William, whenever they met, behaved mostly with wary restraint and only occasionally with direct truth. William had learned very quickly not to tease her, which was his natural inclination, and she had accepted that doling out sarcastic criticism invited a cutting response. They circled each other, in consequence, like exactly matched opponents unwilling to declare open war.

For as long as he could remember William had been irresistibly attracted to horses and had long affirmed his intention to be a jockey, of which Sarah strongly and I mildly disapproved. Security, William said, was a dirty word. There were better things in life than a safe job. Sarah and I, I suppose, were happier with pattern and order and achievement. William increasingly as he grew through thirteen, fourteen, and now fifteen, seemed to hunger for air and speed and uncertainty. It was typical of him that he proposed to spend the week's mid-term break in riding horses instead of working for the eight 'O' Level exams he was due to take immediately afterwards.

I left his letter on my desk to remind myself to send him a cheque and un-locked the cupboard where I kept my guns.

The air-gun that I'd taken to school was little more than a toy and needed no licence or secure storage, but I also owned two Mauser 7.62s, an Enfield No. 4 7.62 and two Anschütz .22s around which all sorts of regulations bris-tled, and also an old Lee Enfield .303 dating back from my early days which was still as lethal as ever if one could raise the ammunition for it. The little I had, I hoarded, mostly out of nostalgia. There were no more .303 rounds being made, thanks to the army switching to 7.62 mm in the sixties.

I put the air-gun back in its rack, checked that everything was as it should be, and locked the doors on the familiar smell of oil.

The telephone bell rang downstairs and Sarah answered it. I looked at the pile of exercise books which would all have to be read and corrected and handed out to the boys again on Monday, and wondered why I didn't have a fixed-hours job that one didn't have to take home. It wasn't only for the pupils that homework was a drag.

I could hear Sarah's telephone-answering voice, loud and bright.

'Oh. Hallo, Peter. How nice . . .'

There was a long pause while Peter talked, and then from Sarah a rising wail.

'Oh, *no*! Oh my *God*! Oh, no, Peter . . .'

Horror, disbelief, great distress. A quality, anyway, which took me straight downstairs.

Sarah was sitting stiffly upright on the sofa, holding the telephone at the end of its long cord. 'Oh no,' she was saying wildly. 'It can't be true. It just *can't*.'

She stared at me unseeingly, neck stretched upwards, listening with even eyes.

'Well, of course . . . of course we will . . . Oh, Peter, yes, of course . . . yes, straight away. Yes . . . yes . . . we'll be there . . .' She glanced at her watch. 'Nine o'clock. Perhaps a bit later. Will that do? . . . All right then . . . and Peter, give her my love . . .'

She clattered the receiver down with shaking hands.

'We'll have to go,' she said. 'Peter and Donna-'

'Not tonight,' I protested. 'Whatever it is, not tonight. I'm damned tired and I've got all those books . . .'

'Yes, at once, we must go at once.'

'It's a hundred miles.'

'I don't *care* how far it is. We must go *now. Now!*'

She stood up and practically ran towards the stairs. 'Pack a suitcase,' she said. 'Come on.'

I followed her more slowly, half exasperated, half moved by her urgency. 'Sarah, hold on a minute, what exactly has happened to Peter and Donna?'

She stopped four stairs up, and looked down at me over the bannister. She was already crying, her whole face screwed into agonized disorder.

'Donna.' The words were indistinct. 'Donna . . .'

'Has she had an accident?'

'No . . . not . . .'

'What, then?'

The question served only to increase the tears. 'She . . . needs . . . me.'

'You go, then,' I said, feeling relieved at the solution. 'I can manage without the car for a few days. Until Tuesday anyway. Monday I can go by bus.'

'No. Peter wants you, too. He begged me . . . both of us.'

'Why?' I said, but she was already running again up the stairs, and wouldn't answer.

I won't like it, I thought abruptly. Whatever had happened she knew that I wouldn't like it and that my instincts would all be on the side of non-involvement. I followed her upwards with reluctance and found her already gathering clothes and toothpaste on to the bed.

'Donna has parents, hasn't she?' I said. 'And Peter, too? So if something terrible's happened, why in God's name do they need *us*?'

'They're our friends.' She was rushing about, crying and gulping and dropping things. It was much, much more than ordinary sympathy for any ill that might have befallen Donna: there was a quality of extravagance that both disturbed and antagonized.

'It's beyond the bounds of friendship,' I said, 'to go charging off to Norfolk hungry and tired and not knowing why. And I'm not going.'

Sarah didn't seem to hear. The haphazard packing went ahead without pause and the tears developed into a low continuous grizzle.

Where once we had had many friends, we now had just Donna and Peter, notwithstanding that they no longer lived five miles away and played squash on Tuesdays. All our other friends from before and after marriage had either dropped away or coupled and bred; and it was only Donna and Peter who, like us, had produced no children. Only Donna and Peter who never talked nursery, whose company Sarah could bear.

She and Donna had once been long-time flat-mates. Peter and I, meeting for the first time as their subsequent husbands, had got on together amicably enough for the friendship to survive the Norfolk removal, though it was by now more a matter of birthday cards and telephone calls than of frequent house-to-house visits. We had spent a boating holiday together once on the canals. 'We'll do it again next year,' we'd all said: but we didn't.

'Is Donna ill?' I asked.

'No . . .'

'I'm not going,' I said.

The keening grizzle stopped. Sarah looked a mess, standing there with vague reddened eyes and a clumsily folded nightdress. She stared down at the pale green froth that she wore against the chill of separate beds and the disastrous news finally burst out of her.

'She was arrested,' she said.

'Donna . . . arrested?' I was astounded. Donna was mouse-like. Organized. Gentle. Apologetic. Anything but likely to be in trouble with the police.

'She's home now,' Sarah said. 'She's . . . Peter says she's . . . well . . . *suicidal. He says he can't cope with it.*' Her voice was rising. 'He says he needs us . . . now . . . this minute. He doesn't know what to do. He says we're the only people who can help.'

She was crying again. Whatever it was, was too much.

'What,' I said slowly, 'has Donna done?'

'She went out shopping,' Sarah said, trying at last to speak clearly. 'An she stole . . . She stole . . .'

'Well, for heaven's sake,' I said, 'I know it's bloody for them, but thousands of people shoplift. So why all this excessive drama?'

'You don't listen,' Sarah shouted. 'Why don't you *listen*?'

'I—'

'She stole a *baby*.'

2

We went to Norwich.

Sarah had been right. I didn't like the reason for our journey. I felt a severe aversion to being dragged into a highly-charged emotional situation where nothing constructive could possibly be done. My feelings of friendship towards Peter and Donna were nowhere near strong enough. For Peter, perhaps. For Donna, definitely not.

All the same, when I thought of the tremendous forces working on that poor girl to impel her to such an action it occurred to me that perhaps the unseen universe didn't stop at the sort of electro-magnetics that I taught. Every living cell, after all, generated electric charges: especially brain cells. If I put baby-snatching on a par with an electric storm, I could be happier with it.

Sarah sat silently beside me for most of the way, recovering, re-adjusting, preparing. She said only once what must have been in both our minds.

'It could have been me.'

'No,' I said.

'You don't know . . . what it's like.'

There was no answer. Short of having been born female and barren, there was no way of knowing. I had been told about five hundred times over the years in various tones from anguish to spite that I didn't know what it was like, and there was no more answer now than there had been the first time.

The long lingering May evening made the driving easier than usual, although going northwards out of London in the Friday night exodus was always a beast of a journey.

At the far, far end of it lay the neat new box-like house with its big featureless net-curtained windows and its tidy oblong of grass. One bright house in a street of others much the same. One proud statement that Peter

371

...ad reached a certain salary-level and still aspired to future improvement. A place and a way of life that I understood and saw no harm in: where William would suffocate.

The turmoil behind the uninformative net curtains was much as expected in some ways and much worse in others.

The usually meticulously tidy interior was in much disarray, with unwashed cups and mugs making wet rings on every surface and clothes and papers scattered around. The trail, I came to realize, left by the in-and-out tramp of officialdom over the past two days.

Peter greeted us with gaunt eyes and the hushed voice of a death in the family; and probably for him and Donna what had happened was literally hurting them worse than a death. Donna herself sat in a silent huddle at one end of the big green sofa in their sitting-room and made no attempt to respond to Sarah when she rushed to her side and put her arms round her in almost a frenzy of affection.

Peter said helplessly, 'She won't talk . . . or eat.'

'Or go to the bathroom?'

'What?'

Sarah looked up at me with furious reproach, but I said mildly, 'If she goes off to the bathroom when she feels the need, it's surely a good sign. It's such a *normal* act.'

'Well, yes,' Peter said limply. 'She does.'

'Good, then.'

Sarah clearly thought that this was another prime example of what she called my general heartlessness, but I had meant only to reassure. I asked Peter what exactly had taken place, and as he wouldn't tell me in front of Donna herself we removed to the kitchen.

In there, too, the police and medics and court officials and social workers had made the coffee and left the dishes. Peter seemed not to see the mess that in past times would have set both him and Donna busily wiping. We sat at the table with the last remnants of daytime fading to dusk, and in that gentle light he slowly unlocked the horrors.

It was on the previous morning, he said, that Donna had taken the baby from its pram and driven off with it in her car. She had driven seventy odd miles north-east to the coast, and had at some point abandoned the car with the baby inside it, and had walked off along the beach.

The car and the baby had been traced and found within hours, and Donna herself had been discovered sitting on the sand in pouring rain, speechless and stunned.

The police had arrested her, taken her to the station for a night in the cells, and paraded her before a magistrate in the morning. The bench had called for psychiatric reports, set a date for a hearing a week ahead and, despite protests from the baby's mother, set Donna free. Everyone had assured Peter she would only be put on probation, but he still shuddered from their appalling future of ignominy via the press and the neighbourhood.

After a pause, and thinking of Donna's trancelike state, I said, 'You told Sarah she was suicidal.'

He nodded miserably. 'This afternoon I wanted to warm her. To put her to bed. I ran the bath for her.' It was a while before he could go on. It seemed that the suicide attempt had been in deadly earnest; he had stopped her on the instant before she plunged herself and her switched-on hair-drier into the water. 'And she still had all her clothes on,' he said.

It seemed to me that what Donna urgently needed was some expert and continuous psychiatric care in a comfortable private nursing-home, all of which she was probably not going to get.

'Come on out for a drink,' I said.

'But I *can't*.' He was slightly trembling all the time, as if his foundations were in an earthquake.

'Donna will be all right with Sarah.'

'But she might try . . .'

'Sarah will look after her.'

'But I can't face . . .'

'No,' I said. 'We'll buy a bottle.'

I bought some scotch and two glasses from a philosophical publican just before closing time, and we sat in my car to drink in a quiet tree-lined street three miles from Peter's home. Stars and street lights between the shadowy leaves.

'What are we going to do?' he said despairingly.

'Time will pass.'

'We'll never get over it. How can we? It's bloody impossible.' He choked on the last word and began to cry like a boy. An outrush of unbearable, pent-up, half-angry grief.

I took the wobbling glass out of his hand. Sat and waited and made vague sympathetic noises and wondered what to God I would have done if, like she said, it had been Sarah.

'And to happen now,' he said at length, fishing for a handkerchief to blow his nose, 'of all times.'

'Er . . . oh?' I said.

He sniffed convulsively and wiped his cheeks. 'Sorry about that.'

'Don't be.'

He sighed. 'You're always so calm.'

'Nothing like this has happened to me.'

'I'm in a mess,' he said.

'Well, it'll get better.'

'No, I mean, besides Donna. I didn't know what to do . . . before . . . and now, after, I can't even *think*.'

'What sort of mess? Financial?'

'No. Well, not exactly.' He paused uncertainly, needing a prompt.

'What then?'

I gave him his glass back. He looked at it vaguely, then drank most of the contents in one mouthful.

'You don't mind if I burden you?' he said.

'Of course not.'

He was a couple of years younger than I, the same age as both Donna and Sarah; and all three of them, it had sometimes seemed to me, saw me not only as William's elder brother but as their own. At any rate it was as natural to me as to Peter that he should tell me his troubles.

He was middling tall and thin and had recently grown a lengthy moustache which had not given him the overpoweringly macho appearance he might have been aiming for. He still looked an ordinary inoffensive competent guy who went around selling his computer know-how to small businesses on weekdays and tinkered with his boat on Sundays.

He dabbed his eyes again and for several minutes took slow deep calming breaths.

'I got into something which I wish I hadn't,' he said.

'What sort of thing?'

'It started more or less as a joke.' He finished the last inch of drink and I stretched across and poured him a refill. 'There was this fellow. Our age, about. He'd come up from Newmarket, and we got talking in that pub you bought the whisky from. He said it would be great if you could get racing results from a computer. And we both laughed.'

There was a silence.

'Did he know you worked with computers?' I said.

'I'd told him. You know how one does.'

'So what happened next?'

'A week later I got a letter. From this fellow. Don't know how he got my address. From the pub, I suppose. The barman knows where I live.' He took a gulp from his drink and was quiet for a while, and then went on, 'The letter asked if I would like to help someone who was working out a computer program for handicapping horses. So I thought, why not? All handicaps for horse races are sorted out on computers, and the letter sounded quite official.'

'But it wasn't?'

He shook his head. 'A spot of private enterprise. But I still thought, why not? Anyone is entitled to work out his own program. There isn't such a thing as *right* in handicapping unless the horses pass the post in the exact order that the computer weighted them, which they never do.'

'You know a lot about it,' I said.

'I've learnt, these past few weeks.' The thought brought no cheer. 'I didn't even notice I was neglecting Donna, but she says I've hardly spoken to her for ages.' His throat closed and he swallowed audibly. 'Perhaps if I hadn't been so occupied . . .'

'Stop feeling guilty,' I said. 'Go on about the handicapping.'

After a while he was able to.

'He gave me pages and pages of stuff. Dozens of them. All handwritten in diabolical handwriting. He wanted it organized into programs that any fool could run on a computer.' He paused. 'You do know about computers.'

'More about microchips than programming, which isn't saying much.'

'The other way round from most people, though.'

'I guess so,' I said.

'Anyway, I did them. Quite a lot of them. It turned out they were all much the same sort of thing. They weren't really very difficult, once I'd got the hang of what the notes all meant. It was understanding those which was the worst. So, anyway, I did the programs and got paid in cash.' He stopped and moved restlessly in his seat, glum and frowning.

'So what is wrong?'

'Well, I said it would be best if I ran the programs a few times on the computer he was going to use, because so many computers are different from each other, and although he'd told me the make of computer he'd be using and I'd made allowances, you never can really tell you've got no bugs until you actually try things out on the actual type of machine. But he wouldn't let me. I said he wasn't being reasonable and he told me to mind my own business. So I just shrugged him off and thought if he wanted to be so stupid it was his own affair. And then these other two men turned up.'

'What other two men?'

'I don't know. They just sneered when I asked their names. They told me to hand over to them the programs I'd made on the horses. I said I had done. They said they were nothing to do with the person who'd paid for the job, but all the same I was to give them the programs.'

'And did you?'

'Well, yes – in a way.'

'But, Peter – ' I said.

He interrupted, 'Yes, I know, but they were so bloody *frightening*. They came the day before yesterday – it seems years ago – in the evening. Donna had gone out for a walk. It was still light. About eight o'clock, I should think. She often goes for walks . . .' He trailed off again and I gave his glass a nudge with the bottle. 'What?' he said. 'Oh no, no more, thanks. Anyway, they came, and they were so *arrogant*, and they said I'd regret it if I didn't give them the programs. They said Donna was a pretty little missis, wasn't she, and they were sure I'd like her to stay that way.' He swallowed. 'I'd never have believed . . . I mean, that sort of thing doesn't *happen* . . .'

It appeared, however, that it had.

'Well,' he said, rallying, 'what I gave them was all that I had in the house, but it was really only first drafts, so to speak. Pretty rough. I'd written three or four trial programs out in long-hand, like I often do. I know a lot of people work on typewriters or even straight on to a computer, but I get on better with pencil and rubber, so what I gave them *looked* all right, especially if you didn't know the first thing about programming, which I should think they didn't, but not much of it would run as it stood. And I hadn't put the file names on anyway, or any REMS or anything, so even if they de-bugged the programs they wouldn't know what they referred to.'

Disentangling the facts from the jargon, it appeared that what he had done had been to deliver to possibly dangerous men a load of garbage, knowing full well what he was doing.

'I see,' I said slowly, 'what you mean by a mess.'

'I'd decided to take Donna away for a few days, just to be safe. I was going to tell her as a nice surprise when I got home from work yesterday, and then the police turned up in my office, and said she'd taken ... taken ... Oh Christ, how *could* she?'

I screwed the cap on the bottle and I looked at my watch. 'It's getting on for midnight,' I said. 'We'd better go back.'

'I suppose so.'

I paused with my hand on the ignition key. 'Didn't you tell the police about your two unpleasant visitors?' I said.

'No, I didn't. I mean, how could I? They've been in and out of the house, and a policewoman too, but it was all about Donna. They wouldn't have listened, and anyway ...'

'Anyway what?'

He shrugged uncomfortably. 'I got paid in cash. Quite a lot. I'm not going to declare it for tax. If I told the police . . .well, I'd more or less have to.'

'It might be better,' I said.

He shook his head. 'It would cost me a lot to tell the police, and what would I gain? They'd make a note of what I said and wait until Donna got bashed in the face before they did anything. I mean, they can't go around guarding everyone who's been vaguely threatened night and day, can they? And as for guarding *Donna* – well, they weren't very nice to her, you know. Really rotten most of them were. They made cups of tea for each other and spoke over her head as if she was a lump of wood. You'd think she'd poked the baby's eyes out, the way they treated her.'

It didn't seem unreasonable to me that official sympathy had been mostly on the side of the baby's frantic mother, but I didn't say so.

'Perhaps it would be best, then,' I said, 'if you did take Donna away for a bit, straight after the hearing. Can you get leave?'

He nodded.

'But what she really needs is proper psychiatric care. Even a spell in a mental hospital.'

'No,' he said.

'They have a high success rate with mental illness nowadays. Modern drugs, and hormones, and all that.'

'But she's not – ' He stopped.

The old taboos died hard. 'The brain is part of the body,' I said. 'It's not separate. And it goes wrong sometimes, just like anything else. Like the liver. Or the kidneys. You wouldn't hesitate if it was her kidneys.'

He shook his head, however, and I didn't press it. Everyone had to decide things for themselves. I started the car and wheeled us back to the house, and Peter said as we turned into the short concrete driveway that Donna was unusually happy on their boat, and he would take her away on that.

The weekend dragged on. I tried surreptitiously now and then to mark the inexorable exercise books, but the telephone rang more or less continuously and, as answering it seemed to be the domestic chore I was best fitted for, I slid into a routine of chat. Relatives, friends, press, officials, busybodies, cranks and stinkers, I talked with the lot.

Sarah cared for Donna with extreme tenderness and devotion and was rewarded with wan smiles at first and, gradually, low-toned speech. After that came hysterical tears, a brushing of hair, a tentative meal, a change of clothes, and a growth of invalid behaviour.

When Peter talked to Donna it was in a miserable mixture of love, guilt and reproach, and he found many an opportunity of escaping into the garden. On Sunday morning he went off in his car at pub-opening time and returned late for lunch, and on Sunday afternoon I said with private relief that I would now have to go back home ready for school on Monday.

'I'm staying here,' Sarah said. 'Donna needs me. I'll ring my boss and explain. He owes me a week's leave anyway.'

Donna gave her the by now ultra-dependent smile she had developed over the past two days, and Peter nodded with eager agreement.

'OK,' I said slowly, 'but take care.'

'What of?' Sarah said.

I glanced at Peter, who was agitatedly shaking his head. All the same, it seemed sensible to take simple precautions.

'Don't let Donna go out alone,' I said.

Donna blushed furiously and Sarah was instantly angry, and I said helplessly, 'I didn't mean . . . I meant to keep her safe . . . from people who might want to be spiteful to her.'

Sarah saw the sense in that and calmed down, and a short while later I was ready to leave.

I said goodbye to them in the house because there seemed to be always people in the street staring at the windows with avid eyes, and right at the last minute Peter thrust into my hand three cassettes for playing in the car if I should get bored on the way home. I glanced at them briefly: *The King and I*, *Oklahoma*, and *West Side Story*. Hardly the latest rave, but I thanked him anyway, kissed Sarah for appearances, kissed Donna ditto, and with a regrettable lightening of spirits took myself off.

It was on the last third of the way home, when I tried *Oklahoma* for company, that I found that what Peter had give me wasn't music at all, but quite something else.

Instead of 'Oh What a Beautiful Morning', I got a loud vibrating scratchy whine interspersed with brief bits of one-note plain whine. Shrugging, I would the tape forward a bit, and tried again.

Same thing.

I ejected the tape, turned it over, and tried again. Same thing. Tried *The King and I* and *West Side Story*. All the same.

I knew that sort of noise from way back. One couldn't forget it, once one knew. The scratchy whine was made by two tones alternating very fast so that the ear could scarcely distinguish the upper from the lower. The plain whine indicated an interval with nothing happening. On Oklahoma, fairly typically, the stretches of two-tone were lasting anywhere from ten seconds to three minutes.

I was listening to the noise a computer produced when its programs were recorded on to ordinary cassette tape.

Cassettes were convenient and widely used, especially with smaller computers. One could store a whole host of different programs on cassette tape, and simply pick out whichever was needed, and use it: but the cassettes were still, all the same, just ordinary cassettes, and if one played the tape straightforwardly in the normal way on a cassette player, as I had done, one heard the vibrating whine.

Peter had given me three sixty-minute tapes of computer programs: and it wasn't so very difficult to guess what those programs would be about.

I wondered why he had given them to me in such an indirect way. I wondered, in fact, why he had given them to me at all. With a mental shrug I shovelled the tapes and their misleading boxes on to the glove shelf and switched on the radio instead.

School on Monday was a holiday after the green-house emotions in Norfolk, and Louisa-the-technician's problems seemed moths' wings beside Donna's.

On Monday evening, while I was watching my own choice on the television and eating cornflakes and cream with my feet on the coffee table, Peter telephoned.

'How's Donna?' I said.

'I don't know where she'd be without Sarah.'

'And you?'

'Oh, pretty fair. Look, Jonathan, did you play any of those tapes?' His voice sounded tentative and half apologetic.

'A bit of all of them,' I said.

'Oh. Well, I expect you'll know what they are?'

'Your horse-handicapping programs?'

'Yes ... er ... Will you keep them for me for now?' He gave me no chance to answer and rushed on, 'You see, we're hoping to go off to the boat straight after the hearing on Friday. Well, we do have to believe Donna will get probation, even the nastiest of those officials said it would be so in such a case, but obviously she'll be terribly upset with having to go to court and everything and so we'll go away as soon as we can, and I didn't like the thought of leaving those cassettes lying around in the office, which they were, so I went over to fetch them yesterday morning, so I could give them to you. I mean, I didn't really think it out. I could have put them in the bank, or anywhere. I suppose what I really wanted was to get those tapes right out of my life so that if those two brutes came back asking for the programs I'd be able to say I hadn't got them and that they'd have to get them from the person I made them for.'

It occurred to me not for the first time that for a computer programmer Peter was no great shakes as a logical thinker, but maybe the circumstances were jamming the circuits.

'Have you heard from those men again?' I asked.

'No, thank God.'

'They probably haven't found out yet.'

'Thanks very much,' he said bitterly.

'I'll keep the tapes safe,' I said. 'As long as you like.'

'Probably nothing else will happen. After all, I haven't done anything illegal. Or even faintly wrong.'

The 'if-we-don't-look-at-the-monster-he'll-go-away' syndrome, I thought. But maybe he was right.

'Why didn't you tell me what you were giving me?' I enquired. 'Why *The King and I* dressing, and all that?'

'What?' His voice sounded almost puzzled, and then cleared to understanding. 'Oh, it was just that when I got home from the office, you were all sitting down to lunch, and I didn't get a single chance to catch you away from the girls, and I didn't want to have to start explaining in front of them, so I just shoved them into those cases to give to you.'

The faintest twitch of unease crossed my mind, but I smothered it. Peter's world since Donna took the baby had hardly been one of general common sense and normal behaviour. He had acted pretty well, all in all, for someone hammered from all directions at once, and over the weekend I had felt an increase of respect for him, quite apart from liking.

'If you want to play those programs,' he said, 'you'll need a Grantley computer.'

'I don't suppose . . .' I began.

'They might amuse William. He's mad on racing, isn't he?'

'Yes, he is.'

'I spent so much time on them. I'd really like to know how they work out in practice. I mean, from someone who knows horses.'

'All right,' I said. But Grantley computers weren't scattered freely round the landscape and William had his exams ahead, and the prospect of actually using the programs seemed a long way off.

'I wish you were still here,' he said. 'All the telephone calls, they're really getting me down. And did you have any of those poisonous abusive beastly voices spitting out hate against Donna, when you were answering?'

'Yes, several.'

'But they've never even *met* her.'

'They're unbalanced. Just don't listen.'

'What did you say to them?'

'I told them to take their problems to a doctor.'

There was a slightly uncomfortable pause, then he said explosively, 'I wish to God Donna had gone to a doctor.' A gulp. 'I didn't even *know* . . . I mean, I knew she'd wanted children. But I thought, well, we couldn't have them, so that was that. I never *dreamed* . . . I mean, she's always so quiet and wouldn't hurt a fly. She never showed any signs . . . We're pretty fond of each other, you know. Or at least I thought . . .'

'Peter, stop it.'

'Yes . . .' A pause. 'Of course, you're right. But it's difficult to think of anything else.'

We talked a bit more, but only covering the same old ground, and we disconnected with me feeling that somehow I could have done more for him than I had.

Two evenings later, he went down to the river to work on his two-berth cabin cruiser, filling its tanks with water and fuel, installing new cooking-gas cylinders and checking that everything was in working order for his trip with Donna.

He had been telling me earlier that he was afraid the ship's battery was wearing out and that if he didn't get a new one they would run it down flat with their lights at night and in the morning find themselves unable to start the engine. It had happened once before, he said.

He wanted to check that the battery still had enough life in it.

It had.

When he raised the first spark, the rear half of the boat exploded.

3

Sarah told me.

Sarah on the telephone with the stark over-controlled voice of exhaustion.

'They think it was gas, or petrol vapour. They don't know yet.'

'Peter . . .'

'He's dead,' she said. 'There were people around. They saw him moving . . . with his clothes on fire. He went over the side into the water . . . but when they got him out . . .'

A sudden silence, then, slowly, 'We weren't there. Thank God Donna and I weren't there.'

I felt shaky and slightly sick. 'Do you want me to come?' I said.

'No. What time is it?'

'Eleven.' I had undressed, in fact, to go to bed.

'Donna's asleep. Knock-out drops.'

'And how . . . how is she?'

'Christ, how would you expect?' Sarah seldom spoke in that way: a true measure of the general awfulness. 'And Friday,' she said, 'the day after tomorrow, she's due in court.'

'They'll be kind to her.'

'There's already been one call, just now, with some beastly woman telling me it served her right.'

'I'd better come,' I said.

'You can't. There's school. No, don't worry. I can cope. The doctor at least said he'd keep Donna heavily sedated for several days.'

'Let me know, then, if I can help.'

'Yes,' she said. 'Goodnight, now. I'm going to bed. There's a lot to do tomorrow. Goodnight.'

I lay long awake in bed and thought of Peter and the unfairness of death: and in the morning I went to school and found him flicking in and out of my mind all day.

Driving home I saw that his cassettes were still lying in a jumble on the glove shelf. Once parked in the garage, I put the tapes back into their boxes, slipped them in my jacket pocket, and carried my usual burden of books indoors.

The telephone rang almost at once, but it was not Sarah, which was my first thought, but William.

'Did you send my cheque?' he said.

'*Hell*, I forgot,' I told him why, and he allowed that forgetting in such circs could be overlooked.

'I'll write it straight away, and send it direct to the farm.'

'OK. Look, I'm sorry about Peter. He seemed a nice guy, that time we met.'

'Yes.' I told William about the computer tapes, and about Peter wanting his opinion on them.

'Bit late now.'

'But you still might find them interesting.'

'Yeah,' he said without much enthusiasm. 'Probably some nutty betting system. There's a computer here somewhere in the maths department. I'll ask what sort it is. And look, how would it grab you if I didn't go to university?'

'Badly.'

'Yeah. I was afraid so. Anyway, work on it, big brother. There's been a lot of guff going on this term about choosing a career, but I reckon it's the career that chooses *you*. I'm going to be a jockey. I can't help it.'

We said goodbyes and I put the receiver down thinking that it wasn't much good fighting to dissuade someone who at fifteen already felt that a vocation had him by the scruff of the neck.

He was slim and light: past puberty but still physically a boy, with the growth into man's stature just ahead. Perhaps nature, I thought hopefully, would take him to my height of six feet and break his heart.

Sarah rang almost immediately afterwards, speaking crisply with her dentist's-assistant voice. The shock had gone, and the exhaustion. She spoke to me with edgy bossiness, a left-over, I guessed, from a very demanding day.

'It seems that Peter should have been more careful,' she said. 'Everyone who owns a boat with an inboard engine is repeatedly told not to start up until they are sure that no gas or petrol or petrol vapour has accumulated in the bilge. Boats blow up every year. He must have known. You wouldn't think he would be so stupid.'

I said mildly, 'He had a great deal else on his mind.'

'I suppose he had, but all the same everyone says . . .'

If you could blame a man for his own death, I thought, it diminished the core of sympathy. 'It was his own fault . . .' I could hear the sharp voice of my aunt over the death of her neighbour . . . 'He shouldn't have gone out with that cold.'

'The insurance company,' I said to Sarah, 'may be trying to wriggle out of paying all they might.'

'What?'

'Putting the blame on to the victim is a well-known ploy.'

'But he should have been more careful.'

'Oh sure. But for Donna's sake, I wouldn't go around saying so.'

There was a silence which came across as resentful. Then she said, 'Donna wanted me to tell you . . . She'd rather you didn't come here this weekend. She says she could bear things better if she's alone with me.'

'And you agree?'

'Well, yes, frankly, I do.'

'OK, then.'

'You don't mind?' She sounded surprised.

'No. I'm sure she's right. She relies on you.' And too much, I thought. 'Is she still drugged?'

'Sedated.' The word was a reproof.

'Sedated, then.'

'Yes, of course.'

'And for the court hearing tomorrow?' I asked.

'Tranquillizers,' Sarah said decisively. 'Sleeping pills after.'

'Good luck with it.'

'Yes,' she said.

She disconnected almost brusquely, leaving me with the easement of having been let off an unpleasant task. Once upon a time, I supposed, we would have clung together to help Donna. At the beginning our reactions would have been truer, less complicated, less distorted by our own depressions. I mourned for the dead days, but undoubtedly I was pleased not to be going to spend the weekend with my wife.

On the Friday I went to school still with the computer tapes in my jacket pocket and, feeling that I owed it to Peter at least to try to play them, sought out one of the maths masters in the common-room. Ted Pitts, short-sighted, clear-headed, bi-lingual in English and algebra.

'That computer you've got tucked away somewhere in a cubby hole in the maths department,' I said, 'it's your especial baby, isn't it?'

'We all use it. We teach the kids.'

'But it's you who plays it like Beethoven while the rest are still at chopsticks?'

He enjoyed the compliment in his quiet way. 'Maybe,' he said.

'Could you tell me what make it is?' I asked.

'Sure. It's a Harris.'

'I suppose,' I said unhopefully, 'that you couldn't run a tape on it that was recorded on a Grantley?'

'It depends,' he said. He was earnest and thoughtful, twenty-six, short on humour, but full of good intentions and ideals of fair play. He suffered greatly under the sourly detestable Jenkins who was head of the maths department and extracted from his assistants the reverential attitude he never got from me.

'The Harris has no language built into it,' Ted said. 'You can feed it any computer language, Fortran, Cobol, Algol, Z-80, Basic, you name it, the Harris will take it. Then you can run any programs written in those languages. But the Grantley is a smaller affair which comes all ready pre-programmed with its own form of Basic. If you had a Grantley Basic language tape, you could feed it into our Harris's memory, and then you could run Grantley Basic programs.' He paused. 'Er, is that clear?'

'Sort of.' I reflected. 'How difficult would it be to get a Grantley Basic language tape?'

'Don't know. Best to write to the firm direct. They might send you one. And they might not.'

'Why might they not?'

He shrugged. 'They might say you'd have to buy one of their computers.'

'For heaven's sake,' I said.

'Yeah. Well, see, these computer firms are very awkward. All the smaller personal computers use Basic, because it's the easiest language and also one of the best. But the firms making them all build in their own variations, so that if you record your programs from their machines, you can't run them on anyone else's. That keeps you faithful to *them* in the future, because if you change to another make, all your tapes will be useless.'

'What a bore,' I said.

He nodded. 'Profits getting the better of common sense.'

'Like all those infuriatingly incompatible video-recorders.'

'Exactly. But you'd think the computer firms would have more sense. They may hang on to their own customers by force, but they're sure as Hades not going to persuade anyone else to switch.'

'Thanks anyway,' I said.

'You're welcome.' He hesitated. 'Do you actually have a tape that you want to use?'

'Yes.' I fished in my pocket and produced *Oklahoma*. 'This one and two others. Don't be misled by the packaging, it's got computer noise all right on the tape.'

'Were they recorded by an expert or an amateur?'

'An expert. Does it make any difference?'

'Sometimes.'

I explained about Peter making the tapes for a client who had a Grantley, and I added that the customer wouldn't let Peter try out the programs on the machine they were designed to run on.

'Oh, really?' Ted Pitts seemed happy with the news. 'In that case, if he was a conscientious and careful chap, it's just possible that he recorded the machine language itself on the first of the tapes. TOMS can be very touchy. He might have thought it would be safer.'

'You've lost me,' I said. 'What are TOMS?'

'Computers.' He grinned. 'Stands for Totally Obedient Moron.'

'You've made a joke,' I said disbelievingly.

'Not mine, though.'

'So why should it be safer?'

He looked at me reproachfully, 'I thought you knew more about computers than you appear to.'

'It's ten years at least since I knew more. I've forgotten and they've changed.'

'It would be safer,' he said patiently, 'because if the client rang up and complained that the program wouldn't run, your friend could tell them how to stuff into their computer a brand-new version of its own language, and then your friend's programs would run from that. Mind you,' he added judiciously, 'you'd use up an awful lot of computer space putting the language in. You might not have much room for the actual programs.'

He looked at my expression, and sighed.

'OK,' he said. 'Suppose a Grantley has a 32K store, which is a pretty normal size. That means it has about forty-nine thousand store-slots, of which probably the first seventeen thousand are used in providing the right circuits to function as Basic. That would leave you about thirty-two thousand store-slots for punching in your programs. Right?'

I nodded. 'I'll take it on trust.'

'But then if you feed in the language all over again it would take another seventeen thousand store-slots, which would leave you with under fifteen thousand store-slots to work with. And as you need one store-slot for every letter you type, and one for every number, and one for every space, and comma, and bracket, you wouldn't be able to do a great deal before all the store-slots were used and the whole thing was full up. And at that point the computer would stop working.' He smiled. 'So many people think computers are bottomless pits. They're more like bean bags. Once they're full you have to empty the beans out before you can start to fill them again.'

'Is that what you teach the kids?'

He looked slightly confused. 'Er . . . yes. Same words. One gets into a rut.'

The bell rang for afternoon registration and he stretched out his hand for the tape. 'I could try that,' he said, 'if you like.'

'Yes. If it isn't an awful bother.'

He shook his head encouragingly, and I gave him *The King and I* and *West Side Story* for good measure.

'Can't promise it will be today,' he said. 'I've got classes all afternoon and Jenkins wants to see me at four.' He grimaced. 'Jenkins. Why can't we call him Ralph and be done with it?'

'There's no hurry,' I said, 'with the tapes.'

Donna got her probation.

Sarah reported, again sounding tired, that even the baby's mother had quietened down because of Peter being killed, and Donna had gently wept in court, and even some of the policemen had been fatherly.

'How is she?' I said.

'Miserable. It's just hitting her, I think, that Peter's really gone.' Her voice sounded sisterly, motherly, protective.

'No more suicide?' I asked.

'I don't think so, but the poor darling is so *vulnerable*. So easily hurt. She says it's like living without skin.'

'Have you enough money?' I asked.

'That's just like you!' she exclaimed. 'Always so damned practical.'

'But . . .'

'I've got my bank card.'

I hadn't wanted to wallow too long in Donna's emotions and it had irritated her. We both knew it. We knew each other too well.

'Don't let her wear you out,' I said.

Her voice came back, still sharp, 'I'm perfectly all right. There's no question of wearing me out. I'm staying here for a week or two longer at least. Until after the inquest and the funeral. And after that, if Donna needs me. I've told my boss, and he understands.'

I wondered fleetingly whether I might not become too fond of living alone if she were away a whole month. I said, 'I'd like to be there at the funeral.'

'Yes. Well, I'll let you know.'

I got a tart and untender goodnight: but then my own to her hadn't been loving. We wouldn't be able to go on, I thought, if ever the politeness crumbled.

The building had long been uninhabited, and we were only a short step from demolition.

On Saturday I put the Mausers and the Enfield No. 4 in the car and drove to Bisley and let off a lot of bullets over the Surrey ranges.

During the past few months, my visits there had become less constant, partly of course because there was no delight during the winter in pressing one's stomach to the cold earth, but mostly because my intense love of the sport seemed to be waning.

I had been a member of the British rifle team for several years but now never wore any of the badges to prove it. I kept quiet in the bar after shooting and listened to others analyse their performances and spill the excitement out of their systems. I didn't like talking of my own scores, present or past.

A few years back, I had taken the sideways jump of entering for the Olympics, which was a competition for individuals and quite different from my normal pursuits. Even the guns were different (at that time all small bore) and all the distances the same (300 metres). It was a world dominated by the Swiss, but I had shot luckily and well in the event and had finished high for a Briton in the placings, and it had been marvellous. The day of a lifetime; but it had faded into memory, grown fuzzy with time passing.

In the British team, which competed mostly against the old Commonwealth countries and often won, one shot 7.62 mm guns at varying distances – 300, 500, 600, 900 and 1,000 yards. I had always taken immense delight in accuracy, in judging wind velocity and air temperature and getting the climatic variables exactly right. But now, both internally and externally, the point of such skill was fading.

The smooth elegant Mausers that I cherished were already within sight of being obsolete. Only long-distance assassins, these days, seemed to need totally accurate rifles, and *they* used telescopic sights, which were banned and anathema to target shooters. Modern armies tended to spray out bullets regardless. None of the army rifles shot absolutely straight and in addition, every advance in effective killing-power was a loss to aesthetics. The present standard issue self-loading rifle, with its gas-powered feed of twenty bullets per magazine and its capability of continuous fire, was already a knobby untidy affair with half of it made of plastic for lightness. On the horizon was a rifle without a stock, unambiguously designed to be shot from waist level if necessary with no real pretence at precise aim: a rifle with infra-red sights for night use, all angular protuberances. And beyond cordite and lead, what? Neutron missiles fired from ground launchers which would halt an invading tank army literally in its tracks. A new sort of battery which would make hand-held ray guns possible.

The marksman's special skill was drifting towards sport, as archery had, as swordplay had, as throwing the javelin and the hammer had; the commonplace weapon of one age becoming the Olympic medal of the next.

I didn't shoot very well on that particular afternoon and found little appetite afterwards for the camaraderie in the clubhouse. The image of Peter stumbling over the side of his boat on fire and dying made too many things seem irrelevant. I was pledged to shoot in the Queen's Prize in July and in a competition in Canada in August, and I reflected driving home that if I didn't put in a little more practice I would disgrace myself.

The trips overseas came up at fairly regular intervals, and because of the difficulties involved in transporting guns from one country to another, I had had built my own design of carrying case. About four feet long and externally looking like an ordinary extra-large suitcase, it was internally lined with aluminium and divided into padded shock-absorbing compartments. It held everything I needed for competitions, not only three rifles but all the other paraphernalia; score-book, ear-defenders, telescope, rifle sling, shooting glove, rifle oil, cleaning rod, batman jab, roll of flannelette patches, cleaning brush, wool mop for oiling the barrel, ammunition, thick jersey for warmth, two thin olive-green protective boiler suits and a supporting canvas and leather jacket. Unlike many people, I usually carried the guns fully assembled and ready to go, legacy of having missed my turn once through traffic hold-ups, a firearm still in pieces and fingers trembling with haste. I was not actually supposed to leave them with the bolt in place, but I often did. Only when the special gun suitcase went on to aeroplanes did I strictly conform to regulations, and then it was bonded and sealed and hedged about with red tape galore; and perhaps also because it didn't look like what it was, I'd never lost it.

Sarah, who had been enthusiastic at the beginning and had gone with me often to Bisley, had in time got tired of the bang bang bang, as most wives did. She had tired also of my spending so much time and money and had been only partly mollified by the Games. All the jobs I applied for, she had pointed out crossly, let us live south of London, convenient for the ranges. 'But if I could ski,' I'd said, 'it would be silly to move to the tropics.'

She had a point, though. Shooting wasn't cheap, and I wouldn't have been able to do as much as I did without support from indirect sponsors. The sponsors expected in return that I would not only go to the international competitions, but go to them practised and fit: conditions that until very recently I'd been happy to fulfil. I was getting old, I thought. I would be thirty-four in three months.

I drove home without haste and let myself into the quiet house which was no longer vibrant with silent tensions. Dumped my case on the coffee table in the sitting-room with no one to suggest I take it straight upstairs. Unclipped the lock and thought of the pleasant change of being able to go through the cleaning and oiling routine in front of the television without tight-lipped disapproval. Decided to postpone the clean-up until I'd chosen what to have for supper and poured out a reviving scotch.

Chose a frozen pizza. Poured the scotch.

The front doorbell rang at that point and I went to answer it. Two men, olive skinned, dark haired, stood on the doorstep: and one of them held a pistol.

I looked at it with a sort of delayed reaction, not registering at once because I'd been looking at peaceful firearms all day. It took me at least a whole second to realize that this one was pointing at my midriff in a thoroughly unfriendly fashion. A Walther .22, I thought, as if it mattered.

My mouth, I dare say, opened and shut. It wasn't what one expected in a moderately crime-free suburb.

'Back,' he said.

'What do you want?'

'Get inside.' He prodded towards me with the long silencer attached to the automatic and because I certainly respected the blowing-away power of hand guns, I did as he said. He and his friend advanced through the front door and closed it behind them.

'Raise your hands,' said the gunman.

I did so.

He glanced towards the open door of the sitting room and jerked his head towards it.

'Go in there.'

I went slowly, and stopped, and turned, and said again, 'What do you want?'

'Wait,' he said. He glanced at his companion and jerked his head again, this time at the windows. The companion switched on the lights and then went across and closed the curtains. It was not yet dark outside. A shaft of evening sunshine pierced through where the curtains met.

I thought: why aren't I desperately afraid? They looked so purposeful, so intent. Yet I still thought they had made some weird sort of mistake and might depart if nicely spoken to.

They seemed younger than myself, though it was difficult to be sure. Italian, perhaps, from the south. They had the long straight nose, the narrow jaw, the black-brown eyes. The sort of face which went fat with age, grew a moustache and became a godfather.

That last thought shot through my brain from nowhere and seemed as nonsensical as a pistol.

'What do you want?' I said again.

'Three computer tapes.'

My mouth no doubt went again through the fish routine. I listened to the utterly English sloppy accent and thought that it couldn't have less matched the body it came from.

'What ... what computer tapes?' I said, putting on bewilderment.

'Stop messing. We know you've got them. Your wife said so.'

Jesus, I thought. The bewilderment this time needed no acting.

He jerked the gun a fraction. 'Get them,' he said. His eyes were cold. His manner showed he despised me.

I said with a suddenly dry mouth, 'I can't think why my wife said ... why she thought ...'

'Stop wasting time,' he said sharply.

'But – '

'*The King and I*, and *West Side Story*,' he said impatiently, 'and *Okla-fucking-homa*.'

'I haven't got them.'

'Then that's too bad, buddy boy,' he said, and there was in an instant in him an extra dimension of menace. Before, he had been fooling along in second gear, believing no doubt that a gun was enough. But now I uncomfortably perceived that I was not dealing with someone reasonable and safe. If these were the two who had visited Peter, I understood what he had meant by frightening. There was a volatile quality, an absence of normal inhibition, a powerful impression of recklessness. The brakes-off syndrome which no legal deterrents deterred. I'd sensed it occasionally in boys I'd taught, but never before at such magnitude.

'You've got something you've got no right to,' he said. 'And you'll give it to us.'

He moved the muzzle of the gun an inch or two sideways and squeezed the trigger. I heard the bullet zing past close to my ear. There was a crash of glass breaking behind me. One of Sarah's mementos of Venice, much cherished.

'That was a vase,' he said. 'Your television's next. After that, you. Ankles and such. Give you a limp for life. Those tapes aren't worth it.'

He was right. The trouble was that I doubted if he would believe that I really hadn't got them.

He began to swing the gun round to the television.

'OK,' I said.

He sneered slightly. 'Get them, then.'

With my capitulation he relaxed complacently and so did his obedient and unspeaking assistant, who was standing a pace to his rear. I walked the few steps to the coffee table and lowered my hands from the raised position.

'They're in the suitcase,' I said.

'Get them out.'

I lifted the lid of the suitcase a little and pulled out the jersey, dropping it on the floor.

'Hurry up,' he said.

He wasn't in the least prepared to be faced with a rifle; not in that room, in that neighbourhood, in the hands of the man he took me for.

It was with total disbelief that he looked at the long deadly shape and heard the double click as I worked the bolt. There was a chance he would realize that I'd never transport such a weapon with a bullet up the spout, but then if he took his own shooter around loaded, perhaps he wouldn't.

'Drop the pistol,' I said. 'You shoot me, I'll shoot you both, and you'd better believe it. I'm a crack shot.' There was a time for boasting, perhaps; and that was it.

He wavered. The assistant looked scared. The rifle was an ultra scary weapon. The silencer slowly began to point downwards, and the automatic thudded to the carpet. The anger could be felt.

'Kick it over here,' I said. 'And gently.'

He gave the gun a furious shove with his foot. It wasn't near enough for me to pick up, but too far for him, also.

'Right,' I said. 'Now you listen to me. I haven't got those tapes. I've lent them to somebody else, because I thought they were music. How the hell should I know they were computer tapes? If you want them back, you'll have to wait until I get them. The person I lent them to has gone away for the weekend and I've no way of finding out where. You can have them without all this melodrama, but you'll have to wait. Give me an address, and I'll send them to you. I frankly want to get shot of you. I don't give a damn about those tapes or what you want them for. I just don't want you bothering me . . . or my wife. Understood?'

'Yeah.'

'Where do you want them sent?'

His eyes narrowed.

'And it will cost you two quid,' I said, 'for packing and postage.'

The mundane detail seemed to convince him. With a disgruntled gesture he took two pounds from his pocket and dropped them at his feet.

'Cambridge main post office,' he said. 'To be collected.'

'Under what name?'

After a pause he said, 'Derry.'

I nodded. 'Right,' I said. A pity, though, that he'd given my own name. Anything else might have been informative. 'You can get out, now.'

Both pairs of eyes looked down at the automatic now on the carpet.

'Wait in the road,' I said. 'I'll throw it to you through the window. And don't come back.'

They edged to the door with an eye on the sleek steel barrel following them, and I went out after them into the hall. I got the benefit of two viciously frustrated expressions before they opened the front door and went out, closing it again behind them.

Back in the sitting-room I put the rifle on the sofa and picked up the Walther to unclip it and empty its magazine into an ashtray. Then I unscrewed the silencer from the barrel, and opened the window.

The two men stood on the pavement, balefully staring across twenty feet of grass. I threw the pistol so that it landed in a rose bush not far from their feet. When the assistant had picked it out and scratched himself on the thorns, I threw the silencer into the same place.

The gunman, finding he had no bullets, delivered a verbal parting shot.

'You send those tapes, or we'll be back.'

'You'll get them next week. And stay out of my life.'

I shut the window decisively and watched them walk away, every line of their bodies rigid with discomfiture.

What on *earth*, I wondered intensely, had Peter programmed on to those cassettes?

4

'Who,' I said to Sarah, 'asked you for computer tapes?'

'What?' She sounded vague, a hundred miles away on this planet but in another world.

'Someone,' I said patiently, 'must have asked you for some tapes.'

'Oh, you mean cassettes?'

'Yes, I do.' I tried to keep any grimness out of my voice; to sound merely conversational.

'But you can't have got his letter already,' she said, puzzled. 'He only came this morning.'

'Who was he?' I said.

'Oh!' She exclaimed. 'I suppose he telephoned. He could have got our number from enquiries.'

'Sarah . . .'

'Who was he? I've no idea. Someone to do with Peter's work.'

'What sort of man?' I asked.

'What do you mean? Just a man. Middle-aged, grey-haired, a bit plump.' Sarah herself, like many naturally slim people, saw plumpness as a moral fault.

'Tell me what he said,' I pressed.

'If you insist. He said he was so sorry about Peter. He said Peter had brought home a project he'd been working on for his firm, possibly in the form of handwritten notes, possibly in the form of cassettes. He said the firm wold be grateful to have it all back, because they would have to re-allocate the job to someone else.'

It all sounded a great deal more civilized than frighteners with waving guns.

'And then?' I prompted.

'Well, Donna said she didn't know of anything Peter had in the house, though she did of course know he'd been working on *something*. Anyway, she looked in a lot of cupboards and drawers, and she found those three loose cassettes, out of their boxes, stacked between the gin and the Cinzano in the drinks cupboard. Am I boring you?'

She sounded over-polite and as if boring had been her intention, but I simply answered fervently, 'No, you're not. Please do go on.'

The shrug travelled almost visibly down the wire. 'Donna gave them to the man. He was delighted until he looked at them closely. Then he said they were tapes of musicals and not what he wanted, and please would we look again.'

'And then either you or Donna remembered – '

'I did,' she affirmed. 'We both saw Peter give them to you but he must have got them mixed up. He gave you his firm's cassettes by mistake.'

391

Peter's firm . . .

'Did the man give you his name?' I said.

'Yes,' Sarah said. 'He introduced himself when he arrived. But you know how it is. He mumbled it a bit and I've forgotten it. Why? Didn't he tell you when he rang up?'

'No visiting card?'

'Don't tell me,' she said with exasperation, 'that you didn't take his address. Wait a moment, I'll ask Donna.'

She put the receiver down on the table and I could hear her calling Donna. I wondered why I hadn't told her of the nature of my visitors, and decided it was probably because she would try to argue me into going to the police. I certainly didn't want to do that, because they were likely to take unkindly to my waving a rifle about in such a place. I couldn't prove to them that it had been unloaded, and it did not come into the category of things a householder could reasonably use to defend his property. Bullets fired from a Mauser 7.62 didn't at ten paces smash vases and embed themselves in the plaster, they seared straight through the wall itself and killed people outside walking their dogs.

Firearms certificates could be taken away faster than given.

'Jonathan?' Sarah said, coming back.

'Yes.'

She read out the full address of Peter's firm in Norwich and added the telephone number.

'Is that all?' she said.

'Except . . . you're both still all right?'

'I am, thank you. Donna's very low. But I'm coping.'

We said our usual goodbyes: almost formal, without warmth, deadly polite.

Duty took me back to Bisley the following day: duty and restlessness and dreadful prospects on the box. I shot better and thought less about Peter, and when the light began to fade I went home and corrected the ever-recurring exercise books: and on Monday Ted Pitts said he hadn't yet done anything about my computer tapes but that if I cared to stay on at four o'clock, we could both go down to the computer room and see what there was to see.

When I joined him he was already busy in the small side-room that with its dim cream walls and scratchily polished floor had an air of being everyone's poor relation. A single light hung without a shade from the ceiling, and the two wooden chairs were regulation battered school issue. Two nondescript tables occupied most of the floor-space, and upon them rested the uninspiring-looking machines which had cost a small fortune. I asked Ted mildly why he put up with such cramped, depressing quarters.

He looked at me vaguely, his mind on his task. 'You know how it is. You have to teach boys individually on this baby to get good results. There aren't enough classrooms. This is all that's available. It's not too bad. And anyway, I never notice.'

I could believe it. He was a hiker, an ex-youth-hosteller, an embracer of earnest discomforts. He perched on the edge of the hard wooden chair and applied his own computer-like brain to the one on the tables.

There were four separate pieces of equipment. A box like a small television set with a typewriter keyboard protruding forward from the lower edge of the screen. A cassette player. A large upright uninformative black box marked simply 'Harris', and something which looked at first sight like a typewriter, but which in fact had no keys. All four were linked together, and each to its own wall socket, by black electric cables.

Ted Pitts put *Oklahoma* into the cassette player and typed CLOAD 'BASIC' on the keyboard. CLOAD 'BASIC' appeared in small white capital letters high up on the left of the television screen, and two asterisks appeared, one of them rapidly blinking on and off, up on the right. On the cassette player, the wheels of the tape-reels quickly revolved.

'How much do you remember?' Ted said.

'About enough to know you're searching the tape for the language, and that CLOAD means LOAD from the cassette.'

He nodded and pointed briefly to the large upright box 'The computer already has its own BASIC stored in there. I put it in at lunchtime. Now just let's see . . .' He hunched himself over the keyboard, pressing keys, stopping and starting the cassette player and punctuating his activity with grunts.

'Nothing useful,' he muttered, turning the tapes over and repeating the process. 'Let's try . . .' A fair time passed. He shook his head now and then, and said finally, 'Give me those other two tapes. It must logically be at the *beginning* of one of the sides – unless of course he added it at the end because he had space left . . . or perhaps he didn't do it at all . . .'

'Won't the programs run on your own version of BASIC?'

He shook his head. 'I tried before you came. The only response you get is ERROR IN LINE 10. Which means that the two versions aren't compatible.' He grunted again and tried *West Side Story*, and towards the end of the first side he sat bolt upright and said, 'Well, now.'

'It's on there?'

'Can't tell yet. But there's something filed under "Z". Might just try that.' He flicked a few more switches and sat back beaming. 'Now all we do is wait a few minutes while that . . .' he pointed to the large upright box . . . 'soaks up whatever is on the tape under "Z", and if it should happen to be Grantley Basic, we'll be in business.'

'Why does "Z" give you hope?'

'Instinct. Might be a hundred per cent wrong. But it's a much longer recording than anything else I've found so far on the tapes, and feels the right length. Four and a quarter minutes. I've fed BASIC into the Harris thousands of times.'

His instinct proved reliable. The word READY suddenly appeared on the screen, white and bright and promising. Ted sighed heavily with satisfaction and nodded three times.

'Sensible fellow, your friend,' he said. 'So now we can see what you've got.'

When he ran *Oklahoma* again, the file names came up clearly beside the flashing asterisk at the top right of the screen, and although some of them were mysterious to me, some of them were definitely not.

DONCA EDINB EPSOM FOLKE FONTW GOODW HAMIL HAYDK HEREF HEXHM

'Names of towns,' I said. 'Towns with racecourses.'

Ted nodded. 'Which would you like to try?'

'Epsom.'

'OK,' he said. He rewound the tape with agile fingers and typed CLOAD 'EPSOM' on the keyboard. 'This puts the program filed under EPSOM into the computer, but you know that, of course, I keep forgetting.'

The encouraging word READY appeared again, and Ted said, 'Which do you want to do, List it or Run it?'

'Run it,' I said.

He nodded and typed RUN on the keyboard, and in bright little letters the screen enquired WHICH RACE AT EPSOM? TYPE NAME OF RACE AND PRESS 'ENTER'.

'My God,' I said. 'Let's try the Derby.'

'Stands to reason,' Ted said, and typed DERBY. The screen promptly responded with TYPE NAME OF HORSE AND PRESS 'ENTER'.

Ted typed JONATHAN DERRY and again pressed the double-sized key on the keyboard marked 'Enter', and the screen obliged with:

EPSOM: THE DERBY

HORSE: JONATHAN DERRY.

TO ALL QUESTIONS ANSWER YES OR NO AND PRESS 'ENTER'.

A couple of inches down there was a question:

HAS HORSE WON A RACE?

Ted typed YES and pressed 'ENTER'. The first three lines remained, but the question was replaced with another.

HAS HORSE WON THIS YEAR?

Ted typed NO. The screen responded:

HAS HORSE WON ON COURSE?

Ted typed NO. The screen responded:

HAS HORSE RUN ON COURSE?

Ted typed YES.

There were questions about the horse's sire, its dam, its jockey, its trainer, the number of days since its last run, and its earning in prize money; and one final question:

IS HORSE QUOTED ANTE-POST AT 25-1 OR LESS?

Ted typed YES, and the screen said merely,

ANY MORE HORSES?

Ted typed YES again, and we found ourselves back at

TYPE NAME OF HORSE AND PRESS 'ENTER'.

'That's not handicapping,' I said.

'Is that what it's supposed to be?' Ted shook his head. 'More like statistical probabilities, I should have thought. Let's go through it again and answer NO to ANY MORE HORSES?'

He typed TED PITTS for the horse's name and varied the answers, and immediately after his final NO we were presented with a cleared screen and a new display.

HORSE'S NAME	WIN FACTOR
JONATHAN DERRY	27
TED PITTS	12

'You've *no* chance,' I said. 'You might as well stay in the stable.'

He looked a bit startled, and then laughed. 'Yes. That's what it is. A guide to gamblers.'

He typed LIST instead of RUN, and immediately the bones of the program appeared, but scrolling upwards too fast to read, like flight-information changes at airports. Ted merely hummed a little and typed LIST 10-140, and after some essential flickering the screen presented the goods.

```
LIST 10-140
10 PRINT "WHICH RACE AT EPSOM? TYPE NAME OF RACE AND PRESS
'ENTER'"
20 INPUT A$
30 IF A$="DERBY" THEN 330
40 IF A$="OAKS" THEN 340
50 IF A$="CORONATION CUP" THEN 350
60 IF A$="BLUE RIBAND STAKES" THEN 360
```

The list went down to the bottom of the screen in this fashion, and Ted gave it one appraising look and said, 'Dead simple.'

The dollar sign, I seemed to remember, meant that the Input had to be in the form of letters. Input A, without the dollar sign, would have asked for numbers.

Ted seemed perfectly happy. He typed LIST 300-380 and got another set of instructions.

At 330 the program read: LET A=10: B=8: C=6: D=2: DI=2.

Lines 332, 334, and 336 looked similar, with numbers being ascribed to letters.

'That's the weighting,' Ted said. 'The value given to each answer. Ten points for the first question, which was ... um ... has the horse won a race. And so on. I see that 10 points are given also for the last question, which was about ... er ... ante-post odds, wasn't it?'

I nodded.

'There you are, then,' he said. 'I dare say there's a different weighting for every race. There might of course be different *questions* for every race. Ho hum. Want to see?'

'If you've the time,' I said.

'Oh sure. I've always got time for TOMS. Love 'em, you know.'

He went on typing LIST followed by various numbers and came up with such gems as:

```
520 IF N$="NO" THEN GOTO 560: X=X+B
530 INPUT N$: AB=AB+1
540 IF N$="NO" THEN GOTO 560: X=X+M
550 T=T+G2
560 GOSUB 4000
```

'What does all that mean?' I asked.

'Um ... well. It's much easier to *write* a program than to read and understand someone else's. Programs are frantically individual. You can get the same results by all sorts of different routes. I mean, if you're going from London to Bristol you go down the M4 and it's called M4 all the way, but on a computer you can call the road anything you like, at any point on the journey, and *you* might know that at different moments L2, say, or RQ3 or B7(2) equalled M4, but no one else would.'

'Is that also what you teach the kids?'

'Er, yes. Sorry, it's a habit.' He glanced at the screen. 'I'd guess that those top lines are to do with skipping some questions if previous answers make them unnecessary. Jumping to later bits of program. If I printed the whole thing out on to paper I could work out their exact meaning.'

I shook my head. 'Don't trouble. Let's try a different racecourse.'

'Sure.'

He rewound the tape to the beginning and typed CLOAD 'DONCA', and when the screen said READY, typed RUN.

Immediately we were asked WHICH RACE AT DONCASTER? TYPE NAME OF RACE AND PRESS 'ENTER'.

'OK,' Ted said, pressing switches. 'What about further down the tape? Say, GOODW?'

We got WHICH RACE AT GOODWOOD? TYPE NAME OF RACE AND PRESS 'ENTER'.

'I don't know any races at Goodwood,' I said.

Ted said, 'That's easy,' and typed LIST 10-140. When the few seconds of flickering had stopped, we had:

```
LIST 10-140
10 PRINT "WHICH RACE AT GOODWOOD? TYPE NAME OF RACE AND
PRESS 'ENTER'"
20 INPUT A$
30 IF A$="GOODWOOD STAKES" THEN 330
40 IF A$="GOODWOOD CUP" THEN 340
```

There were fifteen races listed altogether.

'What happens if you type in the name of a race there's no program for?' I asked.

'Let's see,' he said. He typed RUN, and we were back to WHICH RACE AT GOODWOOD? He typed DERBY, and the screen informed us THERE IS NO INFORMATION FOR THIS RACE.

'Neat and simple,' Ted said.

We sampled all the sides of the three tapes, but the programs were all similar. WHICH RACE AT REDCAR? WHICH RACE AT ASCOT? WHICH RACE AT NEWMARKET?

There were programs for about fifty racecourses, with varying numbers of races listed at each. Several lists contained not actual titles of races but general categories like STRAIGHT 7 FURLONGS FOR 3 YR OLDS AND UPWARDS, OR THREE MILE WEIGHT-FOR-AGE STEEPLECHASE: and it was not until quite late that I realized with amusement that *none* of the races were handicaps. There were no questions at all about how many lengths a horse had won by, while carrying such and such a weight.

All in all, there was provision for scoring for any number of horses in each of more than eight hundred named races, and in an unknown quantity of *un*named races. Each race had its own set of weightings and very often its own set of questions. It had been a quite monumental task.

'It must have taken him days,' Ted said.

'Weeks, I think. He had to do it in his spare time.'

'They're not complicated programs, of course,' Ted said. 'Nothing really needing an expert. It's more organization than anything else. Still, he hasn't wasted much space. Amateurs write very long programs. Experts get to the same nitty-gritty in a third of the time. It's just practice.'

'We'd better make a note of which side of tape contains the Grantley Basic,' I said.

Ted nodded. 'It's at an end. After York. Filed under "Z".' He checked that he had the right tape, and wrote on its label in pencil.

For no particular reason I picked up the other two tapes and briefly looked at the words I had half-noticed before: the few words Peter had pencilled on to one of the labels.

'Programs compiled for C. Norwood.'

Ted, glancing over, said, 'That's the first side you're looking at. Ascot and so on.' He paused. 'We might just as well number the sides properly, one to six. Get them in order.'

Order, to him as to me, was a habit. When he'd finished the numbering he put the cassettes back in their gaudy boxes and handed them over. I thanked him most profoundly for his patience and took him out for a couple of beers; then over his pint he said, 'Will you be trying them out?'

'Trying what out?'

'Those races, of course. It's the Derby next month, some time. If you like we could work out the scores for all the Derby horses, and see if the program comes up with the winner. I'd actually quite like to do it. Wouldn't you?'

'I wouldn't begin to know the answers to all those questions.'

'No.' He sighed. 'Pity. The info must be *somewhere*, but unearthing it might be a bore.'

'I'll ask my brother,' I said, explaining about William. 'He sometimes mentions form books. I'd guess the answers would be in those.'

Ted seemed pleased with the idea, and I didn't immediately ask him which he was keener to do, to test the accuracy of the programs or to make a profit. He told me, however.

He said tentatively, 'Would you mind very much . . . I mean . . . would you mind if I took a *copy* of those tapes?'

I looked at him in faint surprise and he smiled awkwardly.

'The fact is, Jonathan, I could do with a boost to the economy. I mean, if those tapes actually come up with the goods, why not use them?' He squirmed a little on his seat, and when I didn't rush to answer he went on, 'You know how bloody small our salaries are. It's no fun with three kids to feed, and their clothes, their shoes cost a bomb, and the little devils grow out of them before you've paid for them, practically. I'm never under my limit on my credit cards. Never.'

'Have another beer,' I said.

'It's better for you,' he said gloomily, accepting the offer. 'You've no children. It isn't so hard for you to manage on a pittance. And you earn more anyway, with being a head of department.'

I said thoughtfully, 'I don't see why you shouldn't make copies, if you want to.'

'Jonathan!' He was clearly delighted.

'But I wouldn't use them,' I said, 'without finding out if they're any good. You might lose a packet.'

'I'll be careful,' he said, but his eyes gleamed behind his black-rimmed spectacles and I wondered uneasily if I were seeing the birth of a compulsion. There was always a slight touch of the fanatic about Ted. 'Can you ask your brother where I can get a form book?' he said.

'Well . . .'

He scanned my face. 'You're regretting saying I could copy them. Do you want them for yourself, now, is that it?'

'No. I just thought . . . gambling's like drugs. You can get addicted and go down the drain.'

'But all I want – ' He stopped and shrugged. He looked disappointed but nothing more.

I sighed and said, 'OK. But for God's sake be sensible.'

'I will,' he said fervently. He looked at me expectantly and I took the tapes out of my pocket and gave them back to him.

'Take good care of them,' I said.

'With my life.'

'Not that far.' I thought briefly of gun-toting visitors and of much I didn't understand, and I added slowly, 'While you're about it, make copies for me too.'

He was puzzled. 'But you'll have the originals.'

I shook my head. 'They'll belong to someone else. I'll have to give them back. But I don't see why, if copies are possible, I shouldn't also keep what I return.'

'Copies are dead easy,' he said. 'Also they're prudent. All you do is load the program into the computer, from the cassette, like we did, then change to a fresh cassette and load the program back from the computer on to the new tape. You can make dozens of copies, if you like. Any time I've written a program I especially don't want to lose, I record it on to several different tapes. That way, if one tape gets lost or some idiot re-records on top of what you've done, you've always got a back-up.'

'I'll buy some tapes, then,' I said.

He shook his head. 'You give me the money, and I'll get them. Ordinary tapes are OK if you're pushed, but special digital cassettes made for computer work are better.'

I gave him some money, and he said he would make the copies the following day, either at lunch time or after school. 'And get the form book,' he reminded me, 'won't you?'

'Yes,' I said; and later, from home, I telephoned the farm and spoke to William.

'How's it going?'

'What would you say if I tried for a racing stable in the summer?'

'I'd say stick to farms,' I said.

'Yeah. But the hunters are all out at grass in July and August, and this riding school here's cracking up. They've sold off the best horses, there's nothing much to ride, and there's weeds and muck everywhere. Mr Askwith's taken to drink. He comes roaring out in the mornings clutching the hard stuff and swearing at the girls. There are only two of them left now, trying to look after fourteen ponies. It's a mess.'

'It sounds it.'

'I've been reduced to doing some revision for those grotty exams.'

'Things must be bad,' I said.

'Thanks for the cheque.'

'Sorry it was late. Listen, I've a friend who wants a racing form book. How would he get one?'

William, it transpired, knew of about six different types of form book. Which did my friend want?

One which told him a horse's past history, how long since it had last raced and whether its ante-post odds were less than 25 to 1. Also its sire's and dam's and jockey's and trainer's history, and how much it had won in prize money. For starters.

'Good grief,' said my brother. 'You want a combination of the form book and *The Sporting Life*.'

'Yes, but *which* form book.'

'*The* form book,' he said. '*Raceform* and *Chaseform*. *Chaseform*'s the jumpers. Does he want jumpers as well?'

'I think so.'

'Tell him to write to Turf Newspapers, then. The form book comes in sections; a new updated section every week. Best on earth. I covet it increasingly, but it costs a bomb. Do you think the trustees would consider it vocational training?' He spoke, however, without much hope.

I thought of Ted Pitts's financial state and enquired for something cheaper.

'Hum,' said William judiciously. 'He could try the weekly *Sporting Record*, I suppose.' A thought struck him. 'This wouldn't be anything to do with your friend Peter and his betting system, would it? You said he was dead.'

'Same system, different friend.'

'There isn't a system born,' William said, 'that really works.'

'You'd know, of course,' I said drily.

'I do read.'

We talked a little more and said goodbye in good humour, and I found myself regretting, after I'd put down the receiver, that I hadn't asked him if he'd like to spend the week with me rather than on the farm. But I didn't suppose he would have done. He'd have found even the drunken Mr Askwith more congenial than the decorum of Twickenham.

Sarah telephoned an hour later, sounding strained and abrupt.

'Do you know anyone called Chris Norwood?' she said.

'No, I don't think so.' The instant I'd said it I remembered Peter's handwriting on the cassette. 'Program compiled for C. Norwood.' I opened my mouth to tell her, but she forestalled me.

'Peter knew him. The police have been here again, asking questions.'

'But what – ' I began in puzzlement.

'I don't *know* what it's all about, if that's what you're going to ask. But someone called Chris Norwood has been shot.'

5

Ignorance seemed to surround me like a fog.

'I thought Peter might have mentioned him to you,' Sarah said. 'You always talked with him more than to Donna and me.'

'Doesn't Donna know this Norwood?' I asked, ignoring the bitter little thrust.

'No, she doesn't. She's still in shock. It's all too much.'

Fogs could be dangerous, I thought. There might be all manner of traps waiting, unseen.

'What did the police actually say?' I said.

'Nothing much. Only that they were enquiring into a death and wanted any help Peter could give.'

'Peter!'

'Yes, Peter. They didn't know he was dead. They weren't the same as the ones who came before. I think they said they were from Suffolk. What does it matter?' She sounded impatient. 'They'd found Peter's name and address on a pad beside the telephone. This Norwood's telephone. They said that in a murder investigation they had to follow even the smallest lead.'

'Murder . . .'

'That's what they said.'

I frowned and asked, 'When was he killed?'

'How do I know? Sometime last week. Thursday. Friday. I can't remember. They were talking to Donna, really, not to me. I kept telling them she wasn't fit, but they wouldn't listen. They wouldn't see for ages that the poor darling is too dazed to care about a total stranger, however he died. And to crown it all, when they did finally realize, they said they might come back when she was better.'

After a pause I said, 'When's the inquest?'

'How on earth should I know?'

'I mean, on Peter.'

'Oh.' She sounded disconcerted. 'On Friday. We don't have to go. Peter's father is giving evidence of identity. He won't speak to Donna. He somehow thinks it was her fault that Peter was careless with the boat. He's been perfectly beastly.'

'Mm,' I said noncommittally.

'A man from the insurance company came here, asking if Peter had ever had problems with leaking gas lines and wanted to know if he always started the engine without checking for petrol vapour.'

Peter hadn't been careless, I thought. I remembered that he'd been pretty careful on the canals, opening up the engine compartment every morning to let any trapped vapour escape. And that had been diesel, not petrol: less inflammable altogether.

'Donna said she didn't know. The engine was Peter's affair. She was always in the cabin unpacking food and so on while he was getting ready to start up. And anyway,' Sarah said, 'why all this fuss about vapour? It isn't as if there was any actual *petrol* sloshing about. They say there wasn't.'

'It's the vapour that explodes,' I said. 'Liquid petrol won't ignite unless it's mixed with air.'

'Are you serious?'

'Absolutely.'

'Oh.'

There was a pause: a silence. Some dying-fall goodbyes. Not with a bang, I thought, but with a yawn.

On Tuesday, Ted Pitts said he hadn't yet had a chance to buy the tapes for the copies and on Wednesday I sweet-talked a colleague into taking my games duty for the afternoon and straight after morning school set off to Norwich. Not to see my wife, but to visit the firm where Peter had worked.

It turned out to be a three-room two-men-and-a-girl affair tucked away in a suite of offices in a building on an industrial estate: one modest component among about twenty others listed on the directory-board in the lobby: MASON MILES ASSOCIATES, COMPUTER CONSULTANTS rubbing elbows with DIRECT ACCESS DISTRIBUTION SERVICES and SEA MAGIC, DECORATIVE SHELL IMPORTERS.

Mason Mile and his Associates showed no signs of overwork but neither was there any of the gloom which hangs about a business on the brink. The inactivity, one felt, was normal.

The girl sat at a desk reading a magazine. The younger man fiddled with a small computer's innards and hummed in the manner of Ted Pitts. The older man, beyond a wide open door labelled Mason Miles, lolled in a comfortable chair with an arm-stretching expanse of newspaper. All three looked up without speed about five seconds after I'd walked through their outer unguarded defences.

'Hallo,' the girl said. 'Are you for the job?'

'Which job?'

'You're not, then. Not Robinson, D.F.?'

'Afraid not.'

'He's late. Dare say he's not coming.' She shrugged. 'Happens all the time.'

'Would that be Peter Keithly's job?' I asked.

The young man's attention went back to his eviscerated machine.

'Sure is,' said the girl. 'If you're not for his job, how can we help you?'

I explained that my wife, who was staying in Peter's house, was under the impression that someone from the firm had visited Peter's widow, asking for some tapes he had been working on.

The girl looked blank. Mason Miles gave me a lengthy frown from the distance. The young man dropped a screwdriver and muttered under his breath.

The girl said, 'None of us has been to Peter's house. Not even before the troubles.'

Mason Miles cleared his throat and raised his voice. 'What tapes are you talking about? You'd better come in here.'

He put down the newspaper and stood up reluctantly, as if the effort was too much for a weekday afternoon. He was not in the least like Sarah's description of a plump grey-haired ordinary middle-aged man. There was a crinkly red thatch over a long white face, a lengthy stubborn-looking upper lip and cheekbones of Scandinavian intensity; the whole extra-tall body being, as far as I could judge, still under forty.

'Don't let me disturb you,' I said without irony.

'You are not.'

'Would anyone else from your firm,' I asked, 'have gone to Peter's house, asking on your behalf for the tapes he was working on?'

'What tapes were those?'

'Cassettes with programs for evaluating racehorses.'

'He was working on no such project.'

'But in his spare time?' I suggested.

Mason Miles shrugged and sat down again with the relief of a traveller after a wearisome journey. 'Perhaps. What he did in his spare time was his own affair.'

'And do you have a grey-haired middle-aged man on your staff?'

He gave me a considering stare and then said merely, 'We employ no such person. If such a person has visited Mrs Keithly purporting to come from here, it is disturbing.'

I looked at his totally undisturbed demeanour and agreed.

'Peter was writing the programs for someone called Chris Norwood,' I said. 'I don't suppose you've ever heard of him?' I made it a question but without much hope, and he shook his head and suggested I ask his Associates in the outer office. The Associates also showed nil reactions to the name of Chris Norwood, but the young man paused from his juggling of microchips long enough to say that he had put everything Peter had left concerning his work in a shoe-box in a cupboard, and he supposed it would do no harm if I wanted to look.

I found the box, took it out, and began to sift through the hand-written scraps of notes which it contained. Nearly all of them concerned his work and took the form of mysterious memos to himself. 'Remember to tell RTT of modification to PET.' 'Pick up floppy discs for LMP.' 'Tell ISCO about L's software package.' 'The bug in R's program must be a syntax error in the subroutine.' Much more of the same, and none of it of any use.

There was a sudden noise and flurry at the outer door, and a wild-eyed breathless heavily flushed youth appeared along with a suitcase, a hold-all, an overcoat and a tennis racket.

'Sorry,' he panted. 'The train was late.'

'Robinson?' the girl said calmly. 'D.F.?'

'What? Oh. Yes. Is the job still open?'

I looked down at another note, the writing as neat as all the others: 'Borrow Grantley Basic tape from GF.' Turned the piece of paper over. On the back he'd written, 'C. Norwood, Angel Kitchens, Newmarket.'

I persevered to the bottom of the box, but there was nothing else that I understood. I put all the scrappy notes back again, and thanked the Associates for their trouble. They hardly listened. The attention of the whole firm was intently fixed on D.F. Robinson, who was wilting under their probing questions. Miles, who had beckoned them all into the inner office, was saying, 'How would you handle a client who made persistently stupid mistakes but blamed *you* for not explaining his system thoroughly?'

I sketched a farewell which nobody noticed, and left.

Newmarket lay fifty miles to the south of Norwich, and I drove there through the sunny afternoon thinking that the fog lay about me as thick as ever. Radar, perhaps, would be useful. Or a gale. Or some good clarifying information. Press on, I thought: press on.

Angel Kitchens, as listed in the telephone directory in the post office, were to be found in Angel Lane, to which various natives directed me with accuracy varying from vague to absent, and which proved to be a dead-end tarmac tributary to the east of the town, far from the mainstream of the High Street.

The Kitchens were just what they said: the kitchens of a mass food-production business, making frozen gourmet dinners in single-portion foil pans for the upper end of the market. 'Posh nosh' one of my route-directors had said. 'Fancy muck,' said another. 'You can buy that stuff in the town, but give me a hamburger any day' from another, and 'Real tasty' from the last. They'd all known the product, if not the location.

At a guess the Kitchen had been developed from the back half and out-houses of a defunct country mansion; they had that slightly haphazard air, and were surrounded by mature trees and the remnants of a landscaped garden. I parked in the large but well-occupied expanse of concrete outside a new-looking white single-storey construction marked Office, and pushed my way through its plate-glass double-door entrance.

Inside, in the open-plan expanse, the contrast to Mason Miles Associates was complete. Life was taken at a run, if not a stampede. The work in hand, it seemed, would overwhelm the inmates if they relaxed for a second.

My tentative enquiry for someone who had been a friend of Chris Norwood reaped me a violently unexpected reply.

'That *creep*? If he had any friends they'd be down in Veg Preparation, where he worked.'

'Er, Veg Preparation?'

'Two-storey grey stone building past the freezer sheds.'

I went out to the car park, wandered around and asked again.

'Where them carrots is being unloaded.'

Them carrots were entering a two-storey grey stone building by the sack-load on a fork-lift truck, the driver of which mutely pointed me to a less cavernous entrance round a corner.

Through there one passed through a small lobby beside a large changing-room where rows of outdoor clothing hung on pegs. Next came a white-tiled scrub-up room smelling like a hospital, followed by a swing door into a long narrow room lit blindingly by electricity and filled with gleaming stainless steel, noisily whirring machines and people dressed in white.

At the sight of me standing there in street clothes a large man wearing what looked like a cotton undervest over a swelling paunch advanced with waving arms and shooed me out.

'Cripes, mate, you'll get me sacked,' he said, as the swing-door swung behind us.

'I was directed here,' I said mildly.

'What do you want?'

With less confidence than before I enquired for any friend of Chris Norwood.

The shrewd eyes above the beer-stomach appraised me. The mouth pursed. The chef's hat sat comfortably over strong dark eyebrows.

'He's been murdered,' he said. 'You from the press?'

I shook my head. 'He knew a friend of mine, and he got both of us into a bit of trouble.'

'Sounds just like him.' He pulled a large white handkerchief out of his white trousers and wiped his nose. 'What exactly do you want?'

'I think just to talk to someone who knew him. I want to know what he was like. Who he knew. Anything. I want to know why and how he got us into trouble.'

'I knew him,' he said. He paused, considering. 'What's it worth?'

I sighed. 'I'm a schoolmaster. It's worth what I can afford. And it depends *what* you know.'

'All right then,' he said judiciously. 'I finish here at six. I'll meet you in the Purple Dragon, right? Up the lane, turn left, quarter of a mile. You buy me a couple of pints and we'll take it from there. OK?'

'Yes,' I said. 'My name is Jonathan Derry.'

'Akkerton.' He gave a short nod, as if sealing a bargain. 'Vince,' he added as an afterthought. He gave me a last unpromising inspection and barged back through the swing doors. I heard the first of the words he sprayed into the long busy room, 'You, Reg, you get back to work. I've only to take my eyes off you . . .'

The door closed discreetly behind him.

I waited for him at a table in the Purple Dragon, a pub a good deal less colourful than its name, and at six-fifteen he appeared, dressed now in grey trousers and a blue and white shirt straining at its buttons. Elliptical views of hairy chest appeared when he sat down, which he did with a wheeze and a licking of lips. The first pint I bought him disappeared at a single draught, closely followed by half of the second.

'Thirsty work, chopping up veg,' he said.

'Do you do it by hand?' I was surprised, and sounded it.

'Course not. Washed, peeled, chopped, all done by machines. But nothing hops into a machine by itself. Or out, come to that.'

'What, er . . . veg?' I said.

'Depends what they want. Today, mostly carrots, celery, onions, mushrooms. Regular every day, that lot. Needed for Burgundy Beef. Our best seller, Burgundy Beef. Chablis Chicken, Pork and Port, next best. You ever had any?'

'I don't honestly know.'

He drank deeply with satisfaction. 'It's good food,' he said seriously, wiping his mouth. 'All fresh ingredients. No mucking about. Pricey, mind you, but worth it.'

'You enjoy the job?' I asked.

He nodded. 'Sure. Worked in kitchens all my life. Some of them, you could shake hands with the cockroaches. Big as rats. Here, so clean you'd see a fruit fly a mile off. I've been in Veg three months now. Did a year in Fish, but the smell hangs in your nostrils after a while.'

'Did Chris Norwood,' I said, 'chop up veg?'

'When we were pushed. Otherwise he cleaned up, checked the input, and ran errands.' His tongue was assured and positive: a man who had no need to guard his tongue.

'Er, checked the input?' I said.

'Counted the sacks of veg as they were delivered. If there were twenty sacks of onions on the day's delivery note, his job was to see twenty sacks arrived.' He inspected the contents of the pint glass. 'Reckon it was madness giving him that job. Mind you, it's not millionaire class, knocking off sacks of carrots and onions, but it seems he was supplying a whole string of bleeding village shops with the help of the lorry drivers. The driver would let the sacks fall off the lorry on the way here, see, and Chris Norwood would count twenty where there was only sixteen. They split the profits. It goes on everywhere, that sort of thing, in every kitchen I've ever worked in. Meat too. Sides of ruddy beef. Caviar. You name it, it's been nicked. But Chris wasn't just your usual opportunist. He didn't know what to keep his hands off.'

'What didn't he keep his hands off?' I asked.

Vince Akkerton polished off the liquid remains and put down his glass with suggestive loudness. Obediently I crossed to the bar for a refill, and once there had been a proper inspection of the new froth and a sampling of the first two inches, I heard what Chris Norwood had stolen.

'The girls in the office said he pinched their cash. They didn't cotton on for ages. They thought it was one of the women there that they didn't like. Chris was in and out all the time, taking in the day-sheets and chatting them up. He thought a lot of himself. Cocky bastard.'

I looked at the well-fleshed worldly-wise face and thought of chief petty officers and ships' engineers. The same easy assumption of command: the ability to size men up and put them to work. People like Vince Akkerton were the indispensable getters of things done.

'How old,' I said, 'was Chris Norwood?'

'Thirtyish. Same as you. Difficult to say exactly.' He drank. 'What sort of trouble did he get you in?'

'A couple of bullies came to my house looking for something of his.'

Fog, I thought.

'What sort of thing?' said Akkerton.

'Computer tapes.'

If I'd spoken in Outer Mongolian, it couldn't have meant less to him. He covered his bewilderment with beer and in disappointment I drank some of my own.

'Course,' said Akkerton, rallying, 'there's a computer or some such over in the office. They use it for keeping track of how many tons of Burgundy Beef and so on they's got on order and in the freezers, stuff like that. Working out how many thousands of ducks they need. Lobsters. Even coriander seeds.' He paused and with the first glint of humour said, 'Mind you, the results are always wrong, on account of activities on the side. There was a whole shipment of turkeys missing once. Computer error, they said.' He grunted. 'Chris Norwood with his carrots and onions, he was peanuts.'

'These were computer tapes to do with horseracing,' I said.

The dark eyebrows rose. 'Now that makes more sense. Every bleeding thing in this town practically is to do with horseracing. I've heard they think the knacker's yard has a direct line to our Burgundy Beef. It's a libel.'

'Did Chris Norwood bet?'

'Everyone in the firm bets. Cripes, you couldn't live in this town and not bet. It's in the air. Catching, like the pox.'

I seemed to be getting nowhere at all and I didn't know what else to ask. I cast around and came up with, 'Where was Chris Norwood killed?'

'Where? In his room. He rented a room in a council house from a retired old widow who goes out cleaning in the mornings. See, she wasn't supposed to take in lodgers, the council don't allow it, and she never told the welfare, who'd been doling out free meals, that she was earning, so the fuss going on now is sending her gaga.' He shook his head. 'Next street to me, all this happened.'

'What *did* exactly happen?'

He showed no reluctance to tell. More like relish.

'She found Chris dead in his room when she went in to clean it. See, she thought he'd have gone to work; she always went out before him in the mornings. Anyway, there he was. Lot of blood, so I've heard. You don't know what's true and what isn't, but they say he had bullets in his *feet*. Bled to death.'

Christ Almighty . . .

'Couldn't walk, you see,' Akkerton said. 'No telephone. Back bedroom. No one saw him.'

With a dry mouth I asked, 'What about . . . his belongings?'

'Dunno, really. Nothing stolen, that I've heard of. Seems there were just a few things broken. And his stereo was shot up proper, same as him.'

What do I do, I thought. Do I go to the police investigating Chris Norwood and tell them I was visited by two men who threatened to shoot my television and my ankles? Yes, I thought, this time I probably do.

'When . . .' My voice sounded hoarse. I cleared my throat and tried again. 'Which day did it happen?'

'Last week. He didn't show up on Friday morning, and it was bloody inconvenient as we were handling turnips that day and it was his job to chop the tops and roots off and feed them into the washer.'

I felt dazed. Chris Norwood had been dead by Friday morning. It had been *Saturday afternoon* when I'd flung my visitors' Walther out into the rose

bush. On Saturday they had been still looking for the tapes, which meant . . .
dear God . . . that they hadn't got them from Chris Norwood. They'd shot
him, and left him, and they still hadn't got the tapes. He would have given
them to them if he'd had them: to stop them shooting him; to save his life.
The tapes weren't worth one's life: they truly weren't. I remembered the in-
souciance with which I faced that pistol, and was in retrospect terrified.

Vince Akkerton showed signs of feeling it was time he was paid for his
labours. I mentally tossed between what I could afford and what he might
expect and decided to try him with the least possible. Before I could offer it,
however, two girls came into the bar and prepared to sit at the next table.
One of them, seeing Akkerton, changed course abruptly and fetched up at
his side.

'Hullo, Vince,' she said. 'Do us a favour. Stand us a rum and coke and I'll
pay you tomorrow.'

'I've heard that before,' he said indulgently, 'but this friend of mine's buying.'

Poorer by two rum and cokes, another full pint and a further half (for
me), I sat and listened to Akkerton explaining that the girls worked in the
Angel Kitchens office.

Carol and Janet. Young, medium bright, full of chatter and chirpiness, expecting from minute to minute the arrival of their boyfriends.

Carol's opinion of Chris Norwood was straightforwardly indignant. 'We
all worked out it had to be him dipping into our handbags, but we couldn't
prove it, see? We were just going to set a trap for him when he got killed, and
I suppose I should feel sorry for him, but I don't. He couldn't keep his hands
off anything, I mean, not anything. He'd take your last sandwich when you
weren't looking and laugh at you while he ate it.'

'He didn't see anything wrong in pinching things,' Janet said.

'Here,' Akkerton said, leaning forward for emphasis, 'young Janet here,
she works the computer. You ask her about those tapes.'

Janet's response was a raised-eyebrow thoughtfulness.

'I didn't know he had any actual tapes,' she said. 'But of course he was
always around. It was his job, you know, collecting the day-sheets from all
the departments and bringing them to me. He'd always hang around a bit,
especially the last few weeks, asking how the computer worked, you know? I
showed him how it came up with all the quantities, how much salt, you
know, and things like that, had to be shifted to each department, and how all
the orders went through, mixed container loads to Bournemouth or Birmingham, you know. The whole firm would collapse you know, without the
computer.'

'What make is it?' I said.

'What *make?*' They all thought it an odd question, but I'd have gambled
on the answer.

'A Grantley,' Janet said.

I smiled at her as inoffensively as I knew how and asked her if she would have let Chris Norwood run his tapes through her Grantley if he'd asked her nicely, and after some guilty hesitation and a couple of downward blushes into her rum and coke, said she might have done, you know, at one time; before they discovered, you know, that it was Chris who was stealing their cash.

'We should have guessed it ages ago,' Carol said, 'but then the things he took, like our sandwiches and such, and things out of the office, staples, envelopes, rolls of sticky tape, well we *saw* him take those, we were used to it.'

'Didn't anyone ever complain?' I said.

Not officially, the girl said. What was the use? The firm never sacked people for nicking things, if they did there would be a strike.

'Except that time, do you remember, Janet?' Carol said. 'When that poor old lady turned up, wittering on about Chris stealing things from her house. *She* complained, all right. She came back three times, making a fuss.'

'Oh sure,' Janet nodded. 'But it turned out it was only some odd bits of paper she was on about, you know, nothing like money or valuables, and anyway Chris said she was losing her marbles, and had thrown them away, most like, and it all blew over, you know.'

I said, 'What was the old lady's name?'

The girls looked at each other and shook their heads. It was weeks ago, they said.

Akkerton said he hadn't known of that, he'd never heard about the old lady, not down with his Veg.

The girls' boyfriends arrived at that moment and there was a general reshuffle round the tables. I said I would have to be going, and by one of those unspoken messages Akkerton indicated that I should see him outside.

'O'Rorke,' said Carol suddenly.

'What?'

'The old lady's name,' she said. 'I've remembered it. It was Mrs O'Rorke. She was Irish. Her husband had just died, and she'd been paying Chris to carry logs in for her fire, and things like that that she couldn't manage.'

'I don't suppose you remember where she lived?'

'Does it matter? It was only a great fuss over nothing.'

'Still . . .'

She frowned slightly with obliging concentration, though most of her attention was on her boyfriend, who was tending to flirt with Janet.

'Stetchworth,' she exclaimed. 'She complained about the taxi fare.' She gave me a quick glance. 'To be honest, we were glad to be rid of her in the end. She was an awful nuisance, but we couldn't be too unkind because of her old man dying, and that.'

'Thanks very much,' I said.

'You're welcome.' She moved away from me and sat herself decisively between her boyfriend and Janet, and Akkerton and I went outside to settle our business.

He looked philosophically at what I gave him, nodded and asked me to write my name and address on a piece of paper in case he thought of anything else to tell me. I tore a page out of my diary, wrote, and gave it to him thinking that our transaction was over, but when I'd shaken his hand, said goodbye and walked away from him he called after me.

'Wait, lad.'

I turned back.

'Did you get your money's worth?' he said.

More than I'd bargained for, I thought. I said, 'Yes, I think so. Can't really tell yet.'

He nodded, pursing his lips. Then with an uncharacterstically awkward gesture he held out half of the cash. 'Here,' he said. 'You take it. I saw into your wallet in the pub. You're nearly cleaned out. Enough's enough.' He thrust his gift towards my hand, and I took it back with gratitude. 'Teachers,' he said, pushing open the pub door. 'Downtrodden underpaid lot of bastards. Never reckoned much to school myself.' He brushed away my attempt at thanks and headed back to the beer.

6

By map and in spite of misdirections, I eventually found the O'Rorke house in Stetchworth. Turned into the driveway. Stopped the engine. Climbed out of the car, looking at what lay ahead.

A large rambling untidy structure; much wood, many gables, untrained creeper pushing tendrils on to the slated roof, and sash window frames long ago painted white. The garden in the soft evening light seemed a matter of grasses and shrubs growing wherever they liked; and a large bush of lilac, white and sweet-scented, almost obliterated the front door.

The bell may have rung somewhere deep inside in response to my finger on the button, but I couldn't hear it. I rang again, and tried a few taps on the inadequate knocker, and when the blank seconds mounted to minutes, I stepped back a few paces, looking up at the windows for signs of life.

I didn't actually see the door open behind the lilac bush, but a sharp voice spoke to me from among the flowers.

'Are you Saint Anthony?' it said.

'Er, no.' I stepped back into the line of sight and found standing in the shadowy half-open doorway a short white-haired old woman with yellowish skin and wild-looking eyes.

'About the fate?' she said.

'Whose fate?' I asked, bewildered.

'The church's, of course.'

'Oh,' I said. 'The *fête*.'

She looked at me as if I were totally stupid, which from her point of view I no doubt was.

'If you cut the peonies tonight,' she said, 'they'll be dead by Saturday.'

Her face was distinguishably Irish, but with the pure vowels of education, and her words were already a dismissal. She was holding on to the door with one hand and its frame with the other, and was on the point of irrevocably rejoining them.

'Please,' I said hastily, 'show me the peonies . . . so that I'll know which to pick . . . on Saturday.'

The half-begun movement was arrested. The old woman considered for a moment and then stepped out past the lilac into full view, revealing a waif-thin frame dressed in a rust-coloured jersey, narrow navy blue trousers, and pink and green checked bedroom slippers.

'Round the back,' she said. She looked me up and down, but apparently saw nothing to doubt. 'This way.'

She led me round the house along a path whose flat sunken paving stones merged at the edges with the weedy overgrowth of what might once have been flowerbeds. Past a shoulder-high stack of sawn logs, contrastingly neat. Past a closed side door. Past a greenhouse filled with the straggly stalks of many dead geraniums. Past a wheelbarrow full of cinders, about whose purpose one could barely guess. Round an unexpected corner, through a too-small gap in a vigorously growing hedge. and finally into the riotous mess of the back garden.

'Peonies,' she said, pointing, though indeed there was no need. Around the ruin of a lawn huge swathes of the fat luxurious blowsy heads, pink, crimson, frilly white, raised themselves in every direction from a veritable ocean of glossy dark leaves, the sinking sun touching all with gold. Decay might lie in the future but the present was a triumphant shout in the face of death.

'They're magnificent,' I said, slightly awed. 'There must be thousands of them.'

The old woman looked around without interest. 'They grow every year. Liam couldn't have enough. You take what you like.'

'Um.' I cleared my throat. 'I'd better tell you I'm not from the church.'

She looked at me with the same sort of bewilderment as I'd recently bent on her. 'What did you want to see the peonies for, then?'

'I wanted to talk to you. For you not to go inside and shut your door when you learned what I want to talk about.'

'Young man,' she said severely, 'I'm not buying anything. I don't give to charities. I don't like politicians. What do you want?'

'I want to know,' I said slowly, 'about the papers that Chris Norwood stole from you.'

Her mouth opened. The wild eyes raked my face like great watery searchlights. The thin body shook with powerful but unspecified emotion.

'Please don't worry,' I said hastily. 'I mean you no harm. There's nothing at all to be afraid of.'

'I'm not afraid. I'm angry.'

'You did have some papers, didn't you, that Chris Norwood took?'

'Liam's papers. Yes.'

'And you went to Angel Kitchens to complain?'

'The police did nothing. Absolutely nothing. I went to Angel Kitchens to make that beastly man give them back. They said he wasn't there. They were lying. I know they were.'

Her agitation was more than I was ready to feel guilty for. I said calmly. 'Please, could we just sit down . . .' I looked around for a garden bench, but saw nothing suitable. 'I don't want to upset you. I might even help.'

'I don't know you. It's not safe.' She looked at me for a few more unnerving seconds with full beam, and then turned and began to go back the way we had come. I followed reluctantly, aware that I'd been clumsy but still not knowing what else to have done. I had lost her, I thought. She would go in behind the lilac and shut me out.

Back through the hedge, past the cinders, past the cemetery in the greenhouse: but not past the closed side door. To my slightly surprised relief she stopped there and twisted the knob.

'This way,' she said, going in. 'Come along. I think I'll trust you. You look all right. I'll take the risk.'

The house was dark inside and smelled of disuse. We seemed to be in a narrow passage, along which she drifted ahead of me, silent in her slippers, light as a sparrow.

'Old women living alone,' she said, 'should never take men they don't know into their houses.' As she was addressing the air in front of her, the admonishment seemed to be to herself. We continued along past various dark-painted closed doors, until the passage opened out into a central hall where such light as there was filtered through high-up windows of patterned stained glass.

'Edwardian,' she said, following my upward gaze. 'This way.'

I followed her into a spacious room whose elaborate bay window looked out on to the glory in the garden. Indoors, more mutedly, there were deep-blue velvet curtains, good-looking large rugs over the silver-grey carpet, blue velvet sofas and armchairs – and dozens and dozens of seascapes crowding the walls. Floor to ceiling. Billowing sails. Four-masters. Storms and seagulls and salt spray.

'Liam's,' she said briefly, seeing my head turn around them.

When Liam O'Rorke liked something, I thought fleetingly, he liked a lot of it.

'Sit down,' she said, pointing to an armchair. 'Tell me who you are and why you've come here.' She moved to a sofa where, to judge from the book and glass on the small table adjacent, she had been sitting before I arrived, and perched her small weight on the edge as if ready for flight.

I explained about Peter's link with Chris Norwood, saying that Chris Norwood had given what I thought might be her husband's papers to Peter for him to organize into computer programs. I said that Peter had done the job, and had recorded the programs on tape.

She brushed aside the difficult technicalities and came straight to the simple point. 'Do you mean,' she demanded, 'that your friend Peter has my papers?' The hope in her face was like a light.

'I'm afraid not. I don't know where the papers are.'

'Ask your friend.'

'He's been killed in an accident.'

'Oh.' She stared at me, intensely disappointed.

'But the tapes,' I said. 'I do know where those are – or at least I know where copies of them are. If the knowledge that's on them is yours, I could get them for you.'

She was a jumble of renewed hope and puzzlement. 'It would be wonderful. But these tapes, wherever they are, didn't you bring them with you?'

I shook my head. 'I didn't know you existed until an hour ago. It was a girl called Carol who told me about you. She works in the office of Angel Kitchens.'

'Oh, yes.' Mrs O'Rorke made a small movement of embarrassment. 'I screeched at her. I was so *angry*. They wouldn't tell me where to find Chris Norwood in all those buildings and sheds. I'd said I'd scratch his eyes out. I've an Irish temper, you know. I can't always control it.'

I thought of the picture she must have presented to those girls, and reckoned their description of her 'making a fuss' had been charitable.

'The trouble is,' I said slowly, 'that someone else is looking for those tapes.' I told her a watered-down version of the visit to my house of the gunmen, to which she listened with open-mouthed attention. 'I don't know who they are,' I said, 'or where they come from. I began to think that so much ignorance might be dangerous. So I've been trying to find out what's going on.'

'And if you know?'

'Then I'll know what *not* to do. I mean, one can do such stupid things, with perhaps appalling consequences, just through not knowing some simple fact.'

She regarded me steadily with the first glimmer of a smile. 'All you're asking for, young man, is the secret that has eluded *homo sapiens* from day one.'

I was started not so much by the thought as by the words she phrased it in, and as if sensing my surprise she said with dryness, 'One does not grow

413

silly with age. If one was silly when young, one may be silly when old. If one were acute when young, why should acuteness wane?'

'I have done you,' I said slowly, 'an injustice.'

'Everyone does,' she said indifferently. 'I look in my mirror. I see an old face. Wrinkles. Yellow skin. As society is now constituted, to present this appearance is to be thrust into a category. Old woman, therefore silly, troublesome, can be pushed around.'

'No,' I said. 'It's not true.'

'Unless, of course,' she added as if I hadn't spoken, 'one is an *achiever*. Achievement is the saviour of the very old.'

'And you are not . . . an achiever?'

She made a small regretful movement with hands and head. 'I wish I were. I am averagely intelligent, but that's all. It gets you nowhere. It doesn't save you from rage. I apologize for my reaction in the garden.'

'But don't,' I said. 'Theft's an assault. Of course you'd be angry.'

She relaxed to the extent of sitting back into the sofa, where the cushions barely deflated under her weight.

'I will tell you as much as I can of what has happened. If it saves you from chasing Moses across the Red Sea, so much the better.'

To know what *not* to do . . .

I grinned at her.

She twitched her lips and said, 'What do you know about racing?'

'Not a great deal.'

'Liam did. My husband. Liam lived for the horses all his life. In Ireland, of course, when we were children. Then here. Newmarket, Epsom, Cheltenham, that's where we've lived. Then back here to Newmarket. Always the horses.'

'Were they his job?' I asked.

'In a way. He was a gambler.' She looked at me calmly. 'I mean a professional gambler. He lived on his winnings. I still live on what's left.'

'I thought it wasn't possible,' I said.

'To beat the odds?' The words sounded wrong for her appearance. It was true, I thought, about what she'd said about categories. Old women weren't expected to talk gambling; but this one did. 'In the old days it was perfectly possible to make a good living. Dozens did it. You worked on a profit expectation of ten per cent on turnover, and if you had any judgement at all, you achieved it. Then they introduced the Betting Tax. It took a slice off all winnings, reduced the profit margin to almost nil, killed off all the old pros in no time. Your ten per cent was all going into the Revenue, do you see?'

'Yes,' I said.

'Liam had always made more than ten per cent. He took a pride in it. He reckoned he could win one race out of three. That means that every third bet, on average, would win. That's a very high percentage, day after day, year after year. And he *did* beat the tax. He tried new ways, added new factors. With his statistics, he said, you could always win in the long run. None of the bookies would take his bets.'

'Er, what?' I said.

'Didn't you know' She sounded surprised. 'Bookmakers won't take bets from people who repeatedly win.'

'But I thought that's what they were in business for. I mean, to take people's bets.'

'To take bets from ordinary mug punters, yes,' she said. 'The sort who may win occasionally but never do in the end. But if you have an account with almost any bookie and you keep winning, he'll close your account.'

'Good grief,' I said weakly.

'At the races,' she said, 'all the bookies knew Liam. If they didn't know him to talk to, they knew him by sight. They'd only let him bet in cash at starting price, and then as soon as he'd got his money on they'd tic-tac it round the ring and they'd all reduce the price of that horse to ridiculously small odds, making the starting price very low, so that he wouldn't win much himself, and so that the other racegoers would be put off backing that horse, and stake their money on something else.'

There was a longish pause while I sorted out and digested what she'd said.

'And what,' I said, 'about the Tote?'

'The Tote is unpredictable. Liam didn't like that. Also the Tote in general pays worse odds than the bookies. No, Liam liked betting with the bookies. It was a sort of war. Liam always won, though most times the bookies didn't know it.'

'Er,' I said, 'how do you mean?'

She sighed. 'It was a lot of work. We had a gardener. A friend, really. He lived here in the house. Down that passage where we came in just now, those were his rooms. He used to like driving round the country, so he'd take Liam's cash and drive off to some town or other, and put it all on in the local betting shops, bit by bit, and if the horse won, which it usually did, he'd go round and collect, and come home. He and Liam would count it all out. So much for Dan – that was our friend – and so much for the working funds, and the rest for us. No more tax to pay, of course. No income tax. We went on for years like that. Years. We all got on so well together, you see.'

She fell silent, looking into the gentle past with those incongruously wild eyes.

'And Liam died?' I said.

'Dan died. Eighteen months ago, just before Christmas. He was ill for only a month. It was so quick.' A pause. 'And Liam and I, we didn't realize until after – We didn't know how much we depended on Dan, until he wasn't there. He was so strong. He could lift things . . . and the garden . . . Liam was eighty-six, you see, and I'm eighty-eight, but Dan was younger, not over seventy. He was a blacksmith from Wexford, way back. Full of jokes, too. We missed him so much.'

The golden glow of sunlight outside had faded from the peonies, the great vibrant colours fading to greys in the approaching dusk. I listened to the young voice of the old woman telling the darker parts of her life, clearing the fog from my own.

415

'We thought we'd have to find someone else to put the bets on,' she said. 'But who could we trust? Some of the time last year Liam tried to do it himself, going round betting shops in places like Ipswich and Colchester, places where they wouldn't know him, but he was too old, he got dreadfully exhausted. He had to stop it, it was too much. We had quite a bit saved, you see, and we decided we'd have to live on that. And then this year a man we'd heard of, but never met, came to see us, and he offered to buy Liam's methods. He said to Liam to write down how he won so consistently, and he would buy what he'd written.'

'And those notes,' I said, enlightened, 'were what Chris Norwood stole?'

'Not exactly,' she said, sighing. 'You see there was no need for Liam to write down his method. He'd written it down years ago. All based on statistics. Quite complicated. He used to update it when necessary. And, of course, add new races. After so many years, he could bet with a thirty-three per cent chance of success in nearly a thousand particular races every year.'

She coughed suddenly, her white thin face vibrating with the muscular spasm. A fragile hand stretched out to the glass on the table, and she took a few tiny sips of yellowish liquid.

'I'm so sorry,' I said. 'Making you talk.'

She shook her head mutely, taking more sips, then put down the glass carefully and said, 'It's great to talk. I'm glad you're here, to give me the opportunity. I have so few people to talk to. Some days I don't talk at all. I do miss Liam, you know. We chattered all the time. He was a terrible man to live with. Obsessive, do you see? When he had something in his mind he'd go on and on and on with it. All these sea pictures, it drove me mad when he kept buying them, and now he's gone, well, they seem to bring him close again, and I won't move them, not now.'

'It wasn't so very long ago, was it, that he died?' I said.

'On March 1st,' she said. She paused, but there were no tears, no welling distress. 'Only a few days after Mr Gilbert came, Liam was sitting there . . .' she pointed to one of the blue armchairs, the only one which showed rubbed dark patches on the arms and a shadow on its high back, '. . . and I went to make us some tea. Just a cup. We were thirsty. And when I came back he was asleep.' She paused again. 'I thought he was asleep.'

'I'm sorry,' I said.

She shook her head. 'It's the best way to go. I'm glad for him. We'd both loathed the thought of dying in hospital stuck full of tubes. If I'm lucky and if I can manage it I'll die here too, like that, one of these days. I'll be glad to. It is comforting, do you see?'

I did see, in a way, though I had never before thought of death as a welcome guest to be patiently awaited, hoping that he would come quietly when one was asleep.

'If you'd like a drink,' she said in exactly the same matter-of-fact tone, 'there's a bottle and some glasses in the cupboard.'

'I have to drive home . . .'

She didn't press it. She said, 'Do you want to hear about Mr Gilbert? Mr Harry Gilbert?'

'Yes, please. If I'm not tiring you.'

'I told you. Talking's a *pleasure*.' She considered, her head to one side, the white hair standing like a fluffy halo round the small wrinkled face. 'He owns bingo halls,' she said, and there was for the first time in her voice the faintest hint of contempt.

'You don't approve of bingo.'

'It's a mug's game.' She shrugged. 'No skill in it.'

'But a lot of people enjoy it.'

'And pay for it. Like mug punters. The wins keep them hooked but they lose in the end.'

The same the world over, I thought with amusement: the professional's dim view of the amateur. There was nothing amateur, however, about Mr Gilbert.

'Bingo made him rich,' the old woman said. 'He came here one day to see Liam, just drove up one day in a Rolls and said he was buying a chain of betting shops. He wanted to buy Liam's system so he'd always be six jumps ahead of the mugs.'

I said curiously, 'Do you always think of a gambler as a mug?'

'Mr Gilbert does. He's a cold man. Liam said it depends what they want. If they want excitement, OK, they're mugs but they're getting their money's worth. If they want profit and they still bet on instinct, they're just mugs.'

She coughed again, and sipped again, and after a while gave me the faint smile, and continued.

'Mr Gilbert offered Liam a lot of money. Enough for us to invest and live on comfortably for the rest of our days. So Liam agreed. It was wisest. They argued a bit about the price, of course. They spent almost a week ringing each other up with offers. But in the end it was settled.' She paused. 'Then before Mr Gilbert paid the money, and before Liam gave him all the papers, Liam died. Mr Gilbert telephoned me to say he was sorry, but did the bargain still stand, and I said yes it did. It certainly did. I was very pleased to be going to be without money anxieties, do you see?'

I nodded.

'And then,' she said, and this time with anger, 'that *hateful* Chris Norwood stole the papers out of Liam's office ... Stole all his life's work.' Her body shook. It was the fact of *what* had been stolen which infuriated her, I perceived, more than the fortune lost. 'We'd both been glad to have him come here, to carry coal and logs and clean the windows, and then I'd begun to wonder if he'd been in my handbag, but I'm always pretty vague about how much I have there ... and then Liam died.' She stopped, fighting against agitation, pressing a thin hand to her narrow chest, squeezing shut those wide-staring eyes.

'Don't go on,' I said, desperately wanting her to.

'Yes, yes,' she said, opening her eyes again. 'Mr Gilbert came to collect the papers. He brought the money all in cash. He showed it to me, in a briefcase. Packets of notes. He said to spend it, not invest it. That way there would be no fuss with tax. He said he would give me more if I ever needed it, but there was enough, you know, for years and years, living as I do . . . And then we went along to Liam's office, and the papers weren't there. Nowhere. Vanished. I'd put them all ready, you see, the day before, in a big folder. There were so many of them. Sheets and sheets, all in Liam's spiky writing. He never learned to type. Always by hand. And the only person who'd been in there besides Mrs Urquart was Chris Norwood. The only person.'

'Who,' I said, 'is Mrs Urquart?'

'What? Oh, Mrs Urquart comes to clean for me. Or she did. Three days a week. She can't come now, she says. She's in trouble with the welfare people, poor thing.'

Akkerton's voice in the pub floated back: '. . . she never told the welfare she was earning . . .'

I said 'Was it in Mrs Urquart's house that Chris Norwood lodged?'

'Yes, that's right.' She frowned. 'How did you know?'

'Something someone said.' I sorted through what I had first said to her to explain my visit and belatedly realized that I'd taken for granted she'd known something which I now saw that perhaps she didn't.

'Chris Norwood . . .' I said slowly.

'I'd like to strangle him.'

'Didn't your Mrs Urquart tell you . . . what had happened?'

'She rang in a great fuss. Said she wasn't coming any more. She sounded very upset. Saturday morning, last week.'

'And that was all she said, that she wasn't coming any more?'

'We hadn't been very good friends lately, not with Chris Norwood stealing Liam's papers. I didn't want to quarrel with her. I needed her, for the cleaning. But since that hateful man stole from us, she was very defensive, almost rude. But she needed the money, just like I needed her, and she knew I'd never give her away.'

I looked out towards the peonies, where the greys were darkening to night, and debated whether or not to tell her what had befallen Chris Norwood. Decided against, because hearing of the murder of someone one knew, even someone one disliked, could be incalculably shattering. To thrust an old lady living alone in a big house into a state of shock and fear couldn't do any possible good.

'Do you read newspapers?' I said.

She raised her eyebrows over the oddness of the question but answered simply enough. 'Not often. The print's too small. I've good eyes, but I like big-print books.' She indicated the fat red-and-white volume on her table. 'I read nothing else, now.' She looked vaguely round the dusk-filled room. 'Even the racing pages. I've stopped reading those. I just watch the results on television.'

'Just the results? Not the races?'

'Liam said watching the races was the mug's way of betting. Watch the results, he said, and add them to statistical probabilities. I do watch the races, but the results are more of a habit.'

She stretched out a stick-thin arm and switched on the tablelight beside her, shutting out the peonies instantly into blackness and banishing the far corners of the room into deep shadow. On herself the instant effect was to enhance her physical degeneration, putting skin-folds cruelly back where the dusk had softened them, anchoring the ageless mind into the old, old body.

I looked at the thin, wizened yellow face, at the huge eyes that might once have been beautiful, at the white unstyled hair of Liam O'Rorke's widow, and I suggested that maybe, if I gave her the computer tapes, she could still sell the knowledge that was on them to her friend Mr Gilbert.

'It did cross my mind,' she said, nodding, 'when you said you had them. I don't really understand what they are, though. I don't know anything about computers.'

She'd been married to one, in a way. I said, 'They are just cassettes – like for a cassette player.'

She thought for a while, looking down at her hands. Then she said, 'If I pay you a commission, will you do the deal for me? I'm not so good at dealing as Liam, do you see? And I don't think I have the strength to haggle.'

'But wouldn't Mr Gilbert pay the agreed price?'

She shook her head doubtfully. 'I don't know. That deal was struck three months ago, and now it isn't the papers themselves I'm selling, but something else. I don't know. I think he might twist me into corners. But you *know* about these tapes, or whatever they are. You could talk to him better than me.' She smiled faintly. 'A proper commission, young man. Ten per cent.'

It took me about five seconds to agree. She gave me Harry Gilbert's address and telephone number, and said she would leave it all to me. I could come back and tell her when it was done. I could bring her all the money, she said, and she would pay me my share, and everything would be fine.

'You trust me?' I said.

'If you steal from me, I'll be no worse off than I am at present.'

She came with me to the lilac-shrouded front door to let me out, and I shook her thistledown hand, and drove away.

The Red Sea parted for Moses, and he walked across.

7

On Thursday I trundled blearily round school, ineffective from lack of the sleep I'd forfeited in favour of correcting the Upper V's exercise books. They too, like William, had decisive exams ahead. One of the most boring things about myself, I'd discovered, was this sense of commitment to the kids.

Ted Pitts didn't turn up. Jenkins, when directly asked, said scratchily that Pitts had laryngitis, which was disgraceful as it put the whole Maths department's timetable out of order.

'When will he be back?'

Jenkins gave me a sour sneer, not for any particular reason but because it was an ingrained mannerism.

'His wife telephoned,' he said. 'Pitts has lost his voice. When he regains it, doubtless he will return.'

'Could you give me his number.'

'He isn't on the telephone,' Jenkins said repressively. 'He says he can't afford it.'

'His address, then?'

'You should ask in the office,' Jenkins said. 'I can't be expected to remember where my assistant masters live.'

The school secretary was not in his office when I went to look for him during morning break, and I spent the last two periods before lunch (Five C, magnetism; Four D, electrical power) fully realizing that if I didn't send the computer tapes to Cambridge on that very day they would not arrive by Saturday: and if no computer tapes arrived at Cambridge main post office by Saturday I could expect another and much nastier visit from the man behind the Walther.

At lunchtime, food came low on the priorities. Instead I first went out of school along to the nearest row of shops and bought three blank sixty-minute cassettes. They weren't of the quality beloved by Ted Pitts, but for my purpose they were fine. Then I sought out one of Ted Pitts's colleagues and begged a little help with the computer.

'Well,' he said hesitantly. 'OK, if it's only for ten minutes. Straight after school. And don't tell Jenkins, will you?'

'Never.'

His laugh floated after me as I hurried down the passage towards the coin-box telephone in the main entrance hall. I rang up Newmarket police station (via Directory Enquiries) and asked for whoever was in charge of the investigation into the murder of Chris Norwood.

That would be Detective Chief Superintendent Irestone, I was told. He wasn't in. Would I care to talk to Detective Sergeant Smith? I said I supposed so, and after a few clicks and silences a comfortable Suffolk voice asked me what he could do for me.

I had mentally rehearsed what to say, but it was still difficult to begin. I said tentatively, 'I might know a bit about why Chris Norwood was murdered and I might know perhaps roughly who did it, but I also might easily be wrong, it's just that . . .'

'Name, sir?' he said interrupting. 'Address? Can you be reached there, sir? At what time can you be reached there, sir? Detective Chief Superintendent Irestone will get in touch with you, sir. Thank you for calling.'

I put the receiver down not knowing whether he had paid extra-fast attention to what I'd said, or whether he had merely given the stock reply handed out to every crackpot who rang up with his/her pet theory. In either case, it left me with just enough time to catch the last of the hamburgers in the school canteen and to get back to class on the dot.

At four, I was held up by Louise's latest grudge (apparatus left out all over the benches – Martin would never do that) and I was fearful as I raced along the corridors the boys were not allowed to run in, and slid down the stairs with both hands on the bannisters and my feet touching only about every sixth tread (a trick I had learned in my far-back youth), that Ted Pitts's colleague would have tired of waiting, and gone home.

To my relief, he hadn't. He was sitting in front of the familiar screen shooting down little random targets with the zest of a seven-year-old.

'What's that?' I said, pointing at the game.

'"Starstrike". Want to have a go?'

'Is it yours?'

'Something Ted made up to amuse and teach the kids.'

'Is it in BASIC?' I asked.

'Sure, BASIC, graphics and special characters.'

'Can you List it?'

He typed LIST, and Ted's game scrolled up the screen to seemingly endless flickering rows.

'There you are,' Ted's colleague said.

I looked at part of the last section of the program, which was now at rest on the screen:

410 RESET (RX, RY): RX = RX − RA: RY = RY − 8
420 IF RY > 2 SET (RX, RY): GOTO 200
430 IF ABS (I * 8 − RX) > 4 THEN 150
460 FOR Q = I TO 6: PRINT @ 64 + 4 * Vv, "****";

A right load of gibberish to me, though poetry to Ted Pitts.

To his colleague I said, 'I came down here to ask you to record something . . . anything . . . on these cassettes.' I produced them. 'Just so they have computer noises on them, and a readable program. They're for, er, demonstration.'

He didn't query it.

I said, 'Do you think Ted would mind me using his game?'

He shrugged. 'I shouldn't think so. Two or three of the boys have got tapes of it. It's not secret.'

He took the cassettes out of my hands and said, 'Once on each tape?'

'Er, no. Several times on each side.'

His eyes widened. 'What on earth for?'

'Um.' I thought in circles. 'To demonstrate searching through file names.'

'Oh. All right.' He looked at his watch. 'I'd leave you to do it, but Jenkins goes mad if one of the department doesn't check the computer's switched off and put the door key in the common-room. I can't stay long anyway, you know.'

He put the first of the tapes obligingly into the recorder, however, typed CSAVE 'A', and pressed 'Enter'. When the screen announced READY, he typed CSAVE 'B', and after that CSAVE 'C', and so on until the first side of the tape was full of repeats of 'Starstrike'.

'This is taking ages,' he muttered.

'Could you do one side of each tape, then?' I asked.

'OK.'

He filled one side of the second tape and approximately half of a side on the third before his growing restiveness overcame him.

'Look, Jonathan, that's enough. It's taken nearer an hour than ten minutes.'

'You're a pal.'

'Don't worry, I'll hit you one of these days for my games duty.'

I picked up the cassettes and nodded agreement. Getting someone else to do games duty wasn't only the accepted way of wangling Wednesday afternoons off, it was also the coin in which favours were paid for.

'Thanks a lot,' I said.

'Any time.'

He began putting the computer to bed and I took the cassettes out to my car to pack them in a padded envelope and send them to Cambridge, with each filled side marked 'Play this side first.'

Since there was a Parents' Evening that day, I went for a pork pie with some beer in a pub, corrected books in the common-room, and from eight to ten, along with nearly the whole complement of staff (as these occasions involved a three-line whip) reassured the parents of all the fourth forms that their little horrors were doing splendidly. The parents of Paul apple-on-the-head Arcady asked if he would make a research scientist. 'His wit and style will take him far,' I said noncommittally, and they said, 'He enjoys your lessons', which was a nice change from the next parent I talked to who announced belligerently, 'My lad's wasting his time in your class.'

Placate, agree, suggest, smile: above all, show concern. I supposed those evenings were a Good Thing, but after a long day's teaching they were exhausting. I drove home intending to flop straight into bed but when I opened the front door I found the telephone on the boil.

'Where have you been?' Sarah said, sounding cross.

'Parents' meeting.'

'I've been ringing and ringing. Yesterday too.'

'Sorry.'

With annoyance unmollified she said, 'Did you remember to water my house plants?'

Hell, I thought. 'No, I didn't.'

'It's so *careless*.'

'Yes. Well, I'm sorry.'

'Do them now. Don't leave it.'

I said dutifully, 'How's Donna.'

'Depressed.' The single word was curt and dismissive. 'Try not to forget,' she said acidly, 'the croton in the spare bedroom.'

I put the receiver down thinking that I positively didn't want her back. It was an uncomfortable, miserable, thought. I'd loved her once so much. I'd have died for her, literally. I thought purposefully for the first time about divorce and in the thinking found neither regret nor guilt, but relief.

At eight in the morning when I was juggling coffee and toast the telephone rang again, and this time it was the police. A London accent, very polite.

'You rang with a theory, sir, about Christopher Norwood.'

'It's not exactly a theory. It's . . . at the least . . . a coincidence.' I had had time to cut my words down to essentials. I said, 'Christopher Norwood commissioned a friend of mine, Peter Keithly, to write some computer programs. Peter Keithly did them, and recorded them on cassette tapes which he gave to me. Last Saturday, two men came to my house, pointed a gun at me, and demanded the tapes. They threatened to shoot my television set and my ankles if I didn't hand them over. Are you, er, interested?'

There was a silence, then the same voice said, 'Wait a moment, sir.'

I drank some coffee and waited, and finally a different voice spoke in my ear, a bass voice, slower, less stilted, asking me to repeat what I'd said to the inspector.

'Mm,' he said, when I'd finished. 'I think I'd better see you. How are you placed?'

School, he agreed, was unavoidable. He would come to my house in Twickenham at four-thirty.

He was there before me, sitting not in a labelled and light-flashing police car, but in a fast four-door saloon. When I'd braked outside the garage he was already on his feet, and I found myself appraising a stocky man with a craggy young-old face, black hair dusting grey, unwavering light brown eyes and a sceptical mouth. Not a man, I thought, to save time for fools.

'Mr Derry?'

'Yes.'

'Detective Chief Superintendent Irestone.' He briefly produced a flip-over wallet and showed me his certification. 'And Detective Inspector Robson.' He indicated a second man emerging from the car, dressed casually like himself in grey trousers and sports jacket. 'Can we go inside, sir?'

'Of course.' I led the way in. 'Would you like coffee – or tea?'

They shook their heads and Irestone plunged straight into the matter in hand. It appeared that what I'd told them so far did indeed interest them intensely. They welcomed, it seemed, my account of what I'd learned on my trek via Angel Kitchens to Mrs O'Rorke. Irestone asked many questions, including how I persuaded the gunmen to go away empty-handed.

I said easily, 'I didn't have the tapes here, because I'd lent them to a friend. I said I'd get them back and post them to them and luckily they agreed to that.'

His eyebrows rose, but he made no comment. It must have seemed to him merely that I'd been fortunate.

'And you'd no idea who they were?' he said.

'None at all.'

'I don't suppose you know what sort of pistol it was?'

He spoke without expectation, and it was an instant before I answered: 'I think . . . a Walther .22. I've seen one before.'

He said intently, 'How certain are you?'

'Pretty certain.'

He reflected. 'We'd like you to go to your local station to see if you can put together Identikit pictures.'

'Of course, I will,' I said, 'but you might be able to see these men themselves, if you're lucky.'

'How do you mean?'

'I did send them some tapes, but not until yesterday. They were going to pick them up from Cambridge main post office, and I should think there's a chance they'll be there tomorrow.'

'That's helpful.' He sounded unexcited, but wrote it all down. 'Anything else?'

'They aren't the tapes they wanted. I still haven't got those back. I sent them some other tapes with a computer game on.'

He pursed his lips. 'That wasn't very wise.'

'But the real ones morally belong to Mrs O'Rorke. And those gunmen won't come stampeding back here while they think they've got the goods.'

'And how long before they find out?'

'I don't know. But if they're the same two people who threatened Peter, it might be a while. He said they didn't seem to know much about computers.'

Irestone thought aloud. 'Peter Keithly told you that two men visited him on the Wednesday evening, is that right?' I nodded. 'Christopher Norwood was killed last Friday morning. Eight and a half days later.' He rubbed his chin. 'It might be unwise to suppose it will take them another eight and a half days to discover what you've done.'

'I could always swear those were the tapes Peter Keithly gave me.'

'And I don't think,' he said flatly, 'that this time they'd believe you.' He paused. 'The inquest on Peter Keithly was being held today, wasn't it?'

I nodded.

'We consulted with the Norwich police. There's no room to doubt your friend's death was an accident. I dare say you've wondered?'

'Yes, I have.'

'You don't need to. The insurance inspector's report says the explosion was typical. There were no arson devices. No dynamite or plastics. Just absence of mind and rotten bad luck.'

I looked at the floor.

'Your gunmen didn't do it,' he said.

I thought that maybe he was trying to defuse any hatred I might be brewing, so that my testimony might be more impartial, but in fact what he was giving me was a kind of comfort, and I was grateful.

'If Peter hadn't died,' I said, looking up, 'they might have gone back to him when they found what they'd got from him was useless.'

'Exactly,' Irestone said drily. 'Do you have friends you could stay with for a while?'

On Saturday morning, impelled, I fear, by Mrs O'Rorke's ten per cent promise, I drove to Welwyn Garden City to offer her tapes to Mr Harry Gilbert.

Not that I exactly had the tapes with me as they were still locked up with Ted Pitts's laryngitis, but at least I had the knowledge of their existence and contents, and that should be enough, I hoped, for openers.

From Twickenham to Welwyn was twenty miles in a direct line but far more in practice and tedious besides, round the North Circular Road and narrow shopping streets. In contrast, the architects' dream city, when I got there, was green and orderly, and I found the Gilbert residence in an opulent cul-de-sac. Bingo, it seemed, had kept poverty a long long way from his doorstep, which was reproduction Georgian, flanked with two pillars and surrounded by a regular regiment of windows. A house of red, white and sparkle on a carpet of green. I pressed the shiny brass doorbell thinking it would be a bore if the inhabitants of this bijou mansion were out.

Mr Gilbert, however, was in.

Just.

He opened his front door to my ring and said whatever I wanted I would have to come back later, as he was just off to play golf. Clubs and a cart for transporting them stood just inside the door, and Mr Gilbert's heavy frame was clad appropriately in check trousers, open-necked shirt and blazer.

'It's about Liam O'Rorke's betting system,' I said.

'What?' he said sharply.

'Mrs O'Rorke asked me to come. She says she might be able to sell it to you after all.'

He looked at his watch; a man of about fifty, in appearance unimpressive, more like a minor official than a peddlar of pinchbeck dreams.

'Come in,' he said. 'This way.'

His voice was no-nonsense middle-of-the-road, nearer the bingo hall than

Eton. He led me into an unexpectedly functional room furnished with a desk, typewriter, wall maps with coloured drawing pins dotted over them, two swivel chairs, one tray of drinks and five telephones.

'Fifteen minutes,' he said. 'So come to the point.' He made no move to sit down or offer me a seat, but he was not so much rude as indifferent. I saw what Mrs O'Rorke had meant about him being a cold man. He didn't try to clothe the bones of his thoughts with social top-dressing. He'd have made a lousy schoolmaster, I thought.

'Liam O'Rorke's notes were stolen,' I began.

'I know that,' he said impatiently. 'Have they turned up?'

'Not his notes, no. But computer programs made from them, yes.'

He frowned. 'Mrs O'Rorke has these programs?'

'No. I have. On her behalf. To offer to you.'

'And your name?'

I shrugged. 'Jonathan Derry. You can check with her, if you like.' I gestured to the rank of telephones. 'She'll vouch for me.'

'Did you bring these . . . programs with you?'

'No,' I said. 'I thought we should make a deal first.'

'Humph.'

Behind his impassive face, a fierce amount of consideration seemed to be taking place, and at length I had a powerful feeling that he couldn't make up his mind.

I said, 'I wouldn't expect you to buy them without a demonstration. But I assure you they're the real thing.'

It produced no discernible effect. The interior debate continued; and it was resolved not by Gilbert or myself but by the arrival of someone else.

A car door slammed outside and there were footsteps on the polished parquet in the hall. Gilbert's head lifted to listen, and a voice outside the open door called 'Dad?'

'In here,' Gilbert said.

Gilbert's son came in. Gilbert's son, who had come to my house with his pistol.

I must have looked as frozen with shock as I felt; but then so did he. I glanced at his father, and it came to me too late that this was the man Sarah had described – middle-aged, ordinary, plump – who had gone to Peter's house asking for the tapes. The one to whom she had said, 'My husband's got them.'

I seemed to have stopped breathing. It was as if life itself had been punched out of me. To know what *not* to do . . .

For all my instinct that ignorance was dangerous, I had not learned enough. I hadn't learned the simple fact that would have stopped me from walking into that house: that Mr Bingo Gilbert had a marauding Italian-looking son.

It was never a good idea to pursue Moses across the Red Sea . . .

'My son, Angelo,' Gilbert said.

Angelo made an instinctive movement with his right hand towards his left armpit as if reaching for his gun, but he wore a bloused suede jerkin over his jeans, and was unarmed. Thank the Lord, I thought, for small mercies.

In his left hand he carried the package I had sent to Cambridge. It had been opened, and he was holding it carefully upright to save the cassettes from falling out.

He recovered his voice faster than I did. His voice and his arrogance and his sneer.

'What's this mug doing here?' he said.

'He came to sell me the computer tapes.'

Angelo laughed derisively. 'I told you we'd get them for nothing. This mug sent them. I told you he would.' He lifted the package jeeringly. 'I told you you were an old fool to offer that Irish witch any cash. You'd have done better to let me shake the goods out of her the minute her old man died. You've no clue, Dad. You should have cut me in months ago, not tell me when it's already a mess.'

His manner, I thought, was advanced son-parent rebellion: the young bull attacking the old. And part of it, I suspected was for my benefit. He was showing off. Proving that even if I'd got the better of him the last time we'd met, it was he, Angelo, who was the superior being.

'How did this creep get here?' he demanded.

Gilbert either ignored the peacockery or indulged it. 'Mrs O'Rorke sent him,' he said.

Neither of them thought to ask the very awkward question of how I knew Mrs O'Rorke. I'd have given few chances for my health if they'd worked it through. I reckoned that this was one exceptional occasion when ignorance was emphatically the safest path, and that in prudence I should be wholly ignorant of the life and death of Chris Norwood.

'How come he still has the tapes to sell,' Angelo said cunningly, 'if he's already sent them to me?'

Gilbert's eyes narrowed and his neck stiffened, and I saw that his unprepossessing exterior was misleading: that it was indeed a tough bull Angelo was challenging, one who still ruled his territory.

'Well?' he said to me.

Angelo waited with calculation and triumph growing in his eyes and throughout his face like an intoxication, the scarifying lack of inhibition ballooning as fast as before. It was his utter recklessness, I thought, which was to be feared above all.

'I sent you a copy,' I said. I pointed to the package in his hand. 'Those are copies.'

'Copies?' It stopped Angelo for a moment. Then he said suspiciously, 'Why did you send copies?'

'The originals belonged to Mrs O'Rorke. They weren't mine to give you. But I certainly didn't want you and your friend coming back again waving your gun all over the place, so I did send some tapes. I had no idea I would ever see you again. I just wanted to be rid of you. I had no idea you were Mr Gilbert's son.'

'Gun?' Gilbert said sharply. *'Gun?'*

'His pistol.'

'Angelo – ' There was no mistaking the anger in the father's voice. 'I've forbidden you – *forbidden* you, do you hear, to carry that gun. I sent you to ask for those tapes. To ask. To buy.'

'Threats are cheaper,' Angelo said. 'And I'm not a child. The days when I took your orders are over.'

They faced each other in unleashed antagonism.

'That pistol is for protection,' Gilbert said intensely. 'And it is mine. You are not to threaten people with it. You are not to take it out of this house. You still depend on me for a living, and while you work for me and live in this house you'll do what I say. You'll leave that gun strictly alone.'

God in Heaven, I thought: *he doesn't know about Chris Norwood.*

'You taught me to shoot,' Angelo said defiantly.

'But as a sport,' Gilbert said, and didn't understand that sport for his son was a living target.

I interrupted the filial battle and said to Gilbert, 'You've got the tapes. Will you pay Mrs O'Rorke?'

'Don't be bloody stupid,' Angelo said.

I ignored him. To his father I said, 'You were generous before. Be generous now.'

I didn't expect him to be. I wanted only to distract him, to keep his mind on something trivial, not to let him *think*.

'Don't listen to him,' Angelo said. 'He's only a mug.'

Gilbert's face mirrored his son's words. He looked me up and down with the same inner conviction of superiority, the belief that everyone was a mug except himself.

If Gilbert felt like that, I thought, it was easy to see why Angelo did. Parental example. I would often at school know the father by the behaviour of the son.

I shrugged. I looked defeated. I let them get on with their ill-will. I wanted above all to get out of that house before they started putting bits of knowledge together and came up with a picture of me as a real towering threat to Angelo's liberty. I didn't know if Gilbert would stop his son – or *could* stop him – if Angelo wanted me dead: and there was a lot of leafy Welwyn Garden City lying quietly in the back garden.

'Mrs O'Rorke's expecting me,' I said, 'to know how I got on.'

'Tell her nothing doing,' Angelo said.

Gilbert nodded.

I edged past Angelo to the door, looking suitably meek under his scathing sneer.

'Well,' I said weakly, 'I'll be going.'

I walked jerkily through the hall, past the attendant golf clubs and out of the open front door, taking with me a last view of Gilbert locking psychological horns with the menace that would one day overthrow him.

I was sweating. I wiped the palms of my hands on my trousers, fumbled open the car door, put a faintly trembling hand on the ignition key and started the engine.

If they hadn't been so busy fighting each other . . .

As I turned out of the drive into the cul-de-sac itself I had a glimpse of the two of them coming out on to the step to stare after me, and my mouth was uncomfortably dry until I was sure Angelo hadn't leapt into his car to give chase.

I had never felt my heart flutter that way before. I had never, I supposed, felt real fear. I couldn't get it to subside. I felt shaky, restless, short of breath, slightly sick.

Reaction, no doubt.

8

Somewhere between Welwyn and Twickenham, I pulled into a parking space to work out where to go.

I could go home, collect my guns, and drive to Bisley. I looked down at my hands. On present form, I'd miss the target by a yard. No point in wasting money on the ammunition.

It should take a fair while for the Gilberts to discover that they had 'Starstrike' instead of racing programs, but not as long as that to work out that while I had the original tapes, they had no exclusive control of Liam's system. I needed somewhere they wouldn't find me when they came looking. Pity, I thought, that Sarah and I had so few friends.

I walked across the road to a public telephone box and telephoned to William's farm.

'Well, of course, Jonathan,' Mrs Porter said. 'Of course, I'd have you. But William's got fed up with no horses to ride here and he packed up and went off to Lambourn this morning. He'd a friend there, he said, and he's going straight back to school from there tomorrow evening.'

'Was he all right?'

'So much *energy*!' she said. 'But he won't eat a thing. Says he wants to keep his weight down, to be a jockey.'

I sighed. 'Thanks anyway.'

'It's a pleasure to have him,' she said. 'He makes me laugh.'

I rang off and counted the small stack of coins I had left, and public-spiritedly spent them on the Newmarket police.

'Chief Superintendent Irestone isn't here, sir,' they said. 'Do you want to leave a message?'

I hesitated, but in the end all I said was, 'Tell him Jonathan Derry called. I have a name for him. I'll get in touch with him later.'

'Very good, sir.'

I got back into the car, consulted a slip of paper in my wallet and drove to Northolt to visit Ted Pitts, knowing that quite likely he wouldn't be pleased to see me. When I had finally tracked down the school secretary, he had parted with the requested information reluctantly, saying that the masters' addresses were sacrosanct to save them from over-zealous parents. Ted Pitts, he said, had particularly made him promise not to divulge.

'But I'm not a parent.'

'Well, no.'

I'd had to persuade, but I got it. And one could see, I thought, why Ted wanted to guard his privacy, because where he lived, I found, was in a mobile home on a caravan site. Neat enough, but not calculated to impress some of the social-climbers in the P.T.A.

Ted's wife, who opened the door to my knock, looked surprised but not unwelcoming. She was as earnest as Ted, small, bright-eyed, an occasional visitor to school football matches, where Ted tore up and down the pitches refereeing. I sought for a name and thought 'Jane', but wasn't sure. I smiled hopefully instead.

'How's Ted?' I said.

'Much better. His voice is coming back.' She opened the door wider. 'He'd like to see you, I'm sure, so do come in.' She gestured to the inside of the caravan, where I couldn't yet see, and said – 'It's a bit of a mess. We didn't expect visitors.'

'If you'd rather I didn't – '

'No. Ted will want you.'

I stepped up into the van and saw what she meant. In every direction spread an untidy jumble of books and newspapers and clothes and toys, all the normal clutter of a large family but condensed into a very small space.

Ted was in the minuscule sitting-room with his three little girls, sitting on a sofa and watching while they played on the floor. When he saw me he jumped to his feet in astonishment and opened his mouth, but all that came out was a squeaky croak.

'Don't talk,' I said. 'I just came to see how you are.' Any thoughts I had about cadging a bed from him had vanished. It seemed silly, indeed, to mention it.

'I'm better.' The words were recognizable, but half a whisper, and he gestured for me to sit down. His wife offered coffee and I accepted. The children squabbled and he kicked them gently with his toe.

'Jane will take them out soon,' he said huskily.

'I'm being a nuisance.'

He shook his head vigorously. 'Glad you came.' He pointed to a ledge running high along one wall and said, 'I bought your new tapes. They're up there, with your cassettes, out of reach. The children climb so. Haven't done the copying yet, though. Sorry.' He rubbed his throat as if massage would help, and made a face of frustration.

'Don't talk,' I said again, and passed on William's information about form books. He seemed pleased enough but also subdued, as if the knowledge no longer interested.

Jane returned with one mug of coffee and offered sugar. I shook my head and took a sip of the liquid which looked dark brown but tasted weak.

I said, more to make conversation than anything else, 'I don't suppose either of you know where I could put up for a night or two? Somewhere not too expensive. I mean, not a hotel.' I smiled lopsidedly. 'I've spent so much on petrol and other things this week that I'm a bit short.'

'End of the month,' Ted said, nodding. 'Always the same.'

'But your house!' Jane said. 'Ted says you've got a house.'

'Er . . . um . . . er . . . I haven't been getting on too well with Sarah.' The convenient half-truth arrived just in time and they made small sad noises in sympathetic comprehension. Ted, all the same, shook his head, sorry not to be able to help.

'Don't know of anywhere,' he said.

Jane, standing straight, tucking her elbows into her sides and clasping her hands tightly together said, 'You could stay here. On the sofa.'

Ted looked extremely surprised but his wife very tersely said, 'Would you pay us?'

'Jane!' Ted said despairingly: but I nodded.

'In advance?' she said rigidly, and I agreed again. I gave her two of the notes I'd got from the bank earlier and asked if it was enough. She said yes, looking flushed, and bundled the three children out of the room, out of the caravan, and down towards the road. Ted, hopelessly awkward and embarrassed, stuttered a wheezy apology.

'We've had a bad month . . . they've put the land rent up here . . . and I had to pay for new tyres, and for the car licence. I must have the car and it's falling to bits – and I'm overdrawn . . .'

'Do stop, Ted,' I said. 'I know all about being broke. Not starving broke. Just penniless.'

He smiled weakly. 'I suppose we've never had the bailiffs . . . but this week we've been living on bread mostly. Are you sure you don't mind?'

'Positive.'

So I stayed with the Pitts. Watched television, built bright brick towers for the children, ate the egg supper my money had bought, took Ted for a pint. The talking couldn't have done his throat much good, but between the froth and the dregs I learned a good deal about the Pitts. He'd met Jane one summer in a youth hostel in the Lake District, and they'd married while he was still at college because the oldest of the little girls was imminent. They were happy, he said, but they'd never been able to save for a deposit for a house. Lucky to have a mobile home. Hire purchase, of course. During the holidays, he looked after the children while Jane took temporary secretarial jobs. Better for the family income. Better for Jane. He still went hiking on his own, though, one week every year. Backpacking. Sleeping in a tent, in hilly country; Scotland or Wales. He gave me a shy look through the black-framed glasses. 'It sorts me out. Keeps me sane.' It wasn't everyone, I thought, who was his own psychotherapist.

When we got back, the caravan was tidy and the children asleep. One had to be quiet, Ted said, going in: they woke easily. The girls all slept, it appeared, in the larger of the two bedrooms, with their parents in the smaller. There was a pillow, a car travelling rug and a clean sheet awaiting me, and although the sofa was a bit short for comfort it was envelopingly soft.

It was only on the point of sleep, far too late to bother, that I remembered that I hadn't called back to Irestone. Oh well, I thought, yawning, tomorrow would do.

In the morning I did call from a telephone box near the public park where Ted and I took the children to play on the swings and seesaw.

Irestone, as usual, wasn't in. Wasn't he *ever* in, I asked. A repressive voice told me the Chief Superintendent was off-duty at present, and would I please leave a message. I perversely said that no, I wouldn't, I wanted to speak to the Chief Superintendent personally. If I wanted to leave a number, they said, he would in due course call me. Impasse, I thought: Ted Pitts had no telephone.

'If I call you at nine tomorrow morning,' I said, 'will Chief Superintendent Irestone be there? If I call at ten? At eleven? At midday?'

I was told to wait and could hear vague conversations going on in the background, and going on for so long that I had to feed more coins into the box, which scarcely improved my patience. Finally, however, the stolid voice returned. 'Detective Chief Superintendent Irestone will be in the Incident Room tomorrow morning from ten o'clock onwards. You may call him at the following number.'

'Wait a minute.' I unclipped my pen and dug out the scrap of paper which held Ted's address. 'OK.'

He gave me the number, and I thanked him fairly coolly, and that was that.

Ted was pushing his tiniest girl carefully round on a sort of turntable, holding her close to him and laughing with her. I wished quite surprisingly fiercely that I could have had a child like that, that I could have taken her to a sunny park on Sunday mornings, and hugged her little body and watched her grow. Sarah, I thought. Sarah – this is the way you've ached, perhaps;

and for the baby to cuddle, and the young woman to see married. This is the loss. This, that Ted Pitts has. I watched his delight in the child and I envied him with all my heart.

We sat on a bench a bit later while the girls played in a sandpit, and for something to say I asked him why he'd lost his first intense interest in the racing form-books.

He shrugged, looking at his children, and said in a husky voice which was slowly returning to normal, 'You can see how it is. I can't risk the money. I can't afford to buy the form books. I couldn't even afford to buy a set of tapes for myself this week, to copy the program onto. I bought some for you with the money you gave me, but I just didn't have enough . . . I told you, we've been down to counting pennies for food, and although next month's pay will be in the bank tomorrow I still haven't paid the electricity.'

'It's the Derby soon,' I said.

He nodded morosely. 'Don't think I haven't thought of it. I look at those tapes sitting up on that shelf, and I think, shall I or shan't I? But I've had to decide not to. I can't risk it. How could I possibly explain to Jane if I lost? We need every pound, you know. You can see we do.'

It was ironic, I thought. On the one hand there was Angelo Gilbert, who was prepared to kill to get those tapes, and on the other, Ted Pitts, who had them and set them lower than a dust-up with his wife.

'The programs belong to an old woman called O'Rorke.' I said. 'Mrs Maureen O'Rorke. I went to see her this week.'

Ted showed only minor signs of interest.

'She said a few things I thought you'd find amusing.'

'What things?' Ted said.

I told him about the bookmakers closing the accounts of regular winners, and about the system the O'Rorkes had used with the gardener, Dan, going round the betting shops to put their money on anonymously.

'Great heavens,' Ted said. 'What a palaver.' He shook his head. 'No, Jonathan, it's best to forget it.'

'Mrs O'Rorke said her husband could bet with an overall certainty of winning once every three times. How does that strike you statistically?'

He smiled. 'I'd need a hundred per cent certainty to bet on the Derby.'

One of the children threw sand in the eyes of another and he got up in a hurry to scold, to comfort, to dig around earnestly with the corner of his handkerchief.

'By the way,' I said, when order was restored, 'I took some copies of your game "Starstrike". I hope you don't mind.'

'You're welcome,' he said. 'Did you play it? You have to type in F or S at the first question mark. I haven't written the instructions out yet, but I'll let you have them when I do. The kids,' he looked pleased and a touch smug, 'say it's neat.'

'Is it your best?'

'My best?' He smiled a fraction and shrugged, and said, 'I teach from it. I had to write it so that the kids could understand the program and how it worked. Sure, I could write a far more sophisticated one, but what would be the point?'

A pragmatist, Ted Pitts, not a dreamer. We collected the children together, with Ted brushing them down and emptying sand from their shoes, and drove back to the caravan to home-made hamburgers for lunch.

In the afternoon under Ted's commiserating eyes I corrected the load of exercise books which I happened not to have carried into my house on Friday night. Five B had Irestone to thank for that. And on Monday morning with Ted's voice in good enough shape, he thought, to quell the monsters in the third form, we both went back to school.

We each drove our own cars. I felt I'd used up my welcome in the caravan and although Jane said I could stay if I liked I could see I was no longer a blessing from heaven. The new pay cheque would be in the bank. There would be more than bread this week, and I would have to think of somewhere else.

Ted stretched up in the last minutes before we left and plucked the six cassettes from the high shelf. 'I could do these at lunchtime today,' he said, 'if you like.'

'That would be great,' I said. 'Then you can keep one set and the others will be Mrs O'Rorke's.'

'But don't you want some yourself?'

'Maybe later I could get copies of yours, but I can't see me chasing round betting shops for the rest of my life.'

He laughed. 'Nor me. Though I wouldn't have minded a flutter . . .' A sort of longing gleamed in his eyes again, and was quickly extinguished. 'Ah well,' he said, 'forward to the fray.' He kissed Jane and the little girls, and off we went.

During the mid-morning break I yet again tried to reach Chief Superintendent Irestone, this time from the coin box in the common-room. Even with the new number, I got no joy. Chief Superintendent Irestone wasn't available at that time.

'This is boring,' I said. 'I was told he would be.'

'He was called away, sir. Will you leave a message?'

I felt like leaving a couple of round oaths. I said, 'Tell him Jonathan Derry called.'

'Very good, sir. Your message timed at ten thirty-three.'

To hell with it, I thought.

I had taken about five paces down the room in the direction of the coffee machine when the telephone bell rang behind me. It was the time of day when masters' wives tended to ring up to get their dear ones to run errands on their way home, and the nearest to the bell answered its summons as a matter of course. My wife, at least, I thought, wouldn't be calling, but someone shouted, 'Jonathan, it's for you.'

Surprised, I retraced my steps and picked up the receiver.

'Hallo,' I said.

'*Jonathan*,' Sarah said. 'Where *have* you been? Where in God's name have you *been*?'

She sounded hysterical. Her voice was high, vibrating with tension, strung higher than I'd ever heard before. Near snapping point. Frightening.

'What's happened?' I asked. I was aware that my voice sounded too calm, but I couldn't help it. It always seemed to come out that way when there was a jumbled turmoil going on inside.

'Oh my *Christ*!' She still had time to be exasperated with me, but no time to say more.

After the shortest of pauses another voice spoke, and this time every hair of my body rose in protest.

'Now you listen to me, creep . . .'

Angelo Gilbert.

'You listen to me,' he said. 'Your little lady wifey's sitting here snug as you like. We tied her to a chair so's not to hurt her.' He sniggered. 'Her friend too, the wet little bird. Now you listen, mug, because you're going to do just what I tell you. Are you listening?'

'Yes,' I said. I was in fact listening with all my might and with one hand clamped over my other ear because of the chatter and coffee cups all around me. It was macabre. It also seemed to have divorced me from any feeling in my feet.

'That was your last runaround, that was,' Angelo said, 'sending us those duff tapes. This time you'll give us the real ones, get it?'

'Yes,' I said mildly.

'You wouldn't like to get your little wifey back with her face all smashed up, would you?'

'No.'

'All you got to do is give us the tapes.'

'All right,' I said.

'And no bloody runaround.' He seemed disappointed that I'd shown so little reaction to his dramatics but even in that dire moment it seemed second nature to use on him the techniques I'd unconsciously developed in the years of teaching: to deflate the defiance, to be bored by the super-ego, to kill off the triumphant cruelty by an appearance of indifference.

It worked on the kids, it worked a treat on Jenkins, and it had already worked twice on Angelo. He should have learned by now, I thought, that I didn't rise to sneers or arrogance: not visibly anyway. He was too full of himself to believe that someone might not show the fear he felt the urge to induce. He might not be ultra-bright, but he was incalculably dangerous.

He held the receiver to Sarah's mouth, and against her I had fewer defences.

'Jonathan . . .' It was half anger, half fright: high and vehement. 'They came yesterday. *Yesterday*. Donna and I have been tied up here all *night*. Where have you damned well *been*?'

435

'Are you in Donna's house?' I said anxiously.

'*What*? Yes, of *course*. Of *course*, we are. Don't ask such damn silly questions.'

Angelo took the phone back again. 'Now you listen, mug. Listen good. This time there's to be no messing. This time we want the real McCoy, and I'm telling you, it's your last chance.'

I didn't answer.

'Are you there?' he said sharply.

'Sure,' I said.

'Take the tapes to my father's house in Welwyn. Have you got that?'

'Yes. But I haven't got the tapes.'

'Then *get* them.' His voice was nearly a screech. 'Do you hear?' he demanded. 'Get them.'

'It'll take some time,' I said.

'You haven't got time, creep.'

I took a deep breath. He wasn't safe. He wasn't reasonable. He wasn't a schoolchild. I simply couldn't play him too far.

'I can get the tapes today,' I said. 'I'll take them to your father when I get them. It might be late.'

'Sooner,' he said.

'I can't. It's impossible.'

I didn't know exactly why I wanted to delay. It was an instinct. To work things out; not to rush in. This time the Egyptians would have more sense.

'When you get there,' he said, seeming to accept it, 'my father will test the tapes. On a computer. A Grantley computer. Get it, mug? My father bought a Grantley computer, because that's the sort of computer those tapes were written for. So no funny tricks like last time. He'll try the tapes, see? And they'd better be good.'

'All right,' I said again.

'When my father is satisfied,' he said, 'he'll ring me here. Then I'll leave your little wifey and the wet chick tied up here, and you can come and rescue them like a right little Galahad. Got it?'

'Yes,' I said.

'Don't you forget, creep, any funny stuff and your little wifey will keep the plastic surgery business in work for years. Starting with her nice white teeth, creep.'

He apparently again held the receiver for Sarah because it was her voice which came next. Still angry, still frightened, still high.

'For God's sake, get those tapes.'

'Yes I will,' I said. 'Has Angelo got his pistol?'

'Yes. Jonathan, do as he says. *Please* do as he says. Don't fool about.' It was an order just as much as a prayer.

'The tapes,' I said with an attempt at reassurance, 'are not worth a tooth. Keep him calm if you can. Tell him I'll do what he says. Tell him I've promised you.'

She didn't answer. It was Angelo who said, 'That's all creep. That's enough. You get those tapes. Right?'

'All right,' I said, and the line abruptly went dead.

I felt pretty dead myself.

The common-room had emptied and I was already going to be late for the Lower VI. I picked up the necessary books mechanically and propelled myself on unfelt feet along the passages to the laboratories.

Get the tapes . . .

I couldn't get them until I could find Ted Pitts, which would probably not be until lunchtime at twelve fifteen. I had an hour and a half until then in which to decide what to do.

The Lower VI were studying radioactivity. I told them to continue the set of experiments with alpha particles that they had started last week and I sat on my high stool by the blackboard from where I often taught, and watched the Geiger counters counting with my mind on Angelo Gilbert.

Options, I thought.

I could yet once again ring the police. I could say an unstable man is holding my wife hostage at gunpoint. I could say I thought it was he who had killed Christopher Norwood. If I did, they might go chasing out to the Keithly house and try to make Angelo surrender – and then Sarah could be a hostage not for three little cassettes, but for Angelo's personal liberty. An escalation not to be thought of.

No police.

What, then?

Give Harry Gilbert the tapes? Trust that Angelo would leave Sarah and Donna undamaged. Do, in fact, precisely what I'd been told, and believe that Angelo wouldn't wait for me to walk into Donna's house and then leave three dead bodies behind when he walked out of it.

It wasn't logically likely, but it was possible.

It would have been better if I could have thought of a good valid logical reason for the murder of Chris Norwood. He hadn't given Angelo the finished computer programs because if he had there would have been no need for Angelo to come to me. I had speculated, not for the first time, on exactly what had happened to Liam O'Rorke's original notes, and what had happened to the tapes Peter told me he had sent to the person who had commissioned them. To C. Norwood, Angel Kitchens, Newmarket.

To Chris Norwood, comprehensive thief. Cocky little bastard. Akkerton had said. Vegetable chief Akkerton, feeding his paunch in the pub.

I supposed that Chris Norwood, when first faced with Angelo, had simply said that Peter Keithly was writing the programs and had all the notes, and that Angelo should get them from *him*. Angelo had then gone threateningly to Peter, who had been frightened into giving him programs which he knew were incomplete. By the time the Gilberts discovered they were useless, Peter was dead. Back Angelo must have gone to Chris Norwood, this time waving a gun. And again Chris Norwood must have said Peter Keithly had the programs on tapes. That if he was dead, they were in his house. He would have told him that, I thought, *after* Angelo had shot up the stereo. He would have begun to be really frightened: but he would have still wanted to keep the programs if he could, because he knew they were a meal ticket for life.

Chris Norwood, I guessed, had twice not given Angelo what he wanted; and Chris Norwood was dead.

I also had fooled and obstructed Angelo twice, and I couldn't be sure that I wasn't alive because I'd had a handy rifle. Without his father there to restrain him, Angelo could still be as volatile as the petrol vapour that had killed Peter, even if he thought he finally had his hands on the treasure he'd been chasing for so long.

Some of the Lower VI were getting their nuclei into knots. Automatically I descended from the heights of the stool and reminded them that cloud chambers didn't cloud if one neglected to add dry ice.

No more runarounds, Angelo had said.

Well . . .

What tools did I have, I thought. What skills that I could use?

I could shoot.

I couldn't on the other hand shoot Angelo. Not while he had a Walther to Sarah's head. Not without landing myself in jail for manslaughter at the least.

Shooting Angelo was out.

I had the knowledge that Physics had given me. I could construct a radio, a television, a thermostat, a digital clock, a satellite tracker and, given the proper components, a laser beam, a linear accelerator and an atomic bomb. I couldn't exactly make an atomic bomb before lunch.

The two boys who were using the alpha-particle-scattering analogue were arguing over the apparatus, which consisted of one large magnet bombarded by a host of small ones. One boy insisted that the power of permanent magnets decays with time and the other said it was rubbish, permanent meant permanent.

'Who's right, sir?' they asked.

'Permanence is relative,' I said. 'Not absolute.'

There was a flash of impermanent electrical activity at that moment in my brain. The useful knowledge was to hand.

God bless all boys, I thought.

9

Ted Pitts hunched over the Harris all through lunchtime, making and test-ing the copies on the new tapes.

'There you are,' he said finally, rubbing his neck. 'As far as I can see they're perfect.'

'Which set do you want?' I said.

He peered at me earnestly through the black frames. 'Don't you mind?'

'Choose which you like,' I said. 'I'll take the others.'

He hesitated, but decided on the originals. 'If you're sure?'

'Certain,' I said. 'But give me the original boxes, *Oklahoma* and so on. It might be better if I hand them over in the right wrappings.'

I slid the copies into the gaudy boxes, thanked Ted, returned to the com-mon-room, and told my four long-suffering lieutenants that I had developed a stupefying sick shivery headache and would they please take my afternoon classes between them. There were groans, but it was a service we regularly did for each other when it was unavoidable. I was going home, I said. With luck, I would be back in the morning.

Before I left I made a detour to the prep room where Louisa was counting out springs and weights for the 2nd form that afternoon. I told her about the headache and got scant sympathy, which was fair. While she took the load of batteries through into one of the laboratories to distribute them along the benches I opened one of her tidy cupboards and helped myself to three small objects, hiding them smartly in my pocket.

'What are you looking for?' Louisa asked, coming back and seeing me in front of the still open doors.

'Nothing particular,' I said vaguely. 'I don't really know.'

'Get home to bed,' she said sighing, casting herself for martyrdom. 'I'll cope with the extra work.'

My absence meant in reality less work for her, not more, but there was nothing to be gained by pointing it out. I thanked her profusely to keep her in a good mood for the others, and went out to the car to drive home.

No need to worry about Angelo being there: he was in the Keithlys' house a hundred miles away in Norfolk.

Everything felt unreal. I thought of the two girls, tied to the chairs, un-comfortable, scared, exhausted. Don't fool about, Sarah had said. Do what Angelo says.

Somewhere in one of the sideboard drawers we had a photograph album, thrust out of sight since we had lost the desire to record our joyless life. I dug it out and turned the pages, looking for the picture I had taken once of Peter, Donna and Sarah standing out on the pavement in front of Peter's house. The sun had been shining, I found. All three were smiling, looking happy. A pang to see Peter's face, no moustache, looking so pleased with himself and young. Nothing special about that photograph: just people, a house, a street. Reassuring to me, however, at that moment.

I went upstairs to my own small room, unlocked the gun cupboard and took out one of the Mauser 7.62s and also one of the Olympic-type rifles, the Anschütz .22. Packed them both into the special suitcase along with some ammunition of both sizes. Carried the case down to the car and locked it into the boot.

Reflected and went upstairs to fetch a large brown bathtowel from the linen cupboard. Locked that also in the boot.

Locked the house.

After that I sat in the car for three or four minutes thinking things out, with the result that I went back into the house yet again, this time for a tube of extra-strength glue.

All I didn't have enough of, I thought, was time.

I started the engine and set off not to Welwyn, but to Norwich.

Propelled by demons, I did the trip in a shorter time than usual, but it was still four-thirty when I reached the city outskirts. Six hours since Angelo had telephoned. Six long hours for his hostages.

I drew up beside a telephone box in a shopping parade not far from Donna's house and dialled her number. Praying, I think, that Angelo would answer: that all would be at least no worse than it had been in the morning.

'Hallo,' he said. Eagerly, I thought. Expecting his father.

'It's Jonathan Derry,' I said. 'I've got the tapes.'

'Let me talk to my father.'

'I'm not at your father's house. I haven't got there yet. It's taken me all day to get the tapes.'

'Now you listen, creep . . .' He was roughly, nastily angry. 'I warned you . . .'

'It's taken me all day, but I've got them,' I interrupted insistently. 'I've got the tapes. I've got the tapes.'

'All *right*,' he said tautly. 'Now take them to my father. Take them there, do you hear?'

'Yes,' I said. 'I'll go there straightaway, but it'll take me some time. It's a long way.'

Angelo muttered under his breath and then said, 'How long? Where are you? We've been waiting all fucking night and all fucking day.'

'I'm near Bristol.'

'*Where?*' It was a yell of fury.

'It'll take me four hours,' I said, 'to reach your father.'

There was a brief silence. Then Sarah's voice, tired beyond tears, numb with too much fright.

'Where are you?' she said.

'Near Bristol.'

'Oh my God.' She sounded no longer angry, but hopeless. 'We can't stand much more of this . . .'

The receiver was taken away from her in mid-sentence, and Angelo came back on the line.

'Get going, creep,' he said; and disconnected.

Breathing space, I thought. Four hours before Angelo expected the message from his father. Instead of pressure mounting inexorably, dangerously, in that house, there would at worst, I hoped, be a bearable irritation, and at best a sort of de-fusing of suspense. They wouldn't for another four hours be strung up with a minute-to-minute expectation.

Before getting back into the car I opened the boot, took the telescope and the two rifles out of their non-jolt beds in the suitcase and wrapped them more vulnerably in the brown towel. Put them into the car on the brown upholstery of the back seat. Put the boxes of bullets beside them, also hidden by towel. Looked then at my fingers. No tremors. Not like in my heart.

I drove round into the road where the Keithly house stood and stopped at the kerb just out of sight of the net-curtained window. I could see the roof, part of a wall, most of the front garden – and Angelo's car in the driveway.

There weren't many people in the street. The children would be home from school, indoors having their tea. The husbands wouldn't be back yet from work: there was more space than cars outside the houses. A peaceful suburban scene. Residential street, middle-income prosperous, not long built. An uncluttered street with no big trees and no forests of electricity and telegraph poles: new-laid cables tended to run underground for most of their journey, emerging only occasionally into the daylight. In the photograph of Peter's house, there had been one telegraph pole nearby with wires distributing from it to the individual houses all around, but not much else. No obstructions. Near flat asphalt pavements, white kerbstones, tar-and-chipping roadway. A few neat little hedges bordering some of the gardens. A lot of neat green rectangular patches of repressed grass. Acres of net curtains ready to twitch. I-can-see-out-but-you-can't-see-in.

The first essential for pin-point rifle shooting was to know how far one was from the target. On ranges the distances were fixed, and always the same. I was accustomed to precisely three, four, and five hundred yards. To nine hundred and a thousand yards, both of them further than half a mile. The distance affected one's angle of aim: the longer the distance, the further above the target one had to aim in order to hit it.

Olympic shooting was all done at three hundred metres, but from different body positions: standing, kneeling and lying prone. In Olympic shooting also one was allowed ten sighters in each position – ten chances of adjusting one's sights before one came to the forty rounds which counted for scoring.

In that street in Norwich I was not going to get ten sighters. I could afford barely one.

No regular lines of telegraph poles meant no convenient help with measuring the distance. The front gardens, though, I reckoned, should all be of more or less the same width because all the houses were identical, so as inconspicuously and casually as possible I slipped out of the car and paced slowly along the street, going away from Peter's house.

Fourteen paces per garden. I did some mental arithmetic and came up with three hundred yards meaning twenty-two houses.

I counted carefully. There were only twelve houses between me and my target – say one hundred and seventy yards. The shorter distance would be to my advantage. I could reckon in general to hit a target within one minute of a degree of arc: or in other words to hit a circular target of about one inch wide at a hundred yards, two inches wide at two hundred, three inches wide at three hundred, and so on to a ten-inch dinner plate at a thousand.

My target on that evening was roughly rectangular and about four inches by six, which meant that I mustn't be further away from it than four hundred yards. The main problem was that from where I stood, even if I used the telescope, I couldn't see it.

An old man came out of the house against whose kerbstone I was parked and asked if I wanted anything.

'Er, no,' I said. 'Waiting for someone. Stretching my legs.'

'My son wants to park there,' he said, pointing to where my car was. 'He'll be home soon.'

I looked at the stubborn old face and knew that if I didn't move he would be staring at me through the curtains, watching whatever I did. I nodded and smiled, got into the car, reversed into his next-door driveway, and left the street by the way I'd come.

All right, I thought, driving around. I have to come into the street from the opposite end. I have to park where I can see the target. I do not, if possible, park outside anyone's house fully exposed to one of those blank-looking one-way viewing screens. I do not park where Angelo can see me. I count the houses carefully to get the distance right; and above all I don't take much time.

It's a cliché in movies that when an assassin looks through the telescopic sight, steadies the crossed lines on the target and squeezes the trigger, the victim drops dead. Quite often the assassin will perform this feat while standing up, and nearly always it will be with his first shot: all of which makes serious marksmen laugh, or wince, or both. The only film I ever saw that got it right was *The Day of the Jackal*, where the gunman went into a forest to pace out his distance, to strap his rifle to a tree for steadiness, to adjust his sights and take two or three trial shots at a head-sized melon before transferring it all to the place of execution. Even then, there was no allowance for wind – but one can't have everything.

I drove into the top end of Peter's road, with which I was less familiar, and between two of the houses came across the wide entrance gates to the old estate upon which the new estate had been built. The double gates themselves, wrought iron, ajar, led to a narrow road that disappeared into parkland, and they were set not flush with the roadway or even with the fronts of the houses, but slightly further back. Between the gates and the road there was an area of moderately well-kept gravel and a badly weathered notice board announcing that all callers to the Paranormal Research Institute should drive in and follow the arrows to Reception.

I turned without hesitation on to the gravel area and stopped the car. It was ideal. From there, even with the naked eye, I had a clear view of the target. A slightly sideways view certainly, but good enough.

I got out of the car and counted the houses which stretched uniformly along the street: the Keithlys' was the fourteenth on the opposite side of the road and my target was one house nearer.

The road curved slightly to my right. There was a slight breeze from the left. I made the assessments almost automatically and eased myself into the back of the car.

I had gone through long patches of indecision over which rifle to use. The 7.62 bullets were far more destructive, but if I missed the target altogether with the first shot, I could do terrible damage to things or people I couldn't see. People half a mile away, or more. The .22 was much lighter: still potentially deadly if I missed the target, but not for such a long distance.

In a car I obviously couldn't lie flat on my stomach, the way I normally fired the Mauser. I could kneel, and I was more used to kneeling with the .22. But when I knelt in the car I wouldn't have to support the rifle's weight . . . I could rest it on the door and shoot through the open window.

For better or worse I chose the Mauser. The stopping power was so much greater, and if I was going to do the job, it was best done properly. Also I could see the target clearly and it was near enough to make hitting it with the second shot a certainty. It was the *first* shot that worried.

A picture of Paul Arcady rose in my mind. 'Could you shoot the apple off my head, sir?' What I was doing was much the same. One slight mistake could have unthinkable results.

Committed, I wound down the rear window and then fitted the sleek three-inch round of ammunition into the Mauser's breech. I took a look at the target through the telescope, steadying that too on the window ledge, and what leapt to my eye was a bright, clear, slightly oblique close-up of a flat shallow box, fixed high up and to one side on the telegraph pole: grey, basically rectangular, fringed with wires leading off to all the nearby houses.

The junction box.

I was sorry for all the people who were going to be without telephones for the rest of that day, but not too sorry to put them out of order.

I lowered the telescope, folded the brown towel, and laid it over the door frame to make a non-slip surface. Wedged myself between the front and rear seats as firmly as possible, and rested the barrel of the Mauser on the towel.

I thought I would probably have to hit the junction box two or three times to be sure. 7.62 mm bullets tended to go straight through things, doing most of the damage on the way out. If I'd cared to risk shooting the junction box *through the pole* one accurate bullet would have blown it apart, but I would have to have been directly behind it, and I couldn't get there unobserved.

I set the sights to what I thought I would need for that distance, lowered my body into an angle that felt right, corrected a fraction for the breeze, and squeezed the trigger. Hit the pole, I prayed. High or low, hit the pole. The bullet might indeed go through it, but with the worst of its impetus spent.

7.62 calibre rifles make a terrific noise. Out in the street it must have cracked like a bull whip. In the car it deafened me like in the old days before ear-defenders.

I re-loaded. Looked through the telescope. Saw the bullet hole, round and neat, right at the top of the grey junction box casing.

Allelujah, I thought gratefully, and breathed deeply from relief.

Lowered the sight a fraction, keeping my body position unchanged. Shot again. Reloaded. Shot again. Looked through the telescope.

The second and third holes overlapped, lower down than the first, and maybe because I wasn't shooting at it directly face-on but from a little to one side, the whole casing seemed to have split.

It would have to do. It was all too noisy.

I put the guns and telescopes on the floor with the towel over them and scrambled through on to the front seat.

Started the engine, reversed slowly on to the road and drove away at a normal pace, seeing in the rear-view mirror a couple of inhabitants come out inquiringly into the street. The net curtains must all have been twitching, but no one shouted after me, no one pointed and said 'That's the man.'

And Angelo – what would he think? And Sarah – who knew the sound of a rifle better than church bells? I hoped to God she'd keep quiet.

Going out of Norwich I stopped for petrol and used the telephone there to ring Donna's number.

Nothing.

A faint humming noise, like wind in the wires.

I blew out a lungful of air and wondered with a smile what the repair men would say when they climbed the pole on the morrow. Unprintable, most like.

There were perhaps ways of interfering with incoming calls by technical juggling, by ringing a number, waiting for it to be answered, saying nothing, waiting for the receiver to be put down, and then not replacing one's own receiver, leaving the line open and making it impossible for the number to ring again. I might have trusted that method for a short while, but not for hours: and with some exchanges it didn't work.

Further along the road I again stopped, this time to tidy and reorganize the car. I returned the Mauser and the telescope to their beds in the suitcase in the boot, along with the 7.62 mm ammunition; then broke all my own and everyone else's rules and loaded a live .22 round into the breech of the Anschütz.

I laid the towel on the back seat and rolled the Olympic rifle in it lengthways, and then stowed it flat on the floor behind the front seats. The towel blended well enough with the brown carpet, and I reckoned that if I didn't accelerate or brake or corner too fast, the gun should travel without moving.

Next I put four extra bullets into my right-hand pocket, because the Anschütz had no magazine and each round had to be loaded separately. After so many years of practice I could discharge the spent casing and load a new bullet within the space of two seconds, and even faster if I held the fresh bullet in my right palm. The two rifles were physically the same size, and I'd have taken the Mauser with its available magazine if it hadn't been for its horrific power in a domestic setting. The .22 would kill, but not the people in the next house.

After that I juggled around a bit with the cassettes and their boxes and the glue and the bits I'd pinched from school, and finally drove on again, this time to Welwyn.

Harry Gilbert was expecting me. From the way he came bustling out of his house the moment I turned into his driveway he had been expecting me for a long time and had grown thoroughly tired of it.

'Where have you *been*?' he said. 'Did you bring the tapes?'

He had come close to me as I emerged from the car, thrusting his chin forward belligerently, sure of his power over a man at a disadvantage.

'I thought you didn't approve of Angelo threatening people with your pistol,' I said.

Something flickered in a muscle in his face.

'There are times when only threats will do,' he said. 'Give me the tapes.'

I took the three tapes out of my pocket and showed them to him; the three tapes themselves, out of their boxes.

I said, 'Now ring Angelo and tell him to untie my wife.'

Gilbert shook his head. 'I try the tapes first. Then I ring Angelo. And Angelo leaves your wife tied up until you yourself go to release her. That is the arrangement. It's simple. Come into the house.'

We went again into his functional office, which this time had an addition in the shape of a Grantley computer sitting on his desk.

'The tapes.' He held his hand out for them, and I gave them to him. He slotted the first one into the recorder which stood beside the computer and began to fumble around with the computer's typewriter-like keys in a most disorganized fashion.

'How long have you had that computer?' I said.

'Shut up.'

He typed RUN, and not surprisingly nothing happened, as he hadn't fed the program in from the cassette. I watched him pick up the instruction book and begin leafing through it, and if there had been all the time in the world I would have let him stew in it longer. But every minute I wasted meant one more dragging minute for Donna and Sarah, so I said, 'You'd better take lessons.'

'Shut *up*.' He gave me a distinctly bull-like glare and typed RUN again.

'I want Angelo out of that house,' I said, 'so I'll show you how to run the tapes. Otherwise we'll be here all night.'

He would have given much not to allow me the advantage, but he should have done his homework first.

I ejected the tape to see which side we'd got, then re-inserted it and typed CLOAD "EPSOM", The asterisks began to blink at the top right hand corner as the computer searched the tape, but at length it found "EPSOM", loaded the Epsom program, and announced READY.

'Now type RUN and press "ENTER",' I said.

Gilbert did so, and immediately the screen said:

WHICH RACE AT EPSOM?

TYPE NAME OF RACE AND PRESS 'ENTER'.

Gilbert typed DERBY, and the screen told him to type the name of the horse. He typed in "ANGELO", and made the same sort of fictional replies Ted Pitts and I had done. Angelo's win factor was 46, which must have been maximum. It also said quite a lot about Gilbert's estimate of his son.

'How do you get Ascot?' he said.

I ejected the tape and inserted the first side of all. Typed CLOAD "ASCOT", pressed 'Enter', and waited for READY.

'Type RUN, press "Enter",' I said.

He did so, and at once got WHICH RACE AT ASCOT? TYPE NAME OF RACE AND PRESS 'ENTER'.

He typed GOLD CUP and looked enthralled by the ensuing questions, and I thought that he'd played with it long enough.

'Telephone Angelo,' I said. 'You must surely be satisfied that this time you've got the real thing.'

'Wait,' he said heavily. 'I'll try all the tapes. I don't trust you. Angelo was insistent that I don't trust you.'

I shrugged. 'Test what you like.'

He tried one or two programs on each of the sides, finally realizing that CLOAD plus the first five letters of the racecourse required, inserted between inverted commas, would unlock the goodies.

'All right,' I said at length. 'Now ring Angelo. You can run the programs all you like when I've gone.'

He could find no further reason for putting it off. With a stare to which his own natural arrogance was fast returning he picked up one of the telephones, consulted a note pad beside it, and dialled the number.

Not surprisingly he didn't get through. He dialled again. Then, impatiently, again. Then, muttering under his breath he tried one of the other telephones with ditto nil results.

'What is it?' I said.

'The number doesn't ring.'

'You must be dialling it wrong,' I said. 'I've got it here.'

I fished into my pocket for my diary and made a show of fluttering through the leaves. Came to the number. Read it out.

446

'That's what I dialled,' Gilbert said.

'It can't be. Try again.' I'd never thought of myself as an actor but I found it quite easy to pretend.

Gilbert dialled again, frowning, and I thought it time to be agitated and anxious.

'You *must* get through,' I said. 'I've worried and rushed all day to get those tapes here, and now you *must* ring Angelo, he *must* leave my wife.'

In experience of command he had tough years of advantage, but then I too was accustomed to having to control wily opponents, and when I took a step towards him it was clear to both of us that physically I was taller and fitter and quite decisively stronger.

He said hastily, 'I'll try the operator,' and I fidgeted and fumed around him in simulated anxiety while the operator tried without success and reported the number out of order.

'But it can't be,' I yelled. '*You've got to ring Angelo.*'

Harry Gilbert simply stared at me, knowing that it was impossible.

I cut the decibels a shade but looked as furious as I could, and said, 'We'll have to go there.'

'But Angelo said . . .'

'I don't give a damn what Angelo said,' I said forcefully. 'He won't leave that house until he knows you've got the tapes, and now it seems you can't tell him you have. So we'll bloody well have to go there and tell him. And I'm absolutely fed up with all this buggering about.'

'You can go,' Gilbert said. 'I'm not coming.'

'Yes you are. I'm not walking up to that house alone with Angelo inside it with that pistol. He said I was to give the tapes to *you*, and that's what I've done, and you've got to come with me to tell him so. And I promise you,' I said threateningly, warming to the part, 'that I'll take you with me one way or another. Knocked out or tied up or just sitting quietly in the front seat beside me. Because you're the only one Angelo will listen to.' I snatched up the cassettes lying beside the computer. 'If you want these tapes back you'll come with me.'

He agreed to come. He hadn't much choice. I pulled the cases for the tapes out of my pockets and showed him the labels, *Oklahoma, The King and I, West Side Story.* Then I ejected the cassette which was still in the recorder and put all three of the tapes into their cases. 'And we'll take these,' I said, 'to prove to Angelo that you have them.'

He agreed to that also. He came out with me to my car, slamming his own front door behind him, and sat in the front passenger seat.

'I'll hold the tapes,' he said.

I put them, however, on the glove shelf out of his immediate reach and told him he could have them once we got to Norwich.

It was a strange journey.

He was a far more powerful man than I would normally have thought of opposing, yet I was discovering that I had probably always thought of myself as being weaker than I was. For the whole of my life I had gone in awe of headmasters; as a pupil, as a student, as a teacher. Even when I'd disagreed or despised or rebelled, I'd never tried actively to defeat. One could easily be chucked out of school and out of college and out of the better jobs in physics.

Harry Gilbert couldn't chuck me out of anything, and perhaps that was the difference. I could face his belief in his own superiority and not be intimidated by it. I could use my wits and my muscles to get him to do what I wanted. It was heady stuff. Have to be careful, I reflected, not to develop delusions of grandeur of my own.

Angelo, I thought suddenly, feels just as I do. Feels the spreading of the wings of internal power. Feels he can do more than he realized. Sees his world isn't as constricting as he thought. Angelo too was emerging into a new conception of ability ... but in him there were no brakes.

'There is someone there with Angelo,' I said. 'My wife said "they".' I spoke neutrally, without aggression.

Gilbert sat heavily silent.

'When Angelo came to my house,' I said, 'there was another man with him. Very like Angelo in looks. Did what Angelo told him.'

After a pause Gilbert shrugged and said, 'Eddy. Angelo's cousin. Their mothers were twins.'

'Italian?' I said.

Another pause. Then, 'We are all Italian by descent.'

'But born in England?'

'Yes. Why do you ask?'

I sighed. 'Just to pass the journey.'

He grunted, but gradually a good deal of his resentment of my behaviour subsided. I had no idea whether or not he considered it justified.

Anxiety on my part didn't need to be acted. I found myself drumming my fingers on the steering wheel when stopped by red lights and cursing long lorries which delayed my passing. By the time we got to Norwich, it would be over the four hours I'd warned Angelo to expect, and of all things that I didn't want, was Angelo ballooning into premature rage.

'Will you pay Mrs O'Rorke anything for these tapes?' I said.

A pause. 'No.'

'Not even without Angelo's knowledge?'

He gave me a fierce sideways glare. 'Angelo does what I tell him. Whether I pay or don't pay Mrs O'Rorke is nothing to do with him.'

If he believed all that, I thought, he was deluding himself. Or perhaps he still wanted to believe what had so far been true. Perhaps he truly didn't see his days of domination over Angelo were ticking away fast.

Just let them last, I thought, for another two hours.

10

The long lingering evening was slowly dying by the time we reached Norwich, though it wouldn't be totally dark for another hour. I drove into the Keithlys' road from the direction that would place Gilbert nearest to the house when I pulled up at the kerb: Angelo had seen my car at his father's house as I had seen his, and the sight of it would alarm him.

'Please get out of the car as soon as I stop,' I said to Gilbert. 'So that Angelo can see you.'

He grunted, but when I pulled up he opened the door as I'd suggested, and gave any watchers from behind the curtains a full view of his lumbering exit from the front seat.

'Wait,' I said, standing up on my own side and talking to him across the top of the car. 'Take the tapes.' I reached across the top of the car and gave them to him. 'Hold them up,' I said, 'so that Angelo can see them.'

'You give too many orders.'

'I don't trust your son any more than he trusts me.'

He gave me a bullish stare of fully revived confidence, but he did in fact turn and lift the tapes, showing them to the house.

Behind his back I leant down and picked up the towel-wrapped rifle, holding it longways with the stock to my chest and the flap of my jacket falling over it.

Angelo opened the front door, shielding himself half behind it.

'Go in,' I said to Gilbert. 'This street is full of people watching through the curtains.'

He gave an automatically alarmed look at being spied on and began to walk towards his son. I slid round the car fast and walked close behind him, almost stepping on his heels.

'Explain,' I said urgently.

His head lifted ominously, but he said loudly to Angelo, 'Your telephone's out of order.'

'*What?*' Angelo exclaimed, opening the door a fraction wider. 'It can't be.'

Gilbert said impatiently. 'It is. Don't be a fool. Why else would I come all this way?'

Angelo turned away from the door and strode into the sitting-room, which was where the telephone was located. I heard him pick up the receiver and rattle the cradle, and slam the instrument down again.

'But he brought the tapes,' Gilbert said, walking to the sitting-room door and showing the bright cases. 'I tried them. All of them. This time they're the real thing.'

'Come in here, you, creep,' Angelo called.

I propped the wrapped rifle, barrel downwards to the carpet, against the small chest of drawers which stood within arm's reach of the sitting-room door, and showed myself in the doorway.

The sitting-room furniture was all pushed awry. Sarah and Donna sat back-to-back in the centre of the room, with their wrists and ankles strapped to the arms and legs of two of the chairs from the dining-room. To one side stood Angelo, holding the Walther, with, beyond the two girls, his look-alike, Eddy. There were glasses and plates sprinkled about, and the smell of long hours of cigarette smoke.

Sarah was facing me.

We looked at each other with a curious lack of emotion, I noticing almost distantly the dark smudges under her eyes, the exhausted sag of her body, the strain and pain around her mouth.

She said nothing. No doubt she considered I was showing too little concern and was too calm as usual: the message on her face wasn't love and relief but relief and disgust.

'Go home,' I said wearily to Angelo. 'You've got what you wanted.'

I prayed for him to go. To be satisfied, to be sensible, to be ruled by his father, to be approximately normal.

Harry Gilbert began to turn from his son back towards me, saying, 'That's it, then, Angelo. We'd best be off.'

'No,' Angelo said.

Gilbert stopped. 'What did you say?' he said.

'I said, no,' Angelo said. 'This creep's going to pay for all the trouble he's put me to. You come here, creep.'

Gilbert said, 'No, Angelo.' He gestured to the girls. 'This is enough.'

Angelo pointed his pistol with its bulbous silencer straight at Donna's head. 'This one,' he said viciously, 'has been screaming at me for hours that they'll report me to the police, the stupid little bitch.'

'They won't,' I said quickly.

'Dead right they won't.'

Even to Gilbert his meaning was clear. Gilbert made movements of extreme disapproval and active fear and said, 'Put down the gun. Angelo, put it down.' His voice thundered with parental command and from long long habit Angelo began to obey. Even in the same second he visibly reversed his instinct; and I knew that for me it was then or never.

I stretched out my right arm, thrust my hand down into the towel and grasped the stock of the rifle. Swung the towel off the barrel and in the same fluid movement stood in the doorway with the barrel pointing straight at Angelo and the safety catch unlocking with a click.

'Drop it,' I said.

They were all utterly astounded but perhaps Angelo most of all because I'd twice played the same trick on him. The three men stood there as if frozen, and I didn't look at Sarah, not directly.

'Drop the pistol,' I said. He was still pointing it towards Donna.

He couldn't bear to drop it. Not to lose that much face.

'I'll shoot you,' I said.

Even then he hesitated. I swung the barrel to the ceiling and squeezed the trigger. The noise crashed in the small room. Pieces of plaster fell from the ceiling. The sharp smell of cordite prevailed over stale cigarette, and all the mouths were open, like fish. The rifle was pointing back at his heart with the next round in the breech almost before he'd moved an inch, and he looked at it with dazed disbelief.

'Drop the pistol,' I said. *'Drop it.'*

He was still undecided. I'll have to hit him, I thought despairingly. I don't want to. Why won't he drop the bloody thing, there's nothing he can gain.

The air seemed to be still ringing with the aftermath of explosion, but it was into silence that Sarah spoke.

With a sort of sullen ferocity, which seemed as much directed at me as at Angelo, she said loudly, 'He shot in the Olympic Games.'

Angelo's eyes developed doubt.

'Drop the pistol,' I said quietly, 'or I'll shoot your hand.'

Angelo dropped it.

His face was full of fury and hate and I thought him capable of flinging himself upon me regardless of consequences. I looked at him stolidly, showing no triumph, showing nothing to inflame.

'You've got the tapes,' I said. 'Get in the car, all three of you, and get out of my life. I'm sick of your faces.' I stepped back a pace into the hall and nodded with my head towards the front door.

'Just get out,' I said. 'One at a time. Angelo first.'

He came towards me with his dark eyes like pits in the olive face, the light too dim now to give them wicked life. I stood back a few steps further and followed his progress to the front door, as in my own house, with the black barrel.

'I'll get you,' he said.

I didn't answer.

He pulled open the door with the force of rage and stepped outside.

'Now you,' I said to Harry Gilbert.

He was almost as angry as his son, but perhaps it was fanciful of me to guess that there was also some recognition that I'd been able to stop Angelo where he couldn't, and that that had been a good thing.

He followed Angelo out on to the driveway and I saw them both opening the doors of Angelo's car.

'Now you,' I said to Eddy. 'You pick up Angelo's gun. Pick it up by the silencer. Do you know how to unload it?'

Eddy the carbon-copy nodded miserably.

'Do it, then,' I said. 'Very very carefully.'

He looked at the rifle and at Angelo getting into the car, and shook the bullets out of the clip, letting them drop on the carpet.

'Right,' I said. 'Take the pistol with you.' I gestured with the rifle barrel and jerked my head towards the open front door, and of the three of them it was Eddy who left with the least reluctance and the most speed.

From inside the hall I watched Angelo start the engine, slam the gears into reverse and make a rough exit into the road. Once there he deliberately side-swiped my car, damaging his own rear wing in the process, and accelerated down the street as if to prove his superior manhood.

With a feeling of terrible tension I closed the front door and went into the sitting-room. Crossed to Sarah, looked at the rubber straps which fastened her wrists and unbuckled them. Unbuckled those round her ankles. Then those round Donna.

Donna started crying. Sarah shoved herself stiffly off the chair and collapsed on to the softer contours of the sofa.

'Do you realize how long we've been sitting there?' she demanded bitterly. 'And before you damned well ask, yes, they did untie us now and then for us to go to the bathroom.'

'And to eat?'

'I hate you,' she said.

'I really wanted to know.'

'Yes, to eat. Twice. He made me cook.'

Donna said between sobs, 'It's been awful. Awful. You've no idea.'

'They didn't . . . ?' I began anxiously.

'No they didn't,' Sarah said flatly. 'They just sneered.'

'*Hateful*,' Donna said. 'Called us mugs.' She hobbled across the carpet and lowered herself gingerly into an armchair. 'I hurt all over.' Tears trickled down her cheeks. I thought of Angelo's description of 'wet chick' and stifled it quickly.

'Look,' I said, 'I know you don't feel like it, but I'd be much happier if you'd stuff a few things into a suitcase and we all left this house.'

Donna helplessly shook her head, and Sarah said 'Why?' with mutiny.

'Angelo hated having to go. You saw him. Suppose he comes back? When he thinks we're off guard . . . he might.'

The idea alarmed them as much as me and also angered Sarah. 'Why did you give them the pistol?' she demanded. 'That was *stupid*. You're such a *fool*.'

'Are you coming?'

'You can't expect us . . .' Donna wailed.

I said to Sarah, 'I have to make a phone call. I can't do it from here.' I indicated the dead telephone. 'I'm going away in the car to do it. Do you want to come, or not?'

Sarah took stock of that rapidly and said that yes, they were coming, and despite Donna's protests she drove her stiffly upstairs. They came down a few minutes later carrying a hold-all each, and I noticed that Sarah had put on some lipstick. I smiled at her with some of the old pleasure in seeing her resurfacing briefly, and she looked both surprised and confused.

'Come on, then,' I said, and took the hold-alls from them to put in the boot. 'Best be off.' I fetched the rifle, once again wrapped loosely in the towel to confuse the neighbours, and stowed it in the suitcase. Checked that Donna had brought the door keys: shut the front door; drove away.

'Where are we going?' Sarah asked.

'Where would you like?'

'What about *money*?'

'Credit cards,' I said.

We drove a short way in a silence broken only by Donna's occasional sniffs and sobs, going along now with lights on everywhere and the long soft evening turning to full dark.

I pulled up beside a telephone box and put through a reversed charge call to the Suffolk police.

'Is Detective Chief Superintendent Irestone there?' I said. Hopeless question, but had to be asked.

'Your name, sir?'

'Jonathan Derry.'

'One moment.'

I waited through the usual mutterings and clicks, and then a voice that was still not Irestone's said, 'Mr Derry, Chief Superintendent Irestone left instructions that if you telephoned again, your message was to be taken down in full and passed on to him directly. Chief Superintendent Irestone asked me to say that owing to . . . er . . . a hitch in communications he was not aware that you had tried to reach him so often, not until this afternoon. I am Detective Inspector Robson. I came to your house with the Chief Superintendent, if you remember.'

'Yes,' I said. A man nearing forty, fair-headed, reddish skin.

'If you tell me why you rang, sir?'

'You'll take notes?'

'Yes, sir. And a recording.'

'Right. Well – the man who came to my house with a pistol is called Angelo Gilbert. His father is Harry Gilbert who runs bingo halls all over Essex and north-east London. The man who came with Angelo is his cousin Eddy – don't know his last name. He does what Angelo tells him.'

I paused and Inspector Robson said, 'Is that the lot, sir?'

'No, it isn't. At this moment all three of them are travelling from Norwich in Angelo's car.' I told him the make, the colour, the number, and that it had a bashed-in nearside rear wing. 'They are probably going to Harry Gilbert's house in Welwyn Garden City. I think Angelo also lives there, but perhaps not Eddy.' I gave him the address. 'They should arrive there in about an hour and a quarter to an hour and a half. In the car there is a Walther .22 pistol with a silencer. There may or may not be bullets in it. It may or may not be the pistol which Angelo waved at me, but it looks identical. It might be the pistol which killed Christopher Norwood.'

'That's very useful, sir,' Robson said.

'There's one more thing . . .'

'Yes?'

'I don't think Harry Gilbert knows anything at all about Chris Norwood's death. I mean, I don't think he even knows he's dead. If you go to arrest Angelo, Harry Gilbert won't know why.'

'Thank you, sir.'

'That's all,' I said.

'Er,' he said, 'the Chief Superintendent will be in touch with you.'

'All right, but – ' I hesitated.

'Yes, sir?'

'I'd be glad to know . . .'

'Just a minute, sir,' he interrupted, and kept me hanging on through some lengthy unintelligible background talk. 'Sorry, sir, you were saying?'

'You remember I sent Angelo some computer tapes with games on?'

'Yes, I do. We went to Cambridge main post office and alerted the man whose job it was to hand out letters-to-be-called-for, but unfortunately he went for his tea-break without mentioning it to anyone, and during that short period your package was collected. A girl clerk handed it over. We didn't find out until it was too late. It was . . . infuriating.'

'Mm,' I said. 'Well, Angelo came back with more threats, demanding the real tapes, and I've just given them to him. Only . . .'

'Only what, sir?'

'Only they won't be able to run them on their computer. I think when they get home they might try those tapes straight away, and when they find they don't work they might . . . well they might set out to look for me. I mean – '

'I know *exactly* what you mean,' he said drily.

'So, er, I'd be glad to know if you plan to do anything about Angelo this evening. And if you think there's enough to hold him on.'

'Instructions have already gone off,' he said. 'He'll be picked up tonight as soon as he reaches the house in Welwyn. We have some fingerprints to match . . . and some girls who saw two men arrive at Norwood's. So don't worry, once we've got him, we won't let him go.'

'Could I ring up to find out?'

'Yes.' He gave me a new number. 'Call there. I'll leave a message. You'll get it straight away.'

'Thank you,' I said gratefully, 'very much.'

'Mr Derry?'

'Yes?'

'What's wrong with the tapes this time?'

'Oh, I stuck magnets into the cases.'

He laughed. 'I'll see you later, perhaps,' he said. 'And thanks. Thanks a lot.'

I put the receiver down smiling, thinking of the three powerful Magnadur magnets distorting the programs on the tapes. The permanent magnets which were black and flat; two inches long, three-quarters of an inch wide, three-sixteenths of an inch thick. I'd stuck one into the inside of each case, flat on the bottom, black as the plastic, looking like part of the case itself. I'd taken the tapes and the cases separately to Harry Gilbert's – the tapes in the one pocket, the cases in another – and only after he'd played them had I married them all together. Sandwiching electro-magnetic recording tapes between such magnets was like wiping a blackboard roughly with a wet sponge: there would be traces of what had been recorded there, but not enough to make sense.

It might take Angelo all the way home to see what I'd done, because the magnets did look as if they belonged there.

Or it might not.

I drove wearily in the direction of home. I seemed to have been driving for ever. It had been a very long day. Extraordinary to think it was only that morning that I'd set out from Ted Pitts'.

Both of the girls went to sleep as the miles unrolled, the deep sleep of release and exhaustion. I wondered briefly what would become of us in the future, but mostly I just thought about driving and keeping my own eyelids apart.

We stayed in a motel on the outskirts of London and slept as if dead. The alarm call I'd asked for dragged me from limbo at seven in the morning and, yawning like a great white shark, I got through to the number Inspector Robson had given me.

'Jonathan Derry,' I said. 'Am I too early?'

It was a girl's voice which answered, fresh and unofficial. 'No, it's not too early,' she said. 'John Robson asked me to tell you that Angelo Gilbert and his cousin Eddy are in custody.'

'Thank you very much.'

'Any time.'

I put the receiver down with a steadily lightening heart and shook Sarah awake in the next bed.

'Sorry,' I said, 'but I've got to be in school by nine o'clock.'

II

There was a period when Sarah went back to work and Donna drooped around our house trying to come to terms with the devastation of her life. Sarah's manner to her grew gradually less over-protective and more normal, and when Donna found she was no longer indulged and pampered every waking minute she developed a pout in place of the invalid smile, and went home. Home to sell her house, to collect Peter's insurance money, and to persuade her Probation Officer to take Sarah's psychological place.

On the surface, things between myself and Sarah continued much as before: the politeness, the lack of emotional contact, the daily meetings of strangers. She seldom met my eye and seemed only to speak when it was essential, but I slowly realized that the deeply embittered set of her mouth, which had been so noticeable before the day we set off to Norwich, had more or less gone. She looked softer and more as she had once been and although it didn't seem to have altered her manner towards me it was less depressing to look at.

In my inner self a lot had changed. I seemed to have stepped out of a cage. I did everything with more confidence and more satisfaction. I shot better. I taught with zest. I even found the wretched exercise books less of a drag. I felt that one day soon I would stretch the spreading wings, and fly.

One night as we lay in the dark, each in our frostily separate cocoon, I said to Sarah, 'Are you awake?'

'Yes.'

'You know that at the end of term I'm going to Canada with the rifle team?'

'Yes.'

'I'm not coming back with them.'

'Why not?'

'I'm going to the United States. Probably for the rest of the school holidays.'

'Whatever for?'

'To see it. Perhaps to live there, eventually.'

She was silent for a while: and what she said in the end seemed only obliquely to have anything to do with my plans.

'Donna talked to me a lot, you know. She told me all about the day she stole that baby.'

'Did she?' I said noncommittally.

'Yes. She said that when she saw it lying there in its pram, she had an overpowering urge to pick it up and cuddle it. So she did. She just did. Then when she had it in her arms she felt as if it belonged to her, as if it was hers. So she carried it to her car, which was just there, a few steps away. She put the baby on the front seat beside her and drove off. She didn't know where she was going. She said it was a sort of dream, in which she had at last the baby she'd pined for for so long.'

She stopped. I thought of Ted Pitts's little girls and the protective curve of his body as he held his smallest one close. I would have wept for Sarah, for Donna, for every unwillingly barren parent.

'She drove for a long way,' Sarah said. 'She got to the sea and stopped there. She took the baby into the back of the car and it was perfect. She was in utter bliss. It was still like a dream. And then the baby woke up.' She paused. 'I suppose it was hungry. Time for its next feed. Anyway it began to

456

cry, and it wouldn't stop. It cried and cried and cried. She said that it cried for an hour. The noise started driving her mad. She put her hand over its mouth, and it cried harder. She tried to hug its face into her shoulder so that it would stop, but it didn't. And then she found that its nappies were dirty, and the brown stuff had oozed down the baby's leg and was on her dress.'

Another long pause, then Sarah's voice, 'She said she didn't know babies were like that. Screaming and smelly. She'd thought of them as sweet and smiling at her all the time. She began to hate that baby, not love it. She said she sort of threw it down on to the back seat in a rage, and then she got out of the car and just left it. Walked away. She said she could hear the baby crying all the way down the beach.'

This time the silence was much longer.

'Are you still awake?' Sarah said.

'Yes.'

'I'm reconciled now to not having a child. I grieve . . . but it can't be helped.' She paused and then said. 'I've learned a lot about myself these past weeks, because of Donna.'

And I, I thought, because of Angelo.

After another long while she said, 'Are you still awake?'

'Yes.'

'I don't really understand, you know, all that happened. I mean, I know that that hateful Angelo has been arrested for murder, of course I do, and that you have been seeing the police, but you've never told me exactly what it was all about.'

'You seriously want to know?'

'Of course I do, otherwise I wouldn't ask.' The familiar note of impatience rang out clearly. She must have heard it herself because she immediately said more moderately, 'I'd like you to tell me. I really would.'

'All right,' I said, and I told her pretty well everything, starting from the date that Chris Norwood set it all going by stealing Liam O'Rorke's notes. I told her events in their chronological order, not in the jumbled way I learned of them, so that a clear pattern emerged of Angelo's journeyings in search of the tapes.

When I'd finished, she said slowly, 'You knew all through that day when he had us tied up that he was a murderer.'

'Mm.'

'My God.' She paused. 'Didn't you think he might kill us? Donna and me?'

'I thought he *might*. I thought he might do it any time after he knew his father had the tapes. I thought he might kill all of us, if he felt like it. I couldn't tell . . . but couldn't risk it.'

A long silence. Then she said, 'I think, looking back, that he did mean to. Things he said . . .' She paused. 'I was glad to see you.'

'And angry.'

'Yes, angry. You'd been so *long* . . . And Angelo was so bloody *frightening*.'

'I know.'

'I heard the rifle shots. I was in the kitchen cooking.'

'I was afraid you might tell Angelo you heard them.'

'I only spoke to him when I absolutely had to. I loathed him. He was so *arrogant.*'

'You shook him,' I said, 'telling him I'd shot in the Games. It was the clincher.'

'I just wanted to . . . to kick him in the ego.'

I smiled in the darkness. Angelo's ego had taken quite a pummelling at the hands of the Derrys.

'Do you realize,' I said, 'that we haven't talked like this for months?'

'Such a lot has happened. And I feel . . . different.'

Nothing like a murderer, I thought, for changing one's view of the world. He'd done a good job for both of us.

'Do you want to come, then,' I said, 'to America?'

To America. To go on together. To try a bit longer. I didn't really know which I wanted: to clear out, cut loose, divorce, start again, remarry, have children, or to make what one might of the old dead love, to pour commitment into the shaky foundations, to rebuild them solid.

It was Sarah, I thought, who would have to decide.

'Do you want us to stay together?' I asked.

'You've thought of divorce?'

'Haven't you?'

'Yes.' I heard her sigh. 'Often, lately.'

'It's pretty final, being divorced,' I said.

'What then?'

'Wait a bit,' I said slowly. 'See how we go. See what we both really want. Keep on talking.'

'All right,' she said. 'That'll do.'

Interval

Letter from Vince Akkerton to Jonathan Derry.

Angel Kitchens,
Newmarket.
July 12th

Dear Mr Derry,

You remember you were asking about Chris Norwood, that day back in May? I don't know if you're still interested in those computer tapes you were talking about, but they've turned up here at the Kitchens. We were clearing out the room we change from outdoor clothes in, prior to it being repainted, you see, and there was this bag there that everyone said didn't belong to them. So I looked in it, and there were a lot of old papers of writing and three cassettes. I thought I'd give them a run on my cassette player, because they didn't have any labels on saying what was on them, but all that came out was a screeching noise. Well, a mate of mine who heard it said don't throw them away, because I was going to, that's a computer noise, he said. So I took the tapes in to Janet to see what she could make of them, but she said the firm has got rid of their old computer, it wasn't big enough for all it was having to do, and they've now got a company computer or something with disc drives, she says, and it doesn't use cassettes.

So, anyway, I remembered about you all of a sudden, and I found I'd still got your address, so I thought I'd ask you if you thought this was what you were talking about. I threw the pages of writing into the rubbish, and that's that, they're gone, but if you want these tapes, you send me a tenner for my trouble and you can have them.

Yours truly,
Vince Akkerton

Letter from the executors of Mrs Maureen O'Rorke to Jonathan Derry.

September 1st

Dear Sir,

We are returning the note you wrote to Mrs O'Rorke, together with your enclosure of three cassettes.

Unfortunately Mrs O'Rorke had died peacefully in her sleep at home three days before your gift was posted. In our opinion, therefore, the contents of the package should be regarded as belonging to yourself, and we herewith return them.

We are,

Yours faithfully,

Jones, Pearce and Block, Solicitors

Letter from the University of Eastern California selection board to Jonathan Derry.

London
October 20th

Dear Mr Derry,

Subsequent to your interview in London last week, we have pleasure in offering you a three-year teaching post in the Department of Physics. Your salary for the first year will be Scale B (attached) to be reviewed thereafter. One full semester's notice is to be given in writing on either side.

We understand that you will be free to take up the post on January 1st next, and we await your confirmation that you accept this offer.

Further details and instructions will be sent to you upon receipt of your acceptance.

Welcome to the University!

Lance K. Barowska, D.Sc.

Director of Selections, Science Faculty,

University of Eastern California

Letter from Harry Gilbert to Marty Goldman Ltd, Turf Accountants.

October 15th

Dear Marty

In view of what has happened, I'm asking you to release me from the transfer that we had agreed. I haven't the heart, old friend, to build any more kingdoms. With Angelo jailed for life, there's no point in me buying all your betting shops. You knew, of course, that they were for him – for him to manage, anyway.

I know you had some other offers, so I hope you won't be coming after me for compensation.

Your old friend,

Harry

Excerpt from a private letter from the Governor of Albany Prison, Parkhurst, Isle of Wight to his friend the Governor of Wakefield Prison, Yorkshire.

Well, Frank, we're letting Angelo Gilbert out on parole this week, and I wish between you and me that I felt better about it. I'd like to have advised against it, but he's served fourteen years and there's been a lot of pressure from the Reformers group on the Home Sec. to release him. It's not that Gilbert's actively violent or even hostile, but he's been trying hard to get this parole so for the last two years there's been no breath of trouble.

But as you know with some of them they're never stable however meek they look, and I've a feeling Gilbert's like that. You remember, when you had him about five years ago, you felt just the same. It isn't on the cards, I suppose, to keep him locked up for life, but I just hope to God he doesn't go straight out and shoot the first person who crosses him.

See you soon Frank,

Donald

Part Two

William

12

I put my hand on Cassie's breast, and she said 'No, William. No.'

'Why not?' I said.

'Because it's never good for me, twice, so soon. You know that.'

'Come on,' I said.

'No.'

'You're lazy,' I said.

'And you're greedy.' She picked my hand off and gave it back to me. I replaced it. 'At least, let me hold you,' I said.

'No.' She threw my hand off again. 'With you, one thing leads to another. I'm going to get some orange juice and run the bath, and if you're not careful, you'll be late.'

I rolled on to my back and watched her walk about the bedroom, a tall thin girl with too few curves and very long feet. Seen like that in all her angular nakedness, she still had the self-possessed quality which had first attracted me; a natural apartness, a lack of cling. Her self-doubts, if any, were well hidden, even from me. She went downstairs and came back carrying two glasses of orange.

'William,' she said, 'stop staring.'

'I like to.'

She walked to the bathroom to turn on the taps and came back brushing her teeth.

'It's seven o'clock,' she said.

'So I've noticed.'

'You'll lose that cushy job of yours if you're not out on the gallops in ten minutes.'

'Twenty will do.'

I rose up, however, and pinched the bath first, drinking the orange juice as I went. Count your blessings, I said to myself, soaping. Count Cassandra Morris, a better girl than I'd ever had before; seven months bedded, growing more essential every day. Count the sort of job that no one expects to be given at twenty-nine. Count enough money, for once, to buy a car that wasn't everyone's cast-off held together by rust and luck.

The old ache to be a jockey was pretty well dead, but I supposed there would always be regret. It wasn't as if I'd never ridden in races; I had, from sixteen to twenty, first as an amateur, then a professional, during which time I'd won eighty-four steeplechases, twenty-three hurdle races, and wretchedly cursed by unstoppably lengthening body. At six foot one I'd broken my leg in a racing fall, been imprisoned in traction for three months, and grown two more inches in bed.

It had been practically the end. There *had* been very tall jump jockeys in the past, but I'd progressively found that even if I starved to the point of weakness I couldn't keep my weight reliably below eleven stone. Trainers began saying I was too tall, too heavy, sorry lad, and employing someone else. So at twenty I'd got myself a job as an assistant trainer, and at twenty-three I'd worked for a bloodstock agent, and at twenty-six on a stud farm, which kept me off the racecourse too much. At twenty-seven I'd been employed in a sort of hospital for sick racehorses which went out of business because too many owners preferred to shoot their liabilities, and after that there had been a spell of selling horse cubes, and then a few months in the office of a bloodstock auctioneer, which had paid well but bored me to death; and each time between jobs I'd spent the proceeds of the last one in wandering round the world, drifting homewards when the cash ran out and casting round for a new berth.

It had been at one of the points of no prospects that Jonathan had sent the cable.

'Catch the next flight. Good job in English racing possible if you interview here immediately. Jonathan.'

I'd turned up on his Californian doorstep sixteen hours later and early the next morning he had sent me off to see 'a man I met at a party'. A man, it transpired, of middle height, middle years and middling grey hair: a man I knew instantly by sight. Everyone in racing, worldwide, knew him by sight. He ran his racing as a big business, taking his profits in the shape of blood-stock, selling his stallions for up to a hundred times more than they'd earned on the track.

'Luke Houston,' he said neutrally, extending his hand.

'Yes, sir,' I said, retrieving some breath. 'Er . . . William Derry.'

He offered me breakfast on a balcony overlooking the Pacific, eating grapefruit and boiled eggs and giving me smiling genial glances which were basically as casual as X-rays.

'Warrington Marsh, my racing manager in England, had a stroke four days ago,' he said. 'Poor guy, he's doing well – I have bulletins every a.m. – but it is going to be some time, a long time, I'm afraid, before he'll be active again.' He gestured to my untouched breakfast. 'Eat your toast.'

'Yes, sir.'

'Tell me why I should give you his job. Temporarily, of course.'

Good grief, I thought. I hadn't the experience of the connections of the stricken revered maestro. 'I'd work hard,' I said.

'You know what it entails?'

'I've seen Warrington Marsh everywhere, on the racecourse, at the sales. I know what he does, but not the extent of his authority.'

He cracked his second egg. 'Your brother says you've gotten a lot of general know-how. Tell me about it.'

I listed the jobs, none of which sounded any more impressive than they had in fact been.

He said, 'College degrees?' pleasantly.

'No, I left school at seventeen, and didn't go to university.'

'Private income?' he said. 'Any?'

'My godfather left some money for my schooling. There's still enough for food and clothes. Not enough to live on.'

He drank some coffee and hospitably poured me a second cup.

'Do you know which trainers I have horses with in the British Isles?'

'Yes, sir. Shell, Thompson, Miller, and Sandlache in England and Donavan in Ireland.'

'Call me Luke,' he said. 'I prefer it.'

'Luke,' I said.

He stirred sweetener into his coffee.

'Could you handle the finance?' he said. 'Warrington always has full responsibility. Do millions frighten you?'

I looked out at the vast blue ocean and told the truth. 'I think they do in a way, yes. It's too easy in the upper reaches to think of a nought or two as not mattering one way or another.'

'You need to spend to buy good horses,' he said. 'Could you do it?'

'Yes.'

'Go on,' he said mildly.

'Buying potentially good horses isn't the problem. Looking at a great yearling, seeing it move, knowing its breeding is as near perfect as you can predict, and being able to afford it, that's almost easy. It's picking the excellent from among the second rank and the unknowns, that's where the judgement comes in.'

'Could you guarantee that every horse you bought for me, or advised my trainers to buy, would win?'

'No, I couldn't,' I said. 'They wouldn't.'

'What percentage would you expect to win?'

'About fifty per cent. Some would never race, others would disappoint.'

He unaggressively, quietly, slowly and without pressure asked me questions for almost an hour, sorting out what I'd done, what I knew, how I felt about taking ultimate powers of decision over trainers who were older than myself, how I felt about dealing with the racing authorities, what I'd learnt about book-keeping, banking and money markets, whether I could evaluate veterinarian and nutritive advice. By the end I felt inside out; as if no cranny of my mind stayed gently unprobed. He would choose someone older, I thought.

'How do you feel,' he said finally, 'about a steady job, nine to five, weekends off, pension at the end of it?'

I shook my head from deep instinct, without thinking it out. 'No,' I said.

'That came from the heart, fella,' he observed.

'Well . . .'

'I'll give you a year and a ceiling beyond which you're not to spend. I'll be looking over your shoulder, but I won't interfere unless you get in a fix. Want to take it?'

I drew a deep breath and said, 'Yes.'

He leaned smilingly forward to shake my hand. 'I'll send you a contract,' he said, 'but go right on home now and take over at once. Things can fall apart too fast with no one in charge. So you go straight to Warrington's house, see his wife Nonie, I'll call her you're coming, and you operate from the office he's gotten there until you find a place of your own. Your brother told me you're a wanderer, but I don't mind that.' He smiled again. 'Never did like tame cats.'

Like so much else in American life the contract, when it swiftly followed me over the Pond, was in complete contrast to the relaxed approach of the man who offered it. It set out in precise terms what I must do, what I had discretion to do, what I must not do. It stated terms of reference I'd never have thought of. He had given me a great deal of freedom in some ways and none at all in others; but that, I supposed, was fair enough. He wouldn't want to stake his whole British operation on an unknown factor without enforceable safeguards. I took it to a solicitor who read it and whistled and said it had been drawn up by corporation lawyers who were used to munching managers as snacks.

'But do I sign it?' I said.

'If you want the job, yes. It's tough, but as far as I can see, fair.'

That had been eight months ago. I had come home to widespread and understandable disbelief that such a plum should have fallen my way. I had survived Nonie Marsh's resentment and Warrington's incoherent unhelpfulness; had sold several of Luke's unpromising two-year-olds without great loss, had cajoled the trainers into provisionally accepting me and done nothing sweat-makingly disastrous. Despite all the decisions and responsibility, I'd enjoyed every minute.

Cassie appeared in the doorway.

'Aren't you going to get out of that bath?' she demanded. 'Just sitting there smiling.'

'Life's good.'

'And you'll be late.'

I stood up in the water and as she watched me straighten she said automatically, 'Mind your head.' I stepped out on to the floor, and kissed her, dripping down my neck.

'For God's sake, get dressed,' she said. 'And you need a shave.' She gave me a towel. 'The coffee's hot, and we're out of milk.'

I flung on a few clothes and went downstairs, dodging beams and low doorways on the way. The cottage we'd rented in the village of Six Mile Bottom (roughly six miles south of Newmarket) had been designed for seventeenth-century man, who hadn't suffered the dietetic know-how of the twentieth. And would seven feet, I wondered, ducking into the kitchen, be considered normal in the twenty-fifth?

We had lived in the cottage all summer and in spite of its low ceilings it suited us fine. There were apples now in the garden, and mists in the mornings, and sleepy wasps trying to find warm cracks in the eaves. Red tiled floors and rugs downstairs, dining-room surrendered to office, sitting-room cosy round an as yet untried hearth; red-checked curtains, rocking chairs, corn dollies and soft lights. A townspeople's country toy, but enough, I sometimes thought, to make one want to put down roots.

Bananas Frisby had found it for us. Bananas, long-time friend, who kept a pub in the village. I'd called in there one day on my way back to Newmarket and told him I was stuck for somewhere to live.

'What's wrong with your old boat?'

'I've grown out of it.'

He gave me a slow glance. 'Mentally?'

'Yeah. I've sold it. And I've met a girl.'

'And this one,' he suggested, 'isn't ecstatic about rubbing down dead varnish?'

'Far from.'

'I'll keep it in mind,' he said, and indeed he called me a week later at Warrington's house and said there was a tarted-up cottage down the road from him that I could go and look at: the London-based owners didn't want to sell but could do with some cash, and they'd be willing to let it to someone who wouldn't stay for ever.

'I told them you'd the wanderlust of an albatross,' he said. 'I know them, they're nice people, don't let me down.'

Bananas personally owned his almost equally old pub, which was very slowly crumbling under his policy of neglect. Bananas had no family, no heirs, no incentive to preserve his worldly goods; so when each new patch of damp appeared inside his walls he bought a luxurious green potted plant to hide it. Since I'd known him, the shiny-leafed camouflage had multiplied from three to eight: and there was a vine climbing now through the windows. If anyone ever remarked about the dark patches on the walls, Bananas said the plants had caused then, and strangers never realized it was the other way round.

Bananas' main pride and joy was the small restaurant, next door to the bar, in which he served *cuisine minceur* of such perfection that half the passing jockeys of England ate there religiously. It had been over his dried, crisp, indescribable roast duck that I'd first met him, and like a mark well hooked had become an addict. Couldn't count the *délices* I'd paid for since.

He was already up as usual when I waved to him on my way to the gallops: sweeping out, cleaning up, opening his windows wide to get rid of the overnight fug. A fat man himself, he nonetheless had infinite energy, and ran the whole place with the help of two women, one in the bar and one in the kitchen, both of whom he bossed around like a feudal lord. Betty in the kitchen cooked stolidly under his eagle eye and Bessie in the bar served drinks with speed bordering on sleight-of-hand. Bananas was head-waiter and every other sort of waiter, collecting orders, delivering food, presenting bills, cleaning and relaying tables, all with a deceptive show of having all day to chat. I'd watched him at it so often that I knew his system; he practically never wasted time by going into the kitchen. Food appeared from Betty through a vast serving hatch shielded from the public view, and dirty dishes disappeared down a gentle slide.

'Who washes up?' I'd said once in puzzlement.

'I do,' Bananas said. 'After closing time I feed it all through the washer.'

'Don't you ever sleep?'

'Sleep's boring.'

He needed, it seemed, only four hours a night.

'And why work so hard? Why not have more help?'

He looked at me pityingly. 'Staff cause as much work as they do,' he said. And I'd found out later that he closed the restaurant every year towards the end of November and took off to the West Indies, returning in late March when the Flat racing stirred back to life. He hated the cold, he said: worked at a gallop for eight months for four months' palm trees and sun.

That morning on the Limekilns, Simpson Shell was working his best young prospect and looking smug. The eldest of Luke Houston's five trainers, he had been resigned to me least and still had hang-ups which showed on his face every day.

'Morning, William,' he said, frowning.

'Morning, Sim.' I watched him with the rangy colt upon whom the Houston hope of a classic next season was faintly pinned. 'He's moving well,' I said.

'He always does.' The voice was slighting and impatient. I smiled to myself. Neither compliments nor soft soap, he was saying, were going to change his opinion of the upstart who had overruled him in the matter of selling two two-year-olds. He had told me he disagreed strongly with my weeding-out policy, even though I'd put it to him beforehand and discussed every dud to be discarded. 'Warrington never did that,' he'd thundered, and he'd warned me he was writing to Luke to complain.

I never heard the result. Either he'd never written or Luke had backed me up; but it consolidated his Derry-wards hostility, not least because although I had saved Luke Houston a stack of pointless training fees I had at the same time deprived Simpson Shell. He was waiting, I knew, for the duds to win for their new owners so that he could crow, and it was my good luck that so far they hadn't.

Like all Luke's trainers, he trained for many other owners besides. Luke's horses at present constituted about a sixth of his string, which was too high a percentage for him to risk losing them altogether: so he was civil to me, but only just.

I asked him about a filly who had had some heat in her leg the previous evening, and he grumpily said it was better. He hated me to take a close interest in his eight Houston horses, yet I guessed that if I didn't, another letter would be winging to California complaining that I was neglecting my duties. Sim Shell, I thought ruefully, couldn't be pleased.

Over in the Bury Road, Mort Miller, younger, neurotic, fingers snapping like fire crackers, told me that Luke's ten darlings were eating well and climbing the walls with eagerness to slaughter the opposition. Mort had considered the sale of three no-gooders a relief, saying he hated the lazy so-and-sos and grudged them their oats. Mort's horses were always as strung up as he was, but they certainly won when it mattered.

I dropped in on Mort most days because it was he, for all his positive statements, who in fact asked my opinion most.

Once a week, usually fitting in with race meetings, I visited the other two trainers, Thompson and Sandlache, who lived thirty miles from each other on the Berkshire Downs, and about once a month I spent a couple of days with Donavan in Ireland. With them all, I had satisfactory working arrangements, they on their part admitting that the two-year-olds I'd got rid of were of no benefit to themselves, and I promising that I would spend the money I'd saved on the training fees on extra yearlings in October.

I would be sorry, I thought, when my year was over.

Driving home from Mort's, I stopped in the town to collect a radio I'd been having repaired, and again to fill up with petrol, and again at Bananas' to pick up some beer.

Bananas was in the kitchen prodding some marinating veal. Opening time still lay an hour ahead. Everything in the place was gleaming and fresh and the plants grew damply in their pots.

'There was a fellow looking for you,' Bananas said.

'What sort of fellow?'

'Big man. Didn't know him. I told him where your cottage was.' He scowled at Betty, who was obliviously peeling grapes. 'I told him you were out.'

'Did he say what he wanted?'

'Nope.'

He shed an apron and took his bulk into the bar. 'Too early for you?' he said, easing behind the counter.

'Sort of.'

He nodded and methodically assembled his usual breakfast; a third of a tumbler of brandy topped up with two scoops of vanilla-walnut ice cream.

'Cassie went off to work,' he said, reaching for a spoon.

'You don't miss much.'

He shrugged. 'You can see that yellow car a mile off, and I was out front cleaning the windows.' He stirred the ice cream into the brandy and with gourmand enjoyment shovelled the first instalment into his mouth. 'That's better,' he said.

'It's no wonder you're fat.'

He merely nodded. He didn't care. He told me once that his size made his fat customers feel better and spend more, and that his fat customers in search of a miracle outnumbered the thin.

He was a natural eccentric, himself seeing nothing unusual in anything he did. In various late-night sessions, he'd unbuttoned a little of his inner self, and under the surface geniality I'd had glimpses of a deep pessimism, a moroseness which looked with despair at the inability of the human race to live harmoniously on the beautiful earth. He had no politics, no god, no urge to agitate. People, he said, were known to starve on rich fertile tropical earth; people stole their neighbour's lands; people murdered people from racial hate; people tortured and murdered in the name of freedom. It sickened him, he said. It had been going on from pre-history, and it would go on until the vindictive ape was wiped out.

'But you yourself seem happy enough,' I'd once said.

He looked at me darkly. 'You're a bird. Always on the wing. You'd be a sparrowhawk if you hadn't such long legs.'

'And you?'

'The only option is suicide,' he said. 'But right now it's not necessary.' He'd deftly poured himself another brandy, and lifted the glass in a sort of salute. 'Here's to civilization, damn it.'

His real fore-names, written over the pub doorway, were John James, but his nickname was a pudding. 'Bananas Frisby', a hot fluffy confection of eggs, rum, bananas and orange, was an item nearly always on his menu, and 'Bananas' he himself had become. It suited his outer persona well, but his inner, not at all.

'You know what?' he said.

'What?'

'I'm growing a beard.'

I looked at the faint shadow on the dark jaw. 'It needs compost,' I said.

'Very funny. The days of the big fat slob are over. What you see is the start of the big fat distinguished innkeeper.' He took a large spoonful of ice cream and drank some of the liquid as a chaser, wiping the resulting white moustache off on the back of his hand.

He wore his usual working clothes: open-necked shirt, creaseless grey flannels, old tennis shoes. Thinning dark hair scattered his scalp haphazardly, with one straight lock falling over an ear, and as Frisby in the evenings wasn't all that different from Frisby in the mornings I couldn't see a beard transforming the image. Particularly not, I thought interestedly, while it grew.

'Can you spare a tomato or two?' I said. 'Those Italian ones?'

'For your lunch?'

'Yeah.'

'Cassie doesn't feed you.'

'It's not her job.'

He shook his head over the waywardness of our domestic arrangements, but if he had had a wife I wondered which one of them would have cooked. I paid for the beer and the tomatoes, promised to bring Cassie to admire the whiskers, and drove home.

Life for me was good, as I'd told Cassie. Life at that moment was a long way from Bananas' world of horrors.

I parked in front of the cottage and walked up the path juggling radio, beer and tomatoes in one hand and fishing for keys with the other.

One doesn't expect people to leap out of nowhere waving baseball bats. I had merely a swift glimpse of him, turning my head towards the noise of his approach, seeing the solid figure, the savagery, the raised arm. I hadn't even the time to think incredulously that he was going to hit me before he did it.

The crashing blow on my moving head sent me dazed and headlong, shedding radio, beer cans, tomatoes on the way. I fell half on the path and half on a bed of pansies and lay in a pulsating semi-consciousness in which I could smell the earth but couldn't think.

Rough fingers twined themselves into my hair and pulled my head up from its face-down position. As if from a great distance away from my closed eyes a harsh deep voice spoke nonsensical words.

'You're not – ' he said. *'Fuck it.'*

He dropped my head suddenly and the second small knock finished the job. I wasn't aware of it. In my conscious mind, things simply stopped happening.

The next thing that impinged was that someone was trying to lift me up, and that I was trying to stop him.

'All right, lie there,' said a voice. 'If that's how you feel.'

How I felt was like a shapeless form spinning in a lot of outer space. He tried again to pick me up and things inside the skull suddenly shook back into order.

'Bananas,' I said weakly, recognizing him.

'Who else? What happened?'

I tried to stand up and staggered a bit, trampling a few more long-suffering pansies.

'Here,' Bananas said, catching me by the arm, 'come into the house.' He semi-supported me, and found the door was locked.

'Keys,' I mumbled.

'Where are they?'

I waved a vague arm, and he let go of me to look for them. I leant against the doorpost and throbbed. Bananas found the keys and came towards me and said in anxiety. 'You're covered in blood.'

I looked down at my red-stained shirt. Fingered the cloth. 'That blood's got pips in,' I said.

Bananas peered at my chest. 'Your lunch.' He sounded relieved. 'Come on.'

We went into the cottage where I collapsed into a chair and began to sympathize with migraine sufferers. Bananas searched in random cupboards and asked plaintively for the brandy.

'Can't you wait until you get home?' I said without criticism.

'It's for you.'

'None left.'

He didn't press it. He may have remembered that it had been he, a week ago, who'd emptied the bottle.

'Can you make tea?' I said.

He said resignedly, 'I suppose so,' and did.

While I drank the resulting nectar, he told me that he'd seen a car driving away from the direction of the cottage at about eighty miles an hour down the country road. It was the car, he said, of the man who'd asked for me earlier. He had been at first puzzled and then disquieted, and had finally decided to amble down to see if everything was all right.

'And there you were,' he said, 'looking like a pole-axed giraffe.'

'He hit me,' I said.

'You don't say.'

'With a baseball bat.'

'So you saw him,' Bananas said.

'Yeah. Just for a second.'

'Who was he?'

'No idea.' I drank some tea. 'Mugger.'

'How much did he take?'

I put down the tea and patted the hip pocket in which I carried a small notecase. The wallet was still there. I pulled it out and looked inside. Nothing much in there, but also nothing missing.

'Pointless,' I said. 'What did he want?'

'He asked for you,' Bananas said.

'So he did.' I shook my head which wasn't a good idea as it sent little daggers in all cranial directions. 'What exactly did he say?'

Bananas gave it some thought. 'As far as I can remember, he said, "Where does Derry live?"'

'Would you know him again?' I asked.

He pensively shook his head. 'I shouldn't think so. I mean, I've a general impression – not young, not old, roughish accent – but I was busy, I didn't pay all that attention.'

Oddly enough, though I'd seen him for only a fraction of the time Bananas had, I had a much clearer recollection of my attacker. A freeze view, like a snapshot, standing framed in my mind. A thick-set man with yellowish skin, greyish about the head, intent eyes darkly shadowed. The blur on the edge of the snapshot was the downward slash of his arm. Whether the memory was reliable, or whether I'd know him again, I couldn't tell.

Bananas said, 'Are you all right to leave?'

'Sure.'

'Betty will finish those grapes and stare into space,' he said. 'The old cow's working to rule. That's what she says. Working to rule, I ask you. She doesn't belong to a union. She's invented her own bloody rules. At the moment rule number one is that she doesn't do anything I don't directly tell her to.'

'Why not?'

'More pay. She wants to buy a pony to ride on the Heath. She can't ride, and she's damn near sixty.'

'Go on back,' I said smiling. 'I'm OK.'

He semi-apologetically made for the door. 'There's always the doctor, if you're pushed.'

'I guess so.'

He opened the door and peered out into the garden. 'There are beer cans in your pansies.'

He went out saying he would pick them up, and I shoved myself off the chair and followed him. When I got to the door he was standing on the path holding three beer cans and a tomato and staring intently at the purple and yellow flowers.

'What is it?' I said.

'Your radio.'

'I've just had it fixed.'

He looked at me. 'Too bad.'

Something in his tone made me totter down the path for a look. Sure enough, my radio lay in the pansies: what was left of it. Casing, dials, circuits, speaker, all had been comprehensively smashed.

'That's nasty,' Bananas said.

'Spite,' I agreed. 'And a baseball bat.'

'But *why*?'

'I think,' I said slowly, 'that maybe he thought I was someone else. After he'd hit me, he seemed surprised. I remember him swearing.'

'Violent temper,' said Bananas, looking at the radio.

'Mm.'

'Tell the police,' he said.

'Yeah.'

I took the beer from him and sketched a wave as he walked briskly up the road. Then I stared for a while at the shattered radio thinking slightly disturbing thoughts: like what would my head have looked like if he hadn't stopped after one swipe.

With a mental shiver, I went back indoors and applied my concussion to writing up my weekly report sheet for Luke Houston.

13

I never did get around to consulting the doctor or calling the police. I couldn't see anything productive coming from spending the time.

Cassie took the whole affair philosophically but said that my skull must be cracked if I didn't want to make love.

'Double ration tomorrow,' I said.

'You'll be lucky.'

I functioned on two cylinders throughout the next day and in the evening Jonathan rang, as he sometimes did, keeping a long-distance finger on little brother's pulse. He had never grown out of the *in loco parentis* habit and nor, to be honest, did I want him to. Jonathan, six thousand miles away, was still my anchor, my most trusted friend.

A pity about Sarah, of course. I would have seen more of Jonathan if I could have got on better with Sarah. She irritated me like an allergy rash with her bossiness and her sarcasm, and I'd never been able to please her. I'd thought at one time that their marriage was on the way to the cemetery and I hadn't grieved much, but somehow or other they'd retreated from the brink. She certainly seemed softer with Jonathan nowadays, but when I was around the old acid rose still in her voice, and I never stayed long in their house. Never staying long in one place was in fact, according to her, one of my least excusable faults. I ought to buckle down, she said, and get a proper job.

She was looking splendid these days, slender as a girl and tawny with the sun. Many, I supposed, seeing the fair hair, the good bones, the still tight jawline, the grace of movement, would have envied Jonathan his young-at-forty-five wife. And all, as far as I knew, without the plastic surgeon's knife.

'How's Sarah?' I said automatically. I'd been asking after her religiously most of my life, and not caring a jot. The truce she and I maintained for Jonathan's sake was fragile; a matter of social form, of empty politeness, of unfelt smiles, of asking after health.

'She's fine,' he said. 'Just fine.' His voice after all these years had taken on a faint inflection and many of the idioms of his adopted country. 'She sends you her best.'

'Thanks.'

'And you?' he said.

'Well enough considering some nutter hit me on the head.'

'What nutter?'

'Some guy who came here and lay in wait, and took a bash at me.'

'Are you all right?'

'Yeah. No worse than a racing fall.'

'Who was he?' he asked.

'No idea. He asked for directions from the pub, but he'd got the wrong man. Maybe he asked for Terry . . . it sounds much the same. Anyway, he blasted off when he found he'd made a slight error, so that's that.'

'And no harm done?' he asked insistently.

'Not to me, but you should see my radio.'

'What?'

'When he found I was the wrong guy, he took it out on my radio. I wasn't awake, mind you, at that point. But when I came round, there it was, smashed.'

475

There was a silence on the other end, and I said, 'Jonathan? Are you still there?'

'Yes,' he said. 'Did you see the man? What did he look like?'

I told him: fortyish, greyish, yellowish. 'Like a bull,' I said.

'Did he say anything?'

'Something about me not being who he expected, and fuck it.'

'How did you hear him if you were knocked out?'

I explained. 'But all that's left is a sore spot for the hair brush,' I said, 'so don't give it another thought.'

We talked about this and that for the rest of our customary six minutes, and at the end he said, 'Will you be in tomorrow night?'

'Yes, I should think so.'

'I might call you back,' he said.

'OK.' I didn't bother to ask him why. He had a habit of not answering straightfoward questions with straightforward answers if it didn't suit him, and his noncommittal announcement told me that this was one of those times.

We said amicable goodbyes and Cassie and I went to bed and renewed our normal occupation.

'Do you think we'll ever be tired of it?' she said.

'Ask me when we're eighty.'

'Eighty is impossible,' she said, and indeed it seemed so to us both.

Cassie went to Cambridge every day in her little yellow car to spend eight hours behind a building society desk discussing mortgages. Cassie's mind was full of terms like with-profits endowment and early redemption charges, and I thought it remarkable, sometimes, that she'd never suggested a twenty-five year millstone around my own neck.

I'd once before tried living with someone: nearly a year with a cuddly blonde who wanted marriage and nestlings. I'd felt stifled and gone off to South America and behaved abominably, according to her parents. But Cassie wasn't like that: if she wanted the same things she didn't say so, and maybe she realized, as I did, that I always came back to England, that the homing instinct was fairly strong. One day, I thought, one *distant* day . . . and maybe with Cassie . . . I might, just perhaps, and with all options open, buy a house.

One could always sell it again, after all.

Jonathan did telephone again the following evening, and came straight to the point.

'Do you,' he said, 'remember the summer when Peter Keithly got killed in his boat?'

'Of course, I do. One doesn't actually forget one's own brother being tangled up in a murder.'

'It's fourteen years ago,' he said doubtfully.

'Things that happen when you're fifteen stay sharp in your mind for ever.'

'I guess you're right. Anyway, you know who I mean by Angelo Gilbert.'

'The bumper-off,' I said.

'As you say. I think the man who hit you on the head may be Angelo Gilbert.'

A great one, my brother, for punching the air out. On a distinctly short breath I said, 'You sound very calm about it.' But then of course he would. He was always calm. In the scariest crisis it would be Jonathan who spoke and acted as if nothing unusual was happening. He'd carried me out of a fire once as a small child and I'd thought that somehow nothing was the matter, nothing was really wrong with the flames and the roaring and crashing all around us, because he'd looked down at me and smiled.

'I checked up,' he said. 'Angelo Gilbert got out of prison seventeen days ago, on parole.'

'Out – '

'It would take him a while to orientate himself and to find you. I mean, if it was him, he would have thought you were me.'

I sorted my way through that and said, 'What makes you think it was him?'

'Your radio, really. He seemed to enjoy destroying things like that. Televisions. Stereos. And he'd be forty now, and his father reminded me of a bull. What you said took me right back.'

'Good grief.'

'Yes.'

'You really think it was him?'

'I'm afraid it's possible.'

'Well,' I said, 'now that he knows he got the wrong guy, maybe he won't bother me again.'

'Monsters don't go away if you don't look at them.'

'What?'

'He may come back.'

'Thanks very much.'

'William, take it seriously. Angelo was dangerous in his twenties and it sounds as if he still is. He never did get the computer programs he killed for, and he didn't get them because of me. So take care.'

'It might not have been him.'

'Act as if it was.'

'Yeah,' I said. 'So long, Professor.' The wryness in my voice must have been plain to him.

'Keep off horses,' he said.

I put the receiver down ruefully. Horses, to him, meant extreme risk.

'What's the matter?' Cassie said. 'What did he say?'

'It's all a very long story.'

'Tell it.'

I told it on and off over the next few hours, remembering things in pieces and not always in the order they'd happened, much as Jonathan had told it to me all those years ago. Before going off to Canada to shoot he had collected me straight from school at the end of that summer term and we'd

477

gone to Cornwall, just the two of us, for a few days' sailing. We'd had great holidays there two or three times before, but that year it blew a gale and poured with rain continuously, and to amuse me while we sat and stared through the dripping yacht club windows waiting for the improvement which never came, he'd told me about Mrs O'Rorke and Ted Pitts and the Gilberts, and how he'd stuck magnets in the cassettes. I'd been so fascinated that I hadn't minded missing the sailing.

I wasn't sure that I'd been shown every alley of the labyrinth; my quiet schoolmasterly brother had been reticent in patches and I'd always guessed that it was because probably in some way he'd used his guns. He never would let me touch them, and the only thing I ever knew him to be scared of was having his precious firearms certificate taken away.

'So there you are,' I said finally. 'Jonathan got Angelo tossed into clink. And now he's out.'

Cassie had listened with alternating alarm and amusement, but it was doubt that remained in the end.

'So what now?' she said.

'So now, if Angelo's on the rampage, hostilities may be resumed.'

'Oh no.'

'And there are certain disadvantages that Derry number two may have to contend with.' I ticked them off on my fingers. 'One, I can't shoot. Two, I know practically nothing about computers. And three, if Angelo's come charging out of jail intending to track down his lost crock of gold, I've no idea where it is or even if it still exists.'

She frowned. 'Do you think that's what he wants?'

'Wouldn't you?' I said gloomily. 'You spend fourteen years in a cell brooding over what you lost and dreaming of vengeance and yes, you're going to come out looking for both – and a small detail like having attacked the wrong man isn't going to put you off.'

'Come to bed,' Cassie said.

'I wonder if he thinks the way he used to.' I looked at her increasingly loved face. 'I don't want him busting in here to hold you hostage.'

'With no Jonathan to cut the telephone wires and send for the posse? Come to bed.'

'I wonder how he did it?'

'What?'

'Cut the wires. It isn't that easy.'

'Climbed the pole with a pair of scissors,' she said.

'You can't climb a pole. There aren't any footholds except at the top.'

'Why are you wondering about it after all these years? Come to bed.'

'Because of a bang on the head.'

She said, 'Are you really anxious?'

'Uneasy.'

'You must be. I've mentioned bed three times and you're still sitting down.'

I grinned at her and rose to my feet – and at that moment an almighty crash on the front door burst it open with splintering wood and a broken lock.

Angelo stood in the gap. Stood for less than a second regaining his balance from the kick which had brought him in, stood with the baseball bat swinging and his face rigid with ill intent.

Neither Cassie nor I had time to protest or yell. He waded straight in, laying about him, smashing anything near him, a lamp, some corn dollies, a vase, a picture . . . the television. Like a whirlwind demented, he devastated the pretty interior, and when I leapt at him I met a fist in the face and a fast knee which missed my groin, and I smelled his sweat and heard his breath rasp from exertion and took in what he was grittily saying: and it was just my name and Jonathan's, over and over.

'Derry – Derry – Fucking *Derry*.'

Cassie tried to help me, and he slashed at her with the heavy wooden bat and connected with her arm. I saw her stumble from the pain of it and in a fury I put one of my own arms round his neck and tried to yank his head back, to hurt him enough to make him drop his weapon and probably if the truth were told to throttle him. But he knew more about dirty fighting than I'd ever learned and it took him about two elbow jabs and a scrunching backhand jerk of my fingers to prise me loose. He shook me off with such a force that I half fell, but still clung to his clothes with octopus tentacles, not wanting to be thrown clear so that he could get another swing with that bat.

We crashed around the broken room with me sticking to him with at least his equal ferocity and him struggling to get free; and it was Cassie, in the end, who finished it. Cassie who had grabbed the brass coal scuttle from the hearth by its shining handle and swung it in an arc at arm's length, aiming at Angelo's head. I saw the flash of its gleaming surface and felt the jolt through Angelo's body: and I let go of him as he fell in a sprawl on the carpet.

'Oh, God,'Cassie was saying. 'Oh, God.' There were tears on her face and she was holding her left arm away from her body in a way I knew all too well.

Angelo was visibly breathing. Stunned only. Soon to awake.

'Have to tie him,' I said breathlessly. 'What've we got?'

Cassie painfully said, 'Washing line,' and before I could stop her she'd vanished into the kitchen, returning almost at once with a new line still in its package. Wire wrapped in plastic, the bright label said. Strong enough, indeed, for a bull.

While I was still uncoiling it with unsteady fingers, there was the sound outside of someone thudding up the path and I had time for a feeling of absolute despair before I saw who it was.

Bananas came to the dark doorway with a rush and there stood stock still taking in the ravaged scene.

'I saw his car come back. I was just closing up . . .'

'Help me tie him,' I said, nodding at Angelo, who was stirring ominously. 'He did all this. He's coming round.'

Bananas turned Angelo on to his face and held his hands together behind his back while I built knots around the wrists, and then continued with the job himself, leading the line down from the wrists to join it to two more knots round the ankles.

'He's broken Cassie's arm,' I said.

Bananas looked at her and at me and at Angelo, and walked purposefully over to where the telephone stood miraculously undamaged on its little table.

'Wait,' I said. 'Wait.'

'But Cassie needs a doctor. And I'll get the police . . .'

'No,' I said, 'not yet.'

'But you must.'

I wiped my nose on the back of my hand and looked remotely at the resulting smear of blood. 'There's some pethidine and a syringe in the bathroom,' I said. 'It'll do a lot to stop Cassie hurting.'

He nodded in understanding and said he would fetch it.

'Bring the box marked "Emergency". It's on the shelf over the bath taps.'

While he went and came back with his ever-surprising speed, I helped Cassie to sit on a chair and to rest her left arm on a cushion which I put on the telephone table. It was the forearm, I found, which was broken: both bones, probably, from the numb uselessness of her hand.

'William,' she said whitely, 'don't. It hurts. Don't.'

'Darling . . . darling . . . It has to have support. Just let it lie there. Don't fight it.'

She did mutely what I said and looked paler than ever.

'I didn't feel it,' she said. 'Not like this . . . not at first.'

Bananas brought the emergency box and opened it. I tore the syringe out of its sterile package and filled it from the ampoule of pethidine. Pulled Cassie's skirt up high over the sun-browned legs and fed the muscle-relaxing pain-killer into the long muscle of her thigh.

'Ten minutes,' I said, pulling the needle out and rubbing the place with my knuckle. 'A lot of the pain will go. Then we'll be able to take you to the casualty department of Cambridge hospital to get it set. Nowhere nearer will be open at this time of night.'

She nodded slightly with the first twitch of a smile, and on the floor Angelo started trying to kick.

Bananas again walked towards the telephone and again I stopped him.

'But William – '

I looked around at the jagged evidence of a passionate need for revenge; the explosion of fourteen years of pent-up hate.

I said, 'He did this because my brother got him jailed for murder. He's out on parole. If we call the police he'll be back inside.'

'Then, of *course*,' Bananas said, picking up the receiver.

'No,' I said. 'Put it down.'

480

He looked bewildered. Angelo on the floor began mumbling as if in delirium; a mixture of atrocious swear words and loud incomprehensible unfinished sentences.

'That's stir talk,' said Bananas, listening.

'You've heard it before?'

'You hear everything in the end in my trade.'

'Look,' I said. 'I get him sent back to jail and then what happens? It wouldn't be so long next time before he was out, and he'd have a whole new furious grudge to avenge. And by that time he might have learned some sense and not come waving a piece of wood and going off half-cock, but wait until he'd managed to get a pistol, and sneak up on me one day three, four years from now, and finish me off. This . . .' I waved a hand, 'isn't an act of reason. I'm only Jonathan's brother. I myself did him no harm. This is anger against life. Blind, colossal, ungovernable rage. I can do without him focusing it all on me personally in the future.' I paused. 'I have to find a better . . . a final solution. If I can.'

'You can't mean . . .' Bananas said tentatively.

'What?'

'To . . . to . . . No, you couldn't.'

'Not that final solution, no. Though it's quite a thought. Cement wellingtons and a downwards trip in the North Sea.'

'Tankful of piranhas,' Cassie said.

Bananas looked at her with relief and almost laughed, and finally put the telephone receiver back in its cradle.

Angelo stopped mumbling and came fully awake. When he realized where he was and in what condition, the skin, which had until then been pale, became redly suffused: the face, the neck, even the hands. He rolled halfway over onto his back and filled the room with the intensity of his rage.

'If you start swearing,' I said, 'I'll gag you.'

With an effort he said nothing, and I looked at his face squarely and fully for the first time. There wasn't a great deal left of the man whose picture I had once pored over in a newspaper; not youth, not black hair, not narrow jaw, not long thin nose. Age, heredity, prison food, all had given him fatty deposits to blur the outlines of the head and bulk the body.

Average brains, Jonathan had said. Not clever. Relies on his frightening-power, and gets results from that. Despises everyone. Calls them creeps and mugs.

'Angelo Gilbert,' I said.

He jerked, and looked surprised, as if he had thought I wouldn't know him: and nor would I have, if Jonathan hadn't called.

'Let's get it straight,' I said. 'It was not my brother who sent you to prison. You did it to yourself.'

Cassie murmured, 'Criminals in jail are there voluntarily.'

Bananas looked at her in surprise.

'My arm feels better,' she said.

I stared down at Angelo. 'You chose jail when you shot Chris Norwood. Those fourteen years were your own fault, so why take it out on *me*?'

It made no impression. I hadn't really thought it would. Blaming one's troubles on someone else was average human nature.

Angelo said, 'Your fucking brother tricked me. He stole what was mine.'

'He stole nothing of yours.'

'He did.' The words were bass-voiced, fierce and positive, a growl in the throat. Cassie shivered at the menace Angelo could generate even tied up in ignominy on a cottage floor.

The crock of gold, I thought suddenly, might have its uses.

Angelo seemed to be struggling within himself but in the end the words tore out of him, furious, frustrated, still bursting with an anger that had nowhere to go. '*Where is he?*' he said. 'Where's your fucking brother? I can't find him.'

Saints alive . . .

'He's dead,' I said coldly.

Angelo didn't say whether or not he believed me but the news did nothing for his general temper. Bananas and Cassie displayed a certain stillness, but thankfully kept quiet.

I said to Bananas, 'Could you watch him for a minute while I make a phone call?'

'Hours if you like.'

'Are you all right?' I asked Cassie.

'That stuff's amazing.'

'Won't be long.' I picked the whole telephone off the table beside her and carried it into the office, closing the door as I went.

I called California, thinking that Jonathan would be anywhere but home, that I'd get Sarah, that it would be siesta time under the golden sun. But Jonathan was in, and he answered.

'I just had a thought,' I said. 'Those tapes that Angelo Gilbert wanted, have you still got them?'

'Good grief,' he said. 'I shouldn't think so.' A pause while he reflected. 'No, we cleared everything out when we left Twickenham. You remember, we sold the furniture and bought new out here. I got rid of pretty well everything. Except the guns, of course.'

'Did you throw the tapes away?'

'Um,' he said. 'There was a set I sent to Mrs O'Rorke and got back again. Oh yes, I gave them to Ted Pitts. If anyone still has them it would be Ted. But I shouldn't think they'd be much use after all these years.'

'The tapes themselves, or the betting system?'

'The system. It must be long out of date.'

It wouldn't matter too much, I thought.

'There are a lot of computer programs out here now for helping you win on horses,' Jonathan said. 'Some of them work, they say.'

'You haven't tried them?'

'I'm not a gambler.'

'Oh yeah?'

'What do you want the tapes for?' he said.

'To tie Angelo up in knots again.'

'Take care.'

'Sure. Where would I find Ted Pitts?'

He told me doubtfully to try the East Middlesex Comprehensive, where they'd both been teaching, but said it was unlikely he was still there. They hadn't been in touch with each other at all since he'd emigrated. Perhaps I could trace Ted through the Schoolmasters Union, who might have his address.

I thanked him and disconnected, and went back into the sitting-room, where everyone looked much as I'd left them.

'I have a problem,' I said to Bananas.

'Just one?'

'Time.'

'Ah. The essence.'

'Mm.' I stared at Angelo. 'There's a cellar under this cottage.'

Angelo had no fear: one had to give him that. I could see quite clearly that he understood I meant not to let him go, yet his only reaction was aggressive and set him struggling violently against the washing line.

'Watch him,' I said to Bananas. 'There's some stuff in the cellar. I'm going to clear it out. If he looks like getting free, give him another bash on the head.'

Bananas looked at me as if he'd never seen me before; and perhaps he hadn't. I put a quick apologetic hand on Cassie's shoulder as I went, and in the kitchen opened the latched wooden door which led to the steps to the cellar.

Down there it was cool and dry: a brick-lined room with a concrete floor and a single light bulb swinging from the ceiling. When we had come to the cottage we had found the garden chairs stacked in there, but they were now outside on the grass, leaving only oddments like a paraffin stove, some tins of paint, a step-ladder and a stack of fishing gear. I carried everything in relays up the steps and dumped it all in the kitchen.

When I'd finished there was nothing in the cellar to help a captive; yet I would still have to keep him tied because of the nature of the lockless door. It was made simply of upright planks with bracing bars across the top, centre and bottom, the whole screwed together with the screwheads thankfully on the kitchen side. Across near the top there were six thumb-sized holes, presumably for ventilation. A good enough barrier against most contingencies, but not to be trusted to withstand the sort of kick with which the enemy had battered his initial way in.

'Right,' I said, going back into the sitting-room. 'Now you, Angelo, are going into the cellar. Your only alternative is an immediate return to jail, as all this . . .' I indicated the room '. . . and that . . .' Cassie's arm '. . . will cancel your parole and send you straight back behind bars.

'You bloody can't,' he said furiously.

'I bloody can. You started this. You damn well take the consequences.'

'I'll get you *busted*.'

'Yeah. You try it. You got it wrong, Angelo. I'm not my brother. He was clever and wily and he tricked you silly, but he would never use physical force; and I will, you mug, I will.'

Angelo used words that made Bananas wince and glance apprehensively at Cassie.

'I've heard them before,' she said.

'You've a choice, Angelo,' I said. 'Either you let my friend and me carry you carefully down the steps without struggling, or you struggle and I pull you down by the legs.'

The loss of face in not struggling proved too much. He tried to bite me as I bent down to put my arms under his armpits, so I did what I'd said; grasped the line tying his ankles and dragged him feet foremost out of the sitting-room, through the kitchen and down the cellar steps, with him yelling and swearing the whole way.

14

I tugged him well away from the stairs, let go of his legs and returned to the kitchen. He shouted after me blasphemously and I could still hear him when the door was shut. Let him get on with it, I thought callously; but I left on the single light, whose switch was outside on the kitchen wall.

I wedged the latch shut by sliding a knife handle through the slot, and for good measure stacked the step-ladder, the table and a couple of chairs into a solid line between the refrigerator and the cellar door, making it impossible for it to open normally into the kitchen.

In the sitting-room and without hustling, I said, 'OK. Decision time, mates.' I looked at Bananas. 'It's not your fight. If you'd rather, you can go back to your dishwashing and forget this ever happened.'

He looked resignedly round the room. 'I promised you'd leave this place as you found it. Practically pledged my soul.'

'I'll replace what I can. Pay for the rest. And grovel. Will that do?'

'You can't manage that brute on your own.' He shook his head. 'How long do you mean to keep him?'

'Until I find a man called Pitts.' I explained to him and Cassie what I wanted to do and why, and Bananas sighed and said it seemed fairly sensible in the circs, and that he would help where he could.

We shoe-horned Cassie gently into my car and I drove her to Cambridge while Bananas in his effective way set himself to tidy the sitting-room. There wasn't a great deal one could do at that point about the splintered and unclosable front door, and he promised to stay in the cottage until we got back.

In the event it was only I who returned. I sat with Cassie through the long wait in the silent hospital while they tried to find someone to X-ray her arm, but it seemed that after midnight the radiology department was firmly shut, with all the radiologists asleep in their own homes, and only the direst surgical emergency would recall them.

Cassie was given a careful splint from shoulder to fingernails and also another pain-killer and a bed: and when I kissed her and left she said, 'Don't forget to feed the bull,' which the nurses put down to drug-induced lightheadedness.

Bananas was asleep when I got back, flat out on the sofa and dreaming I dare say of palm trees. The mess I'd left behind was miraculously cleared with every broken fragment out of sight. There were many things missing but overall it looked more like a room the owners would recognize. Gratefully I went quietly into the kitchen and found my barricade altered and strengthened with four planks which had been lying in the garage, the door now wedged shut from top to bottom.

The light switch was up. Except for whatever dim rays were crawling through the ventilation holes, Angelo was lying in the dark.

Although I'd been quiet I'd woken Bananas, who was sitting up pinching the bridge of the nose and blinking heavy eyelids open and shut.

'All the pieces are in the garage,' he said. 'Not in the dustbin. I reckoned you might need them, one way or another.'

'You're great,' I said. 'Did Angelo try to get out?'

Bananas made a face. 'He's a horrible man, that.'

'You talked to him?'

'He was shouting through the door that you'd stopped his circulation by tying his wrists too tight. I went to see, but you hadn't, his fingers were pink. He was halfway up the stairs and he tried to knock me over. Tried to sweep my legs from under me and make me fall. God knows what he thought it would achieve.'

'Probably to scare me into letting him go.'

Bananas scratched himself around the ribs. 'I came up into the kitchen and shut the door on him, and switched his light off, and he went on howling for ages about what he'd do to you when he got out.'

Keeping his courage up, I thought.

I looked at my watch. Five o'clock. Soon be light. Soon be Friday with all its problems. 'I guess,' I said yawning, 'that a couple of hours shut-eye would do no harm.'

'And that one?' He jerked his head towards the kitchen.

'He won't suffocate.'

'You're a revelation to me,' Bananas said.

I grinned at him and I think he thought me as ruthless as our visitor. But he was wrong. I was fairly sure that Angelo that night had come back to kill, to finish off what he had earlier started, knowing by then who I was and not expecting a Cassie. I was soft compared with him.

Bananas walked home to his dishwasher and I took his place on the sofa, feeling the bedroom too far away out of touch. Despite the hectic night I went to sleep immediately and woke with mind-protesting reluctance to switch off the alarm clock at seven o'clock. The horses would be working on the Heath. Simpson Shell had set up a trial of two late-developing three-year-olds, and if I wasn't there to watch he'd be writing to Luke Houston to say I was a shirker . . . and I wanted anyway, Angelo or no Angelo, to see how those horses went.

I loved the Heath in the early mornings with the manes blowing under the wide skies. My affection for horses was so deep and went back so far that I couldn't imagine life without them. They were a friendly foreign nation living in our land, letting their human neighbours tend them and feed them, accepting them as servants as much as masters. Fast, fascinating, essentially untamed, they were my landscape, my old shoes, the place to where my heart returned, as necessary to me as the sea to sailors.

Even on that morning they lifted my spirits and I watched the trial with a concentration Angelo couldn't disrupt. One of the three-year-olds finished most decisively fast and Simpson said with careful civility that he hoped I would report to Luke how well the colt was looking.

'I'll tell Luke you've done wonders with him. Remember how unbalanced he looked in May? He'll win next week, don't you think?'

He gave me the usual ambivalent stare, needing my approbation but hating it. I smiled internally and left him to drive the short distance to where Mort was directing his string.

'All OK?' I asked.

'Well, yes,' Mort said. 'Genotti's still shaping up well for the Leger.' He flicked his fingers six times rapidly. 'Can you come back to the house for breakfast? The Bungay filly is still not eating well, and I thought we might discuss what we could do. You sometimes have ideas. And there's Luke's bill. I want to explain one or two items before you query them.'

'Mort,' I interrupted him regretfully, 'could we postpone it for a day or two? Something's come up that I'll have to deal with first.'

'Oh? Oh,' he sounded put out, because I'd never refused him before. 'Are you sure?'

'Really sorry,' I said.

'I might see you this afternoon,' he said, fidgeting badly.

'Um, yes. Of course.'

He nodded with satisfaction and let me go with good grace, and I doubted whether I would in fact turn up on Newmarket racecourse for that day's programme, even though three of Luke's horses were running.

On my way through the town I stopped at a few shops which were open early and did some errands on my prisoner's account, buying food and one or two small comforts. Then I rocketed the six miles to the village and stopped first at the pub.

Bananas, looking entirely his usual self, had done the dishes, cleaned the bar, and put Betty's back up by saying she was too old to start learning to ride.

'The old cow's refusing to make the celery mousse for lunch. Working to her stupid rules.' He disgustedly assembled his breakfast, adding chopped ginger as a topping to the ice cream and pouring brandy lavishly over the lot. 'I went down to the cottage again. Not a peep from our friend.' He stirred his mixture with anticipation. 'You can't hear him from outside, however loud he yells. I found that out last night. You'll be all right if you keep any callers in the garden.'

'Thanks.'

'When I've finished this, I'll come and help you.'

'Great.'

I hadn't wanted to ask him, but I was most thankful for his offer. I drove on down to the cottage and unloaded all the shopping into the kitchen, and Bananas appeared in his tennis shoes while I was packing food into a carrier. He looked at the small heap of things I'd put ready by the door.

'Let's get it over,' he said. 'I'll carry this lot.'

I nodded. 'He'll be blinded at first by the light, so even if he's got himself free we should have the advantage.'

We began to remove the barricade from against the door, and when it would open satisfactorily I took the knife out of the latch, picked up the carrier, switched on the cellar light and went into the cage.

Angelo was lying face down in the middle of the floor, still trussed the way we'd left him: arms behind his back, white clothes line leading slackly between tied wrists and tied ankles.

'It's morning,' I said cheerfully.

Angelo barely moved. He said a few low words of which 'turd' was the only one distinguishable.

'I've brought you some food.' I dumped in one corner the carrier bag which in fact contained two sliced loaves, several cartons of milk, some water in a plastic bottle, two large cooked chickens, some apples and a lot of various candy bars and chocolate. Bananas silently dumped his own load which consisted of a blanket, a cheap cushion, some paperback books and two disposal polystyrene chamber pots with lids.

'I'm not letting you out,' I said to Angelo, ' but I'll untie you.'

'Fuck you,' he said.

'Here's your watch.' I had slipped it off his wrist the evening before to make the tying easier. I took it out of my pocket and put in on the floor near his hand. 'Lights out tonight at eleven,' I said.

It seemed prudent at that point to search Angelo's pockets, but all he was carrying was money. No knives, no matches, no keys: nothing to help him escape.

I nodded to Bananas and we both began to untie the knots, I the wrists, Bananas the ankles, but Angelo's struggles had so tightened our original work that it took time and effort to remove it. Once Angelo was free we coiled the line and retreated up the stairs, from where I watched him move stiffly into a kneeling position with his arms loose and not yet working properly.

The air in the cellar had seemed quite fresh. I closed the door and fixed the latch and Bananas restacked the barricade with methodical thoroughness.

'How much food did you give him?' he asked.

'Enough for two to four days. Depends on how fast he eats it.'

'He's used to being locked up, there's that about it.'

Bananas, I thought, was busy stifling remaining doubts. He shoved the four planks into place between the cellar door and the refrigerator, casually remarking that during the night he'd sawn the wood to fit.

'More secure that way,' he said. 'He'll not get out.'

'Hope you're right.'

Bananas stood back, hands on hips, to contemplate his handiwork, and indeed I was as sure as one could be that Angelo couldn't kick his way out, particularly as he would have to try it while standing on the stairs.

'His car must be here somewhere,' I said. 'I'll look for it after I've phoned the hospital.'

'You phone, I'll look,' Bananas said, and went on the errand.

Cassie, I was told, would be having her arm set under anaesthetic during the morning. I could collect her at six that evening if all went well.

'May I speak to her?'

'One moment.'

Her voice came slowly and sleepily on to the line. 'I'm pie-eyed with pre-med,' she said. 'How's our guest?'

'Happy as a kangaroo with blisters.'

'Hopping . . . mad?'

'That pre-med isn't working,' I said.

'Sure is. My body's floating but my brain's fizzing along in zillions of sparks. It's weird.'

'They say I can fetch you at six.'

'Don't . . . be late.'

'I might be,' I said.

'You don't love me.'

'Yeah.'

'Sweet William,' she said. 'A pretty flower.'

'Cassie, go to sleep.'

'Mm.'

She sounded infinitely drowsy. 'Goodbye,' I said, but I don't think she heard.

I telephoned next to her office, told her boss she'd fallen down the cellar steps and broken her arm, and that she'd probably be back at work sometime the next week.

'How irritating,' he said. 'Er . . . for her, of course.'

'Of course.'

Bananas came back as I was putting down the receiver and said that Angelo's car was parked harmlessly at the top of the lane where the hard surface petered out into muddy cart track. Angelo had left the keys in the ignition. Bananas dumped them on the table.

'Want anything, shout,' he said. I nodded gratefully and he padded off, a power-house in a suit of blubber.

I set about the task of finding Ted Pitts, telephoning first to Jonathan's old school, the East Middlesex Comprehensive. A female voice there crisply told me that no one of that name was presently on the staff, and that none of the present staff could help me as they were not there: the new term would not start for another week. The only master who had been teaching in the school fourteen years ago would be, she imagined, Mr Ralph Jenkins, assistant headmaster, but he had retired at the end of the summer term and in any case it would be unlikely that any of his past assistants would have kept in touch with him.

'Why not?' I asked curiously.

After the faintest of hesitations the voice said levelly, 'Mr Jenkins himself would have discouraged it.'

Or in other words, I thought, Mr Jenkins had been a cantankerous old bastard. I thanked her for as little as I had realiztically expected and asked if she could tell me the address of the Schoolmasters Union.

'Do you want their number as well?'

'Yes please.'

She told me both, and I put through a call to their offices. Ted Pitts? Edward? I suppose so, I said. Could I wait? Yes, I could.

The answering voice, a man's this time, shortly told me that Edward Farley Pitts was no longer a member. He had resigned his membership five years previously. His last known address was still in Middlesex. Did I want it? Yes please, I said.

Again I was given a telephone number along with the address. Another female voice answered it, this time with music and children's voices loud in the background.

'What?' she said, 'I can't hear you.'

'Ted Pitts,' I shouted. 'Can you tell me where he lives?'

'You've got the wrong number.'

'He used to live in your house.'

'What? Wait a minute . . . shut up, you lousy kids. What did you say?'

'Ted Pitts . . .'

'Terry, shut off that bleeding stereo. Can't here myself think. Shut it off. Go on, shut it off.'

489

The music suddenly stopped.

'What did you say?' she said again.

I explained that I wanted to find my lost friend, Ted Pitts.

'Guy with three daughters.'

'That's right.'

'We bought this house off him. Terry, you knock Michelle's head on that wall one more time and I'll rattle your teeth. Where was I? Oh yes, Ted Pitts. He gave us an address to send things on to but it's years ago and I don't know where my husband put it.'

It was really important, I said.

'Well if you hold on I'll look. Terry, *Terry*!' There was the sound of a slap and a child's wail. The joys of motherhood, I thought.

I held on for an age listening to the scrambled noise of the squabbling siblings, held on for so long I thought she had forgotten all about me and simply left me off the hook, but in the end she did come back.

'Sorry I've been so long, but you can't put your hand on a thing in this house. Anyway, I've found where he moved to.'

'You're a doll,' I said, writing it down.

She laughed in a pleased fashion. 'Want to call round? I'm fed up to the teeth with these bloody kids.'

'School starts next week.'

'Thank the Lord.'

I disconnected and tried the number she had given me, but to this one there was no reply. Ten minutes later, again no reply.

I went to the kitchen. All quiet from the cellar. I ate some cornflakes, padded restlessly about and tried the number again.

Zilch.

There was something, I thought, looking at it, that I could immediately do about the front door. It wouldn't at the moment even fit into the frame, but given a chisel and some sandpaper . . . I fetched them from the tool-rack in the garage and reduced the sharply splintered patches to smooth edges, shutting the door finally by totally removing the broken lock. It looked all right from the outside but swung inward at a touch: and we had sweet but inquisitive neighbours who called sometimes to sell us honey.

I again dialled Ted Pitts's possible number. No reply.

Shrugging, I tugged a small chest of drawers across inside the front door and climbed out through the dining-room window. Drove down to the pub: told Bananas the way in.

'Do you expect *me* – ?'

'Not really. Just in case.'

'Where are you going?' he asked.

I showed him the address. 'It's a chance.'

The address was in Mill Hill on the northern outskirts of London. I drove there with my mind resolutely on the traffic and not on Cassie, unconscious, and Angelo, captive. Crunching the car at that point could be the ultimate disaster.

The house, when I found it, proved to be a middle-sized detached affair in a street of trees and somnolence; and it was empty.

I went up the driveway and looked through the windows. Bare walls, bare floors, no curtains.

With sinking spirits I rang the bell of the house next door, and although it was clearly occupied there was no one in there either. I tried several more houses, but none of the people I spoke to knew anything more of Ted Pitts than yes, perhaps they had seen some girls going in and out, but of course with all the shrubs and trees one was shielded from one's neighbours, which meant, of course, that also one couldn't see them.

It was in one of the houses obliquely opposite, from where only a corner of the Pittses' front garden was visible, that in the end I found some help. The front door was opened a foot by a large woman in pink hair rollers with a pack of assorted small dogs roaming round her legs.

'If you're selling, I don't want it,' she said.

I exercised on her the story I had by then invented, saying that Ted Pitts was my brother, he'd sent me his new address but I'd lost it, and I wanted to get in touch with him urgently. After six repetitions, I almost believed it.

'I didn't know him,' she said, not opening the door any wider. 'He didn't live there long. I never even saw him, I don't think.'

'But, er, you noticed them move in . . . and out.'

'Walking the dogs, you see.' She looked fondly down at the pack. 'I go past there every day.'

'Do you remember how long ago they left?'

'It must be ages. Funny your brother didn't tell you. The house was for sale for weeks after they'd gone. It's only just been sold, as a matter of fact. I saw the agents taking the board down just last week.'

'You don't happen to remember,' I said carefully, 'the name of the agents?'

'Goodness,' she said. 'I must have walked past it a hundred times. Just let me think.' She stared at her pets, her brow wrinkled with concentration. I could still see only half of her body but I couldn't tell whether the forbidding angle of the door was designed to keep the dogs in or me out.

'Hunt bleach,' she exclaimed.

'What?'

'Hunt comma B L E A C H.' She spelled it out. 'The name of the agents. A yellow board with black lettering. You'll see it all over the place, if you look.'

I said fervently, 'Thank you very much.'

She nodded the pink rollers and shut herself in, and I drove around until I found a yellow board with Hunt, Bleach's local address: Broadway, Mill Hill.

The brother story brought its by now familiar crop of sympathetic and/or pitying looks, but finally gained results. A slightly sullen-looking girl said she thought the house had been handled by their Mr Jackman who was now away on his holidays.

'Could you look in the files?'

She took advice from various colleagues, who doubtfully agreed under my urging that perhaps in the circumstances she might. She went into an inner office, and I heard cabinet drawers begin to open and shut.

'Here you are, Mr Pitts,' she said, returning, and it took me a fraction to realize that of course I too would be Pitts. 'Ridge View, Oaklands Road.'

She didn't give a town. I thought: he's still *here.*

'Could you tell me how to get there?' I said.

She shook her head unhelpfully, but one of the colleagues said, 'You go back up the Broadway, right round the roundabout until you're pointing towards London, then first left, up the hill, turn right, that's Oaklands Road.'

'Terrific.' I spoke with heartfelt relief which they took as appropriate, and I followed their directions faithfully and found the house. It looked a small brown affair; brownish bricks, brown tiled roof, a narrow window each side of an oak front door, bushes screening much else. I parked in what seemed an oversized driveway outside a closed double garage, and doubtfully rang the doorbell.

There was no noise from inside the house. I listened to the distant hum of traffic and the nearer hum of bees round a tub of dark red flowers, and pressed the bell again.

No results. If I hadn't wanted to find Ted Pitts so much I would have given up and driven away at that point. It wasn't even the sort of road where one could enquire at a neighbour's: there were houses only on one side, with a steep wooded hillside rising on the other, and the houses themselves were far-spaced and reclusive, drawing themselves back from public view.

I rang a third time out of indecisiveness, thinking that I could wait, or come back, or leave a note begging Pitts to call me.

The door opened. A pleasant-looking girl-woman stood there; not young, not yet middle-aged, wearing a loosely flowing green sundress with broad straps over suntanned shoulders.

'Yes?' she said enquiringly. Dark curly hair, blue eyes, the brown glowing face of summer leisure.

'I'm looking for Ted Pitts,' I said.

'This is his house.'

'I've been trying to locate him. I'm the brother of an old friend of his. A friend he had years ago, I mean. Could I see him, do you think?'

'He isn't here at the moment.' She looked at me doubtfully. 'What's your brother's name?'

'Jonathan Derry.'

After the very slightest pause her face changed from watchfulness to welcome; a smile in remembrance of time past.

'Jonathan! We haven't heard from him for years.'

'Are you . . . Mrs Pitts?'

She nodded. 'Jane.' She opened the door wide and stepped back. 'Come in.'

'I'm William,' I said.

492

'Weren't you . . .' she frowned, 'away at school?'

'One does tend to grow.'

She looked up at me, 'I'd forgotten how long it was.' She led me across a cool dark hall. 'This way.'

We came to a wide stairway of shallow green-carpeted steps leading downwards, and I saw before me what had been totally invisible from the higher roadway, that the house was large, ultra-modern, built into the side of the hill and absolutely stunning.

The stairs led directly down to a huge room whose ceiling was half-open to the sky and whose floor was partly green carpet and partly swimming pool. There were sofas and coffee tables nearest the stairs and lounging chairs, bamboo with pink, white and green cushions, dotting the far poolside, out in the sun; and on either side wings of house spread out protectively, promising bedrooms and comfort and a life of delight. I looked at the spectacular and pretty room and thought no schoolmaster on earth could afford it.

'I was sitting over there,' Jane Pitts said, pointing to the sunny side. 'I nearly didn't answer the doorbell. I don't always bother.'

We walked around there, passing white trellised alcoves filled with plants and cushioned bamboo sofas with bathing towels casually thrown down. The pool water looked sea-green and peaceful, gleaming and inviting after my trudging search.

'Two of the girls are around somewhere,' Jane said. 'Melanie, our eldest, is married, of course. Ted and I will be grandparents quite soon.'

'Incredible.'

She smiled. 'We married at college.' She gestured to the chairs and I sat on the edge of one of the loungers while she spread out voluptuously on another. Beyond the house the lawn sloped grassily away to a wide sweeping view over north-west London, the horizon lost in misty purples and blues.

'This place is fantastic,' I said.

She nodded. 'We were so lucky to get it. We've only been here three months, but I think we'll stay for ever.' She pointed to the open roof. 'This all closes over, you know. There are solar panels that slide across. They say the house is warm all winter.'

I admired everything sincerely and asked if Ted were still teaching. She said without strain that he sometimes taught University courses in computer programming and that unfortunately he wouldn't be home until quite late the following evening. He would be so sorry to have missed me, she said.

'I would quite urgently like to talk to him.'

She gently shook her head. 'I don't honestly know where he is, except somewhere up near Manchester. He went this morning, but he didn't know where he'd be staying. In a motel somewhere, he said.'

'What time would he be back tomorrow?'

'Late. I don't know.'

She looked at the concern which must have shown plainly on my face and said apologetically, 'You could come early on Sunday, if you like, if it's that important.'

15

Saturday crawled.

Cassie wandered around with her plastered arm in a sling and Bananas jogged down to the cottage three or four times, both of them worried by the delay and not saying so. It had seemed reasonable on Thursday night to incarcerate Angelo with his handiwork still appalling us in the sitting-room and Cassie in pain, but by Saturday evening she and Bananas had clearly progressed through reservations and uneasiness to downright anxiety.

'Let him go,' Bananas said when he came late after closing time. 'You'll be in real trouble if anyone finds out. He knows now that you're no pushover. He'd be too scared to come back.'

I shook my head. 'He's too arrogant to be scared. He'd want his revenge, and he'd come back to take it.'

They stared miserably at each other. 'Cheer up,' I said. 'I was ready to keep him for a week – two weeks – as long as it took.'

'I just don't know,' Bananas said, 'how you could calmly go to the races.'

I'd gone uncalmly to the races. Also to the gallops in the morning and to Mort's for breakfast, but no one I had seen could have guessed what was going on at home. Behind a public front I found it fairly easy to hide an ongoing crime: hundreds of people did it, after all.

'I suppose he's still alive,' Cassie said.

'He was up by the door swearing at four o'clock.' Bananas looked at his watch. 'Nine and a half hours ago. I shouted at him to shut up.'

'And did he?'

'Just swore back.'

I smiled. 'He's not dead.'

As if to prove it Angelo started kicking the door and letting go with the increasingly familiar obscenities. I went into the kitchen and stood close to the barricade, and when he drew breath for the next verbal onslaught I said loudly, 'Angelo.'

There was a brief silence, then a fierce growling shout: *Bastard.*

'The light's going out in five minutes,' I said.

'I'll kill you.'

Maybe the heavily savage threat should have raised my goose bumps, but it didn't. He had been murderous too long, was murderous by nature, and I already knew it. I listened to his continuing rage and felt nothing.

'Five minutes,' I said again, and left him.

In the sitting-room Bananas was looking mildly piratical in his open-necked shirt and his sneakers and his four days' growth of harsh black beard, but he himself would never have made anyone walk the plank. The gloom and doom in his mind deplored what I was doing even while he condoned it, and I could almost sense him struggling anew with the old anomaly that to defeat aggression one might have to use it.

He sat on the sofa and in short order drank two stiff brandies with his arm round Cassie, who never minded. He was tired, he'd said, of us being out of his favourite tipple: he'd brought the bottle himself. 'Have some ice cream with it?' Cassie had suggested, and he'd said seriously, 'What flavour?'

I gave Angelo his five minutes and switched off the light, and there was a baleful silence from the cellar.

Bananas gave Cassie a bristly kiss, said she looked tired, said every plate in the pub needed washing, said 'Barbados!' as a toast, and tossed back his drink. 'God rest all prisoners. Good night.'

Cassie and I watched his disappearing back. 'He's half sorry for Angelo,' she said.

'Mm. A fallacy always to think that because you feel sorry for the tiger in the zoo he won't eat you, given the chance. Angelo doesn't understand compassion. Not other people's for him. He feels none himself. In others he sees it as a weakness. So never, my darling, be kind to Angelo expecting kindness in return.'

She looked at me. 'You mean that as a warning, don't you?'

'You've a soft heart.'

She considered for a moment, then found a pencil and wrote a message to herself in large letters on the white plaster.

REMEMBER TIGERS.

'Will that do?'

I nodded. 'And if he says his appendix is bursting or he's suffering from bubonic plague feed him some aspirins through the ventilation holes, and do it in a roll of paper, and not with your fingers.'

'He hasn't thought of that yet.'

'Give him time.'

We went upstairs to bed but as on the previous night I slept only in brief disturbed snatches, attuned the whole time to any noise from the cellar. Cassie slept more peacefully than before, the cast becoming less of a problem as she grew used to it. Her arm no longer hurt, she said; she simply felt tired. She said play would be resumed when the climate got better.

I watched the dark sky lighten to streaks of navy-blue clouds across a sombre orange glow, a strange brooding dawn like the aura of the man downstairs. Never before, I thought, had I entered a comparable clash of wills; never tested so searchingly my willingness to command. I had never thought of myself as a leader, and yet, looking back, I'd never had much stomach to be led.

In recent months I had found it easier than I'd expected to deal with Luke's five trainers, the power seeming to develop as the need arose. The power to keep Angelo in the cellar, that too had arisen, not merely physically, but also in my mind. Perhaps one's capacity always expanded to meet the need: but what did one do when the need was gone? What did generals do with their full-grown hubris when the war was over? When the whole world no longer obeyed when they said jump?

I thought: unless one could adjust one's power-feeling perpetually to the current need, one could be headed for chronic dissatisfaction with the fall of fate. One could grow sour, power-hungry, despotic. I would shrink back, I thought, to the proper size, once Angelo was solved, once Luke's year was over. If one saw that one had to, perhaps one might.

The fierce sky slowly melted to mauve-grey clouds drifting over a sea of gold and lingeringly then to gentle white over palest blue, and I got up and dressed, thinking that the sky's message was false: the problems didn't fade with the sun and Cain was still downstairs.

Cassie's eyes, when I left, were saying all that her tongue wasn't. Hurry. Come back. I don't feel safe here with Angelo.

'Sit by the telephone,' I said. 'Bananas will run.'

She swallowed. I kissed her and drove away, burning up the empty Sunday-early roads to Mill Hill. It was still only eight-thirty when I turned into Oaklands Road, the very earliest that Jane Pitts had said I could arrive, but she was already up and in a wet bathing dress to answer the doorbell.

'Come in,' she said. 'We're in the pool'

'We' were two lithely beautiful teenage girls and a stringy man going bald who swam without splashing, like a seal. The roof was open to the fair sky and a waiting breakfast of cereals and fruit stood ready on one of the low bamboo tables, and none of the Pittses seemed to mind or notice that the new day was still cool.

The stringy man slithered out on to the pool's edge in a sleek economical movement and stood shaking the water from his head and looking approximately in my direction.

'I'm Ted Pitts,' he said, holding out a wet hand. 'I can't see a damn thing without my glasses.'

I shook the hand and smiled into the unfocused eyes. Jane walked round with some heavy black frames which converted the brown fish into an ordinary short-sighted mortal, and he dripped round the pool beside me to where his towel lay on a lounging chair.

'William Derry?' he said, blotting water out of his ears.

'That's right.'

'How's Jonathan?'

'Sends his regards.'

Ted Pitts nodded, towelled his chest vigorously and then stopped abruptly and said, 'It was you who told me where to get the form books.'

All those years ago . . . information so casually given. I glanced around the amazing house and asked the uppermost question. 'The betting system on those tapes,' I said. 'Did it really work?'

Ted Pitts's smile was of comprehensive contentment. 'What do you think?' he said.

'All this – '

'All this.'

'I never believed in it,' I said, 'until I came here the other day.'

He towelled his back. 'It's fairly hard work, of course. I shunt around a good deal. But with this to come back to . . . most rewarding.'

'How long . . .' I said slowly.

'How long have I been gambling? Ever since Jonathan gave me the tapes. That first Derby . . . I borrowed a hundred quid with my car as security to raise some stake-money. It was madness, you know. I couldn't have afforded to lose. Sometimes in those days we had hardly enough to eat. It was pretty well desperation that made me do it, but of course the system looked mathematically OK and it had already worked for years for the man who invented it.'

'And you won?'

He nodded. 'Five hundred. A fortune. I'll never forget that day, never. I felt so sick.' He smiled vividly, the triumph still childlike in its simplicity. 'I didn't tell anybody. Not Jonathan. Not even Jane. I didn't mean to do it again, you see. I was so grateful it had turned out all right, but the *strain* . . .' He dropped the damp towel over the arm of a chair. 'And then you know, I thought, why not?'

He watched his daughters dive into the pool with their arms round each other's waists. 'I only taught for one more term,' he said calmly. 'I couldn't stand the head of the Maths department. Jenkins, his name was.' He smiled. 'It seems odd now, but I felt oppressed by that man. Anyway, I promised myself that if I won enough during the summer holidays to buy a computer, I would leave at Christmas, and if I didn't, I'd stay and use the school's computer still, and be content with a wager now and then.'

Jane joined us, carrying a pot of coffee. 'He's telling you how he started betting? I thought he was crazy.'

'But not for long.'

She shook her head, smiling. 'When we moved out of our caravan into a house – bought it outright with Ted's winning – then I began to believe it would last, that it was safe. And now here we are, so well off it's embarrassing, and it's all thanks to your dear brother Jonathan.'

The girls climbed dripping out of the pool and were introduced as Emma and Lucy, hungry for breakfast. I was offered bran flakes, natural yoghurt, wheat germ and fresh peaches, which they all ate sparingly but with enjoyment.

I ate as well, but thought inescapably of Angelo and of Cassie alone with him in the cottage. Those planks would hold . . . they'd kept him penned in for two whole days. No reason to think they'd fail this morning . . . no reason, just a strong feeling that I should have persuaded her to wait with Bananas.

It was over coffee, when the girls were again swimming and Jane had disappeared into the house, that Ted said, 'How did you find me?'

I looked at him. 'Don't you mean why?'

'I suppose so. Yes.'

'I came to ask you to let me have copies of those tapes.'

He breathed deeply and nodded. 'That's what I thought.'

'And will you?'

He looked at the shimmering pool for a while and then said, 'Does Jonathan know you're asking?'

'Yeah. I asked him where the tapes were now, and he said if anyone knew, you would. You and only you, he said.'

Ted Pitts nodded again and made up his mind. 'It's fair. They're his, really. But I haven't any spare tapes.'

'I brought some,' I said. 'They're out in the car. Can I fetch them?'

'All right.' He nodded decisively. 'I'll change into dry clothes while you're getting them.'

I fetched the computer-type tapes I'd brought for the purpose, and he said, 'Six? You'll only need three.'

'Two sets?' I suggested.

'Oh. Well, why not?' He turned away. 'The computer's downstairs. Would you like to see it?'

'Very much.'

He led the way into the body of the house and we went down some carpeted stairs to a lower floor. 'Office,' he said succinctly, leading the way into a normal-sized room from which one could see the same wide view of London as upstairs. 'It's a bedroom really. Bathroom through there,' he pointed. 'Spare bedroom beyond.

The office was more accurately a sitting-room with armchairs, television, bookshelves and pinewood panelling. On an upright chair by one wall stood a pair of well-used mountain climbing boots, with the latest in thermal sleeping bags still half in its carton on the floor beside them. Ted followed my glance. 'I'm off to Switzerland in a week or two. Do you climb?'

I shook my head.

'I don't attempt the peaks,' he said earnestly. 'I prefer walking, mostly.' He pulled open a section of the pine panelling to reveal a long counter upon which stood a host of electronic equipment. 'I don't need all this for the racing programs,' he said, 'but I enjoy computers . . .' and he ran his fingers caressingly over the metal surfaces with the ardour of a lover.

'I've never seen those racing programs,' I said.

'Would you like to?'

498

'Please.'

'All right.' With the speed of long dexterity he fed a tape into a cassette re-corder and explained he was putting the machine to search for the file 'Epsom'. How much do you know about computers?' he said.

'There was one at school, way back. We played "Space Invaders" on it.'

He glanced at me pityingly. 'Everyone in this day and age should be able to write a simple program. Computer language is the universal tongue of the new world, as Latin was of the old.'

'Do you tell your students that?'

'Er . . . yes.'

The small screen suddenly announced 'READY?' Ted pressed some keys on the keyboard and the screen asked 'WHICH RACE AT EPSOM?' Ted typed DERBY, and the screen in a flash presented:

EPSOM: THE DERBY.

NAME OF HORSE?

He put in his own name and randomly answered the ensuing questions, ending with:

TED PITTS. WIN FACTOR: 24

'Simple,' I said.

He nodded. 'The secret is in knowing which questions to ask, and in the weighting given to the answers. There's nothing mysterious about it. Anyone could evolve such a system, given the time.'

'Jonathan says there are several of them in the United States.'

Ted nodded. 'I've got one of them here.' He opened a drawer and brought out what looked like a pocket calculator. 'It's a baby computer with quite elegant programs,' he said. 'I bought it out of curiosity. It only works on American racing of course, because one of its bases is that all tracks are iden-tical in shape, left-handed ovals. It is geared chiefly to prize money. I understand that if you stick to its instruction book religiously you can cer-tainly win, but of course like Liam O'Rorke's system you have to work at it to get results.'

'And never back a hunch?'

'Absolutely not,' he said seriously. 'Hunches are hopelessly unscientific.'

I looked at him curiously. 'How often do you go to the races?'

'To the races themselves? Practically never. I watch them, of course, on television, sometimes. But you don't need to to win. All you need are the form books and objectivity.'

It seemed to me a dry view of the world where I spent my life. Those beautiful creatures, their speed, their guts, their determination, all reduced to statistical probabilities and microchips.

'These copies of yours,' he said, 'do you want them open, so that anyone can use them?'

'How do you mean?'

'If you like, you can have them with passwords, so that they wouldn't work if anyone stole them from you.'

'Are you serious?'

'Of course,' he said, as if he were never anything else. 'I've always put passwords on all my stuff.'

'Er, how do you do it?'

'Easiest thing in the world. I'll show you.' He flicked a few switches and the screen suddenly announced 'READY?'

'You see that question mark,' Ted said. 'A question mark always means that the computer operator must answer it by typing something. In this case, if you don't type in the correct sequence of letters the program will stop right there. Try it. See what happens.'

I obediently typed EPSOM. Ted pressed the key marked 'Enter'.

The screen gave a sort of flick and went straight back to 'READY?'

Ted smiled. 'The password on this tape is QUITE. Or it is at the moment. One can change the password easily.' He typed QUITE and pressed 'Enter' and the screen flashed into WHICH RACE AT EPSOM?

'See the question mark?' Ted said. 'It always needs an answer.'

I thought about question marks and said I'd better not have passwords, if he didn't mind.

'Whatever you say.'

He typed BREAK and LIST 10-80, and the screen suddenly produced a totally different looking format.

'This is the program itself,' Ted said. 'See Line 10?'

Line 10 read INPUT A$: IF A$="QUITE" THEN 20 ELSE PRINT "READY?"

Line 15 read GO TO END.

Line 20 read PRINT "WHICH RACE AT EPSOM?"

'If you don't type QUITE,' Ted said, 'You never get to line 20.'

'Neat,' I agreed. 'But what's to prevent you looking at the program, like we are now, and seeing that you need to type QUITE?'

'It's easy to make it impossible for anyone to List the program. If you buy other people's programs, you can practically never List them. Because if you can't List them you can't make copies, and no one wants their work pinched in that way.'

'Um,' I said. 'I'd like tapes you *can* List, and without passwords.'

'OK.'

'How do you get rid of the password?'

He smiled faintly, typed 10 and then pressed 'Enter'. Then he typed LIST 10-80 again, but this time when the program appeared on the screen there was no Line 10 at all. Line 20 was the first.

'Elementary, you see,' he said.

'So it is.'

'It will take me quite a while to get rid of the passwords and make the copies,' he said. 'So why don't you go and sit by the pool. To be honest, I'd get on faster on my own.'

Pleased enough to agree, I returned to the lazy bamboo loungers and listened to Jane talking about her daughters. An hour crawled by before Ted reappeared bearing the cassettes, and even then I couldn't leave without an instructional lecture.

'To run those tapes, you'll need either an old Grantley personal computer, and there aren't many of them about nowadays, they're obsolete, or any type of company computer, as long as it will load from a cassette recorder.'

He watched my incomprehension and repeated what he'd said.

'Right,' I said.

He told me how to load Grantley BASIC, which was the first item on Side 1 of the tapes, into a company computer, which had no language of its own built in. He again told me twice.

'Right.'

'Good luck with them,' he said.

I thanked him wholeheartedly, and Jane also, and as quickly as decently possible set off on the drive home.

Half a mile down the road, compelled by a feeling of dread, I stopped by a telephone box and called Cassie. She answered at the very first ring and sounded uncharacteristically shaky.

'I'm so glad it's you,' she said. 'How long will you be?'

'About an hour.'

'Do hurry.'

'Is Angelo . . . ?'

'He's been banging ever since you left and wrenching at the door. I've been in the kitchen. He's shaking those planks, he'll have the door off its hinges if he goes on and on. I can't strengthen the barricade. I've tried, but with one arm – '

'Cassie,' I said. 'Go up to the pub.'

'But – '

'Darling, go. Please do.'

'What if he gets out?'

'If he gets out I want you safe up the road with Bananas.'

'All right.'

'I'll see you,' I said, and disconnected. Drove like the furies towards home, taking a chance here and there and getting away with it. Across Royston Heath like a streak, weaving through pottering Sunday-outing traffic. Through the town itself; snarling down the last stretch crossing the M11 motorway, and finally branching off the main road into Six Mile Bottom village.

Wondering all the way what Angelo would do if he did get free. Smash up the cottage? Set fire to it? Lie in wait somewhere for me to return.

The one thing he would not do was to go meekly away.

16

I walked carefully up the path to the lockless front door which we now no longer guarded with the chest because Cassie found climbing through the window too difficult.

The birds were singing in the garden. Would they sing if Angelo were among them, hidden in the bushes? No they wouldn't. I reached the door and pushed it open.

The cottage lay silent as if long deserted, and with spirits sinking I went through to the kitchen.

Angelo had ripped away one of the main timbers of the door and had dislodged two of the extra planks which had been wedging it shut. The door in fact was still closed, but the knife had gone from the latch.

The hole in the door was large enough to shove an arm through, but not to allow the passage of a grown man. The table and chairs and the two lowest planks hadn't shifted, but with the progress he'd made their stopping power was temporary. I had come not a minute too soon.

'Angelo,' I said.

He appeared almost instantly at the hole in the door, scowling furiously at my return. He put both hands into the gap and violently tried to wrench away the wood from each side, and I saw that he had already been bleeding from his exertions.

'I'm going to let you out,' I said. 'You can save your strength.'

'I'll get you.' The deep growl again. The statement of intent.

'Yeah,' I said. 'I dare say. Now listen, because you'll want to hear.'

He waited, eyes black with ferocity in the shadows.

I said, 'You believe that my brother cheated you out of some computer tapes. They weren't yours to start with, but we'll not argue about that. At this moment *I* have those tapes. They're here in the cottage. It's taken me a good while to get them, which is why you've stayed here this long in the cellar. I'll give you those tapes. Are you listening?'

He wouldn't say so, but his attention was riveted.

'You spent fourteen years brooding over the fortune you lost. I'll give it to you. Fourteen years swearing to kill my brother. He's dead. You came here to do violent damage, and for that you could lose your parole. I'm prepared not to report you. In return for the computer tapes and for your continued freedom you can clear out of here and henceforward leave me strictly alone.'

He stared through the door with little change of expression; certainly without joy.

I said, 'You may have been brooding over your revenge for so many years that you can't face not having the prospect of it there any longer to keep you going. You may fall apart from lack of purpose.' I shrugged. 'But *if* I give you liberty and the treasure you want, I'll expect the slate to be wiped clean between you and me.' I paused. 'Do you understand?'

He still said absolutely nothing.

'If you agree that what I'm offering is OK,' I said, 'you can throw out that knife you took from the door latch, and I will give you the three tapes and the keys to your car, which is still where you left it.'

Silence.

'If you choose not to accept that offer,' I said, 'I'll telephone to the police to come and fetch you, and they'll hear about you breaking my friend's arm.'

'They'll have you for keeping me in here.'

'Maybe. But if they do, you'll never get those tapes. And I mean it. *Never.* I'll destroy them immediately.'

He went away from behind the door but after a long minute he reappeared.

'You'll trick me,' he said. 'Like your brother.'

I shook my head. 'It's not worth it. I want you out of my life altogether and permanently.'

He made a fierce thrusting movement with his unshaven chin, a gesture which could be taken as assent.

'All right, then,' he said. 'Hand them over.'

I nodded. Turned away from him. Went into the sitting-room and sorted out one copy of each tape, shutting the three spares into a chest drawer. When I returned Angelo was still standing by the door; still suspicious, still wary.

'Tapes,' I showed him. 'Car keys.' I held them up. 'Where's the knife?'

He raised his hand and let me see it: a dinner knife, not very sharp, but destructive enough to be counted.

I laid the three cassettes on a small tray and held it out to him, and he put his arm through the hole to snatch them up.

'Now the knife,' I said.

He dropped it out on to the tray. I slid it into my hand and replaced it with the keys.

'All right,' I said. 'Go down the steps. I'll undo the barricade. Then you can come up and go out. And if you've any thoughts of rushing me, just remember your parole.'

He nodded sullenly.

'Have you still got that computer you bought fourteen years ago?'

'Dad smashed it. When I got sent down. Out of rage'

Like son, like father ... 'The tapes are still in the same computer language,' I said. 'Grantley Basic. The language itself is there, on Side 1. You'll need to know that.'

He scowled. Beyond him entirely to be placated, let alone pleased.

'Go on,' I said. 'I'll unbar the door.'

He disappeared from the impromptu window and I tugged away the effective planks and pulled the table and chairs from their stations, and stood finally out of his arms' reach behind them.

'Come up,' I called. 'Undo the latch and be on your way.'

He came out fast, clutching the cassettes in one bloodstained hand and the keys in the other: gave me a brief hard stare which nonetheless held little of the former menace, and disappeared through the sitting-room towards the front door. I followed and watched him go down the path, first quickening his step and almost running as he turned into the lane and then fairly sprinting out of sight towards where he'd left his car. In a short time he came blasting back again, driving as if he feared I would still somehow stop him; but in truth all I did want was to be rid of him once and for all.

The empty cellar stank like a lair of an animal.

I looked into it briefly and decided it was a job for a shovel, a hose, a broom and some strong disinfectant, and while I was collecting those things Bananas and Cassie waked anxiously along from the pub.

'We saw you come,' she said, 'and we saw him go. I wanted to be here but Bananas said it might snarl things up.'

'He was right.' I kissed her soundly, both from love and tension released. 'Angelo hates to lose face.'

'You gave him the tapes?' Bananas said.

'Yeah.'

'And may they choke him,' Cassie said.

I smiled. 'They may not. I'd guess Ted Pitts is worth a million.'

'Really?' Her eyebrows shot up. 'Then why don't we – ?'

'It takes time and work. Ted Pitts lives right at the London end of the M1, half a mile off the country's biggest artery. I'll bet he spends countless days beating up that road to towns in the north, traipsing round betting shops, sucking his honey. It's what I guess he does, anyway. He was near Manchester yesterday, his wife said. A different town every day, so that no one gets to know him.'

'What difference would that make?' Bananas said.

I explained what happened to constant winners. 'I'll bet there isn't a single bookie who knows Ted Pitts by sight.'

'If you did it,' Bananas said thoughtfully, 'I suppose they'd know you at once.'

I shook my head. 'Only on the racecourse. Round the backstreet betting shops in any big town I'd be just another mug.'

They both looked at me expectantly.

'Yeah,' I said. 'I can just see me spending my life that way.'

'Think of the loot,' Bananas said.

'And no tax,' said Cassie.

I thought of Ted Pitts's splendid house and of my own lack of amassed goods. Thought of him walking the upper slopes of Swiss mountains, restoring his spirit, wandering but coming home. Thought of my lack of a settled life-pattern and my hatred of being tied down. Thought of the way I'd enjoyed the past months, making decisions, running a business, knowing all the time it was just for a year, not a lifetime, and being reassured by such impermanency. Thought of spending hot summer days and wet winter afternoons in betting shops, playing the percentages, joylessly, methodically making a million.

'Well?' Bananas said.

'Maybe one day, when I'm hungry.'

'You've no sense.'

'You do it then,' I said. 'Give up the pub. Give up the cooking. Take to the road.'

He stared at me while he thought about it, then grimaced and said, 'There's more to life than making money. Not a lot, but some.'

'One of these days,' said Cassie with sweet certainty, 'You'll both do it. Not even a saint could sit on a goldmine and be too lazy to pick up the nuggets.'

'You think it's just lazy – ?'

'I sure do. Where's your buccaneering heart? Where's the glint of piracy? What about the battlecry of those old north-country industrialists – where there's muck there's brass?' She looked alight with enthusiasm, a glow I guessed derived as much from Angelo's absence as from the thought of an available fortune.

'If you feel the same when I've finished for Luke Houston,' I said, 'I'll give it a trial. Just for a while.'

'Picky,' she said. 'That's what you are.'

All the same it was in better spirits that I set about cleaning the cellar and making it fit for fishing gear to live in; and in the later afternoon, all three of us sat in the sun on the cottage grass while Cassie and Bananas discussed how they would spend the lolly they thought I would inevitably chase.

They already felt as I did that Angelo's revengeful lust had been at last dissipated, and they said he had even done us a favour as without his violent attack I would never have sought out Ted Pitts.

'Good can come of bad,' Cassie said with satisfaction.

And bad of good, I thought. Jonathan's conjuring tricks had trapped Angelo thoroughly and made it certain that he would be convicted empty handed. Had ensured that for fourteen years Angelo would be unable to kill anyone else. But that particular good sequence of actions which had seemed so final at the time had proved to be only a plug for a simmering volcano. The psychopathic young man had at length erupted as a full-blown coarsened thug, no longer as Jonathan had described him, occasionally high on the drug of recklessness, but more plainly, comprehensively, violent.

Time changed perspectives. From disasters could come successes, and from successes, disasters. A pity, I thought, that one could never perceive whether to weep or cheer at the actual event.

Our lives gradually quietened to sensible proportions. Cassie went back to work in a sling and Bananas invented a new delight involving liquid spiced beef: and I began a series of forays to stud farms to take preliminary peeks at the yearlings soon to be offered at the sales, all too aware that the climax of my year was approaching, the test by which Luke would judge me, looking back. To buy young stock that would win would be satisfactory; to buy a colt to sire a dynasty would be luck. Somewhere between the two lay an area in which judgment would turn out to have been good, indifferent or absent, and it was there that I hoped to make as few mistakes as possible.

For about a week I mosied around all over the place with detours to race meetings and to Luke's two trainers in Berkshire, and spent every spare waking minute with the Stud Book. Sim Shell said severely that he wished to be present and in full consultation whenever I bought anything for him personally to train, and Mort with every nerve twitching asked for Sir Ivor, Nijinsky and Northern Dancer, all at once, and at the very least.

Cassie came with me to the evening session on the first day of the sales, roaming about on the forever legs and listening engrossed to the gossip. Every year Newmarket sale ring saw fortunes lost quicker than crashing stock markets, but the talk was all of hope and expectation, of slashing speed and breeding potential, all first-day euphoria and unspent cheques.

'What excitement,' Cassie said. 'You can see it in every face.'

'The joy of acquisition. Disillusion comes next week. Then optimistic gloom. Then, if you're lucky, complacent relief.'

'But today . . .'

'Today,' I nodded. 'There's still the chance of buying the winner of the Derby.'

I bought two colts and a filly on that evening for staggering sums, reassured to a point by having competed against top echelons of bloodstock agents but pursued by the sapping fear that it was I who had pressed on too far, not they who had stopped too soon.

We stayed to the end of the programme, partly because of Cassie's fascination with a new world but also because it was when the big buyers had gone home that a bargain sometimes arose, and I did in fact buy the last lot of the day, a thin-looking pony-like creature, because I liked his bright eyes.

The breeder thanked me. 'Is it really for Luke Houston?'

'Yes,' I said.

'He won't be sorry. He's intelligent, that little colt.'

'He looks it.'

'He'll grow, you know,' he told me earnestly. 'His dam's family are all late growers. Come and have a drink. It isn't every day I sell one to Luke Houston.'

We went back, however, to drink and eat with Bananas, and from there to the cottage, where I sent off a telexed report to Luke, for whom our midnight was three in the afternoon.

Luke liked telexes. If he wanted to discuss what I'd sent he would telephone after his evening dinner, catching me at six in the morning before I'd left for the gallops, but more normally he would reply by telex or not at all.

The dining-room was filled with equipment provided by Luke: a video-disc recorder for re-watching and analysing past races, a print-out calculator, photo-copier, a row of filing cabinets, an electric typewriter, the telex machine and a complicated affair which answered the telephone, took messages, gave messages, and recorded every word it heard, including my own live conversations. It worked on a separate line from the telephone in the sitting room, a good arrangement which most simply divorced our private calls from his business, allowing me to pay for one and him the other. All he hadn't given me – or had had me collect from an unwilling Warrington Marsh – was a computer.

When I came down the following morning I found the telex had chattered during the night.

'Why didn't you buy the Fisher colt? Why did you buy the cheap colt? Give my best to Cassie.'

He had never actually met Cassie but only talked to her a few times on the telephone. The politeness was his way of saying that his questions were simply questions, not accusations. Any telexes which came without 'best to Cassie' were jump-to-it matters.

I telexed back. 'Two private owners who detest each other, Schubman and Mrs Crickington, beat each other up to three hundred and forty thousand for the Fisher colt, way beyond its sensible value. The cheap colt might surprise you yet. Regards, William.'

Cassie these days was being collected and brought back by a slightly too friendly man who lived near the pub and worked a street away from Cassie in Cambridge. She said he was putting his hand on her knee instead of the steering wheel increasingly often and she would be extremely glad to be rid of both him and the plaster. In other respects than driving the cast had been accommodated, and our night-time activities were back to their old joy.

By day we slowly repaired or replaced everything which had been smashed, using as reference the pieces Bananas had stacked in the garage. Television, vases, lamps, all as near as possible to the originals. Even six corn dollies hung again in their mobile group, dollies freshly and intricately woven from the shiny stalks of the new harvest by an elderly ethnic-smock lady who said you had to cut the corn for them specially nowadays by hand, because the combine harvesters chopped the straw too short.

Bananas thought that replacing the corn dollies might be going too far, but Cassie said darkly that they represented pagan gods who should be placated – and deep in the countryside *you never knew*.

I carpentered new pieces into both the damaged doors and fitted a new lock to the front. All traces of Angelo gradually vanished, all except his baseball bat which lay along the sill of the window which faced the road. We had consciously kept it there to begin with as a handy weapon in case he should come back, but even as day after peaceful day gave us a growing sense of ease we let it lie: another hostage to the evil eye, perhaps.

Jonathan telephoned me one evening and although I was sure he wouldn't approve of what I'd done I told him everything that had happened.

'You kept him in the *cellar*?'

'Yeah.'

'Good God.'

'It seems to have worked.'

'Mm. I can't help being sorry that Angelo has that system after all.'

'I know. I'm sorry too, after all you did to keep it from him. I really hated giving it to him. But you were right, he's dangerous, and I don't want to vanish to California, the life I want is right here on the English turf. And about the system . . . Don't forget, it isn't enough just to possess it, you'd have to operate it discreetly. Angelo knows just about nothing about racing, and he's impetuous and undisciplined, not cunning and quiet.'

'He may also,' Jonathan said, 'think that the system gives a winner every time, which it doesn't. Old Mrs O'Rorke said it steadily gave an average of one winner in three.'

'Angelo versus the bookies should be quite a match. And by the way, I told him you were dead.'

'Thanks very much.'

'Well you didn't want him turning up one day on your sunny doorstep, did you?'

'He'd never get a visa.'

'You can walk across the Canadian border,' I said, 'without anyone being the wiser.'

'And the Mexican,' he agreed.

I told him in detail about Ted Pitts's house, and he sounded truly pleased.

'And the little girls? How are they?'

'Grown up and pretty.'

'I envied him those children.'

'Did you?' I said.

'Yes. Well . . . there you are. It's the way life turns out.'

I listened to the regret in his voice and understood how much he himself had wanted a daughter, a son . . . and I thought that I too would regret it one day if I didn't . . . and that maybe it would be terrific fun if Cassie . . .

'Are you still there?' he said.

'Yeah. If I get married, will you come over to the wedding?'

'I don't believe it.'

'You never know. I haven't asked her yet. She might not want to.'

'Keep me posted.' He sounded amused.

'Yeah. How's Sarah?'

'Fine, thanks.'

'So long,' I said, and he said, 'So long,' and I put down the receiver with the usual feeling of thankfulness that I had a brother, and specifically that he was Jonathan.

More days passed. By the end of the first week's sales I'd bought twelve yearlings for Luke and lost five more to higher bidders, and I'd consulted with Sim until he was sick of it and given Mort a filly that was on her toes if not actually a dancer, and spent two evenings in the Bedford Arms with the Irish trainer Donavan, listening to his woes and watching him get drunk.

'There's more good horses in Ireland than ever come out,' he said, wagging an unsteady finger under my nose.

'I'm sure.'

'You want to come over, now. You want to poke around them studs, now, before you go to the sales.'

'I'll come over soon,' I said. 'Before the next sales, two weeks from now.'

'You do that.' He nodded sagely. 'There's a colt I have my eye on, way down below Wexford. I'd like to train that colt, now. I'd like for you to buy that little fella for Luke, that I would.'

In that particular year, as a trial, the first Newmarket Yearling Sales had been held early, at the beginning of September. The Premium Sales, when most of the bluest-blooded youngsters would come under the hammer, were as usual at the end of the month. The colt Donavan had his eye on was due to be sold two weeks ahead, but unfortunately not only Donavan had his eye on it. The whole of Ireland and most of England seemed also to have their optics swivelled that way. Even allowing for Irish exaggeration, that colt seemed the best news of the season.

'Luke would want that fella, now,' Donavan said.

'I'll bid for it,' I said mildly.

He peered boozily into my face. 'What you want to do, now, is to get Luke to say there's no ceiling. No ceiling, that's the thing.'

'I'll go to Luke's limit.'

'You're a broth of a boy, now. And it's write to Luke I did, I'll admit it, to say you were as green as a pea and no good to man nor horse, not in the job he'd given you.'

'Did you?'

'Well now, if you get me that little colt I'll write again and say I was wrong.' He nodded heavily and half fell off the bar stool. He was never drunk on the gallops or at the races or indeed by the sale ring itself, but at all other times – probably. The owners didn't seem to mind and nor did the horses: drunk or sober. Donavan produced as many winners year by year as anyone in Ireland. I didn't like or dislike him. I did business with him before ten in the morning and listened intently in the evenings, the time when through clouds of whisky he spoke the truth. Many thought him uncouth, and so he was. Many thought Luke would have chosen a smoother man with tidier social manners, but perhaps Luke had seen and heard Donavan's intimate way with horses, as I now had, and preferred the priceless good to a gaudier package. I had come to respect Donavan. Two solid days of his company were quite enough.

When the flood of purchasing trainers and agents and go-it-alone owners had washed out of the town temporarily, Sim gave a brown short-necked filly a final work-out and afterwards rather challengingly told me she was as ready as could be to win the last race on St Leger day, on Saturday.

'She looks great,' I said. 'A credit to your care.'

Sim half scowled. 'You'll be going to Doncaster, I suppose?'

I nodded. 'Staying up there, Friday night. Mort's running Genotti in the St Leger.'

'Will you help me saddle mine up?' Sim said.

I tried to hide my astonishment at this olive branch of epic proportions. He usually attempted to keep me as far from the runners as possible.

'Be glad to,' I said.

He nodded with customary brusqueness. 'See you there, then.'

'Good luck.'

He was going up on the Wednesday for the whole of the four-day meeting but I didn't particularly want to, not least because Cassie still found it difficult to manage on her own with the rigid arm. I left her on the Friday, though, and drove to Doncaster, and almost the first person I saw as I walked through the racecourse gates was Angelo.

I stopped abruptly and turned aside, willing him not to spot me, not to speak.

He was buying two racecards from one of the booths near the entrance, holding up the queue while he sorted out coins.

I supposed it was inevitable I would one day see him if he took to racegoing at all often, but somehow it was still a shock. I was glad when he turned away from the booth in the opposite direction to where I stood: there might be a truce between us but it was fragile at best.

I watched while he barged his way through the swelling crowd with elbows like battering rams and thighs like rocks: he was heading not to anywhere where he could place a bet but towards the less populated area near the rails of the track itself, where supporters had not yet flocked to see the first race. Reaching the rails, he stopped beside an elderly man in a wheelchair and unceremoniously thrust one of the racecards into his hands. Then he turned immediately on his heel and bulled his way purposefully towards the serried ranks of bookmakers inside the stands, where I lost sight of him, thankfully, for the rest of the day.

He was back, however, on the Saturday. Although I seldom bothered with gambling, I decided to have a small bet on Genotti in the St Leger, infected no doubt by Mort's fanatical eagerness, and as I stood near a little Welsh bookmaker whom I'd long known, I saw Angelo, thirty feet away, frowning heavily over a small notebook.

'Genotti,' my bookmaker friend said to his clerk who wrote down (in the book) every transaction, 'Three tenners at fives, William Derry.'

'Thanks, Taff,' I said.

Along the row Angelo began arguing about a price on offer, which was apparently less than he thought fair.

'Everyone else is at five to one.' His voice was a growl which I knew all too well.

'Try someone else, then. It's fours to you, *Mister* Gilbert.'

With half my mind I was satisfied that Angelo was indeed rushing in stupidly with the system where Liam O'Rorke and Ted Pitts had taken care not to tread, but also I was uneasy that he should be arousing opposition so soon. I positively needed for him to win for a while. I'd never envisaged him sticking to the anonymous drudgery required for long-term success, but the honeymoon period should not have been over.

Taff-the-bookmaker glanced over his shoulder at the altercation and gave his clerk an eyes-to-heaven gesture.

'What's all the fuss about?' I asked.

'He's a right git, that man.' Taff divided his comment impartially between him, his clerk, and the world in general.

'Angelo Gilbert.'

Taff's gaze sharpened on me directly. 'Know him, do you?'

'Somebody pointed him out . . . he murdered somebody, years ago.'

'That's right. Just out of jug, he is. And *stupid* – you wouldn't credit it.'

'What's he done?'

'He came up to York last week with a fistful of banknotes, laying it about as if there were no tomorrow, and us not knowing who he was at that moment. And there's us thinking we were all taking lollipops off a baby when whammo, this outsider he'd invested about six big ones on comes cantering in from nowhere and we're all paying out and wincing and scratching our heads over where he got the info, because the trainer hadn't as much as a quid on, as far as we knew. So Lancer, that bloke along there arguing with this Gilbert, he asks the geezer straight out who'd put him on to the winner, and the stupid git smirked and said Liam O'Rorke did.'

Taff peered at my face, which I felt must have mirrored my feeling of inner shock, but apparently it merely looked blank because Taff, who was a good sixty-plus, made a clicking sound with his mouth and said, 'Before your time, I suppose.'

'What was?'

Taff's attention was torn away by several customers who crowded to place bets, and he seemed vaguely surprised to see me still there when they'd gone.

'Are you that interested?' he asked.

'Got nothing else to do.'

Taff glanced along to where Angelo had been, but Angelo had gone. 'Thirty years ago. Thirty-five. Time does go quick. There was this old Irishman, Liam O'Rorke, he'd invented the only system I ever knew that would guarantee you'd win. Course, once we'd cottoned to him we weren't all that keen to take his bets. I mean, we wouldn't be, would we, knowing he had the edge on us somehow. Anyway, he would never part with his secret, how he did it, and it went with him to the grave, and good riddance, between you and me.'

'And now?'

'And now here's this geezer rocking us back on our heels with this huge win at York and then he's sneering at us and calling us mugs and saying we

don't know what's hit us yet, and what he's using on us is Liam O'Rorke's
old system resurrected, and now he's all indignant and complaining that we
won't give him a good price. Acting all hurt and angry.' Taff laughed con-
temptuously. 'I mean, how stupid can you get?'

17

Genotti won the St Leger by an easy four lengths.

Mort's excitement afterwards seemed to levitate him visibly off the
ground, the static electricity about him crackling in the dry September sunshine. He wrung my hand with bone-scrunching enthusiasm and danced
round the unsaddling enclosure giving rapturous responses to all who congratulated him, reacting with such uncomplicated delight to his victory that
he had all the crowd smiling. It was easy, I reflected, to think of Mort as
simple through and through, whereas, as I had gradually discovered, he traversed mental mazes of tortuous routes where pros battled cons like moves
on a chessboard, and the plans and solutions which seemed so obvious once
they had turned out to be right were the fruits of the mazes.

I collected my winnings from Taff, who gloomily said he would never have
given anyone five to one if he'd known beforehand that Genotti was Angelo
Gilbert's fancy.

'Did Angelo win?' I asked.

'Of course, he did. He must have had a grand on. None of us would take
his money at the finish.'

'So he didn't get fives?'

'More like evens,' he said sourly.

At evens, Angelo would still have doubled his money, but for Angelo that
might not be enough. Grievance, I could see, might raise a very ugly head.

'No system could win every single time,' I said. 'Angelo won't.'

'I dare say not,' Taff said with obstinacy. 'But you can take it from me that
no bookie on the racecourse will in future give that arrogant so-and-so much
more than evens, even if what he's backing is lame on three legs, carrying
two stone overweight and ridden by my old dad.'

'At evens, he wouldn't win over all,' I said.

'So who's crying? We're not in the loving-kindness business, you know.'

'Fleece the mugs?'

'You got it.'

He began paying out other successful punters with the rapidity of long practice but it was seldom that he would go home from a racetrack with less cash than he'd brought. Few bookmakers were gamblers at heart and only the good mathematicians survived.

I drifted away from him and drank some champagne with the similarly fizzing Mort and a little later helped Sim to saddle the filly, who made it another hooray-for-Houston day by a short head. Sim took it more calmly than Mort, but with a satisfaction at least as deep, and he seemed to be admitting and acknowledging at last that I was not an ignorant bossy upstart but a well-meaning colleague and that all Luke's successes worked for our joint good. I wasn't sure how or why his attitude had changed, I knew only that a month earlier a friendly drink together in a racecourse bar to celebrate a Houston winner would have been unthinkable.

Thinking more of Mort and Sim and the horses than of the still active spectre of Angelo, I drove from Doncaster to collect Cassie, and from there to a late dinner with Bananas. He too, it appeared, had backed Genotti, more than doubling my own winnings.

'I had a hundred on,' he said.

'I didn't know you ever bet.'

'On the quiet, now and then. Hearing all I do, how could I not?'

'So what did you hear about Genotti?'

He looked at me pityingly. 'Every time you've seen that colt work on the gallops, you've come back like a kid with tickets to the Cup Final.'

'More to the point,' Cassie said, 'if you'd used Liam O'Rorke's system, would it have come up with Genotti?'

'Ah.' I read Bananas's new menu and wondered what he meant by Prisoner Chicken. Said casually, 'Angelo Gilbert backed him.'

'What?'

I explained about Angelo, the bookmakers, and stupidity in general.

'He's blown it,' Cassie said, not without satisfaction.

I nodded. 'Into fragments.'

Bananas looked at me thoughtfully. 'What's it going to do for the dear man's temper?'

'It's not William's fault,' Cassie said.

'That trifle didn't stop him before.'

Cassie looked frowningly alarmed. 'What's Prisoner Chicken?' I said.

Bananas smirked. 'Breast of chicken marinated in lemon juice and baked under match-stick thin bars of herb pastry.'

'It sounds dry,' I said with jaundice.

'Bread and water are optional extras.'

Cassie laughed and Angelo retreated a little. We ate the Prisoner Chicken which was predictably a delight of juice and flavour and reminded us not at all of its inspiration.

'I'm going to Ireland tomorrow,' I said to Cassie. 'Like to come?'

'Ireland? There and back?'

I nodded. 'To see a man about a horse.'

'What else?'

So we spent some of my winnings on her fare, and went down south of Wexford to see the colt the world wanted: and half the world, it seemed, was there on the same errand, standing around an untidy stable yard with blank faces all carefully not expressing identical inner thoughts.

Cassie watched as the beautifully coupled brown yearling skittered around under the calming hands of the stud groom and unprofessionally pronounced him 'sweet'.

'A money machine on the hoof,' I said. 'Look at the greed in all those shuttered faces.'

'They just seem uninterested to me.'

'Enthusiasm puts the price up.'

One or two of the bored-looking onlookers advanced to run exploratory hands down the straight young bones, stepping back with poker-player non-committal eyes, the whole procedure hushed as if in church.

'Aren't you going to feel its legs?' Cassie asked.

'Might as well.'

I took my turn in the ritual, and found like everyone else that the young limbs were cool and firm with tendons like fiddle strings in all the right places. There was also a good strong neck, a well-shaped quarter and most importantly a good depth of chest. Quite apart from his pedigree, which resounded with Classic winners, one couldn't, I thought, even imagine a better-looking animal: all of which meant that the bidding at the sale on Wednesday would rise faster than Bananas Frisby.

We flew thoughtfully back to England and I sent a telex to Luke. 'Bidding for the Hansel colt will be astronomical. I've seen him. He's without fault. How high do you want me to go?'

To which, during the night, I received a reply. 'It's your job, fella. You decide.'

Ouch, I thought. Where is the ceiling? How high is disaster?

Newmarket filled up again for the new week of sales, the most important programme of yearling sales of the whole season. Everyone in racing with money to spend brought determination and dreams, and the four-legged babies came in horse-boxes from just up the road, from Kent and the Cotswolds, from Devon and Scotland, from across the Irish Sea.

The Hansel colt from Wexford was due to be sold at the prime time of seven-thirty on the Wednesday evening and by seven the high-rising banks of seats of the sale ring were invisible under a sea of bodies, Cassie somewhere among them. Down near the floor in the pen reserved for probable bidders, Donavan was breathing heavily at my elbow as he had been all afternoon, determinedly sober and all the gloomier for it.

'Now you get that little colt, now, you get him for me.' If he'd said it once he'd said it a hundred times, as if repetition of desire could somehow make the purchase certain.

They brought the colt into the ring in the sudden hush of a host of lungs holding back their breath all at once, and the light gleamed on the walking gem and he did in truth look like a prince who could sire a dynasty.

The bidding for him started not in thousands but in tens of thousands, leaping in seconds to the quarter million and racing away beyond. I waited until the first pause and raised the price by a giant twenty-five thousand, to be immediately capped by a decisive nod from an agent along to my right. I raised another twenty-five and lost it as quickly, and another, and another: and I could go on nodding, I thought, until my head fell off. Nothing easier in the world than spending someone else's money as fast as noughts running through the meter on a petrol pump.

At eight hundred thousand guineas I just stopped. The auctioneer looked at me enquiringly. I didn't blink. 'Against you, sir,' he said.

'Go on,' said Donavan, thinking I'd merely overlooked that it was my turn. 'Go on, go on.'

I shook my head. Donavan turned and literally punched me on the arm in an agony of fear that my dithering would lose him the colt. 'Go on, it's you. Bid, you bugger, bid.'

'Any more, sir?' the auctioneer said.

I again shook my head. Donavan kicked my leg. The auctioneer looked around the silent sale ring. 'All done, then?' he said: and after a lifetime's pause his gavel came down sharply, the clap of opportunity gone for ever. 'Sold to Mr O'Flaherty. Next lot, please.'

Under the buzz of comment that followed the super-colt out of the ring, Donavan thrust a furious purple face towards mine and yelled uninhibitedly, 'You buggering *bastard*. Do you know who bought that colt?'

'Yes I do.'

'I'll kill you, so I will.'

Shades of Angelo . . .

'There's no reason,' I said, 'why Luke should pay for your feud with Mick O'Flaherty.'

'That colt will win the Derby.'

I shook my head. 'You're *afraid* it will.'

'I'll write to Luke, so I will. I'll tell him it's you who's afraid. Bloody English. I'd kill the lot of you.'

He stalked away with rage pouring visibly from every pore, and I watched him with regret because I would indeed have liked to buy him his little fellow and seen him croon over him to make him a champion.

'Why did you stop?' Cassie asked, taking my arm.

'Does it worry you?'

She blinked. 'You know what they're saying?'

'That I didn't have the nerve to go on?'

'It was just that I heard . . .'

I smiled lop-sidedly. 'My first big battle, and I retreated. Something like that?'

'Something.'

'O'Flaherty and Donavan hate each other so much it curdles their judgment. I meant to go as far as seven hundred and fifty thousand guineas and I thought I'd get the colt. I really did, because that's an extremely high price for any yearling. I went one bid higher still, but it wasn't enough. O'Flaherty was standing behind his agent prodding him in the back to make him carry on. I could see him. O'Flaherty was absolutely determined to buy the colt. To spite Donavan, I think. It isn't sense to go on bidding against someone compelled by raw emotion, so I stopped.'

'But what if he *does* win the Derby?'

'About ten thousand thoroughbred colts were born last year in the British Isles alone. Then there's France and America too. *One* colt from that huge crop will win the Derby the year after next, when he's three. The odds are against it being this one.'

'You're so cool.'

'No,' I said truthfully. 'Bruised and disgruntled.'

We drove home and I sent the telex to Luke. 'Regret under-bidder at eight hundred and forty thousand pounds excluding tax for Hansel colt. Donavan's deadly rival Mick O'Flaherty successful at eight hundred and sixty-six thousand two fifty. Donavan furious. Sack me if you like. Regards, William.'

The return message came within an hour. 'If the colt wins the Derby you owe me ten million pounds otherwise you are still employed. Best to Cassie.'

'Thank God for that,' she said. 'Let's go to bed.'

Two busy days later I dropped her at work and drove on south-westwards to Berkshire to visit Luke's other trainers during the morning and to go on to see three of their horses race at Newbury in the afternoon; and there again on the racecourse was Angelo.

This time he saw me immediately before I had time to dodge: came charging across a patch of grass, took roughly hold of my lapel, and told me the betting system didn't work.

'You sold me a pup. You'll be sorry.' He looked quickly around as if hoping to find us both on deserted moorland, but as there was only concrete well populated, he smothered his obvious wish to slaughter me there and then. He was physically tougher, I thought. Less pale, less puffy; the effects of long imprisonment giving way to a healthy tan and tighter muscles, the bull-like quality of his body intensifying it. The black eyes . . . cold as ever. I looked at his re-emerging malevolence and didn't like it a bit.

I pulled his hand off my lapel and dropped it. 'There's nothing wrong with the system,' I said. 'It's not my fault you've been tramping all over it like a herd of elephants.'

His voice came back in the familiar bass register, 'If I'm still losing by five tomorrow, I'll *know* you've conned me. And I'll come after you. That's a promise.'

He turned away abruptly and strode off towards the stands, and in a while I went in search of Taff among the bookmakers.

'The latest on Angelo Gilbert?' He looked down at me from his raised position on an inverted beer crate. 'He's nuts.'

'Are you still offering him rotten odds?'

'Look you, Mr Derry, I'm too busy to talk now.' He was indeed surrounded by eager customers holding out cash. 'If you want to know, buy me a pint after the last race.'

'Right,' I said, 'it's a deal.' And at the end of the afternoon he came with me into the crowded bar and shouted the unexpected news into my attentive ear.

'That man Angelo's gone haywire. He won big money at York, like I told you, and a fair amount at Doncaster, but before York it seems he lost a packet at Epsom and last Monday he kissed goodbye to a fortune at Goodwood, and today he's plunged on two horses who finished out of sight. So we're all back to giving him regular odds. Old Lancer – he works for Joe Glickstein, Honest Joe, you must have seen his stands at all the tracks?' I nodded. 'Well, Old Lancer, he took a thousand in readies this afternoon off that Angelo on Pocket Handbook, what couldn't win if it started yesterday. I mean, the man's a screwball. He's no more playing Liam O'Rorke's system than I'm a bleeding fairy.'

I watched him drink his beer, feeling great dismay that Angelo couldn't manage the system even to the extent of letting it find the right horses. He had to be guessing some of the answers to the multifarious questions instead of looking them up accurately in the form books: skipping the hard work out of laziness and still trusting the scores which the computer returned. But a computer couldn't advise him, couldn't tell him that omitting an answer here and an answer there would upset all those delicately balanced weightings and inevitably distort the all-important win factors.

Angelo was dumb, dim, stupid.

Angelo would think it was my fault.

'They say his father's getting tired of it,' Taff said.

'Who?'

'That Angelo person's father. Old Harry Gilbert. Made a packet out of bingo halls, they say, before he got struck.'

'Er, struck?'

Taff brought a lined brown outdoor face out of the beer mug. 'Struck down with arthritis, I think it is. He can't hardly walk, anyway. Comes to the races sometimes in a wheelchair, and it's him what has the cash.'

Enlightened, I thought back to the previous week at Doncaster, seeing in memory Angelo giving a racecard to an elderly chairbound man. Angelo's father, still indulgent, still supportive, still paying for his deadly middle-aged son.

I thanked Taff for his information. 'What's this Angelo to you?' he said.

'A long-time no friend of my brother's.'

He made an accepting motion with his head, looked at his watch and finished his beer at a gulp, saying he'd left his clerk looking after the day's takings and he'd be happier having his mitts on them himself. 'We've all had a good day,' he said cheerfully, 'with those two odds-on favourites getting stuffed.'

I drove homewards and collected Cassie who was waiting at the hospital after what they had called a progress assessment.

'Plaster off next week,' she complained. 'I wanted it off this afternoon, but they wouldn't.'

The plaster was by then itching badly, the 'REMEMBER TIGERS' was fading, Cassie was insisting that her arm *felt* mended and impatience had definitely set in.

We again went to the sales: I seemed to have spent half a lifetime round the sale ring, and Luke now owned twenty-eight yearlings he had not yet seen. I had signed cheques on his behalf for nearly two million pounds and was tending to dream about it at night. There was only the Saturday morning left now, an undistinguished programme according to the catalogue, the winding down after the long excitements of the week. I went early by habit and with only short premeditation bought very cheaply the first lot of the day, an undistinguished-looking liver chestnut colt whose blood lines were sounder to the inspection than his spindly legs. One couldn't have foretold on that misty autumn morning that *this* was the prince who would sire a dynasty, but that in the end was what happened. My mind, as I signed for him and arranged for him to be sent along the road to Mort's stable, was more immediately on the conversation I'd had with Jonathan on the telephone the evening before.

'I want to talk to Angelo's father,' I said. 'Do you remember where he lived?'

'Of course I do. Welwyn Garden City. If you give me a minute, I'll find the street and the number.' There was a pause while he searched. 'Here we are. Seventeen, Pemberton Close. He may have moved, of course, and don't forget, William, he won't be in the least pleasant. I heard he was threatening all sorts of dire revenges against me after Angelo was convicted, but I didn't hang around long enough for him to get going.'

'Angelo seems to depend on him for cash,' I said.

'That figures.'

'Angelo's making a right balls-up of the betting system. He's losing his father's money and he's blaming me for it, and stoking up again towards volcanic eruption with me as the designated target for the lava flow.'

'He's an absolute pest.'

'He sure is. How does one rid oneself of a monster that won't go away? Don't answer that. Engineering Angelo back into jail permanently is all I can think of, and even then I would need to do it so that he didn't know who'd done it, and would it even on the whole be fair?'

'Provocation? Put a crime in his way and invite him to commit it?'

'As you say.'

'No, it wouldn't exactly be fair.'

'I was afraid you wouldn't think so,' I said.

'Nothing much short of murder would put him back inside for the whole of his life. Anything less and he'd be out breathing fire again, as you said before. And however could you line up a living victim?'

'Mm,' I said, 'it's impossible. I still think the only lasting solution is to make Angelo prosper, so I'll see if I can persuade his old dad to that effect.'

'His old dad is an old rattlesnake, don't forget.'

'His old dad is in a wheelchair.'

'Is he?' Jonathan seemed surprised. 'All the same, remember that rattlesnakes don't have legs.'

I reckoned that on that Saturday afternoon Angelo would still be blundering around the bookies on Newbury racecourse and that his father might have stayed at home, so it was then that I drove to Welwyn Garden City, leaving Cassie wandering around the cottage with a duster and an unaccustomedly domestic expression.

The house at number seventeen Pemberton Close proved to be inhabited not by Harry Gilbert but by a stockbroker, his chatty wife and four noisy children on roller skates, all of them out in the garden.

'Harry Gilbert?' said the wife, holding a basket of dead roses. 'He couldn't manage the stairs with his illness. He built himself a bungalow full of ramps.'

'Do you know where?'

'Oh sure. On the golf course. He used to play, poor man. Now he sits at a window and watches the foursomes go by on the fourteenth green. We often wave to him, when we're playing.'

'Does he have arthritis?' I said.

'Good Lord, no.' She made a grimace of sympathy. 'Multiple sclerosis. He's had it for years. We've seen him slowly get worse . . . We used to live four doors away, but we always liked this house. When he put it up for sale, we bought it.'

'Could you tell me how to find him?'

'Sure.' She gave me brisk and clear instructions. 'You do know, don't you, not to talk about his son.'

'Son?' I said vaguely.

'His only son is in prison for murder. So sad for the poor man. Don't talk about it, it distresses him.'

'Thanks for warning me,' I said.

She nodded and smiled from a kind and unperceiving heart and went back to tidying her pretty garden. Surely goodness and mercy all thy days shall follow thee, I thought frivolously, and no monsters who won't go away shall gobble thee up. I left the virtuous and went in search of the sinner, and found him, as she'd said, sitting in his wheelchair by a big bay window, watching the earnest putters out on the green.

The wide double front doors of the large and still new-looking one-storey building were opened to me by a man so like Angelo at first sight that I thought for a fearsome moment that he hadn't after all gone to the races; but it was only the general shape and colouring that was the same, the olive skin, greying hair, unfriendly dark eyes, tendency to an all-over padding of fat.

'Eddy,' a voice called. 'Who is it? Come in here.'

The voice was as deep and harsh as Angelo's, the words themselves slightly slurred. I walked across the polished wood of the entrance hall and then across the lush drawing-room with its panoramic view, and not until I was six feet away from Harry Gilbert did I stop and say I was William Derry.

Vibrations could almost be felt. Eddy, behind me, audibly hissed from the air leaving his lungs. The much older version of Angelo's face which looked up from the wheelchair went stiff with strong but unreadable emotions, guessed at as anger and indignation, but possibly not. He had thinning grey hair, a grey moustache, a big body in a formal grey suit with a waistcoat. Only in the lax hands was the illness visible, and only then when he moved them; and from his polished shoes to the neat parting across his scalp it seemed to me that he was denying his weaknesses, presenting an outwardly uncrumbled façade so as to announce to the world that authority still lived within.

'You're not welcome in my house,' he said.

'If your son would stop threatening me, I wouldn't be here.'

'He says you have tricked us like your brother.'

'No.'

'The betting system doesn't work.'

'It worked for Liam O'Rorke,' I said. 'Liam O'Rorke was quiet, clever, careful and a statistician. Is Angelo any of those things?'

He gave me a cold stare. 'A system should work for everyone alike.'

'A horse doesn't run alike for every jockey,' I said.

'There's no similarity.'

'Engines run sweetly for some drivers and break down for others. Heavy-handedness is always destructive. Angelo is trampling all over the system. No wonder it isn't producing results.'

'The system is wrong,' he said stubbornly.

'It may,' I said slowly, 'be slightly out of date.' Yet for Ted Pitts it was purring along still: but then Ted Pitts too was quiet, clever; a statistician.

It seemed that I had made the first impression upon Harry Gilbert. He said with a faint note of doubt, 'It should not have changed with the years. Why should it?'

'I don't know. Why shouldn't it? There may be a few factors that Liam O'Rorke couldn't take into account because in his time they didn't exist.'

A depressed sort of grimness settled over him.

I said, 'And if Angelo has been hurrying through the programs, skipping some of the questions or answering them inaccurately, the scores will come out wrong. He's had some of the answers right. You won a lot at York, so I'm told. And you'd have won more on the St Leger if Angelo hadn't scared the bookmakers with his boastfulness.'

'I don't understand you.' The slur in his speech, the faint distortion of all his words was, I realized, the effect of his illness. Articulation might be damaged but the chill awareness in his eyes said quite clearly that his intelligence wasn't.

'Angelo told all the bookmakers at York that he would henceforth fleece them continually, because it was he who possessed Liam O'Rorke's infallible system.'

Harry Gilbert closed his eyes. His face remained unmoved.

Eddy said belligerently, 'What's wrong with that? You have to show people who's boss.'

'Eddy,' Harry Gilbert said, 'you don't know anything about anything and you never will.' He slowly opened his eyes. 'It makes a difference,' he said.

'They gave him evens on the St Leger winner. The proper price was five to one.'

Harry Gilbert would never thank me: not if I gave him life-saving advice, not if I helped him win a fortune, not if I kept his precious son out of jail. He knew, all the same, what I was saying. Too much of a realizt, too old a businessman, not to. Angelo in too many ways was a fool, and it made him more dangerous, not less.

'What do you expect me to do?' he said.

'I expect you to tell your son that if he attacks me again, or any of my friends or any of my property, he'll be back behind bars so fast he won't know what hit him. I expect you to make him work the betting system carefully and quietly, so that he wins. I expect you to warn him that the system guarantees only one win in three, not a winner every single time. Making the system work is a matter of strict application and careful persistence, not of flamboyance and anger.'

He stared at me expressionlessly.

'Angelo's character,' I said, 'is as far different from Liam O'Rorke's as it's possible to get. I expect you to make Angelo aware of that fact.'

They were all expectations, I saw, that were unlikely to be achieved. Harry Gilbert's physical weakness, though he disguised it, was progressive, and his imperfect control of Angelo would probably only last at all for exactly as long as Angelo needed financing.

A tremor shook his body but no emotion showed in his face. He said however with a sort of throttled fury, 'All our problems are your brother's fault.'

The uselessness of my visit swamped me. Harry Gilbert was after all only an old man blindly clinging like his son to an old obsession. Harry Gilbert was not any longer a man of reason, even if he had ever been.

I tried all the same, once more. I said, 'If you had paid Mrs O'Rorke all those years ago, if you had bought Liam's system from her, as you had agreed, you would legally have owned it and could have profited from it ever since. It was because you refused to pay Mrs O'Rorke that my brother saw to it that you didn't get the system.'

'She was too old,' he said coldly.

I stared at him. 'Are you implying that her age was a reason for not paying her?'

He didn't answer.

'If I stole your car from you,' I said, 'would you consider me justified on the grounds that you are too ill to drive it?'

'You prattle,' he said. 'You are nothing.'

'Mug,' Eddy said, nodding.

Harry Gilbert said wearily, 'Eddy, you are good at pushing wheelchairs and cooking meals. On all other subjects, shut up.'

Eddy gave him a look which was half-defiant, half-scared, and I saw that he too was dependent on Harry for his food and shelter, that it couldn't be all that easy out in the big cynical world for murderer's assistants to earn a cushy living, that looking after Harry wasn't a job to be lightly lost.

To Harry Gilbert I said, 'Why don't you do what you once intended? Why don't you buy Angelo a betting shop and let the system win for him there?'

I got another stretch of silent unmoving stare. Then he said, 'Business is a talent. I have it. It is, however, uncommon.'

I nodded. It was all the answer he would bring himself to make. Certainly he wouldn't admit to me of all people that he thought Angelo would bankrupt any sensible business in a matter of weeks.

'Keep your son away from me,' I said. 'I've done more for you in getting you that system than you deserve. You've no rights to it. You've no right to demand that it makes you a fortune in five minutes. You've no right to blame me if it doesn't. You keep your son away from me. I can play as rough as he does. For your own sake, and his, you keep him off me.'

I turned away from him without waiting for any sort of answer, and walked unhurriedly out of the room and across the hall.

Footsteps pattered after me on the polished wood.

Eddy.

I didn't look round. He caught up with me as I opened the front door and stepped outside, and he put his hand on my arm to make me pause. He looked back guiltily over his shoulder to where his uncle sat mutely by his splendid window, knowing the old man wouldn't approve of what he was doing. When he saw Harry was looking out again steadfastly to the golf, he turned on me a nasty self-satisfied smirk.

'Mug,' he said, speaking with prudent quietness, 'Angelo won't like you coming here.'

'Too bad.' I shook his hand off my sleeve. He sneered back in a poisonous mixture of slyness and malice and triumph, and half-whispered his final enjoyable words.

'Angelo's bought a pistol,' he said.

18

'Why are you so thoughtful?' Cassie asked.

'Uneasy.'

We were sitting as so often at a table in Bananas' dining room with him moving about light-footedly in his sneakers seeming never to hurry yet keeping everyone fed. The plants grew with shining healthy leaves in the opulent gloom of his designedly intimate lighting, glasses and silverware gleaming in candlelight and mould spreading slowly in the dark.

'It's not like you,' Cassie said.

I smiled at her thin sun-tanned uncomplicated face and said that I didn't want above all things a return visit from Angelo.

'Do you really think he'd come?'

'I don't know.'

'We'd never get any more corn dollies,' she said. 'It's too late now for decent straw.'

Her arm in its plaster lay awkwardly on the table. I touched the bunched fingertips peeping out. 'Would you consider leaving me for a while?' I asked.

'No, I wouldn't.'

'Suppose I said I was tired of you?'

'You're not.'

'Are you so sure?'

'Positive,' she said contentedly. 'And anyway, for how long?'

I drank some wine. For how long was an absolute puzzle. 'Until I get Angelo stabilized,' I said. 'And don't ask me how long, because I don't know. But the first thing to do, I think, is persuade Luke he needs a computer right here in Britain.'

'Would that be difficult?'

'It might be. He has one in California . . . he might say he didn't need two.'

'What do you want it for, the betting system?'

I nodded. 'I think,' I said, 'that I'll try to rent one. Or some time on one. I want to find out what the winners should be according to O'Rorke, and what Angelo's doing wrong. And if I can put him right, perhaps that will keep him quiet.'

'You'd have thought just giving him the tapes would be enough.'

'Yes, you would.'

'He's like a thistle,' she said. 'You're sure you've got rid of him and he grows right back.'

Thistles, I thought, didn't go out to buy guns.

Bananas reverently bore his eponymous soufflé to the people at the next table, the airy peaks shining light and luscious and pale brown. The old cow, whose skill had produced it, must have stopped working to rule: Bananas himself, joining us later for coffee, gloomily admitted it. 'She took an hour to shred carrots. Did them by hand. Ten seconds in the processor. She said processors were dangerous machinery and she'd have to negotiate a new rate for all jobs with machinery.'

Bananas' new beard had grown curly which was unforseen in view of the lank straight locks further up but seemed to me to be in accord with the doubleness of his nature.

'Historically,' he said, 'it's seldom a good idea to appease a tyrant.'

'The old cow?'

'No. Angelo Gilbert.'

'What do you suggest, then? I asked. 'Full-scale war?'

'You have to be sure you'll win. Historically, full scale war's a toss up.'

'The old cow might leave,' Cassie said, smiling.

Bananas nodded. 'Tyrants always want more next time. I dare say next year she'll turn to motor racing.'

'I suppose you don't know anyone who has a computer you can feed any language into?' I said.

'Turkish? Indo-Chinese? That sort of stuff?'

'Yeah. Gibberish, double-speak, jargonese and gobble-de-gook.'

'Try the sociologists.'

I tried, however, Ted Pitts, early the following morning, and reached Jane instead.

'Ted isn't here,' she said. 'I'm afraid he's still in Switzerland. Can I help?'

I explained I wanted to borrow a good computer to run a check on the racing programs and she said sadly that she couldn't really lend me Ted's, not without him being there; she knew he was working on a special program for his classes and if anyone touched the computer at present his work could be lost, and she couldn't risk that.

'No,' I agreed. Did she know of anyone else whose computer I could use?'

She thought it over. 'There's Ruth,' she said doubtfully. 'Ruth Quigley.'

'Who?'

'She was a pupil of Ted's. Actually he says there's nothing he can teach her now, and when she comes here I can't understand a word they say to each other, it's like listening to creatures from outer space.'

'Would she have a computer of her own?'

'She's got everything,' Jane said without envy. 'Born rich. Only child. Only has to ask, and it's hers. And on top of that, she's brainy. Doesn't seem fair, does it?'

'Beautiful as well?'

'Oh.' She hesitated. 'Not bad. I don't really know. It's not the sort of thing you *notice* about Ruth.'

'Well, um, where could I find her?'

'In Cambridge. That's why I thought of her, because she lives over your way. She writes programs for teaching-machines. Would you like me to ring her? When do you want to go?'

I said 'Today', and half an hour later I'd had my answer and was on my way, seeking out a flat in a modern block on the outskirts of the town.

Ruth Quigley proved to be young: very early twenties, I guessed. I could see also what Jane meant about not noticing her looks, because the first, overpowering and lasting impression she gave was of the speed of her mind. There were light eyes, light brown extra-curly hair and long slender neck, but mostly there was an impatient jerk of the head and a stumblingly rapid diction as if to her utter disgust her tongue couldn't speak her thoughts fast enough.

'Yes. Come in. Did you bring your tapes?' She wasted no precious words on any other greeting. 'This way. Old Grantley Basic, Jane said. You've got the language with you. Do you want to load it, or shall I?'

'I'd be glad if – '

'Hand them over, then. Which side?'

'Er, first program on Side 1.'

'Right. Come along.'

She moved with the same inborn rapidity, disappearing down a short passage and through a doorway before I'd even managed a step. She must always find, I thought, that the rest of the world went along intolerably in slow motion.

The room into which I finally followed her must originally have been designed as a bedroom, which it now in no way resembled. There was a quiet, felt-like pale green floor covering, track-lighting with spotlights, a roller blind at the window, matt white walls – and long benches of machines more or less like Ted Pitts's, only double.

'Workroom,' Ruth Quigley said.

'Eh, yes.'

It was cooler in there than out on the street. I identified a faint background hum as air-conditioning, and remarked on it.

She nodded, not lifting her eyes from the already almost completed job of loading Grantley Basic into a machine that would accept it. 'Dust is like gravel to computers. Heat, damp, all makes them temperamental. They're thoroughbreds, of course'

Racing programs . . . thoroughbred computers. Excellence won. Pains taken gave one the edge. I was beginning to think like her, I thought.

'I'm wasting your time,' I said apologetically.

'Glad to help. Always do anything for Jane and Ted. They know that. Did you bring the form books? You'll need them. Simple programs, but facts must be right. Most teaching-machines, just the same. They bore me quite often. Multiple-choice questions. Then the child takes half an hour to get it right and I put it in a bright remark like, "Well done, aren't you clever." Nothing of the sort. Encouragement, they say, is all. What do you think?'

'Are they gifted children?'

She gave me a flashing glance. 'All children are gifted. Some more so. They need the best teaching. They often don't get it. Teachers are jealous, did you know?'

'My brother always said it was intensely exciting to have a very bright boy in the class.'

'Like Ted, generous. There you are, fire away. I'll be in and out, don't let me disturb you. I'm working on a sort-listing of string arrays. They said it was taking them eighteen minutes, I ask you. I've got it down to five seconds, but only one dimension. I need two dimensions if I'm not to scramble the data. I'm poking a machine-language program into the memory from BASIC, then converting the machine code into assembly-language economics. Am I boring you?'

'No,' I said. 'I just don't understand a word of it.'

'Sorry. Forgot you weren't like Ted. Well, carry on.'

I had brought in a large briefcase the tapes, the racing form books, all sorts of record books and all the recent copies of a good racing paper, and with a feeling that by Ruth Quigley's standards it was going to take me a very long time I set about working out which horses were *likely* to have won according to Liam O'Rorke, and checking them against those which had actually reached the post first. I still needed a list of the horses which Angelo had backed, but I thought I might get that from Taff and from Lancer on the following day: and *then* I might be able to figure out where Angelo had messed everything up.

FILE NAME?

CLOAD DONCA, I typed. Pressed the 'Enter' key, and watched the asterisks; waited for READY. Pressed 'Enter' again and got my reward.

WHICH RACE AT DONCASTER?

ST LEGER, I typed.

DONCASTER: ST LEGER. TYPE NAME OF HORSE AND PRESS 'ENTER'.

GENOTTI, I typed. Pressed 'Enter'.

DONCASTER: ST LEGER.

GENOTTI.

ANSWER ALL QUESTIONS YES OR NO WITH A NUMBER AND PRESS 'ENTER'.

HAS HORSE WON AS A TWO YEAR OLD?

YES, I typed. The screen flashed a new question leaving the headings intact.

HAS HORSE WON AS A THREE YEAR OLD?

YES, I typed.

HOW MANY DAYS SINCE HORSE LAST RAN?

I consulted the daily newspaper which always gave that precise information, and typed in the number which had appeared there on St Leger day: 23.

HAS HORSE WON OVER DISTANCE: ONE MILE SIX FURLONGS?

NO, I typed.

HAS HORSE RUN OVER DISTANCE: ONE MILE SIX FURLONGS?

NO.

TYPE LONGEST DISTANCE IN FURLONGS OVER WHICH HORSE HAS WON.

12

HAS HORSE RUN ON COURSE?

NO.

TYPE IN PRIZE MONEY WON IN CURRENT SEASON.

I consulted the form books and typed Genotti's winnings, which had been fairly good but not stupendous.

HAS HORSE'S SIRE SIRED WINNERS AT THE DISTANCE?

I looked it up in the breeding records, which took much longer, but the answer was YES.

DAM ditto?

YES.

IS HORSE QUOTED ANTE-POST AT TWELVE TO ONE OR LESS?

YES

HAS JOCKEY PREVIOUSLY WON A CLASSIC?

YES.

HAS TRAINER PREVIOUSLY WON A CLASSIC?

YES.

ANY MORE HORSES?

YES.

I found myself back at the beginning and repeated the program for every horse which had run in the race. The questions weren't always precisely the same, because different answer produced alternative queries, and for some horses there were far more questions than for others. It took me a good hour to look everything up, and I thought that if I ever did begin to do it all seriously I would make myself a whole host of more easily accessible tables than those available in the record books. When I at last answered NO to the final question ANY MORE HORSES? I got the clear reply that left no doubt about Liam O'Rorke's genius.

Genotti headed the win factor list. An outsider turned up on it in second place, with the horse that had started favourite in third: and the St Leger result had been those three horses in that order exactly.

I could hardly believe it.

Ruth Quigley said suddenly, 'Got the wrong result? You look flummoxed.'

'No – the right one.'

'Disturbing.' She grinned swiftly. 'If I get the results I expect, I check and check and check. Doesn't do to be complacent. Like some coffee?'

I accepted and she made it as fast as she did everything else.

'How old are you?' I said.

'Twenty-one. Why?'

'I'd have thought you'd have been at the university.'

'Degree at twenty plus one month. Nothing unusual. Cheated my way in, of course. Everything's so slow nowadays. Forty years ago, degrees at nineteen or less were possible. Now they insist on calendar age. Why? Why hold people back? Life's terribly short as it is. Masters degree at twenty plus six months. Did the two courses simultaneously. No one knew. Don't spread it around. Doing my doctorate now. Are you interested?'

'Yes,' I said truthfully.

She smiled like a summer's day, come and gone. 'My father says I'm a bore.'

'He doesn't mean it.'

'He's a surgeon,' she said, as if that explained much. 'So's my mother. Guilt complexes, both of them. Give to mankind more than you take. That sort of thing. They can't help it.'

'And you?'

'I don't know yet. I can't give much. I can't get jobs I can do. They look at the years I've been alive and make judgments. Quite deadly. Time has practically nothing to do with anything. They'll give me the jobs when I'm thirty that I could do better now. Poets and mathematicians are best before twenty-five. What chance have they got?'

'To work alone,' I said.

'My God. Do you understand? You're wasting time, get on with your programs. Don't show me what I should do. I've got a research fellowship. What do I seek for? What is there to seek? Where is the unknown, what is not known, what's the question?'

I shook my head helplessly, 'Wait for the apple to fall on your head.'

'It's true. I can't contemplate. Sitting under the apple trees. Metaphorical apple trees. I've tried. Get on with your nags.'

Philosophically I loaded YORK and worked through the three races for which there were programs, and found that in two of them the highest-scoring horse had won. Three winners from the three races I'd worked through. Incredible.

With a feeling of unreality I loaded EPSOM and went painstakingly through the four races for which there were programs; and this time came up with no winners at all. Frowning slightly I loaded NEWBU for Newbury and from a good deal of hard accurate work came up with the win factors of the race in which Angelo had backed the absolute no-hoper Pocket Handbook.

Pocket Handbook, who had finished exhausted and tailed-off by at least thirty lengths, was at the top of the win-factor list by a clear margin.

I stared distrustfully at the rest of the scores, which put the race's actual winner second from the bottom with negligible points.

'What's the matter?' Ruth Quigley said, busy at her own machine and not even glancing my way.

'Parts of the system are haywire.'

'Really?'

I loaded GOODW and sorted through five races. All the top scorers were horses which in the events had finished no nearer than second.

'Are you hungry?' Ruth said. 'Three-thirty. Sandwich?'

I thanked her and went with her into her small kitchen where I was interested to see that her speed stopped short of dexterity with slicing tomatoes. She quite slowly, for her, made fat juicy affairs of cheese, chutney, tomatoes and corned beef which toppled precariously on the plate and had to be held in both hands for eating.

'Logical explanations exist,' she said, looking at my abstracted expression. 'Human logic's imperfect. Absolute logic isn't.'

'Mm,' I said. 'Ted showed me how easy it is to add and delete passwords.'

'So?'

'It would be pretty easy, wouldn't it, to change other things besides?'

'Unless it's in ROM. Then it's difficult.'

'ROM?'

'Read only Memory. Sorry.'

'He showed me how to List things.'

'You've got RAM, then. Random Access Memory. Change what you like. Kids' stuff.'

We finished the sandwiches and returned to the keyboards. I loaded the Newbury file, chose the Pocket Handbook race and listed the program piece by piece.

LIST 1200-1240 I typed, and in front of the resulting screenful of letters, numbers and symbols sat figuring out the roots of the trouble.

```
1200 PRINT "TYPE IN PRIZE MONEY IN CURRENT SEASON"
1210 INPUT W: IF W<1000 THEN T = T + 20
1220 IF W>1000 THEN T = T: IF W>5000 T = T
1230 IF W>10000 THEN T = T: IF W>15000 THEN T = T
1240 GOSUB 6000
```

Even to my ignorant and untutored eyes it was nonsense. Liam O'Rorke wouldn't have meant it, Peter Keithly wouldn't have written it, Ted Pitts would never have used it. In plain language, what it was saying was that if the season's winnings of a horse were *less* than one thousand pounds, the win factor score should be increased by 20, and if they were *more* than one thousand, and however much more, the win factor score would not increase at all. The least successful horses would therefore score most highly on that particular point. The weighting was topsy-turvy and the answers would come out wrong.

With the hollow certainty of what had happened staring me in the face, I loaded the Epsom file and searched the Lists of the programs for the four races on which Angelo had lost. In two cases the weightings for prize money were upside down.

Tried Goodwood. In three of the five listed races, the same thing.

Depressed beyond measure, I loaded the files for Leicester and Ascot, where races were to be held during the week ahead. Typed in the names of all the races to be run there and found there were programs for eight of them: one at Leicester, seven at Ascot. Listed each of the eight programs in sections, and found that in four of them the score for amassing much prize money was nought, and the score for prize money of under one thousand pounds was anything up to 20.

There were programs for some races at all the tracks which I knew for a certainty were not fourteen years old. Modern races, introduced since Liam O'Rorke had died.

The programs were no longer pure O'Rorke, but O'Rorke according to Pitts. O'Rorke updated, expanded, renewed. O'Rorke, on these particular tapes, interfered with, falsified, mangled. Ted Pitts – one had to face it – had wrecked the system before he'd handed it to me ... and had delivered me defenceless to the wrath of Angelo Gilbert.

I thanked the frustrated and brilliant Miss Quigley for her day-long patience and drove home to Cassie.

'What's the matter?' she said immediately.

I said wearily, 'The ess aitch I tee has hit the fan.'

'What do you *mean*?'

'Angelo thinks I've tricked him. That the betting system I gave him is wrong. That it produces too many losers. Well so it does. Normally it must be all right but on these tapes it's been altered. Ted Pitts has rigged so many of the programs that anyone using them will fall flat on his greedy face.' And I explained about the reversed scores for winning, which produced scatty results. 'He may also have changed some of the other weightings to get the same effect. I've no way of knowing.'

She looked as stunned as I felt. 'Do you mean Ted Pitts did it on *purpose*?'

'He sure did.' I thought back to the time he'd taken to make me 'copies'; to the hour I'd spent sitting by his pool talking to Jane, leaving him, at his own request, to work alone.

'But why?' Cassie said.

'I don't know.'

'You didn't tell him, did you, what you wanted the tapes for?'

'No, I didn't.'

She said doubtfully, 'Perhaps it might have been better if you'd said how vital they were.'

'And perhaps he wouldn't have given them to me at all if he'd known I had Angelo locked in the cellar. I mean, I thought he might not want to be *involved*. Most people wouldn't, with something like that. And then, if he was like Jonathan, he might have changed the weightings anyway, jut to prevent Angelo from profiting. You never know. Jonathan himself would somehow have tricked Angelo again. I'm sure of it.'

'You don't think Ted Pitts asked Jonathan what he should do, do you?'

I thought back and shook my head. 'It was before nine in the morning when I went to the Pitts's house. That would make it about one a.m. in California. Even if he had his number, which I doubt, I don't think he would have telephoned Jonathan in the middle of the night ... and Jonathan anyway sounded truly disappointed when I told him I'd given Angelo the tapes. No, Ted must have done it for his own reasons, and by himself.'

'Which doesn't help much.'

I shook my head.

I thought of the certainty with which I'd gone to Harry Gilbert's house on the previous day. Hell's teeth, how wrong could one be, how naïve could one get?

If I warned Angelo not to use the tapes in the week ahead he would be sure I had tricked him and was scared to death of his revenge.

If I didn't warn him not to use the tapes, he would most likely lose again and be more sure than ever that I'd tricked him . . .

If I wrung the right answers out of Ted Pitts and told them to Angelo, he would still think I had deliberately given him useless tapes – on which he had already lost.

Ted Pitts was in Switzerland walking up mountains.

'Would you care,' I said to Cassie, 'for a long slow cruise to Australia.'

19

Jane Pitts on the telephone again, 'No, terribly sorry, he moves about and stops in different places every night. Quite often he sleeps in his tent. Is it important?'

'Horribly,' I said.

'Oh dear. Could I help?'

'There's something wrong with those tapes he made for me. Could you by any chance lend me his own?'

'No, I simply can't. I'm frightfully sorry but I don't know where he keeps anything in that room and he positively hates his things being touched.' She thought for a few minutes, puzzled but not unwilling, friendly, anxious to help. 'Look, he's sure to call me one day soon to say when he'll be home. Would you like me to ask him to ring you?'

'Yes please,' I said fervently. 'Or ask him where I can reach him, and I'll call him. Do tell him it's really urgent, beg for me, would you? Say it's for Jonathan's sake more than mine.'

'I'll tell him,' she promised, 'as soon as he rings.'

'You're unscrupulous,' Cassie said as I put down the receiver. 'It's for your sake, not Jonathan's.'

'He wouldn't want to weep on his brother's grave.'

'William!'

'A joke,' I said hastily. 'A joke.'

Cassie shivered, however. 'What are you going to do?'

'Think.'

The basic thought was that the more Angelo lost, the angrier he would get, and that the first objective was therefore to stop him betting. Taff and the others could hardly be persuaded not to accept such easy pickings, which left the source of the cash, Harry Gilbert himself. Precisely what, I wondered, could I say to Harry Gilbert which would cut off the stake money without sending Angelo straight round to vent his rage?

I could tell him that Liam O'Rorke's system no longer existed: that I'd got the tapes in good faith but had been tricked myself. I could tell him a lot of half-truths, but whether he would believe me, and whether he could restrain Angelo even if he himself were convinced, of those imponderables there was no forecast.

Realistically there was nothing else to do.

I didn't particularly want to try to trap Angelo into being sent back to jail: fourteen years was enough for any man. I only wanted, as I had all along, for him to leave me alone. I wanted him deflated, defused ... docile. What a hope.

A night spent with my mind on pleasanter things produced no cleverer plan. A paragraph in the *Sporting Life*, read over a quick breakfast after an hour with the horses on the Heath, made me wish that Angelo would solve my problems himself by bashing someone else on the head: about as unlikely as him having a good week on the system. Lancer the bookmaker, said the paper, had been mugged on his own doorstep on returning from Newbury races on Friday evening. His wallet, containing approximately fifty-three pounds, had been stolen. Lancer was OK, police had no leads: poor old Lancer, too bad.

I sighed. Who, I wondered, could I get Angelo to bash?

Besides, of course, myself.

On account of the knee-groper, I was driving Carrie to work whenever possible, and on that morning after I'd dropped her I went straight on to Welwyn Garden City, not relishing my prospects but with not much alternative. I hoped to persuade both Harry Gilbert and Angelo that the havoc the years had caused to the O'Rorke system couldn't be undone, that it was blown, no longer existed, couldn't be recovered. I was going to tell them again that any violence from Angelo would find him back in a cell; to try to make them believe it ... to fear it.

I was taller than Angelo and towered over a man in a wheelchair. I intended slightly to crowd them, faintly to intimidate, certainly to leave a physical impression that it was time for them to back off. Even on Angelo, who must have known how to frighten from childhood, it might have some effect.

Eddy opened the front doors and tried at once to close them again when he saw who had called. I pushed him with force out of my way.

'Harry isn't dressed,' he said fearfully, though whether the fear was of me or of Harry wasn't clear.

'He'll see me,' I said.

'No. You can't.' He tried to bar my way to one of the wide doors at the side of the entrance hall, thereby showing me which way to go, and I walked over there with Eddy trying to edge me out of my path by leaning on me.

I thrust him again aside and opened the door, and found myself in a short passage which led into a large bedroom which was equipped first and most noticeably with another vast window looking out to the golf.

Harry Gilbert lay in a big bed facing the window, ill and growing old but still in some indefinable way not defenceless, even in pyjamas.

'I tried to stop him,' Eddy was saying ineffectually.

'Take this tray and go away,' Harry Gilbert said to him, and Eddy picked off the bedclothes the half-eaten breakfast which I had interrupted. 'Shut the door.' He waited until Eddy had retreated and then frostily to me said, 'Well?'

'I've discovered,' I said with urgency, 'that Liam O'Rorke's betting system has the equivalent of smallpox. It should be treated like the plague. It'll bring trouble to all who touch it. The old system has been through too many hands, been adulterated by the years. It's gone bad. If you want to save your cash, you'll stop Angelo using it, and it's pointless getting angry with me on any counts. I got the system for you in good faith and I'm furious to find it's useless. Bring Angelo in here and let me tell him.'

Harry Gilbert stared at me with his usual unreadable face, and it was without any visible consternation that he said in his semi-slurred way, 'Angelo isn't here. He is cashing my cheque at the bank. He is going to Leicester races.'

'He will lose,' I said. 'I didn't need to warn you. I'm warning you. Your money will be lost.'

Thoughts must have traversed the brain behind the cold eyes but nothing much showed. Finally, and it must have been with an inner effort, he said, 'Can you stop him?'

'Stop the cheque,' I said. 'Call the bank.'

He glanced at a clock beside him. 'Too late.'

'I can go to Leicester,' I said. 'I'll try to find him.'

After a pause he said, 'Very well.'

I nodded briefly and left him, and drove towards Leicester feeling that even if I had managed to convince Harry, which was in itself uncertain, I was facing the impossible with Angelo. The impossible all the same had to be tried: and at least, I thought, he wouldn't actually attack me on a busy race-course.

Leicester races on that cold autumn day turned out to be as busy as a well-smoked beehive, with only a scattering of dark-coated figures trudging about doggedly, head down to the biting wind. As sometimes happened on city-based tracks on weekdays, the crowd was thin to the point of embarrassment, the whole proceedings imbued with the perfunctory and temporary air of a ritual taking place without fervour.

Taff was stamping about by his beer crate, blowing on his fingers and complaining that he would have done better business if he'd gone to the day's other meeting at Bath.

'But there's the Midlands Cup here,' he said. 'It'll be a good race. I thought it would pull them – and look at them, not enough punters to sing auld lang syne round a tea-pot.' The Welsh accent was ripe with disgust.

'What are you making favourite?' I said smiling.

'Pink Flowers.'

'And what about Terrybow?'

'Who?'

'Runs in the Midlands Cup,' I said patiently. Terrybow, the computer's choice, top of the win factors. Terrybow with a habit of finishing tenth of twelve, seventh of eight, or fifteenth of twenty: never actually last but a long way from success.

'Oh, Terrybow.' He consulted a notebook. 'Twenties, if you like.'

'Twenty to one?'

'Twenty-five then. Can't say fairer than twenty-five. How much do you want?'

'How much would you take?'

'Whatever you like,' he said cheerfully. 'No limit. Not unless you know something I don't, like it's stuffed to the eyeballs with rocket dust.'

I shook my head and looked along the row of cold disgruntled book-makers who were doing a fraction of their usual trade. If Angelo had been among them I would have seem him easily, but there was no sign of him. The Midlands Cup was the fourth race on the programme and still an hour ahead, and if Angelo was sticking rigidly to the disaster-laden system, Terry-bow would be the only horse he would back.

'Have you see Angelo Gilbert here today, Taff?' I asked.

'No.' He took a bet from a furtive-looking man in a raincoat and gave him a ticket. 'Ten at threes, Walkie-Talkie,' he told his clerk.

'How's Lancer?' I asked. 'Can't see him here.'

'Cursing muggers and rubbing a lump.' He took another tenner from a purposeful woman in glasses. 'Ten at eights, Engineer. Some kids rolled old Lancer on his own doorstep. I ask you, he carried thousands around the racecourse, pays it in to his firm at the end of the day, and then goes and gets himself done for fifty quid.'

'Did he see who robbed him?'

'One of Joe Glick's other boys who's here says it was a bunch of teen-agers.'

Not Angelo, I thought. Well, it wouldn't have been. But if only he *would* . . .

I looked speculatively at Taff, who worked for himself and did carry his takings home at the end of the day. Pity one couldn't catch Angelo in the act of trying to retrieve his stake money after Terrybow had lost . . . pity one couldn't arrange for the police to be on hand when Angelo mugged Taff on the way home.

I'm down to fantasies, I thought: it's depressing.

The time passed and Angelo, who had been so ubiquitous when I had been trying to avoid him, was nowhere to be seen. I walked among the bookmakers and asked others besides Taff, but none of them had seen Angelo at all that afternoon, and there was still no sign of him during the run-up to the Midlands Cup. If he had gone to Bath after all, I thought, I was wasting my time – but the only race that day on the O'Rorke tapes was the Midlands Cup; its only designated horse, Terrybow.

With less than five minutes to go, when the horses were already cantering down to the start, a tremendous burst of tic-tac activity galvanized the men with white gloves high on the stands who semaphored changes of odds. With no direct link like telephones or radio the bookmakers relied on tic-tac to tell them if large sums had been placed with their firms on any particular horse, so that they could bring down the offered price. Taff, watching his man signalling frenziedly, rubbed out the 20 written against Terrybow on his blackboard and with his piece of chalk wrote in 14. Along the row all the other bookies were similarly engaged. Terrybow fell again to 12.

'What's happening?' I said to Taff urgently.

He cast an abstracted eye in my direction. 'Someone down in the cheap ring is piling a stack on Terrybow.'

'*Damn*,' I said bitterly. I hadn't thought of looking for Angelo anywhere but round his usual haunts: certainly not in the comfortless far enclosure away down the course where the entrance fee was small, the view of the races moderate, and the expectation of the few bookmakers trading there modest to the point of not being worth standing in the cold all afternoon. And even if I'd thought of it I wouldn't have gone there, because it would have meant risking missing Angelo in the paddock. Damn and blast, I thought. Damn Angelo today and all days and for the whole of his life.

'You knew something about this Terrybow,' Taff said to me accusingly.

'I didn't back it,' I said.

'Yeah, that's right, so you didn't. So what's going on?'

'Angelo Gilbert,' I said. 'He's betting where he isn't known in case you wouldn't give him a good price up here.'

'What? Really?' He laughed, rubbed out the 12 against Terrybow and replaced it with 20. A small rush of punters resulted and he took their money with relish.

I went up on the stands and watched in a fury while Terrybow ran true to his form and drifted in twelfth of fifteen. Ted Pitts, I thought bleakly, might as well have shoved me under the wheels of a truck.

I did see Angelo that afternoon, and so did practically everyone else who hadn't gone home before the sixth race.

Angelo was the angrily shouting epicentre of a fracas going on near the weighing-room; a row involving several bookmakers, a host of racegoers and some worried looking officials. Disputes between bookmakers and clients were traditionally dealt with on that spot by one particular Jockey Club official, the Ring Inspector. Angelo appeared to have punched him in the face.

The milling crowd parted a little and shifted and I found myself standing near the front of the onlookers with a clear view of the performance. The Ring Inspector was holding his jaw and trying to argue round his winces, six bookmakers were declaring passionately that money once wagered was lost for ever, and Angelo, waving his hard bunched fist, was insisting they gave it back.

'You tricked me,' he shouted. 'The whole bloody lot of you, you stole my cash.'

'You bet it fair and square,' yelled a bookmaker, wagging a finger forcefully in Angelo's face.

Angelo bit the finger. The bookmaker yelled all the harder.

A man standing next to me laughed but most of the onlookers had less objectively taken sides and it seemed that a general brawl needed only a flashpoint. Into the ugliness and among the angrily gesturing hands and violent voices walked two uniformed policemen, both very young, both slight, both looking poor opponents in size and in forcefulness for the prison-taught Angelo. The Ring Inspector said something to one of them which was inaudible to me in the hubbub and to his immense and visible surprise Angelo suddenly found himself wearing, on the wrist he happened not to be waving in the air at that moment, a handcuff.

His bellow of rage fluttered the pigeons off the weighing room roof. He tugged with his whole weight and the boy-policeman whose own wrist protruded from the other cuff was jerked off his feet on to his knees. It looked not impossible that Angelo could pick him up bodily and simply run off with him, but the second constable came to his rescue, saying something boldly to Angelo and pulling his radio-communicator out of the front of his uniform jacket to bring up reinforcements.

Angelo looked at the ring of spectators through which he had little real hope of pushing and at his unexpectedly adroit captor, now rising from his knees, and at the seething bookmakers who were showing signs of satisfaction, and finally straight at me.

He took a step towards me with such strength that the half-risen policeman lost his balance again and fell on his back, his arm twisting awkwardly over his head, stretching in the handcuff. There was about Angelo suddenly such an extraordinary growth of menace, something so different from a mere racecourse argument, that the thronging voices fell away to silence and eyes looked at him with age-old fright. The monstrous recklessness seemed to swell his whole body, and even if his words were banal his gritty voice vibrated with a darkness straight out of myth.

'You,' he said deliberately, 'you and your fucking brother.'

There was an awareness in his face of the attentive crowd of witnesses around us and he didn't say aloud what was in his mind, but I could hear it as clearly as if he'd woken the sleeping hills.

536

I'll kill you. *I'll kill you.*

It was a message not so much new as newly intense. More than ever implacable. A promise, not a threat.

I stared back at him as if I hadn't heard, as if it wasn't there looking at me out of his eyes. He nodded however as if savagely satisfied and turned with a contemptuous shrug to the rising policeman, jerking him the last few inches upright; and he went, after that, without fighting, walking away between the two constables towards a police car which was driving in through the gates. The car halted. They put him in the back seat between them and presently rolled away, and the now strangely quiet crowd began to spread open and disperse.

A voice in my ear, the Welsh voice of Taff, said, 'You know what set all that off?'

'What?' I said.

'The bookies down in the cheap ring told Angelo he was a right mug. They were laughing at him, it seems. Joshing him, but friendly like to start with. They said they'd be happy to keep on taking his money because if he thought he'd bought Liam O'Rorke's old system he'd been robbed, duped, bamboozled, made a fool of and generally conned from here to Christmas.'

Dear God.

'So then this Angelo sort of exploded and started trying to get his stake back.'

'Yes,' I said.

'Well,' Taff said cheerfully. 'It all makes a change, though I reckon those goons in the cheap ring would have done better to keep their mouths shut. That Angelo was a bit of a golden goose and after this he won't lay no more golden eggs.'

I drove home with a feeling that the seas were closing over my head. Whatever I did to try to disentangle myself from Angelo it seemed that I slid further into the coils.

He was never, after this, going to believe that I hadn't tricked him on purpose. Even if I could at last get him the real correct system, he wouldn't forgive me the bets lost, the sneers of the bookmakers, the click of those handcuffs.

The police might hold him overnight, I thought, but not much longer: I doubted if one punch and a few yells would upset his parole. But to the tally in his mind would be added a night in the cells to rankle with those in my cellar – and if he'd come out of prison angry enough to attack me with nothing against me but the fact of my being Jonathan's brother, how much more would he now come swinging.

Cassie had long been home when I finally got there and was buoyantly pleased with the prospect of having the plaster off her arm on the following afternoon. She had arranged a whole day off from work and had thanked the groper for the last time, confident that she would be able to drive more or less at once. She was humming in the kitchen while I cooked some spaghetti for supper and I kissed her abstractedly and thought of Angelo and wished him dead with all my heart.

Before we had finished eating, the telephone rang and most unexpectedly, it was Ted Pitts calling from Switzerland. His voice, on the whole, was as cool as the Alps.

'Thought I'd better apologize,' he said.

'It's kind of you.'

'Jane's disgusted with me. She told me to ring you at once. She said it was urgent. So here I am. Sorry, and all that.'

'I just wondered,' I said hopelessly, 'why you did it.'

'Mashed up the weightings?'

'Yes.'

'You'll think I'm mean. Jane says I'm so mean she's ashamed of me. She's furious. She says all our wealth is due to Jonathan, and I've played the most rotten trick on Jonathan's brother. She's hardly speaking to me she's so cross.'

'Well . . . *why*?' I said.

He did at least seem to want me to understand. He spoke earnestly, explaining, excusing, telling me the destructive truth. 'I don't know. It was an impulse. I was making those copies and I suddenly thought I don't want to part with this system. I don't want anyone else to have it. It's mine. Not Jonathan's, just mine. He didn't even want it, and I've had it to myself all these years, and I've added to it and made it my own. It belongs to me. It's *mine*. And there you were, just asking for it as if I would give it to you as of right, and I suddenly thought why should I? So I just quickly changed a lot of the weightings. I didn't have time to test them. I had to guess. I altered just enough, I thought, but it seems I did too much. Otherwise you wouldn't have checked . . . I intended that when you used the system, you wouldn't win enough to think it worth all the work, and you'd get tired of it.' He paused. 'I was jealous of you having it, if you really want to know.'

'I wish you'd told me . . .'

'If I'd said I didn't want to give it to you, Jane would have made me. She says I must now. She's so cross.'

'If you would,' I said, 'you might have saved me a lot of grief.'

'Make your fortune, you mean.' The apology, it seemed, hadn't come from the heart: he still sounded resentful that I should be learning his secrets.

I thought again about telling him about Angelo but it still seemed to me that he might think it the best reason for *not* giving me the system that I could devise, so I said merely, 'It could work for two people, couldn't it? If someone else had it, it wouldn't stop you yourself winning as much as ever.'

'I suppose,' he said grudgingly, 'that that's true.'

'So . . . when do you come home?'

'The week after next.'

I was silent. Appalled. By the week after next heaven knew what Angelo would have done.

Ted Pitts said with half-suppressed annoyance, 'I suppose you've betted heavily on the wrong horse and lost too much, and now you need bailing out a lot sooner than the week after next?'

I didn't dispute it.

'Jane's furious. She's afraid I've cost you more than you can afford. Well, I'm sorry.' He didn't truly sound it.

'Could she find the tapes to give to me?' I said humbly.

'How soon do you need them?'

'More or less at once. Tonight, if possible.'

'Hmph.' He thought for a few moments. 'All right. All right. But you can save yourself the journey, if you like.'

'Er, how?'

'Do you have a tape recorder?'

'Yes.'

'Jane can play the tapes to you over the telephone. They'll sound like a lot of screeching. But if you've a half-way decent recorder the programs will run all right on a computer.'

'Good heavens.'

'A lot of computer programs whiz round the world on telephones every day,' he said. 'And up to the satellites and down again. Nothing extra-ordinary in it.'

To me it did seem extraordinary, but then I wasn't Ted Pitts. I thanked him with more intensity than he knew for his trouble in ringing me up.

'Thank Jane,' he said.

I did thank her, sincerely, five minutes later.

'You sounded in such *trouble*,' she said. 'I told Ted I'd sent you to Ruth because you'd wanted to check the tapes, and he *groaned*, so I asked him why . . . and when he told me what he'd done I was just *furious*. To think of you wasting your precious money when everything we have is thanks to Jonathan.'

Her kindness made me feel guilty. I said, 'Ted said you could play the real tapes to me over the telephone – if you wouldn't mind.'

'Oh yes, all right. I've seen Ted do it often. He and Ruth are always swopping programs that way. I've got the tapes here beside me. I made Ted tell me where to find them. I'll go and get the recorder now, if you'll hang on, and then I'll play them to you straight away.'

I had called her from the office because of the message-recorder already fitted to that telephone, and when she returned I recorded the precious programs on Luke's supply of fresh unused tapes which might not have been of prime computer standard but were all the same a better lot, I reckoned, than trying to record new machine language on top of old.

Cassie came into the office and listened to the scratchy whining noises running on and on and on.

'Horrible,' she said: but to me, sweet music. A ransom to the future. Passport to a peaceful world. In a sudden uprush of optimism entirely at variance with the gloom of my drive home from Leicester, I convinced myself that this time, now that we had the genuine article, our troubles would come to an end. The solution was still, as it had always been, to make Angelo rich, and at last it could be done.

'I'll give these tapes to Angelo,' I said, 'and we'll go away from the cottage for just a while, a few weeks, just until he's won enough not to want his revenge. And we'll be free of him at last, thank God.'

'Where shall we go?'

'Not far. Decide tomorrow.'

When three tapes were full and the noises fell quiet I switched off the recording part of the machine and spoke again to Jane.

'I'm very grateful,' I said. 'More than I can say.'

'My dear William, I'm so sorry . . .'

'Don't be,' I said. 'You've saved my life.' Quite literally, probably, I thought. 'Everything,' I said, 'will be all right.'

One shouldn't say such things. One really shouldn't.

20

Cassie came with me in the early morning to see the horses work on the Heath, shivering a little in boots, trousers and padded husky jacket, but glad, she said, to be alive in the free air and the wide spaces. Her breath, like mine, like that of all the horses, spurted out in lung-shaped plumes of condensing vapour, chilled and gone in a second and quickly renewed, cold, transformed to heat within the miracle of bodies.

We had already in a preliminary fashion left the cottage, having packed clothes and necessaries and stowed the suitcases in my car. I had also brought along a briefcase containing the precious tapes and a lot of Luke's paperwork and had re-routed my telephone calls by a message on the answer-system, and it remained only to make a quick return trip to pick up the day's mail and arrange for future postal deliveries to be left at the pub.

We hadn't actually decided where we would sleep that night or for many nights to come, but we did between us have a great many friends who might be cajoled, and if the traditional open-house generosity of the racing world failed us, we could for a while afford a hotel. I felt freer and more light-hearted than I had for weeks.

Sim was positively welcoming on the gallops and Mort asked us to break-fast. We shivered gratefully into his house and warmed up with him on toast and coffee while he slit open his letters with a paperknife and made comments on what he was at the same time reading in the *Sporting Life*. Mort never did one thing at a time if he could do three.

'I've re-routed my telephone messages to you,' I told him. 'Do you mind?'

'Have you? No, of course not. Why?'

'The cottage,' I said, 'is at the moment uninhabitable.'

'Decorators?' He sounded sympathetic and it seemed simplest to say yes.

'There won't be many calls,' I promised. 'Just Luke's business.'

'Sure,' he said. He sucked in a boiled egg in two scoops of a spoon. 'More coffee?'

'How are the yearlings settling in?' I asked.

'Come and see them. Come this afternoon, we'll be lungeing them in the paddock.'

'What's lungeing?' Cassie said.

Mort gave her a fast forgiving smile and snapped his fingers a few times. 'Letting them run round in a big circle on the end of a long rein. Gives them exercise. No one rides them yet. They've never been saddled. Too young.'

'I'd like that,' Cassie said, looking thoughtfully at the plaster and clearly wondering about the timing.

'Where are you staying?' Mort asked me. 'Where can I find you?'

'Don't know yet,' I said.

'Really? What about here? There's a bed here, if you like.' He crunched his teeth across half a piece of toast and ate it in one gulp. 'You could answer your own phone calls. Makes sense.'

'Well,' I said. 'For a night or two . . . very grateful.'

'Settled then.' He grinned cheerfully at Cassie. 'My daughter will be pleased. Got no wife, you know. She scarpered. Miranda gets bored, that's my daughter. Sixteen, needs a girl's company. Stay for a week. How long do you need?'

'We don't know,' Cassie said.

He nodded briskly. 'Take things as they come. Very sensible.' He casually picked up the paperknife and began cleaning his nails with it, reminding me irresistibly of Jonathan who throughout my childhood had done his with the point of a rifle bullet.

'I thought I'd go to Ireland at the weekend,' I said, 'and try to make peace with Donavan.'

Mort gave me a blinding grin, 'I hear you're a turd and an ignorant bas-tard, and should be dragged six times round the Curragh by your heels. At the least.'

The telephone standing on the table by his elbow rang only once, sharply, before Mort was shouting 'Hallo?' down the receiver. 'Oh,' he said, 'Hallo,

Luke.' He made signalling messages to me with his eyebrows. 'Yes, he's here right now, having breakfast.' He handed over the receiver, saying, 'Luke rang your number first, he says.'

'William,' Luke said, sounding relaxed and undemanding. 'How are the new yearlings?'

'Fine. No bad reports.'

'Thought I'd come over to see them. See what you've gotten me. I feel like a trip. Listen fella, do me a favour, make me some reservations at the Bedford Arms for two nights, fourteenth and fifteenth October?'

'Right,' I said.

'Best to Cassie,' he said. 'Bring her to dinner at the Bedford on the fourteenth, OK? I'd sure like to meet her. And fella, I'll be going on to Dublin. You aiming to go to the Ballsbridge Sales?'

'Yeah, I thought to. Ralph Finnigan died . . . they're selling all his string.'

Luke sounded appreciative. 'What would you pick, fella? What's the best?'

'Oxidise. Two years old, well bred, fast, a prospect for next June's Derby and bound to be expensive.'

Luke gave a sort of rumbling grunt. 'You'd send it to Donavan?'

'I sure would.'

The grunt became a chuckle. 'See you, fella, on the fourteenth.'

There was a click and he was gone. Mort said, 'Is he coming?' and I nodded and told him when. 'Most years he comes in October,' Mort said.

He asked if we'd like to see the second lot exercise but I was anxious to be finished at the cottage so Cassie and I drove the six miles back to the village and stopped first at the pub. Mine host, who had been invisible earlier, was now outside in his shirtsleeves sweeping dead leaves off his doorstep.

'Aren't you cold?' Cassie said.

Bananas, perspiring in contrast to our huskies, said he had been shifting beer barrels in his cellar.

We explained about going away for a while, and why.

'Come inside,' he said, finishing the leaves. 'Like some coffee?'

We drank some with him in the bar but without the ice cream and brandy he stirred into his own. 'Sure,' he said amiably. 'I'll take in your mail. Also papers, milk, whatever you like. Anything else?'

'How absolutely extravagantly generous are you feeling?' Cassie said.

He gave her a sideways squint over his frothy mugful, 'Spill it,' he said.

'My little yellow car is booked in today for a service and its road test, and I just wondered . . .'

'If I'd drive it along to that big garage for you?'

'William will bring you back,' she said persuasively.

'For you, Cassie, anything,' he said. 'Straightaway.'

'Plaster off this afternoon,' she said happily, and I looked at her clear grey eyes and thought I loved her so much it was ridiculous. Don't ever leave me, I thought. Stay around for ever. It would be lonely without you . . . it would be agony.

We all went in my car along to the cottage and left it out in the road because of Cassie wanting Bananas to back her little yellow peril out of the garage on to the driveway. She and he walked towards the garage doors to open them and I, half watching them, went across to unlock the front door and retrieve the letters which would have fallen on the mat just inside.

The cottage lay so quiet and still that our precautions seemed unnecessary, like crowd barriers on the moon.

Angelo is unpredictable, I told myself. Unstable as Mount St Helens. One might as well expect unreasonable behaviour from an earthquake, even if one does ultimately wish him to prosper.

REMEMBER TIGERS.

There was a small banging noise out by the garage. Nothing alarming. I paid little attention.

Six envelopes lay on the mat. I bent down, picked them up, shuffled through them. Three bills for Luke, a rate demand for the cottage, an advertisement for books and a letter to Cassie from her mother in Sydney. Ordinary mundane letters, not worth dying for.

I gave one final glance round the pretty sitting-room, seeing the red check frills on the curtains and the corn dollies moving gently in the breeze through the door. It wouldn't be so long, I thought, before we were back.

The kitchen door stood open, the light from the kitchen window lying in a reflecting gleam on the white paint: and across the gleam a shadow moved.

Bananas and Cassie, I thought automatically, coming in through the kitchen door. But they couldn't. It was locked.

There was hardly enough time even for alarm, even for primaeval instinct, even for rising hair. The silencer of a pistol came first into the room, a dark silhouette against the white paint, and then Angelo, dressed in black, balloon-high with triumph, towering with malice, looking like the devil.

There was no point in speech. I knew conclusively that he was going to shoot me, that I was looking at my own death. There was about him such an intention of action, such a surrender to recklessness, such an intoxication of destructiveness, that nothing and no one could have talked him out of it.

With a thought so light-fast that it wasn't even conscious, I reached out to the baseball bat which still lay on the window sill. Grasped its handle end with the dexterity of desperation and swung towards Angelo in one continuous movement from twisting foot through legs, trunk, arm and hand to bat, bringing the weight of the wood down towards the hand which held the pistol with the whole force of my body.

Angelo fired straight at my chest from six feet away. I felt a jerking thud and nothing else and wasn't even astonished and it didn't even a fraction deflect my swing. A split second later the bat crunched down on to Angelo's wrist and hand and broke them as thoroughly as he'd broken Cassie's arm.

I reeled from the force of that impact and spun across the room, and Angelo dropped the gun on the carpet and hugged his right arm to his body, yelling one huge shout at the pain of it and doubling over and running awkwardly out of the front door and down the path to the road.

I watched him through the window. I stood in a curious sort of inactivity, knowing that there was a future to come that had not yet arrived, a consequence not yet felt but inexorable, the fact of a bullet through my flesh.

I thought: Angelo has finally bagged his Derry. Angelo has taken his promised revenge. Angelo knows his shot hit me straight on target. Angelo will be convinced that he has done right, even if it costs him a lifetime in prison. In Angelo, despite his smashed wrist, despite his prospects, there would be at that moment an overpowering, screaming, unencompassable delirium of joy.

The battle was over, and the war. Angelo would be satisfied that in every physical, visible way, he had won.

Bananas and Cassie came running through the front door and looked enormously relieved to see me standing there, leaning a little against a cupboard but apparently unhurt.

'That was Angelo,' Cassie said.

'Yeah.'

Bananas looked at the baseball bat which lay on the floor and said, 'You bashed him.'

'Yeah.'

'Good,' Cassie said with satisfaction. 'His turn for the dreaded plaster.'

Bananas saw Angelo's gun and leaned to pick it up.

'Don't touch it,' I said.

He looked up enquiringly, still half bent.

'Fingerprints,' I said. 'Jail him for life.'

'But – '

'He shot me,' I said.

I saw the disbelief on their faces begin to turn to anxiety.

'Where?' Cassie said.

I made a fluttery movement with my left hand towards my chest. My right arm felt heavy and without strength, and I thought unemotionally that it was because some of the muscles needed to lift it were torn.'

'Shall I get an ambulance?' Bananas said.

'Yes.'

They didn't understand, I thought, how bad it was. They couldn't see any damage, and I was concerned mostly about how to tell them without frightening Cassie to death.

It wasn't that at that point it felt so terrible, but I still knew in a detached fashion that it soon would be. There was an internal disintegration going on like the earth shifting, like foundations slipping away. Accelerating, but still slowly.

I said, 'Ring Cambridge hospital.'

It all sounded so calm.

I slid down, without meaning to, to my knees, and saw the anxiety on their faces turn to horror.

'You're really hurt,' Cassie said with spurting alarm.

'It's ... er ... er ...' I couldn't think of what to say.

She was suddenly beside me, kneeling, finding with terrified scarlet fingers that the entry wound that didn't show through the front of my padded husky jacket led to a bigger bleeding exit at the back.

'Oh my *God*,' she said in stunned absolute shock.

Bananas strode over for a look and I could see from both their faces that they did know now, there was no longer any need to seek the words.

He turned grim-faced away and picked up the telephone, riffling urgently through the directory and dialling the number.

'Yes,' he was saying. 'Yes, it's an emergency. A man's been shot. Yes, I did say shot ... through the chest ... Yes, he's alive ... Yes, he's conscious ... No, the bullet can't be in him.' He gave the address of the cottage and brief directions. 'Look, stop asking damn fool questions ... tell them to shift their arse ... Yes, it does look *bloody* serious, for God's sake stop wasting time ... *My* name? Christ Almighty, John Frisby.' He crashed the receiver down in anger and said, 'They want to know if we've reported it to the police. What the hell does it matter?'

I couldn't be bothered to tell him that all gunshot wounds had to be reported. Breathing, in fact, was becoming more difficult. Only words that needed to be said were worth the effort.

'That pistol,' I said. 'Don't put it ... in a plastic bag. Condensation ... destroys ... the prints.'

Bananas looked surprised and I thought that he didn't realize I was telling him because quite soon I might not be able to. I was beginning to feel most dreadfully ill, with clamminess creeping over my skin and breaking into a sweat on my forehead. I gave a smallish cough and wiped a red streak from my mouth on to the back of my hand. An enveloping wave of weakness washed through me and I found myself sagging fairly comprehensively against the cupboard and then half lying on the floor.

'Oh, William,' Cassie said. 'Oh *no*.'

If I'd ever doubted she loved me, I had my answer. No one could have acted or feigned the extremity of despair in her voice and in her body.

'Don't ... worry,' I said. I tried a smile. I don't suppose it came off. I coughed again, with worse results.

I was trying to breathe, I thought, through a lake. A lake progressively filling, fed by many springs. It was happening faster now. Much faster. Too fast. I wasn't ready. Who was ever ready?

I could hear Bananas saying something urgent but I didn't know quite what. My wits started drifting. Existence was ceasing to be external. I'm dying, I thought, I really am. Dying too fast.

My eyes were shut and then open again. The daylight looked odd. Too bright. I could see Cassie's face wet with tears.

I tried to say, 'Don't cry,' but I couldn't get the breath. Breathing was becoming a sticky near-impossibility.

Bananas was still talking, distantly.

There was a feeling of everything turning to liquid, of my body dissolving, of a deep subterranean river overflowing its banks and carrying me away.

Dim final astringent thought . . . I'm drowning. God damn it, in my own blood.

21

Cassie's face was the next thing I saw, but not for more than a day, and it was no longer weeping but asleep and serene. She was sitting by a bed with me in it, surrounded by white things and glass and chromium and a lot of lights. Intensive care, and all that.

I woke by stages over several hours to the pain I hadn't felt from the shot, and to tubes carrying liquids into and away from my log of clay and to voices telling me over and over that I was lucky to be there; that I had died and was alive.

I thanked them all, and meant it.

Thanked Bananas, who had apparently picked me up and put me in my own car and driven me at about a hundred miles an hour to Cambridge because it was quicker than waiting for an ambulance.

Thanked two surgeons who it seemed had worked all day and then again half the night to staunch and tidy the wreckage of my right lung and stop blood dripping out of the drainage as fast as the transfusions flowed into my arm.

Thanked the nurses who clattered about with the deft hands and noisy machinery, and in absentia thanked the donors of blood type 'O' who had refilled my veins.

Thanked Cassie for her love and for sitting beside me whenever they'd let her.

Thanked the fates that the destructive lump of metal had missed my heart. Thanked everyone I could for anything I could think of in gratitude for my life.

The long recurring dreams that had come during unconsciousness faded, receded, seemed no longer to be vivid fact. I no longer saw the Devil pacing beside me, quiet but implacable, the master waiting for my soul. I no longer saw him, the Fallen Angelo, the Devil with Angelo's face, the yellow face with frosted hair and black empty holes where the eyes should have been.

The Presence had gone. I was back to the daft real enjoyable world where tubes were what mattered, not concepts of evil.

I didn't say how close I had been to death because they were saying it for me, roughly every five minutes. I didn't say I had looked on the spaces of eternity and seen the everlasting Darkness and had known it had a meaning and a face. The visions of the dying and the snatched-from-death were suspect. Angelo was a living man, not the Devil, not an incarnation or a house or a dwelling place. It was delirium, the confusion of the brain's circuits, that had shown me the one as the other, the other as the One. I said nothing for fear of ridicule: and later nothing from feeling that I had in truth been mistaken and that the dreams were indeed . . . merely dreams.

'Where is Angelo?' I said.

'They said not to tire you.'

I looked at the evasion in Cassie's face. 'I'm lying down,' I pointed out. 'So give.'

She said reluctantly, 'Well . . . he's here.'

'*Here*?' In this hospital?'

She nodded. 'In the room next door.'

I was bewildered. 'But why?'

'He crashed his car.' She looked at me anxiously for signs I supposed of relapse, but was seemingly assured. 'He drove into a bus about six miles from here.'

'After he left the cottage?'

She nodded. 'They brought him here. They brought him into the emergency unit while Bananas and I were waiting there. We couldn't believe it.'

It wasn't over. I closed my eyes. It was never ever going to be over. Wherever I went, it seemed that Angelo would follow, even on to the slab.

'William?' Cassie said urgently.

'Mm?'

'Oh. I thought . . .'

'I'm all right.'

'He was nearly dead,' she said. 'Just like you. He's still in a coma.'

'What?'

'Head injuries,' she said.

I learned bit by bit over the next few days that the hospital people hadn't believed it when Bananas and Cassie told them it was Angelo who had shot me. They had fought as long and hard to save his life as mine, and apparently we had been placed side by side in the Intensive Care Unit until Cassie told them I'd have a heart attack if I woke and found him there.

The police had more moderately pointed out that if it was Angelo who woke first he might complete the job of murdering me: and Angelo was now in his unwaking sleep along the hallway, guarded by a constable night and day.

It was extraordinary to think of him being there, lying there so close. Unsettling in a fundamental way. I wouldn't have thought it would have affected me so badly, but my pulse started jumping every time anyone opened the door. Reason said he wouldn't come. The subconscious feared it.

Bodies heal amazingly quickly. I was free of tubes, moved to a side ward, on my feet, walking about within a week: creeping a bit, sure, and stiff and sore, but positively, conclusively alive. Angelo too, it seemed, was improving. On the way up from the depths. Opening unseeing eyes, showing responses.

I heard it from the nurses, from the cleaners, from the woman who pushed a trolley of comforts, and all of them watched me curiously to see how I would take it. The piquancy of the situation hit first the local paper and then the national dailies, and the constables guarding Angelo started drifting in to chat.

It was from one of them that I learned how Angelo had lost control of his car while going round a roundabout, how a whole queue of people at a bus stop had seen him veer towards the bus as if unable to turn the steering wheel, how he'd been going too fast in any case, and how he had seemed at first to be *laughing*.

Bananas, when he heard it, said trenchantly, 'He crashed because you broke his wrist.'

'Yes,' I said.

He sighed deeply. 'The police must know.'

'I expect so.'

'Have they bothered you?'

I shook my head. 'I told them what happened. They wrote it down. No one has said much.'

'They collected the pistol.' He smiled. 'They put it in a paper bag.'

I left the hospital after twelve days, walking slowly past Angelo's room but not going in. Revulsion was too strong even though I knew he was still lightly unconscious and wouldn't be aware I was there. The damage he had caused in my life and Cassie's might be over but my body carried his scars, livid still and still hurting, too immediate for detachment.

I dare say I hated him. Perhaps I feared him. I certainly didn't want to see him again, then or ever.

For the next three weeks I mooched around the cottage doing paperwork, getting fitter every day and persuading Bananas at first to drive me along to the Heath to watch the gallops. Cassie went to work, the plastered arm a memory. My blood had washed almost entirely off the sitting-room carpet and the baseball bat was in the cellar. Life returned more or less to normal.

Luke came over from California, inspected the yearlings, met Cassie, listened to Sim and Mort and the Berkshire trainers, visited Warrington Marsh, and went off to Ireland. It was he, not I, who bid for Oxidise at Ballsbridge and sent the colt to Donavan, and he who in some way smoothed the Irish trainer's feelings.

He came back briefly to Newmarket before leaving for home, calling in at the cottage and drinking a lunchtime scotch.

'Your year's nearly through,' he said.

'Yeah.'

'Have you enjoyed it?'

'Very much.'

'Want another?'

I lifted my head. He watched me through a whole minute of silence. He didn't say, and nor did I, that Warrington Marsh was never going to be strong enough again to do the job. That wasn't the point: the point was permanence . . . captivity.

'One year,' Luke said. 'It's not forever.'

After another pause I said, 'One year, then. One more.'

He nodded and drank his drink, and it seemed to me that somewhere he was smiling. I had a presentiment of him coming over again the next year and offering the same thing. One year. One year's contract at a time, leaving the cage door open but keeping his bird imprisoned: and as long as I could go, I thought, I might stay.

Cassie, when she came home, was pleased. 'Mort told him he'd be mad to lose you.'

'Did he?'

'Mort likes you.'

'Donavan doesn't.'

'You can't have everything,' she said.

I had quite a lot, it was true; and then the police telephoned and asked me to see Angelo.

'No,' I said.

'That's a gut reaction,' a voice said calmly. 'But I'd like you to listen.'

He talked persuasively for a long time, cajoling again every time I protested, wearing down my opposition until in the end I reluctantly agreed to do what he wanted.

'Good,' he said finally. 'Wednesday afternoon.'

'That's only two days – '

'We'll send a car. We don't expect you to be driving yet.'

I didn't argue. I could drive short distances but I tended to get tired. In another month, they'd said, I'd be running.

'We're grateful,' the voice said.

'Yeah . . .'

I told Cassie and Bananas, in the evening.

'How awful,' Cassie said. 'It's too much.'

The three of us were having dinner alone in the dining-room as the restaurant didn't officially open these days on Mondays: the old cow had negotiated Mondays off. Bananas had done the cooking himself, inventing a soufflé of white fish, herbs, orange and nuts to try out on Cassie and me: a concoction typically and indescribably different, an unknown language, a new horizon of taste.

'You could have said you wouldn't go,' Bananas said, heaping his plate to match ours.

'With what excuse?'

'Selfishness,' Cassie said. 'The best reason in the world for not doing things.'

'Never thought of it.'

Bananas said, 'I hope you insisted on a bullet-proof vest, a six-inch-thick plate glass screen and several rolls of barbed wire.'

'They did assure me,' I said mildly, 'that they wouldn't let him leap at my throat.'

'Too kind,' Cassie murmured.

We poured Bananas' exquisite sauce over his soufflé and said that when we had to leave the cottage we would camp in his garden.

'And will you bet?' he asked.

'What do you mean?'

'On the system.'

I thought blankly that I'd forgotten all about that possibility: but we did have the tapes. We did have the choice.

'We don't have a computer,' I said.

'We could soon pay for one,' Cassie said.

We all looked at each other. We were happy enough with our own jobs; with what we had. Did one always, inevitably, stretch out for more?

Yes, one did.

'You work the computer,' Bananas said, 'and I'll do the betting. Now and then. When we're short.'

'As long as it doesn't choke us.'

'I don't want diamonds,' Cassie said judiciously, 'or furs, or a yacht . . . but how soon can we have a pool in our sitting-room?'

Whatever Luke said to my brother when he got home to California I never knew, but it resulted in Jonathan telephoning that night to say he would be arriving at Heathrow on Wednesday morning.

'What about your students?'

'Sod the students. I've got laryngitis.' His voice bounced the distance strong and healthy. 'I'll see you.'

He came in a hired car looking biscuit-coloured from the sun and anxious about what he would find, and although I was by then feeling well again it didn't seem to reassure him.

'I'm alive,' I pointed out. 'One thing at a time. Come back next month.'

'What exactly happened?'

'Angelo happened.'

'Why didn't you tell me?' he demanded.

'I'd have told you if I'd died. Or someone would.'

He sat in one of the rockers and looked at me broodingly.

'It was all my fault,' he said.

'Oh, sure.' I was ironic.

'And that's why you didn't tell me.'

'I'd probably have told you one day.'

'Tell me now.'

I told him, however, where I was going that afternoon, and why, and he said in his calm positive way that he would come with me. I had thought he would: had been glad he was coming. I told him over the next few hours pretty well everything which had happened between Angelo and me, just as he had told me all those years ago in Cornwall.

'I'm sorry,' he said, at the end.

'Don't be.'

'You'll use the system.'

I nodded. 'Pretty soon.'

'I think old Mrs O'Rorke would be glad. She was proud of Liam's work. She wouldn't want it wasted.' He reflected for a bit and then said, 'What make of pistol, do you know?'

'I believe . . . the police said . . . a Walther .22?'

He smiled faintly. 'True to form. And just as well. If it had been a .38 or something like that you'd have been in trouble.'

'Ah,' I said drily. 'Just as well.'

The car came for us as threatened and took us to a large house in Buckinghamshire. I never did discover exactly what it was: a cross between a hospital and a civil service institution, all long wide corridors and closed doors and hush.

'Down there,' we were directed. 'Right along at the end. Last door on the right.'

We walked unhurriedly along the parquet flooring, our heels punctuating the silence. At the far end there was a tall window, floor to ceiling, casting not quite enough daylight; and silhouetted against the window were two figures, a man in a wheelchair with another man pushing him.

Those two and Jonathan and I in due course approached each other, and as we drew nearer I saw with unwelcome shock that the man in the wheelchair was Harry Gilbert. Old, grey, bowed, ill Harry Gilbert who still consciously repelled compassion.

Eddy, who was pushing, faltered to a halt, and Jonathan and I also stopped, we staring at Harry and Harry staring at us over a space of a few feet. He looked from me to Jonathan glancing at him briefly at first and then looking longer, more carefully, seeing what he didn't believe.

He switched to me. 'You said he was dead,' he said.

I nodded slightly.

His voice was cold, dry, bitter, past passion, past hope, past strength to avenge. 'Both of you,' he said. 'You destroyed my son.'

Neither Jonathan nor I answered. I wondered about the genetics of evil, the chance that bred murder, the predisposition which lived already at birth. The biblical creation, I thought, was also the truth of evolution. Cain existed, and in every species there was survival of the ruthless.

551

It was only by luck that I had lived; by Bananas' speed and surgeons' dedication. Abel and centuries of other victims were dead: and in every generation, in many a race, the genes still threw up the killer. The Gilberts bred their Angelos for ever.

Harry Gilbert jerked his head back, aiming at Eddy, signalling that he wanted to go; and Eddy the look-alike, Eddy the easily led, Eddy the sheep from the same flock, wheeled his uncle quietly away.

'Arrogant old bastard,' Jonathan said under his breath, looking back at them.

'The breeding of racehorses,' I said, 'is interesting.'

Jonathan's gaze came round very slowly to my face. 'And do rogues,' he asked, 'beget rogues?'

'Quite often.'

He nodded and we went on walking along the corridor, up to the window, to the last door on the right.

The room into which we went must once have been finely proportioned but with the insensitivity of government departments it had been hacked into two for utility. The result was one long narrow room with a window and another inner long room without one.

In the outer room, which was furnished only by a strip of mud-coloured carpet on the parquet leading to a functional desk and two hard chairs, were two men engaged in what looked like unimportant passing of the time. One sat behind the desk, one sat on it, both fortyish, smallish, smooth, bored-looking and with an air of wishing to be somewhere else.

They looked up enquiringly as we went in.

'I'm William Derry,' I said.

'Ah.'

The man sitting on the desk rose to his feet, came towards me, shook hands, and looked enquiring at Jonathan.

'My brother, Jonathan Derry,' I said.

'Ah.'

He shook hands with him too. 'I don't think,' he said neutrally, 'that we'll need to bother your brother.'

I said, 'Angelo is more likely to react violently to Jonathan than to me.'

'But it was you he tried to kill.'

'Jonathan got him jailed . . . fourteen years ago.'

'Ah.'

He looked from one of us to the other, his head tilted slightly back to accommodate our height. We seemed to be in some way not what he'd expected, though I didn't know why. Jonathan did certainly look pretty distinguished, especially since age had given him such an air of authority, and he had always of the two of us had the straighter features; and I, I supposed, looked less a victim than I might have. I wondered vaguely if he'd been expecting a shuffling little figure in a dressing gown and hadn't reckoned on clothes like his own.

'I think I'll just go and *explain* about your brother,' he said at last. 'Will you wait?'

We nodded and he opened the door to the inner room parsimoniously and eeled himself through the gap, closing it behind him. The man behind the desk went on looking bored and offered no comment of any sort, and presently his colleague slid back through the same sized opening and said they were ready for us inside and would we please go in.

The inner room was lit brightly and entirely by electricity and contained four people and a great deal of electrical equipment with multitudinous dials and sprouting wires. I saw Jonathan give them a swift sweep of the eyes and supposed he could identify the lot, and he said afterwards that they had all seemed to be standard machines for measuring body changes – cardiograph, encephalograph, gauges for temperature, respiration and skin moisture – and there had been at least two of each.

One of the four people wore an identifying white coat and introduced himself quietly as Tom Course, a doctor. A woman in similar white moved among the machines, checking their faces. A third person, a man, seemed to be there specifically as an observer, since that was what he did, without speaking, during the next strange ten minutes.

The fourth person, sitting in a sort of dentist's chair with his back to us, was Angelo.

We could see only the top of his bandaged head, but also his arms, which were strapped by the wrists to the arms of the chair.

There was no sign of any plaster on the arm I'd broken: mended no doubt. His arms were bare and covered sparsely with dark hairs, the hands lying loose, without tension. From every part of his body it seemed that wires led backwards to the machines, which were all ranked behind him. In front of him there was nothing but a stretch of empty brightly lit room.

Dr Course, young, wiry, bolstered by certainties, gave me an enquiring glance and said in the same quiet manner, 'Are you ready?'

As ready, I supposed, as I ever would be.

'Just walk round in front of him. Say something. Anything you like. Stay there until we tell you it's enough.'

I swallowed. I had never wanted to do anything less in all my life. I could see them all waiting, polite, determined, businesslike ... and too damned understanding. Even Jonathan, I noticed, was looking at me with a sort of pity.

Intolerable.

I walked slowly round the machines and the chair and stopped in front of Angelo, and looked at him.

He was naked to the waist. On his head, below a cap of fawn crêpe bandage, there was a band of silvery metal like a crown. His skin everywhere gleamed with grease and to his face, his neck, his chest, arms and abdomen were fastened an army of electrodes. No one, I imagined, could have been more comprehensively wired; no flicker of change could have gone un-monitored.

He seemed as well-fleshed and as healthy as ever, despite his earlier two weeks in a coma. The muscles looked as strong, the trunk as tank-like, the mouth as firm. The hard man. The frightener. The despiser of mugs. Apart from his headdress and the wires he looked just the same. I breathed a shade deeply and looked straight into his black eyes, and it was there that one saw the difference. There was nothing in his eyes, nothing at all. It was extraordinary, like seeing a stranger in a long-known face. The house was the same . . . but the monster slept.

It was five weeks all but a day since we had last faced each other; since we had brought each other near death, one way or another. Even though I had been prepared, seeing him again affected me powerfully. I could hear my heart thudding: could actually hear it in the expectant room.

'Angelo,' I said. My tongue felt sticky in my dry mouth. 'Angelo, you shot me.'

In Angelo, nothing happened.

He was looking at me in complete calm. When I took a pace to one side, his eyes followed. When I stepped back he still watched.

'I am . . . William Derry,' I said. 'I gave you . . . Liam O'Rorke's betting system.' I said the words slowly, clearly, deliberately, trying to control my own uneven breath.

From Angelo there was no reaction at all.

'If you hadn't shot me . . . you'd have been free now . . . and rich.'

Nothing. Absolute nothing.

I found Jonathan standing beside me and after a pause Angelo's gaze wandered from me to him.

'Hallo, Angelo,' Jonathan said. 'I'm Jonathan, do you remember? William told you I was dead. It wasn't true.'

Angelo said nothing.

'Do you remember?' Jonathan said. 'I tricked you sideways.'

Silence. A dull absence of all we had endured for so long. No fury. No sneers, no threats, no towering hurricane of hate.

Silence, it seemed to me, was all that was appropriate. Jonathan and I stood there together in front of the shell of our enemy and there was nothing in the world left to say.

'Thank you,' Tom Course said, coming round the chair to join us. 'That should do it.'

Angelo looked at him.

'Who are you?' he said.

'Dr Course. We talked earlier, while we were fixing the electrodes.'

Angelo made no comment but instead looked directly at me.

'You were talking,' he said. 'Who are you?'

'William Derry.'

'I don't know you.'

'No.'

His voice was as deep and as gritty as ever, the only remnant, it seemed, of the old foe.

Dr Course said heartily, 'We'll take all those wires off you now. I expect you'll be glad to get rid of them.'

'Who did you say you are?' Angelo said, frowning slightly.

'Dr Course.'

'Who?'

'Never mind. I'm here to take the wires off.'

'Can I have tea?' Angelo said.

Dr Course left the taking-off of the wires to his woman colleague and led us round to look at the results on the machines. The observer, I noticed, was also consulting them acutely, but Course paid him scant attention.

'There we are,' he said, holding out a yard long strip of paper. 'Not a flicker. We had him stabilized for an hour before his visitors came. Breathing, pulse rate, everything rock steady. Quiet in here, you see. No interruptions, no intrusions, no noise. That mark, that's the point at which he saw *you*,' he nodded at me, 'and as you can see, nothing altered. This is the skin temperature chart. Always rises if someone's lying. And here . . .' he moved across to a different machine. 'Heart rate unchanged. And here . . .' to another. 'Brain activity, very faint alteration. He couldn't have seen *you*, his hated victim, suddenly and unexpectedly standing in front of him, and yet show no strong body or brain changes, not if he'd known you. Absolutely impossible.'

I thought of my own unrecorded but pretty extreme responses, and knew that it was true.

'Is this state permanent?' Jonathan asked.

Tom Course gave him a swift look. '*I* think so. It's *my* opinion, yes. See, they dug pieces of skull out of his brain tissue. Brilliant repair job on the bone structure, have to hand it to them. But there you are, you can see, no memory. Many functions unimpaired. Eat, talk, walk, he can do all that. He's continent. He'll live to be old. But he can't remember anything for longer than about fifteen minutes, sometimes not even that. He lives in the absolute present. Loss of capacity for memory is not all that rare, you know, after severe brain damage. But with this one, there were *doubts*. Not *my* doubts, official doubts. They said he was faking, that he knew he'd go to a hospital, not a prison, if he could persuade everyone he'd lost his memory.'

Tom Course waved a hand around the machines. 'He couldn't have faked today's results. Conclusive. Settle the arguments once and for all. Which is why we're all here, of course. Why they gave us this facility.'

His woman colleague had taken the silver band off Angelo's forehead and the straps off his wrists, and was wiping the grease from his skin with pieces of cotton wool.

'Who are you?' he said to her, and she answered, 'Just a friend.'

'Where will he go?' I said.

Tom Course shrugged. 'Not my decision. But I'd be careful. I'm not a civil servant. My advice, I don't suppose, will be taken.' His remark was clearly aimed at the observer, who remained obstinately impassive.

I said slowly, 'Could he still be violent?'

Tom Course gave me a swift sideways glance. 'Can't tell. He might be. Yes, he might be. He looks harmless. He'll never *hate* anyone, he can't remember anyone long enough. But the sudden impulse . . .' he shrugged again. 'Let's say, I wouldn't turn my back on him if we were alone.'

'Not ever?'

'How old is he? Forty?' He pursed his mouth. 'Not for another ten years. Twenty perhaps. You can't tell.'

'Lightning?' I said.

'Just like that.'

The woman finished wiping the grease and was holding out a grey shirt for Angelo to put on.

'Have we had tea?' he said.

'Not yet.'

'I'm thirsty.'

'You'll have tea soon.'

I said to Tom Course, 'His father was outside . . . did Angelo see him?'

Course nodded. 'No reaction. Nothing on the machines. Conclusive tests, the whole lot of them.' He looked slyly at the observer. 'They can stop all the arguing.'

Angelo stood up out of the chair, stretching upright, seeming strong with physical life but fumbling with the buttons of his shirt, moving without total coordination, looking around vaguely as if not quite sure what he should be doing next.

His wandering gaze came to rest on Jonathan and me.

'Hallo,' he said.

The doors from the outer room opened wide and two white-coated male nurses and a uniformed policeman came through it.

'Is he ready?' the policeman said.

'All yours.'

'Let's be off, then.'

He fastened a handcuff round Angelo's left wrist and attached him to one of the nurses.

Angelo didn't seem to mind. He looked at me uninterestedly for the last time with the black holes where the eyes should have been and walked as requested to the door.

Diminished, defused . . . perhaps even docile.

'Where's my tea?' he said.